The Golden Fleece

Robert Graves was born in 1895 in Wimbledon, the son of Irish writer Perceval Graves and Amalia Von Ranke. He went from school to the First World War, where he became a captain in the Royal Welch Fusiliers and was seriously wounded at the Battle of the Somme. After that, apart from a year as Professor of English Literature at Cairo University in 1926, he earned his living by writing. His mostly historical novels include *I, Claudius*; *Claudius the God*; *Count Belisarius*; *Wife of Mr Milton*; *Sergeant Lamb of the Ninth*; *Proceed, Sergeant Lamb*; *The Golden Fleece*; *They Hanged My Saintly Billy*; and *The Isles of Unwisdom*. He wrote his autobiography, *Goodbye to All That*, in 1929, and it was soon established as a modern classic. *The Times Literary Supplement* acclaimed it as 'one of the most candid self-portraits of a poet, warts and all, ever painted', as well as being of exceptional value as a war document. His two most discussed non-fiction works are *The White Goddess*, a study of poetic inspiration, and *The Nazarine Gospel Restored* (with Joshua Podro), an examination of primitive Christianity. He also translated or co-translated Apuleius, Lucan, Suetonius and *The Rubáiyát of Omar Khayyám* for Penguin, and compiled the first modern dictionary of Greek Mythology, *The Greek Myths*. He was elected Professor of Poetry at Oxford in 1961 and made an Honorary Fellow of St John's College, Oxford, in 1971.

Robert Graves died on 7 December 1985 in Majorca, his home since 1929. On his death *The Times* wrote of him, 'He will be remembered for his achievements as a prose stylist, historical novelist and memoirist, but above all as the great paradigm of the dedicated poet, "the greatest love poet in English since Donne".' His *Complete Poems*, as well as many of his novels, is published in Penguin Classics.

D1293555

ROBERT GRAVES

The Golden Fleece

PENGUIN BOOKS

PENGUIN CLASSICS

Published by the Penguin Group
Penguin Books Ltd, 80 Strand, London WC2R ORL, England
Penguin Group (USA) Inc., 375 Hudson Street, New York, New York 10014, USA
Penguin Group (Canada), 90 Eglinton Avenue East, Suite 700, Toronto, Ontario,
Canada M4P 2Y3 (a division of Pearson Penguin Canada Inc.)
Penguin Ireland, 25 St Stephen's Green, Dublin 2, Ireland (a division of Penguin Books Ltd)
Penguin Group (Australia), 250 Camberwell Road, Camberwell, Victoria 3124, Australia
(a division of Pearson Australia Group Pty Ltd)
Penguin Books India Pvt Ltd, 11 Community Centre, Panchsheel Park,
New Delhi – 110 017, India
Penguin Group (NZ), 67 Apollo Drive, Rosedale, Auckland 0632, New Zealand
(a division of Pearson New Zealand Ltd)
Penguin Books (South Africa) (Pty) Ltd, 24 Sturdee Avenue, Rosebank, Johannesburg 2196,
South Africa

Penguin Books Ltd, Registered Offices: 80 Strand, London WC2R ORL, England

www.penguin.com

First published by Cassell 1944
Published in Penguin Classics 2011
1

Copyright © Robert Graves, 1944
All rights reserved

The moral right of the author has been asserted

Printed in England by Clays Ltd, St Ives plc

ISBN: 978-0-141-19764-7

www.greenpenguin.co.uk

MIX
Paper from
responsible sources
FSC
www.fsc.org   FSC™ C018179

Penguin Books is committed to a sustainable
future for our business, our readers and our
planet. This book is made from paper certified
by the Forest Stewardship Council.

THE GOLDEN FLEECE

INVOCATION

Ancaeus, Little Ancaeus, oracular hero, last survivor (it is said) of all the Argonauts who sailed to Colchis with Jason in search of the Golden Fleece, speak to us visitants, speak clearly from your rocky tomb by the Goddess's fountain in cool Hesperidean Deia. First tell us how you came there, so far from your home in Flowery Samos; and next, if it pleases you, unfold the whole story of that famous voyage, starting from the very beginning. Come, we will pour you libations of honey water to sweeten your throat! But remember, no lies! The dead may speak the truth only, even when it discredits themselves.

ANCAEUS AT THE ORANGE-GROVE

Ancaeus the Lelegian, of Flowery Samos, was marooned one summer evening on the sandy southern shore of Majorca, the largest of the Islands of the Hesperides, or, as some call them, the Islands of the Slingers, or the Islands of the Naked Men, which lie close together in the far west of the sea, not above a day's sail from Spain when the wind is fair. The islanders, astonished by his appearance, refrained from putting him to death and conducted him, with undisguised contempt for his Greek sandals, short travel-stained tunic, and heavy seaman's cloak, to the Chief Priestess and Governess of Majorca, who lived in the cave of the Drachë, the most distant from Greece of the many entrances to the Underworld.

Since she happened to be preoccupied with some work of divination, the Chief Priestess sent Ancaeus across the island to be judged and disposed of by her daughter, the Nymph of the sacred orange-grove at Deia. A party of naked Goat men escorted him across the plain and over the rough mountains; but by the order of the Chief Priestess they refrained from conversing with him by the way. They did not pause for a moment in their trotting journey, except to prostrate themselves at a massive cromlech, standing beside their path, where as boys they had been initiated into the rites of the Goat fraternity. Three times they came to places where three ways met, and each time made a wide circuit to avoid the triangular thicket marked out with stones. Ancaeus was pleased to find such respect paid to the Triple Goddess, to whom these enclosures are sacred.

Very weary and footsore by the time that he reached Deia, Ancaeus found the Orange Nymph seated upright on a stone near a copious spring of water which burst from the granite rock and watered the grove. Here the mountain, which was shaggy with wild olive and esculent oak, sloped sharply down to the sea, five hundred feet below, at that time dappled with small banks of mist, like sheep grazing, as far as the horizon-line.

Ancaeus, when the Nymph had addressed him, replied reverently, using the Pelasgian language and keeping his eyes fixed on the ground. Every priestess of the Triple Goddess has the double-eye which, as Ancaeus knew, can turn a man's spirit to water and his body to stone and can blast to death any animal that crosses her path. The oracular serpents which these priestesses tend have the same terrible power over birds, mice, and rabbits. Ancaeus also knew that he should say nothing to the Nymph except in answer to her questions, and then speak briefly and in the humblest possible tones.

The Nymph dismissed the Goat men, who went a little apart and perched in a row on the edge of a rock until she should summon them again. They were a calm, simple people, with blue eyes and short muscular legs. Instead of warming their bodies with clothes, they smeared them with the juice of the mastic plant mixed with hogs' grease. Each wore at his side a goat-skin wallet full of wave-worn stones, and held a sling in his hand, with another sling wound about his head, and a third serving as a loin strap. They expected that the Nymph would soon give them orders to despatch the stranger, and already were debating in a friendly fashion among themselves who should have the first cast, and who the second, and whether they should allow him a fair start in a lively hunt down the mountain-side, or whether they should knock him to pieces as he approached them, each aiming at a different part of his body.

The orange-grove, which contained fifty trees, surrounded a rock shrine inhabited by an unusually large serpent, which the other nymphs, the fifty Hesperides, fed daily with barley-flour worked into a very thin paste with goats' milk. The shrine was sacred to an ancient hero who had brought the orange into Majorca from some land or other on the distant shores of the Ocean. His name was forgotten and they spoke of him only as 'The Benefactor'; the serpent, being bred from the marrow of his spine and animated by his ghost, went by the same name. The orange is a round, scented fruit, unknown elsewhere in the civilized world, which grows green at first, then golden, with a hot rind and cold, sweet, sharp flesh. It is found on a smooth tree with glossy leaves and prickly branches, and ripens in mid-winter, unlike any other fruit. It is not eaten indiscriminately in Majorca, but once a year only, at the winter solstice, after ritual chewing of buckthorn and other purgative herbs; thus eaten, it confers long life. At other times, the slightest taste of an orange will result in immediate death, so sacred a fruit is it; unless the Orange Nymph herself dispenses it.

In these islands, by virtue of the orange, both men and women live as long as they please; in general, it is only when they find that they are becoming burdensome to their friends, because of the slowness of their movements or the dullness of their talk, that they decide on death. Then, for the sake of politeness, they do not say goodbye to their dear ones, nor make any commotion in the cave – for they all live in caves – but slip out quietly and fling themselves head-foremost from a rock; as is pleasing to the Goddess, who hates any unnecessary grief or complaint, and who rewards these suicides with distinguished and joyful funerals.

The Orange Nymph was tall and beautiful. She wore a flounced bell-shaped skirt in the Cretan fashion, of linen dyed the colour of orange with heather dye, and no upper garment, except a short-sleeved green waistcoat that did not fasten in front but showed the glory of her full breasts. Her badges of office were a belt of countless small pieces of gold linked together in the form of a serpent with jewelled eyes, a necklace of dried green oranges, and a high caul-cap embroidered in pearls and surmounted by the golden disc of the Full Moon. She had borne four handsome girls, the youngest of whom would one day succeed to her office, as she herself, being the youngest of her sisters, would one day succeed her mother, the Chief Priestess at Drachë. These four girls, not being yet old enough to be nymphs, were maiden huntresses, very skilful slingers, who went out with the men to bring them good luck in the chase. Maiden, Nymph, and Mother are the eternal royal Trinity of the island, and the Goddess, who is worshipped there in each of these aspects, as New Moon, Full Moon, and Old Moon, is the Sovereign Deity. It is she who induces fertility in those trees and plants upon which human life depends. Is it not well known that all green things shoot while the Moon waxes and cease while the Moon wanes, that only the hot rebellious onion does not obey her monthly phases? Yet the Sun, her man-child, yearly born and yearly dying, assists her with his warm emanations. It was for this reason that the only man-child born to the Orange Nymph, being the Sun incarnate, had been sacrificed to the Goddess, as the custom was, and his torn morsels thereupon mixed with the seed-barley to ensure a bountiful harvest.

The Nymph was surprised to find that the Pelasgian language, which Ancaeus spoke, closely resembled that of the Islands. Though she was pleased that she could question him without the troublesome necessity of gesturing and scratching pictures on clay with a stick, she was a little troubled in her mind that he might have been conversing with the Goat men on matters about which it was her policy, and that of her mother's, to keep them in innocence. She asked first: 'Are you a Cretan?'

He answered: 'No, Holy One, I am a Pelasgian from the island of Samos, in the Aegean Sea, and therefore no more than a cousin of the Cretans. But my overlords are Greeks.'

'You are an ugly little old wretch,' she said.

'Forgive me, Holy One,' he answered. 'I have led a hard life.'

When she asked why he had been set ashore on Majorca, he answered that he was exiled from Samos because of his obstinate adherence to the ancient ritual of the Goddess – the Samians having lately introduced new Olympian ritual which vexed his religious soul – and that, being aware that in Majorca the Goddess was worshipped with primitive innocence, he had asked the master of the vessel to set him ashore there.

'Indeed,' remarked the Nymph. 'Your story reminds me of a champion named Hercules, who visited our island many years ago when my mother was the Nymph of this grove. I cannot tell you the ins and outs of his story, because my mother was secretive about it in my childhood, but this much

I know: Hercules was being sent around the world by his overlord, King Eurystheus of Mycenae (wherever Mycenae may be), to perform a number of seemingly impossible Labours, and all because, so he said, of his obstinate devotion to the ancient ritual of the Goddess. He landed on the island from a canoe and announced with surprising boldness that he was come in the name of the Goddess to fetch a basketful of sacred oranges from this grove. He was a Lion man, which made him conspicuous in Majorca, where we have no Lion fraternity or sorority, and also gifted with colossal strength and a miraculous appetite alike for food, drink, and the pleasures of love. My mother took a fancy to him, and freely gave him the oranges, and also did him the honour of companying with him at the spring sowing. Have you ever heard tell of this Hercules?'

'I was once a shipmate of his, if you mean Hercules of Tiryns,' replied Ancaeus. 'That was when I sailed to the Stables of the Sun aboard the famous *Argo*, and I am sorry to tell you that the old rogue must have deceived your mother. He had no right to ask for the fruit in the name of the Goddess, who detested him.'

The Nymph was amused by his heat and assured him that she was now satisfied with his credentials: he might lift his eyes to her face and converse with her a trifle more familiarly, if he pleased. But she was careful not to put him formally under the protection of the Goddess. She asked him to what fraternity he belonged, and he answered that he was a Dolphin man.

'Ah,' said the Nymph. 'The very first time that I was initiated into nymph-hood and companied with men, in the open furrow of the field after the sowing, it was with nine Dolphin men. The first of my choice became Sun Champion, or War King, for the ensuing year, as is customary here. Our Dolphins are a small, very ancient fraternity, and distinguished for musical skill even above the Seals.'

'The dolphin is delightfully responsive to music,' Ancaeus agreed.

The Nymph continued: 'Yet, when I bore my child, it was not a girl, to be preserved, but a boy; and in due course back he went, torn in pieces, to the furrow from which he had sprung. The Goddess gave and the Goddess took away again. I have never since had the heart to company with a Dolphin man, judging that the society is an unlucky one for me. No male child of our family is permitted to live beyond the second sowing season.'

Ancaeus was bold enough to ask: 'Has no nymph or other priestess ever (since priestesses are so powerful in this island) smuggled away her own male child to a foster-mother and reared this mother's female child in his place, so that both might live?'

She answered severely: 'A trick of this sort may be practised in your island, Ancaeus, but not in ours. No woman here ever deceives the Triple Goddess.'

Ancaeus said: 'Indeed, Holy One, nobody can possibly deceive the Goddess.' But he asked again: 'Is it not perhaps your custom, if a royal nymph has an inordinate affection for her male child, to sacrifice a male calf or kid in his stead, swaddling it in infant's clothing and putting sandals on its feet? In my island it is supposed that the Goddess will turn a blind eye to the substitution and that the fields will yield no less abundantly. It is only after a bad season, when the corn is stunted or blighted, that a male child is sacrificed at the next sowing. And even so, he is a child of poor parents, not of the royal stock.'

The Nymph answered again in the same severe voice: 'Not in our island. No woman here ever trifles with the Triple Goddess. That is the reason why we prosper. Ours is the island of innocence and of calm.'

Ancaeus assented that it was by far the most pleasant island of all the hundreds that he had visited in his travels, his own island of Samos, called The Flowery Island, not excepted.

The Nymph then said: 'I am at leisure to hear a story, if it is not tedious. How is it that your cousins the Cretans have ceased to visit these islands as they once did, in my great-grandmother's time, conversing with us politely in a language which, though not our own, we could readily understand? Who are these Greeks, your overlords, who come in the same ships as the Cretans once used, and with the same goods for sale – vases and olive oil and dyes and jewels and linen and emery whetstones and fine bronze weapons – but use the Ram, not the Bull for their figure-heads and speak an unintelligible language, and bargain in a rude and threatening fashion, and leer shamelessly at the women and pilfer any small object that they find lying about? We are not eager to trade with them and often send them away empty-handed breaking their teeth with sling-shot and dinting their brazen helmets with large stones.'

Ancaeus explained that the mainland, to the north of Crete, which had once been known as Pelasgia, was now named Greece after its new overlords. It was inhabited by a remarkably mixed population. The most ancient people were the earthborn Pelasgians, said to have sprung from the scattered teeth of the Serpent Ophion when the Triple Goddess had torn him into shreds. To these were added, first, Cretan settlers from Cnosssos; next, Henetian settlers from Asia Minor, mixed with Aethiopians from Egypt, whose rich King Pelops gave his name to the southern part of the land, the Peloponnese, and who built cities with enormous stone walls, and white marble tombs in the bee-hive shape of African huts; lastly, the Greeks, a barbarous pastoral people from the north, beyond the river Danube, who came down by way of Thessaly, in three successive invasions, and eventually possessed themselves of all the strong Pelopian cities. These Greeks ruled the other peoples in an insolent and arbitrary manner. 'And alas, Holy One,' said Ancaeus, 'our overlords worship the Father God as their sovereign Deity and secretly despise the Triple Goddess.'

The Nymph wondered whether she had misheard his words. She asked: 'Who may the *Father God* be? How can any tribe worship a *Father*? What

are fathers but the occasional instruments that a woman uses for her pleasure and for the sake of becoming a mother?' She began to laugh contemptuously and cried: 'By the Benefactor, I swear that this is the most absurd
story that ever I heard. Fathers, indeed! I suppose that these Greek fathers
suckle the children and sow the barley and caprify the fig-trees and make
the laws and, in short, undertake all the other responsible tasks proper to
women?' She tapped impatiently with her foot on a stone and the hot blood
darkened her face.

When the Goat men observed this, each silently took a pebble from his
wallet and laid it in the leathern pocket of his sling. But Ancaeus answered
mildly and gently, casting down his eyes again. He remarked that there
were many strange customs in this world, and many tribes who seemed to
others to be insane. 'I should like to show you the Mosynoechians of the
Black Sea coast, Holy One,' he said, 'with their wooden castles and their
enormously fat tattooed boys, fed on chestnut cakes. They live next to the
Amazons, who are as queer as they... As for the Greeks, they argue as
follows: since women are dependent on men for their maternity – for the
wind alone will not quicken their wombs as it quickens those of Iberian
mares – men are consequently more important than they.'

'But that is an insane argument,' cried the Nymph. 'You might as well
pretend that this splinter of pine-wood is of more importance than myself,
because I employ it to pick my teeth. The woman, not the man, is always
the principal: she is the agent, he the tool always. She gives the orders, he
obeys. Is it not the woman who chooses the man, and overcomes him by
the sweetness of her perfumed presence and orders him to lie down in the
furrow on his back, and there riding upon him, as upon a wild horse tamed
to her will, takes her pleasure of him and, when she has done, leaves him
lying like a dead man? Is it not the woman who rules in the cave, and if any
of her lovers displeases her by his surly or lazy behaviour, gives him the
three times repeated warning to take up all his gear and begone to his
fraternity lodge?'

'With the Greeks,' said Ancaeus in a low, hurried voice, 'the custom is
exactly the contrary. Each man chooses the woman whom he wishes to
make the mother of his child (as he calls it) and overcomes her by the
strength of his desire, and orders her to lie upon her back wherever it may
suit him best, and then, mounting, takes his pleasure of her. In the house
he is the master, and if the woman vexes him by her nagging or lewd behaviour he beats her with his hand, and if that does not make her alter her ways
he packs her back to her father's house with all the gear that she has
brought and gives her children to a slave woman to rear for him. But, Holy
One, do not be angry, I charge you by the Goddess! I am a Pelasgian; I
detest the Greeks and their ways, and am dutifully obeying your instructions by answering these questions.'

The Nymph contented herself by saying that the Greeks must be the

most impious and disgusting people in the world, worse than African apes
– if Ancaeus were not indeed mocking her. She questioned him again
about the sowing of barley and the caprification of figs: how did the men
of the Greeks manage to obtain bread or figs without the intervention of
the Goddess?

He answered: 'Holy One, when the Greeks first arrived in Pelasgia they
were a pastoral people, living only on roast meat, cheese, milk, honey, and
wild salads. They therefore knew nothing of the ritual of planting barley
or of the cultivation of any fruits whatever.'

She asked, interrupting him: 'These insane Greeks, then (I suppose),
came down from the North without their own women, as sometimes the
drones, who are the idle fathers among the bees, make a sortie from the hive
and form a colony apart from their Queen and eat filth instead of honey?'

'No,' said Ancaeus, 'they brought their own women with them; but
these women were accustomed to what will seem to you a topsy-turvy and
indecent way of life. They tended the cattle, and were bought and sold by
the men as though they were themselves cattle.'

'I refuse to believe that men could ever buy and sell women,' cried the
Nymph. 'You have evidently been misinformed on this point. But did the
filthy Greeks continue long in this way of life, once they were settled in
Pelasgia?'

Ancaeus answered: 'The first two tribes of invaders, the Ionians and the
Aeolians, who were armed with bronze weapons, soon yielded to the might
of the Goddess when she consented to adopt their male gods as her sons.
They relinquished many of their barbarous ways. And when they were
presently persuaded to eat the bread baked by the Pelasgians, and when
they found that it had an agreeable taste and holy qualities, one of them,
named Triptolemus, asked leave of the Goddess to plant barley himself,
for he was confident that men could do so almost as successfully as women.
He said that he wished, if possible, to spare the women needless labour and
anxiety; and the Goddess indulgently consented.'

The Nymph laughed until the sides of the mountain re-echoed with the
noise, and the Goat men laughed sympathetically from their rock, rolling
about in merriment, though they had not the least idea why she laughed.
She said to Ancaeus: 'A fine crop indeed this Triptolemus must have
reaped – all poppy and henbane and thistle!'

Ancaeus was wise enough not to contradict her. He began to tell her
about the third tribe of Greeks, the iron-weaponed Achaeans, and of their
insolent bearing towards the Goddess and how they instituted the Divine
Family of Olympus; but he observed that she was not listening, and
desisted. She asked with a sneer: 'Come now, Ancaeus, tell me, how are
clans reckoned among the Greeks? You surely will not tell me that there
are male clans instead of female, with the generations reckoned through
the fathers rather than the mothers?'

Ancaeus nodded his head slowly, as though forced into admitting an absurdity by the shrewdness of the Nymph's cross-examination. 'Yes,' said he, 'since the coming of the iron-weaponed Achaeans, which happened many years ago, male clans have supplanted female clans in most parts of Greece. The Ionians and Aeolians had already introduced great innovations; the arrival of the Achaeans turned everything upside-down. The Ionians and the Aeolians had by then learned to reckon descent from the mother; but to the Achaeans paternity was, and is, the only consideration in tracing genealogy, and they have lately converted most of the Aeolians and some of the Ionians to their view.'

The Nymph cried: 'No, no, that is manifestly absurd. Though it is plain and indisputable, for example, that little Korë is my daughter forasmuch as the midwife drew her out of my body, how can it be known certainly who was her father? For the impregnation does not necessarily come from the first man whom I enjoy at our sacred orgies. It may come from the first or it may come from the ninth.'

'That uncertainty the Greeks attempt to dispel,' said Ancaeus, 'by each man choosing what he calls a wife – a woman who is forbidden to company with any but himself. Then, if she conceives, his own paternity is not to be disputed.'

The Nymph looked earnestly into Ancaeus's face and said: 'You have an answer for everything. But do you expect me to believe that women can be so ruled and watched and guarded as to be prevented from enjoying any man whom they please? Suppose that a young woman became wife to an old, ugly, or blemished man like yourself: How could she ever consent to company with him?'

Ancaeus, meeting her gaze, answered: 'The Greeks profess that they can so control their wives. But, I grant you, it often happens that they cannot, and that a woman secretly mates with a man to whom she is not wife. Then her husband is jealous and tries to kill both the wife and her lover, and if both the men are kings, their peoples are drawn into war and great bloodshed ensues.'

'That I can well imagine,' said the Nymph. 'They should not tell lies in the first place, nor afterwards undertake more than they can perform, and so give themselves occasion for jealousy. I have often noticed that men are absurdly jealous: indeed, next to their dishonesty and talkativeness, it appears to be their chief characteristic. But tell me, what happened to the Cretans?'

'They were overthrown by Theseus the Greek, who was helped to victory by one Daedalus, a famous craftsman and inventor,' said Ancaeus.

'What did he invent?' asked the Nymph.

'Among other things,' Ancaeus replied, 'he constructed brazen bulls that bellowed artificially when a fire was lighted beneath their bellies; also, lifelike wooden statues of the Goddess, the jointed limbs of which could be moved in any direction, so that it seemed a miracle – and what was more, the eyes could be made to open and shut by the pulling of a concealed cord.'

'Is this Daedalus still living?' asked the Nymph. 'I should like to make his acquaintance.'

'Alas, no,' replied Ancaeus. 'All these events happened long before my time.

She pressed him: 'Yet can you tell me how the joints of the statues were constructed, so that the limbs could be moved in any direction whatsoever?'

'Doubtless they rolled in ball-sockets,' he said, doubling his right fist and rolling it in the clasp of the fingers of his left hand, so that she readily understood his meaning. 'For Daedalus invented the ball-socket. At all events, it was by means of a Daedalian invention that the navy of the Cretans was destroyed, so that they no longer visit your island, but only the Greeks and a few chance Pelasgians and Thracians and Phrygians.'

'I heard from my mother's mother,' said the Nymph, 'that though the Cretans worshipped the Goddess almost as reverently as ourselves, they differed from us in many religious particulars. For example, the Chief Priestess did not choose a Sun Champion for one year only. The man she chose reigned sometimes for nine years or more, refusing to resign his office, on the ground that experience brings sagacity. He was called the Priest of Minos, or the Bull King. For the Bull fraternity had become supreme on the island: the Stag men and Horse men and Ram men and such-like never dared to contend for the war-kingship, and the Chief Priestess companied only with Bull men. Here my mother and I distribute our favours evenly among all the fraternities. It is not wise to let any one fraternity secure the supremacy, nor to let a king reign beyond two or three years at the utmost: men have a great capacity for insolence if they are not kept in their proper place, and fancy themselves to be almost the equals of women. By insolence they destroy themselves and cause vexation to the women into the bargain. I do not doubt but that the same happened in Crete.'

Still conversing, she secretly signed to the Goat men that they should take Ancaeus and lead him away from her sight, and then hunt him to death with their slings. For she decided that a man who could relate such disturbing and indecent stories must not be allowed to remain alive on the island, even for a short time longer, now that he had told her what she wished to know about the principle of jointing the wooden statues. She feared what mischief he might do by unsettling the minds of the men. Besides, he was a bent, bald, ugly old fellow, an exile, and a Dolphin man, who would bring no luck to the grove.

The Goat men prostrated themselves in reverence before the Orange Nymph and then, rising up, obeyed her command with joy. The chase was not a long one.

CHAPTER ONE

THE PARCHING OF THE BARLEY

When the first body of invading Greeks, the Ionian tribe, moving down from the upper reaches of the Danube through Istria and Illyria, passed at last into Thessaly, all the natives, such as Satyrs, Lapiths, Aethics, Phlegyans and Centaurs, withdrew into their mountain fastnesses. The invaders, who were very numerous, brought their own gods with them and all the sacred instruments of worship. The Centaurs, the aboriginal inhabitants of Mount Pelion, watched them move slowly with their flocks and herds into the plain of Pagasae, far below to the west, where they remained for a few days; but then, lured by reports of yet richer pasturage to the southward, the Ionians resumed their journey towards the fortress of Phthia and passed out of sight. At Iolcos, near the foot of Pelion, stood an ancient college of Fish nymphs whose Chief Priestess legislated in sacred matters for the whole of Phthiotis. They did not run off at the approach of the Ionians but made Gorgon grimaces at them, sticking out their tongues and hissing; the Ionians prudently passed on into Boeotia.

The Ionians found a hospitable race living in Pelasgia, as Greece was then called: of native Pelasgians mixed with Henetian and Cretan and Egyptian settlers, all of whom worshipped the Triple Moon Goddess under one name or another. Envoys, sent out from Mycenae, Argos, Tiryns, and the other cities to the venerable shrine of the Goddess at Olympia, were instructed by her to make the Ionians welcome, but on the strict condition that they respected the religious customs prevailing in her dominions. The Ionians were impressed by the civility and firm bearing of the envoys and by the colossal walls of the cities from which they had been sent out. Loth to return to Thessaly, yet despairing of conquest, they prudently allowed their gods to make submission to the Goddess and to become her sons by adoption. The first Ionian chieftain to urge this submission was named Minyas, whom the Goddess thereafter favoured beyond all others; his father, Chryses, had founded the settlement of Aeaea, on the island of that name opposite to Pola, at the head of the Adriatic Sea. When Minyas died, the Goddess awarded him the title of hero and instructed fifty nymphs to tend his great white shrine at the Boeotian city of Orchomenos, beside Lake Copaïs, and to legislate in sacred matters for the whole countryside. These nymphs did not marry but took lovers on days of festival, in the Pelasgian style. Cecrops the Egyptian had already brought the institution of marriage into Attica, and the Goddess had condoned the innovation only so long as it should be practised without disrespect to herself or injury to her Pelasgian people; the Ionians practised marriage too, but finding that the most honourable of the natives considered the custom indecent, most of them discontinued it from shame.

Presently followed another Greek invasion, this time by the Aeolian tribe, who were more vigorous than the Ionians, and came by way of Thrace. They passed Iolcos by, as the Ionians had done, but seized the Boeotian city of Orchomenos, which they found unguarded at a time of festival. Their chieftains won the right to be considered the military guardians of the land by persuading the nymphs of the shrine of Minyas to accept them as husbands; and thereafter called themselves Minyans. They became the aristocracy of that part of eastern Greece, but were unable to press into Attica or the Peloponnese because the strong city of Cadmean Thebes barred their passage. Aeolus, their great ancestor, was also awarded the title of hero, and from the Thracian cave, or cleft in the earth, in which his bones were buried would graciously send out snake-tailed winds at the request of his visitants. This power over the winds was delegated to him by the Triple Goddess.

When Theseus, King of Ionian Athens, had secretly built a fleet and sacked Cnossos in Crete, the Minyans also took to the sea. They fitted out a hundred ships or more, which they drew up near Aulis on the protected beaches of the Euboean Gulf. Theseus, rather than engage them in a naval war, made a treaty with them by which the two states peaceably shared the carrying trade that had been wrested from the Cretans and took joint action against pirates. The Athenians traded with the south and the east – with the cities of Egypt, Africa, Phoenicia and Asia Minor, and with Phrygian Troy, the prime market of the far east; the Minyans traded with Thessaly and Thrace in the north, and with Sicily, Corfu, Italy, and Gaul in the west. For convenience of their western trade the Minyans stationed a part of their fleet at Sandy Pylos, a possession of theirs on the western side of the Peloponnese, and by this means avoided the difficult circuit of Cape Malea. The winds supplied by Aeolus, which the nymphs who tended his shrine had the art of confining in pigs' bladders, were of great service to the masters of the Minyan ships.

The Minyans grew rich, and were not at first disturbed in the enjoyment of their kingdom, chiefly because they did as much as possible to please the Goddess. Their Sky God, Dios, whom they worshipped on Mount Laphystios in the form of a ram, they publicly acknowledged to be the son of the Mother Goddess. She therefore renamed him Zagreus, or Zeus, after the child whom, it was said, she used to bear every year, as a proof of her fertility, in the Dictean Cave of Crete, but who was yearly sacrificed for the good of the land. This sacrifice was now discontinued and Zeus enjoyed the privileges of adult godhead. Though in some matters he was granted precedence of the Nymph Goddess and the Maiden Goddess, her daughters, the Mother Goddess remained the sovereign Deity.

The next event in the history of the Minyans, as it concerns this Argonautic story, was that they extended their kingdom to the Pagasaean Gulf and as far northward as Larisa in Thessaly. A haughty Minyan King named Athamas invited Ino, the Chief Priestess of the college at Iolcos, to celebrate a marriage with him, and her nymphs a simultaneous marriage with his chieftains. Ino could not well refuse to marry Athamas, a tall, fine, yellow-haired man, because he brought great gifts for her and the other women, and because the Minyans were more numerous and better armed than her own people of Phthiotis. Yet if she consented to the marriage this would be an infringement of the rights of the Centaurs of Pelion: the Centaurs of the Horse fraternity had always been the chosen lovers of the Fish nymphs of Iolcos, just as the Centaur College of Wryneck nymphs who tended the shrine of the hero Ixion took lovers only from the Leopard fraternity of the Magnesians. Ino consulted the Goddess, asking whether she and her nymphs should destroy their husbands on the bridal night, as the Danaids of Argos had done long before in similar circumstances, or whether they should destroy themselves by leaping into the sea, as the Pallantids of Athens had done. Or what other orders had the Goddess to give? The Goddess answered in a dream: 'Pour unmixed wine to the Horse men and leave the rest to my contrivance.'

The marriage was celebrated with great splendour, and upon Ino's insistence the Horse men were invited down from their mountain caves to join in the festivities. When they arrived, brimming cups of Lemnian wine were dispensed to them. The Centaurs honour a Thessalian hero, named Sabazius, as the inventor of barley-ale, their ritual drink, which causes great jollity at first and then sends the worshippers fast asleep. They now assumed this unfamiliar liquor, wine, to be a sort of ale, seeing that it was of a pale golden colour, though of a sharper scent than ale and not needing to be drunk through straws, as they drank ale, since it had no mash floating thickly about in it. They tossed the wine off unsuspectingly, crying out 'Io Sabazius, Io, Io!'; found that it tasted sweet and called for more. But instead of sending them to sleep the wine presently inflamed them, so that they bucked about uncontrollably, rolling their eyes and whinnying for lust. The Fish nymphs felt the pangs of pity, and suddenly quitting the sober Minyans, who had mixed their wine with four parts of water, darted out into the woods and there companied with the Centaurs in love.

This capricious behaviour vexed the Minyan husbands, who pursued their wives and killed a dozen Centaurs with their bronze swords. The next day Athamas led an attack on the Centaurs' mountain fastness. They withstood him as best they could with their pine-wood spears and with boulders sent toppling down the mountain-side; but he defeated and drove them away to the northward. To discourage their return he removed from her shrine the mare-headed image of the White Goddess and, taking it down to Iolcos to the Fish College, daringly rededicated the shrine on Pelion to Zeus the Ram, or Rain-Making Zeus. For a time he broke the spirit of the Centaurs; but Ino, by the hand of one of her nymphs, secretly conveyed the mare-headed image to a cave in a wooded valley half-way to Mount Ossa, where the Centaurs reassembled and prayed to her for revenge.

King Athamas was unaware that Ino had restored the image to the Centaurs; otherwise he would have addressed her even more insolently than he did. 'Wife,' he said, 'I have banished your horsey lovers from Mount Pelion, because they profaned our bridal night. If any of them, seeking out the image of the Goddess, dares to descend again into the meadows of Iolcos he will be destroyed without pity. Mount Pelion has now become the abode of our Aeolian God, Zeus; it is worthier of him than Mount Laphystios, which by comparison is inconsiderable in height.'

'Be careful what you say, husband,' replied Ino, 'if husband I must call you. How will the Goddess regard your driving her down from Pelion? And how do you suppose that the barley will grow, if the Horse men are not present at the sowing festival to company with me and my Fish women in the sight of the White Goddess?'

Athamas laughed and replied: 'The Goddess will not grudge Pelion to her son. And now that each of your women has a husband from among my followers, and you have me, what more can you desire? We are all tall, sturdy men, immeasurably superior in every way to those mad and naked Centaurs; and we shall be pleased to company with you in the fields at the sowing festival if the itch customarily takes you at that season.'

Ino asked: 'Are you so ignorant as to believe that our Goddess will allow us to accept the embraces of your Ram men on so holy an occasion as that? She will never bless the barley if we do so. No, no! We are content to be your wives for the better part of the year, but if our affairs are to prosper we must company not only with the Centaurs in the sowing season, but with the visiting Satyr Goat men at the ceremony of caprification, when we ripen the figs by the stinging of the gall-insect; and with lovers from other fraternities upon such appropriate occasions as may from time to time be revealed to me by the Goddess.'

Athamas answered: 'Are you so ignorant as to believe that any right-minded Greek would allow his wife to enjoy the embraces of another man, either at the sowing festival or at any other? Your chatter is nonsensical. Figs ripen by themselves without artificial aid, as may be observed in deserted orchards where the ceremony has been omitted. And what need of women have we Minyans, even for the sowing of our barley? The hero

Triptolemus demonstrated that men can sow barley as successfully as women.'

'He did so by gracious permission of the Goddess,' said Ino, 'whose luminary, the Moon, is the power that makes all seeds grow and all fruits ripen.'

'It was unnecessary to ask her permission,' said Athamas. 'The Goddess has no true power over grain or fruits of any sort. All that is necessary is that the barley-corns should be planted carefully while the strength of the sun is languishing, in the furrows of a well-ploughed field, and then harrowed over with a thorn-harrow, and then rained upon in due season. Zeus will supply the rain at my intercession and the revived Sun will genially ripen the ears. The Moon is cold and dead: she has no creative virtue at all.'

'And what of the holy dew?' asked Ino. 'I suppose that the dew is also a gift of the Sun?'

'At least it is no gift of the Moon,' he answered, 'who often does not rise before the grass is hoary with dew.'

'I wonder,' said Ino, 'that you dare speak in this way of the Goddess; as I wonder that without asking my leave you have removed her venerable white image from its shrine and replaced it with the image of her adopted son. A terrible fate is in store for you, Athamas, if you do not mend your ways before another day passes and do not approach the Goddess as a peni-tent. If the sowing of Triptolemus was rewarded with a good harvest, you may be sure that this was because he had first gained the Goddess's favour by his humility, and because he did not omit any of the usual love-cere-monies at the sowing. Besides, it is untrue that figs ripen in deserted orchards without caprification. There is a complete register of fig-trees in this country, and each tree is tended by one of my nymphs, however lonely or remote its place of growth may be.

'I am not accustomed to be ruled by women,' Athamas answered passionately. 'My Boeotian wife, Nephele, who waits for me at Orchomenos, has learned by experience to avoid my displeasure and to busy herself with her own affairs, leaving me to mine. I would be a fool indeed if I visited the shrine where you are Chief Priestess, and asked you (of all women) to intercede with her for my pardon.'

Ino pretended to be overawed by Athamas's male violence. Caressing his head and stroking his beard, she cried: 'Forgive me, husband, for confessing my religious scruples. I will obey you in all things. But grant me this, that your followers will themselves sow the barley, in the manner of Triptolemus, without the help of my women. We all fear the anger of our Goddess if we plant the barley without the customary fertility rites, for which the loving company of the Centaurs seems to us essential.'

She thus placated Athamas. He had insufficient respect for the Goddess and trusted rather in the power of Zeus, who in his former name of Dios had been the chief deity of his tribe when first they came down into Thessaly. To the newly dedicated shrine of Rain-Making Zeus on Pelion he transferred a particularly holy object from Mount Laphystios. This was the figure of the Ram God, carved from an oak root, over which was hooked a great ram's fleece, dyed with sea-purple to match the colour of those rain-clouds which it could magically conjure up even at the height of summer. Because of the saying 'rain is gold,' and also because of the golden pollen which colours the fleeces of the sheep on Ida, where Zeus is said to have been reared by shepherds, a precious fringe had been sewn along the edges of the fleece, of thinly drawn gold wire arranged in locks like wool, so that it became known as the Golden Fleece. Huge, curling golden horns were attached to the head of the Fleece, which fitted over the wooden stump of the image's head. This Golden Fleece was wonderful to look at, and never failed to draw down rain, whenever the appropriate sacrifice was made to the God. The priests declared that Zeus levitated the image on such occasions: it rose they said, on the smoke of the sacrifice through the smoke-hole in the roof of the shrine, and presently descended again, wringing wet with the first drops of rain.

At Iolcos the harvest was brought in and the season of autumn sowing approached. Ino waited for a sign from the White Goddess, who presently appeared again to her in a dream and said: 'Ino, you have done well, but you shall do better. Take all the seed-barley from the jars where it is stored in my sacred precinct, and secretly distribute it among the women of Phthiotis. Order them to parch it in front of their domestic fires, each of them two or three harvest-baskets full, but not to let any of the men know what is being done, under pain of my deathly displeasure.'

Ino in the dream trembled and asked: 'Mother, can you ask me to do this? Will not the fire destroy the life in the sacred seed?'

The Goddess replied: 'Do it, nevertheless. At the same time poison the water of the Minyan sheep-troughs with agaric and spotted hemlock. My son Zeus has robbed me of my home on Pelion and I will punish him by destroying his herds.'

Ino obeyed the Goddess faithfully, though with some disquiet of heart. The women carried out the tasks assigned to them, and not unwillingly, because they hated their Minyan conquerors. The Minyans did not suspect, when their sheep died, that it was these women who had poisoned them, but complained among themselves against Athamas. Since their law forbade the eating of any beast that had died except by ritual slaughter, they were forced to eat more bread than was their custom, and whatever game they could hunt down in the forests; but they did not excel in hunting.

Ino said to Athamas: 'I hope, husband, that you will have good luck with your sowing. Here is the barley-seed, stored in these jars. Look and smell how excellently dry it is: mildewed seed, as perhaps you know, does not raise plentiful crops.'

The moon was on the wane; yet Minyan men, with Athamas at their head, sowed the seed in the furrows of ploughed earth. They did so without any ceremony or prayer, while Ino's nymphs watched from a distance and laughed silently together. It happened to be an unusually dry season, and when the barley did not show green above the soil at the expected time, Athamas with a few companions ascended the mountain, and invoked Rain-Making Zeus. This they did with rain-rattles and bull-roarers, and with the sacrifice of a black ram, burning the sacred thigh-bones rolled in fat and merrily eating every morsel of the carcase.

That same evening a pleasant shower of rain fell. 'It will bring up the barley, wife, never fear,' said Athamas to Ino.

Ten days went by and still there was no glint of green in the fields. Ino told Athamas: 'The shower which Zeus sent was insufficient. It did not sink far enough into the soil. You planted the seed too deep, I fear. You must invoke Zeus again; and why not send to the Thracian shrine of your ancestor Aeolus for a few puffs of the rain-bringing northeastern wind?'

Athamas, growing anxious, again ascended Pelion. This time he propitiated the God with a sacrifice of fifty white rams and one black one, burning them to cinders on pine-wood bonfires, and not himself eating anything, to demonstrate his humility of heart; he whirled the bull-roarer and rattled the rain-gourd until his arms ached. Zeus that night duly thundered and lightened, and a deluge of rain fell, so that Athamas and his people were nearly smothered by it on their return to Iolcos. The Anauros brook rose in a sudden flood and washed away the foot-bridge by which they had crossed, so that they had to wait for the waters to subside before they could regain the city.

A week later the fields, though thick with weeds which the rain brought up, did not show a single barley-blade. Ino said to Athamas: 'Since you have persuaded me that the omission of the fertility rites of which I spoke cannot have caused a failure of the crops, I must conclude that Zeus has sent the wrong sort of rain. If by the next new moon no barley is showing, some of us must die of starvation. It is too late to sow another crop, most of your flocks are dead, and your men have made greedy inroads on our stores of grain. As for the fish, they have all deserted the gulf since the arrival of your Minyans, as was only to be expected: they regard our College as desecrated.'

At Ino's instigation her nymphs, who had pretended the greatest reverence for their husbands, now prompted them to demand from Athamas the performance of a third and final sacrifice. For the Minyans believed that if Zeus were unwilling to send rain when offered a single ram, or even when offered fifty, this was a sign that he greedily demanded something better still – the sacrifice of the Ram Priest's own children. The husbands agreed with the women that this sacrifice must now be made, and they came in a crowd to Athamas one day as he stood gloomily poking his staff into the unfruitful earth of a barley-field. The eldest among them said: 'Athamas, we pity you, but we call on you to perform your duty without flinching. Sacrifice your son Phrixus and your daughter Helle to Father Zeus, and the divine rain that must then fall will awaken the barley-seed and save our lives.'

At first Athamas refused to listen to them. When they threatened him with violence he agreed to sacrifice the children only if the Oracle at Delphi so ordered; Delphi then being for the Greeks the chief court of appeal in sacred matters. The Oracle was managed by a priestess of the White Goddess; originally she had received oracular inspiration from a sacred python, the ghost of the dead hero Dionysus, who was in the Goddess's closest confidence and whose navel-string and jaw-bone were laid on a table in his shrine behind a hedge of spears. But this python, when the Greeks first came down from Thessaly, was said to have made some slighting remarks about their new God, Apollo the Archer. Apollo, formerly a Mouse demon from the island of Delos, with the power of raising and allaying pestilence, had been taken as a god by Henetian colonists to Tempe in Thessaly, where the Aeolians were saved from plague by him. The archers of Apollo, when they heard that Dionysus had denied their God's divinity and had asserted 'I will swallow down that little mouse', marched furiously to Delphi from their valley home in Tempe, entered the enclosure of Dionysus and knocked three times on the door of the round white tomb. Out darted the python in a rage and the archers transfixed it with arrows. They then burned the navel-string and jaw-bone of Dionysus on a fire made of the sacred spear-shafts; and fled back to Tempe. To expiate his crime, Apollo consented, though unwillingly, to become bondman to the White Goddess and, entering the empty tomb at Delphi, to undertake the work formerly done by Dionysus; and he founded the Pythian Games in memory of the python. It was no longer, therefore, from the serpent's intelligent writhings that the priestess read and disclosed the past or future, though she was still known as the Pythoness. Instead, she chewed leaves of laurel, the tree sacred to Apollo, which induced in her a prophetic intoxication. Shiploads of young laurel trees from Tempe were brought to Delphi and planted about the shrine so that presently their branches met and formed a dense shade. The place was still named Pytho, or the Navel Sanctuary, but Apollo's priests explained that it had its name from the central position that it occupied in Greece; the memory of Dionysus lapsed, and was not revived for a long time.

Athamas expected a favourable reply from the Pythoness, because, as he said, 'Apollo will sympathize with me in my predicament: he will understand that the Goddess is the cause of my trouble – she refuses obstinately to let the seed grow. Despite his pretended loyalty to her, he will find some means of absolving me from my cruel obligations; he owes much to us Aeolians. Why should I sacrifice my children to Zeus merely because his Mother is behaving with her usual female perversity?'

Ino sent to Delphi too, by the hand of a Boeotian shepherd who knew the shortest tracks across the rugged mountains and thorny valleys, and warned the Pythoness that Athamas had not only behaved very disrespectfully to the Goddess, to whom both Apollo and she owed allegiance, but had refused to placate Zeus in the customary way, and that his obstinacy threatened to bring boundless misery on his own tribe and on the Centaurs too. Therefore when Athamas arrived and tried to propitiate Apollo with the offering of a golden tripod, the Pythoness refused it; she ordered him to sacrifice his two children on Mount Pelion to Rain-Making Zeus, and without delay.

By the same shepherd, her emissary, Ino was informed of Apollo's answer in good time, four or five days before her husband's return.

CHAPTER TWO

THE LOSS OF THE FLEECE

Ino sent for Helle, and warned her that Athamas intended to take her life. 'Daughter,' she asked, 'how do you like this? Why should your father barbarously sacrifice you and your dear brother Phrixus, in the bloom of life, merely because Apollo so orders it? Apollo is an intruder on Mount Parnassus, a Delian waif who was picked up by your tribe in an unlucky hour long after the decease of your great ancestor Aeolus. Not one trustworthy oracle has come from the Navel Shrine since the python of Dionysus was impiously killed by him. Apollo is not in the Goddess's confidence, as he pretends to be, and gives out guesses and equivocations instead of the truth.'

Helle, trembling and weeping, answered: 'Apollo fears Zeus, and so do my brother Phrixus and myself. Die we must, Holy One.'

Ino answered: 'If the sacrifice were necessary, why did not Zeus himself order it? Consider, Daughter, how your father came to make this cruel decision. First, he insulted the White Goddess, who is the Sovereign Deity alike of Phthiotis and Magnesia, by trying to deprive my Iolcan Fish nymphs of their sacred autumn tryst with the Centaur Horse men. She was naturally vexed and put it into the hearts of the Horse men to disturb the wedding that he and his Minyans forced upon us. In revenge, your father cast her roughly out of her shrine, which he rededicated to her greedy son Zeus. This was to meddle in divine matters, which no mortal has any right to do. The Goddess was then more vexed than ever and began poisoning his flocks, and when all love-ceremonies were omitted at the sowing of barley she refrained from fertilizing the seed, so that no amount of rain that Zeus may send will ever make it grow. Zeus himself has not commanded this cruel sacrifice of Phrixus and yourself; for it is not his wrath that starves the fields, but his Mother's.'

'Yet Apollo has commanded it,' said Helle, sobbing.

Ino answered: 'Apollo has always been a trouble-maker. He commands the sacrifice in the hope of making Zeus a laughing-stock for our tribe and yours: he knows that though a whole hecatomb of girls and boys may be sacrificed on the rugged shoulder of Pelion, not one blade of barley will sprout until your father has humbled himself before the Goddess and restored the ancient purity of her worship.' And Ino added, using an ancient formula: 'It is not my word, but my Mother's word.'

Though Helle would have gone to the death-trench without a thought of disobedience had Zeus so ordered it, yet Ino's review of the matter encouraged her to hope that her fate might somehow be averted. She sought out Phrixus, whom the news of the impending sacrifice had stunned into a miserable apathy. He had never disobeyed his father in the least thing, and held Zeus in the profoundest awe: whenever there was thunder and lightning on the hills, he would stop his ears with beeswax, and bandage his eyes with a linen cloth, and creep away under a pile of blankets until his servants assured him that the sky was clear again. But Helle asked him privately: 'Brother, why should we consent to give up our lives in this senseless fashion? Or why, because our father Athamas has committed sacrilege, should we be made the instruments of embittering the ill-feeling already existing among the Immortal Gods?'

Phrixus, pale and thin from fasting, replied: 'Who are we to question our fate? We can do nothing but submit.'

Helle smiled and stroked his cheeks. She told him: 'Fasting has weakened your resolution. Our loving stepmother Ino will find us a legitimate means of escape.' So insistent was Helle that at last Phrixus consented to be guided by her, and thus saved his life.

Ino further reasoned with them both that neither had Zeus ordered the sacrifice nor had Athamas wished to perform it. 'Nor yet,' said she, 'has either of you been warned by your father himself of his intention. Nothing would please him better, when he returns from Delphi, travelling as slowly as possible, than to find you both gone: for with all his faults he is a most affectionate father, as I am bound to admit.'

'But where are we to flee?' asked Phrixus. 'Our father Athamas is a man of importance in Greece, and wherever we go he will certainly fetch us back. He must obey the Oracle of Delphi, whether he likes it or not; and if we take refuge at Athens, or Thebes, or Argos, the city governors will voluntarily send us back to Iolcos as soon as they hear that Apollo has demanded our deaths.'

'Greece is not the whole world,' said Ino. 'The power neither of Apollo nor of Zeus extends beyond Greece and its colonies. The Triple Goddess alone has universal power. If you consent to put yourself under her protection, she will find a safe and pleasant home for you beyond the seas. But, children, you must hasten your decision, for your father, however slowly he may travel, must already be well on his way home.

It happened that Nephele, the Boeotian wife of Athamas, arrived at Iolcos that very day, on a visit to her children Phrixus and Helle. Ino treated her with exemplary courtesy, and by feigning solicitude for the fate of the children, convinced her that they should throw themselves on the mercy of the Goddess and obey her divine orders implicitly, whatever they might be. Nephele mistrusted the genuineness of the Delphic Oracle and agreed that the Goddess, though slighted by Athamas, might pity his children if they approached her piously. Ino tempted her into coming with the Fish nymphs on their next moonlight orgy over Pelion. Nephele wreathed her head with an ivy garland, took a fir-cone wand in her hand and, clad only in a fawn-skin, went raging across the mountain-side with the rest of the rout, doing great things. Her feet seemed to be furnished with wings, and never in all her life had she experienced such holy rapture. Athamas had slighted her by his marriage with Ino, and this was her revenge; for she found among the Centaurs several more attentive lovers than he.

Between them, Ino, Nephele, and Helle overcame the religious scruples of Phrixus. One man, unless he resorts to violence, cannot long resist the reiterated arguments of three women. That evening he and Helle ritually purified themselves, and Ino gave them an infusion of sacred herbs which caused them to sleep; and in their sleep a voice, which they took for the Goddess's own, offered them their lives on condition that they obeyed certain orders. When they awoke, each reported to the other what the voice had said, and the two messages tallied exactly. These were the words:

'Children of Athamas, why should you die for your father's sin? It is I alone who have blasted the barley-fields and made them barren. No rain, no sun, no dew can restore them to fertility. I am offended by the intrusion of my son Zeus into my ancient sanctuary on Mount Pelion, and by the removal of my mare-headed image. I am the Triple Mother of Life, the mistress of all the Elements, the original Being, the Sovereign of Light and Darkness, the Queen of the Dead, to whom no God is not subject. I rule the starry skies, the boisterous green seas, the many-coloured earth with all its peoples, the dark subterrene caves. I have names innumerable. In Phrygia I am Cybele; in Phoenicia, Ashtaroth; in Egypt, Isis; in Cyprus, the Cyprian Queen; in Sicily, Proserpina; in Crete, Rhea; in Athens, Pallas and Athena; among the pious Hyperboreans, Samothea; Anu among their dusky serfs. Others name me Diana, Agdistis, Marianaë, Dindymene, Hera, Juno, Musa, Hecate. And in the Stables of the Sun in Colchis, at the further end of the Black Sea, under the shadow of the towering Caucasus, where I propose to send you, I am named "The Bird-headed Mother" or "Brimo", or "The Ineffable". It is I who have inspired the sentence of the Delphic Oracle. Your mother does wrong to doubt its authenticity; but it is uttered with the intention of bringing ruin upon your father rather than upon yourselves.

'Tonight you must both climb together in the moonlight up the steep path which winds to the shoulder of Pelion, until you come to my sacred enclosure. Phrixus shall enter first, wearing the ritual mask of a horse, and finding the guardians of the shrine asleep he shall cry without fear: "In the name of the Mother!" He shall then unhook the sacred Fleece from the Ram's image and wrap it in a dark-coloured blanket and go out. Next Helle shall enter, wearing a similar mask and, finding the blanket but not unwrapping it, shall convey it out of the shrine. Then both of you shall re-enter and together drag out the guardians by their feet and daub their hair with horse-dung and leave them lying outside the enclosure. Then you shall return together and take out the naked image itself and lay it upside-down, with its trotters in the air, between the sleeping guardians. Next, you shall spill a skinful of wine over the image, and cover it with your cloaks. Then, standing apart, you shall watch my mare-headed image restored to the shrine, in a solemn procession of my Centaur people, with waving of torches, with pipe and drum. When the door of the shrine is shut, you shall return in haste to Iolcos, carrying the Fleece by turns.

'Outside the gate, a messenger with a white wand will meet you and you shall say to him no more than this: "In the name of the Mother!" He will conduct you both to the sandy beach of Pagasae, where the ship-yard is, and put you aboard a Corinthian galley which is bound for the City of Cyzicus by the Sea of Marmora. You must preserve a holy silence throughout the voyage, and when you are within a day's sail of my holy island, Samothrace, Phrixus shall hook the glittering Fleece across the bows of the ship. From Cyzicus you shall go by land to the kingdom of the Mariandynians on the southern coast of the Black Sea, and there demand, in my name, a sea passage to Colchis. When you are at last set ashore at Colchian Aea you shall together present the Fleece to Aeëtes the Colchian King and say to him: "A gift from the Mother, the Ineffable. Guard it well." Your lives will thereafter be free and happy so long as you continue to be my servants. If Aeëtes by any chance fears the wrath of Zeus and asks you: "Did you steal the Fleece from the shrine of Zeus?" you, Phrixus, shall answer, "By the power of the Goddess, I swear that I did not steal the Fleece out of the shrine, nor did I prevail on anyone else to do so for me." And you, Helle, shall answer, "By the power of the Goddess, I swear that I never so much as saw the Fleece until we came within a day's sail of Samothrace." Thus by telling the exact truth you shall yet deceive him.'

These instructions Phrixus and Helle unswervingly obeyed, though not without fear and heart-searching. It was Cheiron the wise Centaur, son of Philara the priestess of the oracular shrine of Ixion, who led the triumphal procession of the returning Goddess. Afterwards, concealed among the rocks, he watched the drugged guardians awake and saw the horror on their faces when they found the Ram God lying naked and drunken between them on the stony bed outside the enclosure. They hastily sprang up, fetched water and washed the image clean. They dried it with their own garments and were for bringing it back again to the shrine; but there the Mare-headed Goddess sat in her old place and a neighing voice came from her mouth: 'Guardians,' she said, 'take away my drunken Son, and let him not return until he is clothed and sober.' The priests abased them-selves before her in terror, ran off groaning and between them brought the image down to Iolcos on a rough litter of pine branches, covered. with their cloaks. There they explained to the Minyan chieftains that the God had invited them to drink wine with him, which they had at first refused, since he customarily drank only water, or water mixed with honey; but that he had overcome them by his importunity. They remembered no more until they found themselves lying with him in one bed, their heads aching and wine soaking their garments.

There was a hue-and-cry after the Fleece, even before Athamas returned. When it was known that Phrixus and Helle had disappeared at about the same time, it was rumoured that, going up the mountain to worship the God (for a shepherd had seen them setting out along the path), they had come upon the Fleece lying on the ground where the God had discarded it in his drunkenness, and had thought to restore it to the shrine; but that there they had received orders from the Goddess to dispose of it in some other way.

A further rumour that they had been seen making their way northward in the direction of Mount Ossa was put about by Ino to set the pursuers on a false scent. The truth was that Phrixus and Helle, coming down the mountain with the Fleece just as the moon set, and avoiding discovery, had met the man with the white wand. He had guided them to Pagasae, and there put them into the Corinthian ship, which was to sail at dawn. The master had welcomed them in the name of the Goddess, and they kept a holy silence; and on the third day, as they coasted by the headland of Actaean Athos with a favouring wind, Phrixus took the Golden Fleece from the dark blanket in which it was wrapped and hooked it across the bows, to the amazement of the master and the crew.

Then they sailed on and entered the narrow strait, once called the Dardanian Strait, which leads from the Aegean Sea into that of Marmora. It was a windless day, and they were rowing with all their might against a strong current, which nevertheless pressed the ship back. Here Helle, seated in the bows, forgot her instructions. She leaped to her feet and, breaking silence, cried out: 'O Phrixus, Phrixus, we are lost!' For she saw that the ship was heading directly for the Dardanian rocks. A sudden flaw of wind struck the ship, heeled her over and bellied out the sail; they were saved from the rocks and sailed on. But Helle was flung overboard by the sudden tossing of the ship and carried off by the tide beyond hope of rescue, and drowned. The strait is called by the Greeks the Hellespont, or the water of Helle, to this day.

Phrixus by a closer observance of the Goddess's desires reached Colchis in safety, presented the Fleece to King Aeëtes, and answered his questions in the manner prescribed. Aeëtes suspended the Fleece from a cypress-tree in a sacred enclosure, the home of an immense oracular python. In this python resided the spirit of the ancient Cretan hero Prometheus, who is said to have first discovered and explained to mankind how to make fire by

the moon-wise twirling of a fire-wheel, or fire-drill, and thus to have originated the arts of pottery, metallurgy and the rest, besides becoming the
first cook and the first baker. He was held in high esteem in Attica and
Phocis; but his navel-string and jaw-bone and other wonder-working relics
had been for many years laid up at Corinthian Ephyra, from where his
descendant Aeëtes removed them when he emigrated to Colchis. There
was a long-standing dispute between the worshippers of Zeus and the
worshippers of Prometheus; for the lightning of Zeus was held by the
Greeks to be the original source of fire, and the priests at Dodona accused
Prometheus of having stolen a spark of it from one of the other sanctuaries
of Zeus, and put it to smoulder unseen in the pith of a fennel-stalk. And
indeed there is a sort of giant fennel, as tall as a man, in the dried stalk of
which a spark can be carried for a mile or more and afterwards blown to a
flame with the mouth. Whichever story was true, the committing of the
Golden Fleece of Zeus to the charge of Cretan Prometheus was a further
sign of the White Goddess's implacable mood. But Phrixus was hospitably
entertained by Aeëtes, who allowed his daughter Chalciope to marry him
and ask for no bride-gift in return. He lived prosperously in Colchis for
many years.

When Athamas returned to Iolcos and learned what had happened in
his absence he considered himself hated by all the Gods. He lay down on
his couch, covered his head with the skirt of his robe and groaned. Ino
came to console him. 'Husband,' she said, 'one of the Centaurs, who still
range Mount Pelion in sportive defiance of your orders, has reported that
very early in the morning of that fatal day he saw your son and daughter
climbing slowly towards the shrine of the Ram God, from which
proceeded loud sounds of drunken revelry. He saluted them and ran on.
What may have happened when they reached the enclosure and found the
debauched Son lying naked between his guardians, and the Mother in
sober possession of the shrine, who can tell? They may have been
converted by her into rocks or trees in punishment of some unconsidered
words that they spoke. Or they may have touched the Fleece as it lay on
the ground, and been converted by the Son into bats or weasels. Or they
may have run mad and, catching up the Fleece at the instigation of the
Mother, have run down the further slope of Pelion and plunged with it into
the sea. These are enigmas, and have as yet no solution.'

Athamas did not answer, but continued to groan.

Ino continued: 'Dearest of men, this is my advice to you. First make
your peace with the White Goddess, abasing yourself before her in her
shrine on Pelion, and offering her the richest sacrifices possible, in the
hope of averting her wrath and then return to this room and behave as one
already dead. Unless you do this your people, who believe that you have
smuggled away your children in defiance of Apollo's oracle, will demand
your own sacrifice. Be dead until the next sowing season, when my women

and I will plant what barley-seed we have saved, with the customary rites, and all will be well. Meanwhile, let your brother Cretheus act as your regent in military and naval matters, while I rule the land again in all else, as formerly. Though we may go hungry, the Goddess will doubtless preserve us from starvation.'

Athamas was too low-spirited to dissent. While he was visiting Pelion and making abject supplications to the Goddess, Ino called a conference of Minyan chieftains and acquainted them with his decisions. The disgrace that had overtaken their Ram God weighed so heavily on their minds that whatever Ino told them in the name of the Goddess seemed ungainsayable. They swore to obey Cretheus as their war king and as priest of Zeus during the temporary death of Athamas, and to obey Ino as their law-maker and Governess. This Cretheus was an easy-going, feeble-bodied man, over whom Ino had perfect ascendancy.

The Centaurs were then invited to return to Mount Pelion and promised indemnification for the slaughter of their kinsmen, as well as restoration to all their ancient privileges. The White Goddess smiled on them with her mare's teeth; but the naked image of the Ram God was reclothed in a plain black fleece and conducted quietly back to his former shrine on Mount Laphystios. Cretheus did not punish the guardians for their negligence, since they pleaded that they had merely obeyed the God when he offered them wine to drink and that his excesses were no fault of theirs.

As for Athamas, as soon as he returned to the royal mansion under cover of darkness, he died and remained dead for a full year; eating only the red food of the dead, which living men may not eat except on certain solemn occasions: lobster, crayfish, blood pudding, boiled bacon and ham, the pomegranate, and barley-cakes soaked in the juice of berries. When he came to life again, after the autumn sowing had been conducted by Ino with the full ritual, he was found to be deranged in his wits. Three years later he killed Learchus, one of the two infant sons born to Ino and himself, shooting him with bow and arrow from a window that overlooked the courtyard. The Minyans then decided to depose him and grant the priesthood and kingship to Cretheus.

But Ino was already dead. The madness of Athamas had entered into her when she saw Learchus dying in the courtyard: she had caught up her other son, Melicertes, from the harvest basket in which he was cradled and, dressed all in white, had rushed yelling triumphantly up the slopes of Pelion. There at the shrine of the Goddess she tore her child in pieces, and hastening onwards and upwards, with a light froth on her lips, she crossed the topmost ridge of Pelion and ran down the opposite slope. She came at last to a sea-cliff and flung herself into the sea. The crew of a Corinthian ship found both bodies floating in the water, and brought them to Corinth for burial, where King Sisyphus instituted the Isthmian Games in honour of Melicertes. Ino, because of her suicide and murder of her son, became one with the Goddess whom she had served, and was worshipped both in Corinth and Megara as the White Goddess, Ino, thus adding yet another name to the countless others with which the Mother of All Things is honoured. But Athamas was ordered by the Goddess to travel towards the sunset and settle wherever he should be entertained by wild beasts. He travelled to the mountains behind Halos, where he fell in with a pack of wolves devouring a flock of sheep. They fled at his approach and left the carcases for his eating. So there he settled and called the place Athamantia, and raised a new family; but he was dead before ever the *Argo* sailed to Colchis.

The land of Phthiotis was at peace for some years and a firm friendship arose between the Minyans and Centaurs, because when Cretheus recalled the Centaurs to their caves on Mount Pelion they doled out grain and edible acorns to the hungry Minyans from their hidden stores and supplied them with venison and other game. Then, when sometimes the Iolcan Fish nymphs stole out of their huts at night to join the Horse men in customary love-orgies on the mountain, their Minyan husbands did not dare to show resentment; and during the sowing festival, and the festival of caprifica-tion, these Minyans went out for a holiday to the seashore and did not return until all was over.

Cretheus died and was succeeded by his son Aeson, whose wife Alcimede was now Priestess in Ino's place. At the funeral games given in honour of Cretheus a drunken Centaur tried to kill Aeson with a huge earthenware wine jar; Aeson defended himself with a golden one and dashed out the Centaur's brains. But otherwise the next few years were passed pleasantly without disturbance, until suddenly everything was turned upside-down by the coming of the iron-weaponed Achaeans under the command of Pelias, son of Poseidon. One early morning Cheiron the Centaur from his cave-mouth on Pelion saw a tall cloud of smoke rising from the city of Iolcos, and a palace servant came stumbling up the mountain-path to warn the Centaurs of their danger. He committed to Cheiron's keeping, in the name of the Goddess, a little fair-haired boy of two years old, dressed in a tunic of purple cloth, who was seated astride his shoulders: Diomedes, the only surviving son of Aeson and Alcimede.

Cheiron was afraid, yet could not refuse the charge. He gave out to his people that the child Diomedes was one of the Magnesians, sent him for initiation into the rites of the Horse men; for between the Leopard men and Horse men this exchange of courtesies was habitual. He renamed him Jason, which means 'The Healer', in the hope though not the confidence that he would one day be the means of restoring peace in Phthiotis.

Such, at least, is the account of these events that has been handed down to us by a succession of trustworthy poets, who contradict one another only in unimportant particulars. And some say that the trade that Jason plied while he was living on Mount Pelion was that of torch-maker to the Goddess: by her sanction he would wound the pine-tree near the root and after thirteen months cut out, from the part about the wound, the wood impregnated with resin, which he shaped into phallic torches. This he did for three years running, and at last cut out the heart of the tree for the same purpose.

CHAPTER THREE

THE RISE OF THE OLYMPIANS

When, moving southward from beyond the river Danube by slow stages, their last headquarters being at Dodona in Epirus, the sturdy Achaean people finally reached the settled parts of Greece, they found many things that displeased their savage hearts as well as many that pleased them. The gracious and well-decorated houses, the strongly walled cities, the swift and commodious ships, inclined them to wonder and even reverence; and they were pleased to vary their diet of roast and boiled meat, milk, cheese, berries, and wild salads, with dried figs, barley-bread, sea-food, and olive oil. But they were astonished and scandalized to find that their cousins, the Ionian and Aeolian Greeks who had entered the country before them, had become softened by long intercourse with the natives. They were not only wearing womanish clothing and jewelry, but seemed to regard women as the holier and more authoritative sex. Almost all the priestly functions were engrossed by women, and even the Greek tribal gods had acknowledged themselves sons and dependents of the Triple Goddess. The Achaeans were disgusted by this discovery, and determined not to fall into the same error as their cousins, over whom their chariots and iron weapons gave them supremacy in battle. In Greece only bronze weapons had been known hitherto, and the horse, a sacred animal, was little used in warfare. The Achaean chariot columns went forward with such speed that each of the walled cities was surprised and occupied in turn before the citizens of the next were fully aware of its danger.

King Sthenelus, the new Achaean overlord of the Peloponnese, justified his seizure of the throne of Mycenae from the Henetian house of Pelops by denying that his predecessor had a valid title to it: he married Nicippe, a matrilinear descendant of Andromeda, sister of Perseus the Cretan who had founded the city, and ruled in her name.

Now, the Triple Goddess, who in her character of Mother Rhea had adopted the Greek Sky God, Dios, as a son and had renamed him Zagreus or Zeus, had kept him under control by making him subject to Cronus, her indolent Cretan lover, and by supplying him with several elder brothers, for the most part ancient Pelasgian heroes, the occupants of oracular shrines. Sthenelus and his Achaeans now disavowed the tutelage of Cronus over Zeus and recognized as elder gods, divine brothers of Zeus, only Poseidon and Hades, who had been, like himself, ancient gods of the Greek people. They also denied that Zeus was Zagreus, son of the Triple Goddess: reverting to the ancient Greek fable that he was Dios and had descended from Heaven upon insensate Earth in the form of a thunderbolt, they declared that Earth was not his mother in the sense that he had ever been dependent upon her, and that he was the Supreme and Original God of All Things. But this view was not well received by the Ionians, Aeolians, and Pelasgians, who insisted that he was indeed Cretan Zagreus, the last of the Goddess's children to be born in the Dictean Cave.

The Chief Priestess of the Mother Goddess Rhea, in alliance with the Chief Priestess of the Maiden Goddess Athena, sent secret envoys to the Chief Priests of Poseidon and Apollo, urging that Zeus should be deposed from his sovereignty at once, lest a sour monotheistic cult, on the model of that recently established in Egypt by the Pharaoh Akhenaton, should destroy the rich complexity of religious life in Greece: she undertook that when Zeus had been deposed, by a sudden raid upon Dodona, his holiest seat, the Mother Goddess would institute a divine republic of gods and goddesses, all of equal standing, under her own benign presidency. This suggestion was accepted by Poseidon and Apollo, but Sthenelus was informed of the plot in good time, and arresting the Chief Priests and the Chief Priestesses brought them in chains to Mycenae. He did not, however, dare to put them to death, but sent for advice to the Oracle at Dodona. The Oracle ordered that Poseidon and Apollo should be banished from Greece for a full year and become hired servants to foreigners; meanwhile their worship was to be wholly discontinued. This punishment was carried out in the persons of the two Chief Priests: Sthenelus sent them to his ally, King Laömedon of Troy, who employed them as stone-masons to build his palace, but in Trojan style, it is said, cheated them of their pay. By order of the Oracle, Rhea and Athena were punished in another way: their Chief Priestesses were hung up publicly to an oak-tree by their hair, with anvils tied to their feet, until they swore to be of good behaviour. But their worship was not discontinued, for the sake of the harvest.

The Achaeans found that the Triple Goddess was too powerful for them either to deny or destroy, as they had at first intended, and were for a while at a loss what to do. Then they decided, on behalf of Zeus, to repudiate his former wife, Dione, and force the Goddess into marriage with him, so that he was now to be the Great Father and she merely the mother of his children, no longer the Great Mother. Their decision was generally accepted by the other Greeks, who were cowed by the vengeance taken on Apollo and Poseidon and Rhea and Athena. It was a decision of the greatest importance, since it authorized all fathers to assume the headship of their households and to have the say in matters which hitherto had been left entirely to the discretion of their wives.

The Thracian War God Ares and a new Smith God, Hephaestus of Lemnos, were declared reborn of this forced union of Zeus and the Triple Goddess. It was further proposed that the God Apollo should be reborn of the same union, but the priestly archers of Apollo opposed this, intending to make the Oracle of Delphi independent of the Goddess, and claimed that he was son to Zeus by another mother, a Quail woman from Ceos named Leto. A similar refusal was made by the adherents of Hermes, formerly a Pelasgian hero charged with authority over his fellow-ghosts, but now promoted to be the Olympian Herald God; they claimed that Hermes was the son of Zeus by a daughter of the Titans named Maia the Arcadian. The Achaeans accepted both these claims, but denied the claim of Ares, who hated Zeus, to have been born to Hera parthenogenetically; for every god but Zeus, they insisted, must have a father. The Triple Goddess, however, controlled the shrines of numerous other heroes throughout Greece, and since it was found impracticable to close all of them, because of the devotion of the Pelasgian peasantry, she was now, in her new character of consort to Zeus, known only as Hera, the protectress of heroes. In order to limit her powers, it was alleged by the adherents of Zeus that he was the father, by other mothers, of many of these heroes. The conflicting claims caused a deal of religious difference in Greece, and it was rumoured that Hera had withdrawn her favour from all heroes who boasted Zeus to be their father. The Greeks complained that she was a jealous wife and a cruel stepmother.

Sthenelus now sent envoys to every part of Greece with notice that he intended to call a grand conference on sacred matters, hoping to compose all outstanding differences between the devotees of the various deities of the land. The place appointed was a township near Pisa in the west of the Peloponnese, named Olympia after a near-by hill, the Lesser Mount Olympus; here was a shrine of Mother Rhea, or Ge, the most venerable in Greece. To the conference came all the Greek and Pelasgian religious leaders; they feasted together more amicably than might have been expected and disputed points of theogony and theology. It was first of all debated which deities were worthy to belong to the Divine Family now installed on the Greater Mount Olympus under the sovereignty of Father Zeus. Among those admitted to senior godhead was the repentant Poseidon. Poseidon had been a god of the forests, but the gradual thinning of the forests in the settled parts of Greece made it proper for him to govern some other department of nature as well. He became God of the Sea (as was natural, since ships are built of forest timber and propelled by wooden oars) and was confirmed in his sovereignty of the Sea by a marriage to Amphitrite, the Triple Goddess in her marine character; she became the mother by him of all the Tritons and Nereids. But the thunderbolt with which he had formerly been armed was taken from him and he was given a trident instead, for the spearing of fish; the thunderbolt was reserved by Zeus for his sole use.

The God Apollo, though not reckoned as a senior, had improved his standing by taking over the greater part of the reverence hitherto owed to the hero Prometheus: he became patron of the Promethean schools of music, astrology, and art which had been founded in the neighbourhood of Delphi long before his arrival there, and adopted the fire-wheel of Prometheus as one of his own emblems.

The Triple Goddess in her gracious character of Nymph could not be excluded from the Olympian family; but she lost her ancient name, Marianaë, and was forced into ignoble marriage with Hephaestus, the lame, dwarfish, sooty-faced Smith God who had hitherto been regarded merely as a Lemnian hero. She was renamed Aphrodite, the Foam-born One. It was also urged by many voices that the Triple Goddess must be represented on Olympus in her third principal character, that of Maiden, and after some dispute she was admitted as the Maiden Huntress and known as Artemis of the New Moon, for Artemis was the chief name of the Triple Goddess among the Pelasgians; but the new Artemis was reborn as a sister of Apollo by Leto. This concession, however, did not satisfy the Boeotians and Athenians, on whose affections the Maiden Goddess had so powerful a hold in her character of Athena that a second seat on Olympus had to be found for her. After much more dispute she was admitted as Athena, but only on condition that she too suffered a rebirth, denying that she was daughter to the Mother Goddess and alleging that she sprang full-armed from the head of Zeus: this was to be proof that Father Zeus could beget children, even females, without having recourse to the female womb, by an independent act of will. Athena repented of her attempt to overthrow Zeus and became the most dutiful and industrious of all his daughters and his most zealous champion against lawlessness.

When the question of the Underworld was raised, an attempt was made on behalf of the Triple Goddess, in her character of Mother Hecate, to claim this as her ancient and inalienable possession; but the claim was rejected by the adherents of Zeus, who feared that she might use it as a base of war against Olympus. They awarded it to gloomy Hades, brother to Zeus. However, since it was impossible to keep the Goddess wholly out of the Underworld, she was admitted as the Maiden Persephone, but forced under the harsh tutelage of her uncle Hades and allowed little say in the government of her former dominions. Mother Hecate was treated even more shamefully. Since sacrifices of dogs had been customarily offered her, she became a three-headed dog kennelled at the gate of Hades, and was renamed Cerberus. This award of the Underworld to Hades caused more dissension in Greece than any other decision of the conference, and his union with Persephone was bewailed by the Pelasgians as a rape rather than a marriage.

The Ionians, when they first acknowledged the authority of the Triple Goddess, had most of them allowed their male children to be initiated into the Pelasgian secret fraternities which assisted in her worship. The Aeolians had done the same. Each fraternity had its demon, incarnate in some beast or bird the flesh of which was death to eat, except on peculiarly solemn occasions; and its members met regularly for festival dances to the demon, in which they imitated the gait and habits of the sacred beast or bird and were disguised in its hide or fur or feathers. Their leader impersonated the demon and was inspired by him. The choice of a fraternity was in some cases made for a child by its mother before birth if a creature, either in dream or in waking life, obtruded itself on her notice; but, in general, the fraternity comprised all the male members of a half-tribe. Thus the Satyrs of Thessaly and the Silenians of Phocis were Goat men; the Centaurs of Pelion, Horse men; some of the Magnesians, Leopard men; the Crisaeans of Phocis, Seal men; and there were Owl men at Athens. The women had similar societies, called sororities, and no woman was permitted by the Goddess to take a lover from the fraternity which matched her sorority – thus Lion might company with Leopardess, and Lioness with Leopard; but not Lion with Lioness or Leopard with Leopardess – which was a rule doubtless designed to bind up the scattered tribes in affectionate harmony, with the pleasant comings and goings that it entailed. But in proof that the demons of each fraternity were subject to the Triple Goddess, there was a yearly holocaust held in her honour: each fraternity sent its sacred male animal, bound, to the nearest of her many mountain sanctuaries, there to be burned alive, all of them together, on a raging bonfire.

The Achaeans showed a natural suspicion of these demons because of their allegiance to the Triple Goddess and because of the promiscuous love-making that they enjoined on their worshippers. It was the policy of Sthenelus to suppress as many as possible of the societies and to subject the demon of each of those that remained to some member of the Olympian Family. Thus he claimed that Zeus had not only a Ram character, his worshippers having been shepherds, but could be appropriately worshipped as Bull, Eagle, Swan, Dove, and Great Serpent. Hera was permitted to retain power over the Lion, Cuckoo, and Wryneck. To Apollo, who had formerly been a Mouse demon, were granted the additional characters of Wolf, Bee, Dolphin, and Falcon. To Athena were granted the Crow, Heron, and Owl, and later she took the Cuckoo from Hera; to Artemis were granted the Fish, Deer, Dog, and Bear; to Poseidon, the Horse and Tunny; to Hermes, the Lizard and Lesser Serpent; to Ares, the Boar; and so on. The Pelasgians were greatly incensed when Poseidon styled himself the Horse God, and in one of their towns an image of the Mare-headed Mother, called the Furious Mare, was set up in protest; for the horse plainly confesses the sovereignty of the Triple Goddess by the moon-shaped imprint of his hoof.

These and other confusing changes in the Greek religion, which included the inauguration of a new calendar, were explained to the assembled visitants at Olympia in the solemn spectacle, arranged by the heralds of the God Hermes, which concluded the conference. There was a pantomimic representation of the castration by Zeus of his supposed father Cronus – after which Zeus was crowned with wild olive and pelted with apple-leaves in congratulation – of the marriage of Hera and Zeus, Poseidon and Amphitrite, Hephaestus and Aphrodite; of the rebirths of Ares, Hephaestus, and Athena; of the Beast and Bird demons making submission each to a new master or mistress – in short, of all the novel mythological happenings now agreed upon. These performances ended with a lively exhibition of the twelve Olympians seated at dinner together, wearing the garbs appropriate to their new characters and attributes. Each deity was represented by some king, priest or priestess; the part of Zeus being taken by Sthenelus of Mycenae, who held in one hand the dog-headed golden sceptre of Perseus, and in the other the Gorgon-faced shield of aversion.

The Olympic festival was made an occasion for grand athletic contests between young men from every city and colony of Greece: funeral games in honour of Cronus. The contests, known as the Olympic Games, were organized by young Alcaeus of Tiryns, the principal male champion of the Triple Goddess and a matrilinear descendant of Andromeda. He won the straight and the all-in wrestling contests himself. Alcaeus, a man of phenomenal size and strength, and leader of the Bull fraternity of Tiryns, had arrived at Olympia bawling out threats against the Goddess's enemies; but, like most strong and hot-tempered men, he was easily hoodwinked. The adherents of Zeus plied him with food and drink and allowed him to believe that he had forced many important concessions from them as to the new status of the Goddess – and indeed he had done for her more than any one else had done. He had threatened to wreck the conference chamber with his brass-bound olive club unless it were agreed that the Goddesses in Olympus should not be outnumbered by the Gods. When the Achaeans therefore introduced Ares, Hephaestus, and Hermes into the Olympian family, Alcaeus introduced the Triple Goddess in two more characters: as Demeter the Corn Mother, mother of Persephone, and as Hestia the Goddess of the Hearth. Thus there were six Gods and six Goddesses[1] in

1   *Olympian Deities*

Zeus (Jupiter)	Hera (Juno)
Poseidon (Neptune)	Athena (Minerva)
Apollo (Apollo)	Demeter (Ceres)
Ares (Mars)	Hestia (Vesta)
Hermes (Mercury)	Aphrodite (Venus)
Hephaestus (Vulcan)	Artemis (Diana)

Underworld Deities

Hades (Pluto)	Persephone (Proserpina)

the new Pantheon. But it was clear to everyone that Alcaeus had been fooled into accepting on behalf of the Triple Goddess far less than her just due; for alike in the Sky, Sea and Underworld, and on the Earth, she was now under male tutelage; and when the Priestess of the Triple Goddess of Olympia sitting, cuckoo-sceptre in hand at the divine feast in Hera's place, asked him whether he had acted in treachery or stupidity, he shot an arrow clean through her two breasts – a disgraceful deed which brought him the worst of luck. Alcaeus later became famous under his new name of Hercules, or Heracles, which means 'Glory of Hera', which he adopted when he quitted the Bull fraternity and became a Lion man, in the hope of placating the Goddess whom he had injured.

Everywhere there was murmuring against this wholesale reformation of religion, but the Achaeans overawed the complainants by force of arms and the Oracles unanimously confirmed the innovations. The weightiest utterances came from Apollo's Oracle at Delphi, the possession of which had ceased to be a humiliation to him and become a source of glory and power; and from Zeus's own Oracle at Dodona in Epirus, where the response to enquiries was given by the rustling leaves of a sacred oak-grove, and by augury of black doves. No sudden outbreaks of armed revolt occurred in Greece: as when, a generation or two before, a band of Pelasgian women, since mistakenly known as the Amazons, had made a sudden armed assault on Athens because they were displeased with the religious innovations of King Theseus the Ionian; or when, in the time of King Pelops the Henetian, the Danaid river-nymphs, forced into wedlock by his Egyptian masons, had murdered all but one of them on their common wedding night. Four kings only refused to recognize the new Olympian order: Salmoneus of Elis, brother of King Athamas; Tantalus, son of the Ionian hero Tmolus, who had lately settled overseas in Lydia; Aeëtes, King of Colchis, but formerly of Corinthian Ephyra, who was of Cretan stock; and Sisyphus of Corinthian Asopia, nephew of Aeëtes.

All four were laid under a curse by the Oracles. To Tantalus, who had ridiculed the feast of the Gods, fire and water were universally denied, so that he starved to death; Salmoneus, who in contempt of Zeus the Rain-Giver had raised a rain-storm of his own by making artificial thunder with the loud clanging of brazen pots, was stoned to death. Sisyphus was forced to work as a labourer in the marble-quarries of Ephyra, where he remained for years until one day a falling stone crushed him. His offence was that he had broken the oath of secrecy which was exacted of all members of the conference: he had sent a timely warning to the College of Asopian Fish nymphs that they were to be carried off by the Achaeans and ceremonially prostituted in the island of Aegina. He had also put in chains a priest of Hades who came to take over an Underworld shrine from a priestess of Hecate; and when Sthenelus, his overlord, sent a herald to release the priest and to remind Sisyphus that Hades was now the sole ruler of the

Underworld, Sisyphus boldly forbade any of his relatives to bury him when he died, preferring, as he said, the liberty of wandering along the banks of the Asopus as a ghost. As for Aeëtes of Colchis, he lived far enough away to be able to laugh at the Oracles.

Some poets have asserted that several conferences were held at Olympia and elsewhere, not one only, before the reformation could be completed; and that many of the incidents represented in the final pantomime had already been engrafted on the national religion in the time of the Aeolians and Ionians. Others deny that any conference at all was held, declaring that all the decisions on matters affecting the Divine Family of Olympus were taken by Zeus in person without any human advice. Who can tell where the truth of all this may lie? At all events, the power of Zeus was now firmly established throughout Greece, and no public oaths were highly valued that were not sworn in his name.

The government of the province of Phthiotis, from Iolcos in the north to Halos in the south, fell to an Achaean named Pelias, who had represented the God Poseidon at the divine feast of Olympia and adjudicated the horse race at the Games. He behaved contemptuously towards the local Minyans after he had killed the most dangerous of them; yet he did not put to death Aeson, son of Cretheus, their King, contenting himself merely with marrying a daughter of Athamas and Nephele and acting as Aeson's regent. Since Aeson had no surviving children (or so it was supposed), Pelias became his heir and expected that his own children would one day succeed him as the unquestioned rulers of the country.

It happened that Pelias could claim to be a Minyan himself, and was indeed a half-brother of Aeson's. Tyro, their mother, wife to King Cretheus, had been visiting a College of Thessalian Heron nymphs on the banks of the Enipeus some years before, when a raiding party of Achaeans carried her off. They prostituted her in a temple of Poseidon, and when she was found to be with child they sent her home on foot to her husband. She was delivered of twin boys by the wayside but, feeling ashamed to bring them back to Cretheus, exposed them; they were found by a horseherd riding by on his mare, who took them home to his wife and called them Pelias and Neleus – Pelias, which means 'dirty', because the mare had kicked a clod of dirt in this child's face; Neleus, which means 'ruthless', because of his staring eyes. Sidero, the horseherd's wife, happened to have just lost a child of her own, and agreed to foster the twins; but had not enough milk for two. That they therefore took turns at the dugs of the shepherd's wolf-hound bitch was afterwards held to account for the fierceness of their natures.

Two days later Tyro returned, intending to bury her sons and so protect herself from their resentful ghosts. When she found them alive at the horseherd's house she was overjoyed, having bitterly repented her deed, and asked for them to be restored to her. But Sidero refused the great rewards that Tyro offered, and sent her off with a beating. When Pelias and Neleus grew to an age of understanding and were told the story in full, they killed their foster-mother Sidero in punishment for her cruelty to Tyro. Then they ran off to the Achaeans, to whom they presented themselves as sons of Poseidon, having been born to a temple prostitute, and were given high rank. When the Achaeans invaded Hellas, Pelias in virtue of his Minyan blood successfully claimed the kingdom of Phthiotis; and Neleus, the other Minyan kingdom of Pylos. But the Mother Goddess hated Pelias, because he had violated one of her sanctuaries: he had killed Sidero as she was clinging to the very horns of the moon altar.

CHAPTER FOUR

JASON CLAIMS HIS KINGDOM

The Centaurs of Mount Pelion were now again forbidden to company with the wives of the Minyans, a practice which Pelias considered indecent and would not condone. But, since 'even such pitiful savages cannot live without the occasional company of women', as he said, he encouraged them to steal brides from their old enemies, the Lapiths of Thessaly, who were now ruled by a Minyan aristocracy. Pelias had found the Lapiths restless and insolent neighbours, and was pleased to assist the Centaurs in their raids.

One day he paid the Centaurs a ceremonial visit, meeting Cheiron, their leader, in the enclosure of the Mare-headed White Goddess on Pelion. Cheiron persuaded Pelias to enter the shrine and consult the Oracle. It amused Pelias to ask the Goddess how he should die; his reason for posing this question, he told his companions, was not that he needed enlightenment but that he wished to test the Goddess's veracity. He had already been informed of the exact manner of his death by the Oracle of Father Zeus at Dodona; and who could presume to contradict All-mighty, All-knowing Zeus?

The answer that the Goddess returned was: 'How shall I tell you, Pelias, what you pretend to have heard already from my Son? Yet let me warn you to beware of the one-sandalled man: he will hate you, and before he has done his hatred will make mince-meat of you.'

Pelias paid little attention to the maunderings of this 'old three-souled woman', for so he blasphemously called her, whose religion, as he said, was now everywhere in decay; especially since he could not reconcile her prophecy with the solemn assurance of Zeus that no man's hand should ever be raised against him in violence and that, in old age, he should be given the choice of the hour and manner of his death. Nevertheless, he prudently gave orders that no Aetolians should be allowed to enter Phthiotis on any pretext whatsoever; because the Aetolians, for good luck when they march or dance, go shod on their left foot only.

A few days later, Pelias had a curious reminder of the power of Zeus. The Chief Priest of Apollo came on foot through Iolcos, once more in the dress of a hired servant, and refused the richer portions of roast meat and the better drink, due to his distinguished rank, that Pelias offered him; he sat beside the hearth with the menials and ate umbles. He was on his way to the fortress of Pherae, in Thessaly, where Admetus the Minyan lived, son-in-law to Pelias; carrying out in his own person a second punishment of his divine master decreed by the Oracle of Zeus. This was the story:

The priests of Hades complained at Dodona that a new school of medicine had been founded at Delphi by one of Apollo's sons, born of a temple prostitute, named Aesculapius. They charged Apollo with encouraging the study of medicine and surgery in order to decrease the number of dead, especially children, and thus to deprive the Infernal priesthood of their fees and perquisites. It seems that Aesculapius, at the request of a poor widow, had attended the funeral of her only son who had been drowned. The howling lament was already being raised by the priests of Hades; yet Aesculapius refused to regard the boy as dead, and by emptying him of water and moving his arms about, as if he were still alive, brought back the breath into his body. He sat up and sneezed, and Aesculapius thereupon dedicated him to the service of Apollo.

The Dodonan Oracle gave a response favourable to the complainants by ordering the school to be closed, but Aesculapius refused to accept the decision as genuinely oracular. He protested that Hades caught every soul in the end, and that the more lives of children Apollo saved, the more children would be born in the course of nature: all of whom would eventually become the prey of Hades. This argument vexed Zeus, because it was unanswerable except by violence. A party of temple guards were at once sent from Dodona to Delphi, where they killed both Aesculapius and the boy whose life he had saved. A retaliatory raid was made on Dodona by Apollo's archers, who shot to death all the Sons of Cyclops, the smiths of Dodona who made the sacred furniture for the shrines of Zeus, Poseidon, and Hades, and who were called the One-Eyed men because they worked with one eye shaded against the sparks flying from their anvils.

The Oracle of Zeus then threatened Apollo with extinction if he would not abase himself and once more serve as a menial for a full year: this time his servitude was to be in the wildest province of Greece – which the Chief Priest took to be the Minyan kingdom of Pherae; during that year the Oracle was to be silent and all sacrifices, vows, and prayers to Apollo were to be discontinued. The Chief Priest had no choice but to submit. It is possible that he chose Pherae as his place of servitude because Admetus, King of Pherae, was under an obligation to him; Admetus had once unwittingly offended Apollo's sister, the Maiden Goddess Artemis, by omitting the propitiatory sacrifice to her when he married Alcestis, the eldest daughter of King Pelias. The Goddess had punished Admetus by arranging that when he entered the bridal chamber he should find nothing in the bed but a basketful of snakes; and at first refused ever to give Alcestis back to him. Admetus then went to Delphi with offerings and begged

Apollo to intercede with his divine sister; which he did. So now, in return, Admetus gave the Chief Priest as pleasant a servitude as possible; and earned his abiding gratitude.

It was a long time before any other deity (except the Triple Goddess, who remained implacably hostile) dared dispute the authority of Zeus; but Apollo has never forgotten the insult that he was then forced to swallow, and it has been prophesied among the barbarians that one day he will make common cause with the Triple Goddess, and will castrate his father Zeus as ruthlessly as Zeus once castrated his father Cronus. Apollo, it is prophesied, will use against him the golden sickle laid up in the temple of Zeus at Hyllos in Corfu, which is said to be the authentic instrument used against Cronus. But Apollo has learned to be cautious and bides his time. At the entrance to the Navel Shrine these words are written: 'Nothing in excess.' And he studies the sciences.

At the next winter solstice, when Mount Pelion was capped with snow, and so too was Mount Othrys far across the gulf to the southwestward, Pelias celebrated the customary festival in honour of the deities of the land. He paid especial reverence to his Father Poseidon, and gave precedence over the others to the Maiden Goddess Artemis. Because the Fish was now sacred to Artemis, he had rededicated the College of Fish Nymphs at Iolcos to her, putting it under the charge of old Iphias, his maternal aunt, daughter of a King of Argos. Pelias was obliged to make three strange omissions from the list of immortal guests whom he invited to share in the rich public feast of roast beef, mutton, and venison, The first omission was the name of Zeus himself. This was because, some years before, in the time of King Athamas, the God had unfortunately (as Pelias put it) been discovered on Pelion by the Mare-headed Mother, sleeping off the effects of a pleasant debauch; embarrassed to find himself naked – for he had flung off his Golden Fleece to cool his heated body – he had yielded his shrine to her and retired, in a new sober suit of black wool, to Mount Laphystios. 'Until Father Zeus publicly returns to Pelion and sends the Mare-headed One packing,' said Pelias, 'I consider it wise to offer only private sacrifices to him.' Since, however, he did not wish to seem an ally of the Mother in her quarrel with Zeus, the second and third omissions from his list were the names of the Goddess in her characters of Hera and Demeter. He made this omission – which was even stranger than the omission of Zeus, because the mid-winter festival had originally been sacred to the Goddess alone – without offering her any propitiation. He wished to show her that he neither feared her oracles nor intended to curry favour with her. But he propitiated Zeus with a private sacrifice in his dining-hall, in which he burned the whole carcass of a fine ox and ate not a morsel of it himself.

In the confidence that he had averted the Father's displeasure, Pelias then went down into the market-place, where the bonfires of dried pine-logs were already crackling, ready to roast the carcases of the beautiful beasts that he had chosen for sacrifice to the other Olympians. Among the crowd of holiday-makers he noticed a remarkable stranger – young, tall and handsome, with features that he seemed to recall as from a dream, armed with two bronze-bladed spears. To judge from his close-fitting deer-skin tunic and breeches and his leopard-skin cape, he was a Magnesian of the Leopard fraternity, come down from the mountains above Lake Boebe; yet the long mane of yellow hair that he wore proved him to have been initiated into the Centaur Horse fraternity. 'Strange,' thought Pelias. 'I might have taken him for a Greek with that yellow hair, that fine straight nose and those large limbs.' The stranger was gazing at Pelias intently and disconcertingly, but Pelias did not deign to greet him.

Pelias ordered the garlanded victims to be led to the great altar, on which he had set several equal heaps of roasted barley-grains and one twice as big as the rest. He sprinkled the polls of the beasts with salt calling out the name of each God or Goddess in turn; then his assistant slaughtered them with a pole-axe; then he himself cut their throats with a curved flint knife. He turned their heads upwards as he did so since this was a sacrifice to the Olympians, not to any hero or Underworld deity. Lastly, he made a burnt offering of the thigh-bones, rolled in fat, and part of the entrails; but every morsel of the flesh was for the worshippers' own eating. Salt sprinkled upon sacrificial victims as a seasoning was an innovation of the Achaeans; before their time no deity had called for it, and the Triple Goddess still refuses any salted offering that is made her.

As soon as these sacrifices were completed, the stranger accosted Pelias boldly and asked: 'King Pelias, why do you offer sacrifices to all the other deities, but not to the Great Goddess as she is worshipped by the Pelasgians?

He answered: 'Man without eyes, have you not observed that no sacrifice has been offered to Father Zeus, either? Would it be mannerly to invite the wife to the feast (for you surely know that the Great Goddess is now the consort of Zeus) and not the husband? This sacrifice is for my father Poseidon and the lesser Olympian Gods whose names you have heard me invoke.'

The stranger said: 'Perhaps you are right in making no sacrifice to Zeus, if what I hear is true: that he loathes to appear in these parts since once he uncovered his nakedness to his Mother in a fit of drunkenness.'

Pelias looked the stranger up and down, for this was a speech so bold as almost to be impious, until his eye was suddenly checked at the feet: he saw only one sandal.

He immediately enquired the stranger's name, and he replied: 'Ask me any other question, Greybeard, and I shall do my best to answer it.'

Pelias paused in astonishment and then asked, gasping: 'Stranger, what would you do if you were in my place?' He had never in his life been so affronted.

The stranger laughed insolently, tossed up his rowan-hefted spears, both together, caught them again, and answered: 'I should send out a wool-gathering expedition with orders to the commander not to return until he had found golden wool, even though he had to sail for it to the other end of the world – perhaps to Colchis where the chariot-horses of the Sun are stabled – or to descend into the lowest depths of the Earth where, according to our new theology, the Thirteenth Deity has his dark and horrible empire.'

'A wise suggestion,' said Pelias, hoping that the stranger would destroy himself by a careless answer of the next question. 'And would you perhaps commit the command of the expedition to the boldest man in your dominions?'

'He would need to be the boldest man in all Greece, I believe,' the stranger answered, with the same impudence, 'to undertake that task.'

'You are the very man,' cried Pelias.

'I?' asked the stranger, taken aback.

'You,' said Pelias. 'To come armed and alone, as you have done, to a festival at which no weapons are permitted, to address the ruler of the city as 'Greybeard' and refuse him your name, to throw random taunts at Father Zeus, who is the King of Heaven and the principal God of Greece – this has proved you the boldest man in the whole world, not merely in my kingdom of Phthiotis.'

He answered hotly: 'I have never in my life shrunk from any adventure. Yet I shall not go in search of the Golden Fleece unless you swear that on my return – for I shall not return empty-handed, you may depend on that – you will yield the regency of this kingdom to me.'

Pelias replied: 'Fool, I cannot make any such absurd undertaking. This kingdom by law can only be ruled by a Minyan, a member of the royal family. When my brother Aeson dies I shall succeed him in the title as well as in the power of kingship, because I am now his nearest heir of Minyan blood – my comrades killed his two sons and two brothers who stood nearer than I did; and when I die the kingdom will duly pass to Acastus, my eldest son.'

The stranger shook his head slowly. 'I think,' said he, 'that it will not.'

Pelias asked: 'Why do you shake your head and say that you think it will not? Not even a God can alter the laws of inheritance.'

The stranger explained: 'At the age of two years I was secretly rescued by a palace servant from the sack of this city, and given into the safe-keeping of the Centaurs, who took good care of me. Now for sixteen years I have been under the tutorship of Cheiron son of Philara. I have today come down to Iolcos, to the festival, where I had hoped to participate in the sacrifice to the Goddess. I beg you to excuse my rough appearance: this deer-skin tunic of mine was torn on an acanthus bush during my swift descent, and I seem to have lost one sandal – perhaps in the mud of the swollen Anauros as I forded it. I am Diomedes, the only surviving son of your brother Aeson; but Cheiron has renamed me Jason. I, not you, am the nearest heir to the Minyan throne.'

'Do not vex the Gods with your nonsense,' cried Pelias sharply. 'It is well known that Diomedes died in the burning palace and was duly mourned and buried.'

'It was not Diomedes who died,' said Jason, 'but a slave-boy, and here in my wallet are my infant garments of purple wool, unscorched by fire, to prove my story true.'

Pelias's heart sank in him, but he feared to display anger or to do Jason any injury on such a sacred occasion. He contented himself with saying dryly that Jason must think every ill of his courage if he expected him to resign all his wealth of gold, jewels, cattle, and grain without a struggle.

Jason answered: 'Why, Uncle, I said nothing about taking your wealth from you. Keep it, it is yours to do as you please with. All I ask is that you acknowledge me my father's heir. And since my father has not thought fit to avenge on you the murder of his brothers and sons, it would not become me to do so either.' He said this in all innocence, because his rough life in the mountains had not taught him that a king without wealth is like a spear without a shaft. A king must have revenue with which to pay his soldiers and servants and provide hospitality for visiting princes and sacrifices for the Gods; and to spend on a thousand other things.

Pelias did not know whether Jason was very simple or very shrewd and stood silent for a while. Then he laughed aloud and embraced him in the friendliest manner, welcoming him back to his native city with feigned expressions of joy. But as he took him by the arm and led him to the house where Aeson lay bed-ridden, he began to sigh heavily. He said: 'Jason, Jason, why did you not confess at once whose son you are? Then I should never have asked you the question to which, inspired by some God (perhaps by my Father Poseidon himself, the chief guest at our feast), you make an unretractable answer before witnesses. There is nothing for it now, but that you must go in search of the lost Fleece, and when you come back, drawn by the hopes and prayers of this whole people, I shall willingly resign the regency of Phthiotis in your favour and become your loyal and devoted comrade.'

An expression of dismay had settled on Jason's face when he understood how dearly he must pay for his indiscreet words, and Pelias now showed him how seemingly hopeless a task the recovery of the Fleece was, by telling him of King Aeëtes and his hostility to the Greeks.

Two years after Phrixus and Helle had fled from Iolcos, news had come to Cretheus, the regent, that Helle had been drowned in the Trojan Strait, but that Phrixus had presented the Fleece to Aeëtes, son of Heleus, King of Colchis, who had put it under the protection of the hero Prometheus. Upon hearing this news, Cretheus had debated with his chieftains whether or not he should send to Aeëtes demanding the Fleece, for there was a presentiment among them that the good luck of the Minyans was bound up with it; but they decided not to risk the anger of the White Goddess, and therefore nothing was done. However, some years later Aeëtes heard that his nephew Sisyphus, to whom he was bound by the most solemn oaths of friendship, had been deposed and enslaved for refusing to recognize the new subservience of the Triple Goddess to her former sons, Zeus, Poseidon, and Hades. This news angered him excessively, for Sisyphus had been King of Asopia, the western half of the double kingdom of Corinth, whereas the eastern half, including the isthmus and the city of Ephyra, was his own; he had left his lands under the stewardship of his friend Bunus, but Sisyphus had been acting as regent of the people. Aeëtes therefore swore to massacre the first crew of Greek seamen who dared venture into Colchis, unless they brought him news of the release and restoration of his nephew Sisyphus. But so far from releasing Sisyphus or restoring the old religion in Corinth, the new Achaean governor issued a public proclamation denying that the city had, as everyone thought, been founded by a priestess of the Maiden Goddess Ephyra. He asserted, instead, that it had been founded by a champion named Corinthus, a devotee of Zeus, from whom Ephyra had stolen the glory, and that the original name, Corinth, since applied to the whole kingdom, must now be restored to it. He confiscated the lands of King Aeëtes, on the ground that his title to it, which derived from Ephyra, was invalid; and Asopia passed into the possession of his friend Creon who had married Glauce, the daughter of Sisyphus, against her will.

Since that time there had been no direct communication between Colchis and Greece; and the Trojans acted as middlemen for trade. This was a great inconvenience to the Greeks, for whereas the toll that the Trojans had formerly levied was only a fifth part of the agreed value of the cargo, now they sold Colchian goods to the Greek merchant-captains for twice or three times as much as they had paid for them. Troy was a strong fortress, built of huge blocks of stone by Egyptian masons, like Mycenae and the other Greek cities, and well guarded. The Greeks threatened to send an expedition to destroy the place if the Trojans refused to act more reasonably; but did not yet feel strong enough to carry out their threat. King Aeëtes was said to have signed an agreement with the Trojans by which he promised to trade with no other western nation but theirs, on condition that they paid him a fair price for his goods and that they held the straits against any punitive expedition that might be sent against Colchis from Greece.

Pelias told Jason of all these circumstances, sighing deeply throughout his narration. He hoped that Jason, deeply discouraged by the difficulties of his task, would sneak back to Pelion and the company of his fellow-Centaurs; which would so discredit him in the eyes of the Minyans that he would never be able to show his face again in the market-place of Iolcos. Or, better still, he would be stung by shame into attempting a voyage for the recovery of the Fleece, which, Pelias reasoned, could only end in disaster. Even if he eluded the watchful Trojans on the outward voyage, how could Aeëtes be possibly persuaded to give up the Fleece while he still had a powerful army and a powerful fleet? And if, which was almost incredible, Jason should succeed in stealing the Fleece by a sudden bold descent, how would he contrive to pass through the Hellespont a second time? The Trojans would be waiting for him and, after examining his cargo, would hold him until the pursuing Colchian fleet came up; and then he would be killed. For there is no known way out of the Black Sea except by way of the Bosphorus and Hellespont.

Pelias had trapped Jason prettily, as he thought. Nevertheless, Jason put a bold face on the matter, and said to him: 'Dear Uncle, let us leave behind all gloomy thoughts and go together to the house of my parents, whose faces I have not seen since I was a child of two years old. I wish to embrace them and receive their blessing.'

So while the sacrificial meats were still roasting, turned slowly on spits with a pleasant smell and hissing noise over the bonfires in the market-place, Pelias led Jason to the modest house of his parents whom he saluted reverently. Alcimede was overjoyed to see her only child once more, and pressed him feverishly to her bosom; but Aeson, who had started up to a sitting posture from the couch where he lay dozing under a pile of blankets, grew pale, shrank back again and turned his face to the wall. While Jason had been away among the Centaurs, Aeson had thought of him with paternal affection and hope but now that he had come boldly down from the mountain and revealed himself to Pelias, Aeson was overcome by doubts and fears and almost hated him. He expected to be called to account by Pelias for never having confessed to him the fraud of the mock-funeral; and feared that he would seize the first pretext that occurred to him for putting both Jason and himself to death. So Aeson muttered unintelligibly over his shoulder and paid no attention either to the eloquent protestations of loyalty that Pelias uttered or to his congratulations on Jason's return as it were from the dead. When Pelias praised Jason to his face for his strength and beauty and courage Alcimede rejoiced, forgetting what ill-luck such praise brings, forgetting that the Spites are always hovering about, in the form of blue-flies or moths or mosquitoes, and fly off with the news to the jealous Olympian Gods or those of the Underworld; but Aeson continued to groan.

Pelias left Jason with his parents and returned to the market-place. There, when his chief herald had blown on a conch-shell three times, to command silence, he loudly ordered the people to rejoice with him, now that Jason, heir to the throne of Minyan Phthiotis, had unexpectedly returned to them. 'And a most courageous and reverent young man he has proved to be,' said Pelias, 'after his schooling in the cave of honest Cheiron the Centaur, who has all these years concealed him – I do not know why – under a false name and pedigree. Indeed, so courageous and so reverent is this Jason that he refuses to settle tamely among us yet awhile. He must first do great deeds, he declares, and show a deep respect for Father Zeus, the ruler of the Gods, by restoring the lost Fleece to the Ram image of Mount Laphystios. May every God and Goddess,' he said, 'favour his princely intentions! And may no Minyan prince of equal courage with Jason stand back from so glorious an enterprise!' For Pelias hoped to involve twenty or thirty Minyan nobles, the natural enemies of the Achaeans, in the death of his upstart nephew.

The people, who were already intoxicated with mead and beer, cheered Pelias's speech with a prolonged roar, and when they saw Jason coming again into the market-place to take his share of the roast meats, they ran to greet him with cries of admiration. Those who wore garlands of winter flowers and berries crowned him with them, while others drunkenly kissed his hands or stroked his shoulders.

Jason had not a word to say in reply. Already he walked like the uncomprehending victim that is conducted to the sacrifice, wreathed in garlands, white the greedy worshippers smack their lips and shout aloud for joy with: 'Ah, how handsome a beast! How tasty a morsel for the Gods, and for ourselves!'

Pelias was in so cheerful a mood that he feasted Jason at the palace for five days and nights.

CHAPTER FIVE

THE WHITE GODDESS APPROVES THE VOYAGE

Jason returned to Mount Pelion to ask Cheiron's advice. Cheiron was surprised to see him still alive. He knew Jason's hasty temper and had begged him not to make the journey, which he was sure would bring nobody any luck. He shook his head sadly when Jason reported what had happened in the market-place at Iolcos, and said: 'Child, the news that you bring could hardly have been worse. Either you will fail in your enterprise and be killed by the Colchians or their Trojan allies, or else (which is, however, far less likely) you will recover the Fleece and Zeus the Ram will return to this shrine and once more oust our beloved Mother. Oh, your tongue! How often have I told you that a man who ventures alone among enemies must keep his mouth closed and his ears open? You have disgraced my cave.'

Remorsefully Jason begged Cheiron at least to consult the Goddess for him, to learn what course he should follow. He undertook that, if the Goddess ordered him to abandon the enterprise and thereby make himself ridiculous in the eyes of his fellow-Minyans, he would obey her nevertheless and renounce all claims to the throne of Phthiotis.

Cheiron that night purified himself, entered into the Goddess's shrine and laid his head on a pillow of trefoil, which, because of its three leaves joined together in one, is sacred to the Triple Goddess and induces true dreams. At midnight the Goddess, as it seemed to him, stepped down from her throne and spoke as follows:

'Cheiron, to you as my trusty servant I dare reveal more of the truth than I find convenient to reveal to the uninitiated. In the first place, you must understand that the power of a Goddess is circumscribed by the condition of her worshippers. The iron-weaponed Achaeans have brought so great an access of strength to my rebellious son Zeus that I can no longer gain my ends directly. Even in my contest with Athamas the Aeolian, who was a far less formidable opponent than this bitch-suckled Achaean Pelias, I was obliged to contrive a tortuous plot and pretend compliance with his religious innovations. However, I have marked down Pelias for destruction just as surely as I marked down Athamas, and intend to take my revenge on every one of my other human enemies in turn; and upon my husband Zeus too. I am a very long-lived, patient Goddess, and it pleases me to take my time and keep my temper. You know how implacable I was in the case of Theseus the Athenian. I had little cause to complain of him at first when he sacked Cnossos and punished Minos for me; because he treated myself and my priestesses with due respect. But when later in Attica he began to show rebelliousness and furtively removed from their shrines two images of myself as the Maiden Goddess, the one worshipped as Helen and the other worshipped as Persephone, I persuaded his people to banish him. He fled to the isle of Scyros, where he had inherited an estate; but I prompted the King of Scyros to lead him to the highest cliff in the whole island, as if to show him the extent of his property, and then push him down headlong. And Peirithoüs, the trusty companion of Theseus, fared even worse at my hands.

'Now it has suited my humour to enter the Olympian family as Zeus's wife, rather than to remain outside as his enemy; I can lead him an insufferable life by my nagging and spying and mischief-making, just as he was a continual torment to me when he was my surly son and I was in authority over him. And my self-multiplication into his divine sisters and daughters increases his difficulties.

'You must not suppose that it was of Jason's own accord that he taunted his uncle in the market-place of Iolcos. Jason, as you know, is a wild and witless young man, despite your careful education of him, and an easy subject for my unsuspected promptings. Have you heard how he came to lose his sandal? During his descent from Pelion, when he had passed successively through the pine forests and the thickets of arbutus and acanthus, and across the thyme-covered meadows, I appeared to him in the withered person of Iphias, priestess of Artemis, who is in my confidence. I promised him good luck if he carried me over the flooded Anauros. At first he refused, but then thought better of it and took me up on his shoulders. At once I put him into a trance and taught him the very words which he afterwards spoke to Pelias. When he set me down on the further bank I broke the trance and made a Gorgon grimace at him, rolling my eyes and sticking out my tongue. At once he pulled off his sandal and threw it at me to break the spell. I bent aside; the sandal fell into the brook and was carried away.

'This hasty-mouthed Jason, though the meaning of his name may be "Healer", is destined to be a poison in the belly of Greece and a breeder of innumerable wars, like my mad servant Hercules; but let that be the affair of Zeus not mine, since Zeus has usurped my power. I am sending Jason to Colchis for one immediate purpose only: to consign to the earth the ghost of my servant Phrixus which still hovers disconsolately between the jawbones of his unburied skull, so that he may at last enter into the eternal rest that I promised him. If Jason wishes at the same time to recover the Fleece, I care not. The Fleece is nothing in itself – a cast garment – and its return to Zeus will serve to recall the humiliation which I once forced him to accept at my hands. Guard well the secrets that I have revealed to you. Jason needs to be told merely this much: he may go to Colchis with my favour, but upon the one condition, that before he makes his attempt on the Fleece he must demand from Aeëtes the bones of his kinsman Phrixus, and must bury them in a decent manner, wherever I may prompt him to do so.'

Jason was relieved to learn that he had not forfeited the Goddess's favour. Despite his rash tongue he was timorous enough wherever the favour of Gods or Goddesses was concerned. It seemed to him now that he was extraordinarily fortunate: he could count upon the Goddess to raise no obstacles to his journey, even though it was to be made chiefly on behalf of Zeus. Now he must scrupulously avoid any action that might possibly stir the enmity or jealousy of either deity. Since he would be obliged to inform his fellow-Minyans, as a means of persuading them to join him, that the Goddess in a dream had promised him her favour, it would be prudent to consult the Oracle of Zeus as well; otherwise, the priests of Zeus might suspect that the voyage had been undertaken on secret instructions from the Goddess, with some injurious intention.

When Jason told his Uncle Pelias that the Goddess had approved the voyage, he was surprised and said: 'Indeed! And upon what grounds?'

'Upon this ground, that the ghost of my kinsman Phrixus must be set at rest,' Jason answered.

This puzzled Pelias, who had no notion that the ghost of Phrixus was not at rest or even that he had died. But he answered cunningly: 'Alas, yes, the Goddess is right to remind you of the pious duty that you owe your miserable cousin. A few years ago that wretch Aeëtes added to his other crimes by poisoning Phrixus at a banquet and throwing his bones without ceremony into a thicket near the royal dining-hall. Red poppies now peep through the eye-holes of our kinsman's skull and brambles twine about his bones. His ghost will continue to plague every member of his family until it is laid with the proper burial rites. It has already disturbed my sleep on several occasions.'

Jason then told Pelias that he intended to consult the Oracle of Father Zeus at Dodona. Pelias praised him for his piety and asked him which of the three alternative routes from Thessaly to Epirus he proposed to take. The first is by land all the way, across high mountains and deep valleys; the second is partly by land and partly by sea – to take the Delphi road and then to sail through the Corinthian Gulf and up the western coast of the Adriatic Sea as far as the mouth of the river Thyamis, in Epirus, from which a convenient road runs to the plain of Dodona; the third is by sea almost the whole way – to circumnavigate Greece as far as the mouth of the Thyamis, and then to take the Dodona road. This third alternative was the one recommended by Pelias, who promised to supply Jason with a ship and crew free of charge.

Jason had never been on shipboard in his life, and therefore preferred the overland route to the other two; but Pelias warned him that it would lead him through Lapith territory and across the inhospitable ridge of Pindus, which was inhabited by Dolopians, Aethics, and other bloody savages. He persuaded him to abandon his intention, though admitting that the second route was not a promising one either, since he was unlikely to find a ship in the Corinthian Gulf ready to make the Dodona voyage at that time of year. The summer was already nearly over, and the season of storms had begun. 'But,' said Pelias, 'if you take the third route and dare to circumnavigate Greece I can promise you a fine ship and a capable master.'

Jason replied that, since the season was unpropitious, he thought it more prudent to avoid the third route too, even if he sailed in one of Pelias's own ships; for he had heard terrible accounts of the changing winds off the rugged eastern coast of the Peloponnese and of the furious gales encountered by ships which rounded Capes Malea and Taenaros. He reminded Pelias of the proverb, that the shortest cut to the Underworld was to round Cape Taenaros in autumn weather; and said that he intended to take the second route, by way of the Gulf of Corinth – doubtless some God would find him a ship.

Pelias then promised to escort him by land as far as the Crisaean Bay, near Delphi, in the Gulf of Corinth, and there, if possible, to charter a ship for him to continue the journey to Epirus.

Jason started out on his journey with Pelias at about the time of year that olives begin to ripen; sitting at Pelias's side in his polished mule-cart, with an armed escort of Achaeans riding ahead on their ponies. They went by way of the Cephisos river and Daulis and passed through the Cleft Way where Oedipus the Theban long afterwards murdered his father King Laius by mistake. They were soon obliged to dismount from the car and continue on mule-back, because a fall of rock had cut the highway. Delphi lies in a semi-circle, very high up on the olive-rich southern side of Mount Parnassus; above it tower the Shining Cliffs, a rock-wall of prodigious height, and in front, across the valley of the Plistos, the fir-fledged crest of Mount Cirphis shuts off the view of the Corinthian Gulf and protects the town from ill winds in summer. Plentiful rain had recently fallen, and down a gorge near by a hissing cascade of white water leaped giddily, mingling its water with that of the Castalian spring far below – the spring where the priests of Apollo wash their hair – the two waters together flowing into the Plistos valley after another prodigious leap.

At Delphi, a town small in size but great in reputation, the priests of the Navel Shrine commented politely on Jason's handsome appearance and on his generous acceptance by Pelias as the rightful heir to the Phthiotid throne. Jason paid his humble respects to Apollo, in order to win as many deities to his side as possible. He asked the Pythoness, as he presented her with the customary gift of a bronze tripod (supplied by his father Aeson), what advice Apollo had to give him; and the Pythoness, after putting herself into an oracular trance by the chewing of laurel leaves – for humbler visitants she omitted this painful procedure and was content to give uninspired but sensible advice from her own knowledge and experience – began to rave and mutter unintelligible words as she sat on the gift tripod in a recess of the round white tomb.

Presently Jason understood her to say that the voyage which he must undertake would be renowned in song for unnumbered ages, if he took the precaution of sacrificing to Apollo, God of Embarkations, on the day that he launched his ship; and to Apollo, God of Disembarkations, on the night of his return. Then she relapsed into what seemed to be nonsense. The only recurrent phrase that he could catch at was that he should 'take the true Jason' with him. But the Pythoness, when she recovered her sobriety, was unable to tell him who this person might be.

Delphi was renowned for curative lyric music, but Jason, educated only in the stirring music of pipe and drum, despised the gentle twanglings of the tortoise-shell lyre. He had difficulty in preserving the required silence while it was being played to him by the priests of the musical college; and he grieved when he saw the flayed skin of the Pelasgian Marsyas, which the priests of Apollo had cured and nailed up in derision on the door of the college. Marsyas had been a Silenian, leader of the Goat men who made pipe-music in honour of the hero Dionysus; but Apollo's archers had driven out the Goat men, and those who escaped their arrows they hurled down into the gorge. The priests claimed that the lyre was a recent invention of the God Hermes, who had presented it to Apollo. Yet the only difference between the lyre which they used and that which had been used by the priestesses of the Triple Goddess from time immemorial was that they fitted it with four strings instead of three, and that they extended it with a pair of curved horns branching outwards from the tortoise-shell body and connected near the top by a yoke of wood to which the strings were fastened.

Astronomy was another study at Delphi, and the priests were already dividing the stars into constellations and timing their first ascensions above the horizon and their subsequent declensions. A school of image-makers and vase-painters, founded by Prometheus, was also under Apollo's patronage, but Iphitus the Phocian, a famous artist with whom Jason lodged on this occasion and who afterwards became an Argonaut, told him that the name of Prometheus, like that of Dionysus, was no longer honoured at Delphi.

As for the Aesculapian school of medicine, a compromise between the claims of Apollo and Hades had been found. Once the mourning wail had been uttered over a sick person, Apollo's physicians were forbidden to attempt his cure; and in general the art of medicine was to be palliative rather than restorative. But Apollo's physicians have not always kept to their side of the bargain, especially those settled in the island of Cos.

CHAPTER SIX

ZEUS APPROVES THE VOYAGE

From Delphi it was only a short journey to the blue waters of the Crisaean Bay, where Pelias and Jason found a Corinthian trading-ship at anchor; she was conveying a cargo of Phocian pottery and painted ornaments to King Alcinoüs of Corfu, an island which lies opposite the river Thyamis, at a few miles' distance from it. Pelias bargained with the master for Jason's safe conveyance to the Thyamis, and was careful to tell him, as if in confidence: 'This nephew of mine, Jason son of Aeson, proposes to sail to Colchis in the spring, with the bold aim of seizing the Golden Fleece of Zeus from evil-minded King Aeëtes, who has refused to return it to the Achaean rulers of Greece. Jason now hopes to consult the Oracle of Zeus at Dodona and there win the God's approval for his enterprise. It would be the greatest pity if he fell overboard before he reached the coast of Epirus; for, not being yet under the protection of Zeus, it is likely that he would drown and the Fleece would therefore remain in the possession of Aeëtes.' Pelias then paid the master in advance the fare that he demanded, and also gave him a valuable gold ring with these words: 'Take as good care of my nephew as if he were already homeward bound with the Fleece.'

The Corinthian master, as Pelias suspected, reverenced his fellow-countryman King Aeëtes as a champion of the old religion against the new, and cherished the memory of his former patron, generous King Sisyphus of Asopia, whom Zeus and the Achaeans had brought to so cruel an end. The words of Pelias, 'It would be the greatest pity if he fell overboard', rang in his head, and the value of the ring suggested that Pelias trusted in Jason's ability to secure the Fleece and prized him accordingly. The Corinthian therefore decided to murder Jason; which was what Pelias had intended him to do, though he had been careful to remain guiltless in the matter.

The water in the Gulf was calm enough, and the wind fair, but on the third day, as the Corinthian ship coasted past Leucas and met the full fury of the Ionian Sea, Jason fell sick and lay under the shelter of the prow wrapped in his woollen cloak and occasionally rising up to vomit over the side. Then the master, whose brother, the helmsman, knew of his intentions, caught Jason by the legs and heaved him overboard. Nobody but the helmsman saw or heard what was done, for the rowers were hard at work with their backs turned, and the master smothered Jason's feeble cry with a cheerful song; while the helmsman from his end of the ship began cursing one of the oarsmen for not keeping stroke.

This would have been the end of Jason, who was weak from frequent vomiting and being swept along by a powerful current, but for a miraculous intervention. A wild olive-tree, rooted up by the force of a gale or flood from a near-by mountain-side and thrown into the sea, came drifting past. Jason, whose whole life had been spent in the mountains, so that he had never learned to swim, caught at the branches and with a huge effort pulled himself astride the trunk. He clung to this tree until evening, when at last he saw a sail to the northward and presently an Athenian vessel came bowling down the wind, about two bowshots away. The helmsman, observing Jason's signals, steered towards him; and the crew hauled him aboard. When they heard who he was and how he came to be in the water they were astounded; for, not an hour before, they had watched the Corinthian vessel being wrecked with all hands, and beyond possibility of rescue, on the rocks of a lee shore. Judging that Jason, whom they had found surrounded by large, savage fish, must certainly be under the protection of the Gods, the master agreed to turn the helm about, for no reward, and convey him safely to his destination. The name of this Athenian master was Hestor.

Jason thanked Hestor heartily and, kneeling by the mast, prayed aloud to the Goddess Athena, the ship's patroness. He undertook, in gratitude for his preservation from the bellies of the fish, to erect an altar to her at Iolcos and burn most exquisite heifer sacrifices on it. Clearly, the rescue had been from first to last arranged by Athena, for the olive-tree is sacred to her.

Jason came safe to Dodona a few days later, accompanied by Argus, Hestor's eldest son. He was surprised, after hearing so many boasts about this place by the Achaeans, whose fathers had resided there for some years, to find it a mean, straggling village at the head of a lake full of noisy water-fowl. It contained no buildings of lofty height or neat construction, and even the council-chamber was a large tumble-down hut with a turf roof and a floor of rammed earth. However, he had been instructed by Cheiron, whose advice he had now learned to respect, to pretend admiration, in the course of his travels, for even the most miserable buildings, clothes, weapons, cattle and the like that were pointed out to him with pride by their possessors, and at the same time to decry everything that he had left behind at home, except the simplicity and honesty of his fellow-citizens. By these arts he ingratiated himself with the Dodonans, and though the priests at the shrine were disappointed that the gifts which he had intended to present to the God – a great copper cauldron and a sacrificial sickle with an ivory handle – had been lost in the wreck of the Corinthian ship, they were satisfied with his promise to send other gifts of equal value as soon as he returned to Iolcos. As a token of good faith he cut off two long tresses of his yellow hair and laid them before the altar; these would give the priests power over him until the promise had been fulfilled.

The Chief Priest, who was a relative of King Pelias, was delighted to hear of Jason's resolve to recover the Fleece from the hands of foreigners. He informed him that King Aeëtes by long traffic with the kinky-haired Colchian savages, and by marriage with a savage Taurian princess from the Crimea, had become a mere savage himself and tolerated customs in his own family at which it would be shameful even to hint in so sacred a spot as Dodona. 'Is it not terrible,' he asked, 'to think that the Fleece of Zeus, one of the holiest of Greek relics, and one upon which the fertility of all Phthiotis depends, has been hung up by that wretch's filthy hands in the very shrine of Prometheus the fire-thief, the avowed enemy of Zeus, whom the Colchians now identify with their national War God? Let me tell you more about this Aeëtes. He is of Cretan descent and claims to be of the royal blood of those unnaturally inclined Pasiphaë priestesses, who boasted that they were all-navel, that is to say insatiable in their sexual desires, and are believed to have coupled with sacred bulls. Aeëtes practised witchcraft of a peculiarly impious sort while he was a resident of Corinth, having been initiated into the art by his fair-haired sister Circe. Why they suddenly parted, Circe sailing to a remote island off the coast of Istria and Aeëtes to the eastern shore of the Black Sea, is an enigma; but it is suspected that the separation was ordered by the Triple Goddess in punishment for incest or some other crime that they had committed in company.'

'Holy One,' said Jason, 'your report stirs my soul to righteous anger. Consult the God for me, if you will, and let me be assured of his favour.'

The Priest answered: 'Purge yourself with buckthorn, wash yourself in the waters of the lake, abstain from all food, remove all your woollen clothing, and meet me in the oak-grove at grey dawn tomorrow.'

Jason did as he was told. Dressed only in his close-fitting leather tunic and rough sandals, he came at the time appointed and stood in the shadow of the oak-grove. The Priest was already present in his ceremonial dress of ram's wool, with a pair of gilded, curling horns tied on his brow and a yellow branch in his hand. He took Jason by the arm and told him to fear nothing. Then he began softly to whistle two or three notes of a melody and to wave the branch to and fro, until a breeze sprang up and rustled the leaves of the oak, causing those that were scattered on the ground to run round and round as if in ritual dance to the God.

The Priest continued waving his branch and whistling louder and louder. Soon the wind roared through the branches, and Jason seemed to hear the leaves sing all together: 'Go, go, go with the blessing of Father Zeus!' When the Priest ceased his invocation, there was a sudden lull, followed by another furious single gust and a distant roll of thunder. Then a crack sounded above their heads and down tumbled a leafy branch, about the size and form of a man's leg, and fell at Jason's feet.

Seldom had so propitious a sign been granted to any visitant in that grove, the Chief Priest assured Jason. After trimming the branch with a sickle, to remove all the leaves and twigs, he graciously gave it into Jason's hands. 'Here,' said he, 'is something holy to build into the prow of the ship in which you sail to Colchis.'

Jason asked: 'Will the God be benignant enough to supply me with a ship?'

The Chief Priest answered: 'No, no: since the Goddess Athena has already been at pains to rescue you from the sea, let her be in charge of the ship-building too. Father Zeus has other cares. Pray, tell her so.'

When Jason returned in elation to the hut where he was lodged, his comrade Argus asked him whether he proposed to winter at Dodona, now that their ship had sailed homewards and they could not count on finding another; or whether he would try to make his way back to Iolcos over the mountains.

Jason replied that he could not afford to remain idle during the winter, and that the sacred branch of the oak of Zeus would be sufficient protection for any journey. Argus thereupon offered to accompany him. Two days later, carrying wallets stuffed with dried meat, roasted acorns, and other rough food, they set out on their journey, following the valley of the rushing Arachthos river until they came to a rock-strewn pass overshadowed by Mount Lacmon. The heights were bitterly cold and the snow already whitened the peaks; at night they took turns in watching at the camp fire. When the owls hooted, Jason heard their outcry not as an ill augury but as the heartening cry of the Goddess Athena's own bird, and being an initiate of the Leopard fraternity he was equally undisturbed by the howling of the leopards, which are numerous in the Pindus range. But the roaring of the lions terrified him.

From the pass they continued eastward until they came to the headwaters of the Peneus. The Peneus, though a small stream at first, gathers tributaries in its descent to the fertile plains of Thessaly and at last debouches as a noble river into the Aegean Sea at Tempe, between the greater Mount Olympus and Mount Ossa. Game was scarce in this desolate country, and Jason, though famous as a hunter on the slopes of Pelion, was unacquainted with the haunts and habits of the beasts of Pindus. He and Argus tightened their hunger-belts and considered themselves fortunate on the eighth day to cripple a hare and kill a partridge with well-aimed stones. But the knowledge that they were under the protection of so many deities sustained them, and at last they saw a shepherd's hut in the distance, with sheep grazing near by, and hurried towards it in eagerness.

Then arose a furious barking and a Molossian hound, of immense size, came rushing at them, its yellow fangs bared, and without making the least pause leaped at Jason's throat. Argus drove his spear into the belly of the beast as it leaped, and it died howling. The shepherd, who had lived for years in this wilderness without any human companionship, came running out of the hut and saw Argus transfix the hound with his spear. He caught up a javelin and without the least pause rushed at Argus, bent on avenging the death of the hound, his only friend. Argus had not yet disengaged his spear, which was caught between the hound's ribs, and would have been killed in his turn had not Jason, who was carrying the sacred branch, brought it down with a crash upon the shepherd's skull and sent him sprawling.

They carried the stunned shepherd to the hut and tried to restore him by dashing cold water in his face and by burning feathers under his nose. But when his breath came in snores, they knew that he was about to die. They were greatly troubled and each with his lips and eyes began to reproach the other silently, for they feared that the ghost of the dead man, since he was not killed in legitimate warfare, would haunt them stubbornly until his kinsmen had avenged him; but Jason's guilt was the heavier of the two. They rubbed their faces with soot from the hearth, hoping that the ghost would not recognize them again mistaking them for Aethiopians; and Argus washed away in flowing water the hound's blood that had spurted over his hand.

When the shepherd expired at last, they dug a grave at the spot where he had fallen and buried him in it just as he was, with his dog beside him, averting their faces the whole while lest the ghost might recognize them even through the soot, and conversing in squeaky voices. They heaped stones over the grave and poured a libation of milk and honey (which they found in the hut) to placate the ghost. They did not dare touch any of the shepherd's other possessions, and to show their friendly intentions drove his flock into the sheepfold for safety and passed on.

They went forward together in silence for a mile or two until a shining thought came into Jason's mind. He turned to Argus and said: 'I thank you, dear comrade, for saving my throat from the fangs of that furious hound.'

Argus was surprised that a homicide should dare to speak so soon after the event. He answered: 'And I thank you, noble prince, for despatching that furious shepherd.'

Jason said mildly: 'You owe me no gratitude, son of Hestor. Neither you nor I killed the shepherd. It was this sacred oak branch that struck the blow. Let Father Zeus be wholly responsible for the deed. His shoulders are broad enough to sustain any burden of guilt.'

Argus was pleased with this notion. He embraced Jason and, after washing the soot off their faces at a wayside stream, they continued their journey to the nearest settlement, one of five huts belonging to the brigand tribe of Aethics. The inhabitants, women for the most part, were impressed with the resolute bearing and well-made weapons of Jason and Argus and set bowls of milk before them. Jason presently reported having witnessed the death of the shepherd, which, he said, had been caused by an oak branch blown from a tree. The Aethics believed this story (which was true so far as it went), since they knew that several oak-trees grew near the hut, and reasoned that if these strangers had murdered the shepherd they would have concealed the fact as long as possible. When they asked what had become of the dead man's sheep, Jason answered: 'Good people, we are not thieves. The sheep are safe in the fold. The shepherd's red Molossian hound mistook us for enemies and attacked us, and my companion was obliged to spear him. But I thought it wrong to leave the sheep to the mercy of wild beasts; I led them safely into the fold.'

The Aethics praised Jason for his consideration, and sent a boy to fetch the flock down to the settlement, which he did. Since, as it happened, the shepherd was an exile from a distant clan, with no known kinsmen, the flock was thereupon divided equally among all the huts; two sheep that remained over, when each of the huts had been awarded an equal number, were sacrificed to the War God Ares, whom the Aethics principally worship. That evening everyone fed plentifully on roast mutton and sucked beer through barley-straws and danced in honour of Ares, men and women together, and praised the dead shepherd. Jason and Argus expected to be treacherously attacked before dawn, because the Aethics have the reputation of being entirely without moral principles. They therefore drank sparingly of the beer and took turns as usual at keeping armed watch. But nothing untoward happened, and in the morning they were guided by one of their hosts to the house of his maternal kinsman, who lived twenty miles away down the Peneus valley; and there they were treated with equal friendliness.

From the territory of the Aethics their route lay through that of the Lapiths, hereditary enemies of the Centaurs. But Argus undertook to escort Jason safely through if he would braid up his hair in other than Centaur fashion and pretend to be a servant; to which Jason agreed. On their arrival in Lapith territory, where they found fine herds of cattle and horses grazing in the water meadows, Argus immediately made himself known. He claimed matrilinear kinship with Theseus of Athens, who is celebrated by the Lapith balladists for his friendship with their former King, Peirithoüs; these two heroes were allies in a successful war against the Centaurs which had arisen, as usual, from a quarrel about women.

Argus was hospitably entertained by the Lapiths, and all would have been well had not Jason chafed at being treated like a servant: he told his hosts haughtily that he expected better food than husks and gristle. The Lapith chieftain was scandalized and ordered Jason to be beaten for his insolence; so Argus interposed and revealed who this servant really was, but with the warning that he was under the protection not only of the

White Goddess but of the Olympians Apollo, Athena, Poseidon and Zeus. The chieftain, whose name was Mopsus the Minyan, understood that Jason would be of more value to him alive than dead. He thought at first of demanding from Pelias a huge ransom in gold and cattle, but Argus told him plainly that Pelias could not be counted upon to pay so much as a bone button. While Mopsus was still debating the matter with his companions, Jason undertook that if he were set free, without any conditions, he would persuade the Centaurs, over whom he had influence, to make peace with the Lapiths. Mopsus took Jason at his word and set him free; and this was the beginning of their friendship.

When Jason returned safely to Iolcos, by way of Pherae, and boasted of his adventure in the Ionian Sea, Pelias was vexed beyond measure at having overreached himself. If he had not put it into the Corinthian master's mind to attempt murder, Jason would assuredly have lost his life on the rocks. But Pelias knew well how to conceal such vexedness of heart under the cloak of flattery or congratulation, and feasted Jason as nobly as before.

Jason presently visited Cheiron and submitted to him the proposals of Mopsus, which were that hostilities between the Lapiths and Centaurs should cease at once; that Pelias should be restrained by the Centaurs from continuing the Lapith war on his own account; and that the Centaurs should have free passage through Lapith territory whenever they wished to go courting the Aethic women of Pindus. These proposals Cheiron accepted; and after a while he persuaded Pelias, by gifts of hides and timber, to make peace likewise. Thus Jason was the means of healing the ancient feud between Centaurs and Lapiths and justified the name that Cheiron had given him.

CHAPTER SEVEN

THE BUILDING OF THE *ARGO*

When Jason had sacrificed a pair of white heifers to the Goddess Athena in fulfilment of his promise he sent out heralds, royally clothed, to all the chief cities of Greece. Each herald carried in his right hand four twigs of different woods and a miniature double-axe, wound all together with a long thread of yellow wool; and in his pouch he carried a fir-cone. Whenever he came to the courtyard of any great house where the proprietor was of Minyan blood, he would clap his hands for attention and presently display the axe and the bundle of twigs. He would say: 'The blessings of Olympus fall upon this House! I come in the name of the Immortal Gods. See this twig of ash: the ash is sacred to Poseidon, whose spears and oars are made of its stubborn wood. See this twig of laurel: it is Apollo's own prophetic tree. This twig of olive is Athena's; I need not remind you of the virtues of the olive, that fertile cow among trees. Look finally at this twig of oak, sacred to Zeus himself, whose axe of power is here enclosed in the bundle. My lords, what does this strand of yellow wool signify? It signifies the common purpose of four great Greek deities in the matter of the Golden Fleece, which is the ancient property of Zeus and has been unjustly and impiously withheld from him by Aeëtes the Corinthian, now King of Colchis, who reigns in Caucasian Aea, where the swift horses of the Sun are stabled, at the furthest end of the Black Sea. This priceless object must be won back from Aeëtes either by persuasion, fraud, or force, and must be restored to the Father's holy oaken image on Mount Laphystios.

'I am the herald of Jason the Minyan, son of King Aeson who rules at Iolcos in Phthiotis, or (as some now call it) Haemonia. Let the ash witness: in the market-place of Iolcos during a well-thronged festival of sacrifice to the God Poseidon, this Jason was inspired to propose the expedition to Colchis. Let the laurel witness: the God Apollo afterwards publicly confirmed Jason in his resolution. Let the olive witness: the Goddess Athena, when she saw Jason struggling in a boisterous sea off the island of Leucas, rescued him in a miraculous manner and set him safely ashore at her Father's gate. Lastly, let the oak witness: Almighty Zeus accepted the offer of Jason's services and tossed him as a token of favour an oak branch from his own sacred tree. Is this not wonderful?

'Come, my lord, and you, and you, will you not join Jason in this holy quest and thus earn glory – glory which will not only shine for you garland-wise throughout your life, however long that may be, but after your death, will confer dignity on your house and city and on your latest posterity? When you die, my lords, you will all assuredly become heroes, and offerings will be heaped and poured to your ghosts, so that you will never wander hungry and disconsolate through the gloomy caverns of the Underworld as lesser beings are fated to do. You will drink from cups of the largest size and ride on white ghost horses and assist the seeds that your children have planted in your ancestral fields to germinate and bear rich and abundant fruit. The blessed Olympians all favour this expedition, which cannot but be successful, however hazardous it may seem. For Zeus has charged his dutiful daughter Athena to build the ship, and has charged his loyal brother Poseidon to calm the waters of the sea; and Apollo his son has obscurely prophesied other good things.

'And for what worthier leader than Jason could you hope, since Hercules of Tiryns is busied with his Labours and cannot come? It is reported – doubtless with truth, for who would have dared to invent so improbable a tale – that Jason before his rescue by the Maiden Athena was seven days and seven nights in the water, fighting alone against a swarm of sharp-toothed sea-monsters, of which the largest ran at him open-mouthed and engulfed him; yet so manful is this Jason that he cut his way out of the creature's massive side with his sharp Magnesian hunting-knife.

'Listen further: there is not only imperishable glory to be won at Colchis, but treasure. Is not the merchants' road through the Caucasian mountains guarded by the impious Aeëtes, who levies a toll of a fifth part or more on all the merchandise that comes heaped in wheeled carts from Persia, Chaldea, Bactria, Sogdiana, India, and the uttermost ends of Asia? Are not his palace rooms and cellars bursting with riches? When Aeëtes is destroyed and the Fleece regained, what will prevent you from each carrying away as much gold dust and as many gold ingots and silver ingots and bales of carpets and bags of balsam-drops and caskets of jewels as he pleases?

'Come, my lords, how do you say? But let me warn you that none but sturdy young noblemen of undoubted Minyan blood will be accepted for this expedition, and no more than a ship's complement of these. Many will necessarily be turned away. Come quickly, my lords, to Iolcos.'

This speech seldom failed to rouse the spirits of the Minyans who heard it, especially those who chafed at their peaceful occupations and at the taunts of their Achaean overlords: for the Achaeans had a poor opinion of them, declaring that they had become enervated by the easy life that they led in Greece and were unfit for any dangerous enterprise. Some of these Minyans immediately engaged themselves to join the expedition, but others were more circumspect and asked: 'Is it not true, gracious Herald, that the Fleece of which you speak was stolen long ago from the Ram of Mount Laphystios by the Mare-headed Mother, in revenge for his having usurped her shrine on Mount Pelion? Do you invite us to side in this quarrel with the Ram God, who is now named Father Zeus, against the Great Triple Mother whom he has since forced to become his wife Hera? We are Minyans, descendants of that Minyas whom the Mother loved and honoured above all other Greeks because it was he who first counselled the Ram God to become subject to her. Should we not be dishonouring the memory of our ancestor, to whose glorious hive-shaped tomb at Orchomenos we still send yearly gifts, if we attempted to undo the work of the Goddess? Was it not by her own order that the stolen Fleece was committed to the hands of King Aeëtes?'

This was the herald's answer: 'I praise you for your continued devotion to the Goddess. But now look at the other true token which I carry in my pouch. It is a fir-cone from Mount Pelion and is enclosed, as you see, in a white hair-mesh woven from the mane of the Goddess's sacred mare. This token answers all your questions: from it you can read plainly that the Goddess approves the voyage. For though the recovery of the Fleece may be no concern of hers, yet she promises her blessing to whatever Minyans will sail to Colchis with Jason and there give rest to the ghost of her servant Phrixus, which still clings disconsolately to his unburied bones. Let me warn you, noble Minyans, not to find in the forgotten quarrel between the former Triple Goddess and him who was once her son a reason against your sailing to Colchis in search of the Fleece. To do so would be to forget what calamities have come upon your clan since this Fleece was stolen away. Athamas the Minyan was the guardian of the precious relic, and for his loss of it he was punished by Father Zeus with the loss of his reason; to such madness was he driven by the Furies that he transfixed his own son Learchus with an arrow, mistaking him for a beast of chase in the very courtyard of his own palace. Since Athamas was deposed, the Minyan power has declined. First, the seven champions who went against Thebes were beaten from its walls by Hercules of Tiryns. Then the ailing Aeson could not hold the north-eastern gateway of Greece against the invading Achaeans; and then it was not long before his uncles, the Minyan Kings Perieres of Messene and Salmoneus of Elis, ended their lives miserably. But Aeson's son Jason, lately returned from a Centaur's dark cave as if from the dead, is a man of extraordinary courage and wisdom: it is his opinion that, until the Fleece is recovered, the Minyans will never regain the favour of Zeus and must sit still with complaisant smiles while their proud overlords taunt them with indolence and cowardice.'

This speech convinced a few of the waverers, but by no means all.

Meanwhile, Jason had visited the illustrious city of Athens, sailing in fine weather through the sheltered Euboean Gulf. There he paid his devotions to the Goddess Athena and humbly conveyed to her the orders of her Father Zeus. The King and Queen Archons, who together govern the religious life of Attica, made him welcome and showed the greatest interest in his project. After a short consultation they offered him all the help that they could command, but extracted a promise from him in return not to offer any insult or violence to the inhabitants of Troy, with whom the Athenians were on excellent terms, but to obey any reasonable request that the Trojan King might make. When Jason had confirmed his promise with oaths of so solemn a nature that only a madman would have ventured to break them, he learned with pleasure that Athena had accepted her Father's charge, and that the building of the ship was to be entrusted to Argus, son of Hestor, who was not only a descendant of Daedalus the inventor but almost his equal in the shipbuilding art.

Jason returned to Iolcos and told King Pelias of his successful interview with the Archons. Pelias, feigning pleasure, offered him hewn timber and nails and cordage and all the resources of his ship-yards. Jason thanked him ceremoniously but referred him to Argus, in whose hands the whole task of ship-building rested; and then, in private, reminded Argus that, since Pelias was secretly ill-disposed to the expedition, no gift of his would bring any luck – to use even a strand or two of Iolcan cordage would be to rig the ship with curses. Argus thereupon declined the offer of Pelias, though protesting gratitude, on the ground that the Goddess Athena had stipulated that every least cord used on the ship should have been twisted on the rope-walk of Athens, and that every length of timber should have been hewn in the Goddess's name

Argus went in search of pine wood and found what he needed near the foot of Mount Pelion, where a row of tall trees had been felled by a gale; some of their roots were still fast in the soil, so that they had withered slowly and the wood was tough. Here was sufficient timber for the planking of a single-masted, narrow-beamed, thirty-oared ship of war, which was in his opinion the most handy build of vessel for a raid on Colchis. His men trimmed these pines with axes and then stripped them of what bark remained on them; the logs, none of which was found in the least degree rotten, were hauled down to the shore in ox-drawn wooden cradles, then lashed together as a raft and floated across the bay to the broad beach of Pagasae opposite.

Not far off, at Methone, Argus found oak timber suitable for the ribs of the ship, selecting crooked limbs of large trees, and one tall straight oak for the keel. When he had floated these too to Pagasae, the work of building could begin. Some of his carpenters smoothed the pine timbers with adzes into planking, others with saws and axes cut the oak ribs, then dove-tailed them into the keel and bored bolt-holes for fastening them with olive-wood pegs to the stout oaken bulwark. Soon the skeleton of the ship took shape, and by the time that the prow and stern-post were fitted, the planking was ready to be nailed to the ribs with copper nails; but first each plank was made pliant by steaming it over cauldrons filled with boiling sea-water. The ship measured sixty paces in length, at the water-line, with a beam of five paces; some seamen of experience thought that a wider beam would be needed for a passage of the Black Sea, which had the reputation of throwing up huge waves from every quarter at the same time; but Argus obstinately maintained that speed was a more important consideration than the comfort of the crew.

The mast was stowed away in a crutch, but was easily pulled out and stepped into its socket with the aid of massive oaken wedges. The sail was a square of coarse white linen, brought from Egypt, and the hawsers were of plaited horse-hair wound about with hemp. The ash oars, each twice the length of a man, had narrow blades; but the blades of the two oar-rudders, one fixed to port and the other to starboard of the helmsman's seat, were broad. The benches were of oak, with well-fitting lockers under them, and the oar-holes were lined with bull's leather on the under part.

The prow, into which the sacred oak branch from Dodona was firmly fitted, curved up gracefully like the neck of a swan, but ended in a carved ram's head; the stem curved up similarly, so that the helmsman from his raised seat would have a clear view over the oarsmen's heads. A stout wickerwork shield, lined outside with leather, was fixed above the bulwarks to protect the rowers against rain and boisterous waves; and, in order that the sacred tree of each of the deities who had sponsored the voyage should be used in the construction of the vessel, the uprights of this shield were made of laurel wood cut from Apollo's grove at Delphi.

The ship was built in ninety days' time, and before work on the stern was completed the proofing and adorning of the prow and sides had already begun. After being caulked with hot beeswax, the sides were blackened inside and out with tar distilled from the pines of Pelion; and the cheeks of the prow were painted vermilion with cinnabar bought in the summer market at Troy. On each side of this prow, high up, a great eye was painted with white and green earths, and curling black lashes were added with the tar brush. Flat anchor stones were also found, pierced to take a hawser, and chipped into a circular shape so that they could easily be trundled up a plank and heaved overboard; poles were cut for fending the ship off rocks or pushing her off a sandbank if she grounded; and two ladders were made for the convenience of embarking and disembarking. Leather thongs secured the oars to the bulwarks so that they should not slip through the oar-holes and be lost.

All who examined the ship – and hundreds of people travelled from far and near for a view of it – declared that they had never in their lives seen anything so handsome. She was named *Argo* in honour of Argus, and he grew so proud of her that he declared that he could not bear to be parted from his handiwork and would sail in her wherever she went.

The palace at Iolcos was filled that winter with brisk young men who had assembled in response to the heralds' invitation. Most of them were Minyans, but not all; for it was thought that Jason would perhaps accept likely men with no Minyan blood in their veins if they consented to become Minyans by adoption. Pelias could not refuse hospitality to these visitors, but complained to Jason that they were wasting his substance like locusts, and that the sooner the voyage began the better he would be pleased; being men of distinction, they had to be fed appropriately to their rank, and most of them came accompanied by several retainers. Aeson, the father of Jason, though nominally King of Phthiotis, was living in such poverty that he could not lodge more than six men; which struck the adventurers as so odd that half of them decided after all not to make the voyage. They concluded that Pelias, not Aeson, was the real ruler of the kingdom and that it was he, not any god, who had prompted Jason to make this voyage in the hope of ridding himself of a rival. Nevertheless, they did not immediately return to their homes, since they found good sport at Iolcos in hunting, quoit-throwing, boxing, wrestling, dicing, and running races, and Pelias for the honour of his house did not stint them of food or drink.

The more energetic of them asked Argus what they should do to prepare themselves for the voyage. He answered that they had no need to ask him a question which they could themselves answer in a moment: they would be best employed in learning the art of rowing unless they were already perfect in it, which he doubted. For unless the winds were more favourable than they had any right to expect, it would be only by hard rowing that they would either stem the strong currents of the Hellespont and Bosphorus, or escape from the pursuing Colchian fleet when they had landed and carried off the Fleece. As it happened, a few of them were already practised oarsmen, who had made the Sicilian or the Italian voyage and knew almost everything that was to be known about the handling of ships; but most of them had been more concerned with horse-breeding and fighting than with seafaring and had seldom or never been aboard a ship except as passengers in calm summer weather. Then Jason borrowed from Pelias a pair of twenty-oared war-galleys which had been hauled up for the winter, and there in the sheltered waters of the gulf he and his new acquaintances rowed races for wagers, under the guidance of two well-known helmsmen, Ancaeus of Tegea and Tiphys of Thisbe. They learned to turn the oars in the oar-holes as a key turns in a lock and to keep time to the helmsman's chant. Their hands grew hard and their shoulders muscular, and from this exercise, taken together every day, grew a bond of comradeship which restrained them from armed conflict at night over their wine-cups and dice.

One evening Jason went to Pelias and said to him privately: 'Uncle something is weighing upon my mind, I am ashamed to tell you what.'

'Let me hear the worst, Boy,' said Pelias benignly.

Jason hesitated a while and then told him: 'A lying rumour is going about the palace. Your guests are saying that you hate and fear me, and that you are sending me out on this voyage only to be rid of me; some even hint that you plan to sink our ship by some mechanical or magical device as soon as we are clear of the Pagasaean Gulf. How shamelessly the rascals talk! Nevertheless, I fear that unless you can reassure them that you are as favourably disposed to me, and to the ship *Argo*, as I know in my heart that you are, there will be no volunteers for the voyage, or not enough to man the ship. Then you will have been caused all this expense needlessly, and the *Argo* will become a by-word throughout Greece. Worse, when kings and priests chat together and say to one another, "Tell me, why did the *Argo* not sail after all? There had been so much boasting beforehand and such lavish preparations of all sorts" – this will be the answer: "It was known that Pelias meditated some treachery; this was the true reason why the *Argo* never sailed, not the evil omens that they pretended to find when they sacrificed." And consider, Uncle, whether the Gods will be pleased when the same rumour reaches high Olympus.'

Pelias was disturbed. He called all the adventurers together and told them: 'My lords, some madman has been tarnishing my good name. May Father Zeus blast him with a thunderbolt from a clear sky and the Harpies carry off the writhing remnants! Which of you, my honoured guests, will dare to repeat to my face the base lies that he whispers behind my back? I tamper with the hull of the *Argo* or plot against the life of her crew? How can you think that I have so little respect for the Gods and for my fellow-men? Oh, some rascals will believe anything. But now let me give you proof of my honest intentions towards you. There sits my only son, the Prince Acastus, whom I love dearly. Although I have need of him here to lead my men in war – for I myself am past the age of fighting, even from a chariot – I herewith cheerfully devote him to the sacred quest of the Fleece. He shall go with you, he shall be your comrade, and any trouble or disaster that may strike the *Argo* shall strike my son Acastus at the same time, and myself because of him.'

He spoke deceitfully, intending at the last moment to detain Acastus on some pretext or other but the speech reassured many of the doubtful ones. Acastus, who had just been drunkenly complaining that his father was unkind to forbid him an adventure from which no Minyan prince could decently abstain, uttered a yell of delight. He staggered across the hall to embrace the knees of Pelias and ask his blessing. Pelias was obliged to grant the blessing and conceal his displeasure.

Now, among the chieftains of Phthiotis was a young nobleman of Corinthian stock who had fled to Iolcos from his island of Aegina after killing a stepbrother with a quoit; but it was not clear whether this was murder or manslaughter. He had then married the daughter of a cousin to

Pelias, the leader of the Myrmidon clan, and at Phthia was given a thorough ritual purification to cheat the stepbrother's ghost. After the ceremony he changed his name to Peleus – his original name is now forgotten – and was initiated into the Ant fraternity. Peleus then went with his father-in-law to Arcadia to take part in the famous hunt of the Calydonian boar. When the boar suddenly broke cover, Peleus threw his javelin at it; but it glanced off the boar's shoulders and transfixed the father-in-law. He went to Iolcos for a further purification, which was performed by Acastus, but retained the name of Peleus; and then returned to Phthia to take over his father-in-law's lands, and the leadership of the Myrmidon clan. While he was still at Iolcos, the wife of Acastus fell in love with him, or so he afterwards said, and made advances to him. When he rejected them she secretly accused him to Acastus of having made advances to her which she had rejected. Acastus was friendly with Peleus, but the Achaeans set so much store on the chastity of their wives that he felt bound to avenge his honour. However, he shrank from killing Peleus outright, because the ceremony of purification was, he knew, a troublesome one and not always effective. Instead he took Peleus hunting on Mount Pelion in a part of the forest reserved by treaty for the Centaurs, and presently put him to sleep by giving him several draughts of beer on an empty stomach. Then he took away his sword and left him, hoping that either wild beasts or Centaurs would kill him.

The Centaurs were the first to discover Peleus, but fortunately old Cheiron happened to come up in time to call off his hot-headed tribesmen, reminding them that if they killed one Achaean twenty Centaur lives would be exacted in vengeance. Peleus guessed who had taken his sword and why, and persuaded Cheiron to send down a report to Iolcos that his body had been found mangled by wild beasts. The wife of Acastus then publicly boasted that her husband had avenged her honour; and Acastus, growing alarmed, shut himself in his room and would not eat, and daubed his face with filth and tore all his garments to make himself unrecognizable to the vengeful ghost of his friend. When Peleus returned safe and sound a few days later and gave his own version of the story everyone laughed at Acastus; but Acastus could at least laugh at his wife. He and Peleus became blood-brothers and swore eternal friendship. So it was that when Acastus was given leave to sail in the *Argo*, Peleus decided to come too.

The spring equinox was approaching, which was the earliest time at which it was considered safe to begin the voyage, and at last Jason, who had sent to the shrine of Zeus the Ram on Mount Laphystios to enquire a favourable day for sailing, was able to announce that their adventure would begin on the fourth day after the next new moon.

At this a great cheer was raised in the hall, but it was noticed that several of those who had been foremost in feasting and quoit-playing and racing were silent: and presently they began to make excuses why they could not sail. Some pretended to have injured their arms in rowing, others took to their beds in what seemed to be high fever, others went off in the night without any goodbye or polite excuse. It seemed unlikely that a sufficient ship's company would, after all, be found, and Jason went about with a gloomy look on his face, which had a dampening effect on the spirits of his comrades.

CHAPTER EIGHT

THE ARRIVAL OF HERCULES

On the evening of the new moon a messenger came hurrying into the palace and told King Pelias: 'An ancient enemy of the Minyans is marching along the road from Halos. Who he is you may easily guess when I tell you of the brass-bound club of olive wood he carries over his shoulder, the enormous bow slung at his back, the lion-skin tunic and the long unkempt mane, like a lion's. However, he has informed travellers on the road that he comes on a peaceful errand, and it is seldom that he troubles to tell a lie.'

There was a stir in the hall, and Erginus of Miletos, formerly of Orchomenos, put his hand to his sword and would have run out to do battle, but his comrades restrained him. The gloomy-featured Melampus, Poseidon's son from Pylos, said: 'Erginus, we know that you have had cause to curse the name of Hercules of Tiryns since he fought against you at Thebes, after first cutting off the ears and noses of your tribute-gatherers from Orchomenos. Yes, the tribute was no unjust one: we all know that it was exacted by you in compensation for your father's death at the hands of the Thebans. Yet if, as I suppose, Hercules has heard of our proposed expedition and wishes to take part in it, will you not have cause at last to bless his name? There is no bolder or more experienced fighter in the world than Hercules. Let us Minyans hurry out of this hall, not with swords to oppose his coming, but with garlands and cups of wine to greet him. Many years ago by his defence of Thebes he checked our attempt to subjugate Boeotia; but this old injury should be forgotten, now that the Achaeans have made themselves the overlords of all Greece and Hercules himself is become a bond-servant to King Eurystheus of Mycenae. You have all heard the saying "Nothing without Hercules", and it is true that he has been absent from no great military exploit of the last thirty years. I regard his coming as a most fortunate sign. Let us heal the old feud by inviting him to join us as our leader.'

These words were applauded by everyone present except Jason, who, despite his complete ignorance of seamanship and navigation, had counted on the glory of commanding the expedition. Only he and Argus, who had lamed himself with an axe, stayed behind in the hall when the other adventurers ran out to welcome Hercules.

Pelias, observing this, asked Jason with a sneer: 'Why do you sit brooding there in your leopard-skin, nephew? Do you not know that the Lion is the King of Beasts?' When Jason made no reply, he added: 'I advise you to run hurriedly after your companions and overtake them and be the first to welcome Hercules. If you do not, they will be vexed and sail without you, and then you will be the laughing-stock of Greece.'

Pelias hoped that Hercules would consent to command the expedition: for Jason would thereby lose his glory. Besides, Hercules, who was subject to fits of madness, had the reputation of being as terrible to his friends as to his enemies. He was capable of suddenly snatching up his massive brass-bound club, because of some imagined insult or injury, and knocking five or six of his companions stone dead; and then he would bellow remorsefully and beat his great head against a wall.

Jason took his uncle's advice and hurried out. When he had gone, Pelias could not refrain from saying to Argus: 'I doubt whether your ship, well bolted though she may be, will long sustain the weight of a champion as massive as Hercules.'

Jason, who was very swift of foot, soon outstripped the other Minyans. He came panting and alone an hour later to Pagasae, where he found Hercules with Hylas, his young squire, in a hut not far from the shining *Argo*, drinking with the ship's carpenters and painters. 'Most noble Prince Hercules,' he gasped, 'I am Jason of Iolcos, where the glad news has already come of your arrival in these parts. I have run ahead of all my companions to be the first to greet you. It is with the greatest readiness that I resign the leadership of our enterprise into your famous hands.'

Hercules, a pig-eyed, bull-necked man of extraordinary muscularity and height – he was nearly seven foot tall – sat gnawing at a shoulder of mutton. He grunted in answer, stripped off a little more of the roasted meat with a wrench of his huge, dirty hands and crammed it into his mouth. Then suddenly he flung the blade-bone through the open doorway, where Jason stood, at a diving-duck which was bobbing about in the water a few paces from the shore. The bone whistled by Jason's ear, flew the full breadth of the beach and, striking the bird on the head, killed it instantly. 'I hit her every time,' Hercules chuckled to himself. He wiped his greasy fingers in his grizzled, stubbly hair, belched resonantly and presently asked: 'Huh! what enterprise is this, my fine boy? You speak as though everyone in the world knew the gossip of your small corner of Thessaly. Have the wolves of Mount Haemon been stealing your bony sheep? Or have the Centaurs of Pelion broken out again and begun kissing your bony women?'

This was his usual banter; he knew well enough what enterprise Jason meant. He had just completed the sixth of the famous Twelve Labours imposed on him by King Eurystheus of Mycenae (the son and successor of King Sthenelus), which was to capture alive the wild-boar that had been terrorizing the slopes of Mount Erymanthos. The news of Jason's projected voyage reached him in the market-place of Mycenae just as he was hauling down the boar, securely fettered, from the handcart in which he had wheeled it all the way from the bleak and cypress-shadowed valley of Arcadian Psophis. The citizens were shouting for wonder at the beast's terrific tusks, almost like an African elephant's, and at its glaring, blood-shot eyes. Young Hylas told the citizens: 'My master Hercules made short work of the creature: he chased it into a deep snowdrift and then caught it in a hempen net as it floundered.' Then, as it happened, one of Jason's heralds came into the market-place and began making his speech about the twigs and the wool and the axe to a group of Minyans whom he found there. Hercules cried out: 'Good people, take this boar to King Eurystheus with my compliments and tell him that I will return for further orders when I have been to Colchis and settled this little matter of the lost Fleece. Come, Hylas my child, reach me down my wallet from the cart, and off we go again on our travels.

Hercules prolonged his Labours by a number of voluntary ones, many of them more extraordinary than those imposed by Eurystheus. He did this to show his contempt for his master. That Eurystheus had any power at all over Hercules may seem surprising; but this is the story. After his victory over the Minyans of Orchomenos, Hercules (then known as Alcaeus) had been rewarded by the King of Thebes with the hand of his eldest daughter Megara, but four years later in one of his drunken fits killed his children by her, and a couple of his nephews at the same time, mistaking them for snakes or lizards. Their ghosts began to haunt him. The customary rites of purification were ineffective because the ghosts of a man's own children cannot be easily deceived, and he therefore went to Delphi to ask Apollo's advice, complaining of sudden tweaks at his legs and tunic and of childish voices ringing in his head. The Chief Priest had not forgotten what hostility Hercules had shown to the new religion, and ordered him to become a servant for a Great Year to King Eurystheus, whose father Sthenelus had been murdered by Hyllus, a son of Hercules. He was to do everything, within reason or without, that Eurystheus ordered; and was promised that at the end of the year these tweaks and voices would entirely cease. Meanwhile the sacred physicians prescribed palliatives. A Great Year is nearly eight years long, and by the end of it sun, moon, and planets are all back again where they were when it began.

Eurystheus was pleased at first with this arrangement, which flattered his power and gave him hope of avenging his father's murder on Hercules, who had instigated it; but he soon became aware of the disadvantages of having so unusual a servant. Hercules when he had successfully accomplished his first task, that of strangling the Nemean Lion, frightened Eurystheus nearly to death by playfully tossing the corpse into his lap.

Eurystheus refused him further audience and built himself a brass refuge-tomb under his throne, into which he could slip if Hercules ever broke into the palace again, pulling a trap-door down over his head and feigning death. Then he thought out a series of almost impossible tasks, which his herald Talthybius would order Hercules to perform, and which were designed to keep him out of Mycenae for as long as possible. Hercules used to greet Talthybius with: 'Holloa, Dung-man, what is the latest filth that you bring from your master?' But his respect for heralds kept him from ever beating him or breaking his teeth.

Jason had once been warned by his tutor Cheiron that it was always wiser to drink with Hercules than to quarrel with him. He therefore answered his banter mildly. He said: 'Indeed? Can it really be that you have not yet heard what all Greece is buzzing with? No doubt you have been abroad or in some inaccessible district of Greece for the last few months. But, by my Leopard's spots, I swear that these carpenters and painters have been wonderfully discreet: I wonder what scruples have kept them from telling you what vessel this is that they have been working at, and to what purpose it is dedicated.'

Hercules growled: 'Ugh! They did begin to tell me some foolish story about a pack of young Minyans who boast that they are sailing her to Scythia – or was it India? – in search of treasure guarded by gryphons. To be honest with you, I ceased to listen when I heard that it was a Minyan enterprise. I have never felt the least interest in what the Minyans may do since I gave them such a beating at Thebes some years ago.'

Jason kept his temper. 'I fear,' he said, 'most noble Hercules, that you did not see my fellow-Minyans at their best on that occasion.'

'I fear not, Boy,' answered Hercules. 'Indeed, they made a pitiable showing. I believe that my Hylas here could have routed them with his little sling and dagger. Could you not, my sweet?'

Hylas blushed, and Jason said: 'Pray excuse me if I admire the looks of your young companion, Hercules. I feel bound to declare him the hand-somest child I ever saw.'

Hercules drew Hylas to him and gave him three or four smacking kisses on the neck and face. 'He is all the world to me,' he cried, 'and as brave a boy as walks. I intend in a year or two, now that he has attained to puberty, to initiate him into the Lion fraternity. There are not many of us, but Holy Serpents, we make our presence felt in the world!' Hercules had originally been a Bull man, but quitted the fraternity when it was announced that Zeus had taken it over from the Mother Goddess. 'If a Ram can turn into a Bull,' he said, 'a Bull can become a Lion'; then, to propitiate the Goddess for the injury he had done to her High Priestess at Olympia, and also for the death of her Nemean Lion, which he had strangled, he went to visit Queen Circe of Aeaea, who managed affairs of this sort, and enrolled himself in the Lion fraternity. She ordered him to bite off one of his own fingers to placate the ghost of the lion, and this he fearlessly did and, what is more, instituted the Nemean Games in its honour.

Jason was pleased to have found a soft side to the rugged nature of Hercules. 'I am sure that your Hylas will prove worthy of you,' he said. 'Already he carries his head like a king. How does he come to be in your service? He is not one of your innumerable bastards, is he?'

Hercules sighed gustily. 'The poor child is an orphan. I killed his father myself. This was what happened. I was wandering through western Thessaly on some expedition or other, and one day I happened to feel hungry. I came across a Dryopian farmer ploughing a fallow field in a sheltered valley, and uttering, for luck, the usual obscene imprecations. I saluted him with: "My lucky ploughman, I am so hungry that I could eat an ox." He answered, with a smile, but continuing to curse, that I should at any rate not eat his ox until the field had been ploughed and harrowed too. "Holy Serpents," I cried, losing patience, "I will, if I like." "Hold hard," said he. "I am Theiodamas the Dryopian. I must ask you not to speak to me in that peremptory way." I answered: "To the crows with your 'peremptory'. I am Hercules of Tiryns and I always say, do, and get, just whatever I please. At Delphi the other day I told the Pythoness exactly what I have just told you; but she refused to believe me. I pulled the sacred tripod from under her and carried it out of the shrine. 'Now,' said I, 'if needs must I will have an oracle of my own.' Ho, ho! That soon brought her to her senses." But Theiodamas either had never heard of me or else could not believe that I was I. He threatened me with his ox-goad so I gave him a friendly tap with my club and cracked his skull like an egg-shell. Alas, I never meant to kill him. I never know my strength, that is my curse. The same thing happened to me when I was a boy learning to play the lyre, and my music-teacher, a pompous fool named Linus, rapped my knuckles and told me that my fingering was incorrect. I gave him a playful whack with the lyre and dashed out his brains. A pure accident, that I swear! I pleaded self-defence and the affair blew over, but I have never touched a lyre since.

'Well, as I was saying, I was strangely hungry that day. I killed the ox, skinned it, started a fire with the wooden plough and the goad, and fed it with a few dry logs pulled from the side of a barn near by. While my meat was roasting, I piously dedicated the corpse of Theiodamas to the Corn Mother and scattered pieces of it along the furrows to improve the crop; which was a cunning way of escaping the attentions of his ghost, I considered. I was about to sit down to dinner when I heard a little whining noise from the side of the barn – whee, whee, wow, whee! There sat a pretty child of two years old who had been sleeping on his father's coat in the warm sun. The crunching of my jaws must have awakened him. Yes, you have guessed right: it was Hylas. I took a fancy to him at once. I gave him a marrow-bone to suck and toasted him a tit-bit of ox-tongue at the fire. He and I soon grew so friendly that I carried him off in my wallet. He has come with me on all my adventures ever since. They say that his mother died of grief at her double loss. If so, she was a silly woman: Theiodamas was an obstinate mule, and she should have known better than to grudge Hylas an education that most mothers would have paid anything to provide for their sons. Never you mind, my darling Hylas; Hercules is your father and mother now. Hercules will always take care of you.'

Jason asked: 'May I enquire what you are doing in Phthiotis, most noble Hercules? Are you perhaps engaged on another of your world-famous Labours?'

'No, no. I had just completed the sixth of them – or was it the seventh? – no matter – when it occurred to me to take a holiday in Thessaly, show Hylas his paternal lands, and pay a visit to my old friend Cheiron the Centaur on the way. One of these days I will put Hylas on the Dryopian throne if he likes. Eh, darling?' He caught up Hylas again and began hugging him. When Hylas yelped with pain, Hercules immediately desisted. 'There, you see,' he said. 'I never know my own strength. I cracked a couple of his ribs a few months ago and he had to lie up. Truly, I meant no harm; I have a very warm nature, you know.'

'Since you are, then, somewhat at leisure,' said Jason, 'we Minyans, who are by no means so degenerate as you judge us to be, will esteem it the very greatest honour if you will accompany us to Colchis as captain of this ship. For we intend there to recover the Golden Fleece of Zeus.'

Hercules considered a moment. 'Colchis, Colchis, did you say? I remember the place. You sail to Troy first, and have your usual disagreement with the sulky Trojans, and break a few heads. Then you keep along the southern shore of the Black Sea, trudging up and down hills for a few hundred miles – some of the tribes you meet have the most peculiar manners – until you reach the country of the Amazons, to the north of Armenia. I went there not so long ago, on a Labour, to fetch back Queen Hippolyte's girdle: it was not at all an easy task, for the Amazons fight like wild cats, and I was obliged to humour them. However, I got what I came to get. After Amazonia, another hundred miles or so, and at last you see the Caucasian mountains on the horizon and the Black Sea ends. That is Colchis. I remember a wide, slimy river and a tangle of wild vines in the forests, and tree-frogs of the colour of emeralds, and some kinky-headed natives at the port, and a number of odd-looking Indian trees. I started up the river in a canoe for I had business at the shrine of Prometheus, some distance upstream but I was forced to turn back again as usual because of the children's voices in my head. I should like to try again. I should like to visit the land of perpetual snow at the top of Caucasus, where the garlic-eating Soanians slide down the snow-chutes on skin toboggans faster than the diving swallow, or climb up slippery ice pinnacles with their spiked shoes of raw hide. I have heard that the snow falls in flat cakes like little knives not in stars and flowers as with us; I wonder is that so? Very well, I will come to Colchis with you. Our Thessalian holiday can wait – eh, Hylas?'

'How generous you are, Prince Hercules,' cried Jason, wishing him dead and securely buried under a towering barrow of earth and stone.

Hercules silenced him. 'Listen, Boy, I am very careful in my choice of messmates. If I consent to lead the expedition, I insist on deciding who goes with me and who stays behind.'

'That will save me a great deal of embarrassment,' said Jason, 'so long as you consent to include me among those who go.'

'I cannot say that I like the look of you,' said Hercules with severity. 'You call yourself a Minyan, you swear by the Leopard's spots like a Magnesian, and you wear your hair in a mane as though you were a Centaur. You remind me of the Chimaera, the lion-headed she-goat of Caria with the snake's tail. I have never met her myself. I do not expect to do so either. I believe that half the accounts one hears of her are fraudulent. Who are you?'

Jason gave a brief account of himself When Hercules heard that he was one of Cheiron's pupils he cried, 'Good, good!' and treated him with greater affability. 'Cheiron is the last of my old friends,' he said 'He and his wise mother Philara once doctored a nasty wound of mine. I will never forget it. I had feared to lose an arm.'

They spoke no more about the expedition, but drank together jovially and soon the other Minyans came bursting into the hut and greeted Hercules with wild cheers. He roared at them to go away, saying that he was busy with his cups, and slammed the door in their faces so hard that part of the roof fell in. They slouched back in chagrin to Iolcos.

Jason flattered Hercules and plied him with wine, a fresh jar of which he fetched from a farmhouse near by, and at last incautiously asked leave to imprint a chaste kiss on the cheek of Hylas.

Hercules bellowed with indignant laughter and waggled his great horny forefinger at Jason. 'You had best do nothing of the sort,' he said. 'The boy is mine, not yours!' An iron crow-bar lay among the carpenters tools in a corner of the hut. Hercules picked it up and began bending it into a collar for Jason's neck, but Hylas pleaded for Jason's forgiveness; so, instead, Hercules twisted the crow-bar into a coiled snake, with head raised ready to strike, and set it on the floor facing Jason, hissing himself in a threatening way. His face had grown fiery red with his exertions, for he was already in his fiftieth year and his strength was declining somewhat; he looked terrible.

CHAPTER NINE

THE CHOOSING OF THE ARGONAUTS

The next morning Hercules slept off his drink. He awoke about noon in an irritable mood; but Hylas was waiting for him with a huge basin of wine and a beef-steak or two which Jason had prepared, and presently he consented to be ferried over to Port Iolcos in a boat. They were half-way across when the two racing-galleys came threshing past; and their wash set the boat rocking. Hercules shouted out a curse, seized and strung his bow, and leaping up, stamped furiously with his foot. He would have sent a volley of arrows after the galleys, but that he had stamped a great hole in the bottom of the boat, which instantly filled and sank. Hylas could swim like a fish and struck out for the Iolcan shore, which he soon reached, but Jason bitterly regretted that he had not learned from his previous adventure to take swimming as well as rowing lessons. He managed to keep his mouth above water with the help of an oar and yelled to Hercules for help. Then he knew no more for a long time. Hercules, not wishing to be dragged down by Jason's frantic struggles, had taken the precaution of stunning him with his fist. It was fortunate that Jason's thick skull was protected by the coils of his braided hair and a leather helmet.

When eventually he came to, with a violent headache, he heard a heavy tread near him, and half-opening his eyes saw Hercules gazing down at him in a puzzled manner. 'You are not dead, are you?' Hercules asked.

Jason looked painfully about him and saw that he was in the hall of Pelias again, not in the caverns of the Underworld as he had supposed. 'No, I am still alive,' he answered. 'What hit me?'

Hylas tittered, Hercules chuckled, and soon the whole hall rang with a tremendous roar of laughter. 'What hit him? Ha! Ha! What hit him?' For Hercules had just been giving a display of strength, in the course of which he had challenged Augeas, the young King of Elis with the famous stable of horses, to a wrestling match, and then catching him by both knees had tossed him up to the roof; his belt caught on the peg of a cross-beam where he hung like a flitch of dried goat-meat. Hercules had also left his mark on the place, as he always did, by dealing a right-handed punch at a great copper cauldron, so that the marks of his knuckles showed in a dint four inches deep. 'What hit him? Ha! Ha! What hit him?' King Augeas of Elis echoed from the rafters, congratulating himself on being alive and uninjured. He was in no haste to descend.

The next evening after supper Jason, still weak but able to stagger about with the help of a stick, asked Hercules whether he had yet chosen the crew for the *Argo*. The business had escaped Hercules's memory, but he attended to it without delay. He clapped his hands for silence, and even King Pelias, who was giving some detailed instructions to his cup-bearer, thought it wise to obey. Hercules, wherever he went, seemed to be king.

'First of all,' he began in his booming voice, 'I order all those guests of King Pelias who wish to sail with me to Colchis in the what's-her-name to range themselves on my right hand; and those who do not wish to sail to range themselves on my left hand.'

After a moment of hesitation, fifty men stepped to the right, a few of them Minyans; and thirty to the left, most of them Minyans.

'Next,' said Hercules, 'I order you thirty cowards who hang back from the voyage even when you know that Hercules is sailing, to lay down your weapons and divest yourselves of all your clothes. You are to leave them lying there as a grateful return to King Pelias for the hospitality that he has shown you, and to go home at once without so much as a pair of leather breeches among you.'

There was a roar of laughter from the fifty and a cry of indignation from the thirty, who brandished their weapons and refused to do what Hercules ordered. But when he reached for his brass-bound club and spat on his palms the thirty thought better of their defiance and began laying down their swords, spears, and javelins, and undoing their buttons. The daughters and women guests of King Pelias blushed and went out by a side door; the King himself was alarmed, fearing that a dozen wars might grow out of the incident. But Hercules would not relent and the young men went stark naked out of the hall into the cold night, leaving their clothes and weapons and jewels behind them. The fifty bolder men hooted after them.

Then Hercules said genially to Jason: 'I am an unlucky man, I always have been so. They say that I am no judge of men, and perhaps they are right. Let my Hylas choose the crew for me. He knows better than I the sort of man that is needed; he is a clever youngster, is Hylas. But first let all the volunteers who are of Minyan blood stand aside; for the heralds have promised them the first places in the ship.' The adventurers who were not Minyans resented that the choice should be made by a mere boy, but none dared to oppose the wishes of Hercules.

The fourteen Minyans (there were no more) stood aside. Conspicuous among them was Mopsus the Lapith, who, having lately been assured by an old hen-stork that he would die in the deserts of Libya, was perfectly confident that he would survive the voyage, which would take him in the other direction. For Mopsus claimed to understand the language of birds, though admitting that they sometimes talked as nonsensically as humans. He wore a starling crest, and the tip of his tongue was slit with a knife. Near him stood honest Coronus the Lapith, of the Crow fraternity; gloomy Melampus of Argos, a cousin of Jason, who wore the Magpie crest; and hot-tempered Erginus of Miletos, whose cloak was striped like a tunny-fish in honour of his father Poseidon, and who wore a belt of plaited horse-hair. Next to Erginus stood another son of Poseidon, the wizard Periclymenus, from Sandy Pylos; he wore the same sort of belt as did Erginus, but had been born during an eclipse of the sun and was therefore free to wear whatever badges he pleased – he was even permitted to eat the food of the dead. His mother, Chloris, was now wife to Neleus, the cruel brother of Pelias. Next to Periclymenus stood taciturn Ascalaphus, a son of the God Ares by Astyoche, whose arms were tattooed with lizards. These three men had come to have divine parentage because their mothers' distinguished birth had marked them out for election as temple prostitutes. The other Minyans were Jason, son of Aeson; Acastus, son of Pelias; Eurydamas the Dolopian from Lake Xynias in Thessaly, a stalwart horse-breeder; Tiphys the helmsman, from Thisbe in Boeotia; two men from Halos whose names are now forgotten; and a pair of brothers, grand-sons of Perieres the former King of Messenia, named Idas and Lynceus. Idas and Lynceus wore caps of lynx-skin which they never removed from their heads; they were tall men in the prime of life, and cared nothing for any man.

Hylas went up and down the ranks of the volunteers who were not of Minyan blood. Two magnificently tall champions, twins by the look of them, with bulging muscles, swan's-feather head-dresses and cloaks of swan's-down, caught his eye first. He tapped them on the shoulders.

'Your names, if you please,' said Hercules.

'Castor and Pollux,' they answered in one breath. 'We are the sons of Leda by Father Zeus, and princes of Sparta.'

'I fancied that I recognized you,' said Hercules, 'though upon my soul I could never tell you apart. Which of you is the horse-tamer and wrestler – the one whom I threw far over the ropes into the crowd at Olympia, and who afterwards tried to teach me the art of fencing?'

Castor smiled and answered: 'I am Castor. I was a fool to enter the ring with you. Yet I had never been thrown before and have never been thrown since. I well remember those fencing lessons… In the end I advised you to stick to your club.'

'I am Pollux,' said Pollux. 'I won the boxing contest at the Games. It was lucky for me that you did not enter.'

'I was too beastly drunk,' said Hercules, 'which was lucky for both of us: once I am in the ring I can never remember that I am fighting a friendly match – can I, Hylas my child?'

Castor and Pollux, though not Minyans, were cousins to Idas and

Lynceus, and brought up with them since childhood; there was deadly rivalry between the two pairs of brothers.

Hylas then tapped two wild-looking Northerners, another pair of twins, who wore feathered head-dresses of kite-plumes stained with sea-purple. The face of each was tattooed with thin blue interlocking rings.

'Your names, if you please,' said Hercules.

'Calaïs and Zetes,' Calaïs answered. 'Our mother, Oreithyia of Athens, when a girl, was carried off by Thracian pirates as she was dancing in honour of Artemis, on the banks of the Ilissos. They made her a prostitute at the Oracle of the North Wind, on the bank of the Erginos river, and we were born to her there. Afterwards, blind King Phineus of Thynia took Oreithyia as his wife and begot two more sons on her; we are thus known as the sons of Phineus. But we are, properly, the sons of the North Wind.'

Hylas next chose Euphemus, the son of Europa, from Taenaron, which lies on the southernmost promontory of the Peloponnese. He was the best swimmer in all Greece. Compared with others, he seemed to skim along the surface of the water like the swallow, which happened to be his badge. Poets have therefore celebrated him as a son of Poseidon; but his father was Ctimenus the Phocian.

The truth was that Hylas had a fancy for feather head-dresses and was choosing all the men who belonged to bird fraternities. His next choice was Idmon of Argos, who wore the golden crest of the hoopoe. Idmon was heir to the King of Argos, but his mother, Calliope, had become pregnant of him after a pleasurable visit to the Oracle at Delphi, and he thus ranked as a son of Apollo. He wore scarlet boots and tunic and a white cloak embroidered with laurel leaves in his divine father's honour. Like Mopsus, he was a student of augury.

The next man chosen was Echion, a son of the God Hermes by Antianeira of Alope; he wore a snake's badge in his father's honour and a gorgeous heraldic robe embroidered with myrtle-leaves. He had been one of the heralds employed by Jason and had persuaded himself to volunteer for the voyage by the force of his own eloquence.

Just as Hylas was choosing Echion, in came a splendid-looking Thessalian, dressed in a cloak and tunic made from the skins of lambs cast untimely. He was one of the boldest of the adventurers, but had been away on a short visit to his home, which was not far off. No sooner had he seen Hercules than he uttered a cry of joy and came running to embrace him. He was Admetus of Pherae, the Thessalian King with whom Apollo had been condemned by Zeus to serve as a menial. One day, some twelve years before this, he had accidentally trespassed in an enclosure newly consecrated to the God Hades, where a stag which he had been pursuing was harboured. The priest of Hades then warned Admetus that either he or one of his relatives must, within seven days, offer himself as a victim to the offended God; otherwise a curse would fall on the whole country. His wife

Alcestis, one of the daughters of Pelias, went at once to the shrine and offered herself in place of Admetus; for she was the best of wives. However, Hercules, passing through Thessaly with the infant Hylas on his shoulders, happened to hear the story. Protesting that Hades had no shadow of right to the shrine which had recently been stolen from the Goddess Persephone, he ran in with his club, terrified the Infernal priests and rescued Alcestis in the nick of time. Hercules had a high regard for Alcestis, and used to say regretfully that no woman had ever loved him well enough to have offered her life for his. He now gave Admetus a friendly slap that sent him spinning across the hall, and told Hylas: 'Count Admetus in!' For Admetus was a Minyan, son of Aeson's brother Pheres.

Hylas continued to choose from the remaining volunteers, and when he had chosen a full ship's company, all but three, Hercules waved his hand and said: 'Enough. Now let the remainder strip themselves to the buff and fight it out among themselves for our diversion, wrestling or boxing with nothing barred. The last three men to remain upon their feet shall come with us.'

Then ensued a battle that was at once very fierce and very mild, for not all the twenty contestants were whole-heartedly set upon making the voyage; the rest had volunteered from shame and wished for nothing so much as to be rejected. Some fell down and lay like logs at the first feeble tap that was dealt them; others fought with terrible vigour, punching, kicking, gouging, and biting. The spectators yelled encouragement to their kinsmen, and one or two could not be restrained from running into the fight and taking part. Hylas squealed and Hercules roared with laughter to see two enormous fighters, who had blacked each other's eyes, break off their fight by mutual consent and go in search of easier game; and to watch the antics of leather-helmeted Little Ancaeus of Flowery Samos – not Great Ancaeus of Tegea, the helmsman, who wore a broad-brimmed Arcadian hat. Little Ancaeus pretended to be fighting with the utmost fury, but was merely darting in and out of the scrimmage, dodging blows and dealing none, in order to reserve his strength for the final tussle.

Gradually the hall cleared. Now only seven contestants remained on their feet: four in a struggling mass; two together, whose names were Phalerus and Butes, sparring cautiously apart; and Little Ancaeus. Little Ancaeus ran up to Phalerus and Butes. 'Break away, Athenians,' he cried. 'You, like myself, are still fresh and strong. Let us fall, all three together, on the other bloody-nosed fools, and sweep them away like a mountain torrent.'

Phalerus the archer and Butes the bee-master were as shrewd as one expects Athenians to be: they knew that their best chance of being chosen was to stage a sham fight, exchanging noisy but ineffective blows, and trusting that their reputation as boxers would keep other fighters away. One young Arcadian from Psophis, who had a grudge against Athens, did indeed try to make a three-cornered fight of it, but Phalerus jerked his knee into the Arcadian's groin, so that he fell groaning.

At the invitation of Ancaeus the Athenians dropped their fists, and all ran together to the other end of the hall, where three of the combatants were trying to fell the fourth. Ancaeus crouched down behind the knees of one of them, a Mycenaean, whom Butes caught by the hair and dragged backwards. As the Mycenaean toppled and fell, Phalerus drove a great fist into his midriff. This trick they repeated with one of the remaining pair, both Cadmeans from Thebes; and the survivor they picked up bodily and swung out through the open door of the hall into the muddy road. So Butes, Phalerus, and Little Ancaeus were the victors.

However, the names of the thirty oarsmen, the helmsman, and the supernumeraries, who eventually sailed in the *Argo* do not correspond with those of the ship's company chosen by Hylas and Hercules. For a couple of Minyans, those from Halos, slipped away on the last night and two Aetolian new-comers, a man and a woman, unexpectedly took their places. Since, therefore, there has been so much vain boasting by pretended Argonauts who never so much as saw the *Argo* riding at anchor in a sheltered harbour, the authentic roll will be given in full; but not yet.

CHAPTER TEN

THE *ARGO* IS LAUNCHED

The day appointed by the Oracle for the launching of the ship was now close at hand, and the chosen crew practised rowing together in the same galley – all but Hercules, who went off with Hylas on a visit to his Centaur friends and spent the next three days and the intervening nights in a tremendous carousal with Cheiron. Those of the crew who were not Minyans by birth performed a perfunctory ceremony of becoming so by adoption. Each in turn crept out from between the knees of Jason's mother, Alcimede, and then wailed like a new-born infant until comforted by her with a rag-teat dipped in ewes' milk. After this they were solemnly given their own names again and grew to manhood within the hour.

Jason saw to the provisioning of the ship, but many of the Argonauts were men of wealth and willing to pay their share, or more than their share, of the expense. With the silver and golden ornaments, the jewels and the embroidered robes that they contributed to the common stock Jason was able to purchase from Pelias sacks of grain, sides of cured beef, conical lumps of fig-bread, sun-dried grapes, roast salted filberts, jars of honey, honey-cakes flavoured with thyme and patterned with pine kernels, and all manner of other confections, in large quantities. He found it unnecessary to ballast the ship with stones and sand: instead, enormous earthenware jars, of the length of a man or longer, filled with sweet wine and well stop-pered, were laid in cradles on either side of the kelson. Each Argonaut provided his own arms and bedding, but spare cordage and sails had been found by the Archons of Athens.

At last the fateful morning dawned. The sky was unclouded and the North Wind blew cold from Thessaly, but dropped as the sun rose. In Iolcos a great wailing was heard. Some of it was caused by genuine grief at the departure of so many magnificent young men on an unusually hazardous voyage; but most of it was raised by hired mourners whom the Argonauts had paid to avert the jealousy of any God or Spite who happened to feel maliciously inclined towards the ship – just as beans are planted with curses to keep away the ghosts that gnaw at the young shoots. Pelias, for politeness, wept the loudest of all and kept repeating: 'If only the dark wave which carried Helle away to her death had overwhelmed

Phrixus too! For then the Fleece would never have been conveyed to Colchis, and my very dear nephew Jason would never have had occasion to make this voyage. I fear that it will prove fatal to many, if not all, of the brave men who sail with him.'

Aeson, when Jason came very early to say goodbye, bore himself with dignity, and gave him his blessing. He also undertook to send to Dodona the promised cauldron and ivory-handled sacrificial sickle, though he could ill afford to purchase them. Alcimede wound her arms about Jason's neck, weeping ceaselessly. He managed at last to disengage himself, saying: 'For shame, Mother! Anyone would think that you were an orphan girl, cruelly ill-treated by a stepmother, who sobs around the neck of an old nurse, the only person in the house who still cares for her. These cries are unbecoming in a Queen.'

Crouched on the floor, she sobbed: 'When you are gone, what will become of your dear father and me? You may be sure that you will never find us alive on your return – if ever you do return. Pelias will have been our murderer. Then who will dare to bury us? Our bodies will be thrown into the open fields for the kites to peck at and for the dogs to gnaw. I do not fear death, which is the common fate of mankind, but I do shrink in loathing from the miserable existence of an earth bound ghost, condemned to wander homeless for ever, twittering like a bat, in the cold and rain.'

Jason told her curtly to be of good cheer and went striding out into the market-place. There the people greeted him with cheers of admiration mingled with howls of grief. They strewed his path with the scarlet wind-flower, which is the emblem of youth that is doomed to die. His grand-aunt Iphias, the Chief Priestess, stood in his path. She had fallen in love with him, as aged virgins sometimes do with handsome young men. She seized his right hand and kissed it, but, for all her eagerness to say something, she could not force the words out, because her heart beat so loud against her ribs. Jason passed on, with the crowd yelling beside him, and she was left there by the wayside mumbling spitefully: 'The heartless young man, with no respect for age or virtue! May he one day remember me when his hair is grey and thin and his bones ache; when the fine ship towards which he now hurries so proudly is a rotting skeleton on the beach; when there are no crowds to cheer him and slap his back!' She scratched a secret figure in the dust at her feet.

Jason continued on his way along the curving coast road and at Pagasae found most of his comrades already assembled. They were sitting on the coiled cordage, folded sails, and other gear collected on the beach. Argus, dressed in a long cape of bull's hide, with the black hair worn outside, stood waiting impatiently for permission to launch the ship. Hercules had not yet arrived, but Jason suggested that they should begin to launch the ship without him. Jason had vowed a sacrifice to Apollo, God of Embarkations, and his father Aeson who had supplied a yoke of oxen on each of the three preceding days – for sacrifices to Zeus, Poseidon, and Athena respectively – had promised him yet another yoke, of the small herd still remaining to him; so the company would feast well as soon as the ship had taken to the water. When Jason told them of this they all rose to their feet and began collecting large flat stones which they piled one on top of the other to make an altar, and heaped logs of dry driftwood about it.

When this was done, Jason took off all his clothes except his leather breeches and laid them on a large rock above high-water mark, the others followed his example. Then at the request of Argus they frapped the ship lengthwise from prow to stern with four heavy ropes, which they wetted first and afterwards drew tight with a windlass. As each rope was securely reeved and knotted, Jason called in turn on each of the four Olympian deities who had sponsored the voyage, to guard that rope well.

Argus had mattocks ready, and set his comrades to dig a trench, a little broader than the ship's beam, down the beach into the sea, beginning from her prow. There was a greater depth of water at this point than anywhere else on the coast for half a mile around. Behind them, as they dug, their servants, armed with heavy logs, rammed down the stony sand of the trench to make a level surface. The *Argo* was already resting on a set of rollers which had been in position since her keel was laid. Now it remained to lay others ahead of her in the trench, of stout pine logs with the bark stripped off, and heave her forward upon them. There was no room at the pointed poop for more than two or three men to heave; but Argus reversed the oars in the oar-holes so that the butts protruded a couple of feet beyond the gunwale and the blades pressed against the ribs on the opposite side. Then he posted a man at each of the oars and climbed up into the bows and cried: 'One, two, three – heave!'

The Argonauts heaved with their arms and shoulders and thrust backwards with their feet, while the crowd kept holy silence. The *Argo* shuddered, creaked, and began to slide slowly forward. The men at the oars and those at the stem heaved the harder, and Tiphys kept her straight on her course by shouting: 'Handsomely, you of the starboard side! More muscle, you of the port!' The rollers groaned and a light smoke rose from the friction as she rattled down. Tiphys shouted 'Ho up, ho up! Avast shoving! Hold her now! Handsomely, handsomely all!' Then with a swish her prow took to the water, and her whole length followed. Tiphys, who had a jar of olive oil in readiness, emptied it into the sea, splashing it first upon the prow, as a libation to the God Poseidon and a request for a calm sea.

The *Argo* rode trimly on the water, and the crowd cheered three times for good luck. The crew tied her up in shallow water and, after reversing the oars again and securing them in the oar-holes with the leather loops began lifting stores aboard. Argus saw to the stepping of the mast, to the adjusting of the loops and pulleys for hoisting the yard, and then to the reeving of the rigging; but he did not hoist the sail, for there was no wind.

These tasks were nearly complete when a sudden shout of dismay rose from the shore. Hylas appeared from the direction of Iolcos, beside a rough ox-wagon on which was stretched Hercules, at full length, with a train of mourners following behind. 'He is dead, Hercules our leader is dead,' the Argonauts cried in dismay, and one or two of them added: 'Nothing without Hercules! Hercules is dead; we cannot sail.' But it proved that he was only lying in a drunken stupor and that the hired mourners, after taking refreshment by the way, had come down to Pagasae to give the *Argo* a lucky send-off.

When Hylas revived Hercules with a helmetful of sea-water dashed in his face, he sat up in a fury, seized his club and jumped out of the wagon, which had pulled up close to the newly built altar. The crowd scattered in all directions and the Argonauts clambered up the sides of the vessel and crouched down inside. Hercules suddenly aimed two vicious blows in quick succession on the polls of the white oxen which had been drawing the wagon. They fell down dead upon their horns. Jason, peeping over the stern from the helmsman's seat, called out: 'Well struck, most noble Hercules! You have caused the victims to fall in the most propitious manner possible.'

Hercules rubbed his eyes and woke as if from a trance. Then he began to laugh. The crowd crept out from their hiding-places, the Argonauts vaulted back over the sides of the ship into the water, and all joined in the laughter, even the hired mourners. Then Jason called on Great Ancaeus and one or two others to help him unyoke the fallen oxen and drag them nearer to the altar. They were the very beasts which Aeson had promised for the sacrifice; Hylas had happened to see them being driven down the road towards Pagasae and had borrowed them as draught animals for the conveyance of Hercules.

Standing before the altar, Jason raised his voice and cried out: 'Sun-like Brother of the Moon-like Artemis, Delphic Apollo, Wolfish One, Be-laurelled Apollo of the Embarkations, to whom I vowed this sacrifice six months ago when I visited your holy shrine and city – listen to me! At your prompting, not I but Hercules of Tiryns has felled these oxen in your honour, and unexpectedly soon, for I had not yet poured the lustral water on my hands, nor set your portion of holy barley in the hollow upon the altar. You know, Dear Lord of Mice, how prompt Hercules is in any enter-prise: look with favour, I beseech your musical Majesty, on this reversal of the order of your customary ritual. Now, washing my hands free of any uncleanness, I formally dedicate these fine, unblemished beasts to you, Truth-teller, sprinkling salt on their polls as a seasoning. Guide our ship, I beg you, safe and sound back to this beach of Pagasae, after we have fulfilled our quest; and watch over all who are in her. Upon her return each of us whose life is spared will lay again on this altar bright offerings of bulls' flesh; and other gifts of countless number and priceless value we will bring to your bee-frequented shrines of Delphi or Tempe or Ortygia. Idmon, guest of your own Delphic house, will sail with us; and so also will pious Admetus, King of Pherae, who once showed you a strange reverence when you were his menial and bound to obey his least command. Protect your own, Heavenly Archer of the Unshorn Hair, and grant us a lucky sign when we unreeve the hawsers; intercede also for us with your stern uncle Poseidon, that his sea-horses, the waves, may not rush too restlessly across the deep.'

With that he ladled out the barley-porridge on the altar top, pleased with himself for having introduced into his speech the greater part of the God's divine attributes.

Idmon, as priest of Apollo, then cut the oxen's throats with a sacrificial knife of dark green obsidian. Out gushed the blood into the trench around the altar: warm food to appease any lurking ghosts.

Lynceus, whose eyes were of such keenness that he could distinguish seven Pleiads in the night sky where others saw only six, and was always the first to detect the secret presence of a God, ghost, or Spite, now began to smile. He observed in an undertone to Little Ancaeus: 'How greedily they drink, those ghosts! There is one fierce-looking shepherd among them, an Aethic or Dryopian by his dress, who has shouldered away the crowd from the deeper end of the trench and is drinking far more than his fair share. He has a huge wolf-hound beside him and the two of them are lapping together, tongue to tongue, at the excellent blood before it soaks into the sand.' Jason did not overhear these words, but Little Ancaeus stored them in his memory.

Argus, as a Bull man, was forbidden to eat beef except on one holy day of each year. He built another altar and sacrificed a fine ewe before it to the Goddess Athena, for his own eating and hers. Lynceus nudged Little Ancaeus again and said: 'Bats and owls! What an appetite that Aethic shepherd and his dog have! Now they are at the ewe's blood which seems more to their taste. If they drink any more it will colour them clearly enough for even you to see them. I wonder on what errand they are come here? The shaggy red wolf-hound is baring its fangs at Jason: why, how strange, there is a shadowy bronze spearhead protruding from its back!'

But Jason did not overhear these words, either; he was busy skinning off the white hide of one of the oxen. The noblemen who were watching despised his deftness, for skinning was a task that men of distinguished birth left to their menials. With here a cut and there a jerk and there another cut, Jason had soon drawn the whole hide free of the carcase with not a drop of blood showing on the white hair.

As Jason was thus busied, the ghost of the shepherd came creeping up slowly towards him with murder in his eye. Lynceus, hastily fumbling in his wallet, pulled out three beans, thrust them into his mouth and spat them out again at the ghost. 'Begone, begone, begone!' he whispered. The ghost vanished with a soundless shriek of rage and pain.

Slowly turned on oaken spits, the great joints of meat roasted at the altar fire, while the sacred thigh-bones, rolled in fat, burned with an appetizing stench. Idmon watched the smoke mounting up from the driftwood in dark spirals of good omen, while Jason poured out a libation of milk and honey-water to Apollo; and, as he watched, he was moved to prophesy in Apollo's name and cried: 'Idmon, Idmon, what do you see in the flames?' Then he answered himself: 'I see the small yellow aconite flower. I see death for you, Idmon, death on a flowery meadow, far from your home in lovely Delphi, while the ship sails on eastward without you, to the sound of threshing oars, and the faces of your shipmates shine bright with glory.'

The comrades of Idmon commiserated deeply with him, though relieved that he did not see in the flames destruction for them all. They tried to dissuade him from making the voyage. But Idmon answered: 'A dread of the future is shameful in a priest.'

To Mopsus came two wagtails walking along the beach and stood nervously twittering to him for a few moments before they flew off. Jason took Mopsus aside and asked what they had said. Mopsus answered: 'Wagtails are thoughtful creatures. They reminded me to take salves, vulneraries, febrifuges, and other medicaments in the ship. But I have already tied up in a linen bag all that we are likely to need.'

The feast was ready for eating before the sun had touched the highest peak of the sky, and the last preparations for the voyage had meanwhile been made under the directions of Argus. The company now sat down in a ring about the altar and began voraciously eating the splendid roast meat, which they cut off the hissing joints with their knives, just as they felt inclined. Hylas mixed the fragrant wine for them in patterned drinking-cups of Minyan ware, and bore it around with polite words of praise to each man in turn. It was flavoured with wild mint.

When they were well settled and at ease, Argus rose to his feet and raised his hand for silence. This is what he said: 'My lords, according to the instructions given me by the King and Queen Archons at Athens, who had them from the cuckoo-sceptred Goddess Athena herself, I was to build a ship for Jason the Minyan, heir to the Kingdom of Phthiotis, in which he and his chosen comrades were to sail to Colchis, at the further end of the Black Sea, to fetch back the lost Golden Fleece of the Laphystian Ram. These instructions I have obeyed; for Jason approves of my work, and praises it. But my interest in the ship does not end with her completion. I propose to sail in the *Argo* myself, so proud have I become of her. I cannot think that any of you will grudge me a seat in her, though I was not present when the choice was made; for if ever she is dashed in wreckage upon some rocky coast, who will know so well as I how to patch and refloat her? But tell me, my lords, who of you all is the captain to whom I am to swear the customary oath of obedience? Is it Jason the Minyan, who, after having been marked down for the leadership of the expedition by the will of the

Gods (as some say), sent out heralds who summoned you together? Or is it Hercules, Prince of Tiryns, whose fame and powers immeasurably exceed those of all other men alive today? I have heard some of you say that it would be mad presumption in Jason, or in anyone else, to aspire to the leadership now that Hercules (though no Minyan even by a ceremony of rebirth) has consented to come with us. Although none of us loves to obey where he might command, yet we must agree to choose a leader who will conclude treaties for us at whatever foreign courts we happen to visit, and who will give the casting vote in our councils of war. For my part, I am ready to obey either Jason or Hercules, or whomsoever else you may choose, saying no more to sway your verdict than that it was to Jason that Father Zeus confided the sacred branch; and that King Pelias, perhaps inspired by his father Poseidon, expressed a doubt whether my ship, however strongly built, would bear for long the massive weight of Hercules.'

Then Admetus and Peleus and Acastus shouted 'Give us Hercules!' and the Argonauts all took up the cry: 'Hercules, Hercules!' He would have been a very brave man who had shouted any other name, for it was not known whether Hercules had yet feasted well enough to restore his natural good temper after the debauch on Mount Pelion. Hercules took up the shoulder of mutton which Argus had given him to supplement the great chine of beef provided by Jason, stripped it of what meat still remained on it, crammed the meat into his mouth, wiped his greasy hands in his mane of hair, and began picking his teeth with a dagger. Then, seeing an aquatic bird of ill omen flying across the water with harsh screams, he suddenly hurled the shoulder-blade in its path, and struck it dead. 'I always kill her,' he growled, as a great roar of wonder went up.

There were renewed cries of 'Hercules, Hercules!' But he stretched out his right hand and said: 'No, comrades, it is useless to choose me. I am too often made insensible by drink. Besides, at any moment that accursed herald Talthybius, whom I call the Dung-man, might come creeping up to me on his soft feet and say: "The compliments of King Eurystheus, most noble Prince Hercules! You are to fetch him Poseidon's trident, if you please." Then I would be forced to leave you and go off on the new Labour: for whenever I disobey, the children's voices in my head get louder and louder until they nearly split my eardrums, and unseen hands tweak my nose and pull the short hair by my temples, where the skin is most tender. Choose someone else.'

Then after a pause one cried 'Admetus' and another 'Great Ancaeus' and another 'Castor and Pollux together.' But nobody cried 'Jason'.

Hercules after a while silenced the hubbub with a wave of his hand and said: 'My unlucky friend Cheiron the Centaur told me last night that he trusted in Jason's capacity to lead the expedition, should I myself refuse it. "Oh," said I. "Can you really mean Jason the son of Aeson?" "Yes," said he. "The Olympians have shown him unusual favour, and for my part I am grateful to him for his recent help in composing my differences with the Lapiths. Besides, Jason is a man of this sort: most men either envy or despise him, but most women fall in love with him at first sight. Since women everywhere, both among barbarians and among civilized races, hold the secret reins of power and win their own way in the end, the gift bestowed on Jason by the Nymph Goddess is no poor one. He is a better leader even than you, Hercules, whom all men admire and none envy, and at first sight of whom every woman in her senses gathers up her skirts and runs off yelling." Cheiron's wisdom is justly famed, though he was exaggerating the fear that women have of me; and therefore, while I refuse to lead the expedition myself, I am ready to fight all men, either singly or in a body, who wish to dispute Cheiron's choice. But whether I despise or envy Jason, let no man impudently enquire.'

CHAPTER ELEVEN

THE *ARGO* SAILS

Jason rose to thank Hercules from a full heart, humbly undertaking to ask his advice immediately whenever difficulties or anxieties arose, and always to follow it.

'Very well,' said Hercules. 'But if ever I happen to be asleep or drunken, consult Hylas. His intelligence matches, or even (if that were possible) exceeds, his beauty, and he has twice as much experience of foreign travel as any man present except myself alone.'

Jason thanked Hercules again in the same humble tones and then spoke up briskly. 'My lords,' he said, 'let us now draw lots for the benches. Be good enough, each of you, to hand me a pebble which may be recognized again. I will shake them together in my helmet, and Hylas shall draw them out at random, two at a time. Thus we shall fill all the benches in turn, beginning with the bench nearest the helmsman, and ending with the bow bench. Naturally, I except Hercules: he must take his ease while the rest of you row.'

Soon Jason had pebbles from all of them except Hercules, Hylas, and Tiphys the helmsman. Hylas, with eyes averted, picked them out of the helmet two by two, when Jason had shaken them well together. Holding them up, he asked each time: 'Whose pebbles are these?' But when thirteen pairs had been called there was nothing left in the helmet, and it was clear that four men were missing. Two proved to be the Minyans from Halos; they had gone out from the palace on the evening before, with the excuse of sacrificing to Artemis on the third night of the moon, but had not been seen since. Evidently, they had thought better of the adventure and run off home, leaving all their gear behind them. The other missing pair were Acastus, son of King Pelias, and his friend Peleus the Myrmidon. They had taken part in the launching of the vessel, but shortly afterwards a message had come for Acastus from the King, which he could not disobey, ordering him to return to Iolcos and there answer a complaint from the King's bailiff about some slave-woman whom he was accused of ill-treating. Acastus had thereupon ridden off on a mule; Peleus had followed him a little later.

It was now debated whether the sailing should be delayed until these two returned. Hylas told the company that on his way down to Pagasae in the ox-wagon he had been stopped by a company of palace guards drawn up about a mile from the city; they had lifted the blanket from the face of Hercules and quickly put it back again when they recognized him, explaining that they had strict orders to prevent Prince Acastus from embarking on the *Argo*. Thus the Argonauts understood that the matter of the slave-woman and the bailiff was a pretext invented by Pelias to prevent his son from sailing.

Idas, brother of keen-sighted Lynceus, said: 'Acastus may well be as guilty as his father. He is a coward at heart, I believe. But I had not thought that Peleus the Myrmidon would desert us so shamefully though, indeed, he is the unhandiest javelin-man that ever I saw and as slippery in his dealings as an oiled eel.'

Old Nauplius answered cheerfully: 'Yet it is better perhaps to have a ship even half-full of willing oarsmen than a ship full of unwilling ones.'

Some of his companions murmured a doubtful assent.

The afternoon drew on. The young men began to joke together and tell the witty or obscene tales which are customary in the final stage of a banquet. But Jason continued silent, wrapped in his cloak, without contributing so much as a smile to the merriment. Idas had reached behind the back of Hylas, filled a goblet with unmixed wine, tossed it off, and twice returned for more. He now began a drunken war-dance on the beach. Striking an attitude and pointing sideways at Jason with his thumb, he began to declaim some faulty verses which ran as follows:

Jason, son of Aeson, tell me true:
What has suddenly come over you?
Confess to me what you are brooding about.
If you are afraid to whisper, why do you not shout?

Are you ashamed perhaps of taking command
Of the bravest champions in all this glorious land?
But the bravest of all is Idas, son of Aphareus,
Who owes more to his spear than he does to Zeus.

[Here he brandished his spear dangerously.]

Pluck up your spirits, coward, if it be cowardice
That makes you tuck your head under your arm – like this!

[Here he mimicked Jason's attitude.]

Idas is sailing with you – Idas – do you hear?
The world's finest exponent of the art of the spear.
Idas of Arene, who never lost a fight
And does not care a fig for any God's might,
Not even for Apollo, whom you honour today.

He once tried to steal my Marpessa away
And make her a prostitute in his marble shrine.
But no God may ever seize anything of mine
I ran at his ministrants with my long spear –

At this point Mopsus and Idmon intervened, Idmon catching at his legs and oversetting him while Mopsus twisted the spear from his grasp. Others of the company held him down while Idmon lectured him in some such words as these:

'Insolent boaster, you are inviting trouble. I see by your bowl that you have been drinking unmixed wine, but even this should not have been enough to madden you into insulting the Bright God whose fellow-guest you are. Remember what happened only the other day to the two Aloeid chieftains. They refused to acknowledge Apollo's jurisdiction over the musical Mare nymphs of Mount Helicon, alleging that these had been resident on Helicon, as servants of the Triple Muse, long before Apollo's time. They threatened war on all the Olympians together if Apollo tried to make Helicon his own; and spoke absurdly of piling Pelion upon Ossa, if that were necessary, in order to reach the summit of Olympus and pluck Father Zeus from his seat. But I prophesied against them; and even before my father Apollo could send out his archers the two braggarts were dead. They had quarrelled over a stag which they were hunting and which each claimed to have killed: they had hacked each other to pieces with their swords.'

Idas laughed, but gaspingly, for Pollux the boxer was seated on his chest. 'Come, Argive Frog,' he said, 'prophesy against me if you dare, as you did against the Aloeids, and watch for what will happen. You will be proved a false prophet, you buskined rogue, for I assure you that your dead body will lie and rot here, here on the beach of Pagasae, not on some remote flowery meadow (as you pretend), while the ship sails on without you.'

The quarrel would have ended in bloodshed, for Lynceus was on his way, sword in hand, to the help of his brother Idas, had it not been for a sudden twanging and banging and tinkling behind the altar – a four-stringed lyre played incomparably well. At this sound those who were struggling with Idas relaxed their grip on him. They rose up and began to dance in time with the music. Idas rose too and joined in the dance, without showing any resentment, for drunken men have a short memory; and Lynceus was glad to sheathe his sword and follow. Next Jason started out of his brooding trance and pranced about nimbly, with his arms raised and fingers cracking, for Cheiron had been a stern and accomplished dancing-master. Finally the thud of feet aroused Hercules. He heaved himself up and leaped upon the ox-cart, where he stamped about, keeping time to the music, until it seemed certain that the axle would break. Beside him the train of dancers wound in and out, weaving a holy figure of eight.

With a whack on the belly of the lyre, the music ended as suddenly as it had begun. Mopsus, Idmon, and several more ran to embrace the gaunt wild-eyed Thracian, with the tattooed face and the white linen robe, whose intervention had so narrowly averted bloodshed. 'Orpheus,' they cried, 'Orpheus, you are come again to us from your Egyptian wanderings and your self-imposed exile among the cruel Ciconians?

Orpheus replied: 'I have been instructed in a dream to sail with you. Let us go aboard.'

The arrival of Orpheus prolonged the banquet until evening, when it was too late to sail. Then Jason called for grass to be cut and spread upon the beach for couches, and he and his companions ate and drank until the moon shone high in the sky, and Orpheus entertained them with his music. Ballad after ballad he sang of the good old days of Theseus and Peirithoüs, and still they called for more. At about midnight they fell asleep, one by one; but their retainers kept guard lest Pelias might be meditating treachery. The night was calm, and presently dawn shone clear and bright.

When they had breakfasted on cold meats and a little wine, Jason gladly led the way down to the *Argo*, and the crew clambered aboard and took their allotted seats. Retainers came crowding up with the gear that had been piled on the beach, and their masters hurriedly stowed all in the lockers under the benches. They were anxious to be gone, now that Orpheus was playing the solemn, slow rowing chant, *Slide out to sea, devoted barque* – since famous, then heard for the first time. When Hercules magnanimously volunteered to take the starboard oar on the bench nearest the helmsman, Jason gave orders that the heavier man of each pair of oarsmen abaft the mast should seat himself on the port side to counterpoise the weight of that tremendous pull; this he did on the advice of Argus. The wind blew fitfully from the south.

Tiphys took his high seat in the stern, and Jason shouted to the crowd on the beach to unreeve the hawsers from the pierced anchor-stones. They did so, and flung the rope-ends aboard for Jason to catch. But Argus reproached Jason for wishing to leave behind the stones which the masons had so long laboured to drill and shape. Despite murmurs of impatience from the benches, the stones were taken up from the beach and trundled up a long plank into the ship.

At last Jason gave the signal for departure. Hercules dipped his oar into the water, and heaved. The other oarsmen did likewise, and after a ragged start the beautiful ship began to glide down the gulf, the oars dipping and rising in perfect time. Here was seen the fulfilment of Apollo's prophecy that the true Jason would appear. For, once aboard the *Argo*, Jason was no healer of discord, despite his name; it was Orpheus who was called upon to compose the incessant quarrels of her jealous and unruly crew.

Jason observing a triple wink of sunlight on polished brass from the direction of Methone, a signal that he had been expecting, told Tiphys:

'Steer for Methone, if you please. There I hope to make up our complement.' Tiphys did so, and soon the sound of wailing from the beach of Pagasae came more faintly down the wind.

When they had left Iolcos well astern, Lynceus, casting his eye over his left shoulder, interrupted the music. 'I see something, comrades,' he cried. 'Two men and a woman are running down the spur of Pelion towards Methone, half hidden by the oak thickets. The men you all know: they are Acastus, son of Pelias, and Peleus the Myrmidon, his friend. Many of you also know the woman: she runs and leaps across the bushes with the gliding motion of a deer; and by her braided hair, short tunic, and bow anyone would tell her for a maiden huntress of the Goddess Artemis.'

'Oh, Lynceus, Lynceus, tell me, what is the colour of her tunic?' eagerly asked young Meleager of Calydon, his bench partner. 'It is not saffron-coloured, is it?'

'Saffron-coloured,' replied Lynceus, 'and she wears a necklace of bears' claws. I will not leave you any longer in suspense, Meleager. It is the woman whom you love better than your life; it is Atalanta of Calydon.'

Great Ancaeus cried out angrily: 'She had better not set foot in this ship. No ship is lucky with a woman aboard.'

Be careful,' said Meleager. 'You spoke in the same strain in Calydon before the hunt, and where would you have been without Atalanta? Did she not save your life?'

Great Ancaeus growled some unintelligible reply.

As the *Argo* drew alongside the great rock at Methone which served as a jetty, Atalanta sprang aboard before anyone could prevent her, with a fir branch in her hand. 'In the name of the Maiden Goddess,' she cried. Jason had no choice but to accept her as a member of the ship's company. The silver fir is sacred to Artemis, who, though she has renounced her connexion with the Triple Goddess and acknowledged herself a daughter of Zeus, still keeps most of her former characteristics. It is more dangerous to offend her than almost any other deity, and Jason was relieved that she too favoured the expedition; he had feared that he might have offended her priestess Iphias by his curtness that morning.

But Meleager, who was in love with Atalanta, was bitterly disappointed that she had come in the Goddess's name and was therefore untouchable. Recently he had offered to put away his young wife Cleopatra, the daughter of Idas and Marpessa, and marry Atalanta instead as soon as she had withdrawn from the service of Artemis. This she was free to do if she performed certain unnameable sacrifices at a shrine of the Goddess; but an oracle had warned her that marriage would bring her ill luck, and, besides, she did not wish either to provoke Idas, Cleopatra's father, or to wrong Cleopatra herself, who had been her fellow-huntress. Atalanta had therefore refused to marry curly-haired Meleager, who then swore that at least she could not compel him to remain with Cleopatra: he would go to Iolcos and there volunteer for the voyage to Colchis, and forget them both.

It seemed now that Atalanta did not by any means wish Meleager to forget her. She came to sit on the same bench with him, and Lynceus resigned his oar to her. It was noticed that she had three bloody scalps dangling at her girdle, which caused her neighbours discomfort and anxiety.

Presently Acastus and Peleus came running down to the jetty and sprang aboard, laughing. They sat down together on the bow bench and fixed their oars in the oar-holes, while Jason and Lynceus pushed the ship away from the jetty with poles. As they rowed off, Acastus told his comrades what had happened. It seems that when he reached Iolcos Pelias had told him at once that he had no charge to answer but that guards were posted to prevent his return to Pagasae. Acastus had answered resentfully and made no pretence of submission to his father's will until Peleus arrived. For Peleus came into the hall declaring that he had quarrelled with Jason about the leadership of the expedition, and swore that he, for one, would never think of embarking except under the captaincy of Hercules. 'You were wise,' Pelias told him, 'very wise, for (to be frank with you) I do not expect ever to see the ship again, now that the adventurers have put themselves under the captaincy of my presumptuous nephew.' Then Acastus, feigning a change of heart, said: Since you too have returned, dear Peleus, I do not much care whether I sail or whether I stay. Come, now, let us sit down and feast, and tomorrow morning early we will go up to Pelion to greet Cheiron and persuade him to hunt with us.' To this Pelias made no objection. So the next morning they arose early and went a little way up the mountain and then turned off towards Methone; for Peleus had told Jason of his intention and hoped to find the *Argo* there. Presently they fell in with Atalanta, who had just killed two Centaurs and was engaged in removing their scalps...

'The Centaurs do not recognize the Olympian Artemis,' explained Atalanta. 'They have hated her ever since she took over the College of Fish Nymphs at Iolcos, and so deprived them of their customary pleasures. Three of them lay in wait for me as I came over the mountains from Ossa, and would doubtless have tried to outrage me had I not sprung the ambush with an arrow. I started away at once and laid an ambush myself when I saw that they were following me; from which I shot the remaining two, as Peleus and Acastus have said. To avoid being haunted by their erotic ghosts I scalped them – these horse manes that the Centaurs wear are handy for the purpose – and thus made them powerless against me. All their power lies in their hair. No, no the drops of blood that drip from the scalps will bring the ship good luck, not bad.

Atalanta's story horrified Jason. Whatever she might say, the ghosts of the Centaurs, his kinsmen, would almost certainly call on him for vengeance. Yet he could not risk an offence to Artemis. He said at last: 'So long as you have not killed my stepfather Cheiron, I can forgive you. It would have gone hard with you if you had killed my stepfather Cheiron.'

'Ah! Did I forget to tell you,' Hercules interrupted, 'that my old centaur friend is dead? He died yesterday. He, Hylas, and I were having the happiest of times together, feasting and telling stories, and then… I cannot remember exactly how the trouble began, but I know that some of the other Centaurs began to grow excited and make faces at me. I slapped one of them and must have hit him a trifle too hard, because he did not speak another word. The others grew still more excited and decided to avenge the dead one.'

'Hercules killed about six Centaurs,' said Hylas. 'It was those children's voices in his head again. That man tried to restrain him from exterminating the tribe, but ran into the way of one of his arrows. Hercules was overcome with remorse, as you can imagine, and I had to soothe him with another jar of wine. That was why we were late at the beach.' He called Cheiron 'that man' to avoid invoking his ghost.

'The Centaurs are a pest,' said Coronus the Lapith. 'They set upon my father Caeneus, without provocation, beating him to death with pine logs. My heart always leaps within me when I hear that a Centaur is killed.'

At this Orpheus hastily struck up a soothing melody, and began singing:

Let us forget, comrades, let us forget
    What dark deeds lie behind us.
Let grief not blind us,
Confuse, or bind us.
    There is hope yet.

'Sing that verse again, Thracian,' said Hercules. 'You are right. Let us forget those miserable Centaurs. You bear me no ill will, Jason?'

Jason did not reply until Hercules had repeated his question threateningly, and then he said in a broken voice, the tears starting to his eyes: 'That man was the noblest man of all my acquaintance, and I would think very ill of myself if I did not shed tears at this news; for I see that even the eyes of bold Peleus are streaming, and that his shoulders are heaving with sobs. Nevertheless, I had rather that my dear foster-father and my Centaur comrades had fallen by your hand, most noble Hercules, than by any other. For I know that on your return to Greece you will appease that man's ghost with more magnificent offerings than he could hope from any other man, and that you will not forget the other ghosts either. And that man was not blameless himself: he should have refrained from publicly broaching a cask of wine; wine is the Centaurs' curse, as he himself often said.'

Thus Jason soothed the rising anger of Hercules.

'Comrades,' said Argus, 'I propose that we make good use of the afternoon and row clear out of the Pagasaean Gulf before Pelias sends a galley in pursuit.'

'Sing that song again, Orpheus,' Hercules repeated. 'By the way, Linus the music-master whom in self-defence, long ago, I brained with his own lyre – a tiresome pedant – was he not your brother?'

'Forget those dark deeds, Hercules,' said Orpheus sorrowfully, and presently struck up again.

Yet Methone was not the last place in the Pagasaean Gulf where the *Argo* was made fast: Jason was constrained to touch at a beach in the innermost recess of the gulf, since called Aphetae (or the 'beach of departure'), and there sacrifice to Bright Artemis a kid which he bought from a goatherd for a few lumps of fig-bread. Yet this sacrifice did not delay them long, and Atalanta was persuaded by Meleager to dedicate the Centaurs' scalps at the same altar, which lifted a load from every heart.

This is the story of Atalanta. Jasius the Arcadian, a chieftain of that King Oeneus of Calydon who planted the first vineyard in Aetolia, wished for a son; and when his beloved wife died in childbirth of a girl whom she named Atalanta, he ordered his bailiff to expose the girl on the mountains, there to expiate her mother's murder. However, nobody cares to expose a child, for a child's ghost is far more difficult to shake off than that of a grown person. The bailiff entrusted the task to his under-bailiff, and the underbailiff entrusted it to a swineherd, and the swineherd entrusted it to his wife, and his wife laid Atalanta upon the threshold of a mountain shrine of Artemis the She-Bear and informed the swineherd that the orders of Jasius had been obeyed. It is said that a real she-bear used to come down daily from the mountains to be fed on honey at the shrine, where its visits were welcomed, and would allow Atalanta to drink at her dugs. Atalanta was dedicated to the Goddess and became a famous huntress; when she was fully grown she could run through forest or over broken country faster than anyone in Greece, woman or man, so sure-footed she was.

Presently a great boar began to ravage the fields and orchards of Calydon, in punishment as it was thought for the King's insult to Artemis, Lady of the Wild Things. Oeneus had purposely omitted the Goddess's portion from a sacrifice offered to all the Olympians together, because her foxes had made free with his vineyard. Nobody dared face the boar at first; but at last Meleager, who was the King's son, gathered a band of courageous young men from every part of Greece and went after it. Yet Meleager scrupled to attack the boar unless Artemis should first give her consent, and went to the Bear shrine with a propitiatory gift. The High Priestess approved of Meleager's courage and piety, and not only sanctioned the hunt but sent Atalanta to take part in it. This displeased his companions, who included Idas, Lynceus, Castor, Pollux, Admetus, Great Ancaeus, and Peleus. All of them refused at first to hunt in the company of a woman, declaring that it would bring them bad luck. Meleager replied that if they now abandoned the hunt Artemis would no doubt punish them as severely as she had punished his father Oeneus. So they went hunting, with very bad grace, agreeing that whoever killed the boar should have the pelt.

Atalanta shamed them by being the first to track the boar to the thicket where it was harboured. To show their contempt for her they disobeyed her orders, which were to surround the thicket silently and lie in wait with bows and javelins while she dislodged the boar. Instead, they rushed head-long into the copse, shouting loudly to frighten it. The boar found them bunched together in a crowd, killed two of them and lamed two more, including Great Ancaeus. Atalanta caught Ancaeus up on her shoulders and dragged him to safety while the boar was ravening at the bodies of his companions. She left Peleus the honour of killing the beast with his javelin; but, though the boar was still preoccupied with its filthy task, Peleus succeeded in killing nothing but his father-in-law. The boar ran off unhurt.

When Atalanta had bound up the wound of Great Ancaeus she continued her pursuit of the boar and once more discovered its harbourage. This time the huntsmen obeyed her signals and remained under cover. She crept up close behind the boar and drove an arrow deep into its ham. Out it limped with horrid squeals into a clearing and was met there by a flight of arrows from the bowmen whom Atalanta had posted all around. One arrow struck it full in the left eye and it began to run around in slow circles, foaming at the mouth. Meleager dared to come in on the blind side and drove his javelin through its heart.

The boar fell, and then several other men, who had kept out of the way while it was still dangerous, rushed up to stab at it. As might have been expected, a noisy dispute arose as to who had killed the boar and thereby won the pelt. Meleager settled it by declaring that though he had himself struck the death-blow with his javelin, yet he resigned his claim to the pelt and awarded it to Atalanta. For she had first so lamed the boar that it would have died within a few days in any case, and next had driven it into an ambush which she had herself posted.

Meleager's servants then skinned the boar and presented the pelt to Atalanta. She accepted it with gratitude and was slowly returning to the shrine of Artemis when Meleager's uncles, one of whom claimed to have shot the arrow which blinded the boar, tried in their fury not only to seize the pelt but to violate her. Meleager heard her cry out and ran to the rescue, calling upon Artemis to shield him from guilt. He killed both his uncles with the same javelin that had put an end to the boar. Thus the prejudice against hunting with a woman was confirmed, for five men had died that day; and yet one might say with equal truth that it was the prejudice itself that had killed them.

Jasius, on hearing that Atalanta had won the pelt, grew proud at heart, and acknowledged her as his daughter at last. He made her his heiress and piously provided the shrine of Artemis with bronze doors and an iron roasting-jack. But Atalanta would not settle down to the domestic life of a chieftain's daughter or be ruled by him in any way; she went off hunting whenever it pleased her, especially when the moon was bright.

Here now is a roll of the Argonauts who sailed from the Pagasaean Gulf. By no means all completed the voyage, and others won the title of Argonauts by coming aboard the *Argo* when she had already passed through the Clashing Rocks and entered the Black Sea.

Acastus, son of King Pelias of Iolcos, a Minyan.

Admetus, King of Pherae, a Minyan.

Great Ancaeus of Tegea, son of the God Poseidon.

Little Ancaeus, the Lelegian, of Flowery Samos.

Argus of Athens, by birth a Thespian, builder of the *Argo*.

Ascalaphus of Orchomenos, son of the God Ares, a Minyan.

Atalanta of Calydon.

Augeas, son of Phorbas, King of Elis and priest of the Sun.

Butes of Athens, a priest of the Goddess Athena, the most famous bee-master in Greece.

Calaïs, son of the North Wind, from Thracian Thynia.

Castor of Sparta, son of Father Zeus, the wrestler and horseman.

Coronus the Lapith, of Gyrton in Thessaly, a Minyan.

Echion of Mount Cyllene, son of the God Hermes, the herald.

Erginus of Miletos, son of the God Poseidon, a Minyan.

Euphemus of Taenaron, the Phocian swimmer.

Eurydamas the Dolopian, from Lake Xynias in Thessaly, a Minyan.

Hercules of Tiryns.

Hylas the Dryopian, squire to Hercules.

Idas, son of Aphareus of Arene, a Minyan.

Idmon of Argos, son of the God Apollo.

Iphitus of Phocis, a painter and image-maker.

Jason, captain of the *Argo*, son of King Aeson of Iolcos, a Minyan.

Lynceus, the look-out man, brother to Idas, a Minyan.

Meleager, son of King Oeneus of Calydon.

Melampus of Pylos, son of the God Poseidon, a Minyan.

Mopsus the Lapith, a Minyan and an augur.

Nauplius of Argos, son of the God Poseidon, a noted navigator.

Orpheus, the Thracian musician.

Peleus of Phthia, Prince of the Myrmidons.

Periclymenus of Sandy Pylos, the Minyan wizard, son of the God Poseidon.

Phalerus the archer, of the royal house of Athens.

Pollux of Sparta, the noted boxer, brother to Castor.

Tiphys of Boeotian Thisbe, a Minyan, helmsman of the *Argo*.
Zetes the Thracian, brother to Calaïs.

To these were later added Polyphemus the Lapith, a Minyan from Thessalian Larisa; and three Minyan brothers, Phlegyans from Thessalian Tricca, named Deileion, Phlogius, and Autolycus; and the four sons of Phrixus, the Minyan who had brought the Fleece to Colchis, named Phrontis, Melanion, Cytissorus, and Argeus. Thus twenty-one true Minyans in all could style themselves Argonauts, besides those who became Minyans by the ceremony of adoption. As for Dascylus the Mariandynian, who piloted the *Argo* for a stage or two of the outward voyage; and Telamon of Aegina; and Canthus the brother of Polyphemus; and others who, like the two last-mentioned, were passengers for a stage or two of the homeward voyage – these were not concerned in the quest of the Golden Fleece, and are not therefore reckoned as Argonauts by trustworthy poets and heralds. But it is the recent addition of their names to the roll that has brought the number up to fifty and thus given rise to the false report that the *Argo* was a ship of fifty oars.

CHAPTER TWELVE

THE CAMP-FIRES AT CASTANTHAEA

The *Argo* was making good headway: southward by oars through the narrow mouth of the Gulf of Pagasae, and, as the day drew on, north-east-ward by oars and sail through the deep strait which separates the brow of the island of Euboea from the curved foot of Magnesia. When the sail was first hoisted, and bellied out in the breeze, the Argonauts shouted for delight. Old Nauplius cried: 'Of all the craft that ever swam on salt water, Argus, yours is the prettiest.'

'She sits upon the water with the ease and elegance of a cygnet,' Castor said.

'Rather, she resembles the fleet dolphin, darting from wave to wave,' said Little Ancaeus.

And Idmon said: 'To see her climb the rolling swell and clear the rising foam, sprinkling her children with sea-water from her prow, as with lustral water shaken from a green laurel bough, that, dear comrades, is a spectacle to stir the soul.'

So each Argonaut in turn praised the *Argo* in the imagery most natural to his birth and condition. Then all took to their oars again to hurry her on; but it was with great relief that they finally shipped them in the Sciathan Strait between the heel of Magnesia and the well-wooded rocky island of Sciathos, the most westerly of the Sporades. They lolled on the benches, nursing their blistered hands.

The wind now blew dead astern. Tiphys knew this coast well and kept the *Argo* a couple of bowshots off the shore for fear of sunken rocks. Late in the afternoon he pointed to a dark cliff that rose up before them. 'There is Cape Sepias,' he said, 'a happy landmark on the homeward voyage from Thrace; it is easily recognized by the red cliff beyond it. But we must leave it behind, and Cape Ipni as well, before we disembark tonight. While this wind holds, let us for the second time today see Pelion over our left shoulders.'

So they ran on and, though darkness gathered, the young moon rose and the stars shone brightly. Orpheus sang a hymn to the Goddess Artemis, who owned several shrines in the neighbourhood, warning the Argonauts, with a wealth of recent instances, of the danger incurred by those who forget the respect due to her. Between every verse of the hymn, which carried them a good five miles on their course, Idas would lift up his raucous voice, catching at the melody, and cry:

> Meleager, son of Oeneus,
> O, you Meleager, son of Oeneus,
> This warning is for you, Meleager:
> Refrain from the lips of Atalanta!

And the other Argonauts echoed with ribald laughter:

> This warning is for you, Meleager,
> Refrain from the lips of Atalanta!

Meleager did not care, for Atalanta was sitting on the same bench with him and pressed his foot gently with hers to show that she pitied him. In the end she took the lyre from Orpheus and showed herself a skilful enough musician, singing to the same melody a ballad of the dangers incurred by the maiden huntress who forgot her vows of chastity. She told how Callisto the Arcadian huntress, who fathered her child on Zeus himself, could not escape from the jealous anger of Artemis: for Artemis ordered her to be shot full of arrows, though not through the vital parts, and Callisto was left crippled to die in the forest. The constellation of the She-Bear was named after her, as a reminder to women that Artemis has no mercy.

Pelion viewed from the sea in moonlight looked strangely different from the Pelion that Jason had known all his life: at one point it seemed a table-land, so that his mind grew confused. He asked Hercules: 'Ought we not to be disembarking soon, most noble Hercules? I think that we have passed Pelion by.'

'Why ask me? Ask Tiphys or Argus or whom you please,' Hercules replied, 'but do not pester me with foolish questions, as if you were a child.'

Jason was abashed at the laugh that went up, but Tiphys said: 'I, for one, shall be satisfied if we make Castanthaea tonight, where there is safe anchorage and good water.'

'I know the shepherds of Castanthaea well,' said Jason. 'A small present of wine will buy enough mutton from them to last us for two days.'

So they ran on, under the dark shadow of Pelion, and, avoiding the rocks, cleared the promontory of Ipni beyond; then the breeze slackened and they took to their oars again. They did not make Castanthaea until the grey dawn, dog-tired and full of loud complaints against Jason for carrying them, as they said, nearly half-way to Colchis in the first stage. They found safe anchorage and went ashore, with their legs as stiff as oars.

The Magnesian shepherds mistook them for pirates and, catching up their children, rushed off through the pass between the hills. Jason hallooed after them in reassurance, but they did not heed him.

The Argonauts collected dry sticks and built a fire while Hercules went out in search of mutton. He soon came back with a couple of wethers slung over his shoulders and bleating miserably. 'I intend to sacrifice my bleaters to Hestia, Goddess of the Hearth,' he said. 'This place pleases me immeasurably. One day, when I shall have completed my Labours, I will settle down here with Hylas and build myself a house. I shall sit listening to the gentle sound of the waves and watch the broad moon through feathery branches of the lightning-tree; and if Eurystheus sends Talthybius with a message to me, I shall knock pieces out of him with my frying-pan. Holy Serpents, I am hungry! Quick, build me up an altar, fools and lend me a sacrificial flint.'

Eurydamas the Dolopian asked him, instead, to sacrifice at the tomb of his ancestor Dolops, which stood close by; and Hercules magnanimously consented. He knew in his heart that he would never settle down anywhere, however long he might live.

Soon the sheep were sacrificed, flayed, and cut up, and their blood was poured for the thirsty ghost of Dolops. The Argonauts sat about the two large camp-fires, wrapped in their blankets or cloaks, each man toasting over the flame his portion of mutton, cut in slices and skewered on a sharp stick. Hercules had lugged a jar of wine ashore and Hylas went off with his bronze pitcher to draw water. The *Argo* was well secured by hawsers to two rocks, her sail lowered and put away, her prow thrust into the eye of the wind. Melampus of Pylos, Jason's cousin and the most melancholy and taciturn of the Argonauts, remained aboard as watchman; his comrade Periclymenus the wizard brought him a generous portion of meat and drink.

At the smaller camp-fire, Coronus the Lapith remarked to Admetus of Pherae: 'This is not bad mutton by any means. Though the pasture hereabouts is not so rich as in our Thessaly, the sheep come down, I suppose, to lick the salt stones as an appetizer, which helps them to put on flesh.'

'I give my sheep salt to lick regularly,' said Admetus, 'and, though of a small breed, they are something to boast about, now that you have freed them of ticks for me. That was a neighbourly act, Coronus.'

'It was nothing,' replied Coronus. 'Since Athena first adopted the Crow fraternity, we have had wonderful power over our sacred and long-lived bird. It flies for us to whatever flock may need its services. Yes, indeed, your sheep should be in fine condition this year.'

Butes of Athens said with a smile: 'My woolly flocks are not so white as yours, Admetus; but, though you may scarcely credit this, I own five hundred head for every one of yours. They are so intelligent that I need neither dog nor shepherd to watch over them; and they provide my table with infinitely sweeter food than yours.'

Admetus answered courteously: 'Indeed? The mutton of Pherae is generally reckoned the sweetest in Thessaly and I had thought it unrivalled even in Attica. Our grass is tasty as barley-bread, is it not, Coronus? And the fleeces of my sheep (if I may boast) are as soft as any that I have ever seen: only feel the texture of this blanket!'

'My sheep are brown and yellow, and far smaller than yours,' said Butes, smiling broadly now. 'They go streaming out in a cloud from their pens every morning to pasture on Hymettos, and by dusk they are all safely home. They scorn grass and salt but love flowers. They have small horns on their heads, and hairy bellies.'

He was speaking jestingly of his bees, but it was some time before Admetus solved the riddle. At last Butes pulled a jar of Hymettan honey from under his cloak and asked his companions to dip their fingers in it and afterwards lick them.

When they cried out in admiration of the taste he gave them a lecture on bee-keeping and promised that, as soon as the voyage was over, each should have a swarm and no longer be dependent on the chance discovery of wild honey in hollow trees or the clefts of rocks. 'But do not misunderstand me,' he said. 'I have no scorn for wild honey and spend many an enjoyable morning about Hymettos in search of it. I wait at one side of a flowery field until a bee laden with honey makes off for its nest; then I step behind it and stake out his course with sticks, for bees fly exactly straight on their homeward journey. Presently another bee will set off for home from the other side of the clearing. I stake out his course too; and near the point of intersection I meet bees flying from all directions. There is the nest, soon found.' Butes was an amiable man, and whatever conversation he took part in always swung round in the end to bees or honey. It was odd that he was a priest of Athena rather than of Apollo, patron of the bee societies. He kept his head well shaved and dressed only in white garments, because this had a most soothing effect on his bees; or so he imagined.

At the other camp-fires some unseen Spite provoked the company to several angry arguments: about the nature of fire, and about the proper season for sowing sesame, and about bears – whether the Arcadian bears were fiercer than those of Mount Parnes in Attica, and whether the white bears of Thrace were fiercer than either. Hearing the angry cries with which Phalerus and Argus upheld the fierceness of the Attic bear against the Arcadians, Echion and Great Ancaeus, and the gruff expostulations of the Thracians, Calaïs and Zetes, one might have supposed them bears themselves. But Orpheus silenced them all by saying that no bear was naturally fierce, yet all bears could be made to show fierceness: she-bears by a danger to the cubs, he-bears by sexual jealousy, both equally by being disturbed from their winter sleep with the clash of weapons and the baying of hounds. 'Bears are of all beasts the likest to human kind. They fight for what is their own; and love to be young again in play with their cubs; and think no pleasure so sweet as sleep, unless it is to crunch honey-comb.

Come, comrades, overweariness makes for contention. Sleep sweetly where you sit, and take no thought for danger, I will keep watch, not having laboured so hard as any of you others.

Pelias soon learned that the *Argo* had touched at Methone, but the news did not disturb him. He supposed that Argus was taking aboard some of the gear left there when he was cutting timber near by. Then came a messenger from Mount Pelion reporting the death of Cheiron, and he grew suddenly anxious for his son Acastus, fearing that the Centaurs had taken vengeance for the slaughter made by Hercules. He sent out search-parties, one of which brought back news from a swineherd of Methone that Peleus and Acastus had gone aboard the *Argo* and sailed away, laughing. When Pelias understood that he had been tricked he flew into a vile passion, beat the messengers nearly to death, and paced up and down the dining-hall, growling like a wild beast. Finally he caught up an axe and ran from the palace. He went down the street by moonlight to Aeson's house, rehearsing to himself aloud as he went: 'Your cruel and impious son has stolen Prince Acastus from me, whom I love beyond everything in the world, deceiving him with promises of fame and treasure. If any harm comes to Acastus, brother Aeson, you must not expect to live long yourself.'

It was midnight, and the house was barred and shuttered, but Pelias forced his way in with the axe. He surprised Aeson and Alcimede in the inner court of their house while they were completing an altarless sacrifice, by torchlight, to the Maiden Goddess Persephone.

Pelias stood and watched in astonishment, for Aeson was moving about as briskly as a young man. He had just pole-axed and cut the throat of a frightened black bull, its horns bound with night-blue fillets and its poll shaded with yew branches. The blood was gushing out into a stone trough over which Alcimede was bent, waving her hands and muttering. Neither she nor Aeson had heard the noisy entry of Pelias; they had been preoccupied with the difficult task of killing the bull, which despite a ringed nose resisted their attempts to bring it to the trough.

Aeson now called in solemn tone upon Persephone to grant the ghost of his father, Cretheus the Minyan, permission to ascend from the Underworld and drink the rich warm blood, and then to prophesy truthfully what would be the fate of Jason and his companions in their voyage to Colchis. As Pelias watched, a vague cloud began to gather at the shallow end of the trough, like the mist which sometimes clouds the vision of a sick man; it gradually grew substantial and, assuming a pink colour, hardened into the bent head of Cretheus, lapping with his tongue and quivering with delight.

Pelias drew off a sandal and cast it at the ghost to prevent it from prophesying. It immediately scurried off, paling as it went, and the spell was broken. Pelias took off his helmet and handed it to Aeson, saying: 'Dip this in the deeper end of the trough, traitor, scoop up the warm blood and drink!'

Aeson asked: 'And if I refuse, brother?'

'If you refuse,' Pelias answered, 'I will hack you and your wife into pieces with this axe and scatter your bones over Pelion so that your ghosts will never find rest, for your sepulchre will be in the bellies of leopards and wolves and rats.'

'Why do you give me this impious order?' asked Aeson, trembling so hard that he could scarcely stand on his feet.

'Because you have deceived me these twenty years,' Pelias replied: 'first, by pretending to be bedridden, so that I would not fear you; next, by concealing from me the survival of your brat Diomedes, or Jason; lastly, by conspiring with him to destroy my poor foolish son Acastus. Drink, drink, I say, or I will split you into billets like a dry pine log.'

Aeson said: 'I will drink. But first give me time to repeat backwards the charm that has raised my noble father Cretheus from the dead, so that he may return safely again to his home underground.'

Pelias consented. Aeson repeated the charm correctly, though with a faltering voice; and then, stooping, dipped the helmet in the thick bull's blood. He drank, choked and died. Thereupon Alcimede cut her own throat with the sacrificial knife; so that three shades, father, son, and son's wife, went down to the Underworld hand in hand. But first Alcimede spattered the robe of Pelias with her blood as it spurted out, and with her eyes spoke the curse that her gurgling throat could not.

Pelias gave them decent burial and congratulated himself that they had died by their own hands, not by his. He burned his bloody robe and purified himself in the shrine of Poseidon, where the priests laid only a light penance upon him.

CHAPTER THIRTEEN

TO LEMNOS, BY WAY OF ATHOS

The Argonauts spent a day and a night at Castanthaea, passing the time pleasantly in fishing, hunting, and games, but did not wander far from the ship lest the wind should suddenly change and allow them to resume their voyage. Comfort-loving Augeas of Elis, who had blistered hands and sore buttocks from rowing, urged that for the rest of the voyage oars should be used only in an extremity; and that no day's course should be made longer than was pleasant. Tiphys and Argus shook their heads at this, and old Nauplius said: 'Colchis is very far away, King Augeas, and we must be back before the summer is over if we wish to avoid shipwreck on this same rocky coast.'

The shepherds did not venture to return. When finally the time came to weigh anchor, Jason left behind a picture, drawn skilfully by Iphitus of Phocis, to explain matters to them. The picture, done in charcoal on a smooth rock, showed an enormous Hercules, with club and lion pelt, carrying off twelve small sheep – they had eaten at least twelve – and Jason, with a horse's mane and body spotted like a leopard, graciously leaving in the shepherds' cave a fine bronze spear, in payment of the debt, and a small jar of wine. The *Argo* was shown at anchor in the background, and the Argonauts were represented by the various beasts and birds which were their badges. However, this picture proved unintelligible to the returning shepherds, who quitted their pastures in terror, convinced that some frightful curse was hanging over their heads. The spear and the wine-jar remained in the cave untouched for a year or more.

In the early morning of the second day a brisk breeze came up from the south-west and Tiphys advised Jason to let it bear them along the coast as far as the vale of Tempe, sacred to Apollo, where the river Peneus reaches the sea. Jason agreed. All went aboard again, shoved the ship off with their poles, hoisted the sail, and were soon fairly on their way. The waves slapped roughly against the ship's side and made several of them retch or vomit.

The coast was high and steep-to. Soon Ossa's cone-shaped summit towered over them to landward and they passed the settlement of Eurymenae, where the inhabitants ran to arms in fear of a hostile landing, but then waved in farewell when they found themselves mistaken. After the *Argo* had rounded the promontory of Ossa the coast began to wear an inhospitable look, and Tiphys told of ships that he had seen wrecked on those rocks by furious north-eastern gales. But after a while the mountain range trended away, and left between it and the sea a narrow belt of low land, fronted by a sandy beach, which gave them comfort.

At noon they made the mouth of the Peneus, a river of which Jason knew the headwaters only, but which is the noblest in Greece and with its many tributaries waters the whole of fertile Thessaly. They were about to disembark, since Idmon, Iphitus, Orpheus, Mopsus, and others were set upon visiting Apollo's shrine of Tempe, to take part there in a holy mouse-feast, when suddenly the wind veered about and blew off-shore. Then Argus and Tiphys pressed Jason to take advantage of this breeze, a gift of his ancestor Aeolus, and run due east for the Thracian promontories. He consented. Behind them, further up the coast, enormous Olympus showed a wide surface of pale, naked rock; capped in snow as usual, and with its precipitous sides streaked with dark wooded ravines.

'I know how the Gods and Goddesses spend their time up yonder,' said Idas in solemn tones.

'How do they spend it?' asked Coronus of Gyrton, the simple-minded Lapith.

'Playing at snowballs!' Idas cried, roaring with laughter at his own wit. His companions frowned at him for his levity. The majesty of Olympus, seen from a distance of even ten miles, awed their souls.

They ate a meal of goat-cheese and barley-cake, washed down with wine, and passed the time by asking one another riddles. This riddle was asked by Admetus: 'I never lived until I died in honour of the sister of my master's servant; now I go piously with my master in search of my glorious ancestor.' Atalanta guessed the answer: it was the cap of Admetus, which was made from the pelts of lambs cast by the pregnant ewes sacrificed by him to Artemis. For Artemis was sister to Apollo, the former servant of Admetus; and now the cap was going with Admetus in search of the Golden Fleece.

Meleager asked another riddle: 'I never stay long among my own people. I do not know my strength. I knock men down like rotten trees. I spent my childhood among strangers. When did I ever miss my mark with an arrow? I dare to go alone among a company of enemies; nobody prevents me, because all fear me.'

'Hercules,' everyone shouted at once.

'No,' said Meleager. 'Guess again!' When at last they gave up guessing he told them: 'It is Atalanta. For she does not know the strength of her beauty, how it knocks men down like rotten trees. She spent her childhood among the priestesses of Artemis on Mount Aracynthos, just as Hercules did among strangers in Cadmean Thebes and like him she is seldom among her own people. Who ever saw her miss her mark with an arrow? Now she has dared to come among this company of men, who are the natural enemies of women; and none prevents her.'

It grew dark but still the ship drove on, the progress that she made being noiseless as a dream, and when Tiphys grew weary of guiding her, Little Ancaeus took the helm. He kept the Pole Star over his left shoulder for mile after mile, while Tiphys slept and so did all the other Argonauts but Orpheus. Then Orpheus sang a song for Little Ancaeus alone, of such piercing sweetness that he could not restrain his tears. Ever afterwards at night, during any silent watch when the stars were clear, the words and melody ran in his head:

> She tells her love while half asleep,
> In the dark hours,
> With half-words whispered low:
> As Earth stirs in her winter sleep
> And puts out grass and flowers
> Despite the snow,
> Despite the falling snow.

Ancaeus knew the name of the woman in the song: it was Eurydice, the lovely wife of Orpheus, who had accidentally trodden upon a serpent and been stung by it. Not all the glorious music that poured from his Hyperborean lyre could save her; and in anguish he had cast the dust of Greece from his sandals and journeyed to Egypt. But, returning as suddenly as he went, he had lived ever since in self-imposed exile among the savage Ciconians and was their law-giver, arbiter, and beloved friend.

Orpheus softly thrummed the melody for some time after he had ceased singing. Ancaeus as he glanced to port to make sure that he was keeping a straight course saw, as he thought, the dark heads of men swimming alongside. Looking to starboard he saw several more. He grew frightened and whispered: 'Hist, Orpheus; ghosts are following us!' But Orpheus told him not to be afraid: those were seals drawn from far and near by the power of his music.

Presently Ancaeus heard Orpheus heave a deep sigh and asked him: 'Orpheus, why do you sigh?'

Orpheus answered: 'I sigh for weariness.'

'Sleep, then,' said Ancaeus, 'and I will keep the watch alone. Sleep and rest well.'

Orpheus thanked him but said: 'No, dear Lelegian, mine is not the weariness that can be cured by sleep; only perfect rest will cure it.'

Ancaeus asked: 'Since to rest well is to sleep, but to rest perfectly is to die, do you then desire death, Orpheus?'

Orpheus answered: 'Not even death. We are all caught on a wheel, from which there is no release but by grace of the Mother. We are whirled up into life, the light of day, and carried down again into death, the darkness of night; but then another day dawns red and we reappear, we are reborn. And a man is not reborn in his accustomed body but in that of a bird, beast, butterfly, bat, or creeping thing, according to the judgement passed upon him below. Death is no release from the wheel, Ancaeus, unless the Mother should intervene. I sigh for perfect rest, to be taken at last into her benign keeping.'

As dawn brightened, they saw what appeared to be an island ahead of them. Orpheus knew it for Pallene, at that time named Phlegra, the nearest and most fertile of the three peninsulas of Paeonia, and was pleased that they had kept dead on their course. Orpheus and Little Ancaeus waked Tiphys, who took his trick at the helm again, and Tiphys waked Jason to watch with him. Then, as these four breakfasted together on barley-bread and cheese and wine, the sun rose most beautifully out of the sea, gilding the fleecy clouds that raced overhead through a blue sky. The wind freshened. They steered close inshore, not fearing shoals or rocks, and observed several excellent herds of cattle and sheep grazing unattended close to the sea.

'Do not let us disembark yet,' said Tiphys; 'there will be as good booty further on. Let our fellows sleep. Sleeping men are not hungry men.' They ran on, and the sun warmed the sleepers and disinclined them to awake. They sailed along the sole of Pallene's foot and sighted the mountains and wooded peninsula of Sithonia, which ends in a conical hill named Goat Hill. Little Ancaeus and Orpheus were now asleep, but Jason waked the others for breakfast, and watched the third peninsula, that of Acte, loom up to the north-east. Acte is rugged and broken with ravines, and at the foot rises Mount Athos, a great white cone skirted with dark forest. Here they decided to land for water and for the pleasure of walking on dry land, but could not spend long ashore, because weather-wise Coronus, looking at the sky, foretold that the wind would not hold much longer.

The Argonauts were still in holiday mood, careless of what trials and dangers might lie ahead of them. Jason set them a contest, with a jar of wine for a prize: who could bring back the largest living thing to him before the shadow of a stick, that he set up, travelled from one mark to another. The company scattered, and just before the shadow touched the mark Jason blew on a conch and recalled them. Some of them expected that within so short a space of time nobody would have found anything of great size, and therefore exhibited proudly, one, a young sea-bird that he had robbed from its nest on a cliff; another, a mouse that he had trodden upon but not killed; another, a small crab from the beach. But Atalanta had run down a hare, which they were measuring and weighing against a fine fish hooked by Melampus, when a great roaring was heard from over the hill and they saw Hercules, too late for the prize, stalking down the mountain with a half-grown bear struggling in his arms.

Hercules was displeased to find that the contest was already closed. When he had beaten out the creature's brains against the side of the ship, he showed his displeasure by eating the tenderer parts, raw, without offering a morsel to anyone but Hylas. He tossed what was left of the carcase into the sea as they sailed on.

The wind did not fail until dusk. The sail was then lowered and out came the oars; they had a long pull that night before heaving-to for a few hours' sleep. Not long after dawn on the next morning they made Lemnos, a somewhat bleak-looking island of no great elevation. Myrine the principal city, was easy to find, as they rowed in from the west; Tiphys steered for the conspicuous white shrine of Hephaestus, situated on a promontory. This promontory jutted out from the mainland between two bays; Myrine lay, facing north and south, on the narrow isthmus linking the promontory to the land. Tiphys chose the southern bay, which offers a broad sandy beach in the angle nearest to the town and is protected from storms by shoals which break the force of the waves. As they came swinging in towards the city, keeping good time despite the fast stroke set by Hercules, Jason gave them the order to ship their oars. They did so, and the *Argo* continued to rush forward under the motion that they had given her, while they put on their helmets, strung their bows, and seized their spears or javelins. As the ship headed for the shallow water, gradually losing way, out from the whitewashed houses streamed a company of armed Lemnians to oppose their landing.

Jason said to the Argonauts: 'In the name of all the Gods and Goddesses, I implore you to make no hostile sign. Let them attack us first if they will. Echion, Echion, put on heraldic robe and crown, take the olive wand in your hand and assure these Lemnians that our intentions are peaceable.'

Echion put on his splendid insignia, girded up his robe, and, leaping into the water to his knees, waded ashore with olive wand uplifted.

Suddenly Lynceus cried out: 'By the Lynx's pads and tail! I swear that they are all women!'

Eurydamas the Dolopian echoed: 'Mares, foals, and stallions! Not men but women!'

Then Hercules roared: 'Ho, ho! Are the Amazons come to Lemnos?'

The others all exclaimed variously at the strangeness of the sight.

This is the story of the Lemnian women. Originally, the Triple Goddess was devoutly worshipped by the Lemnians, and there were colleges of nymphs and a Maia, or Chief Priestess, who ruled the whole island from her house in the hills above Myrine; but no institution of marriage. Then the new Olympian religion came to disturb the island. The men grew ambitious to be fathers and husbands and thus to have dominion over the nymphs; but the Chief Priestess threatened them with terrible punishment unless they continued in the old ways. They pretended compliance, but not long afterwards sailed off secretly all together in their fishing-boats and made a sudden descent at evening on the coast of Thrace. It was a day when they knew that the young girls of the district would be gathered together on a small island near the coast, sacrificing to a local hero, with no men anywhere near. They surprised these girls, carried them off, and made them their wives. The affair was so dexterously managed that the Thracians concluded that their women had been devoured by sea-monsters, or carried off by Harpies, or engulfed by quicksands.

The Lemnian men settled down with their wives at Myrine and let the Lemnian women know that they needed them no longer, for their new wives would sow the corn and caprify the figs and look after them well. They embraced the new Olympian religion and, being artificers, put them-selves under the patronage of the Smith God Hephaestus – Hephaestus who had hitherto been regarded as a local hero, not a God, but now was deified as son of Hera and Zeus. His hero-shrine, which Tiphys had seen on the promontory, was rededicated as a temple; sacrifices were offered to him on a lofty altar, not on a low hearth; male priests displaced the college of nymphs.

Only one man, the war-king Thoäs, brother of the Chief Priestess, refused to join the renegades; and the Chief Priestess sent him to warn them of the anger of the Triple Goddess. They pelted him with filth and sent him back, with the message: 'Lemnian women, you have a foul stench. But these Thracian girls are like roses.'

A great festival was to be celebrated at Myrine in honour of the Olympians. When the festival day came, the Chief Priestess sent out spies, who reported towards evening that the men were already lying about in the market-place, dead drunken. So it was that the women, having maddened themselves by chewing ivy leaves and dancing naked in the moonlight, ran down at dawn to Myrine and killed all the men without exception, and all the Thracian women too. As for the children, they spared the girls, but cut the throats of all the boys, sacrificing them to the Maiden Goddess Persephone, lest they might attempt acts of vengeance in later years. All this was done in an ecstasy of religion, and the ancient forms of worship were restored to the shrine on the promontory.

In the morning the women grew frightened at what they had done, but could not call back to life the dead men, some of whom had been their brothers, some their sons, some their lovers. They gave them decent burial and purified themselves from guilt as best they could. The Goddess uttered an oracle, taking all the blame on her own head, and ordering them to be merry and perform a dance of victory, which they did. Then all cheerfully undertook the work usually performed by men, except the glazing of pots and the forging of weapons and instruments, which they did not understand, and contrived to catch enough fish for their needs, and to guide the ploughs and break the clods. They also exercised themselves with spear and sword for fear of a hostile landing by the Thracians.

The Chief Priestess's daughter, the Cuckoo Nymph Hypsipyle, had executed the whole plot under her mother's directions; she had also contrived to conceal Thoäs during the massacre, because he was her mother's brother and well disposed to the Goddess. Afterwards she set him adrift in a boat without oars, not wishing to kill him outright, but dared not tell the women what she had done, because of a unanimous vote that had been cast against the sparing of any man whatsoever. Hypsipyle was a dark-eyed, handsome woman, and the other women had a great regard for her. For some months before the arrival of the *Argo* she had been increasingly disturbed for the future of the island; because all the women had an ill-disguised craving for the sight and smell of man. For want of lovers, they were falling into unnatural passions for one another, and longing for children and behaving in a restless and hysterical manner. Hypsipyle was also anxious for the harvest, the barley not having been fertilized by the customary act of love with the Lemnian men. She could get no further guidance from her holy mother, who had been struck down with paralysis and could not speak: an event of very ill omen. However, the Goddess in a dream advised Hypsipyle to remain patient, since all would be well.

When the *Argo* was first sighted, Hypsipyle naturally concluded her to be a Thracian ship and sounded the call to arms; but as soon as she saw the Ram's head, emblem of the Minyans, she felt somewhat reassured.

CHAPTER FOURTEEN

THE WOMEN'S ISLAND

Hypsipyle received Echion in what had been the men's council-chamber. He allowed her to believe that the *Argo* was bound for Thrace on a trading voyage, and told her that Jason the Minyan, her captain, wished to put in at Myrine merely for food, drink, and recreation. Hypsipyle asked under whose auspices the voyage had been undertaken. He told her: 'Of Zeus, of Poseidon, of Apollo, of Athena, of Artemis.' When she replied 'It is well', but in rather a cold voice, he was shrewd enough to add: 'More than all these, the Triple Goddess favours us.' At these words he saw her face light up with pleasure.

Since Echion asked no awkward questions about the absence of all men from the streets and the council-chamber, Hypsipyle conversed with him in a friendly fashion, explaining that, since all the men of Lemnos were away in Thrace on a military expedition, her council must now deliberate whether it would be proper, in their absence, to allow men of another race to land on the island. She hoped that Jason would be patient for an hour or two until the Council had come to a decision. Meanwhile she gave him a jar of honey in token of friendship.

Echion made a handsome show in his herald's robes; he carried his olive wand, with the two shoots at the top twisted across each other and tied with white wool, as though it were a sceptre. As he went out of the chamber, followed by a slender girl staggering under the weight of a huge jar of honey, many women could not refrain from reaching out to stroke his arms and shoulders caressingly. He smiled in pleasant acknowledgement of each favour, which encouraged the women to greater boldness, until Hypsipyle called them to order and reminded them that the person of a herald was sacred and not to be treated with violence of any description.

Echion returned to the ship and told his story, with dry comments on the strangely uncontrolled warmth of Lemnian women, while Butes sampled the honey for the company. Butes pronounced after a pause: 'Not a bad honey, by any means. Mainly heather, some thyme – rosemary? yes, rosemary – and a trace of cyclamen. For a simple island honey, I must admit that it is very well indeed. Attic honey is more exquisite, of course, because the harmony of its contributory savours is more complex: just as a well-played melody on a seven-stringed zither is more satisfying to the ear than a melody equally well played on a lyre of three strings. But were I asked to judge between a melody well played on three strings, and one badly played on seven, I should reply: "Three strings win." This Lemnian honey is perfection compared with what Pelias set before us at Iolcos, boasting that it was pure arbutus honey. Arbutus, indeed! I do not mind the flavour of wild garlic in a dish of mutton boiled with barley, but, by the Owl of Athena, the laws of hospitality demand that it should be kept out of the honey-jar. However, it would be ungrateful in me to criticize our royal host, and unwise to do so in the presence of his son, his nephew, and his son-in-law, all men of distinction. Let the Chief Steward therefore bear the whole weight of my accusation. But what I wish to say is: that if the amenities of Lemnos are of the same simple but excellent sort as this honey, I look forward most eagerly to my stay here.'

Hypsipyle's Council were torn in their hearts between the resolve that they had taken, never to trust men again or allow them in the island, and the surge of amorous passion that the appearance of Echion had evoked. Hypsipyle addressed them thus:

'Dearest Sisters, Aunts, Nieces, Cousins, and you, my little daughter Iphinoë, listen patiently to me, if you please, and then advise me. These Minyans, unless their herald lies (and I hardly think that he would venture to lie after naming so many Gods and Goddesses, and the Great Mother herself), are peaceable in their intentions, and would doubtless be satisfied with gifts of wine, honey, barley-bread, cheese, and our good Lemnian mutton. After coming ashore to stretch their legs – keeping well away, at our request, from the houses of Myrine – they would sail on to Imbros, their next stage on the Thracian voyage. I admit that the build of their ship suggests war rather than trade. It is likely that their business in Thrace is of a somewhat piratical nature; but let that not concern us. The Thracians are far from being allies of ours. To keep the Minyans thus at arms' length is within our power, for we are more numerous than they and could give a good account of ourselves in battle.

'Their herald seemed to accept as true my story of our men being detained in Thrace; so that they would be cautious of attacking us, if our gifts pleased them, for fear of eventual vengeance. Yet to give them the freedom of our city would be dangerous, for one of us is sure to be indiscreet and blurt out the true story of what happened on that night of blood. Then, though these Minyans might not themselves blame us, yet the story of our terrible deed would soon be spread abroad throughout Greece. The Thracians would come to hear of it, and sail here at once to avenge their daughters' deaths on us.'

After a pause, Iphinoë spoke: 'Mother, after I had delivered the honey-jar to the men in the ship and gone away, I crept back down the gully and hid behind a rock to hear what they were saying. The sea-breezes brought every word to me clearly. I heard one man, whom the others addressed as Little Ancaeus, say: "Is that indeed so? Then what Thoäs told me was no fable, but true after all!" Someone asked him, "Who is Thoäs, and what did he say?" He answered: "Thoäs was an old Lemnian whom in the course of my voyage to Iolcos from Samos I picked up adrift in a rudderless boat and put ashore on the islet of Sicinos, near Naxos. He was crazed from thirst and hunger and persisted in saying that the women of Lemnos had killed all the men of the island but himself, and had set him adrift in the boat. This story was strewn with so many other particulars which were obviously untrue, such as that he had a little barley-patch and a couple of milch-ewes in the box under the helmsman's seat, that my comrades and I could not credit a word of it." So, Mother, I see no reason to keep these handsome sailors away, now that they already know the worst. And I must say this: their tall captain, who has yellow braided hair and wears a tunic of spotted skin, is the handsomest man that I ever saw in my life.'

There was silence for a while. Then a feeble old woman, who had been Hypsipyle's foster-nurse, rose up. She said: 'My dears, I am an old woman, long past child-bearing and too wrinkled and yellow and thin for any man's pleasure. Therefore what I now say is said disinterestedly. I am sure that we did right in killing our men and their wives: we were bound to avenge the Goddess's honour. In so doing we repaired an error into which we had fallen of late years: for when my mother was a girl, the insolence of men was checked at puberty by breaking their right legs, in honour of the lame hero Hephaestus. This prevented them from competing with us in battle or the chase and confined them to the plough, the boat, and the anvil. This excellent custom we discontinued, I suppose from misplaced pity, and our javelins were laid aside. I am sure, also, that we did right in killing the male children: to have spared them would have been to nurse adders in our bosoms. But to forbid any men of any sort from entering this island seems to me, on long reflection, an intolerably spiteful action against ourselves. Consider, my dears: even if you are able to defend Lemnos against all comers, what sort of a life are you storing up for your old age? When we old dames gradually die off and you pretty girls take our places on the fireside settles, how will you manage to live? Will the intelligent oxen yoke themselves and plough the fields of their own accord? Will the busy asses take sickles at harvest-time and reap for you? Will the willing fish leap out of the water into the frying-pans? For my part, I hate to think that I shall die and be buried before my ears are greeted again with the yells and bellowing shouts of sturdy little boys playing at pirates in the courtyard; now I hear only the tedious whine of little girls who slyly pinch and scratch one another, and who whisper empty secrets in corners.

'Be women again, beauties of Lemnos, take lovers from among these handsome strangers, confidently place your persons under the protection of their fame – for there seem to be some notable princes among them – and breed up a nobler race of Lemnians than before.'

A sigh of relief and a burst of applause marked the end of the old woman's speech. Iphinoë, dancing for impatience, cried: 'Mother, mother, may I go at once and fetch all those lovely sailors here?'

Hypsipyle put the question to the Council, who signified their approval without a single dissentient voice; and though some of the women suspected Hypsipyle of smuggling Thoäs out of the island, they were too happily excited at the time to charge her with the crime. So Iphinoë was sent off. She raced down to the shore and cried out: 'Dear sailors, you are all welcome to come ashore and stretch your legs. My mother, Queen Hypsipyle, promises you as happy a time as ever you had at home with your wives, whom you must be missing sadly.'

The Argonauts cheered and blew kisses to her, while Idas laughed raucously and drove his elbow into the ribs of his neighbour Argus, with: 'Hey, Argus, how is your lame leg? Will you not come ashore for once and stretch it?'

In the midst of the mirth that greeted this sally, Jason gave the order to beach the ship. All bent to their oars and soon heard the hiss of their long keel as it ploughed into sand. They reversed their oars, taking care not to beat one another over the head in their eagerness; then clambered out and, heaving on the oar-butts, dragged the *Argo* half out of the water. Hercules tumbled the anchor-stones overboard.

Iphinoë's keen eye searched among the company for a handsome boy to make her own (for she was already nubile), and it fell on Hylas. She smiled at him meaningly; he blushed and smiled shyly back.

'Lead on, dear child,' cried Jason to Iphinoë. 'We are with you to a man.' He unbraided his long mane of hair and took in hand a javelin that Atalanta had given him at Methone in token of fidelity to his leadership, it was iron-headed, and the heft was ornamented with three thin bands of gold. Then he put on his best mantle, dyed with sea-purple; it was embroidered with emblems that told the story of the lost Fleece, though nobody unacquainted with the conventions of art would have understood their meaning. For in the first panel Phrixus and Helle were shown flying through the air on the back of a golden ram, with Helle in the act of tumbling off into the arms of Tritons and Nereids, while their mother Nephele in cloud shape puffed them forward by flapping her cloak, and the Triple Goddess, represented by three graceful women arm in arm, trampled on prostrate Athamas, their father. The ram seemed to be addressing Phrixus over its shoulder. A vulture was tearing at the liver of a man whom anyone would have supposed to be Prometheus, from the fire-wheel in his hand and the snowy mountain; but it was intended for Phrixus, long after his arrival at Colchis. The fire-wheel recorded the dedication of the Fleece in the shrine of Prometheus, and the vulture signified that Phrixus had not been given decent burial. The picture of Jason himself brandishing a spear in the cave of Cheiron, who was shown as half man, half horse, and playing a pipe, was equally mysterious; Jason seemed to be a pigmy attacked by a monster with a blow-pipe.

The other Argonauts also primped and preened themselves, and a very wonderful company they looked when they had done. Jason asked: 'Who stays to guard the ship against treachery? You, Melampus? You, little Ancaeus?'

These two were prepared to stay, though disappointed not to follow with the others, but Hercules unexpectedly said: 'Go, you two! I stay here with Hylas. He is not yet old enough for a jaunt of the sort that this promises to be. If I left him in the company of that hot little wench yonder she would seduce him as quickly as butter melts in the sun.'

Hylas's eyes grew cloudy with resentment. He pleaded: 'O Hercules, let me go! I will come to no harm. I am nearly a man now, you know!'

Atalanta, who had a kind heart, said: 'Yes, Hercules, let him go, and go yourself. I will take the guard duty. I admit that I was looking forward to a chat with those handsome Lemnian girls, and a really well-cooked meal for once. But I might as well stay as go: I can take no part in the love-making that is likely to follow the banquet, and will only be in the way of the others. So go, Hercules: you can best keep Hylas from harm by setting him an example of chastity.'

Jason interrupted: 'One woman is an insufficient guard for the *Argo*.'

Atalanta controlled her anger. 'Meleager can stay with me if he likes,' she said.

Hercules laughed in her face: 'You are in love with Meleager, and jealous of his companying with some Lemnian woman. You wish to keep him for yourself. But I will not leave you alone with him. To do so would be to invite ill luck. You do not trust Meleager away from your side; I do not trust him at your side, lest you vex your mistress Artemis by yielding to his importunities. No, no! Hylas and I stay here, do we not, my darling boy?'

He caught Hylas up in his bear-like embrace and hugged him until he squeaked: 'Yes, yes, Hercules! Put me down! I will do anything that you say. Only, put me down!'

'Very well,' said Atalanta. 'Let it be as you wish.'

Meleager lagged behind the company and whispered to her: 'Sweetheart, let us speak again to Hercules. Let us offer to take care of Hylas while he himself goes up with the others to a feast which he would be sorry to miss. Hylas would enjoy nothing so much as to be free for a few hours from his foster-father's company. With Hylas as a witness of our chaste behaviour, Hercules could not object to our staying behind together.'

Atalanta nodded, and Meleager went back to make his new offer. But

Hercules wagged his finger at him. 'No, no!' he cried. 'I see through your trickery. You intend to make love to Atalanta under the pretence of guarding this ship and of doing me a service; but as soon as my back is turned you will throw Hylas into Iphinoë's arms and afterwards declare that he was with you all the time. No, no, I stay here, do you understand? I have no particular desire to go to Myrine. I am not so fond of the act of love as you might suppose from the great number of women with whom I have performed it... Heigh, ho! Time after time I have the same ill luck. *She* always wants a son by me, as tall and strong as I am, and I always want a daughter by her, as slim and pretty as she is. Every time I lose, and she wins. I think that it must be due to Hera's spite – only think, two or three hundred sons and not a single daughter! Holy Serpents, did you ever hear anything to equal it? I have a good mind to abandon the contest... But what were we discussing a moment ago?'

Atalanta answered shortly: 'Meleager and I offered to guard the *Argo* and look after Hylas while you went up to Myrine. You refused the offer. Come, Meleager!'

As they went off together, Hercules said to Hylas: 'What an evil temper that girl Atalanta has! But no worse, I suppose, than most women's. Well, now, my darling, you are safe from that greedy little Lemnian girl, safe with your dear, affectionate Hercules. I feel a little hungry. What about something good to eat?'

Hylas called to Atalanta as she went: 'Tell Iphinoë that if she brings my foster-father something good to eat it will be a kindness to us both. Tell her that he needs at least a whole roast sheep and a three-gallon jar of wine.'

Iphinoë led Jason and the rest of the Argonauts, two by two, through the city gate. A great cry of admiration and welcome went up from the women. But Great Ancaeus sent the word down the column: 'Eyes to your front, hands tight on your weapons!'

They came to the council-chamber, where armed girls opened the folding-doors studded with bronze lion-heads, and invited them to sit down on the benches; or if they should care to perform their necessities, there was a handsome privy along the corridor, with seats in the Cretan style, flushed with water from a cistern on the roof, and a bag of goose feathers hanging from the wall beside each seat.

Presently Jason was ushered into Hypsipyle's presence. She was seated in a well-furnished upper room with a window facing south. This had been the private apartment of the Cretan governor before the sack of Cnossos by Theseus, which had been followed by the revolt of all the Cretan colonies, including Lemnos. The walls were painted with pictures of Rhea's Lion tearing her naked enemies into pieces, and of boys riding on the backs of dolphins, and of two ladies exchanging gifts of flowers in the market-place of Cnossos.

Jason greeted Hypsipyle with grave respect. 'Beautiful Queen, I have already heard news of your misfortunes from old Thoäs, a native of Lemnos, whom one of my comrades rescued from an oarless boat not far from Naxos. He reported that you had long been plagued by your men-folk and put under the bitter necessity of killing most of them.'

Hypsipyle answered cautiously: 'I am rejoiced that the noble Thoäs, my mother's brother, is still alive, though I cannot conceive how he came to be drifting about the Naxian Sea. He was somewhat unbalanced in his wits when we last met, and did not quite understand what was happening around him. The truth is that a year ago, when the sailing season came round, our men, instead of fishing in their customarily peaceful way, began raiding the Thracian coast and bringing us back gifts of cattle and sheep. We women did not wish to become involved in a war with the Thracians, and my mother, the Chief Priestess, therefore asked them to desist. They pleaded that fish was scarce and, when caught, not so appetizing as beef and mutton. My mother replied that the raids must cease, unless they wished her to refuse them our customary love at the festivals in honour of the Goddess. For the Goddess had advised her to give them exactly this reply. They informed my mother very insolently that where they went was no business of hers; and sailed off to Thrace with the next southerly breeze. There they found a company of Thracian girls celebrating their new-moon festival apart from the men. They carried them off and made wives of them, against the custom of this island, where wives had until then been unknown, and told us nymphs "to go to the crows".

'My mother pleaded with them to return to sanity and restore the girls to their unhappy mothers, but no! they answered that we nymphs stank and that they needed us no longer. Worse than this, they forcibly removed the ancient black image of the Goddess from her unroofed temple a few miles from here and replaced it with one of the Smith God which they had made themselves. We have nothing against the Smith God, though we prefer to consider him a hero rather than a deity, but why did they eject the Ancient One for his sake? Well, one night they were all lying about the streets, shamelessly drunken, and the Goddess inspired us with desperate courage: we would assault the city by night and disarm them, threatening them with death unless they would quit the island for ever. We fought and were victorious. Finding themselves at our mercy, they agreed to sail away with their wives, but only on condition that we gave them all our male children; they said, however, that we might keep the girls. We agreed to that condition, but we made them sail without weapons or armour, since we did not trust them not to return at night and attack us. That was nearly a year ago, and we have not heard a word about them since. Thoäs went after them in a boat one night: he missed male society and we could not persuade him to stay. Lately, my daughter Iphinoë had a vivid dream in which she watched our men land at the mouth of a Thracian river; but the angry Thracians at once set on them and hacked them to pieces. So, alas, we may in a sense be responsible for their deaths, as Thoäs suggested. Who knows?'

Hypsipyle drew a long breath and began to weep. Jason kissed her hand to comfort her and she drew him closer to her. He kissed her neck instead of her hand, whispering that he pitied her.

She gently repelled him, sobbing: 'Do not kiss me from pity, my lord! I would rather by far be kissed in love than in pity. And, O Jason, let me confess to you: I am in the deepest anxiety about our barley harvest. The seed was sown without the usual fertility rites, and though the barley and millet has shown up very thick and green, because we did what we could – sacrificing male kids and lambs to the Mother and making our usual prayers – what if it should prove to be all straw? We should starve.'

Jason asked: 'Is it already too late to save your millet and barley crops by a rite of the amatory sort that I suppose you to practise here? I believe not, and certainly my comrades as well as I –'

'You are a most generous, pious man,' cried Hypsipyle. 'Come, dare to kiss me on the mouth. Do you know, I looked out of the window as you came marching down the street at the head of your glorious men, and I asked myself, "What does he most resemble?"'

'What did I most resemble, my dear?' asked Jason, squeezing her soft arm.

Hypsipyle answered: 'A bright star which a girl at an upper window watches as it rises out of the midnight sea – a girl who, the next day, is to be initiated into the secret of womanhood and can hardly sleep for longing.'

'Is that indeed how I seem to you?' said Jason. 'Let me tell you in return that your clear black eyes are like two midnight pools by the seashore, in which the same star glitters.'

'And I do not stink?' asked Hypsipyle, her lip quivering. 'They said that our bodies stank.'

'You are all violet and rose, and your breath is as sweet as that of Hera's sacred cow,' cried Jason gallantly. 'On the instant that I first set eyes upon you my heart began a golden dance. Do you know how a sunbeam quivers on the whitewashed ceiling of an upper room – as it might be this – thrown up there by a great cauldron of lustral water in the courtyard, whose surface the wind stirs? That is exactly how my heart danced and is dancing now.'

An alcove close to where they were sitting formed a little chapel of Our Lady of Myrine, as the Mother Goddess was there styled. The calm, blue-aproned figure of the Mother, in glazed earthenware, smiled benignly down on the chubby infant Zagreus at her feet – he who was doomed to die miserably for the good of the people – and beside her rose a plain, squat cross, cut from white marble, with twin hollows at its base to receive petty offerings of fruit and nuts. Hypsipyle had spread the table on which the

Goddess stood with sea-sand and cockle-shells and in the costly silver vases on either side of the cross shone the scented lily flowers that the Goddess loved. Only the little spotted snake that she held in her left hand, and the silver moon that dangled on her bosom, reminded visitants of her darker aspects. Her coronal was of stars.

Hypsipyle asked Jason: 'Is it not a pretty shrine? Do you think it possible that Our Lady will ever be extruded from Lemnos? Evil men may neglect or slight her, but will she not always remain with us?'

Jason shook his head. 'The Father has become very powerful,' he said, 'and what his secret intentions may be towards her who was once his mother and is now his wife, who can say? But let us allow no questions of theology to disturb our hearts, which are already sufficiently vexed by the arrows of the cruel Love Spite. Come back with me, radiant Queen, to the council-chamber! Yet before he went, he prudently felt in his wallet and found three hazel nuts and a little lump of hard goats' cheese; with these he propitiated the blue-aproned Goddess, putting them in the hollows at the base of the altar cross.

CHAPTER FIFTEEN

FAREWELL TO LEMNOS

When Jason and Hypsipyle returned to the council-chamber, he with his right arm around her shoulders, she with her left arm around his waist, a roar of applause went up. Hypsipyle was so tall, dark and beautiful, Jason so tall, fair and handsome. Both blushed.

Soon each Argonaut found himself seated at table with a woman on either side of him. The woman on his left hand kept his beech-wood trencher heaped with abundance of food – fish, roast mutton with capers pickled in sour wine, roast beef with sauce of asafoetida, wild game, honey-cakes, stewed dormouse (which, however, the worshippers of Apollo excused themselves from eating), asparagus, dried white figs, barley-bread soaked in olive oil, delicate sheep's-cheese, samphire pickled in brine, and the hard-boiled eggs of sea-fowl. The woman on his right hand filled his goblet with wine and water (and the mixture contained almost as much wine as water), or milk, or beer, whichever he asked for; sometimes she mixed all together and stirred in honey.

Meleager was in a quandary. Though the youngest of the Argonauts, he was one of the tallest and strongest of them all, with curly black hair and regular features, the rather melancholy cast of which made him peculiarly attractive to women. Several made a rush for him, clasping his hands and knees. He disengaged himself with an apologetic but decisive movement. 'Go elsewhere, pretty bees,' he said. 'There is no honey left in this flower.' They smiled and kissed him and went off again, believing him to be less virile than he seemed. Atalanta encouraged this belief: 'Meleager of Calydon is a king's son,' she said, 'but has never yet been able to content a woman as it is proper for women to be contented. His father, King Oeneus, once angered a certain jealous goddess. If you need a lover worthy of you, beautiful girls, go down to the shore and find happiness there!'

Meleager and she sat down together apart from the rest, and helped themselves to whatever they could find boiling in the many smoke-blackened pots by the long hearth, or roasting on the many iron spits. The company paid little attention to them and, after they had eaten and drunken their fill, they took courteous leave of Queen Hypsipyle. She nodded absently to them, entranced by Jason's account of his voyage to

Dodona, and assured them that they were free of the whole island. In some parts of the hall the love-making had already begun in earnest and Atalanta considered it shameful to remain longer.

Iphinoë, who had been mixing wine and water for the pitchers brought to her by the women, slipped out after Meleager and Atalanta. 'O Prince Meleager,' she cried, 'where are you going?'

He answered: 'Atalanta and I are going out to hunt.'

'Dear people,' she said, 'if your hunting takes you down to the beach, I beg you to give that dark-eyed boy a message. Tell him that I will be waiting for him at midnight in the cave above the beach, near the thicket of brambles and caper-bushes.'

'Nothing would please me better,' said Meleager. 'Have you yet sent the food and drink down to Hercules?'

'Yes,' she answered. 'The amorous women whom you rejected have that matter in hand. They are taking down a whole roast sheep, a leg of beef, a goose stewed in barley – no, two geese – and six gallons of wine. The wine is flavoured by me with crushed poppy-seed. If all that does not send him off to sleep, he is a greater wonder even than his frightful appearance declares him.'

Atalanta and Meleager went out through the city gate, confident that the dark forest which spread over the hills behind harboured plenty of game. But first they went down to the *Argo* to deliver Iphinoë's message, if possible. From a distance they saw a great crowd of women buzzing around Hercules like wasps around a fallen piece of honeycomb – not only those whom Meleager had rejected but all who had not been fortunate enough to secure a lover, or the share of a lover, in the hall.

'Alas, poor Hercules,' said Atalanta, smiling. 'He will surely find it difficult enough to please one or two without angering fifty.'

'Hercules has successfully performed more difficult labours even than that,' Meleager answered with a sour smile. 'But I wonder where Hylas can be? Do you see him?'

Atalanta made a wide circuit to escape the notice of Hercules and by swimming and wading came up close to the *Argo*, in which she guessed Hylas to be imprisoned. She peeped over the bulwark, and there was Hylas weeping silently and unable to stir: Hercules, to secure him from the designs of Iphinoë, had seated him in the ship's great copper cauldron and bent the sides over his body, as one might wrap a little fish in a fig leaf. Nobody but Hercules with his hands, or a smith with heavy, clanging blows of a great hammer, could ever release him. Nevertheless, Atalanta whispered her message and returned the way she came. She was still in the water, though a long way from the ship, when something hit her leather helmet with a resounding thud, and knocked it off. She heard the roaring cry of Hercules: 'Ho, ho! I hit her every time.' It was a sheep's shin-bone that he had playfully thrown at her.

Two days later Hercules awoke with a terrible headache and snatched up his club, which he found close to hand. He looked wildly around and saw only the remnants of a feast, some broken combs and torn women's clothes, and a rude altar heaped with charred fruit and grain. Where was his dearest Hylas? He began to rave and bellow, the poppy-seed and wine having clouded his memory and the children's voices in his head sounding particularly shrill and disagreeable. He was rushing off to catch and brain Iphinoë when he heard Hylas calling piteously to him from the *Argo*: 'Hercules, Hercules, let me out, let me out!'

Hercules laughed for delight, vaulted into the ship with a crash, ran to Hylas and wrenched the cauldron back into shape. Then he hugged him, covering his face with slobbered kisses, as a great mastiff will lick the face of his master's little child until he yells for fear. He paused to ask: 'Darling Hylas, how long have I slept?'

'Two whole nights and one whole day,' answered Hylas faintly, 'during which I have sat cramped here in agony, unable to rouse you. Some kind women brought me food and drink and covered my shoulders with this blanket; but that was little comfort. Why, if you truly love me, are you so unkind to me? Why do you imprison and torture your poor Hylas? All the rest of the Argonauts, yourself included, have enjoyed the most wonderful hospitality that a ship's company was ever given since ships were invented.'

'Two nights and one day! And nobody came to release you?' cried Hercules indignantly. 'Oh, the wretches! Why has none of them returned to take over the watch from us? Have those cursed women played the same trick on them as they did on their own kinsfolk? Have they spared only you and me?' But soon he saw Idas and Lynceus sauntering along the beach, each with two women on either side of him, their heads garlanded and their cheeks flushed with wine.

'When are you two idlers coming to relieve me?' he shouted. 'I have been on watch here for two nights and a day.'

'We have no orders,' Idas answered. 'Besides, you rejected Atalanta's offer to go on guard with Meleager. Why do you now complain? We are busy, as you see. We have ladies to love and serve.'

'If you do not come here at once,' snarled Hercules, 'and take over the watch from Hylas and me, I will knock the whole row of you as flat as a threshing-floor.'

They judged it prudent to obey, but brought the women with them. Then Hercules, gripping Hylas by the shoulder with his left hand and the brass-bound club with his right, went raging up into Myrine. At each house-door he rapped with his club and cried: 'Argonauts, turn out!' No door was stout enough to stand against that imperious summons. Either panels and transoms went spinning into the hall or the whole door was

burst from its hinges and came whacking down. Shrill shrieks of alarm and
rage rose from the women of the house, and angry expostulations from the
Argonauts comfortably closeted with them. Hercules went onwards down
the main streets from side to side, methodically knocking at every door
with a fore-handed or backhanded swing and bellowing: 'Argonauts, turn
out!'

At last he came to Hypsipyle's mansion on the bluff and roared out:
'Ahoy there, Jason! Is it not high time to be sailing on in search of that
Fleece of yours? Why do you delay?'

Jason's tousled head appeared at an upper window and Hypsipyle's
beside it. 'Ah, I understand,' said Hercules. 'You are busily employed in
founding a royal house of Lemnos. Good luck attend your efforts, but have
you not nearly done?'

Hypsipyle cried: 'Oh, Hercules, I rejoice to see you. My women bring
me wonderful accounts of your strength and affection. But it was unkind
of you to stay behind on the beach as though the *Argo* were in danger and
to keep that handsome foster-son of yours away from my Iphinoë. The
poor girl has been crying her eyes out in self-pity, and in pity for him. Do,
I beg you, let him run upstairs now and play with her for the rest of the
afternoon.'

Hercules in his anger could think of no suitable answer.

Hypsipyle went on: 'I have almost persuaded Jason to stay with us for
ever and become King of Lemnos. We may as well face the truth now as
later: the worn-out old Mother Goddess cannot compete on equal terms
with these sturdy new Olympians. Kingship is in fashion everywhere, and
Jason is the kingliest man that ever I set eyes upon. Besides, Lemnos is a
glorious island, as you see, with the deepest, moistest soil of any in the
Aegean. Our barley is superb, our wine second only to that of Lesbos, our
hill pastures are not at all to be despised. The forests swarm with game,
too. Jason has promised me to stay for a month at least and meanwhile to
consider –'

'I made no such promise, lovely Hypsipyle,' cried Jason, flushing. 'I
said no more than that I would stay for another day or two and then decide
whether perhaps to stay for another month.'

'He is in love with me, you see,' laughed Hypsipyle, 'and I think,
Hercules, that you will find it something of a Labour to gather a crew
together, for a month or two at least. The men will be loth to leave and the
women will oppose you stoutly – weapon in hand, if need be. After so long
a period of abstinence, they are wallowing in the pleasures of love as
Egyptian crocodiles wallow in the fertile ooze of the Nile.'

A heap of mud scrapings lay piled at the side of the street. Hercules bent
down, scooped up a handful, kneaded it into a mud-pie and with a sudden
heave threw it, flap, into Hypsipyle's face. 'Wallow in that, woman!' he
said gruffly. 'And as for you, my lord Jason, you must descend at once, or

with my club I will knock holes in this mansion through which you could drive four oxen yoked abreast.'

Jason descended, grumbling to himself. 'Now, my lord,' said severe Hercules, 'I counsel you to rally the crew and march them down to the ship. You cannot afford to lose the advantage of this westerly breeze and the calm sea.'

'Allow us an hour or so to say our goodbyes,' Jason pleaded.

Hercules complained: 'What a time you take over things! When as a young man, about your age, I was invited to company with the Thespian nymphs in reward for killing the Beast of Cythaeron, I lay with all fifty in the course of a single night and got every one of them with child. But you! You seem to have spent two days and nights in ineffective dalliance with the same woman. How, at this rate, do you expect ever to win the Golden Fleece? You may be bound that it will not be won by sporting among the barley-fields of Lemnos. By the brass of my club, no man has ever made a fool of me yet, and you will not be the first!'

With angry and obscene taunts he forced Jason away from Hypsipyle's door. Hypsipyle, who had sponged her face clean, ran down into the street, half-naked though she was, and cried after Jason: 'The Blessed Mother bring you back to me, my love, unharmed, victorious, and with all your dear friends alive! You know my promise: you shall be King and as many of your comrades as care to settle in Lemnos shall have as much land and as many cattle as you choose in your wisdom to grant them. Remember your poor Hypsipyle when you are far away. But before you go, tell me, what shall I do if I find myself the mother of your child?'

Jason answered: 'Hypsipyle, you and I have spent two exquisite days and nights together – if only they could have been prolonged to years! But Hercules has spoken to the point. Heavy work lies ahead of us, and we cannot linger here. Nor can I promise to return for good to your lovely Lemnos, because Phthiotis is my kingdom, and it is dangerous for a man to ride upon two horses. The sovereignty of Lemnos must remain in your hands; though if you bear a son, and if he lives to manhood, you may make a king of him by all means; yet remember that he stands next to me in succession to the throne of Phthiotis too, and in the event of my death he must choose, as I do now, between the two thrones. Send word to my old father and mother when you are delivered of the child – for a child I am sure there will be – and if ever you are forced to leave this island they will, for my sake, provide a good home for both of you.' He began to weep.

However, this sad farewell was not to be their last, for Jason could not persuade the other Argonauts, either by threats or promises, to stir from their new homes. Nor was Hercules any longer in a condition to help him; having locked Hylas in a windowless closet near the great kitchen of the council-chamber and leaned his back against the door, he was contentedly gurgling down wine from a large jar of Lesbian that he had found. When

Hypsipyle came into the chamber towards evening and found him there blinking like an owl, she forgivingly brought him bread and a cold roast goose to make the wine go down the sweeter. He caught at her robe in drunken fashion and offered her his sincere condolence upon her union with Jason. 'He is a worthless wretch, Queen Hypsipyle,' he said, 'and if ever you find yourself in trouble will not stretch out a finger to help you. But Hercules of Tiryns is a man of another quality altogether. If ever any disaster overtakes you, whether it be this year, or the next, or twelve years from now, remember that Hercules is your friend. Send for him, either to comfort or avenge you!' She thanked him courteously, keeping a straight countenance, but laughed aloud when she was back with Jason in her bedchamber.

Thus another day passed pleasurably for everyone, except Hylas and Iphinoë. It was the day of the barley-field ceremonies, which were merrily performed.

In the evening Meleager and Atalanta returned to Myrine with Orpheus, who, like them, had taken no part in the revels. They had found him in a clearing of the forest where, as he said, he had been teaching weasels to dance to his lyre. Neither Atalanta nor Meleager saw the dance, for they approached just as the music ceased, but a great many small beasts scuttled past them through the undergrowth. Orpheus played so entrancingly that nobody would have wondered if the trees, stones, and rocks had danced too.

It was Orpheus with his lyre who drew the unwilling Argonauts down to the *Argo* at last, in the early morning of the fourth day. A huge crowd of women accompanied them, and when the ship was afloat in a few feet of water they all tried to clamber over the sides, intending to face the dangers of the voyage at the sides of their lovers. But Hercules, when he had heaved up the anchor-stones, took it upon himself to throw out into the water all the women who had succeeded in getting aboard – twenty or thirty of them, who fought like lynxes.

Iphinoë escaped his notice; she lay under the fold of the sail – for only oars were being used – until the *Argo* was well on her way and the lamentations from the shore sounded less piercingly in the ears of her crew. Then she accidentally sneezed, which was a lucky omen for all but herself. Hercules shipped his oar and had his hands on her in no time. Overboard she went, like a fish that a fisherman rejects from his net as being of the wrong colour or shape. As she struck out for shore she cried to Hylas: 'Hylas, sweetheart, remember me!'

Hercules caught up an anchor-stone and poised it to throw at her, but Hylas yelled suddenly in his ear and he laid it down again; so she escaped death. The lyre's soothing strains carried the ship onwards in rhythmic motion, while the white wake creamed behind her.

Here may be given an account of what happened to the women of Lemnos as a result of the *Argo*'s visit to their hospitable island. Fifty women bore daughters, and no less than one hundred and fifty bore sons. Of these sons, sixty-nine were of the sturdy frame, quick eye, and uncertain temper which proclaimed them sons of Hercules; fifteen favoured Great Ancaeus, who also begot three daughters; twelve sons and five daughters favoured Idas; and so on in descending order of numerousness to Little Ancaeus, who begot one daughter.

Jason begot twin sons on Hypsipyle, by name Euneus and Nebrophonus, of whom Euneus, being the elder, eventually ruled Lemnos as King and married Lalage, daughter of Little Ancaeus, and was famous for his well-planted vineyards. However, the *Argo* never again beached at Myrine and Jason forgot Hypsipyle, as afterwards he forgot other women; but Hylas did not forget Iphinoë, being an impressionable boy.

CHAPTER SIXTEEN

ORPHEUS SINGS OF THE CREATION

A southerly breeze sprang up. Jason wished to sail along the southern coast of Lemnos and then to steer eastward for the Hellespont, but Tiphys would not risk casting the *Argo* away on the rocky flank of Cape Irene. For though a sailing-ship may be steered obliquely to the wind, he feared the reefs of a lee shore; besides, most of the crew were befuddled and in no condition to row. Instead, he proposed Samothrace as the next stage of their voyage.

Jason had heard the name Samothrace, but did not know whether it was a city or an island. Argus told him: 'It is an island, less than half the size of Lemnos, lying at about five hours' sail to the north-east. The inhabitants, like those of Lemnos, are of Pelasgian stock.'

'Let us visit it,' said Jason.

They expected to make Samothrace by the afternoon; but the breeze slackened long before they had lost sight of Lemnos. Mount Scopia was still showing tall on the horizon to the south-west when they were obliged to use their oars. The sun blazed down upon them fiercely and they could put no strength behind their stroke. By evening they had not yet sighted Samothrace, there was a dead calm and they were weary of rowing. A sea-mist gathered and clouded the horizon, obscuring even the acute vision of Lynceus.

The Argonauts ate their meal almost in silence. Most of them were thinking of the women whom they had left behind and reproaching themselves as fools for not having stayed at least a few days longer in that island paradise. Idas, always the first to make an ungracious interruption, suddenly cried out: 'To the fish with this miserable repast! It is the fault of nobody but Orpheus that we are crouched here on these hard benches, with fog in our throats, instead of reclining at ease on dyed sheepskin rugs before a crackling fire and a row of bubbling black pots. Orpheus tricked us aboard with his music. We were happy as kings in Lemnos. Why did he lead us off again on this impossible and thankless quest?'

Castor reproved Idas: 'Consider yourself lucky that Orpheus did so, Idas. You have never shown any moderation since I first knew you as a pugnacious and greedy child. Another few days in Lemnos and you would have been a corpse, overcome by a surfeit of wine, food, and women. For my part, I wish nothing better than to fall again under the compelling charm of that miraculous lyre, listening to which I enjoy greater happiness by far than from a goblet of scented Lemnian wine, from an unbroken chine of tender Lemnian beef, or from the plump white body of a sturdy, love-possessed Lemnian girl.'

Lynceus, twin to Idas, hated Castor and Pollux, whose grandfather Oebalus the Achaean had forcibly married Gorgophone, the Minyan grandmother of Idas and himself, and thus deprived them of a great part of their Messenian inheritance. Gorgophone was the first Greek widow who ever remarried, and this was a lasting shame to their father, Aphareus. Lynceus sneered: 'Yes, Castor, so you say. But these are the words of satiety. Your appetite was never either large or healthy. Confess, you would have spoken in a very different strain a day or two ago.'

Pollux took up the challenge, saying to Lynceus: 'My brother at least did not make a beast of himself as yours did.'

Now, all around, voices were raised, some in protest against this quarrel between the pairs of brothers, some in an attempt to embitter it. Then Hercules growled: 'Had I been in command of this ship I should have begun this morning's voyage by dosing every man-jack of you with a helmet of sea-water to purge your stomach. But Jason commands, not I.'

Then Idmon the augur said in his high voice: 'It is not merely the stomach that should have been purged, but the soul. I heartily wish that our next stage were Apollo's sacred island of Delos, not Pelasgian Samothrace; there would be great work for his priests to perform.'

'Yes,' assented Iphitus the Phocian, 'it would be good indeed if we could land on Delos and there dance the circular dance called The Crane. We would all weave in and out, in and out, for hour after hour, until the monotonous music purged our souls of all desire but to continue dancing in and out, in and out – until we fell fainting.'

'What a jolly entertainment that would be!' said Great Ancaeus scornfully. 'Jump into the water, Iphitus, and show us the steps. Apollo will doubtless bear you up; Apollo can accomplish almost anything.' This made some men laugh, but others grew angry, and still angrier when Idas said: 'Idmon, being an Argive Frog, has webbed feet. He wears buskins to conceal them, but can dance better in the water than on dry land, when he has kicked them off.'

'So holy an island is Delos,' said Idmon, his shrill voice cutting through the general buzz like a sickle through tall grass, 'that nobody may either be born or die there. All impending acts of birth and death are performed on the neighbouring islet of Ortygia.'

'Now I understand,' said Hylas, 'why Hercules has never taken me to Delos. He scatters births and deaths so lavishly wherever he goes that Delos would never be Delos again.'

To the relief of everyone, Hercules took this sally in good part, and repeated it with guffaws as though it were his own.

Ascalaphus of Orchomenos seldom spoke, but whenever he did everyone listened, for his voice came creaking out, as from a door with rusty hinges, seldom used. Now he stood upright upon his bench and raised his hand, saying: 'Orpheus, Thracian Orpheus, sing to us of the Creation of all things. We are as children in knowledge beside you, even the wisest of us. Purge our souls, Orpheus, by a song of the Creation.'

There was silence and then a slow murmur of assent. Orpheus tuned his lyre, put it between his knees, and sang softly but clearly as he plucked the strings.

He sang how the Earth, the Sky, and the Sea were once mingled together in the same form, until a compelling music sounded from nowhere and they separated, yet remained one universe still. This mysterious music announced the birth of the soul of Eurynome; for that was the original name of the Great Triple Goddess, whose symbol is the Moon. She was the universal Goddess and she was alone. Being alone, she presently felt lonely, standing between blank earth, empty water, and the accurately circling constellations of Heaven. She rubbed her cold hands together, and when she opened them again, out slid the serpent Ophion, whom from curiosity she admitted to love with her. From the fearful convulsions of this act of love rivers sprang, mountains rose, lakes swelled; it caused all manner of creeping things and fish and beasts to be born and populate the earth. Immediately ashamed of what she had done, Eurynome killed the serpent and sent his ghost underground; but as an act of justice she banished a mulberry-faced shadow of herself to live underground with the ghost. She renamed the serpent 'Death', and her shadow she named Hecate. From the scattered teeth of the dead serpent sprang up the Sown race of men, who were shepherds, cowherds, and horseherds, but neither tilled the soil nor engaged in warfare. Their food was milk, honey, nuts, and fruit, and they knew nothing of metallurgy. So ended the first Age, that had been the Age of Stone.

Eurynome continued to live in Earth, Sky, and Sea. Her Earth-self was Rhea, with breath of gorse-flower and amber-coloured eyes. As Rhea one day she went to visit Crete. From Sky to Earth is a great distance, the same distance indeed as divides Earth from the Underworld – the distance that a brazen anvil would fall in nine days and nine nights. In Crete, out of sun and vapour, feeling lonely again, Rhea contrived a man–god named Cronus to be her lover. To satisfy her maternal craving, she then every year bore herself a Sun-Child in the Dictean Cave; but Cronus was jealous of the Sun-Children and killed them, one after the other. Rhea concealed her displeasure. She said smilingly to Cronus one day: 'Give me, dear one, the thumb and fingers of your left hand. A single hand is enough for such a lazy god as you are. I will make five little gods out of them to obey your instructions while you recline here with me on the flowery bank. They will guard your feet and legs from unnecessary fatigue.' He accordingly gave her his left thumb and fingers, and out of them she made five little gods called the Dactyls, or Finger Gods, and crowned them with myrtle crowns. They caused him a deal of amusement by their sport and dancing. But Rhea secretly instructed the Dactyls to hide from Cronus the next Sun-Child that she bore. They obeyed her and deceived Cronus, putting an axe-shaped thunder-stone in a sack and pretending that it was Rhea's child which, as usual, they were throwing into the sea for him. This gave rise to the proverb, that the right hand should always be aware of what the left hand is doing. Rhea could not herself suckle the child, whom she named Zagreus, without rousing the suspicions of Cronus; and therefore the Dactyls brought a fat sow to be his foster-mother – a circumstance of which Zagreus afterwards did not like to be reminded. Later, because they found it inconvenient to drown his infant voice with loud drumming and piping whenever he cried, they weaned him from the sow and took him away from Mount Dicte. They consigned him to the care of certain shepherds who lived far to the West, on Mount Ida, where his fare was sheep's cheese and honey. So the second Age, that had been the Golden Age, drew to a close.

Rhea hastened on the new Age by fostering agriculture, and by teaching her servant, Prometheus the Cretan, how to make fire artificially with the fylfot fire-wheel. She laughed long to herself when Zagreus castrated and killed his father Cronus with a golden sickle that Prometheus had forged, and still longer when he tried to disguise himself as a starved and bedraggled cuckoo and pleaded to be nursed back to life in her bosom. She pretended to be deceived, and when he resumed his true shape she allowed him to enjoy her. 'Yes, indeed, my little god,' she said, 'you may be my loving servant if you wish.'

But Zagreus was insolent and answered: 'No, Rhea, I will be your master and instruct you what to do. I am more cunning than you, for I deceived you with my cuckoo disguise. And I am also more reasonable than you. By an act of reason I have just invented Time. Now that Time has begun, with my Advent, we can have dates and history and genealogy instead of timeless, wavering myth. And recorded Time, with its chain of detailed cause and consequence, will be the basis of Logic.'

Rhea was astonished and did not know whether to crush him to atoms with one blow of her sandal or whether to lie back and scream with mirth. In the end she did neither. She said no more than this: 'O Zagreus, Zagreus, my little Sun-Child, what strange notions you have sucked in from the dugs of your foster-mother, the Sow of Dicte!'

He answered: 'My name is Zeus, not Zagreus; and I am a Thunder-Child, not a Sun-Child; and I was suckled by the she-goat Amalthea of Ida, not by the Sow of Dicte.'

'That is a triple lie,' said Rhea smiling.

'I know that,' he answered. 'But I am big and strong enough now to tell triple lies, or even sevenfold lies, without fear of contradiction. If I am of a bilious temper, that is because the ignorant shepherds of Ida fed me with too much honeycomb. You must beware of my masterful ways, Mother, I warn you, for from now onwards I, not you, am the Sole Sovereign of All Things.'

Rhea sighed and answered happily: 'Dear Zagreus, or Zeus, or whatever you care to be called, have you indeed guessed how weary I am of the natural order and tidiness of this manifest universe, and of the thankless labour of supervising it? Rule it, Child, rule it by all means! Let me lie back for a while and meditate at my ease. Yes, I will be your wife and daughter and slave; and whatever strife or disorder you bring into my beautiful universe by any act of reason, as you call it, I will forgive you, because you are still very young and cannot be expected to understand things as well as I do. But pray be careful of the Three Furies that have been born from the drops of blood falling from your father's severed genitals; make much of them or they will one day avenge him. Let us have recorded Time and dates and genealogy and history, by all means; though I foresee that they will cause you far more anxiety and pleasure than they are worth. And by all means use Logic as a crutch for your crippled intelligence and a justification of your absurd errors. However, I must first make a condition: there shall be two islands, one in the Western Sea and one in the Eastern, which I shall retain for my ancient worship. There neither yourself nor any other deity that you may divide yourself into shall have any jurisdiction, but only myself and my serpent Death when I choose to send for him. The western shall be the island of innocence, and the eastern that of illumination; in neither will any record be kept of Time, but every day shall be as a thousand years, and contrariwise.'

Then at once she made the western island rise from the waters, like a garden, at a day's sail from Spain; and she also cast a cloud about the severed member of Cronus, and the Dactyls conveyed it safely to the eastern island, which was already in existence, where it became their companion, the jolly fish-headed god Priapus.

Then Zeus said: 'I accept your condition, Wife, if you agree that your other self, Amphitrite, shall surrender the Sea to my shadow brother Poseidon.'

Rhea answered: 'I agree, Husband, only reserving for my own use the waters that extend for five miles about my two islands; you may also rule in the Sky instead of Eurynome, with possession of all the stars and planets and of the Sun itself; but I reserve the Moon for my own.'

So they clasped hands on the bargain, and to show his power Zeus dealt her a resounding box on the ear, and danced in menace an armed jig, clashing his thunderstone axe against his golden shield, so that the thunder rolled horribly across the vault of Heaven. Rhea smiled. She had not bargained away her control of three most important things, which Zeus never afterwards succeeded in wresting from her: wind, death, and destiny. This is why she smiled.

Presently Zeus scowled and told her to cease smiling and go roast him an ox, for he was hungry. This was the first order that Rhea had ever received, and she stood irresolute because the idea of eating roast flesh disgusted her. Zeus struck her again and shouted: 'Hurry, Wife, hurry! Why do you suppose that I invented fire but that you should use it to roast or boil me tasty food?'

Rhea shrugged her shoulders and did as she was told, but he could not persuade her at first to share the feast.

Then Zeus, to show his power, swept away the greater part of mankind with a flood and formed out of mud a new man named Deucalion and a new woman named Pyrrha, and breathed life into them. With their birth the second Age finally ended, and the third Age, that of Bronze, began. In the Bronze Age, Zeus begot numerous sons on Rhea, whom he had renamed Hera, but did not let her keep them long at her side. As soon as ever they were old enough to fend for themselves he sent his chalky-faced priests, the Tutors, to steal them away from her by night; these Tutors disguised the boys with false beards and masculine clothes, initiated them into masculine arts and customs and gave out they were the sons of mortal women. On every occasion the Tutors first pretended to burn the boys to ashes with a thunderbolt supplied by Zeus, so that Hera would not try to win them back. Hera smiled at the drums and bull-roarers with which they simulated thunder, for the deception was a clumsy one, and she did not want her boys back – as yet. Soon the Iron Age would begin, that is beginning now...

The Argonauts listened in wonder to this story, and when Orpheus had ceased all sighed together with a noise like the rustling of reeds. Idas asked in a small voice, unlike the rude, unmannerly voice of Idas: 'Orpheus, tell us, where does this eastern island lie?'

Orpheus answered: 'The Thracians call it the Isle of Amber; the Trojans call it Dardania; but you Greeks call it Samothrace. The shrine of the Goddess lies below a high-breasted mountain on the northern coast, a coast dangerous to shipping except in calm weather. Sleep now, comrades, wrapped in your blankets; in the early morning we will beach the *Argo* at the feet of the Goddess.'

CHAPTER SEVENTEEN

THE GREAT MYSTERIES OF SAMOTHRACE

At dawn the West Wind stirred and rolled away the mist; first Lynceus and then the others descried mountains far away to the eastward. Argus said: 'Those are the peaks of Samothrace; Tiphys, you have carried us off our course.'

They pulled the ship about, hauled up the sail, and within two hours were sliding through blue water along the rocky northern coast of the island. The priest of the Dactyls, by name Thyotes, came down to meet them on the beach, dressed in his ceremonial robes. He told them: 'Strangers, you are welcome to our island, but only if you accept the laws which preserve its sanctity. I would have you know (if Thracian Orpheus, whom I see among you, has not already told you) that in Samothrace no reverence is paid to the Olympian Gods. Nor, indeed, do we acknowledge any other deities whatsoever, but only the Great Triple Goddess, supreme, omnipotent and changeless, and the six godlings who minister to Her and who are formed from the remnants of old Cronus – namely the five Finger Gods, Her artisans and messengers, and the Phallic God, Priapus, Her lover. Collectively, these deities are known as the Cabeiri. When you set foot on Samothrace you are back again to things as they were before History began. Here Zeus is Zagreus still, an infant yearly born and yearly destroyed. The ceremonial robes and insignia that some of you wear in honour of Apollo or Ares or Poseidon or Hermes – none of these has any meaning for us. Put them off you and let them remain in the ship; wear only your breeches. The Blessed Dactyls will provide you with shirts in good time, to clothe you during your stay with us. Tomorrow you shall all be initiated into the Great Mysteries of the Goddess.'

The Argonauts agreed to do whatever Thyotes instructed them to do – all except Atalanta, who said: 'I am a woman, not a man. What are your intentions towards me, Thyotes?'

Thyotes answered: 'You wear the dress and insignia of the Maiden Huntress, but prolonged maidenhood in a nubile woman is hateful to the Goddess. Tomorrow night the moon will be full. Come then and be initiated by the Owl nymphs into their holy rites. There is no marriage here in Samothrace, but only nymphdom.'

Atalanta answered: 'I am dedicated to the Olympian Artemis, and to do as you suggest would bring a curse on our ship, for she is a jealous Goddess.'

Thyotes answered: 'The Olympian Artemis is not yet born. Lay down your bow and arrow, huntress; unbraid your hair; learn to be the woman that you are.'

Meleager urged her: 'Atalanta, do as Thyotes says.'

She asked him: 'Meleager, am I then to remain in this island all my life with you? For though what I do here may perhaps be no concern of Artemis, what will happen when we resume our voyage? Suppose that my womb should quicken and that on my return to Calydon I were delivered of a child? What then? Would that not be the concern of Artemis? Can a maiden huntress suckle a child and plead that it was begotten on her before Artemis was?'

Meleager replied: 'Doubtless Artemis would be angry, as she was with Callisto when Zeus got her with child. Yet suppose that for love of you I should consent to remain here in Samothrace? Would this not be a good enough land for us? Could we not live here together until old age, happy in each other's love?'

Atalanta answered: 'There is no marriage in Samothrace, but only nymphdom, with no woman bound to any one man. You and I would alike be called upon to company promiscuously with others in honour of the Goddess; then green jealousy would eat you up, and myself too. No, dearest of men, Samothrace is no kinder a place for us two than Lemnos was.'

She remained brooding in the ship, and Meleager stayed to comfort her. All the others but Hylas went off in company of Thyotes – even Hercules, for Meleager swore by his own head to keep Hylas from mischief if Hercules left him behind.

Thyotes and his fellow-priests entertained the Argonauts in the porch of the Dactyls' shrine with grotesque dancing and buffoonery; but did not provide them with food or permit them to offer blood-sacrifices to any deity whatsoever. When Great Ancaeus asked impatiently whether there was famine on the island, Thyotes replied that all things were in abundance, but that this was a night of fast in preparation for the doings of the next day. So saying, he handed each of them a strong, bitter draught to drink, which made them roll about all night clasping their bellies and vomiting – all except Hercules, who felt hardly a twinge.

At dawn the Great Mysteries began. The first part was reserved for male worshippers. It is not lawful to reveal the full formula of the ninefold ritual, which took place in a fir-grove; but much may be told without impropriety. It is no secret that the Goddess Rhea herself appeared, entering into the body of the Priestess of Rhea. She wore a flounced, bell-shaped skirt in Cretan fashion, of linen dyed with sea-purple, but no upper garment except a short-sleeved waistcoat that did not fasten in front and showed the glory of her full breasts. On her head was a high caul cap, surmounted by the disc of the Moon and glittering with amber, and about her neck a necklace of fifty phalluses, carved from yellow ivory. Her eyes were wild, and she was discovered by the Argonauts seated upon a chair of state built from the left horns of Cretan bulls. Her ministrants were the representatives of the Dactyls, the five Finger Gods, and of the God Priapus, her lover. An armed guard kept away women and children and strangers.

All the novices, under pain of death, preserved absolute silence and were stark naked; however, Orpheus, being already an initiate, took his post among the Goddess's musicians, clothed in a white robe into which was worked a jagged streak of golden lightning.

First came the ritual of Creation. Music sounded and the Goddess heaped a circular mound of earth with her own hands and poured water about it in a trench, and danced upon it; this was a slow, rhythmic dance, imitating the monotonous circling of the constellations, and she trod it out with painful exactness. After a weary hour or more the Goddess clapped her hands for the musicians to change the tune, and presently danced again with a huge sacred serpent entwined about her. She danced more and more wildly until the musicians sweated and groaned, trying to keep pace with her postures; while the eyes of the Argonauts stood out from their heads with terror. At last came three loud imperious strokes upon a copper gong, and all hid their eyes while the serpent hissed and screamed. The Goddess uttered a frightful laugh which was like the cold hand of Death gripping at their hearts, and the hair stood out on their napes like the fur of an angry wolf.

When a gentle flute gave them permission to look again, the serpent was gone, and presently the ritual of Domination began with triumphal music. The Dactyls brought the Goddess a live dove, as symbol of the Sky; she strutted and danced, and presently wrung its neck. They brought her a live crab as symbol of the Sea; she strutted and danced and presently tore off its claws. They brought her a live hare, as symbol of the Earth; she strutted and danced, and presently pulled it in pieces.

Rhea issued her first commands; it is not lawful to repeat them.

Next came the ritual of love. Rhea partook of acorns and honey-water, and lovingly offered her fish-faced lover Priapus a share of the meal. She danced with him, disdainfully at first, but afterwards more and more amorously and shamelessly. Then, as before, three warning strokes sounded on the gong and all hid their eyes while a hideous scream rang in their ears as of hyaenas or eagles coupling together.

When the gentle flute sounded again, Priapus was gone, and the worshippers watched the ritual of Birth. Rhea groaned and shrieked and from under her skirt tottered a little black bull-calf and gazed about him wonderingly. Rhea crowned him with a chaplet of flowers. The Argonauts recognized him at once as the child Zagreus, and would have fallen on their faces in adoration but that the Dactyl Gods gestured for them to remain upright.

Next came the ritual of Sacrifice. The naked Dactyls stood behind Rhea, each having a lump of gypsum in either hand. They rubbed these lumps together and powdered their faces and bodies until they were as white as snow. Then they sprang upon the calf from behind. One seized his head and each of the others seized a leg, and while the music raged around them they tore the infant god in pieces, and sprinkled his blood on the Argonauts, to madden them. They rushed forward and ripped the mangled carcase into shreds, eating the flesh greedily, hide and all. Thus by eating of the god they became as gods.

Rhea issued her second commands; it is not lawful to repeat them.

Next came the ritual of Ablution. The Dactyls gave the Argonauts sponges and lustral water in wooden bowls; three times they washed themselves carefully until no speck of blood was to be seen upon any of them.

Next came the ritual of Rebirth and Remembrance. This cannot be told, but ah! how frantically the waters roared in the endless tunnel!

Next came the ritual of Coronation. The reborn Argonauts were crowned with garlands of ivy and anointed with oil and clothed with shirts of purple linen. Rhea gave them each a kiss on the mouth and taught them the formula of prayer by which to address her when in danger of shipwreck; for the snake-tailed winds remain under the control of the Goddess, Zeus having no power over them.

Of the last ritual of all it is not lawful to speak even the name.

Rhea issued her third and last commands, and when she had done the Argonauts were conducted to a cave behind her throne and there fell asleep together.

They slept until midnight, when the latter part of the Great Mysteries, reserved for female worshippers, was nearly over. To assist in the consummation of these they were awakened by a messenger of the God Priapus who ordered them to disrobe and led them into the grove of their initiation. The full, broad moon beamed above them, dappling their skins with tree-shadows. The Owl nymphs treated them cruelly, leaping upon them from burrows in the earth or from hollow trees, savaging them with teeth and nails, and taking their pleasure with a lunatic violence. When dawn shone again the Argonauts thought themselves dead men. Even the huge voice of Hercules came whispering from his swollen and bleeding lips, and he could hardly heave his bulk from the thicket of butcher's broom into which he had been rolled. But the Dactyls came dutifully running up, to anoint them with the fat of adders cupped in leaves of wild fig, and gave them fiery cordials to drink. Then Orpheus charmed them to sleep again in the cave whence they had come.

At noon they awoke refreshed after what seemed to them a sleep of ten
thousand years. They clothed themselves once more in their own breeches
and, reverently taking their leave of Thyotes, returned in silence to the
Argo. But first they dedicated in the Dactyls' shrine five bronze drinking-
bowls with silver rims, which are shown there to this day. And Thyotes
gave Jason, as a parting gift, a charm against the thunderbolt: it was a salve
cunningly compounded of hair, onions, and the livers of pilchards. But
Jason lost it before the voyage was over.

As they went, Orpheus sang them the song of the Cypress and the
Hazel. In this he instructed them how to behave when they were dead, if
they wished to become oracular heroes rather than perennially live out
their existence underground as ignorant and twittering shades. This was
his song:

So soon as ever your mazed spirit descends
From daylight into darkness, Man, remember
What you have suffered here in Samothrace,
What you have suffered.

After your passage through Hell's seven floods,
Whose fumes of sulphur will have parched your throat,
The Halls of Judgement will loom up before you,
A miracle of jasper and of onyx.
To the left hand there bubbles a black spring
Overshadowed with a great white cypress.
Avoid this spring, which is Forgetfulness;
Though all the common rout rush down to drink,
Avoid this spring.

To the right hand there lies a secret pool
Alive with speckled trout and fish of gold;
A hazel overshadows it; Ophion,
Primeval serpent straggling in the branches,
Darts out his tongue. This holy pool is fed
By dripping water; guardians stand before it.
Run to this pool, the pool of Memory,
Run to this pool.

Then will the guardians scrutinize you, saying:
'Who are you, who? What have you to remember?
Do you not fear Ophion's flickering tongue?
Go rather to the spring beneath the cypress,
Flee from this pool.'

Then you shall answer: 'I am parched with thirst.
Give me to drink. I am a child of Earth,

But of Sky also, come from Samothrace.
Witness the glint of amber on my brow.
Out of the Pure I come, as you may see.
I also am of your thrice-blessed kin,
Child of the three-fold Queen of Samothrace:
Have made full quittance for my deeds of blood,
Have been by her invested in sea-purple,
And like a kid have fallen into milk,
Give me to drink, now I am parched with thirst,
Give me to drink!'

But they will ask you yet: 'What of your feet?'
You shall reply: 'My feet have borne me here
Out of the weary wheel, the circling years,
To that still, spokeless wheel: – Persephone.
Give me to drink!'

Then they will welcome you with fruit and flowers,
And lead you toward the ancient dripping Hazel,
Crying: 'Brother of our immortal blood,
Drink and remember glorious Samothrace!'
Then you shall drink.

You shall drink deep of that refreshing draught,
To become lords of the uninitiated
Twittering ghosts, Hell's countless populace –
To become heroes, knights upon swift horses,
Pronouncing oracles from your tall white tombs,
By the nymphs tended. They with honey water
Shall pour libations to your serpent shapes,
That you may drink.

To Atalanta and Meleager and Hylas the returning Argonauts seemed
like gods, not men; a faint nimbus of light shone about each brow. But
when they had climbed up the ladder into the ship and resumed their
garments the glory faded; they were men again, though changed men.

CHAPTER EIGHTEEN

THROUGH THE HELLESPONT

Mountainous white clouds appeared in the direction of Thrace: a sure sign that the north-westerly wind which they needed was at hand. Swiftly they rowed a mile or more out to sea, and there the wind struck them. It was with difficulty that they fetched the *Argo* clear of rock-bound Samothrace, with the waves breaking against her port bulwarks and drenching them with spray. When this danger was past they hoisted the sail and scudded along, with the keel baulking and plunging beneath them like a frightened mule. By noon they were rushing past the western coast of Imbros with its sharp ridges and green valleys. The thought that was now exercising the minds of all was how to elude the vigilance of the Trojans, with whom Jason had promised the Archons of Athens to engage in no armed conflict. For if they could somehow slip through the Hellespont unseen and leave the Trojans unaware of their presence in the Black Sea, they might well slip through a second time on their homeward voyage, assisted by the strong current which flows down from the Sea of Marmora.

The wind slowly veered round to the north and appeared to be settled there. Argus therefore advised Jason to shelter under the lee of Cape Cephalos, which juts out at the south-eastern angle of Imbros. He knew of a little sandy cove where they might anchor for a day or two until the wind, shifting to the south-west or west, blew strongly enough to carry them by night up the whole length of the Hellespont. Tiphys supported Argus, saying that he had closely enquired about the currents in the strait from a helmsman of Percote, a Greek settlement situated in the strait itself. He believed that, given a good south-westerly wind, a moon, and a willing crew, they could bring the *Argo* past Trojan territory in a night. But old Nauplius asked whether the south-westerly wind in this part of the sea differed from that which he had encountered elsewhere; for it would be strange, he said, if such a wind did not bring rain-clouds with it to obscure the moon.

Jason overruled the objection of Nauplius and agreed to run for shelter under Cape Cephalos. The *Argo* was already gliding past the yellowish cliffs of Cephalos and making for the cove of which Argus had spoken when Iphitus of Phocis sprang suddenly to his feet. 'My lords,' he said, 'I see no reason why we should disembark at Imbros. Imbros is, I grant, inhabited by Pelasgians, a race on whose friendship we may count. But the Trojans have coast-guards stationed close to this cove, and whatever story we may tell these guards will not long deceive them. Consider: if we wait there for a clear night and a strong southwesterly breeze, what will they make of us? They will naturally conclude that we are trying to slip past Troy unnoticed. They will follow us in a ship of their own and report our movements to the King of Troy.'

Most of the Argonauts approved this reasoning, but Jason complained: 'It is easy enough, Iphitus, to criticize the decisions of your leader. I am aware of your long experience of seafaring, but unless you have a better plan to offer than Argus and Tiphys have already put forward I advise you to keep your mouth shut, for you will only succeed in setting your comrades against me. I should have thought you wiser than to do that, Iphitus. You now talk as wildly, almost, as Idas. Be silent, if you please!'

Orpheus spoke up on behalf of Iphitus: 'Jason, Jason, have you so soon forgotten what you learned in Samothrace?'

Jason replied: 'I learned in Samothrace how to conduct myself prudently when I am dead. I do not wish to be reminded by you that I may soon have to put this knowledge into practice. Be silent, if you please!'

Orpheus said to Hercules: 'Most noble Hercules, since I am forbidden to address our leader, may I address you? For I understand what Iphitus has in his mind.'

Hercules answered: 'Well, Orpheus, you are an odd-looking anatomy, yet, for a man whose brother I brained with a lyre, you have always treated me well enough. If you have anything sticking in your throat, pray cough it out for me!'

Orpheus answered: 'I cannot speak plainly in the presence of three uninitiated persons; but if, at sunset, they consent to have their ears stopped with wax and their eyes blind-folded for a short time, we may sail through the Hellespont this very night. Let us drive on with the wind until we come to within a few miles of the entrance to the strait, and then we shall do what we shall do.'

Meleager and Atalanta did not object to the proposal, and Hercules undertook that Hylas would obey orders. Thus Jason was overruled in his turn and the *Argo* drove on to the south-east, while all the oarsmen snatched a short sleep. They awoke at evening to find themselves four miles west of the entrance to the Hellespont. No sail had been sighted all day.

Then Orpheus blind-folded Meleager, Atalanta, and Hylas, and stopped their ears with wax. As soon as he could speak freely he reminded Jason that it was foolish for initiates of Samothrace to regard themselves as the helpless sport of the winds: let them put to immediate use the charms and incantations taught them by the Cabeiri in the name of the Great Ones.

Jason neither agreed nor disagreed, but took refuge in gloomy silence while Orpheus, who of all the Argonauts was the least likely to blunder in the Samothracian ritual, invoked the Triple Goddess in her name of Amphitrite. He poured a jar of olive oil upon the waves and in her name respectfully called upon the North Wind to cease. For a while the North Wind, whom his sons Calaïs and Zetes also respectfully invoked, made no response, except for a single furious blast that nearly tore the mast out of the ship, but then gradually ceased. When the air was at peace again, though the waves still heaved sullenly, Orpheus tied an adder's skin to the heel of an arrow and, borrowing a bow from Phalerus, shot the arrow out of sight towards the north-east, calling on the South-West Wind to follow. While they were waiting for the new wind to rise, Peleus, who was the craftiest man aboard, said to Jason: 'My lord, let us lower the sail and stain it black.'

Jason asked: 'For what purpose?'

Peleus answered: 'Otherwise the Trojan watchmen will see it shining in the moonlight as we sail through. A black sail will cheat their sight.'

Argus objected that a tarred sail would be awkward to handle, and that they would be obliged to disembark somewhere and kindle a fire to heat up the ship's tar-pot. But Peleus said: 'I have a better stain than tar.' Among the dainties that he had brought from Lemnos was a jar of costly cuttlefish ink, squeezed from the ink-sacs of hundreds of cuttlefish. This ink, a sweet addition to a stew or to barley-porridge, is of a very dark colour. Augeas, Idas, and the other gluttons resented that so delicious a liquor should be put to so wasteful a use; but it was found that, by mixing it with water, only half the contents of the jar would suffice for dyeing the whole sail to the colour of seaweed.

The Argonauts lowered the sail, painted it on both sides, and hoisted it again. No sooner were the sheets made fast than the South-West Wind could be heard sweeping towards them from the distance, bringing with it rain that whipped the surface of the sea, and soon the sail bellied out and the *Argo* sprang forward. At this they unstoppered the ears and unbound the eyes of the uninitiated. As the darkness grew, they saw indistinctly in the distance the white cliffs of Cape Hellas and felt the speed of the ship slacken as the current of the Hellespont opposed her. At the suggestion of Peleus they muffled their oars and the two rudders with strips of old cloth. 'Fortunately,' said Tiphys, 'the current is weaker on the Thracian than on the Trojan side. It also has fewer eddies, because the coastline runs straighter; yet even on the Thracian side it may well be running at two knots.'

Soon Jason enjoined the whole crew to silence, and they entered the Hellespont itself. The sky was overcast, the moon showing only as a luminous patch behind whirling cloud. Lynceus then served his comrades well. He mounted on the prow and according as the ship approached too near the shore (which for others was a mere wall of darkness) or kept too far away, he signalled to Tiphys by pulling either once or twice at a cord that he held in his hand; for the other end of the cord was tied to the knee of Tiphys. The oarsmen kept a measured stroke, though with no song to help them, and for hours together laboured on in silence, with the wind still fair behind them. Only at one point, the Dardanian narrows, did Tiphys steer into mid-stream, the current being reputedly weaker there than inshore. The oar of Lynceus was taken by a grey-bearded, burly Lapith, an initiate of the Great Mysteries, who had joined the *Argo* from Samothrace: this was Polyphemus of Larisa, who had married the sister of Hercules and was in perpetual exile from his city, having accidentally killed a little girl with his hunting knife. Hercules held him in esteem and affection.

At dawn, the Argonauts found themselves close to Sestos, a bluff headland beyond which lies a little bay with a sandy northern shore, and a stream tumbling into the middle of it. Across the water stretched a low green line of grass-covered coast hills, the district called Abydos. They disembarked by the stream and stretched their limbs, some gathering driftwood for a fire, some playing at leap-frog. Jason disguised the figurehead of the ship, superimposing on the Ram's head another that he had brought with him: the head of a horse made in stout leather painted white; for the White Horse was the figure-head of all the vessels that plied to Troy from Colchis. Now that they were some thirty miles beyond Troy, and in waters not commanded by the Trojans, it would be thought, Jason hoped, that they were subjects of King Aeëtes returning to Colchis from a trading voyage. At Sestos, when they had heaped sober sacrifices to Amphitrite, in gratitude for her help, they decided to rest a day and a night. But the wind veered to the north-east, which is the prevailing quarter for winds in the Hellespont, and blew hard for two days and nights; they could not resume their voyage until the third morning, when it shifted again to the south-west. During all their stay at Sestos nobody came to disturb them, except a shepherd boy who fled like a hare when he saw the glittering company of strangers, and left some of his flock in their hands.

They made fair progress through the narrow strait, hugging the yellowish cliffs of Thrace, and evening found them well within the Sea of Marmora. They sailed on throughout the night, now changing to the opposite shore, for the wind had veered to the south. Great Ancaeus took the helm from Tiphys, who had earned a long sleep.

'Where is our next port of call?' Acastus, son of Pelias, asked the company at large.

Hercules, who was amusing himself by idly twisting the bronze sword of Little Ancaeus into a serpentine shape – without permission – was the first to answer. 'So far as I remember,' he said, 'there is a large rocky island, called Bear Island, not far from here – about a day's sail with a fair wind. It is a peninsula, in reality, not an island. The King is a friend of mine –

what is his name? I have forgotten, but he is a true friend of mine, believe me – and has built a city on the flat isthmus joining the island to the shore. A big clear lake lies in the hills behind, from which a stream runs down to the city. King Aeneus – that is the name, of course – grazes a multitude of fat sheep beside the lake and the stream. His people are the Dolionians, a sort of Achaeans, who worship the God Poseidon. He will welcome us with open arms, I have no doubt. His kingdom extends into the hills behind for a good distance, and along the coast on either side of Bear Island. The inhabitants of the island itself are Pelasgians. Aeneus is always at war with them. When I was last in these parts I went out across the isthmus and killed a few of them for him. They are big men, and I found great pleasure in knocking their skulls together, did I not, dear Hylas?'

With oars and sail they made an excellent run that day. By noon they had sighted Bear Island, with its conspicuous peak, Mount Dindymos, and were coasting past the nearer corn-lands of the Dolionians. The fertile coastal strip slowly narrowed and the hills, covered with low oak-trees and cut with gullies, fell to the water's edge. Here, putting in at a cove, where the beach consisted wholly of shells, the Argonauts removed the Horse from the prow, revealing the Ram, and hoisted the spare white sail instead of the dark one; then they sailed on until they could see the lime-washed walls and tiled roofs of the city of which Hercules had spoken. It was named Cyzicus after its founder – Cyzicus, the father of Aeneus.

They anchored in the snug harbour without fear, and Jason sent out Echion the herald to the palace; where he was received with high honour and assured that all the Argonauts, but especially Hercules, were welcome to remain in Dolionian territory as long as ever they pleased.

CHAPTER NINETEEN

THE WEDDING FEAST OF KING CYZICUS

The Argonauts found that King Aeneus had been dead for several months and that his elder son Cyzicus, a man of about Jason's age, had succeeded him. Cyzicus had just married the most beautiful woman of all Asia. Her name was Cleite, daughter of the King of the Percosians, whose white-walled city on the Trojan side of the Hellespont the Argonauts had passed on their way up from Sestos. Cleite's father, Merops, so far from settling a dowry upon her, which, as he said, would have been like spreading honey on honeycomb, had boldly announced that no man should win her in marriage who would not undertake to pay the heavy tribute lately imposed on Percote by Laömedon of Troy. Cyzicus, who had seen Cleite by chance one day as he sailed down the strait, and could not thereafter banish her image from his mind, presently paid the tribute, which was a great sum in gold dust and cattle, and, as was natural in a young man, considered that he had the best of the bargain. But his brother Alexander called him spend-thrift and absented himself from the wedding, pleading sickness. Perhaps he was jealous. It was on the second of the five days allotted to the festivi-ties that the *Argo* sailed in. Cyzicus, having issued a general invitation to all Greeks to partake of a feast and prepared a superabundance of food, rejoiced to welcome a ship-load of the most distinguished fighting men of Greece, among them the great Hercules, his father's ally.

Within an hour of their landing the Argonauts had been bathed, anointed and perfumed and were reclining in their best clothes upon soft couches, together with numerous other wedding-guests. A hundred beau-tiful boys brought them whatever food and drink they desired and crowned their heads with chaplets of spring flowers, while musicians, seated in the painted gallery above them, played gentle Lydian music. But Phalerus the archer and Idmon the augur kept guard aboard the *Argo*, ready at the least sign of treachery to blow the alarm on conches.

Cleite was as beautiful as report made her. She had pale features, very thick black hair, and grey eyes; but her beauty lay chiefly in her carriage and gestures, in the grave sound of her voice and in her full lips, which never quite smiled. Cyzicus was fair-haired, ruddy-faced, given to laughing heartily, much inclined to adventure. He and Cleite seemed a perfectly matched pair, and as they passed together down the line of couches and courteously enquired from every man whether he was well served, they were followed by unstifled sighs of admiration.

Cyzicus paid the greatest deference to Hercules, whom he concluded to be the true leader of the expedition, whatever Echion had said to the contrary. With his own hands he poured him wine in an embossed goblet on which Hercules himself was depicted with a Bear man in either hand, dashing their skulls together merrily and making the brains fly. When Hercules had rumbled with laughter at this, Cyzicus displayed the other side of the goblet, embossed with a design of men fighting together desperately and of others leaping into the water from a raft. 'Those are the Pelasgians of Proconesos,' he said, 'the allies of the Bear men. They raided our city soon after you had gone away. We lost many of our comrades before we drove them off. If only they would renew the attack while you continue here as my guest – that would be a jape! The surprisers would be surprised indeed.'

Hercules answered: 'King Cyzicus, the visit that I paid to your city while your father Aeneus was still alive, I found singularly pleasant; this visit I am finding no less so. But pray address your wise and flattering speeches to the commander of this expedition, Jason of Iolcos – look yonder, he is the man with the long fair hair – not to me. Leave me to this excellent side of beef, and good luck go with you and your beautiful wife! I am happy to listen to your words while I eat, but as happy simply to eat. You waste your eloquence upon Hercules, the old glutton.'

Cyzicus smiled and passed on. He invited Jason to recline at a gilt-legged table opposite to Cleite and himself. When Jason was well settled, with feather cushions under his head, a richly embroidered rug spread over his knees, and fragrant wine from Lesbos at his elbow Cyzicus pressed him to reveal confidentially the object of his voyage. This, Jason was unwilling to do. He would say no more than that a god had put it into his heart, and the hearts of his comrades, to venture into the Black Sea.

Cyzicus answered politely: 'Indeed! What part of that vast and unfriendly water did the god recommend as worthiest of your interest? Are you perhaps on a visit to the Crimea where the savage Taurians live, who love human sacrifices and adorn the stockades of their towns with human heads? Or is Hercules taking you with him to visit his old enemies, the Amazons? Or is your goal the Olbian country about the outfall of the noble river Boug, where the best honey in the world is produced?'

Jason, evading all these questions, caught at the mention of honey, and beckoned Butes to take part in the conversation, reporting to him what Cyzicus had said about the produce of Olbia. Butes pressed Cyzicus for information about the colour, scent, taste, and viscosity of this honey, and when Cyzicus gave him only vague or random answers, was not offended but chattered learnedly and long about the behaviour of bees. He asked:

'Have you noticed, Majesty, that bees never sip nectar from a red flower? Being givers of life, they avoid the colour of death.' Then, being a little drunk, Butes began to speak bitingly of the God Apollo's patronage of the Bee, which had formerly been the servant of the Cretan Goddess. 'He who was once the Mouse Demon of Delos! Mice are the natural enemies of bees. They invade the hive in winter-time and steal the honey, the shameless thieves! I rejoiced last year when I found a dead mouse in one of my hives. The bees had stung him to death and prettily embalmed him in bee-glue to avoid the stench of death.'

So he ran on; and, when he paused to drink another goblet of wine, Jason began questioning Cyzicus about the navigation of the eastern part of the Sea of Marmora, and about the spring currents in the Bosphorus. But Cyzicus considered himself under no obligation to give any detailed answer, and returned pleasantly to the subject of honey. So the two fenced together for a while, until Jason, in no good humour, excused himself and returned to his former couch. After a while Butes followed him, from good manners.

Cleite said to Cyzicus: 'My darling, have you noticed that this Jason has white eye-lashes? My father Merops once warned me against men with white eye-lashes. They are all untrustworthy, he said. Can it be that this Minyan has come to sack our city, and intends to wait until all your loyal comrades are drowsy tonight from good eating and drinking?'

'My darling,' said Cyzicus, 'it may possibly be so, though I cannot agree that it is probably so.'

'Hercules and Jason both seem to be hiding something from us,' said Cleite, 'as you must admit. And the Bee-man spoke in a very disrespectful way of Apollo, as if tempting us to do the same, and so stir up trouble. Confess that you thought this strange!'

'I did,' said Cyzicus. 'Well, wise one, what do you advise?'

'Warn Jason,' said Cleite, 'that his ship's present anchorage is not safe until she can be provided with heavier anchor-stones. Mention the north-easterly gales. Advise him to shift her berth while your men bore him a couple of really heavy stones. Recommend the protected cove just across the isthmus – Chytos is the name, is it not? Offer him a boat to tow her there. He cannot very well refuse your offer. And if he is planning any sudden treachery he will have to reconsider his plans; for an escape from the palace would not be easy with his ship so far away.'

Cyzicus took her advice and presently made the proposal. Jason considered it a reasonable one and accepted it at once with evident gratitude. But Hercules, shrewdly suspecting that Cyzicus had some motive, other than his alleged one, for shifting the *Argo*'s berth, declared that wherever she went, he and Hylas must also go; and Peleus and Acastus said the same; and Polyphemus said that he did not wish to be parted from Hercules, whom he reverenced above all living men. These five quitted the feast, and were towed in the *Argo* to Chytos cove, where they anchored her; but the merry-making at the palace continued all night.

Cyzicus, from something that Jason incautiously let drop, guessed at first that the purpose of the voyage was to trade at Sinope, or some other Black Sea port, where Eastern goods might be bought at a far lower price than at Troy. But if so, why were so many kings and noblemen aboard? Perhaps something more important was planned. Could they be visiting, in turn, all the petty kingdoms of the Sea of Marmora and the Black Sea, with the intention of building up a sworn confederacy against Troy and Colchis?

He asked Jason this question point blank, and when Jason hesitated to commit himself, declared that if the Greeks made war against Troy, he and his father-in-law, Merops of Percote, with many other neighbouring monarchs, would gladly come forward as allies.

Jason amused himself by allowing Cyzicus to believe that he had guessed correctly. He even hinted that his first port of call after leaving Cyzicus would lie in the territory of King Phineus of Thynia, whose two foster-sons, Calaïs and Zetes, had (he said) come to Greece to propose a war against Troy, and were now returning in the *Argo*.

But Cleite knew by his eyes and hands that he was lying.

At dawn a distant sound of yelling was heard and the blare of war-horns. The Dolionians and the Argonauts immediately sprang to arms each side convinced that the other was behaving treacherously. But the Argonauts were prompter than the Dolionians and overawed them. Jason stood over Cleite with a drawn sword and threatened to kill her unless Cyzicus ordered his men to lay down their arms. This Cyzicus did. Then Echion the herald ran out, followed by Castor, Pollux and Lynceus, to see what was afoot.

The noises proceeded from Chytos cove, across the bay, and Lynceus, straining his eyes, cried: 'A fight is in progress between our guards and a great horde of men who seem to have six hands – for they are dressed in bear-skins with the four paws dangling. To the rescue!'

Echion ran back into the palace with the news, and Jason, when he heard it, sheathed his sword and asked pardon of Cyzicus, which he freely granted. Then all together rushed down to the beach, launched boats and galleys, and rowed hurriedly to the rescue.

When they arrived at Chytos they found that the fight was over. The Bear men had hoped to catch the guards asleep, but Hylas had given the alarm. This came about by chance. Hylas, ever since the departure from Lemnos, had watched for an opportunity of escaping from the tutelage of Hercules and getting back to his Iphinoë. He had not yet found this possible: on Samothrace he would soon have been recaptured, and at Sestos he would have been observed by the two men who were constantly on watch. But now he judged that the hour for his venture had come. He would slip ashore on Bear Island, scramble along the craggy coast, run across the isthmus (as if sent on a message by Hercules), and then strike inland into the Phrygian hills. He hoped to reach Troy within a few days and there, with the bribe of a silver belt-clasp, to persuade some Athenian or Cadmean ship-master to set him ashore on Lemnos.

Hylas had waited until his companions fell asleep one by one. Then he filled a wallet with provisions and his silver belt-clasp and some small gold ornaments, caught up a javelin, and was just lowering himself over the port bulwark near the bows, when he heard someone suppressing a sneeze in the thicket close by. He clambered back again. Thereupon the Bear men, cursing the comrade who had sneezed, rushed forward. One climbed upon the shoulders of another and would have hauled himself over the starboard bulwark had not Hylas run at him and pierced his throat through with the javelin, so that he fell with a great cry. Hylas called out: 'To arms, to arms!' Acastus and Peleus seized their spears and Polyphemus his bronze axe, and standing on the gunwale these three fought the Bear men off. But drunken Hercules dragged himself up to the helmsman's seat and called for his bow and arrows. Hylas brought them to him and he began to shoot. It was strange that the effect of wine on Hercules was to quicken his rate of shooting without impairing the accuracy of his aim. While Acastus and Peleus killed two men apiece with their spears, and Polyphemus another with his axe Hercules transfixed no less than thirty with his arrows before the remainder fed away. They lay dead on the beach or in the water like so many baulks of timber seasoning in the ship-yard of Pagasae.

Hercules swore that he owed his life to the vigilance of his wonderful Hylas and embraced him with the usual violence. Hylas was therefore awarded the spoils of battle: thirty-five fine bear-skins, ten of which were fastened with golden buttons, two well-made Greek helmets which the Bear men had captured from the guards of King Aeneus, a bronze dagger inlaid with green horses at full gallop, three necklaces of bears' claws and one of large painted terra-cotta beads. But the weapons of most of these savages were mere oaken spears, their points sharpened in the fire, rough oaken clubs and jagged stones. Hylas distributed the bear-skins as gifts among the Argonauts. Only Butes refused the skin offered him, saying that if he once put it on, his bees would come to hear of it and never trust him again.

All returned in friendship to the city together. The *Argo* was provided with a heavier anchor-stone, and the light one which it replaced was laid up as a votive offering in the temple of Poseidon, where it may still be viewed. Then blood-sacrifices were offered to all the Olympian Gods and Goddesses in turn. But no offering of any sort was made to the Triple Goddess, because she was worshipped by the Bear men, and by the Pelasgians of Proconesos, and by the Trojans. Cyzicus hated her: only a few days before this he had led an armed expedition into Bear Island, the inhabitants of which fled from him, and there shot one of the lions, sacred to the Goddess in her name of Rhea, that prowl about Mount Dindymos. He had audaciously spread its pelt as a coverlet upon his marriage-bed.

Orpheus urged Jason to go apart with him and a few others and propitiate the Goddess with offerings on her sacred mountain, pleading that the omission of her sacrifice was made for reasons of policy, not in hostility or scorn.

Jason would not listen, protesting that he must gain the perfect confidence of Cyzicus and thus ensure a generous provisioning of the ship; and that to leave the city for a secret journey into Bear Island would certainly be misinterpreted as an act of treason.

So no overtures were made to the Goddess and the marriage-feast continued under Olympian auspices. By the end of it one of the Argonauts, it is not known which, had given away the secret of their mission to Colchis. Several Dolionians at once volunteered for the voyage, but Jason could find no room for them in the *Argo*. Cyzicus himself was anxious to sail and, being a practised helmsman who had twice made the voyage to Colchis, would have been a welcome addition to the crew; for Tiphys was suffering from colic and could not eat or drink anything but sheep's milk and barley-porridge. Cyzicus suggested that Tiphys should remain behind in the palace and be carefully tended, while he took charge of the helm. But Tiphys declared that he was well enough and that he would not resign the helm to Poseidon himself until the voyage had ended, for the Goddess Athena had expressly committed the rudders to his own charge. And Queen Cleite, in private swore that if Cyzicus went off with Jason she would immediately go off to her father's house at Percote and never return: for she would not remain in one house with a fool, and only a fool would trust Jason, with his white eye-lashes.

On the fifth day, therefore, the Argonauts prepared to sail again. Cyzicus called down the blessings of all the Olympians upon the *Argo*, and presented rich presents to the crew: jars of wine and corn, shirts of Egyptian linen, and embroidered cloaks. To Jason he gave a broad-headed spear, with a shaft inlaid with shell, which had belonged to King Aeneus; and Jason in return gave him a golden goblet (one of Hypsipyle's parting gifts) engraved with a continuous design of running stags, and a Thessalian bridle with a silver bit. They clasped hands and became as brothers. But 'I hope never to see that man again,' Cleite muttered as soon as Jason's broad back was turned.

The wind blew fresh from the south-west. When they had trundled the two anchor-stones aboard and Argus had given the hawser-ends to a line of Dolionians to hold until the crew were settled in their seats, a sudden flaw of wind, rushing down from Mount Dindymos, spun the *Argo* about and dragged the men at the hawser-ends into the water. No one was hurt and Cyzicus said, laughing: 'Your *Argo* seems unwilling to leave our hospitable shore. See how she turns her prow about!'

Cleite warned Cyzicus, even before the *Argo* was out of sight: 'Dearest one, see that you keep a vigilant guard for the next few nights. The wind that turned Jason's ship about came as a warning from some god or other that he treacherously intends to return, now that he has spied out our dispositions, and to murder us in our beds.'

Cyzicus replied that had any woman but she spoken in this sense he would have called her an ignorant mischief-maker. Cleite said: 'But, seeing that nobody but myself has done so, what reason have you to disregard the warning?' She insisted on a watch being kept, day and night.

The breeze slackened at dawn, when the *Argo* had travelled a fair distance. No land was to be seen anywhere. The sky was overcast, though the rain had nearly ceased. The *Argo* was surrounded by grey-green waters, with no ship, rock, or reef intervening to break the connected course of the horizon. Neither Tiphys nor Argus nor old Nauplius (whose great-grandfather and namesake was the first Greek ever to steer by the Pole Star) could calculate their position with certainty.

Jason asked Nauplius: 'What sort of weather may we expect today?'

He shook his head: 'I have been at sea, man and boy, for thirty years, throughout each sailing season; yet I cannot undertake to answer you. The sea is to me like the face of an old grandmother to a child. I can never read in her features what is passing in her mind, or what fit she will take next – one moment it may be a calm, the next a storm. Ask Coronus: the Crow, his bird, can foretell the weather infallibly, they say!'

Idas laughed and said: 'Whoever is weather-wise is a fool otherwise.'

Jason put the question to Coronus, who answered simply: 'Expect a squall from the north-east.'

In the middle of the morning the north-eastern horizon began to brighten and sudden gusts of wind blew, now from one quarter and now from another.

Weary Tiphys told his companions: 'Doubtless this is the prelude to the squall that Coronus foretold. By my reckoning we have already come within a day's sail of the Bosphorus. But we cannot hope to sail through in the teeth of a north-easter. And I have heard that, when such a wind has blown for a day or two, the current in the Bosphorus runs at five or six knots; we could make no headway against it even if the wind itself were to drop. When the squall strikes us, let us run before it, coasting past the Besbicos Islands, and make for the sandy beaches at the mouth of the river Rhyndacos which lies to the south-westward This is our wisest course if we wish to avoid shipwreck. Meanwhile let us disguise our ship again with the dark sail and set the White Horse over the Ram.'

The Argonauts began to cry: 'No, no! Why should we not invoke Amphitrite again and obtain from her another sailful of that excellent south-westerly wind? Come, Orpheus, conduct the ceremony!'

Orpheus shook his head. 'Our leader Jason,' he said, 'refused to sacrifice to the Goddess at the time when we honoured the Olympian deities, nor would he take my advice and ascend Mount Dindymos to propitiate her there. He even dared make himself a blood-brother to King Cyzicus, who has killed one of the Goddess's sacred lions and publicly declared himself her enemy. How can we hope by now invoking her in the name of Amphitrite to coax a smile from her? It was not for nothing that the flaw of wind blew down from Dindymos and spun the *Argo* about. I read it at once as a warning from the Goddess that we should not sail until we had earned her pardon; but it was already too late to speak. This is an evil business, and we must all patiently accept the consequences!'

As he spoke, the north-easter came down upon them with the noise of ten thousand whistling arrows, cold and cruel from the distant Scythian steppes. They hastily pulled the ship about and ran before the wind. The sea was soon ridged with white-topped waves across which the *Argo* ran, lifting and sinking, like a frightened deer in full course; but the sail held, and she shipped no water, because of her close-fitting bulwarks. On she sped, hour after hour, and Argus cried: 'Comrades here you see the advantage of a bolted ship! One merely lashed together in the ancient fashion would have been shaken apart long before now, and we should be desperately baling out green water that poured in from ever-widening leaks.'

However, not even Lynceus could sight the Islands of Besbicos, and when at dusk they approached the southern coast it was steep-to and the waves hissed on pitiless rocks. They sailed on, searching for the mouth of the Rhyndacos. It was already night, with the waning moon not yet risen, before they sighted ahead of them what appeared to be a flat plain stretched out between two hills. Some lights twinkled from the foot of the hill on the port bow, and Argus said: 'That will be Dascylion, a small Trojan settlement of about twenty houses. I believe that we shall find the beach flat and without rocks if we steer directly towards it.'

'Boldness is best,' said Peleus. 'Let us spring ashore with a war-cry. We shall take the inhabitants by surprise and overawe them.'

Jason agreed. They put on their helmets and body armour, and soon the wind drove the ship through the surf and upon a sandy and hospitable beach. They hauled her out of reach of the waves and belayed her to a smooth rock, which they found ready to their purpose, then rushed in a body towards the lights, yelling: 'Yield, yield!'

CHAPTER TWENTY

THE FUNERAL OF KING CYZICUS

Armed men poured from the houses on the hill, and battle was joined above the beach. The Argonauts kept together in a body – all except Hercules, who rushed forward laying out to right and left with his terrible club – but the enemy fought in a scattered and disorderly manner. It was Jason's first battle, and a divine fury seized him. He thrust with the gift-spear of Cyzicus at the dark figures that opposed him, while at his right side Polyphemus the Lapith with a long sword, and on his left Little Ancaeus with an axe, hacked their way forward to the houses. It was bloody work and already ten of the enemy were strewn on the field of battle and the rest were in rout, when with a sudden war-cry three tall men came charging together down the hill. Their leader made straight for Jason, who lunged forward with his spear and spitted him through the middle. The spear-head stood out close to the back-bone and Jason could not free it, even by pushing with his foot against his adversary's thighs. Of the other two men, one was struck down by Little Ancaeus, who lopped off his head at the third stroke, and the third fled away shouting: 'We are lost – oh, we are lost – our noble King Cyzicus is killed!'

At this a horror seized the Argonauts and Jason cried: 'A light! A light!'

Young Hylas, who had himself driven a javelin into the bowels of one of the enemy, seized up the smoky pine torch which the dying man let fall and whirled it about his head until it flamed brightly. He ran to Jason, who, bending down to scrutinize the man at his feet, found that it was indeed King Cyzicus, transfixed with the gift-spear, the spear of his own father Aeneus.

Cyzicus looked up and gasped out: 'Cleite, Cleite!' Then the blood gushed from his mouth and he died.

Now they knew at last that they had overshot the Rhyndacos river-mouth by some twenty-five miles, and that the Triple Goddess, for a sour jest, had fetched the Argonauts back to the other side of the same isthmus from which they had sailed two days previously.

Jason ordered Echion the herald to enter the palace, there to make peace on his behalf with Cleite and the brother of Cyzicus and the remaining Dolionian chiefs. Echion courageously accepted this dangerous charge, but when at length he secured admittance and asked to be led to Cleite, he found her hanging from a beam in her bridal chamber. He cut her down, but it was too late.

Morning dawned, bright and gusty. The wind drove huge waves hissing up the beach, which dashed in spray against the *Argo*'s stern. Already the Dolionians had found and claimed their dead, and the sound of mourning rose like the howl of wolves from every house. The Argonauts stood about in little groups, whispering to one another, ill at ease. Only Idas dared speak out. He went up to Jason and said aloud: 'We are free of guilt in this matter. The blood of our dear hosts lies on your head only. Why did you disregard the warning of Orpheus? Why did you not propitiate the Goddess?'

Jason put his hand to his sword and said: 'Idas, you have sworn to obey me as your captain. I now command you to silence. Listen to me. The death of my wretched royal brother weighs heavily on my heart, yet I regard myself as no more to blame for it than yourself. It is clear that the Great Goddess made us all equally the instruments of her vengeance upon him for the death of her sacred lion. Let the Goddess herself, not us, be answerable for this night's work. Not one of our company has been killed or even wounded, except for a scratch or two, which is remarkable and clearly shows that her just anger was turned wholly against the Dolionians.'

Idas was about to make some scoffing retort when Hercules caught him up from behind and tossed him into the air, so that he turned heels over-head and landed on his feet, staggering. 'You have said enough,' said Hercules, twirling his club. Idas choked back his wrath.

Peace was concluded with the Dolionians. Alexander, who succeeded to the throne, accepted Jason's explanation that his men had believed themselves to be at Dascylion; he absolved them of all blame and admitted that he had, for his part, mistaken them for his Pelasgian enemies of Proconesos. It was plain that he felt joy rather than grief at his brother's death. Then, all together, Argonauts and Dolionians heaped pyres and set the twelve corpses upon them, with rosemary and other sweet-smelling herbs to disguise the reek of roasting man-flesh and with all the gifts of food that had been put into the *Argo*, except the wine. Together they danced in armour about each pyre, three times about each, clashing their weapons together, while servants blew on conches and beat drums to frighten off the ghosts of the slain. And always, at the third time about, the dancers threw lighted brands into the pyre and watched while the flames leaped up and the corpse was devoured. The wind made the pyres roar lustily, and soon there was nothing left of the dead men but glowing bones. Over these they heaped high barrows, but the highest barrow of all was heaped for Cyzicus.

The Argonauts washed themselves three times in spring water, and changed their garments. They sacrificed black sheep, the heads turned downwards, and poured the blood upon the barrows, for the ghosts to slake their vengeful thirst; and the gift-wine, too, to make them forget. They also tore out their hair by handfuls. However, the ghost of Cleite was no concern of the Argonauts.

For three days they held funeral games in honour of King Cyzicus, in which the Dolionians also took part; but the Argonauts won every event, as might have been expected.

In the wrestling contest, Great Ancaeus was chosen to represent them, instead of Hercules or Castor. For Hercules had accidentally killed the last two men whom he had met in the ring and was still occasionally plagued by their indignant ghosts, and Castor had injured his thumb as he leaped ashore from the *Argo* on that fateful night. At the first encounter Ancaeus caught the opposing Dolionian about the middle, swung him off his feet, flung him sideways, and touched him down swiftly before he had recovered from the surprise. This won Ancaeus a golden cup, for the Dolionian refused to try a second fall with him.

The weight-lifting contest Hercules won easily. The opposing Dolionian was struggling with two hands to lift the *Argo*'s new anchor-stone upon his shoulders; but while he was still panting and straining ineffectively, Hercules came behind and, seating him on the stone by force, slid one hand underneath it and heaved it above his head with the Dolionian still astride. Then when the Dolionian had leaped off and acknowledged himself beaten, Hercules tossed the stone up and down in his hand, asking whether anyone would play at catch-ball with him. There was no reply, so he heaved the stone through the air like a quoit over the heads of the spectators. Fortunately nobody was hurt. This feat won Hercules a silver cup – silver being more highly prized among the Dolionians than gold.

Castor received a golden helmet-crest for winning the two-horse chariot-race; but the contest itself was not memorable, the local horses being of a poor breed compared with those of Sparta or of Thessaly.

Pollux won a richly woven carpet by his boxing; he was a terrible opponent and played with his man as a wild cat with a mouse. The Dolionian constantly clinched, to the disgust of the Argonauts; for in Greece a clinch is poor sport. But Pollux would let him break away unpunished from each clinch, and then dart after him, planting left-handed jolts on his chin until he grew dazed and sank down miserably on one knee.

The foot-race was waived, because Atalanta had been entered for it; while the Dolionians refused to compete with a woman, Jason would not insult Atalanta by substituting another Argonaut for her.

It was considered only just to let Jason champion the Argonauts in one event at least, and he was permitted to enter for the archery contest, though Phalerus of Athens was a far better archer than he, and Hercules far better than Phalerus. A goose was taken into a field and barley put before it; and at a given signal Jason and his opponent each discharged an arrow at the goose, from a distance of sixty paces. The Dolionian's first arrow wounded the goose in the foot, which pegged it to the ground and made it flutter its wings but Jason's arrow nicked its breast and drew blood. In the second bout both shot wide because of a sudden gust of wind. In the third, the Dolionian's arrow pierced the goose's rump, but Jason's its head. This earned Jason a crown of wild olive, for he refused all other gifts, saying that those he had received before had brought him little luck.

Lastly came the musical competition, and Phoceus, the Dolionian court bard, sang throatily to his lyre a long eulogy of Cyzicus and his dead comrades, detailing the glorious ancestry and valiant deeds of every one of them, and closing each verse with the same sad lament:

> But he died in the night, alas, alas,
> Pierced by the hand of a friend.

He was applauded as he deserved, and then all eyes turned to Orpheus. Orpheus did not, as Phoceus had done, roll out his voice loudly or twang at the strings with ostentatious movements of his hands and wrists, nor were the words he sang empty praise of the fallen. But, turning a troubled face towards Dindymos and plucking at the strings as if each note was pure pain to him, he made the lyre throb with sorrow, and in a clear voice sang:

> Mother, pardon this foolish child, your son –
> So young he scarcely yet can name your name,
> Omnipotent and sober-gifted One!
> For all those wrongs that he today has done,
> Account him not to blame.

> Break short the rudders, shatter the strong hulls
> Of those who hoist their sails of injury,
> And though their ghosts may scream like flocking gulls
> Dance out your night of triumph on their skulls –
> Yet, Mother, smile on me!

> When your snake hisses, when your lion roars...

He could go no further for weeping, and all the Argonauts wept with him. Echion drew from his own right foot a gilt sandal with wings at the heel, emblem of his heraldic office. He gave it to Orpheus with: 'Orpheus, you are a better herald than I can ever be!'

Then with one accord they rose up and went in file down the isthmus into Bear Island. They climbed Mount Dindymos by the path now called Jason's path, bent upon placating the angry Goddess. They had no fear of the Bear men, for Atalanta came with them and, while they stopped their ears, she raised the shrill, mirthless, laughing cry that turns man's blood cold: the cry of the maiden huntress who warns strangers from her path if they would not be metamorphosed into stags. So they came safely to the peak from which, the day being fine, they could view nearly the whole coast of the Sea of Marmora, and Proconesos seemed to lie almost within bow-shot. Lynceus, gazing to the north-west, cried: 'Do you see that silver ribbon in the distance? It is the Bosphorus, through which our way to Colchis lies.' But nobody else could distinguish the strait.

In a hollow, close to the peak, they found the stump of a pine, the top part of which had been taken off by lightning, but it had been so large a tree that two men could not girdle it with outstretched arms. This stump Argus began to cut about with his axe, until it assumed the shape of the Goddess squatting with head between hands and elbows resting on raised knees. When he had done, all the men wreathed their brows with ivy and prostrated themselves before the image. They cut themselves with knives until the blood flowed, and howled in supplication of her pardon, while Atalanta chapleted the image with flowers and addressed her as 'Dear Mistress of the Shining Face'. Then each man went in search of a huge rock, the largest that he could lift or trundle, and Hercules built them into a firm altar. On the altar they set the gifts that they had brought with them – barley, sesame, acorns, pine-kernels, and a precious jar of Hymettan honey, the gift of Butes. When Atalanta had spoken the appropriate prayer, they averted their gaze and waited for a sign. Presently they heard the roar of a lion three times repeated, and knew that all was well.

They returned to the isthmus, two by two, and as they went saw clouds gathering to the south-west. Tiphys said: 'In three days' time we may sail.'

Jason asked: 'Why not tonight?'

Tiphys answered: 'We must allow the wind to run ahead of us and abate the force of the current in the strait.'

That night, which was the last before the new moon, they were plagued with dreams of the dead Dolionians: Little Ancaeus, Peleus, Phalerus, and Erginus of Miletos started up in their sleep and, seizing weapons, would have fought to the death among themselves had not Idmon fortunately been awakened by the noise. He dashed cold water in their faces to bring them to their senses.

In the morning all agreed to sail on as soon as possible, making their next stop at the mouth of the Cios river, which is sheltered from the north by the high ridge of the Arganthonian mountains. Meanwhile Idmon undertook to lay the ghosts more securely than they had been laid at the funeral.

He instructed his comrades to wash themselves three times in the sea and once in spring-water (as he did himself), and to bind their brows with grey-green olive chaplets. Then, standing on the barrow of Cyzicus, dressed in his priestly robes, he made them all pass before him and touched them with a lucky branch of bay. Next came the sacrifice of pigs, first bled upon the barrows, then roasted whole on low hearths until all was devoured by the flames. 'Eat well, dear ghosts!' cried Idmon in his high voice. Next he set up thirty-four oak logs in a row and planted sticks beside them like spears, and called each of the logs by the name of one of the Argonauts. Next, he led the company away on tiptoe across a brook, bare-footed, so that the running water would take away their scent from the keen-nosed ghosts. Next, he came back himself and addressed the ghosts, saying: 'Ghosts, forget your anger and be content at last with your resting-place below. Do not afflict any herds with plague, or any crops with blight. Look, before you in a row, spear in hand, stand those who unwitting killed you. Plague them if you must, but do not visit your anger on their children or other innocents!' He named each of the logs in turn. Finally, covering his head with his cloak, he too stole away and crossed the brook.

'To sea, to sea!' cried the Argonauts. 'Let none of you look back to the barrows,' said Idmon, 'lest the ghosts recognize you and become aware of the deception.' But he had forgotten to put a log of his own in the row and to name it Idmon. The ghost of a Dolionian named Megabrontes, whom he had himself killed in the battle, stole after him, flew aboard the *Argo* and crept into the locker under the helmsman's seat There it lurked in the hope of vengeance. Lynceus saw how it fixed its glowering eyes on Idmon, but said nothing to anyone at the time, not wishing to attract the ghost's atten-tion to himself.

Soon they were at sea again, with the South-West Wind in their sail and Orpheus was playing a wordless melody in honour of the Goddess of Dindymos, so sweet that the sea seemed to every man to bloom with flowers. A shining kingfisher flew from a headland of Bear Island as they rounded it, perched on the yard and began to twitter and shake its short wings.

Orpheus put down his lyre. All began to ask Mopsus: 'What does the bird say? Is it a message from the Goddess?'

Mopsus answered: 'Over and over again it is the same message: "Children, sin no more!"'

But the Dolionians prolonged the term of their mourning for a full month, lighting no fires and subsisting on uncooked foods.

CHAPTER TWENTY-ONE

HYLAS IS LOST

Hercules began to grumble as he rowed: 'King Eurystheus has, I am sure, already sent his herald Talthybius after me with orders for some new Labour. If we meet with any more delays like the last he will catch me, as sure as Fate. I shall not be surprised to find him waiting for me, perched on a rock at the mouth of the Bosphorus. He will say with his insipid smile: "Most noble Hercules, well met! My master, King Eurystheus of Mycenae, your overlord, has sent me to convey you his latest orders. You are to ascend to the Moon and fetch him down some ripe strawberries – be sure that they are ripe!" Pooh! Why should he want strawberries from the Moon? – tell me that! Has he none in his own glens? Holy Serpents, the foolish requests that the long-eared idiot makes! But the worst of the jest is that I have to perform them in all earnest.'

Jason said, to humour him: 'Yes, Prince Hercules, we could ill afford to lose you. We had better make haste, as you say!'

Hercules answered: 'Take an oar yourself for a change, Boy, and let Orpheus be our captain today. He seems to have more intelligence than anyone else in this ship, if I except little Hylas. Take Idmon's oar and let Idmon relieve Tiphys, who has a sick-dog look in his eyes and ought to be lying snug in his blanket.'

Jason took the oar and Tiphys consented to let Idmon steer the ship for him. Tiphys was growing weaker daily; Hercules had been obliged to carry him down from Mount Dindymos on his shoulders.

'Now,' said Hercules, 'let us make haste. I will present the silver cup that I won at the games to the man who can keep stroke with me until we beach our ship tonight. Give us music, Orpheus!'

Orpheus struck up a rowing-song with a low, swinging chant, and began to improvise words about the Sun, who every day crosses the heavens from East to West in a fiery chariot; and every night returns by the Ocean route, conveyed in a golden boat shaped like a water-lily, asleep as he sails. He also sang of Colchian Aea, where are the stables of the Sun's white horses that champ golden corn and fleck the stable-floor with foam. Each verse was a repetition of the preceding one, with only a single new line at the head of it. This cumulative device was a charm that compelled the oarsmen to continue rowing. Hour by hour they pulled away, each boasting to himself that he would be the last to ship his oar.

Hercules sat with glazed eyes, like one who rows in his sleep, yet every now and then he would join in the chorus with a hoarse bellow. So they went on, for verse after verse, and passed the reedy mouth of the Rhyndacos river and its swamps ringing with the cries of wildfowl; and the wooded island of Besbicos, seven miles to the northward. This part of the sea teemed with all manner of fish, some of them unknown to the Greeks and strangely coloured and shaped. The day was hot, and about noon Great Ancaeus said to his neighbour Hercules, breaking the spell of the chant: 'Dear comrade, let us quit rowing for a while and refresh ourselves with a little wine and barley-cake.'

For answer Hercules roared out the next verse of the song at the top of his voice, and neither Ancaeus nor anyone else ventured to mention refreshment again. So they rowed on, for verse after verse, and hour after hour, keeping stroke with Hercules. They passed the Phrygian settlement of Myrlea, built on a flat coast backed by well-cultivated hills; and all longed to disembark there, for they could make out long stretches of carefully tended vines on the terraced slopes behind the city; but the relentless chant kept them at their oars. Eurydamas the Dolopian and his companion, Coronus of Gyrton, were the first to give up, shamefacedly drawing in their oars through the oar-holes. Erginus of Miletos and Ascalaphus, son of Ares, followed their example. When Phalerus the Athenian noted that all four of them were true Minyans, he twitted them, saying: 'If this voyage had been made by Minyans alone, I doubt whether we should ever have seen the coasts of Greece recede over the horizon.'

He thus stirred a spirit of contention between the true Minyans and those who were Minyans only by adoption. Among the next ten men who shipped their oars were Phalerus himself and his comrade Butes. Still the chant rose and fell croakingly as they drove onward into the Cianian Gulf; but those who had given up the contest ceased singing for weariness. Great Ancaeus fainted and fell forward on his oar, which Little Ancaeus made an excuse for shipping his own oar and reviving his namesake with sea-water dashed in his face. To port, across the gulf rose steeply the forbidding mass of the snow-capped, pine-clothed Arganthonian mountains, where bears of gigantic size are found.

When they were still at a distance of five miles from their goal, which was the mouth of the shallow but turbulent Cios river at the head of the gulf, only Castor, Pollux, Jason, and Hercules continued steadfast. As each successive oar had been shipped, the task that fell to the remaining oarsmen had grown heavier, and a strong swell added to their labours. Soon Castor and Pollux ceased rowing together, for neither wished to be preferred to the other and Castor's strength was ebbing. Jason, with hands raw from rowing, continued grimly at his task, hating to yield the supremacy to Hercules. Half a mile more and the contest would be over. But Jason's oar did not bite so deeply into the water as that of Hercules, and Idmon had difficulty in keeping the ship on her course.

Hercules sang more and more loudly; Jason more and more faintly. At last Jason missed a stroke and toppled over backwards. Hercules was left rowing alone. The muddy current of the Cios river pressed against the *Argo*; Hercules stemmed it stoutly and attempted with all his might to drive her onwards. Suddenly came a loud crack, followed by a booming sound. His oar had broken in two and with the butt he had dealt himself so huge a blow on the chest that over he went, flinging Zetes, who sat behind him, into the arms of Meleager, and Meleager into the arms of Nauplius. Hercules recovered himself, glared about him and exclaimed angrily: 'Lions and Leopardesses! Let someone give me a real oar, not another rotten lath like this!'

Argus replied for the others: 'No, noble Hercules! The oar was not at fault. Your wonderful strength matched against this impetuous river would snap the strongest oar in the world. Come, fellow-Minyans one last bout of rowing and we shall camp tonight on those pleasant meadows yonder, starred with white flowers!'

The weary men thrust back their oars through the oar-holes, and Hercules took Jason's oar from his nerveless hands. The *Argo* shot forward again and Idmon steered her into a lagoon. There they anchored stepped ashore on grass and at once began collecting dry driftwood for their camp-fire, which Augeas kindled with his fire-sticks; he was the cleverest man in Greece for kindling a fire in wet or windy weather, though nobody would have guessed it from his fat hands and lazy movements.

They filled the ship's cauldron with river-water, to boil in it the dozen large fish which Tiphys had caught that afternoon by trolling a baited hook on a float behind the ship, but so weak he was, that he had called on Hylas to haul each fish into the boat as he hooked it. Fish chowder prepared with barley-meal and savoury herbs, would warm them well, but Hercules declared that though the mud in the river-water might not spoil the taste of the chowder, he must at least have clean water to mix with his wine. The other Argonauts were too weary to care what they drank; however, Hylas volunteered to find a clear spring and fetch Hercules what he asked. He climbed back into the *Argo* to fetch his pitcher, but at the same time took up the wallet containing his silver belt-clasp, gold ornaments, and provisions of meat and figs. Here was his chance of escape at last. All the Argonauts but Hercules would be too weary to pursue him, and he was confident that he could outwit Hercules.

'Be careful, my darling,' said Hercules. 'Keep to the bank of the river, and if you meet with any danger start back at once and shout for help! Come, kiss me, first!'

Hylas gave Hercules a kiss of unusual fervour, hoping to distract his attention from the wallet. Hercules suspected nothing and, when Hylas disappeared around a turn of the river-path, heaved a huge sigh like the first gust of wind that announces a squall. 'Ah, how that boy loves me,' he cried. 'Do you not envy me, Idas? Do you not envy me, Zetes? Lynceus, you who have the keenest sight of any man living – Argus, Nauplius, Orpheus, my brother Polyphemus, you who (after me) have travelled the furthest of any men of this company – Atalanta, who as a woman can be trusted to speak without prejudice – did any of you ever see a more beautiful, better-mannered, more graceful, or more affectionate boy in all your wanderings?'

'Oh, certainly not, most noble Hercules,' they answered in unison. But Tiphys said gently: 'Be careful, Hercules, or you will make some god envious! It was careless praise of this very sort that tempted Zeus to carry off young Trojan Ganymede. Let me ward off all danger from Hylas by a little disparagement. His nose is somewhat too short, his mouth somewhat too large, and he crooks his little finger affectedly when he drinks.'

'I like short noses, his mouth is perfectly formed, and if you speak another word against the elegant way in which he drinks I will make a pestle of my club and crush you to a paste.'

'Very well,' said Tiphys, 'I recant my words, which were spoken with a good intention.'

'Forget your good intentions and stick to the truth,' said Hercules severely. 'The truth is great and will prevail.' He then remembered the broken oar and told his companions: 'I am going off to cut myself an oar, a real oar that will never snap in two. When Hylas comes back, brother Polyphemus, see that he eats well and drinks a little wine, but not too much. I consider wine in large quantities unwholesome for a child.'

Hercules strode off and rambled around the district, looking for a suitable pine-tree but found none to satisfy him. Each tree that he examined was either too small or too large, or had too many branches, or was crooked. As darkness fell, he came back in a sullen mood and demanded a lighted torch. Polyphemus hurriedly supplied him with one, and he went off again. Two hours or so passed before he found a pine that suited him, a splendid tree, as straight and as smooth as a poplar, growing at the edge of a dark grove. He loosened its roots with his club and then stooping down with straddled legs tugged fiercely at it; it came rushing up at last with a cart-load of earth about its roots. Then, knocking the earth off, he heaved the tree on his shoulder and came blundering back to the camp-fire. 'Let someone give me an axe,' he shouted. 'I intend to trim this oar at once, before I dine. And, Argus, I will trouble you to pierce me a new oar-hole in the ship twice as wide as the other.'

He was whittling and chopping away, with great grunts, when suddenly he called out: 'Hylas, hey you, Hylas my darling, come and see what I am doing!'

'Hylas has not returned yet, noble brother,' said Polyphemus. 'Shall I go out to look for him?'

'Not yet returned! What do you mean by "not yet returned"?' growled Hercules. 'Please do not dare to bait me. I am a touchy man until I have eaten and drunken well.'

'It is no jest,' said Polyphemus. 'Hylas went out with the pitcher and has not yet returned. Shall I go in search of him while you complete your oar?'

'You had better do so, Polyphemus,' said Hercules, 'and, when you have found him, tell him from me that he can expect the worst beating of his life for giving me such anxiety on his account.'

Polyphemus, slinging a faggot of torches behind his back and taking a lighted torch in his hand, set off up the river. As he went he called Hylas by name loudly; but no reply came, except the mocking hoot of an owl. He was a skilled woodman and soon picked up the prints of small, sandalled feet. It was the track of Hylas, who clearly had been running. The toe-marks of the right sandal were not more deeply indented than those of the left: the heavy bronze pitcher must therefore have been counterbalanced by some weight on the other side. Or had Hylas thrown the pitcher into the river? The track led Polyphemus along a small brook which ended in a deep fountain, called the fountain of Pegae, and there he found the sandals and pitcher of Hylas lying by the bank, and his fawn-skin coat, but no Hylas. At that moment the sudden cry of a night bird rang out from the thicket and Polyphemus drew his sword and rushed forward, confused in his wits, thinking that robbers or some wild beast had carried Hylas off. He shouted: 'Hylas, Hylas, what are they doing to you?'

Hercules heard the shout as he sat working by the shore, and seizing his great club came bounding up the valley. Soon he met Polyphemus, who, with chattering teeth and tremulous voice, cried out: 'O dear Hercules – be prepared to hear bad news. Hylas went to the spring up yonder, but there the tracks end. He has left his pitcher and sandals and fawn-skin coat on the grass, but robbers have attacked him, or wild bears, or some jealous god has caught him up into the sky – I heard him cry out!'

Hercules roared with rage and anguish like a monstrous bull stung in some tender part by a gadfly. He ran past Polyphemus and began whirling his club about his head, yelling: 'Hylas, Hylas, my darling, come back to me! Come back, you are forgiven! I never intended to beat you!'

Polyphemus, returning to the Argonauts, warned them what they must expect from Hercules if Hylas could not be found. 'I am sure that he will kill us all – beginning with Tiphys and Jason.'

'What happened is plain enough,' said Erginus of Miletos. 'Hylas ran on until he was hot, drank at the fountain, took off his sandals and fawn-skin for a swim, dived in, found himself out of his depth, and drowned.'

'He could swim like a fish,' Jason objected.

'He must have struck his head against a sunken rock and stunned himself,' said Euphemus of Taenaron. 'The same has happened to many rash swimmers.'

'Hylas was a gallant little fellow,' said Peleus. 'I shall miss him.'

Meleager smiled. 'I do not think that you need speak of him as already dead,' he said. 'From the way in which he spoke to Atalanta and myself the other day in Samothrace, I judge that he has merely run off from his master. And, upon my word, I cannot find it in my heart to blame him.'

Lynceus said: 'I noticed that he had a wallet with him when he started out. If he plunged into the pool for a swim he would have left that behind on the bank as well as his sandals and pitcher.'

'I heard it clink,' said Atalanta.

Polyphemus said: 'A heavy wallet on his left side would account for the evenness of the track. I could not understand why the weight of the pitcher did not depress the toe-marks either on one side or the other.'

'A heavy clinking wallet?' cried Mopsus. 'Then it is as clear as day that the youngster has run off. He is clever enough to give Hercules the slip, for the time being at least. I imagine that he will follow the inland road to Troy, take ship there for Lemnos and find that girl Iphinoë again.'

Argus said: 'Perhaps Pelias was speaking the truth when he suggested that the weight of Hercules would prove too heavy for the *Argo*. When he comes back I fear he will stamp huge holes in her bottom. Has he not gone insane once more? Look at this prodigious oar that he has made. Does he really intend to use it? It is almost as long as the boat. Everyone will laugh at us as we row by.'

Old Nauplius commented sourly: 'This is the oddest oar that ever I saw in all my thirty years of seafaring. It is too long for use even if Hercules were to shift across to the bench on the opposite side. Besides, how could he ever ship it? Should we jettison the mast and put the oar into the mast-crutch instead?'

Hercules could still be heard shouting 'Hylas! Hylas!' in the far distance, but the faint flashes of his torch could no longer be seen. They anxiously discussed whether Hylas would disclose to the Trojans that the *Argo* was on her way to Colchis; for if he did, the consequences would be serious. But Atalanta stood up for Hylas, declaring that he would rather bite out his tongue than betray a comrade, and that he was a wonderfully resourceful little liar when it pleased him. 'I wish him luck with the women,' she said. 'Yet I cannot help feeling anxious about him, now that he is at their mercy – upon my honour I do!'

So the talk ran on. 'Well, I hope now to snatch a little sleep,' said Great Ancaeus. 'This has been an exhausting day for us all. Good night, comrades!'

They all fell asleep but Polyphemus, who did not wish Hercules to think him a shirker. He went up the river again in the direction that Hercules had taken, wearily crying 'Hylas! Hylas!' and waving his torch.

The Cios is the outfall of a large, sacred lake named the Ascanian Lake at the nearer end of which stands an ancient College of Woodpecker nymphs. When Hylas had reached the fountain of Pegae he had surprised the Chief Nymph, whose name was Dryope, bathing naked in it; for this was the evening of the new moon and she was purifying herself for sacrifice. Hylas modestly averted his gaze, but dared ask her to put him on the road to Troy, telling his story with little concealment. Dryope fell in love with him. She told him that, if he pleased, he might come with her to the College, where she would disguise him among her women until the vessel had sailed on. When he thanked her with tears in his eyes, she embraced him, but not in the bear-like fashion of Hercules, and kissed him sweetly. She said that since he had looked on her nakedness, and had not been turned into a fox or stag, the Goddess plainly had arranged this meeting: he might company with her, and welcome. Thus she seduced him without difficulty, for she was a beautiful woman and he was overjoyed to feel himself a man at last and to enjoy the favour of the Goddess. He gave her all his ornaments as a love-token, but she advised him to leave his pitcher, sandals, and coat by the side of the fountain as if he had been drowned; she would take him back with her by a firm, grassy path where his feet would leave no print.

When Hercules went raging to the College to enquire after Hylas, Dryope told him that she knew nothing. He insisted upon searching every nook and she did not oppose his wish, though the College was sacred and he had no right to cross the threshold. He went from room to room, smashing open cupboards and chests with his club and glaring balefully at the terrified nymphs. He passed close by Hylas but did not recognize him in his short green tunic and hood; then with growls, snarls, and curses he went back at dawn to the camp-fire by the lagoon. He shouted out as he approached: 'You traitors have all plotted against me. I will have vengeance. One of you has stolen my darling from me. It is you, Jason; or you, Tiphys. I never trusted either of you.'

But the camp-fire was deserted, and when he looked around for the *Argo*, she was gone. As the sky brightened he could see her, small on the western horizon, coasting along the basalt cliffs of Arganthonios. When he realized that he was marooned he was at first too astonished to be angry. Such a thing had never happened to him before in all his adventures. He searched the shore for his silver cup and other belongings, which he could not doubt but that they had taken out of his locker and left behind for him. But they had left nothing at all behind, except fish-bones and his new oar. O, the pirates! From the woods behind him he could hear the hoarse voice of Polyphemus still crying at intervals: 'Hylas! Hylas! where are you?'

There was a deal of trouble aboard the *Argo*. An hour before dawn a smart breeze had blown down the valley, fanning the spent embers of the camp-fire into a blaze. The smoke made Tiphys cough and sneeze. He awoke and aroused Jason, saying: 'Here is the very breeze that we need. Order all hands into the ship!'

Jason shouted: 'All hands aboard!' The sleepy Argonauts gathered their gear together and stumbled up the ladder into the ship, each to his own bench, except that Meleager went apart from Atalanta and sat down in the seat of Hercules. For during the night a lovers' quarrel had arisen between these two. What was said on either side is not known, but they were now no longer on terms of friendship and if they had any necessary request to make of each other, it was conveyed through Orpheus.

The ladder was drawn up at Jason's command and the Argonauts used the butts of their oars as poles to propel the *Argo* from the lagoon. Then the rapid current of the Cios caught and swept her out into the gulf. 'Up sail!' Jason cried. The mast was hauled from its crutch and stepped, the yard was hoisted, the breeze bellied out the sail. Still half-asleep, the Argonauts watched the misty shore recede.

It was not until they had sailed well out into the gulf that Admetus, who at Iolcos had first urged that Hercules should lead the expedition, suddenly cried: 'Where is Hercules? Why is he not aboard? And where is Polyphemus? What are you doing in the seat of Hercules, Meleager?'

He slewed angrily about to satisfy himself that Hercules was not asleep in the bows. Then he shouted to Tiphys: 'You miserable rascal! You roused us in the half-dark and persuaded Jason to fetch us aboard and push off before we realized that Hercules was not among us. About ship at once, or it will be the worse for you!'

Tiphys made no reply, but smiled grimly back at Admetus.

Admetus shipped his oar and leaped up, weapon in hand. He stumbled cursing down the ship towards Tiphys. But Calaïs and Zetes, sons of the North Wind, caught at him, crying: 'Silence, Admetus! If you have any complaint to make, address it to Jason. He is captain here.'

Admetus struggled with them. 'You are right, Thracians,' he said. 'Jason too is concerned in the plot. He has agreed to maroon Hercules from jealousy. He wishes all the credit for this expedition to come to himself. He knows well that if it is successful everyone with any sense will praise Hercules and forget Jason. About ship, there! Hey, comrades, who is on my side? What hope have we of winning the Fleece without Hercules? Let us return at once and fetch him off, and Polyphemus too. If he punishes Jason and Tiphys as they deserve, I for one will not raise a hand to save them.'

Nobody but Peleus and Acastus supported Admetus. The wind was rough and the previous day's rowing had so exhausted the Argonauts that the thought of lowering the yard and rowing back in the teeth of the wind distressed them. Besides, they were more afraid of meeting Hercules again than of earning the reproach of having deserted him: he had been in a mad enough mood before Hylas had been lost, and they had not even left any food or drink for him at the camping-place.

Idmon said: 'Come, Jason, you are our leader. It is for you to make the decision. Shall we return or shall we proceed?'

Jason sat and glowered, unwilling to say a word.

Phalerus the Athenian taunted him: 'Jason, you are as silent as a fish-monger in the market of Athens, when a customer asks him the price of a fish, reckoned either in oil or barley. He will not name a price fearing to ask less than the customer is prepared to pay. But when the proud fish-monger plays such a trick on me I pick up the wet fish and slap his face with it, though in general I am a patient man.'

Admetus spoke again: 'The wind is bearing us further and further away. Come, Jason, give the word before it is too late.'

Idas mocked raucously: 'Admetus, Admetus, your lamb-skin cap is crooked on your head, and your nose is smudged with tar. Sit down, man, sit down!'

Calaïs said, more gently: 'Admetus, forget about Hercules. Some god or other put it into the mind of Tiphys to rouse us up as he did, and has blinded us to the loss of Hercules until now.'

'And with his unseen finger still seals the lips of Jason, our captain,' put in Zetes. 'Let us sail on, forgetting the mad Tirynthian, and think only of the Fleece.'

Admetus replied: 'Very well. What am I, one man against you all? But bear witness, Acastus and Peleus, that you and I earnestly proposed a return to the camping-place, and that Zetes and Calaïs opposed it. If Hercules cares to be revenged on any of us, let it be upon those two Thracians. Jason, Argus, Tiphys, and the rest seem caught in a divine trance and cannot be held accountable. As for you, Idas, one day you will say one mocking word too many: it will fly back into your mouth as a Spite and sting your tongue.'

They sailed on in a silence which presently was broken by the creaking voice of Ascalaphus of Orchomenos. 'I hear a strange singing noise from the prow. Can it be the oak branch of Zeus?'

'It is only the wind in the cordage,' said Echion.

But Mopsus the soothsayer climbed up into the prow and, beckoning the crew to silence, listened intently. At last he nodded and spoke: The branch says: "Hercules is left behind by the design of Zeus himself. The anger of Hercules will make smooth the path of our return. For Polyphemus, too, Father Zeus has a work to perform at the mouth of the Cios. Cease, my sons, to wrangle among yourselves, but sail on piously in quest of that holy thing which was stolen long ago by a Mare from a Ram."'

This settled the matter, and there was peace again upon the benches.

Hercules, since he could not find the least trace of Hylas in the Cios valley, visited all the neighbouring cities of Mysia, one by one, and accused the rulers of each in turn of having stolen Hylas from him. When they denied the charge, he demanded hostages for their good behaviour and a promise to search for Hylas until they had found him. They consented, knowing that if they refused Hercules anything he would knock their houses to pieces and burn up their crops. To this day the people of Mysia still make search for Hylas everywhere once a year, crying his name vainly up the fertile valleys and through the shaggy woods of their land. But Hercules himself started off for Colchis on foot, hoping to catch the *Argo* there and avenge himself on Jason and his companions.

Polyphemus, being an exile from Larisa, had no fixed home, and when Hercules gave him charge of his thirty young Mysian hostages he decided to settle in the valley of the Cios and build a city there. He did so, and it has since become a place of great importance, and a favourite nesting-place for the holy stork.

CHAPTER TWENTY-TWO

POLLUX BOXES WITH KING AMYCUS

Upon making Cape Poseidon, the Argonauts shaped their course for the north-west, lowering the sail and taking to their oars. The high hills sheltered them from the wind, but they had not yet recovered from their exertions of the previous day, and their progress along the steep and rocky coast was therefore slow.

Nauplius asked Jason: 'Do we attempt the Bosphorus passage this afternoon?'

Jason consulted Tiphys, who answered: 'The current in the strait will still be very strong. Without the help of Hercules I think that we shall hardly be able to stem it.'

'Then why in the world,' cried Admetus, 'did you hurry us away this morning, leaving Hercules behind?'

Idmon said in his high voice: 'Admetus, Admetus, we have already canvassed that question sufficiently, and the speaking branch of Father Zeus has plainly accounted for the action of Tiphys. My advice is that you should go over to Tiphys now and shake him by the hand, to show yourself his friend; and that you should do the same with Jason and Calaïs and Zetes.'

Since everyone approved this suggestion, Admetus was obliged to fall in with it. He rose and solemnly shook hands with his comrades.

'Now, Jason,' Great Ancaeus said, 'if you intend to make no further progress today, why should we not land on the next sheltered beach and complete our interrupted rest?'

'Why, indeed?' Jason assented.

They rowed slowly on for another few miles, until the coast took a westerly turn and the hills receded; then they came up with a prosperous-looking town, where herds grazed on rich meadow grass and a bright stream rushed down from the mountain.

'Does anyone know who these people are?' asked Jason.

Argus answered: 'They are Bebrycians – or rather a mixture of Achaeans, Brygians and Mysians. Two generations ago an Achaean clan settled among the Brygiana at the mouths of the Danube and inter-married with them; they later came here in a fleet of seal-skin rowing-boats accompanied by a number of Brygian fighting men, and soon subjugated the local Mysians. They are a strange people who prefer cow's milk to that of sheep or goats and mix their wine with fresh pine resin. I have heard that their King, who is nearly always at war with the Mariandynians and Bithynians to the north, is a savage creature named Amycus. He claims descent from Poseidon, to whom, in a style now happily abandoned throughout Greece, he offers human sacrifices on the slightest pretext. If Ancaeus of Tegea needs a rest, Amycus is likely to offer him eternal rest.'

Jason put it to the vote: 'Shall we land here, or shall we row on?'

The decision was for landing, by thirty votes to two; so all put on their helmets and armour and, raising a defiant shout, beached the *Argo* opposite what seemed, from its size, to be a royal palace, and there made the hawsers fast to a fine bay-tree.

Echion the herald was the first to go ashore. He advanced with grave and fearless aspect towards the houses. A huge, shaggy, long-armed man with a squat head that looked as though it had been roughly shaped on the anvil with sledge-hammers – King Amycus himself, to judge from his golden ornaments – came out to meet Echion. But instead of greeting him with the formality that every man of honour shows to the herald even of an enemy, he bawled out roughly: 'I suppose that you know who I am. I am King Amycus. No, I do not want to know who you are or where you are bound – and no doubt your mouth is full of lies, in any case – but I would have you understand clearly how you are now circumstanced. No strangers are allowed to land in my kingdom, none at all. Once they have done so, whether by mistake or intentionally, they must accept the consequences. Either they may send out a champion to box with me, in which case I invariably kill him with my famous right-handed swing, or, if they prefer to waive this formality, they may shorten proceedings by an unconditional surrender. In either case, they are subsequently taken up to the top of the headland which you have just rounded and thrown splash into the sea as an offering to my great ancestor, the God Poseidon.'

'I do not box myself,' replied Echion suavely, 'and I regret that Hercules of Tiryns, who was our shipmate until yesterday, is not aboard. He would have given you a pretty fair bout, I believe. Still, we have another champion of fisticuffs here, whom you may enjoy meeting. He is Pollux of Sparta, who won the All-Greece championship at the Olympic Games some years ago.'

Amycus laughed. 'I have never yet set eyes on a Greek who was of any use in the ring. I have, I own, seen Greeks do some very pretty boxing; with neat footwork, ducking and dodging in and out. But what does that profit them? Nothing at all, the fools! I always land my right-handed swing before long and it knocks them in a heap. They cannot hurt me, you must understand. I am nothing but bone and muscle. Hit me and break your wrist.'

They went down together to the *Argo*, and Amycus shouted out in rude tones: 'Where is this mad Spartan, Pollux, who styles himself a boxer?'

Jason said coldly: 'I think that you must have misheard the words of our noble herald, Echion the son of Hermes. I am Jason of Iolcos, leader of this expedition, and I must ask you to address your words of greeting to me first of all.'

Amycus uttered a contemptuous, bleating laugh and said: 'Speak when you are spoken to, Golden-locks! I am the famous and terrible Amycus. I trespass in no man's orchard and allow no man to trespass in mine. Before I pitch you all over the cliff, splash into the sea, one after the other, I wish to meet this All-Greece champion of yours and punch him about for a while. I am in need of exercise.'

The Argonauts looked at one another in a wondering way, but by now the beach was thronged with the armed followers of Amycus. They could not hope to push the *Argo* off and get clear of the shore without heavy losses; and they did not wish to leave Echion behind in the hands of savages who could clearly not be counted upon to respect the inviolability of his person.

'Here I am, King Amycus,' said Pollux, standing up. 'I am somewhat stiff from rowing, but I shall be greatly honoured to meet you in the ring. Where do you usually box? Is it in the courtyard of your fine palace yonder?'

'No, no,' answered Amycus. 'There is a convenient dell under the cliff beyond the village, where I always fight, if you can call it fighting. Usually it is more like a simple blood-sacrifice.'

'Indeed?' said Pollux. 'So you favour the pole-axe style of boxing? Big men like you are often tempted to rise on their toes and deal a swinging downward blow. But do you find it effective against an opponent who keeps his head?'

'You will learn a good many tricks of the ring before I have killed you,' said Amycus, roaring with laughter.

'By the way,' asked Pollux, 'is this to be a boxing match, or an all-in wrestling match?'

'A boxing match, of course,' Amycus replied. 'And I flatter myself that I am a true sportsman.'

'Let me understand you fully,' said Pollux. 'As you may know, codes vary considerably in these outlying kingdoms. First of all: do you permit clinching, handling, or kicking? Or throwing of dust in the other man's eyes?'

'Certainly not,' said Amycus.

'Or biting, butting, hitting below the hip-bone?'

'No indeed!' Amycus indignantly exclaimed.

'And only yourself and myself will be allowed in the ring?'

'Only we two,' said Amycus. 'And the fight is to the finish.'

'Good,' cried Pollux. 'Lead on to the dell!'

Amycus led the way to the dell, which was a very lovely place, where violet, hyacinth, and anemone grew in profusion from the greenest turf imaginable, and the daphne scented the air. His armed followers took up their posts on one side under a row of arbutus-trees, leaving the other side free for the Argonauts. But on the way there, walking apart from the others, Idmon came upon a heartening augury: twin eagles perched upon the carcase of a shaggy black horse, newly dead, of which one was continually thrusting its head between the ribs to tear at the guts, but the other, already satiated, was wiping its curved beak against the horses hoof. Other carrion birds, crows, kites, and magpies, were hopping and fluttering about, intent on sharing the meal. Idmon recognized the twin eagles as Castor and his brother Pollux, the eagle being the bird of their father Zeus; and the horse as Amycus, the horse being sacred to Poseidon; and the other carrion birds were Coronus, Melampus, Calaïs, Zetes, and the rest of the Argonauts.

'This is an unusual sort of ring,' remarked Pollux. 'It allows mighty little room for manoeuvre. And both ends narrow to a point like the bows and stern of a ship.'

'It suits my style of boxing,' said Amycus. 'And I may add that I always box with my back to the cliff. I dislike having the sun in my eyes.'

'I am glad to know that, said Pollux. 'In civilized countries it is more usual to draw lots for position. Come now, my lord, strip yourself, and bind on your gloves!'

Amycus stripped. He was as shapeless as a bear, though longer-legged. The muscles on his shaggy arms stood out like seaweed-covered boulders. His henchmen bound on his gloves for him – huge leather strips weighted with lead and studded with brass spikes

Jason came striding forward to expostulate: 'King Amycus, this will never do! In Greece, studs of metal fixed upon gloves are forbidden as barbarous. This is a boxing match, not a battle.'

'This is not Greece,' said Amycus. 'However, no man must be allowed to question my sportsmanship. Pollux is welcome to my spare set of gloves if he cares to borrow them.'

Jason thanked Amycus, who ordered a slave to fetch gloves for Pollux of the same sort as those that he was wearing himself. Pollux laughed at the slave and shook his head, for Castor had already bound on for him his own supple sparring-gloves, which served to protect his knuckles from swelling and to brace his wrists. The four fingers of each hand were caught in a loop, but the thumb remained free and uncovered.

Jason whispered to Castor: 'Why has your twin rejected those excellent gloves?'

Castor answered: 'The heavier the glove, the slower the blow. You will see!'

The opponents agreed to begin the bout at the blast of a conch. The trumpeter took up his stand on a rock above the dell, and was still pretending to untangle the crossed strings which attached the conch to his neck, when another conch sounded from among the crowd and Amycus rushed at Pollux, hoping to take him off his guard. Pollux leaped back, avoiding the right-handed swing aimed at his ear, sidestepped and turned rapidly about. Amycus, recovering himself, found himself standing with the sun in his eyes.

Amycus was by far the heavier man, and the younger by some years. Enraged at having to face in the wrong direction, he made a bull-like rush at Pollux, hammering at him with both hands. Pollux pulled him up with a straight left-handed punch on the point of his chin, and pressed his advantage, not with the expected right-handed swing but with another jolt from the same fist, which made his teeth rattle.

It took more than this to check Amycus. He ran in, head down, covering up his face against an upper-cut, butted Pollux in the chest and aimed a pair of flailing blows at his kidneys. Pollux broke away in good time and Amycus tried to pursue him into the shaded northern corner of the dell, where the sun did not annoy the eyes of either. But Pollux stood his ground and kept Amycus fighting at a spot where the sun would most trouble him: at one instant it was obscured by a rock and at the next it dazzled out again from above the rock, as Pollux stopped his rushes with hooks, jabs, chopping blows, and upper-cuts. Pollux fought now left-handed and now right-handed, for he was naturally ambidextrous, a wonderful advantage to a boxer.

After the contest had lasted for as long as it would take a man to walk a mile in no great hurry, Pollux was untouched except for a torn shoulder which, forgetting the spikes of Amycus's glove, he had flung up to save his head from a sudden swing; but Amycus was spitting blood from his swollen mouth and both his eyes were nearly closed. Amycus twice tried his pole-axe blow, rising on his toes and swinging downwards with his right fist, but each time he missed, and Pollux caught him off his balance and punished him, for he had drawn his feet too close together.

Pollux now began announcing in what places he intended to strike Amycus, and each warning was immediately followed by a blow. He disdained to strike any body-blows, for that is not the Olympic style, but always made for the head. He cried out: 'Mouth, mouth, left eye, right eye, chin, mouth again.'

Amycus roared almost as loudly as Hercules had roared in his search for Hylas, but when he began bawling obscene threats, Pollux grew angry. He feinted with his right fist, and with the left he landed a heavy blow on the bridge of his enemy's nose; he felt the bone and cartilage crunch under the weight of the blow.

Amycus toppled and fell backwards, Pollux sprang forward to strike him where he lay; for though in the friendly contests of the boxing school it is considered generous to refrain from hitting a prostrate opponent, yet in a public contest a boxer is considered a fool who does not follow up his blow. Amycus rolled over quickly and struggled to his feet. But his blows now came short and wild, his gloves seeming to hum as heavy as anchor-stones; and Pollux did not spare the broken nose, but struck at it continually from either side and from in front

Amycus in desperation snatched with his left hand at the left fist of Pollux, as it came jabbing towards him, and tugged at it, at the same time bringing up a tremendous right-handed swing. Pollux, who had been expecting foul play, threw himself in the same direction as he was tugged; and Amycus, who had expected him to resist the tug and thus fix his head to receive the swing, struck only air. Before he could recover, Pollux had landed a powerful right-handed hook on his temple, followed by a left-handed upper-cut on the point of his chin.

Amycus dropped his guard; he could fight no more. He tottered on his feet, while Pollux methodically swung at his head with rhythmic blows, like those of a woodman who leisurely chops down a tall pine-tree and at last stands aside to watch it crash among the undergrowth. The last blow, a left-handed one that came up almost from the ground, broke the bones of his enemy's temple and knocked him stone dead. The Argonauts roared for wonder and delight.

The Bebrycians had kept pretty quiet during the fight, not believing that Amycus was being worsted. He had often before amused them by staggering about, pretending to be injured by an opponent, and then suddenly springing to life again and pounding him to a bloody pulp. But when Pollux began knocking Amycus about just as he pleased, they grew restive, fingering their spears and twirling their clubs. When at last Amycus fell they rushed forward to avenge him, and a flying javelin grazed Pollux on the hip. The Argonauts ran forward to protect their champion and a short, bloody fight ensued. Pollux joined in, just as he was, and showed himself as well skilled in the art of all-in fighting as he was in pugilism. He kicked, wrestled, bit, punched, butted, and when he had felled the man who threw the spear at him, with a kick in the pit of his stomach, he leapt upon him at once and gouged out his eyes. Castor stood over his brother, and with one blow of a long sword chopped a Bebrycian's skull clean through, so that one might have expected the halves to fall apart across his shoulders.

Idas, at the head of a small body of Argonauts armed with spears, ran along the lip of the dell and took the Bebrycians in the flank. They broke and fled through the arbutus-grove like a swarm of smoked-out bees. Jason, Phalerus, and Atalanta picked off the stragglers with arrows; Meleager pressed hard on the rout with his darting javelin. The Bebrycians streamed inland, leaderless and astonished, leaving forty dead or dying men on the field of battle; but Calaïs and Zetes pursued them a great distance, as kites pursue a flock of wood-pigeons.

Jason rallied his company, of whom three or four were wounded, but none seriously; Iphitus of Phocis had been knocked unconscious with a club, Acastus proudly displayed a spear-cut on the inside of his thigh which bled a good deal and made walking uncomfortable for him, and Phalerus had been bruised on the hip with a rock.

With one accord the Argonauts ran to the palace of Amycus in search of booty. There they found gold and silver and jewels in abundance, which they afterwards distributed by lot among themselves, and great quantities of provisions, including several long jars of Lesbian wine. Hercules had drunk the *Argo* nearly dry, so the wine contented them.

That evening, garlanded with bay leaves from the tree where the *Argo* was moored, they feasted well on tender beef and mutton; and protected themselves against a return of the enemy by arming some captive Mariandynians, whom Amycus had taken in the wars, and posting them all about the town. But the Bebrycians did not venture to the attack.

Jason was deeply concerned not to offend the God Poseidon. The next morning, at his suggestion, old Nauplius of Argos, Periclymenus of Pylos, and Erginus of Miletos, all sons of Poseidon, joined together in preparing a sacrifice for their father. There was no lack of cattle, since all the herds of Amycus were now in the possession of the Argonauts, and what they could not eat they must necessarily leave behind. Making a virtue of necessity, they sacrificed to Poseidon no less than twenty unblemished bulls of the red Thracian breed, burning them utterly and not tasting a morsel, besides what beasts were sacrificed in the ordinary manner to the other gods.

That day, too, the Bebrycian dead were decently buried, King Amycus apart from the rest. The Argonauts did not fear their ghosts since they had died in fair fight.

Butes was delighted with a jar of wild honey that he had found in the private larder of Amycus: it was golden-brown in colour and culled wholly from the pine blossom of the Arganthonian crags. 'Nowhere have I found so pure a pine honey as this,' he declared. 'The Pelion pine honey, so called, is tainted with a variety of other blossoms and flowers; but this has the authentic tang. Nevertheless,' he added, 'it is a curiosity rather than a delicacy.'

CHAPTER TWENTY-THREE

ORPHEUS TELLS OF DAEDALUS

The dining-hall of King Amycus was decorated with coloured frescoes. Among them was one showing Daedalus and Icarus flying on wings from Crete, where a bull-headed man bellowed after them in a death-agony and Theseus of Athens, with an owl perched on his shoulder, brandished a double-headed axe exultantly.

Little Ancaeus said to Orpheus: 'Dear comrade, far-travelled comrade, expound this picture to us, if you will. We undertake to listen attentively and make no interruption.'

This then is the story that Orpheus told them as they sat feasting with bay-garlanded heads in the hall of their defeated enemy.

'It is thought to have been in carelessness rather than wilful disobedience that the leader of the Bull men of Cretan Cnossos, Chief Priest of the Sun God Minos, broke an ancient command of the Triple Goddess, which was that none but native Cretans should be permitted to go aboard any boat or ship which would seat more than five persons. He broke it in the case of Daedalus, a Pelasgian craftsman of Athens, as I will presently explain to you all, dear Argonauts. Theseus the Ionian, King of Athens, had sent Daedalus to Cnossos for the annual Spring Festival, in the company of nineteen other unfortunates, all manacled there to be chased by the sacred bull of the Sun, the Minotaur. Daedalus, a kinsman to Theseus by matrilinear descent, had been sentenced to death by him for the murder of a fellow-craftsman, but Theseus cancelled the sentence when Daedalus offered to enter the bull-ring instead.

'Formerly all the victims of the Minotaur had been Cretan Bull men, volunteers for death, but now the Cretans had grown reluctant to be chased by him, even for the glory of the Goddess. Minos (as the Priest of Minos was styled for short), condoning this reluctance, ordered the bull's twenty victims to be supplied yearly by the Cretan colonies, or by tributary cities. This he did in such a way that he seemed to be conferring a great honour on the place selected; for at the same time the Chief Priestess called for the same number of maidens from it to be priestesses to the Minotaur, an office which brought them wealth and distinction. Usually Minos sent to Mycenae or Tiryns or Pylos or Argos or some other of the cities on the mainland of Greece, but occasionally to the Aegean Islands, or to Asia Minor, or to Sicily; once even to far-off Philistia. These victims were unarmed and usually the Minotaur killed them all in one afternoon without difficulty, since they had no hope of escape except by running and leaping. However, if any man of unusual agility and courage avoided death for a certain length of time, which was reckoned by a trickle of sand falling from a pierced pot, then the nymphs of Ariadne, as the priestesses to the Minotaur were named, came leaping over the barriers, naked except for their python-skin loin-straps, and rescued him from the bull's horns. The Ariadne nymphs had charge of the Minotaur from his calf days and could control him with their voices even when he bellowed and tossed his horns and pawed the sand in a fury. They demonstrated the power of the Triple Goddess by riding on his back, three or four at a time, by turning somer-saults over his head, by ringing his horns with garlands as he playfully charged them, by leaping over him with poles, and by many other pleasing tricks. To conclude the Spring Festival, a mystical act of love was cele-brated between Pasiphaë the Moon-Cow and Minos the Sun-Bull, which was publicly substantiated, after an intricate ritual dance, by the compa-nying of the Ariadne nymphs with the Bull men, who wore their horned disguises. The Minotaur was then ruthlessly slaughtered by the chief Priestess, and the blood that gushed from his throat was caught in a basin and stored in a two-eared jar, together with the tears that the nymphs shed at the death of their horned playmate. Drops of this blood, well diluted with water, were then sprinkled with the tail-feathers of a cuckoo upon the island's countless fruit-trees, to make them yield abundantly: a charm of great virtue.

'Daedalus was remarkable for his ingenuity. Many astonishing inven-tions are credited to him, including the art of casting statues in solid brass by the lost-wax method. It is even claimed that he made artificial wings which he could flap like a bird's and so sustain himself in the air. But what-ever the truth of that story, he did at least outwit the Minotaur in the bull-ring at Cnossos, even though he had drawn the first lot for entering the ring and was lame besides, and no longer a young man, and though none of the nineteen others who went in after him avoided the curved, searching horns. The Minotaur had learned to treat all men as his enemies, and to respect women only; besides, as he galloped out from the dark stall in which he had been enclosed without food or water, a silver pin was each time thrust into his shoulder from above, to stir his anger. Daedalus did not escape from him, as ill-informed balladists pretend, by flying home to Athens on artificial wings. Nor did he burrow into the sand of the bull-ring and hide himself; for the sand on the stone pavement was strewn only thickly enough to prevent the feet from slipping, and to drink up the spilt blood. He contrived another plan of escape.

'He was aware that in the sacred paddocks there were herms set up –

round-headed white pillars ordained by the Goddess as symbols of fertility
to induce vigour in the bulls. The bulls took no heed of these herms,
because they were the familiar furniture of their pasture. The device of
Daedalus was to simulate a herm. The palace room in which he was
confined was walled with white gypsum, a cornice of which he broke off
and powdered in his hands to whiten the gay-coloured clothes with which
he was supplied. He also whitened his hands and feet and face and hair,
and when he was lowered into the ring, just before the Minotaur was let
loose, he hobbled to an altar stone at the side, climbed upon it, covered his
head with a strip torn from his robe, and stood as still as any herm. The
bellowing Minotaur did not notice Daedalus and ran vainly around the
ring in search of a weak spot in the barrier. The smell of men enraged him
and he longed to deal death among the spectators. When the Ariadne
nymphs came running in, as usual, to spurn the corpse with their feet and
play their acrobatic tricks, they found Daedalus still alive. He was drawn
up into safety by the palace guards.

'By his sportiveness and many inventions Daedalus soon earned general
regard at the palace, and the favour of the Chief Priestess. He constructed
for her, among other strange toys, a lifelike statue of the Goddess for
use in the palace shrine, with limbs and eyes that moved, and also a
mechanical man called Talus who went through the motions of a soldier
on sentry-go.

'In the course of the ensuing year Minos grew jealous of Daedalus and
on some pretext or other unjustly confined him in the palace gaol.
However, Daedalus had no difficulty in escaping, with the Chief
Priestess's help, on the evening before the next Spring Festival. At the
same time he released a party of twenty dejected Pelasgians, among them
his sister's son Icarus, who were to have been brought into the bull-ring on
the following afternoon. He led them out through the labyrinthine corridors of the palace and down to the coast, where, as it happened, a new
warship lay ready to be launched at the royal ship-yard. He had fitted it
with a device of his own invention – a quick means of hoisting a sail to catch
the breeze – but the device had not yet been tried and this was the only
ship so rigged. Hitherto, the square Cretan sail had been suspended from
a yard permanently fitted to the mast, and sailors had to climb up the mast
to unhook the sail whenever the wind was contrary; and when the wind was
favourable it had to be hooked up again in the same laborious way. But
Daedalus had invented a method – that now in use throughout Greece –
by which the yard, with the sail attached, could be hauled up or down the
mast by a ring and pulley without any need of climbing, and moreover
could be slewed around slightly to take advantage of a side wind. Minos
had broken the law in permitting Daedalus to set foot on this ship, though
it had not yet been launched; for Daedalus was not a native Cretan.

'The fugitives found the ship-yard deserted, launched the ship by laying rollers underneath, hoisted the sail quickly and were soon driving out to sea, past the island of Dia. An alarm was raised by the watchmen at the harbour-mouth, and a few hours later Minos started out with his fleet in pursuit, expecting to overtake the Pelasgians as soon as the breeze failed, because they were not accustomed to rowing. But the well-rigged ship was already out of sight, and Minos soon found that Daedalus and his companions, before sailing, had sawn all the Cretan rudders half through, so that they broke off when a strain was put on them. He had to return to port and set the carpenters to work at making new rudders. Minos supposed that the fugitives would not dare to return to Attica, for fear of the anger of Theseus; perhaps they would make for Sicily, and there take refuge in one of the several sanctuary shrines of the Goddess.

'Daedalus, delayed by head-winds in the Ionian Gulf, sighted his pursuers just as he was approaching Sicily, and eluded them by boldly sailing through the Strait of Messina, between the rock of Scylla and the whirlpool Charybdis, and then making northward instead of southward. He shook off the pursuit and arrived safely at Cumae in Italy, where he scuttled his ship and dedicated the sail and cordage to the Goddess there. But his sister's son Icarus, the helmsman, had been drowned during the voyage, falling overboard in his sleep one early morning. The sea which engulfed him is since called the Icarian Sea in memory of him. Let no one, from an ignorant misreading of sacred frescoes (such as the one you see before you now), or carved chests, or engraved goblets, believe the foolish fable that Icarus wore wings which Daedalus had attached to his shoulders with wax, and flew too near the Sun so that the wax melted and he was drowned. The wings which they are shown as wearing symbolize the swiftness of their ship; and the melting of the wax in the Sardinian rites now enacted in honour of Daedalus refers only to the ingenious method of casting bronze which he invented.

'From Cumae, Daedalus and his companions travelled on foot through southern Italy and passed over into Sicily. At Agrigentum they were entertained by the Nymph of the shrine of the hero Cocalus, whom Daedalus presented with a small statue of the Goddess, of the same construction as the large one that he had made at Cnossos. She was delighted with the gift and promised him the Goddess's protection. The Cretan fleet, coasting around Sicily in fruitless search of Daedalus, was wrecked off Agrigentum by snake-tailed winds which the Nymph conjured from the earth against them; only Minos himself with a very few of his sailors escaped by swimming ashore. Finding Daedalus and his companions comfortably settled at the shrine of Cocalus, he grew excessively angry and ordered the Nymph, with threatening and unseemly language, to hand them over to him as fugitive slaves. The Nymph was compelled to avenge her own honour and that of the Goddess: instead of warm water, as Minos sat in the bath-tub, her women poured boiling oil or (some say) pitch over him.

'Daedalus repaired one of the wrecked Cretan vessels and boldly sailed to King Theseus at Athens with the news that Minos was dead, showing the seal-ring from his thumb as evident proof. It was a great red carnelian stone, carved with a seated Minotaur and the double-axe of power. Theseus had visited Cnossos, some years before, and competed in the athletic part of the Festival, winning the boxing contest; he considered Cnossos the most wonderful city in the world. When he handled the ring and drew it experimentally upon his thumb, his heart knocked against his ribs for pride and exultation. Daedalus, observing this, privately undertook that if Theseus spared his life and that of his fellow-fugitives he would lead him to the conquest of Crete. Theseus accepted the offer.

'Under the direction of Daedalus a fleet of warships was secretly built, far from any public road, which were swifter and more conveniently rigged than those of the Cretans. No Cretans were allowed to hear of this work. When the new Minos, whose name was Deucalion, sent to Theseus demanding the surrender of Daedalus, Theseus replied that his cousin Daedalus, having been spared by the Minotaur, was a free man and had expiated his original crime of homicide: he was guilty of no other misdeed, so far as was known. The Nymph of Cocalus, Theseus said, had killed Minos on her own account, and Daedalus had taken no part in that atrocious act. It would therefore be unjust to surrender his kinsman to Cretan vengeance as if he were a runaway slave; but let Minos bring proof that Daedalus had participated in any other crime and he would then reconsider the matter. Having thus lulled the suspicions of Minos, Theseus gathered his fleet and sailed to Crete by a roundabout westerly route, taking Daedalus with him as his navigator.

'The Cretans, hitherto the undisputed masters of the seas, had for centuries felt themselves so secure against invasion that even their principal cities remained unwalled. When the watchmen of the coast saw the Greek fleet approaching from the west they concluded that the ships which had sailed to Sicily had not, after all, been sunk, but had been own far out of their course and had now returned, beyond hope. They signalled the news to Cnossos, the populace of which flocked joyfully down to the coast to welcome their comrades; but found themselves deceived. Out from the ships leaped armed Greeks and made a butchery of the holiday crowd, and ran inland to attack the palace. They sacked and burned it, killing Minos and all the principal Bull men. Then they sailed at once to the other harbours of Crete and seized the rest of the island's warships and sacked the remaining towns. But Theseus did not dare affront the Triple Goddess Pasiphaë, or molest any of her priestesses: he entered into a firm alliance with the Chief Priestess, by which she was confirmed in her government of Crete. Then the office of Minos was abolished and the mastery of the seas, which the Cretans had enjoyed for two thousand years, passed suddenly into the hands of the Greeks and their allies.

'Such, at least, is the story that has come down to us, from a succession of trustworthy poets.'

Orpheus then put his lyre between his knees and sang, as he played, of Theseus and the princess whom once he courted and deserted upon the island of Naxos:

High on his figured couch beyond the waves
He dreams, in dream recalling her set walk
Down paths of oyster-shell bordered with flowers
And down the shadowy turf beneath the vine.
He sighs: 'Deep sunk in my erroneous past
She haunts the ruins and the ravaged lawns.'

Yet still unharmed it stands, the regal house
Crooked with age and overtopped by pines
Where first he wearied of her constancy.
And with a surer foot she goes than when
Dread of his hate was thunder in the air,
When the pines agonized with flaws of wind
And flowers glared up at her with frantic eyes.
Of him, now all is done, she never dreams
But calls a living blessing down upon
What he would have mere rubble and rank grass;
Playing the queen to nobler company.

CHAPTER TWENTY-FOUR

KING PHINEUS AND THE HARPIES

Early on the third day the *Argo* sailed off to the northward with a favourable breeze. Aboard her were several Mariandynians of rank, rescued from the Bebrycians, and among them the sister of King Lycus, whom Amycus had made his concubine; for Jason had offered to take them home by sea to their city, which lies on the southern coast of the Black Sea.

They made the mouth of the Bosphorus by noon of the same day; but Argus, Tiphys, and Nauplius, the three most experienced sailors aboard, agreed that the current was dangerously strong. Let the wind blow one day or two longer, they said, and then the passage might be attempted.

Calaïs and Zetes told Jason: 'If you care, meanwhile, to land on the Thracian shore, we promise you a pleasant reception at the Court of our stepfather, King Phineus of the Thynians, whose name we heard you mention to our late host. He rules the whole hilly region of eastern Thrace as far northward as the foot-hills of the Haemos range.'

Jason gladly accepted their suggestion, unaware of the dangers of the adventure to which he was committing himself. The ship ran westward for a couple of miles to where there is a slight break in the line of hills which enclose the Sea of Marmora on all sides, and where the current from the Bosphorus does not tug at shipping. Anchoring near a red cliff, and leaving a guard aboard consisting chiefly of Greeks from the Peloponnese and from the Islands, Jason went ashore with Calaïs and Zetes, Echion the herald, Orpheus, and all the Thessalians, to whom the Thracian language was intelligible.

'King Phineus will still be quartered at Bathynios, his winter capital, which lies beside a lake at about an hour's journey inland from here,' said Zetes. 'He is not accustomed to move up to Salmydessos, his summer capital, until the first figs ripen.' Calaïs and Zetes, who had hitherto disclosed as little as possible about their private affairs, now told Jason, as they went, why they had left Thrace for their recent tour of Greece. It had been partly to learn the arts and customs of their mother's land – Oreithyia had been an Athenian; partly to enter upon any inheritance that might be due to them by the laws of mother-right which still ruled in Attica – but in this they had been disappointed; partly also to avoid the society of their father's new wife. For King Phineus, who was blind, had lately married the daughter of his royal neighbour, the Scythian king who had seized the high land on the southern bank of the Lower Danube; she was named Idaea and proved to have none of the racial virtues of those blameless, milk-drinking Scythians. 'She is, in fact, arrogant, cruel, sly, and lecherous,' said Zetes.

'And to deal honestly with you,' said Calaïs, 'our stepfather as good as banished us when we reproached her, in his presence, for the shame that she had brought on his house. But he is blind and she has infatuated him by her pretended sweetness. He thinks her the best wife in the world.'

'She has a son by him,' added Zetes, 'if indeed the captain of her Scythian bodyguard is not the father of the brat, on whom she clearly intends to confer the kingdom, though we are the heirs-at-law. Her Scythians terrorize the palace guards and the Thynians in general.'

'I cannot venture another step forward with you,' said Jason. 'Why did you not reveal all these circumstances to me before we started out? Now that we have lost Hercules, we are not strong enough to interfere in the domestic politics of every city or kingdom that lies on our route. The chief and almost the only purpose of our voyage is to recover the Golden Fleece. I refuse to be deflected from it.'

'You did not *lose* Hercules,' said Peleus. 'You deliberately marooned him.'

Echion intervened. 'Most noble Jason,' he said, 'you must remember that before our departure from Iolcos all we who have the honour to style ourselves Argonauts gave one another solemn assurances of mutual aid. Since Calaïs and Zetes consented at that time to assist you in your hazardous quest of the Fleece – which, after all, was no direct concern of theirs, for they were not Minyans – it is only just that you should now do whatever lies in your power to make peace between their stepfather and them, as it were oiling the hot hub of a chariot wheel where it screams against the unyielding axle-end.'

The others supported Echion, so on they all went. When they had approached to within half a mile of the palace, a cavalcade was seen riding out westwards beyond the lake. Sharp-sighted Lynceus reported that it consisted of about twenty slant-eyed, bald-headed archers, mounted on sturdy ponies, led by a woman in a coarse black smock and trousers with a jewelled belt about her middle and an embroidered scarf about her head. They were going forward at a fast trot, accompanied by a pack of mastiffs.

'Good. Let us wait here a while until my stepmother and her Scythian guards are out of sight,' said Calaïs. 'But, Orpheus – since you are yourself a Thracian – will you go forward alone as though you were a travelling minstrel and amuse the palace guards and servants in the courtyard? If you do so, the rest of us will pass quietly into the palace by a side-gate. Zetes and I will then have the pleasure of addressing our father Phineus without fear of interruption.'

Nobody in this world could long remain insensible to music which sounded from the lyre of Orpheus, and when now he marched into the palace court, thrumming a lively jig, the sentries laid down their weapons, the cooks left the meat to burn on the spits, the washerwomen abandoned the linen on the flat stones by the lake-side, and all indiscriminately began dancing together in the open court. Caps of fox-skin flew into the air.

The party of Argonauts, stealing softly into the palace, were guided by Calaïs and Zetes to the dining-hall. As they opened a side-door their nostrils were at once affronted by a disgusting stench, a mixture of fresh dung and putrid flesh; and, inside, a marvellously strange sight assailed their eyes. King Phineus was seated before a long gilt-legged table loaded with dishes, among which a covey of twenty or thirty kites were quarrelsomely feeding. Every now and then, with a flutter of wings, another kite would fly in through an open window and join in the feast. They were tearing with their sharp beaks at lumps of offal and putrid flesh laid in the valuable dishes. Though Phineus constantly clapped his hands and shouted at them to begone, they took no notice of him at all but continued greedily at their disgusting repast. Though a man of not more than fifty years of age, Phineus had the emaciated and yellow face of a great-grandfather in his last winter of life.

With one accord the Argonauts made a rush for the table, yelling loudly; and the birds flew away out of the window, first snatching from the dishes whatever they could carry off. Calaïs and Zetes motioned to Echion to speak to the King on their behalf, not wishing to reveal their presence until they had heard his explanation of what had just occurred.

Echion advanced, cleared his throat, and addressed Phineus in his most eloquent style.

'Majesty, I am the herald Echion, an adept of the heralds' college of Mount Cyllene, son of the God Hermes. I believe that I have the honour to address Phineus, King of the famous Thynians whose land extends north-westward from swift-flowing Bosphorus almost to the thousand mouths of tremendous Danube. Majesty, you will (I hope) pardon this unannounced entry, but a travelling musician has just struck up a miserable jig in the courtyard and distracted the attention of all your loyal guards and servitors. They refused to pay the least attention to my comrades and myself when we presented ourselves, and therefore, rather than miss the pleasure of saluting you at our first arrival, we have found our way in by ourselves.'

'Whose herald are you?' asked Phineus, in quavering tones.

Echion replied: 'I represent a party of noble Thessalians come on a trading voyage to your hospitable land. Iolcos is our home port, and we carry a cargo of decorated pottery, white horse-hides and hanks of woollen yarn (dyed in wonderful colours, and ready for the loom), which we hope to trade against the valuable products of your rich land.'

'They are of no use to me,' said miserable Phineus, 'of no use at all. But I would give you all the golden rings and chains that still remain to me in exchange for one little piece of clean bread or a lump of figs or a slice of cheese that has not yet been befouled by these filthy, woman-faced Harpies. Ah, but what is the use of talking? Even if you had such a gift for me, the Harpies would fly back at once and snatch it from my fingers. It is now many months since I had anything clean to eat. For as soon as the rich and tasty meats are brought in, down fly the Harpies through the window and either snatch or spoil them all. My loving wife Idaea has tried every possible means of ridding me of these woman-faced pests, but without the least success. They are sent by some god whom I have unwittingly offended.'

Echion asked: 'If I may be so bold as to ask this question – how do you, a blind man, know what appearance these Harpies wear?'

Phineus replied: 'My loving wife Idaea has often described to me their lean, haggish faces, their withered breasts, and their huge bat-like wings. Besides, I have other senses too, especially ears and nose, and when I hear their cackling laughter and whispering and obscene cries, and the rattle of dishes as they feed, and feel the sough of their wings, and smell their putrid breath and the horrible ordure with which they bespatter the room – why, I need no eyes to see them plainly, and am for once content in my blindness.'

Echion said: 'Gracious King, someone is playing a loathsome trick upon you. Ask any man of our company what he has seen, and what he still sees, and he will tell you the same as I. Those were no woman faced Harpies, but simple kites; and they were not tearing at tasty meats but at lumps of offal and putrid flesh set before them as a lure. Nor did they befoul your table, as you suppose; for this had clearly been done beforehand by your shameless pages who cast the shovellings of the pig-sty and jakes into little heaps here and there on your table, and tainted your dish and cup. As for the cackling laughter and whispering, that doubtless proceeded from certain female slaves concerned in the plot. If your loving wife Idaea has told you that your visitors are Harpies, she is either very wicked or completely mad.'

Peleus, Acastus, Jason, and the rest confirmed Echion's statement, but Phineus found it hard to believe them. He continually reverted to his tale of the Harpies. At last Peleus took from his wallet a piece of barley-bread and another of sheep's cheese, and put them into the King's hand, saying: 'Eat, eat, Majesty. This is wholesome food and nobody will snatch it from you. The kites and the wicked servants are chased away and will not return.'

Phineus tasted doubtfully and then began to eat with relish. Jason pressed on him a lump of figs and a honey-cake or two, and filled a goblet with unmixed wine from a leather bottle at his girdle. The blood flooded back into the King's emaciated cheeks. Then suddenly he began to beat his breast, tear his matted hair and bitterly lament his own credulity, declaring that at last, but too late, he understood how cruelly he had been imposed upon. Why had he ever believed a word of what Idaea told him? Why had he refused to listen to the accusations of his stepsons? They had warned him that she was taking advantage of his blindness to deceive him, but he had stopped his ears against them. In his infatuation he had banished the two eldest, Calaïs and Zetes, and for all he knew their bones might be whitening at the bottom of the sea. The two youngest had lately been accused by Idaea of attempting to rape her in the palace bath; they were now imprisoned in the dungeon, a bronze-doored burial chamber. Guards flogged them daily with whips of bulls' hide until they should confess their sin and plead for pardon.

'But what can I do? What can I do?' he cried in broken tones. 'Idaea rules here, not I; she keeps the prison keys, not I. She commands the guards, not I. I am wholly in her power. Kind Thessalians, in return for your delicious meal, pray take whatever dishes of silver and gold you may fancy, and then go off quickly by the way you came, leaving me here in my distress. I deserve all that I have suffered because of my follies and do not wish to involve you in my wicked wife's vengeance. Alas for my stepsons, Calaïs and Zetes! I charge you, strangers' seek them out wherever they may be; give them my blessing and ask them to forgive me in their hearts for the wrong that I did them. Yet it will be too late for them to deliver their brothers from death under the whip, or myself from slow starvation.'

At this Calaïs and Zetes revealed themselves to Phineus, and the scene of recognition and reconciliation drew tears from every eye. Then Peleus and Coronus ran hastily down to the dungeon chamber and broke open the doors with blows of a heavy hammer. They released the young men, who were nearly dead of hunger and their daily whippings.

From them Calaïs and Zetes learned which of the palace servants were still faithful to Phineus and which were unfaithful. They went out into the courtyard and signalled to Orpheus for the music to cease. Then, rallying the faithful, they seized the unfaithful and sent them down to the prison chamber under escort. Soon the whole palace was in their hands. To be brief, Calaïs next contrived an ambush against the return of Queen Idaea and her bodyguard; into which they presently fell, and were disarmed and taken alive. Idaea was not in any way punished by Phineus for her treachery and spite; he sent her back to her father, the Scythian king, with a plain account of what he had suffered at her hands. The Scythian, who was a just man, as most Scythians are, admired Phineus for the forbearance that he had shown. In token of his admiration he put Idaea to death; but the news of this did not reach Thynia until the *Argo* was well on her way again.

Phineus regarded the Argonauts as his deliverers. He tried to dissuade them from their quest, of which they told him in confidence, but when he could not, he feasted them well and gave them an itinerary of the southern route to Colchis, complete with details of winds, currents, landmarks, and anchorages; and promised them a warm welcome at Salmydessos on their return voyage. He grieved that Calaïs and Zetes were set on remaining aboard the *Argo*, but did not attempt to restrain them when he learned that they were bound by an oath to do so. His younger sons soon set his kingdom into order for him; and the sacred kites, when they were again fed, as formerly, under the meeting-tree of the Kite men (a Thynian fraternity in which Calaïs and Zetes were enrolled), lost the habit, which Idaea had inculcated in them, of swooping in through the windows of the palace dining-hall.

To the question, why did Idaea not murder Phineus outright, rather than plague him as she did? the answer customarily given is: 'No Scythian woman ever murders her husband, for fear of the terrible fate that would be hers in the Underworld.' However, she hoped, by giving Phineus only tainted food, to reduce him to such a lamentable condition that he would end his life voluntarily and not suspect her as the cause of his distress.

CHAPTER TWENTY-FIVE

THE PASSAGE OF THE BOSPHORUS

'The Bosphorus,' Phineus had announced, 'measures some sixteen miles in length from sea to sea, and resembles a rushing river rather than a strait, especially where the channel narrows to less than half a mile from bank to bank: for it receives the outflow of a huge sea nearly a thousand miles long and five hundred miles broad, which is fed by several enormous rivers. O my friends, when the melting snows of the great northern steppes, or of the Caucasian mountains, swell each of those rivers to many times its usual size, and when violent north-easterly gales drive the tremendous mass of waters before them into the Bosphorus you can imagine what a cataract roars down the Narrows! Fortunately the worst season is not yet here and the south-west wind which has now blown for two days will have abated the force of the current. Seize the chance without delay, and may the Gods grant that you win through before the wind swings about again, as by the look of the sky I fear it will soon do.

'The current runs most swiftly in the middle of the strait, and on either side you will find eddies and counter-currents. Remember that unless you make use of these counter-currents your oarsmen's task will be an impossible one; remember, too, that the projecting points of the abrupt and twisted channel provide shelter under their lee, where the current is deflected, and allow you to regain your breath for a renewed effort. But your master and helmsman must be men of the coolest judgement, otherwise you will assuredly be swept against the rocks.

'Begin your ascent from the eastern side, where the coast is bold and you will find deep water close inshore; but beware the entrance to the Narrows, where a shoal fronts the mouth of a mountain torrent and extends off-shore for a hundred paces. Here, as you venture into midstream, your vessel will be whirled about like a chip of wood. Let your helmsman keep her prow pointed straight into the current; and do you put your trust in the Gods and bend to your oars. When you have passed through the Narrows, where the pace of the current today will, I reckon, be that of a man walking very fast, you will find that the strait opens out again, with slack water on either side; on the western shore is Therapeia, a little bay where you may anchor safely, if you wish, for a half-way rest.

Only once more does the passage become difficult; and there lies the greatest danger of all – the Clashing Rocks. You will meet them about two hundred paces off-shore at a narrow point distinguished by a grove of white cypress-trees. As you sail with difficulty along the western side of the strait, where the water is slacker than on the eastern, you will find the counter-current so capricious that your eyes will be tricked. It will seem as though the dark rocks, some of which are awash, are not fixed to the bottom of the channel but swing about and attempt to crush the vessel between themselves and the shore. But let your helmsman fix his gaze on some steady mark across the strait and steer towards it.

'Once you have passed the Clashing Rocks, you may lift up your hearts, for you will have only three more miles to go, and these present no great difficulty. Unless the wind suddenly shifts, you will soon be riding at anchor in the Black Sea, or beached on some pleasant strand.'

They carefully memorized these and other instructions and repeated them to one another as they sailed up the first reach of the strait, not rowing but conserving their strength for the struggle at the Narrows. The water teemed with tunny and swordfish, and the rocks as they passed by were overhung with caper-bushes of a bright green colour.

When they approached the Narrows and took to their oars, Orpheus tuned up for a new song, a sharp satire upon the ship's company, designed to turn away the anger of any jealous god or goddess who might seize this opportunity of injuring them. The chorus went:

> Did ever so strange a company
> Of tall young champions take to sea?

In it he made a jest upon each of the Argonauts in turn. He sung of Lynceus, whose sight was so keen that he could look through an oak and read the thoughts of a beetle crawling on the other side; of Butes, who knew all his bees by name and lineage and wept if one of them did not return to the hive, having perhaps been eaten by a swallow; of Admetus, to whom Apollo came as a menial, but who could think of no better orders for the God than 'Bring me sausages, if you please'; of Euphemus the swimmer, who challenged a tunny to a swimming match around the island of Cythera and would have won but that the fish cheated; of Calaïs and Zetes, who ran so fast that they always arrived at their goal a little before the word 'Go', and who once chased a covey of Harpies down the Sea of Marmora and across the Aegean and Greece to the Strophades Islands; of Periclymenus the wizard, born in an eclipse, who could change at will into any beast or insect that he fancied, but one day got stuck in the shape of an ass's foal too young to remember how to return to human shape; of Mopsus and Idmon, who preferred the conversation of birds to that of any human being, even of each other; of Iphitus, who painted on the interior walls of a house in Phocis so lively a picture of a stag hunt that quarry, hounds, and huntsmen all ran off in the night and disappeared through the smoke-hole in the roof; of Jason, who was so handsome that women fainted at the sight of him and had to be restored with the smell of burning feathers. But Orpheus was careful to satirize himself among the rest: he told how, in an Arcadian valley, a great number of forest trees pulled themselves up by the roots and shuffled along behind him as he thoughtlessly played *Come to a better Country, Come to Thrace.*

These jests carried them safely through the worst of the Narrows, though at one point, even with the most vigorous rowing, it needed three verses of the song to help them gain a hundred paces. They were trembling with their exertions and nearly dead when Tiphys steered them into Therapeia Bay. They cast anchor and refreshed themselves with wine, cheese, and strips of pickled venison which Phineus had given them; but when the wind began to fail they cut short their meal and continued their passage for fear of worse things. But first, to lighten the ship, they disembarked the Mariandynians whom they had rescued from Amycus, and agreed to meet them that same evening, the Gods permitting, on the shores of the Black Sea, to the east of the entrance of the Bosphorus

They sailed slowly up the broader part of the strait, but the wind had died away altogether when they came in view of the cypress headland and from the hissing noise of water they knew that the Clashing Rocks were near. Their mouths were dry with fear and their limbs twitched but Tiphys kept them on their course and Orpheus played cheerfully to them. The current in mid-stream ran at a terrible rate and the eddies close inshore twisted the *Argo* about crazily. The oarsmen saw a heron in flight upstream towards them and gaspingly cheered it, because the bird is sacred to the Goddess Athena; but as it flapped overhead at mast height the cheer changed to a groan of dismay. They faltered in their stroke and lost headway, for a sparrowhawk had stooped at the heron and missed its mark only by a very little. A tail feather fluttered down and was whirled away by the current.

The hawk soared to strike again, and it would have been the worst possible omen had the heron been killed. Phalerus, whose oar Jason had taken at Therapeia because he had not yet recovered from the blow on his hip that a Bebrycian had dealt him, seized up his bow, fitted an arrow to the string and let fly. Down into the boat tumbled the sparrowhawk pierced through the heart, and the heron flew safely on towards the Black Sea.

Seldom was an augury so speedily justified as this. Tiphys, seeing one of the Clashing Rocks uncovered by the tide at some distance away towards mid-stream, judged that he was steering a safe course, but the noise of water had confused him. The sudden tug of an eddy whirled the *Argo* about, and there followed a grinding crash and a shock that made every one aboard think that the voyage had ended untimely and all was lost.

Nevertheless, Orpheus continued with his song, Tiphys regained control of the ship, and they rowed staunchly on, their oars bending like bows from the force of the current. The salt water did not wet their feet, as at every moment they expected it to do; and Phalerus leaning over the side to see what was amiss, shouted that they had merely fouled the base of their stern ornament against a sunken rock. Part had been broken off, much in the same way as the heron had lost her tail feather; but the skin of the boat was not pierced.

Then, lifting up their hearts, they forged ahead, and soon the Black Sea stretched before them. They rounded the eastern headland and passed the white chalk cliff which had been mentioned by King Phineus in his instructions; then they beached the *Argo* a mile or two to the east of it, where yellow cliffs are intersected by small valleys fringed with narrow strips of sand.

No sooner were they ashore than the North-East Wind began to blow and presently rolled monstrous waves down the strait. They laughed, shouted, and pelted one another with handfuls of sand to express their relief and joy. The Athenians, Argus, Butes, and Phalerus, bought sheep from the Bithynian fishermen who lived in the valley near by, presently sacrificing them to Athena in gratitude for her warning sign; but the three sons of Poseidon, not to be surpassed in piety, marked out a plot of sacred ground in honour of their father the Rock-Cleaver, and bought two red bulls for sacrifice to him.

At this beach they were rejoined by the Mariandynians. Here, also Idas rudely revived many jests of Orpheus, especially jeering at Periclymenus the wizard, who had so far not given the Argonauts the least proof of the strange powers generally attributed to him. Periclymenus then exhibited his skill, after first wandering off to collect implements and accessories and calling upon his father Poseidon to grant him inspiration.

Periclymenus displayed a white pebble and a black pebble, and covered each of them with a cockle-shell, in the sight of all; when the shells were removed, the white pebble and the black had changed places.

Next, he took a nut and made magical passes and drove it into the knee of Idas, so that it disappeared without a scar. Then he ordered the nut to grow, which it did, and caused Idas intolerable pain as it put out roots and sprouted, until Idas begged him with tears to remove the growing nut, and asked pardon for his insolence. Periclymenus relented, drawing out the nut-tree by the roots from below and displaying it to the company, with a little blood still clinging to the green shoot.

Next, he turned a stone into a small fish, merely by rubbing it with his hands under a cloth and made a goblet of sea-water boil over without any fire. He even spoke of cutting off Jason's head and bringing him to life again; but Jason would not submit himself to the ordeal, though all his comrades begged him to show his courage and faith.

Last of all, Periclymenus amused and mystified them by throwing his voice about, so that at one moment it seemed as though the fish which had formerly been a stone declaimed a verse of the satiric song – the very one which related to Periclymenus; and at the next it seemed as though Hylas cried merrily from the other side of the rock where they were sitting: 'Here I am again, Argonauts! I have grown a beard since I saw you last and fathered two fine boys.' But nobody was there.

CHAPTER TWENTY-SIX

A VISIT TO THE MARIANDYNIANS

The Black Sea is in outline like the shape of a bent Scythian bow with the string drawn up towards the north, and differs from the Mediterranean in a number of ways. It receives the water of a number of huge rivers, such as the Danube, Dniester, Boug, Dnieper, and Don, each of them greater than any river, except the Nile, that flows into the Mediterranean; and contains no single island of any considerable size. The northern parts are so cold that, incredible though it may seem, even the sea-water freezes, and the great Sea of Azov, which is connected with the Black Sea by a narrow strait, is often frozen two foot deep in winter. The largest rivers of all flow in from the north and north-west, greatly swollen in the spring and summer by melting snow; then their turbid waters move in a mass towards the Bosphorus, where, not being able to enter all at once, they pour in a current along the southern coast of the sea as far as the Caucasian mountains. The whole sea is subject to sudden fogs which blot out all sight of land, and its currents and winds often cause vessels to roll and pitch in a horrible manner even in fine weather; but it abounds in great fish, such as tunny, flounder, and sturgeon, and nowhere are its shores fringed with inhospitable desert sands.

From the middle of the northern coast juts out the Crimean peninsula where the savage Taurians live, who delight in human sacrifice and fix the heads of strangers upon stakes about their houses. Behind the Taurians live the Cimmerians, a small, dark, excitable people, famous for their singing and valiant in war, but addicted to sodomy; and both to the east and west of these Cimmerians live the long-lived, equitable Scythians, who have no homes but their wheeled carts, drink mares' milk and are wonderful archers. Behind these, again, live the black-cloaked cannibal Finns; and the Neurians, many of whom become were-wolves by night; and the hunting Budinians, who paint themselves with red and blue dye, build stockaded wooden cities, and wear beaver-skin caps and tunics; and the Issedonians, who esteem it an act of piety to eat the dead flesh of their parents and make goblets from their skulls; and a bald-headed priestly tribe, the Argippians, who ride on white horses, carry no arms, and feed on milk curdled with cherry juice into a thick paste. On the western coast live the Thynians and Bithynians, who speak the Thracian language; and the lusty beer-swilling Goths; and the agricultural Scythians; and the Brygian fishermen, who wear sealskin breeches; and the tattooed, gold-getting Agathyrsians, who still worship the Triple Goddess with primitive simplicity. On the eastern coast live the Colchians and the mercantile Apsilaeans and the Royal Scythians. On the southern coast live tribes which will be described in order as the *Argo* makes her way past their territory or puts in at their harbours; this southern coast is everywhere backed with high hills and has a climate equal to that of Greece.

On the third day after their entrance into the Black Sea, the Argonauts set sail again, continuing through choppy water but without adventure until towards evening they sighted the headland of Calpe and, close inshore, a rocky islet no more than eighty paces in length, and the height of a man above the level of the sea. On this island – nearly the biggest that they were to see during the whole of their remaining voyage to Colchis – they went ashore and sacrificed a kid to Apollo. The blood of the kid was caught in the hollow of Jason's shield and all dipped their fingers in it, renewing their oaths of loyal comradeship as they did so, and swearing never to desert the ship. Then they poured the blood upon the sand, crying together: 'So may our own blood be spilt if we break this oath.' This ceremony seemed necessary, now that they had come into a sea heaving with perpetual menace and untravelled before by any of them. They also danced the round dance called The Crane to music played by Orpheus, singing:

> Hail Phoebus, Lord of Healing,
>   Phoebus, ever fair…

and Atalanta allowed herself to be reconciled to Meleager again. The Crane was sacred to Artemis, but Apollo and she, being brother and sister, had many emblems and attributes in common.

The Argonauts remained all night on this islet and at dawn a fine westerly wind sprang up, which brought them on the following evening to the boundaries of the Mariandynians, who are a sort of Thracians. They sailed past what seemed to them a sea of trees washing the low hills, and past the mouths of three rivers: the muddy, rushing Sangarios, the Hypios with uneven banks, and the broad Lycos. Soon after leaving the Lycos astern they rounded the Acherusian headland and, recalling the advice of King Phineus, anchored beyond it in a bay protected from the wind by an enormous and inaccessible cliff crowned with plane-trees.

At the head of this bay stands the chief city of the Mariandynians, remarkable for the beauty of its orchards, fields, and gardens. Barley, millet, sesame, and all kinds of vegetables grow in abundance here, with vines, fig-trees, hazels, pears, and all else but olives; for the soil is too rich for the olive. The cliff slopes inland gradually to the valley of the Lycos, and on a hollow glen near the summit is a chasm, one of the main entrances to the Underworld. Here the dangerous stream of Acheron bursts out and flows through a ravine down the cliff face; it is icy-cold water, and a glistening rime frosts the stones at the mouth of the chasm. Nobody has ever descended into this horrible place but only Hercules: he went down a mile or more, years later, at the orders of King Eurystheus, to convey a complaint to the God Hades in person about the ill-treatment that certain distinguished ghosts were said to be receiving at his hands.

King Lycus gave the Argonauts a royal welcome as soon as he learned that his sister and comrades had been rescued by them from a weary captivity among the Bebrycians. Jason, Pollux, and the rest were obliged to refuse more than half the rich gifts that he heaped on them, since the *Argo* was a warship and had no space for cargo.

When they were all seated at a lavish banquet prepared for them which continued, course after course, for twelve whole hours, Lycus asked Jason: 'Tell me, princely saviour of my country, are you acquainted with a Greek champion named Hercules of Tiryns? He is seven foot tall, wears a lion-skin, and is the most wonderful man in the whole world. Some years ago, in the reign of my father, Dascylus, he passed this way on foot from the land of the Amazons, carrying with him as a prize of war the girdle of Queen Hippolyte. My father was at war with the Bebrycians at the time and Hercules offered to subdue them for him, which he did without much trouble, killing their King Mygdon, the brother of Amycus, and seizing all their northern territory, for nothing could stop Hercules when he began swinging his brass-bound club around his head. My wife's younger brother was killed in the course of the fighting, and we held funeral games for him; at these Hercules boxed with our champion, Titias, and not knowing his own strength, crushed in his skull. He was naturally remorseful and offered as a penance to subdue any other hostile tribe that my father chose to name, and he did so – the Henetians to the eastward of us. He would take no reward, either. The Henetians are the obstinate remnants of the great people whom long ago Pelops led into Greece.'

Jason, speaking in an undertone, said: 'King Lycus, this same Hercules was our shipmate for the first part of our voyage, but we lost him by ill luck a few days ago. When we went ashore by the outfall of the river Cios, his adopted son Hylas took the opportunity to run off from him, the ungrateful little wretch, with a jingling wallet at his side; he hoped as we suppose, to reach Troy by the inland track from the Ascanian Lake and thence take ship to Lemnos, where he has a sweetheart named Iphinoë. Hercules did not notice the loss of Hylas for some hours, but then rushed off in a passion of grief to search for him. We followed along the road to Troy for some miles, but he would not heed our shouts and soon outdistanced us; so reluctantly we returned. Calaïs and Zetes yonder, and Tiphys our helmsman, suggested that we should continue our voyage, but how could we desert a comrade? King Admetus of Pherae stressed this point with a warmth that I much admired, and so did Acastus, son of Pelias, and Peleus the Myrmidon. However, the majority were against us, and in the end we had to yield to them. We heaved up our anchor-stones and sailed on, sick at heart. Yet I do not wish to blame either Tiphys or Calaïs or Zetes for this decision. I believe that some god must have made them his mouthpiece.'

Lycus sympathized with Jason: the commander of an expedition, he said, must often make decisions distasteful to him.

Jason confided to Lycus the true reason for the *Argo*'s appearance in the Black Sea, and Lycus applauded his daring and piety. He offered to lend Jason the services of his son Dascylus, who would sail in the ship as far as the river Thermodon, half-way to Colchis, and introduce him, if need be, to all the chieftains and kings of the coast.

Jason accepted this offer with pleasure, and the *Argo* would have sailed the next morning with a fair wind from the west, but for a cruel accident. Idmon, Peleus, and Idas strolled out together by the raised banks of the river Lycus, hoping to walk off the surfeits of their banquet, and Idmon began telling them of an ominous dream that had come to him in the night, of two snakes coupling, which is the unluckiest dream of all. Idas, who set no store by dreams, was mocking at Idmon, when there came a sudden stir among the reeds, and a huge wild boar, which had been wallowing in the mud, charged out upon them. Idas and Peleus sprang aside, but Idmon stood still, unable to move. The boar with its curved white tusks drove at his right thigh, above the scarlet buskin that he wore, and ripped it open. Blood spurted from the wound, and Idmon fell forward with a cry. Peleus hurled a javelin at the boar as it ran back towards the reeds, but with no truer aim than when he had been confronted with the great boar of Calydon. He shouted with vexation, and the boar turned again. This time it charged at Idas, who received it on the point of his spear, aiming between neck and shoulder, and killed it instantly. Idas had often vexed Peleus by his boasts; but the truth was, his spearmanship was unequalled in Greece and has never been excelled to this day. They left the boar lying and hastened to Idmon's side, but could not stop the flow of blood. Mopsus came running up with his vulneraries, which were the juice of mistletoe; a decoction of golden-rod, wound-wort, and yarrow; and clean turpentine. But he came too late. Idmon grew deathly pale and died speechless in the arms of Idas. It was clear that the boar, which had never been seen before in this valley, was no ordinary one; and the Argonauts concluded that it was animated by the ghost of the dead Dolionian, Megabrontes, whom Idmon by mistake had omitted to appease. For the badge of Megabrontes had been the Boar.

King Lycus himself took part in the funeral rites, which lasted for three days. The Argonauts comforted one another with the reminder that Idmon was an initiate of the Great Ones, and would become a ruler among the dead. Flocks of sheep were slaughtered at his tomb and the Mariandynians raised a lofty barrow over him; and on the barrow they planted a wild-olive tree, the leaves of which same ancient tree, laid beneath a pillow, still ensure true dreams.

The Argonauts were again about to sail when they lost another of their comrades, Tiphys the helmsman, who died of a wasting disease, just as his grandfather and father had died before him. A curse had lain on the family ever since the grandfather of Tiphys had accidentally cut down a sacred oak; an Oracle decreed that no male of the family should live longer than the oak had lived, which was forty-nine years. Mopsus administered to dying Tiphys a spoonful of broth made from the heart of a shrew-mouse and the liver of a field-mouse; but even this could not save him, though he rallied wonderfully for a few hours.

Again they mourned and lamented for three days. They raised a second barrow of equal height with the first and began to say to one another: 'The entrance to the Underworld is not far away. Who dies next? Who is the third?' For it was known that such deaths always go by threes. But Great Ancaeus found a rat aboard the *Argo*, nibbling at the stores, and killed it with a stone, and cried out: 'Comrades, let us mourn for the third Argonaut who has died!' This restored them to cheerfulness. But a contention arose, some saying that Nauplius should be helmsman in the place of Tiphys, and some urging the claims of Iphitus, who had for some years been master of a trading vessel; but Jason awarded the post to Great Ancaeus, and this satisfied nearly everyone.

On the eighth day they continued their voyage with a westerly breeze. A recent north-easterly gale had made the sea choppy. They coasted past the mouths of two more rivers, the dark Billaeos, where the beaches are black with coals, washed from the Coaly Headland; and the Parthenios, or river of garlands, so called because of the many flowery meadows through which it flows. Then coming to Henete, famous for boxwood, for wild mules that reproduce their kind, and for the Henetian tree-alphabet, older than the Cadmean, they anchored to leeward of a double peninsula jutting into the sea, and close to an islet with bold yellow shores. But the Henetians fled when they saw the *Argo* approach, and had not reappeared when she sailed on at dawn the next morning.

Next, they passed by a broken and forbidding coast and came to Cape Carambis, a lofty promontory bordered with red cliffs, where Dascylus told them to expect a change of wind; however, it continued westerly. They sailed on all night until by next morning they found themselves half-way to Sinope, sliding past a bluff coast with barren rocks, the land of the Paphlagonians; and since the wind showed no sign of slackening they sailed on all day. At nightfall they anchored in the lee of a reef of rocks, some of which showed above water, a few miles short of Lepte, the great promontory which divides the southern coast of the Black Sea into two shallow gulfs. In three days and two nights they had travelled some two hundred and fifty miles, not relying on the wind and the current alone, but also hurrying the *Argo* along with their oars, to make up for the lost time, in two long spells each day.

On the day that they anchored by this reef, Hercules, journeying towards Colchis on foot, came to the territory of the Mariandynians. King Lycus greeted him with joy, but said: 'Alas, dear Benefactor, if only you had come a day or two earlier, you would have caught up with your comrades the Argonauts, who have been bitterly lamenting your loss – or at least Jason, their captain, has been. I understand from him that when you became separated from them, in the neighbourhood of Ascania, two Thracians, Calaïs and Zetes, and Tiphys the helmsman, dissuaded them from waiting for you.'

'Indeed!' said Hercules. 'I will remember that against them.'

'Tiphys is since dead of a wasting fever,' added Lycus.

'No matter,' said Hercules, 'the two Thracians remain for my vengeance.'

'I will provide you with a war-galley to go in pursuit of them, dear Benefactor,' cried Lycus, 'but first let us be merry and relive old times together in memory.'

'I am so hungry that I could eat an ox,' Hercules roared.

'You shall eat two if you like,' replied Lycus. He was careful to make no enquiries about Hylas until Hercules should have eaten and drunken well.

While they feasted on prime roast beef there was a stir in the hall, and a tall man, a Greek by the look of him, dressed in the royal costume of a herald, came striding up. He saluted Lycus with a flattering address but told him: 'My message is not for you, Majesty. It is for your noble guest, Prince Hercules of Tiryns.'

'Why, upon my soul, if it is not the Dung Man,' cried Hercules. 'You stick as close to me as my own shadow and tread almost as noiselessly.'

Talthybius, with a deep bow, said: 'Most noble Hercules, well met!'

'Well met,' replied Hercules, making a Gorgon face at him.

Talthybius disregarded the insult and, stretching out his serpentine rod of olive, said smoothly: 'The compliments of King Eurystheus of Mycenae, and he requires you to return to Greece at once and there clean out in a single day the filthy stables and byres of King Augeas of Elis.'

Hercules exclaimed: 'Has he sent you half-way across the habitable world to ask me to perform a simple sanitary task in my native Peloponnese? What a man he is!'

'I am only a herald,' Talthybius apologized.

'No, but a Dung Man too,' said Hercules.

Talthybius smiled faintly and replied: 'Alas, most noble Hercules, it is you who are the Dung Man now.'

Hercules roared with laughter, for he was in high good humour again. 'Well answered!' he cried. 'For the sake of this jest I will obey your master. But first I must obtain permission from King Augeas, who is aboard the *Argo*, only a day's sail from here towards the east. I have been promised a swift war galley by the King and will go after her tomorrow.'

'The King's orders are that you shall return to Greece at once,' said Talthybius firmly.

'I cannot clean out the stables and byres of my comrade Augeas without his permission,' said Hercules. 'He may prefer them to remain dirty – who knows?'

He continued obstinate. But no sooner had he set foot in the borrowed galley, the next morning, than his head began to ache and the children's voices shouted discordantly at him: 'Back, back, Hercules! You are killing us! Back, back!' So back he had to go. At the quay-side Lycus dared to ask him what news he had of Hylas, and Hercules gloomily admitted that he had none. He described his fruitless search among the Mysians and how he had taken hostages from their rulers and given these in charge of his brother-in-law who was building a settlement with their help at the mouth of the Cios.

'Well,' said Lycus, 'it may, of course, be that Hylas is somewhere in hiding among the Mysians, but from what one of my guests let fall I gather that the ungrateful boy had for some time been planning an escape by the inland track to Troy. He took a wallet with him, I hear, which jingled; it may have contained gold and silver ornaments to pay his passage to the Island of Lemnos, where he is said to have a sweetheart.'

'WHAT!' bellowed Hercules. 'So that is the story, is it? The heartless wretches, plotting to be rid of me and playing upon my poor boy's adolescent love for the lecherous Iphinoë, loaded him with gold and silver and tempted him to run off! Then as soon as ever I started out after him they sneaked quietly off and marooned me. I shall be even with them one day, you will see; but meanwhile I must find my darling Hylas, who I am sure meant no harm. He is a thoughtless child and of an age when any hot little bitch can lure him to her, even from the side of Hercules who loves him with a huge and enduring love. I thank you, good Lycus, for this information, however painfully it sounds in my ears. You are my loyal friend. Now I am off home to Greece, but I shall pass by way of Troy; and if King Laömedon will neither return my Hylas to me nor tell me where he is to be found, I will tear his proud city to pieces stone by stone. I already owe him a few hard knocks. He cheated me over some man-eating mares which I left in his charge when I last came this way.'

'It will be good news for the whole of Asia if you teach those proud Trojans a lesson,' said Lycus. 'May I suggest that you visit the Dolionians and Percosians and borrow a few war-galleys from them? From all I hear, they are itching for war with the Trojans.'

'That is exactly what I will do,' said Hercules. 'Come, Dung Man, shall we travel along together or separately?'

'It would be an honour to travel in your company, most noble Hercules,' replied Talthybius, 'and a great protection against the insults of barbarians, some of whom have as little respect for a herald as they have for a white maggot in a nut.'

CHAPTER TWENTY-SEVEN

THE MINYANS OF SINOPE

As the Argonauts rounded Cape Lepte, which forms the left horn of a great bull's-head promontory, the wind suddenly changed from west to north-east. They rowed across a gulf of heaving waters bordered with white rocks, and then rounded Cape Sinope, the right horn of the promontory. Cape Sinope has steep sides and a flat top, and from a distance appears to be an island, because the isthmus connecting it to the mainland is a low one. A small whitewashed settlement built on the eastern side of Sinope, near the isthmus, gave the Minyans wistful thoughts of home, for the neat but solid architecture of the houses was identical with that of their own cities in Greece. Jason attempted a landing on the isthmus, but found it protected by sharp limestone reefs full of pot-holes, so he brought the *Argo* back to a small beach on the peninsula itself, and there ran her ashore. The beach was wonderfully protected from both westerly and north-easterly winds.

The Argonauts disembarked and began lighting a fire of driftwood and Echion waved a friendly greeting to a young man who was observing them intently from behind a pinnacle of the low cliff which backed the beach. He waved his hand in reply and presently reappeared, riding a fine Paphlagonian mule at dangerous speed down a ravine towards them. He wore a wolf-skin cap and a necklace of wolves' teeth and was joyfully shouting out the names of the Thessalians, Coronus and Eurydamus, and of Admetus, King of Pherae, whom he had recognized from the cliff-top by their badges and accoutrements. He turned out to be Autolycus of Tricca, a Minyan, whom they had supposed dead. Five years before, he and his two brothers had accompanied Hercules on his expedition to the land of the Amazons but had not returned; when asked what had become of them, Hercules would say no more than that they had fallen behind him on the march and had probably been killed by the Paphlagonians.

This was a happy reunion. Autolycus, whose brothers Phlogius and Deileion were also alive and following close behind him, had not seen a fellow-Greek or heard news of his beloved Thessaly ever since Hercules had deserted them – for Autolycus dared use this hard word of Hercules. It seems that Phlogius had fallen sick on the march and Deileion had sprained an ankle; but Hercules refused to wait for them or even to march at less than his customary rate of thirty-five miles a day. They had been obliged to fall out, and Autolycus had magnanimously remained with them. They were well treated by the Paphlagonians, who are a surly, obstinate but generous race; and repaid the kindness shown them by introducing into the country several useful arts and sciences until then unknown. Especially they showed the Paphlagonians the value of the timber-trees growing plentifully in the hills, such as the maple and the mountain-nut which are highly prized in the West for the making of tables and coffers, and instructed them in the art of seasoning and trimming the timber for export. The brothers also organized a tunny-fishery and taught their hosts the true value of the foreign goods brought overland to this port from Persia and Bactria. Hitherto the Paphlagonians had allowed their allies the Trojans to bargain with the Armenian merchants at a yearly fair, and had been content with a trifling commission on the goods sold, but now Autolycus and his brothers advised them to trade directly with the Armenians at their first entry into the country and make a reasonable profit as middlemen.

These Thessalians had grown rich themselves from the purchase and resale of such goods as tiger-skins, figured carpets, balsam, cinnabar, ruddle, onyx, turquoise, lapis lazuli, and the sheets of Galatian mica-stone with which kings and princes glaze the windows of their bedchambers. Each now possessed a sack of gold dust of nearly his own weight, but all three were homesick for Thessaly. They shrank from the dangers of a return by land, and not being skilled shipwrights had no means of returning by sea, for they would not trust their lives and treasure to the Trojans. Phlogius declared that he would gladly leave all his treasure behind if by so doing he might view once again 'the lovely water-meadows of the Ion and Lethaeos, where brood-mares graze, foals frolic, and the shrill sound of the horseherd's bagpipe sets the sturdy boys dancing under the poplars'.

When Jason told them that the *Argo* was bound for Colchis, where he intended to recover the Golden Fleece from the shrine of Prometheus, the brothers were struck with wonder and dismay. They knew the strength of the Colchian fleet and army and the antipathy of King Aeëtes to the new Olympian religion. But they said: 'If by any chance you should return in peace from Colchis, by way of Sinope, on no account sail back to Greece without us: for we will pay you as passage-money one half of all the gold dust that we possess – gold dust cast up by the gigantic horned ants of India and stolen from them by the dusky Dands – and some wallets full of jewels as well.'

Jason answered: 'Either come with us now and help us to recover the Fleece, or stay where you are and expect nothing at all from us on our homeward voyage. If you come, we shall require neither gold nor jewels as passage-money from you, but only sufficient provisions for another few stages of the voyage.'

But Echion said: 'No, no, son of Aeson. Let them find us provisions and pay us in gold dust besides, as much to each Argonaut as he can grasp in both hands and convey into his wallet without turning the thumb upwards; for that will be no great quantity, yet sufficient to avert jealousy from the sacks. But to show that I have no thirst for gold I shall not dip a finger into the sack myself.'

In the end the three brothers, fortified with Mariandynian wine, decided to come aboard, and agreed to the payment. Echion spread his sacred robe underfoot as a reminder to his comrades that they must not break the treaty by turning up their thumbs or helping themselves twice. Then each of the Argonauts in turn dipped both his hands into a sack and, pulling them out well filled, poured the gold into his wallet. Great Ancaeus, who had the largest hands, pulled out more than anyone, but spilt half of it in fumbling for his wallet, and so did several others; but Little Ancaeus, who had small hands, rubbed them with tallow on both sides as far as the wrist and by great care conveyed all but a few grains into his wallet. Echion warmly praised Little Ancaeus for his sagacity; who praised him warmly in return to see him shake together in a fold of his robe, and gather up as his perquisite, all the dust that had been spilt – enough, as it later proved, to make him a golden sheath for his olive wand and a golden belt engraved with sacred devices.

Jason agreed to wait for two days while the Thessalian brothers put their affairs in order. Dascylus, son of Lycus, then took his leave of the Argonauts, there being no further need of his services: for the new recruits were well acquainted with the coastal tribes as far as Amazonian territory.

Thus the ship's company was again brought to full strength, the places of Hercules, Idmon, and Tiphys being filled by these three Thessalian brothers, who revictualled the ship with flat cakes made of spelt, dried tunny steaks, jars of dolphin oil, and sweet pickled carcases of mutton.

Standing on the headland, Orpheus and the other initiates of the Mysteries of Samothrace now offered sacrifices to the Great Ones and humbly prayed for a north westerly wind; but it did not blow. They concluded that they had made some mistake in the ritual and waited until the next day, when they performed it again. Then the wind slowly veered to the north-west, which suited them, but it did not blow strongly.

During that day they ran across a smooth gulf, past hills fringed with trees to the very shore; far inland rose the double cone of Mount Saramene. Just short of the promontory at the further end of the gulf they passed the delta of the Halys, the largest river of the whole southern sea-board, but not navigable far from its mouth: then as they rounded the promontory they saw, from no great distance, grazing herds of a beautiful sort of deer called the gazelle, which none had seen before except Nauplius when once he was wrecked on the coast of Libya. Gazelles have large eyes, long ears, and slender legs, and are excellent to eat. Atalanta wished to go ashore and hunt them, because Nauplius had provoked her by saying they were so swift that even she could never overtake one; but Jason would not consent and they sailed on. There was a long beach beyond the promontory, backed with low hills, and behind these a marshy lake crowded with water-fowl. They went ashore for an hour or two for recreation, and the Thessalians, now that they were so numerous, gave an exhibition of dancing in full armour to Jason's wild pipe-music. They danced with great agility, leaping marvellously high and whirling their swords about their heads. Two parties in the dance went through a display of mimic warfare, alternately victorious and vanquished, dealing each other what seemed the heaviest of blows, yet with such skill and restraint that not a helmet was dinted.

Meanwhile Atalanta and Meleager ran off together to hunt gazelle, but returned empty-handed and breathless just as the ship was ready to sail.

That night they sailed slowly across yet another gulf and at dawn rounded a low wooded promontory, that of Aricon, where the meandering Iris flows into the sea. 'Here,' said Autolycus, 'is a settlement of curly-bearded, long-robed Assyrians, exiles from their country; and beyond stretches the land of the Chalybeans, a savage tribe famous as iron-workers, with whom I have lately traded. Soon we shall sight an islet, called the Isle of Barter, close to the Chalybean shore, where we of Sinope come in our dug-out canoes and lay out on the rocks painted Minyan pottery and linen cloth from Colchis and sheep-skin coats dyed red with madder, or yellow with heather, such as the Chalybeans prize, and spear-shafts painted with vermilion. Then we row away out of sight behind rocks. As soon as we are gone the Chalybeans venture across to the islet on rafts; they lay down beside our goods broad-bladed, well-tempered spear-heads and axe-heads, also awls and knives and sail-needles, and then go away again. If on our return we are satisfied with their goods, we take them up and make for home; but if we are not satisfied, we remove apart from the rest of our merchandise whatever we think is not covered by their payment. The Chalybeans then return again and pay for this extra heap with a few more iron implements. In the end the barter is complete, unless the Chalybeans in a huff take away all their iron goods and let us sail off empty-handed; for they are a capricious race.'

The *Argo* continued along this coast with a freshening wind, and passed several settlements of huts built of branches, but nowhere did the Argonauts see any flocks or herds, though there was grass sufficient to support them in countless numbers. The hills drew closer to the sea and they passed by the Isle of Barter. The coast then curved sharply to the northward, and after a few miles they came by oars to the low promontory now called Cape Jason. Since it was dusk and the wind was failing, and they did not wish to become involved with the warlike Tibarenians, whose territory began at this cape, they anchored under the lee of another islet. That night was memorable to the Argonauts, for it was then that Nauplius taught them the names of the heavenly constellations, so far as he knew them, such as Callisto the Bear Woman, her son Arcas (usually called the Bear Warden), the Pleiads (which were just rising), and Cassiopeia. Then they amused themselves by naming others for themselves; some of which names gained currency in Greek ports after the return of the *Argo*. Thus the twin stars Castor and Pollux, at the shining of which the roughest seas subside; and the great lumbering constellation of Hercules at Labour; and the Lyre of Orpheus; and the constellation of Cheiron the Centaur (which Jason named) – all these are still remembered. So is the Dolphin of Little Ancaeus: for that evening all but he dined on mutton fried in dolphin oil, which was a food forbidden him; he therefore ate dried tunny instead and named the constellation 'The Dolphin of Little Ancaeus.' It was many years before the *Argo* herself was set in the heavens, low on the southern horizon: a constellation of twenty-three stars. Four stars form the mast, five the port rudder, and four the starboard; five the keel, five the gunwale; but the prow is not shown, because of a homicide that it caused.

The next morning they rowed on, starting out in a dead calm; but the prevailing wind on these coasts is north-westerly, and soon it blew again, taking them at a good rate past the country of the Tibarenians. According to the account given by Autolycus, these savages had not long before dethroned the Mother Goddess and put Father Zeus in her place; but found it difficult to wean themselves entirely of ancient habits which had formed a prime part of their religion. The men gathered together, and one said to the others: 'Seeing that it is the man, the sower of the seed, who creates the child, not the woman, she being only the field in which he sows it, why should she earn his reverence? Let all the pious care hitherto mistakenly bestowed on a woman during her pregnancy and child-bed be bestowed on her husband. He is the parent, not she.' So it was resolved. Now, while his wife is pregnant, each Tibarenian husband eats twice as much as usual, is honoured above his fellows and humoured in strange fancies, and walks abroad with waddling steps; and when his wife is in labour, he lies in bed and groans with his head close bound, and the women tend him pitifully and prepare child-bed baths for him – but the wife is left to her own devices. Like the Chalybeans, these Tibarenians do not till the soil, nor tend sheep or oxen. They live by fishing, hunting, and gathering the fruits of the forest; for the seas are full of fish and the forests of game. Here spontaneously grow immense numbers of apple and pear trees and nuts of various sorts; and the wild vine is hung with heavy clusters of sharp-tasted but refreshing grapes.

At noon the Argonauts approached the marshy outfall of the Cerasos river, beyond which lies the Isle of Ares. The wide sky ahead of them grew suddenly dark with myriads of aquatic birds flying out to sea from the low shores. Mopsus the augur stared at them, his eyes nearly starting from his head, and his mouth as round as an egg. He cried: 'About ship, dear comrades! This is too terrible a sight for an augur's eyes!' But now the birds were streaming past both ahead and astern, and making direct for the *Argo* came a flock of unclean spoonbills. With one accord all the Argonauts seized their weapons and helmets and dishes and copper cauldrons and began clashing them together; and at this hideous noise the birds sheered off, but feathers came raining down. Spoonbills are said to suck the breath of sleeping men, and a flock of them is considered a sure harbinger of the fever. The Second Labour imposed on Hercules was to compel a huge colony of spoonbills to quit the marshes about Stymphalos in Arcadia; he killed some and drove the rest away with discordant cries.

So the Argonauts sailed on, and when they came to the isle of Ares they found it black with little birds, such as larks, wagtails, corncrakes, redstarts, rollers, and even kingfishers in flocks; and these rose in a great cloud as the *Argo* sailed by, but were driven away with the same din as before.

Mopsus stretched out his palms in prayer to Apollo, crying: 'Innumerable perils and innumerable blessings, clouds of whirring doubt. My eye blurs. Darling of Delos, smile upon us, shaking your unshorn locks, and let the good prevail!'

CHAPTER TWENTY-EIGHT

THE FAT MOSYNOECHIANS AND OTHERS

As they sailed past Cape Zephyros that evening, Autolycus cried to his comrades: 'Yonder stretches the territory of the Mosynoechians, and I fear that you will not believe me when I tell you what sort of people they are, for I read incredulity in your eyes as I was describing to you the customs of the Tibarenians. I shall therefore say nothing at all and leave you to base your judgements upon your experiences of this singular folk.'

Soon after Autolycus had said this, they found a beach protected from westerly winds, anchored, disembarked, lighted a fire of driftwood and dined, after having first posted a strong watch. But Autolycus assured them: 'You have nothing to fear from the Mosynoechians, who, when they see our fire, will retire to their wooden castles and remain there all night. In the morning curiosity will tempt them down to us with gifts. It is dangerous to travel through their country, for they dig frequent pitfalls for wild beasts along the forest paths, and if a traveller unluckily falls into one, they consider him fair game and kill him without pity. But they are not dangerous when armed men encounter them in the open.'

The night passed without alarms and, as soon as the sun began to warm the beaches, down came two Mosynoechians to visit them, just as Autolycus had foretold. Their appearance was so droll that the Argonauts burst into a roar of uncontrolled laughter. The Mosynoechians, a man and a boy, were heartened by this evident sign of welcome and began to laugh themselves. The man capered about, the boy clapped his hands. The man carried a shield in the form of an ivy leaf made from the hide of a white ox, a spear of prodigious length with a small spike at the top and a rounded butt, and a basket filled with nuts, fruits, and other dainties. He wore a short white tunic and his face was painted with alternate stripes of yellow and blue dye. On his head was an uncrested leather helmet tied about with the tail of a white ox. He was grossly fat.

The boy was naked and fatter still, prodigiously fat, and could only walk with great difficulty, the sweat pouring from his brow as he did so. His pasty face and dead-white skin suggested that he had been kept in a dark room for weeks on end and fed like a stalled ox, as indeed proved upon enquiry to have been the case. His bulging thighs were gracefully tattooed with flowers and leaves. The man, who was a chieftain, led the boy towards the camp-fire and presented both him and the basket of dainties to Jason with a generous gesture, holding out his hand for some gift in return. Then the Argonauts laughed louder still, for they observed that the boy's plump buttocks were dyed, the one yellow, the other blue, with a staring eye painted upon each in white and black.

Jason was confused. He did not know what to say or do. However, Autolycus, who could speak a few words of the Mosynoechian language, came forward and on Jason's behalf thanked the chieftain for his gift, declaring that the boy was admirably fat.

'And so he should be,' cried the chieftain, 'considering how many measures of boiled chestnuts we cram him with, day after day and night after night.'

Jason asked the chieftain, speaking through Autolycus, what gift would content him in return.

The chieftain answered that he would be content with the woman that the Argonauts had brought with them; though she was not in the first flower of youth and seemed half-starved by her long voyage from Egypt – he said Egypt – he warranted that he would plump her up in a few weeks' time until she resembled a ripe gourd. Meanwhile, to show that he did not despise her for her lean condition, he would company with her before their eyes as a signal compliment.

Autolycus shook his head at this shameless suggestion, but the chieftain with a flourish of his spear, insisted that he must interpret it to Jason. Autolycus did so. His words excited such immoderate laughter that the chieftain innocently concluded that the Argonauts were delighted to be rid of a scraggy woman and acquire a plump boy in exchange. He minced forward towards Atalanta in the first tripping steps of a lecherous dance and tossed off his helmet and tunic.

Atalanta made a Gorgon face at him, but it did not discourage him in the least. When he began unknotting his loin-cloth, she turned and ran. He pursued her, whooping, but Meleager came behind and tripped him up, so that he fell flat on a heap of sharp stones. He raised a yell, and the fat boy screamed like a woman in travail. At this the watching Mosynoechians came running down from their nearest wooden castle, armed with javelins and the same cumbrous spears and white ivy-leaf shields as their chieftain carried. Phalerus, Jason, Admetus, and Acastus, with bows and arrows, stood fast to cover the retreat of their comrades, who quickly launched the ship. But when the savages found that no hurt had been done to their chieftain, and that the fat boy had not been carried off, they did not attack the rear-guard, who climbed safely aboard without wasting their arrows.

Jason still had with him the gift-basket of dainties, which consisted of a flat, soft cake made of spelt; grapes, apples, pears, and chestnuts; some stinking mackerel roes and flounder tails; and a piece of honeycomb. He distributed the cake and fruit among his comrades and threw the fish over-board. But the honeycomb he reserved for Butes. 'I should be glad to hear your opinion of this honey, most noble Butes,' said he. But before Butes could come down the gangway to him, Autolycus and his brother Phlogius had snatched the comb from Jason's hand and flung it into the sea after the stinking fish.

Butes was enraged. 'What, do you rob me of my gift, you pair of Thessalian pirates?' he cried. 'Jason offered me the comb because I know more about honeys than any man in Greece and he wished to have my opinion upon it.'

Autolycus answered: 'That may be, you buzz-brained Athenian. But we are no longer in Greece, as King Amycus reminded us while we were still navigating the Sea of Marmora. My brother Phlogius and I threw away the honeycomb because it was poisonous, and because as loyal Argonauts we valued your life.'

Butes abated his anger. He exclaimed in surprise: 'Hornets and wasps! Did that painted savage indeed wish to poison me? Do I owe my life to your vigilance? Did he perhaps sprinkle the comb with the juice of the deadly aconite which I saw growing in the fields of the Mariandynians?'

'No,' said Autolycus, 'he had no need to do so. The honey here is natu-rally poisonous, being sucked from a plant named goats'-bane. A little of it will craze any man who is not habituated to its use and make him fall senseless to the ground.'

'That is a mere fable and I believe no word of it,' said Butes, growing angry again. 'Bees are sage, sober creatures, far sager and soberer than men, and would never think of storing up poisonous honey in their combs, or manufacturing poisonous bee-bread. Who ever saw an intoxicated bee? Answer me that!'

'Name me liar, if you please,' said Autolycus, 'but at least refrain from sampling any honey of this coast. That of the Moschians, who are tribu-taries of King Aeëtes of Colchis, is equally poisonous. The bees cull it not from goats'-bane but from a beautiful red flower, the Pontic azalea, which grows on northern slopes of the high mountains of Armenia.'

'I will not name you liar, for you are my trusty comrade, but I declare you to be utterly mistaken,' said Butes. 'Bees never visit red flowers and though honey is often employed by criminals, especially female criminals, as a ready means of disguising the poison that they use against their enemies, no pure honey ever harmed a fly even, from whatever flower it was culled. I declare that whoever believes the contrary is a credulous ignoramus.'

Here Orpheus struck up a pleasing melody, Autolycus shrugged his shoulders, and the quarrel ended.

Soon the *Argo* passed by the ravine from which emerges the river Charistotes, and the Argonauts saw a number of three-seated canoes hollowed from tree trunks, being paddled hastily upstream. The occupants were wearing head-dresses of vulture quills. 'The Trojan slave-traders often make sudden descents on this coast,' explained Autolycus. 'They use the men whom they capture as labourers in the stone quarries.'

That day they sailed as far as the Sacred Cape, where the territory of the Mosynoechians ends and that of the Amazons begins. This cape, which is sacred to the Goddess of the Underworld, could be seen by them all, not by Lynceus only, at a distance of sixty miles. A conical hill rises at the extremity, with reddish cliffs about it. But they did not attempt to land, and sailed on all night; because everyone whom they had met had warned them to steer clear of the Amazons.

The Amazons worship the Triple Goddess, and the men of the tribe to which they formerly belonged (but the very name of which has now perished) were of much the same habits as the Centaurs, Aethics, Satyrs or other Pelasgians. But when these men began to speak excitedly of fatherhood – having first heard the word from some Armenian or Assyrian traveller – and exalted Father Zeus at the expense of the Goddess, the women consulted together (much as the women of Lemnos had done) and decided to retain their power, by force if necessary. In a single night they disarmed and killed all their men-folk, or as many as were adult, and offered their severed genitals as a peace-offering to the Mother. Then they conscientiously trained themselves in the arts of war. Their chosen weapons were the short battle-axe and the bow, and they fought from horseback, having a fine tall breed of horses in their plains. They seared away their right breasts to allow themselves to draw the bowstring to the full extent without hindrance; which gave them their name of Amazons, the Breastless Ones. They did not kill the male children, as the Lemnian women had done, but broke their legs and arms instead, to incapacitate them for war, and afterwards taught them how to weave and spin and be useful about the house.

However, they had the same natural longing for the act of love as the women of Lemnos, and scorned to bed with their broken-limbed slaves. So they made war upon the neighbouring tribes and took lovers from the bravest of their captives, afterwards putting them to death without remorse. This policy compelled them gradually to enlarge their kingdom in all directions, further than otherwise suited them: they were not a numerous people and their fertile plain about the river Thermodon was sufficient for their needs. However, they came before long to an understanding with the Macronians, a fierce and handsome tribe who lived in the high hills of the interior. Each spring the young men of the Macronians met with the young women of the Amazons in a frontier valley, and there they companied together; and of the children born of this intercourse, the Amazons kept the girls and handed over the boys to the Macronians.

Such, at least, was the account given by Autolycus, and it confirmed that of Hercules. Hercules had won Queen Hippolyte's girdle without fighting, for she fell in love with him when he came with the Macronians, his friends, to the annual love-making; and he had it from her as a free gift. It was by mere accident that he fell into conflict with her bodyguard, of whom he killed five or six with his arrows: the Macronians were jealous of his success with the Amazons, and had spread the lying report that his secret intention was to kidnap Hippolyte and carry her off as a slave.

The Argonauts sailed on all night, and at noon of the next day, alarmed by the strange aspect of the sky, drew their ship high up on a beach, under the lee of Cape Rhizos, about ninety miles eastward of the Sacred Cape. Cape Rhizos lies in the territory of a tribe named the Bechirians. The hills inland are extremely lofty.

Jason jestingly asked Autolycus: 'What sort of people are these Bechirians? Are they dog-faced? Have they heads growing under their arm-pits? Do they eat sand and drink sea-water? Or what is their peculiarity?'

'The Bechirians,' answered Autolycus, 'have these peculiarities: They speak the truth, are monogamous and faithful to their wives, do not make war on their neighbours and, being wholly ignorant of the existence of any gods or goddesses, spend their lives without fear of retribution for their sins. They believe that when a man dies, he dies utterly, and therefore are unafraid of ghosts. Their land is also free of the fevers which plague their neighbours, and as fertile as one might wish. I have often considered settling among them; only that, when I came to die, my bones would remain unburied, which would be a terrible thing for a Greek as religious-minded as myself.'

From where they had now landed it was only a two-days' sail with a fair wind to the Colchian seaport of Phasis, at the mouth of the Phasis river. In the distance, both to the north and east across the waters, spread an irregular streak of white – the distant snow-capped mountains of the Caucasus.

CHAPTER TWENTY-NINE

THE *ARGO* REACHES COLCHIS

That afternoon a violent north wind sprang up and waves of extraordinary size came hissing up the beach. As the Argonauts gazed out to sea they saw a large vessel, headed east, about a mile off-shore. This was the first ship that they had sighted since quitting the land of the Mariandynians. She was built on Corinthian lines.

Lynceus screwed up his eyes and reported: 'The oarsmen seem from their kinky hair and linen dresses to be Colchians, but some of the passengers, who are bailing out water with helmets and dishes, have a strangely Greek aspect. The ship has sprung a leak, to for'ard I think, and the after-bulwark has been washed away. The oarsmen are exhausted but the master is taking a lash to their backs and forcing them to row on.'

Some of the Argonauts ran up the beach to a little hill, hoping for a clearer view. The Colchian ship was attempting to round the promontory of Rhizos and take refuge in the bay on the other side, which has a long and hospitable beach.

Pollux said with a sigh: 'Alas, poor souls, they will never make it!'

'They will make it comfortably,' cried Idas. 'They are pulling like wild horses.'

'You must not forget the sunken reef past which I steered you,' said Great Ancaeus. 'The trough of every wave will expose it; and there is a rock, awash, about a bowshot off-shore, just beyond the point that they have now reached.'

Ancaeus had hardly finished speaking when a huge wave lifted the ship up and tossed her over its back upon the very rock of which he had made mention. She broke into pieces at once, and down the wind came the shriek of drowning men.

'I was wrong for once,' cried Idas, grinning. 'There they go!'

Lynceus reported: 'The four Greeks are clinging to the mast. One is wounded. With their feet they are fending off two Colchian sailors who have caught hold of the sheets and are trying to pull themselves to safety. There! Look there! That Greek had a knife between his teeth and has cut away the sheets. Now they have a chance of struggling ashore with the mast.'

Euphemus the swimmer was already running towards the point where the ship had struck. He ran swiftly. When he came to the water's edge he plunged in and swam under the waves like an otter or seal until he reappeared close to the four men who clung to the mast. One of them was bleeding from a deep gash on the head and his comrades were supporting him with difficulty. 'Leave him to me,' cried Euphemus, swimming close and performing tricks in the water to show his mastery of it.

'Take him, in the Mother's name!' answered one of them.

Euphemus, swimming on his back, soon brought the wounded man ashore, at a point half a mile away from the wreck. The others, kicking their feet in unison, steered their mast towards the same place of safety. But they would not have been able to scramble ashore but for the help that Euphemus gave them: he plunged in again and hauled them to safety one by one. When they were all ashore at last they embraced him in the most tender manner imaginable, declaring in barbarous Greek that he had earned their undying gratitude.

'You seem to be a sort of Greeks,' said Euphemus.

'We are Greeks,' one of them answered, 'though we have never visited our native land. We are of Minyan blood, which we understand to be of the noblest that Greece can boast.'

'Come before our captain, whose name is Jason, son of Aeson, and tell him your story,' said Euphemus. 'He is a Minyan himself, and so are several of our company.'

Jason welcomed the shipwrecked men, inviting them to dry themselves at the camp-fire. He gave them clothes to wear and warm wine to drink. Mopsus bound up the head of the wounded man with linen bandages, after first dressing it with a vulnerary salve. It was only when his guests were somewhat restored and rested that Jason asked them politely: 'Strangers, who are you? And where, may I ask, were you bound in your ship before this tremendous storm broke her in pieces?'

Their leader replied: 'I do not know whether you have ever heard tell of an Aeolian Greek named Phrixus, who fled from Thessaly, some thirty years ago, because his father, King Athamas, intended to sacrifice him? Well, he came safe to Colchis, and took refuge at the Court of King Aeëtes, an Ephyran, who had been settled there for some years; he married the King's daughter, the Princess Chalciope. We are the four sons of that marriage, but our father, Phrixus, died two years ago and we are not on the best of terms with our grandfather, who is a severe old man. Recently we decided to visit Greece, because our father had told us that a valuable inheritance was waiting to be claimed by us at Orchomenos, namely the Boeotian lands of his father, Athamas. When we petitioned King Aeëtes for permission to sail, he consented grudgingly, and on condition that we should first visit Ephyra to discover what had become of his lands there and register a formal claim to them on his behalf. We agreed to the condition, but had only been at sea for two days when, as you yourself saw, we lost our ship and all our belongings. But for your noble comrade here we should have lost our lives too, likely enough, for he dragged us through the surf when we were exhausted. Our names are Argeus (the one yonder with the gashed head), Melanion (the dark one tending him, who takes after his Colchian grandmother), Cytissorus here (our all-in wrestler), and Phrontis – I am Phrontis, the eldest of the four. We are wholly at your service.'

Jason held out his hand. 'This is a strange meeting. I have treated you as kindly as though you were my own kinsmen, and kinsmen you now prove to be! You and I are cousins-german. Your grandfather Athamas and my grandfather Cretheus were brothers. And you have other cousins among us (I will explain their genealogy later) – Periclymenus and Melampus of Pylos, Admetus of Pherae, Idas and Lynceus of Arene, and Acastus of Iolcos.'

Phrontis, grasping his hand, asked: 'How comes it that you are here on this beach? Have not the Trojans closed the straits against any Greeks wishing to trade here in the Black Sea? They undertook to do so. Our grandfather Aeëtes is an ally of Laömedon, the Trojan King, and has undertaken to help him with ships and men to implement this policy; for, though a Greek himself, he says that the Greeks invariably bring trouble wherever they go. The Amazons, I hear, have made Laömedon a similar undertaking, declaring that the Greeks are too quick with their weapons and too slow with their gifts. There are, by the way, three Thessalian brothers living at Sinope among the Paphlagonians who have brought the Greek name into dishonour: they have the reputation of being out-and-out rogues and skinflints.'

When Jason pressed him for further information about these three brothers, Phrontis answered: 'I have never met them myself, but one of them, Autolycus, is the worst thief in the whole of Asia; according to the Trojans he would steal a man's nose off his face while he slept, or the tripod from under a priestess while she was prophesying. But the Trojans dare not carry these brothers off and put them to death, for the Paphlagonians are deceived into thinking them wonderful men and benefactors of the country and would show their resentment by closing the southern trade route from the East.'

Autolycus said, smiling: 'Never believe what the crooked Trojans tell you, noble Phrontis. Believe the simple Paphlagonians, on whom I and my two brothers have indeed conferred substantial benefits. And do not guard your noses too vigilantly while you sleep; for I swear to you that I will not lay my hands on them, so long as you do not lay your hands on ours. That is what I have always told the Trojans.'

The whole company laughed at this sally, and Phrontis apologized to Autolycus and his brothers, declaring that if they were indeed the three

Thessalians in question, their kindly and frank countenances were in themselves a refutation of the slanders put out against them by their rivals in trade. The brothers granted him their pardon generously, saying that any complaint made against them by the jealous Trojans sounded sweetly in their ears.

Then Jason said: 'Phrontis, these three good Thessalians have come aboard our ship, after settling all their affairs at Sinope, because the glory of our divine quest has fired their hearts with a longing to share it.'

'Indeed?' said Phrontis, relieved to change the subject of the conversation. 'And what, may I ask, is your divine quest?'

Jason answered: 'I will tell you in close confidence: it is to win back the Golden Fleece from King Aeëtes and restore it to the shrine of Laphystian Zeus, to the image from which your father long ago boldly removed it. This is a quest in which you and your brothers should feel the deepest concern; and if you help us to accomplish it, we can promise that your claim to the lands of Athamas will be favourably considered by the rulers of Boeotia, and that the present occupants will be extruded. You must understand that the good luck of the Minyan clan hangs upon the recovery of the Fleece – I believe, indeed, that it was the Triple Goddess herself who cast you upon this shore.'

Phrontis said: 'Your words sound wild and strange to our ears. Our grandfather King Aeëtes will never give up the Fleece willingly, and he commands not only an army of five thousand men but a fleet of thirty swift galleys, each the equal of yours in size; which, if you succeed in seizing the Fleece by a sudden raid, will pursue and overtake you as sure as Fate. Let me warn you, before I go further, that two brazen bulls are set up in the inner hall of our grandfather's palace. They are made after the model of the bull that Daedalus presented to the priestess of Cretan Pasiphaë, but they are dedicated to the savage war god of the Taurians. When our grandfather has caught you he will enclose you, two by two, in the bellies of these bulls and light a sacrificial fire underneath which will roast you to death. Your shouts and yells will issue as roars from the mouths of the bulls and cause him infinite pleasure. And tell me, Cousin, how in the world do you suppose that the Triple Goddess, whom we worship in Colchis as The Bird-headed Mother or The Ineffable One, can favour your rash attempt to undo her work? Why should she consent to restore the Fleece to the rebellious son from whom she filched it?'

Jason answered: 'The great Olympian Deities – Zeus, Poseidon Apollo, Athena, and Artemis – have all personally blessed this enterprise, which is by no means so difficult as many others which you know to have been successfully accomplished. When, for example, Hercules of Tiryns was sent by King Eurystheus of Mycenae to win the girdle of Queen Hippolyte of the Amazons –'

Here Melanion and Cytissorus interrupted: 'O yes, we have all heard of

Hercules, the great Tirynthian. Had Hercules come with you, that would perhaps be a different matter. Even our grandfather Aeëtes fears him.'

Jason said: 'Then let me tell you, and I will confirm this with an oath, if you please, that Hercules is a member of this expedition. If you look in the locker under the bench nearest to the stern you will find some of his possessions, including a helmet the size of a cauldron and a gigantic pair of leather breeches. He disembarked a few stages up the coast on some private business of his own and we fully expect him to overtake us before long, probably in a ship supplied by his friends the Mariandynians. But we do not esteem ourselves less courageous than Hercules, and intend to prosecute our task without him, if he is long delayed. As for the Triple Goddess, we are all sincerely devoted to her, and at Samothrace were initiated into her purest rites. She has given her assent to this expedition and benefited us with the most favourable winds procurable. May I die instantly if I do not speak the truth about her!'

'But what can be her interest in your recovery of the Fleece?' asked Phrontis.

'I do not say that she is interested in it,' replied Jason. 'But at least she does not oppose our quest, for she has a mission of her own for us to perform in Colchis. She wishes us to set at rest the ghost of your father, Phrixus.'

'Indeed?' cried Phrontis. 'I had no idea that he was not at rest. The Colchians gave him a splendid funeral.'

Jason was puzzled. 'I understood that his body was unburied,' he faltered.

'Unburied it is,' said Phrontis. 'We never bury men in Colchis, but only women. Burial of men is forbidden by the Colchian religion, and though King Aeëtes asked permission from his Council of State for our father to be burned on a pyre and interred in the Greek fashion, the Colchian priests refused this, and he did not press the matter. The Sun God is worshipped here, as well as the Triple Goddess, and fire is therefore sacred. Male corpses may not be burned, lest the fire be tainted; nor may they be buried in the earth, which is equally sacred. The Colchian practice, therefore, is to wrap male corpses in untanned ox-hides and hang them from the tops of trees for the birds to feed upon. Our father's body was hung with great reverence and solemnity from the highest branch of the highest tree in the entire river-valley, a gigantic poplar and none of us has ever been troubled by any appearance of his ghost.'

'Is it true that the Fleece hangs in the grove of the hero Prometheus, who is here worshipped as a war god?' asked Jason.

Phrontis replied: 'The story has come to you in a confused version. The Fleece is dedicated in the oracular shrine of Prometheus, not far from the city of Aea, where he is worshipped as a hero, not as a god. I will explain how the war god comes into the story. When, twenty-five years ago, our grandfather Aeëtes married the daughter of the King of the Crimea, a

Taurian, and concluded a military alliance with him, she brought her Taurian bodyguard to Aea. In compliment to her and to his father-in-law, our grandfather awarded the fore-part of the hero's high-walled enclosure to the Taurian war god, reserving the hinder part for the hero's use. Thus, in order to penetrate to the place where the Fleece is hanging, one must pass the scrutiny of a collegeful of armed Taurian priests, who keep watch day and night over the stalls of their sacred bulls. Aeëtes made this award at a time when he feared that Greek raiders might attempt to steal the Fleece. By his Colchian Queen he has a daughter, the Princess Medea, who is now the priestess of Prometheus and feeds the enormous serpent in which the hero is incarnated. This is a python of the Indian variety which kills its prey, whether beast or bird, by first fascinating it with a baleful, unsleeping eye and then crushing it to death in its cold coils. Prometheus resents the presence in his enclosure of anyone at all but the Princess Medea, who sings ancient charms to keep him quiet. No woman envies the Priestess her office.'

Jason's cheek paled when he heard this recital, and his tongue failed him. Nevertheless, he had come too far to be able in honour to turn back. Admetus of Pherae spoke up for him to Phrontis: 'We are none of us discouraged by what you say, Cousin, and you have put yourselves entirely at our leader's disposal. I require you and your brothers to swear that you will loyally follow him until he shall have brought the Fleece safely back to Greece. If you refuse to take this oath I will kill you where you stand, despite our near kinship. For Jason has confided a secret to you which nobody may share who will not actively assist us.'

They took the oath in an unroofed temple of Marianaë which stood not far off. The Amazons had erected it, years before, during one of their raids on this coast. The rude black statue of the Goddess still occupied its niche, and the altar of boulders stood ready to hold their sacrifice. In the three hollows of the topmost boulder they laid round white pebbles, like eggs, and revolved them moon-wise in intercession.

The wind died down during the night. At dawn, though the sea was still rough, they launched the *Argo* and got her under way. With a gentle off-shore breeze they continued their voyage slowly past the lands of the quarrelsome Sapeirians, and of the sure-footed Byzerians, who live next to them, where the mountains draw close to the sea.

They sailed all day and part of the following night, and then hove-to, being becalmed. After rowing all the next day they came to an immense misty plain covered with trees. At dusk that evening they entered the broad Phasis, a river that is navigable for a hundred and twenty miles or more from its mouth; but were too weary to row without a rest. The sons of Phrixus showed them a hidden backwater, where they might pass the night without fear of disturbance. They had come to the Stables of the Sun at last.

But before they put into the backwater, Jason prudently stood up at the prow and poured into the river, from a golden goblet, a libation of honey and pure water, calling upon the deity of the river to be gracious to the *Argo* while she sailed upon that broad and glorious flood.

CHAPTER THIRTY

UP THE PHASIS RIVER

The backwater smelt of fever, and on either side the rotting forest-trees were festooned with creepers to the very tops. The Argonauts were unable to land, because the land was thick black slime rather than earth and covered with a spiny undergrowth. They could not even cast anchor, being warned by the sons of Phrixus that in the morning it would be impossible to free the anchor-stones from the deep mud. Swarms of mosquitoes buzzed spitefully in their ears and stung them in the tenderest places, and grass-green tree-frogs in swarms came hopping along the gunwale and leaped down upon them with clammy feet.

'Alas,' said Peleus, 'that our comrade with the scarlet buskins is no longer with us. Being an Argive, he knew the charm against frogs.'

'Blame your own unhandiness with a javelin,' said Idas, whom the frogs were vexing beyond endurance.

Orpheus tried to comfort Idas by remarking that the frogs came with kindly intentions to rid the ship of mosquitoes; but Idas answered that it were better if the mosquitoes could rid the ship of frogs. He and Lynceus then begged Jason to put to sea again, and Jason consented; but the *Argo* at once grounded on a mud-bank. As they tried to push her off but only stirred up mud of disgusting stench, a thick sea-mist suddenly blew in; not even Lynceus could see his own hand held a foot from his face. They remained fast until morning, in speechless misery.

Two hours after dawn the mist was still fairly thick, but they freed the *Argo* by hauling on two hawsers that Euphemus, swimming across the stream without fear of crocodiles or other monsters, had attached to the roots of trees on the further bank. This was the fiftieth day of the voyage and therefore celebrated with orisons to the Triple Goddess, who favours threes and nines and fifties, just as Zeus favours fours and twelves, and Apollo sevens; but they were careful not to raise their voices loud for fear of discovery. When they had finished their chant, they rowed through the mist past Phasis, the fever-stricken garrison town that King Aeëtes maintained on the left bank of the river; and this was done without trouble, for Argeus, son of Phrixus, answered the challenge of the watchman in his own language, which to the ears of the Argonauts sounded like the twittering of birds. Phasis was built on piles between the river and a lake teeming with grebe and teal and grey duck, and the law was that all foreign ships should put in there, whatever their port of origin, before proceeding under guard to Aea. But Jason preferred to leave the Governor of Phasis ignorant that the *Argo* had sailed up the river.

The mist gradually cleared. They rowed on, hour after hour, between the same creeper-hung trees and banks of tall sedge. When they rested they did not disembark, but ate their meals uncooked. The sons of Phrixus showed them a sort of creeper, the smell of which was obnoxious to insects; they plucked its leaves, bruised them, and rubbed them on their heads and bodies. That night they were not troubled by stings but lay conversing in quiet tones, with the *Argo* secured to a mossy mooring-stake.

Admetus said: 'Comrades, I do not fear death, but I must confess that the nearer we approach the shrine where the Fleece is said to be hanging, the less likely do I think it that I shall ever see my dear wife Alcestis again, or the rich pasture-lands of Pherae, where my fat sheep bleat and my splendid horses whinny.'

Phalerus took up this sentence at once, as though he had been thinking in exactly the same way. He said: 'Or the tall, grey-green olives of Thespiae so neatly planted that broad avenues run straight through the orchards, in wherever direction one chooses to look, whether up or down or diagonally; and under whose shade the sweet-smelling bean-flower shines white in spring. For this is the wildest and gloomiest approach to a city that I have seen in all my life of sailing.'

'Or the shady glens of Sparta,' said Castor, 'where the ground is green but firm, where the two-horse chariot rolls along without creak or jolt, and the booming sound of the sea is never heard. For what is one ship against thirty?'

'Or the flowery slopes of Hymettos,' said Butes, 'where the drowsy buzz of bees sounds at midday, and the young shepherd makes music to his flocks on his jointed pipe. Or Athens crowned at evening with violet light, when the smoke of the evening meal rises at once from every house and hut in the city, redolent with the savour of tasty foods. For what are thirty-six men against five thousand?'

'Or Apollo's navel-shrine gleaming white through the thick laurel-grove,' said Iphitus of Phocis. 'Or the blue waters of the Crisaean Gulf. My comrade of the scarlet buskins perhaps did well to die when he did: he, at least, was buried with full rites, and his ghost by now is a lord of the Underworld, for doubtless he did not forget what he learned in Samothrace. But if we are destroyed by baleful Aeëtes ours will be the miserable fate of Phrixus – to be suspended in untanned ox-hides from the tops of lofty trees, for the crows and kites to peck at.'

Peleus said bitterly: 'If only we had Hercules here, if only you had listened to Admetus and myself –'

'Enough of that, Peleus!' cried Calaïs and Zetes in one breath.

'Have you forgotten, comrades,' asked Mopsus the Lapith, though in a voice that betrayed his lack of confidence, 'that no less than five Olympian deities have blessed our enterprise?'

Melampus of Pylos answered: 'Olympus lies far from here. The law of Zeus does not run beyond Sinope, or the river Lycos even.'

Idas uttered a forced laugh: 'Leave the Olympians to their snowballing, man of Pylos. You have Idas with you – he fears nothing.'

Nobody took Idas up; it was considered that his graceless jokes were best smothered with the wet blanket of silence.

After a pause all looked to Jason to make some reassuring speech, but he sat brooding miserably. At last Orpheus spoke for him: 'Comrades, you have forgotten the Great Goddess whose sovereignty is universal and perpetual (though in Greece she has indulgently divided her powers among her sportive children) and by whose original contrivance we are come here. There is no need to despair while we continue in her service. Forget Zeus and his Fleece for a while; remember the Goddess and her designs. The first object of our voyage is to seek out and inter the bones of Phrixus the Minyan. When we have done this and thereby satisfied the Goddess, we may be permitted to expect her help in the other matter also. Let not another word be said by anyone about the Fleece until the ghost of Phrixus is at peace at last.'

'This must be accepted as an order from myself,' said Jason severely, stirring from his trance.

All the next day they rowed up the river, through the same living-dead forest, and saw not a single human being, but only waterfowl, birds of prey, and a flock of ibis – the filthy Egyptian wading-bird that feeds on snakes and uses its own beak as a clyster-pipe. That evening when they anchored, worn out with the sultry heat, Orpheus delighted them with a song that he had made, incorporating some of the sayings of the previous night, but always with a new turn of his own. This song, beginning

> Grant me at last a safe return
>   To Sparta's cool and grassy glens –

is still sung in the chimney-corners of Greece, and by oarsmen at their benches in foreign waters. In the next verses it is 'Athens, crowned with violets', and 'Thisbe, of the cooing doves', and 'Sandy Pylos, nurse to ships' that are remembered, with numerous other beloved places situated in every region where the Greek language is spoken. These memories are contrasted with the odious sights and sounds of the river Phasis, and each verse ends with the refrain:

> Mother of Destiny, forgive me still
> If I transgress your holy use and will.

Early on the third day of their voyage up the river, the forest thinned and a strong tributary, the Suros, came whirling down between the mountains from the north. At the junction of the streams stood a fair-sized settlement of wattled huts thatched with branches and daubed with mud. Here the Argonauts saw for the first time Colchian peasants with their skinny legs and woolly hair. They were dressed in short, white linen smocks and wore red flowers behind their ears. Argeus, son of Phrixus, said: 'These are a merry and indolent folk, yet think continually of death. Phasis is their Nile and, like their cousins the Egyptians, they venerate the ibis and circumcise their foreskins.'

Herds of buffaloes wallowed in the wet meadows, and on the head of each a small bird was perched, pecking at the swarmed vermin. 'Those buffalo-birds are venerated too,' said Argeus. Towards noon the river-banks grew firmer and the current stronger; but a strong south-westerly wind blew them along without need of oars. More settlements appeared, each with a quay and a row of dug-out canoes moored alongside. They saw horses and cows again and blossoming fields of blue flax, and fields of millet, nearly ripe for the sickle; and women washing by the water-side and naked little children playing at knucklebones, so intent on their game that they did not look up as the ship sailed past. The women painted the edge of their eyelids, in the Egyptian fashion. Here and there were stinking tree-cemeteries: willow-trees hung with shapeless bundles, at some of which the vultures and gryphons were tearing. The Argonauts stuffed their nostrils with leaves of pungent scent as they passed.

The sons of Phrixus called out greetings at each settlement, and since the *Argo* was disguised again with her Colchian figure-head it was supposed that they were returning from the voyage that they had undertaken a few days before, the omens not having been favourable. The Argonauts wondered at the greenness of the plain, which Orpheus pronounced to be far better watered than the valley of the Nile, and of a better climate. Here three crops a year are often taken from the same field, and the vine yields fruit in its second year and requires no digging about its roots or any pruning except once every four years. But the sons of Phrixus warned the Argonauts to beware snakes – for the richer the country, the more poisonous its denizens – and tarantulas, a sort of spider whose bite causes one man to die weeping over the supposed loss of his kinsmen, and another laughing at a joke of his own that nobody else can understand.

'Idas needs no tarantula's bite to make him die laughing at that sort of joke,' Castor bitterly interposed; and this saying had in it something prophetic.

That night the ship was moored to an islet in mid-stream, where they disembarked and lit a camp-fire, knowing that only a few miles lay between them and their goal, the high-walled city of Aea, which stands ringed with mountains, at the confluence of the two great rivers, the Glaucos and the Phasis. They feasted on a buffalo-ox which they caught as it came down to the river to drink; the sons of Phrixus judged that it was a stray beast and therefore legitimate prey. They had not eaten roast meat for some days, and though tough as leather it gave them good heart. Meleager and Atalanta sat together hand in hand, like bride and bridegroom at a marriage-feast, for the fear of death was fuel to their passion and made them reckless.

Jason spoke at last: 'Our trust is in the Gods, but they will not help us unless we help ourselves. Sharpen your weapons, comrades, on my excellent Seriphan whetstone, and strengthen your hearts with faith in the Immortals. Hard trials lie ahead of us.'

Idas made some foolish rejoinder, and a silence followed that at last became unbearable. Nobody had anything to say worth the saying, and so long a silence could only be decently broken by words of the profoundest wisdom. Each man looked at his neighbours, but only blank faces stared back. At last came the creaking voice of Ascalaphus: 'Comrades, listen to me! Though we may make the points of our weapons as sharp as needles and the edges as sharp as razors, there is only one man who can haul us out of this mire, the very man who, like the lanterned Marsh Spite, has led us into it – Jason, son of Aeson. Hercules himself chose him as our captain, and obeyed him faithfully so long as he remained with us. Now why was this? Jason is a skilled archer, but not the equal of Phalerus or Atalanta; he throws the javelin well, but not so well as Atalanta or Meleager or even myself; he can use a spear, but not with the art or courage of Idas; he is ignorant of music, except that of drum and pipe; he cannot swim; he cannot box; he had learned to pull well at an oar, but is no seaman; he is no painter; he is no wizard; his sight is not keen above the ordinary; in eloquence he is below any man here, except Idas, and perhaps myself; he is hasty-tempered, faithless, sulky, and young. Yet Hercules chose him as our captain and obeyed him. I ask again: why was this? Comrades, it was because he possessed a certain power that we others lack; and the noble Centaur told us plainly, by the mouth of Hercules, how that power is manifested.'

Then they all recalled what had been said of Jason's gift of making women fall in love with him; indeed, they had seen it exercised in Lemnos upon Queen Hypsipyle, who was ready to give up her whole kingdom to him after an acquaintance of only two days. At this point Atalanta was inspired by some deity: she called for silence while she recited a ballad, which she composed as she went, accompanying herself prettily on the lyre of Orpheus. The words themselves are forgotten but their substance is as follows:

'I, Atalanta, dreamed that I stood in a doorway of the Divine House on Mount Olympus and, as I stood there, I saw the Goddess Athena crossing the court with a white owl perched upon her shoulder. She was visiting the apartments occupied by the Goddess Hera, she who was once the Sovereign of All Things but has since humbled herself to be the wife of Father Zeus. I followed the bright Goddess into Hera's apartment, where Hera, with large brown eyes like a cow's, reclined brooding on a couch.

'"What news, Athena?" asked Hera.

'Athena replied: "The East Wind brings me a report from Colchis. The *Argo* is moored to an island in the broad Phasis, not far from the city of Aea, and the crew are holding a council of war."

'"I hope," said Hera, "that they do not contemplate an assault on Aea? That would be disastrous for my plans. What are thirty-six men and one woman against five thousand?"

'Athena replied: "They have sharpened their weapons, passing a Seriphan whetstone from hand to hand; but the East Wind tells me that they are also considering stratagems. They propose to deceive Aeëtes with fair words before they make an attempt upon the Fleece."

'"I care nothing for the Fleece," said Hera. "My sole desire is that the bones of Phrixus shall be decently interred."

'Athena answered: "Let me bargain with you, Majesty. If you help Jason to win the Fleece, I undertake to attend to the matter of Phrixus."

'They clasped hands on that bargain. Then Hera struck on a silver bell for Iris her messenger, and when Iris appeared, riding on a rainbow, she said: "Child, summon Aphrodite the Goddess of Love to me instantly."

'Presently Iris returned with Aphrodite, whom she had found seated at her inlaid dressing-table, combing her yellow ringlets; and still she combed them as she entered Hera's apartment.

'"What can I do for you, Majesty?" asked lovely Aphrodite.

'Hera answered: "There is a ship called the *Argo* moored in the Phasis river under the shadow of the Caucasus. I cannot now tell you the whole tangled story of how she comes to be there. To be brief: unless her captain, Jason the Minyan (nephew to one Pelias of Iolcos who has grossly insulted me), can win the affections of the Princess Medea of Colchis, I will be disappointed of the service that he has undertaken to perform for me, and Athena will be disappointed of her dutiful ambition to recover a lost fleece, the property of her father Zeus. You must help us."

'Aphrodite threw up her hands in a gesture of dismay. "Dear Goddesses, I would do anything in the world to serve either of you," she said, "but you surely know that making people fall in love with one another is not my province at all, but that of my naughty son, Eros the Love Spite, over whom I have no control at all. The last time that I tried to make him behave himself properly, and threatened to burn his bow and arrows if he did not, he aimed an arrow at me, his own mother – would you believe it? – and involved me in that shameful scandal with Ares. My poor husband Hephaestus has never forgiven me for it."

'Hera and Athena had difficulty in restraining their laughter when they remembered how foolishly embarrassed Aphrodite and Ares had looked when Hephaestus had caught them in bed together and netted them over with a bronze net.

'"It was not even as though I had ever *liked* Ares," said Aphrodite, nearly weeping. "He is not at all the sort of god in whose company I could have wished to be found. Now, if only it had been Apollo…! But Ares has disgusting Thracian manners, and no talents, and thinks of nothing but war and bloodshed. He is not even handsome. But I could not help myself. It must have been his long mane of hair and his tattooed face."

'Hera said: "Come, my dear, we none of us thought any the worse of you for your adventure. But do your best with your son, I implore you. Bribe him, if you can do nothing else. Promise him what you like – I know – promise him some of the toys with which Zeus used to play long ago in the Dictean Cave of Crete when he was my chubby, spoilt baby. I have preserved them out of foolish sentiment, for he was an affectionate little child, indeed he was, though nobody would believe it now."

'Hera gave Aphrodite the key of her cedar-wood chest and Aphrodite opened it. There she found a wonderful collection of toys – clay men on horseback, little bronze bulls and bronze chariots, big-bottomed female dolls carved in soap-stone, painted wooden ships complete with sails and oars, and some rather improper objects which, as a woman, I hesitate to describe in the hearing of men. Best of all, there was a beautiful ball, perfectly round, of bull's leather stitched over with thin sheet-gold the stitches hidden in a spiral of dark blue enamel made with crushed lapis lazuli; Zeus had been very careful of this toy and the gold was nowhere dinted.

'So Aphrodite took up the ball and went out into the glens of Olympus, tossing it, as she went, from one hand to the other. I followed her, keeping at a safe distance, for Atalanta fears the Love Spite as much as any woman. There under a blossoming almond-tree Eros was playing at dice with the Father's cup-bearer, the boy Ganymede, rolling them down a grassy slope. Eros stood grinning to himself and pressing to his left breast a dozen or more of the golden dice, which he could not otherwise hold in his hand without spilling. The wretched Ganymede was squatting down with a miserable look on his face, shooting off his last pair of dice. The Dog turned up, which is the lowest score in Olympus as it is among us mortals, and Eros greedily scooped up those dice too. The shadow of his mother fell across the grass and he slewed suddenly around with a guilty look, protesting: "No, no, Mother, it is quite fair play; they are not loaded this time, I promise. Whatever you say, I shall never give them back to Ganymede. I won them in fair play, I swear by the Styx."

'Aphrodite looked severely at Eros, caught him by the right hand and led him off. I followed and heard her say: "Dear little Eros, my darling son,

I have a most wonderful plaything for you. If you throw it through the air it shines like the sun and leaves a track like a shooting-star. Hephaestus himself could never have made anything so beautiful. It comes from the land of China, where all the men and women have yellow faces." Then she showed him the ball.

"'Oh! Oh! Oh! Give it to me at once, Mother," he cried. "Ganymede will be jealous, I want to make him jealous."

"'No, child, you must earn it first," said she. Then she told Eros how to find the city of Aea in Colchis, and how to recognize Medea, and what to do when he saw her. He smiled, winked, and placed the golden dice in her lap, counting them carefully first, for he feared that she might return one or two of them to Ganymede; then he spread his wings which resemble those of the hawk-moth, and flew off with the West Wind, his bow in his right hand and his quiver at his left thigh. For, truly, it was the handsomest ball that ever a child saw. Now Eros is hiding behind a pillar in the portico of the royal mansion of Aeëtes; he is pointing his sharpest arrow at Medea, and impatiently awaits the arrival of Jason.'

As Atalanta laid down her lyre, a burst of applause drowned the indignant voice of Ascalaphus, whom she had offended by her reflections on the manners of his divine father, Ares. The applause rang on and on, and Jason blushed red to the neck.

'For my part,' Atalanta whispered in the ear of Meleager, 'I cannot bear the sight of Aeson's son but I know by the very strength of my dislike that he must exercise a strong fascination upon others of my sex.'

As soon as he could make himself heard, Phrontis, son of Phrixus, spoke. 'Medea is famous for her beauty; but she has never yet fallen in love with anyone, so far as I know.'

'No,' his brother Melanion said, 'she never has fallen in love; I am sure of that. Once I spoke with her at length about Greece. She told me that she had never felt herself at home among the dark-skinned Colchians, and also that she hated her mother's savage race. But she hoped that perhaps one day she might visit Greece, which she believed to be a very beautiful and progressive country.'

Cytissorus, the third brother, chimed in: 'She is a strange woman, in whose presence it is difficult to keep one's equanimity: sometimes she behaves like a sweet-tempered child, sometimes like the terrible Mother herself when she dances in ecstasy on her heap of skulls. Our sister Neaera adores Medea, who told her not long ago that no woman of good sense or dignity ever allows herself to be overcome by love of a man, and that men are the inferior sex. This has greatly unsettled Neaera's mind, for she is in love with one of the Taurian priests and does not wish Medea to think ill of her. Yet I cannot complain that Medea has ever treated me badly. She was most gracious to me just before we sailed for Greece and gave me a bag of rare medicines, which unfortunately went down with our ship. She begged me to act prudently at Corinthian Ephyra when I enquired about her father's inheritance there: I was to say nothing at all that would offend the religious feelings of the inhabitants. She told me, by the way, that if anything were to happen to her father, she would willingly resign her share in the Colchian inheritance to her brother Apsyrtus, but only on condition that he gave up his share in the Corinthian inheritance; and that Apsyrtus and she had indeed concluded a private treaty in this sense.'

Here the fourth brother, Argeus, took on the tale. 'It seems that our grandfather Aeëtes left Greece under a cloud at about the same time as his sister Circe also sailed away, and put his Corinthian lands under the stewardship of one Bunus, an Ionian, and his people under the regency of his nephew Sisyphus of Asopia. Then came the Achaean invasion; Bunus was killed in battle at the gate of Ephyra, and Sisyphus died in slavery, and now (so we hear) the Achaeans claim the whole kingdom of Corinth as their own. Creon rules in Asopia, and a governor of Ephyra appointed by King Sthenelus of Mycenae styles himself Corinthus to establish a sort of hereditary title to it. Yet, notwithstanding, Medea has hopes of recovering her father's inheritance; I understand that it has been promised her by the Mother in a dream. Now that Apsyrtus has resigned his claim, she stands the nearest in succession – nearer than us as being the child of Aeëtes, whereas we are only his grandchildren – except for her aunt Circe, who can never return to Ephyra because the Oracle of Asopus sentenced her long ago to perpetual banishment for some nameless crime.'

Jason asked: 'Why is Medea not already married? Has she never had suitors? Does her dislike of men perhaps conceal some incapacity or deformity?'

Argeus answered: 'Many powerful chieftains of Colchis have wished to marry her, not for her beauty and wealth only, but for the peculiar favours that the Bird-headed Mother has shown her. But she has persuaded her father that any such alliance would breed jealousy among the rejected suitors, and that, if she marries, she must marry a foreigner. I do not believe that she is either deformed or incapable of passion; but she has often told Neaera that virginity endows a woman with extraordinary powers in witchcraft and medicine. Wild beasts or serpents have no power to hurt a virgin and she can safely pluck leaves and dig roots that it is death for men or their wives to touch.'

'That is true,' said Atalanta. 'It is the gift of the Goddess Artemis.'

'Medea attributes it to Brimo,' said Argeus, 'but perhaps these are different names for the same aspect of the Ineffable One. Medea is the most skilful physician and witch in the whole kingdom.'

Jason stroked his short, downy beard meditatively. 'She appears to be the very woman for our purpose,' he said. 'Myself, I am not afraid of witches. Cheiron the Centaur taught me an infallible charm against them. She is beautiful, you say, and not very old, though she is your aunt? But "beautiful" to a Colchian may not be "beautiful" to a Greek. I hope that she has not black, kinky hair, flat feet, and inverted shins like your brother Melanion? I could never bring myself to kiss a woman of that sort.'

'Oh, no!' Melanion answered, grinning. 'Her mother was a white Taurian, not a Colchian. Medea has a round chin, yellow ringlets of hair (like those for which her aunt Circe was famous in her girlhood – they are as yellow as mountain cassidony), voluptuous lips, amber-coloured eyes, a slightly hooked nose, and the neatest ankles in Colchis. Her age is about four-and-twenty.'

'That is very well,' said Jason. 'I have always preferred mature women to girls. Now, comrades, to sleep. I wish you all propitious dreams. Our comrade Atalanta has pointed the path for our feet to tread.'

But before he slept he asked Melanion privately: 'Of what does Medea's Colchian inheritance consist? Is she joint-heir with her brother to the throne?'

'No,' he answered. 'She is heir only to a third part of her father's treasure. The kingdom, having been granted to Aeëtes as a reward for his services to the Colchians, is hereditary in the male line, except for the eastern territory, which adjoins the kingdom of Albania. Those wild lands are his only in virtue of his marriage with our Colchian grandmother Ipsia, and at his death will descend in the female line to our sister Neaera.'

Jason said: 'Indeed. Apsyrtus then should be pleased with the bargain that he has struck with her. For Ephyra is nothing to him, and a third part of the treasure that Aeëtes has amassed must amount to a sum sufficient to buy half of Greece.'

CHAPTER THIRTY-ONE

KING AEËTES RECEIVES THE ARGONAUTS

That night King Aeëtes could not sleep, try how he might. Not only had
the Sacred Horses of the Sun been off their feed for some days and unre-
sponsive to the purges duly administered by the Stable Priests, but he was
deeply concerned about an evil omen that he had witnessed in the temple
of the Moon Goddess that evening. Twelve months before this, one of the
temple slaves, whose office it was to provide fish for the sacred black cats
of the Goddess, had suddenly gone mad – though no sign of failing wits
had previously been noted in him – and had rushed out into the forest
caterwauling and shouting ecstatically in a language that nobody understood. The High Priestess had gone out in search of him, fettered him in
sacred fetters, and maintained him for the rest of the year in royal state. At
the annual sacrifice to the Goddess this slave had been sacrificed with the
other victims, being pierced through the heart with an obsidian-tipped
lance; the manner of his fall was expected to provide a heartening omen of
coming events. But, instead of falling forward, a fall which denotes victory,
or backward, which denotes defeat; or sinking in a heap, which denotes
peace – instead of any such fall, the victim chose to whirl around left-
handed three times and die crouching with his hands clasping his belly, a
sight never seen before and one of great horror to all those present.

Aeëtes was reminded by his four wise Councillors of State that the
omen might be significant not of disaster to Colchis, but merely of some
alteration in the Goddess's affairs, a return perhaps to a more primitive
ritual; however, they could not easily reassure him. He prowled about his
palace, which was built of massive well-polished stones, going from room
to room in search of he knew not what: so a house-dog behaves when it is
sickening for rabies, before the madness at last flecks its jaws with foam
and drives it snapping and howling along the streets. Shortly before dawn
he sank down wearily on a couch in the inner hall, not far from the long
basalt pediment on which stood the brazen bulls, and there he dreamed a
most unpropitious dream. First he watched a shining star fall slowly into
the lap of his daughter Medea, who took it in haste down to the Phasis river
and cast it in; the waters whirled it away towards the Black Sea. That part
of the dream did not disquiet him, but next he watched the brazen bulls

being roughly yoked with a red-painted wooden yoke and forced to plough a field. They were indignantly puffing flames from their nostrils and mouths, but the young ploughman cried tauntingly: 'Your flames cannot scorch me. I have been anointed by Medea with Caspian salve.' He spoke in Greek. Aeëtes could not distinguish his face or even his hair, because he was shrouded in a dark cloak; and now he was goading the bulls forward across the field with a javelin. A divine hand scattered serpents' teeth in the crooked furrow behind him, and where they fell armed men sprouted and sprang up. Aeëtes recognized these by their helmets as the priests of the Taurian war god in whose honour he had set up the brazen bulls. The ploughman presently cast a stone at one of them and struck him on the brow; whereupon they began hacking at one another, until all lay dead. At this the ghost of the hero Prometheus wailed aloud with the desolate cry of a night bird, and the hollow valley of Aea rang again with the noise.

Aeëtes awoke in a cold sweat. He stumbled to Medea's bed-chamber and roused her from sleep to tell her his dream, which he forbade her to reveal to a soul, and begged her to tell him what she thought that it portended. She answered: 'Father, I cannot speak with any certainty. I think it probable that you have in some way or other offended the Bird-headed Mother. Propitiate her with rich gifts and perhaps she will inform you in a dream or vision how you have erred and how you may escape the consequences of your error.'

Aeëtes frowned. As King of Colchis he was always in a difficult position because of the religious jealousies and dissensions of his people. His nobles worshipped the gods of Egypt, being descended from the soldiers of Pharaoh Sesostris who had been defeated in futile war with the Goths; but there had been no priests among the broken troops who took refuge in the Phasis valley and established themselves at Aea, and their worship was therefore irregular and debased. When Aeëtes first came to Colchis as a merchant-adventurer he had found a religious war in progress between these Egyptians and their aboriginal neighbours, who worshipped the Caucasian Goddess and Mithras, her fair-haired Sun-Child. He proposed an armistice and offered to reconcile their religious differences. He displayed his own fair hair and amber-coloured eyes in proof to the aboriginals that he was a Sun priest; and satisfied the Egyptians, by an explanation of certain of their own religious observances, that he had a more profound knowledge of the theology of Memphis than they had themselves. They listened to him the more attentively because the oracular jaw-bone of Prometheus which he brought with him had already made several veracious and helpful utterances. Upon their agreeing to abide by the decisions of Prometheus, Aeëtes reformed the national religion of Colchis in a way that enlightened and, for the most part, contented both peoples; for the jaw-bone proclaimed the identity of the Caucasian Goddess with the Bird-headed Goddess, Egyptian Isis. In gratitude, the nobles offered him the throne and swore perpetual loyalty to him and his house. Each people was obliged to yield to the other in some particulars: the aboriginals, who lived in the mountains, submitted to the Egyptian rite of circumcision and the veneration of the ibis; the Colchians, who cultivated the river-valley, submitted to the custom of tree-burial and to the veneration of the white horses of Mithras, his yearly gift from the Mother.

Yet Aeëtes felt that he was treading on the tussocks of a quaking bog that might at any moment engulf him. He now told Medea: 'When, to preserve this country from a Scythian invasion, I allied myself with your grandfather the King of the Taurians, of whom the Scythians stand in awe, I was, as you know, obliged in token of good faith to offer his war god a foot-hold in Aea. I did this reluctantly, well aware that the Mother has no love for this god, who is uncivilized and brutal in the extreme. Likewise my alliance with the Moschians, whose land (as you must agree) is a necessary outpost against the insane Amazons, has involved me in other religious transactions which may have displeased her. But what else could I have done? Let no ignorant person envy me my throne, which is no more comfortable a seat than a thorn-bush spread over with a coverlet of gold tissue.'

'I cannot blame you in the least degree, Father,' replied Medea, who as Priestess of Prometheus, and of Brimo, could sympathize with him in his religious perplexities. 'Yet try to placate the Goddess, and keep your eyes and ears open for a sign from her, which cannot be long in coming. I do not think that the Goddess is offended by your Moschian alliance, but you will know by the sign whether you have insulted her son Mithras, who slew the Bull of Darkness, by introducing the Taurian bulls into your palace, or whether the Goddess herself resents your admission of the Taurian priests to the fore-part of the enclosure of Prometheus. I grant that these acts, which necessity forced upon you, were performed many years ago; and that you propitiated the Goddess most dutifully at the same time; yet this is the first year in which, yielding to the persuasions of my uncle Perses the Taurian, you have dared either to attend the revels of the war god or to garland the bulls with Colchian flowers. You would be wise to consult the Goddess at once. It may be that she is promising that if you are obliged to offend my mother's people by the expulsion of the priests, or the bulls, or both, help will come to you from the land of Greece.'

Aeëtes said: 'This is a possible interpretation, I grant. But what of the serpents' teeth?'

Medea answered: 'The Taurians claim to be sprung from the teeth that fell from the jaws of the snake Ophion, when Eurynome strangled him, and thus to be of an earlier creation than Pyrrha and her lover Deucalion, the clay-formed ancestors of the Greeks. The dream suggests that the Sown men will ruin themselves by their opposition to these Greeks.'

Aeëtes asked again: 'But what of the star that fell into your lap?'

Medea answered: 'Is it perhaps some divine gift conferred on me, which will spread the fame of our house into foreign parts?' She concealed from him the dream which she had been dreaming when he had awakened her, and which, she was convinced, supplemented his own. It was of Circe, his sister who lived in the island of Aeaea at the head of the Adriatic Sea, a proud, falcon-eyed, falcon-nosed crone, beckoning to her and crying: 'Leave all and come to me!'

He asked again: 'But why did the ghost of Prometheus wail?'

She answered: 'How can I tell you that? It may well have been derisive wailing for his Taurian neighbours. He will be pleased enough to see their backs when they are driven from his enclosure.'

Aeëtes pondered on Medea's answers, and approved them in the main. Yet he still felt a grave misgiving, and dared not return to the couch to complete his sleep, for fear of further dreams. Instead, he invited her to come out walking with him in the palace grounds while breakfast was prepared; after breakfast he would avert the evil consequences of his dream by a double precaution – he would wash in the clear water of the Phasis, and he would tell his dream to the Sun so soon as ever it surmounted the eastern peaks.

Medea consented. She dressed herself in one of her finest robes, and adorned her head with care; then she went out with her father along the level walks between the flower-pots and fruit-bushes towards the place where the fifty-jetted fountain played. Wishing to rid his mind of a secret that weighed heavily upon it, he most unseasonably disclosed to Medea a recent decision of his Council of State. They had invited old Styrus, King of the Albanians, to come to Aea with an offer of marriage for her. 'It may be,' he said, 'that my dream of the star is concerned with the fruit of this marriage, which I have planned, as you will understand, solely for the public good. You have always been a prudent girl, avoiding the snares of love which make life so unnecessarily painful for young people; and therefore I trust that you will raise no objections to this marriage (which Styrus himself has proposed through a Moschian intermediary), as you have to others of less political consequence; but, on the contrary, will welcome it. With old Styrus as my son-in-law all our foreign anxieties will end.' For Styrus ruled over a powerful tribe in the mountains to the north of the river Cyrus, and thus not only commanded the trade route upon which much of the prosperity of Colchis depended, but threatened the kingdom's eastern frontiers. And Aeëtes reminded her too: 'Your position in Albania will be one of far greater power than you can ever hope to attain in Colchis when your brother Apsyrtus succeeds me.'

Medea said nothing at all in reply, but inwardly she seethed with rage; for the Albanians are lice-eaters and have disgusting sexual habits, and the Council of State had insulted her by treating with Styrus behind her back.

Aeëtes ironically praised her dutiful silence; but still she said nothing.

Together they watched the distant snowy hills of Moschia take on the reflected radiance of sunrise.

'It is the colour of fresh blood,' said Aeëtes involuntarily; and could not recall these unfortunate words.

As they turned to walk back towards the palace a messenger came running up from the southern watchtower. 'Majesty,' he cried breathlessly, 'a thirty-oared Greek ship has just sailed up the river through the mist and is casting anchor at the Royal Quay. The figurehead is a Ram, and the crew appear, every one of them, to be persons of great distinction. Among them I have discerned your four grandchildren, the sons of Phrixus; of whom one, Prince Argeus, has been wounded in the head.'

Aeëtes strode out at once through the Southern Gate of the city and down towards the quay in an excess of anger, intending to forbid the Argonauts to land; but met Echion the herald already advancing to meet him, olive wand in hand.

Echion was the first to speak:

'Thrice-noble King Aeëtes of Colchis, formerly of glorious Ephyra, we come in the name of The Mother on an errand of piety which our captain will presently disclose to you in better words than I can muster. He is Jason the Minyan, heir to the throne of Phthiotis, and the rest of our ship's company are, similarly, of the best blood to be found in Greece, some of them kings, others of divine parentage. Among them is Augeas, King of Elis, who, like you, is a hereditary priest of the Sun. You need not fear that we come with any evil intent, for The Mother herself has sent us. By her gracious intervention, not many days ago, Jason rescued from drowning your four noble grandsons and now restores them to you, safe and sound. And he rescued not only your grandchildren, but his own kinsmen. For Cretheus, Jason's grandfather, was brother to their grandfather, King Athamas of Orchomenos.'

Aeëtes answered with a lowering look: 'Is it not known throughout Greece that when news was brought to me of the barbarous murder of my nephew Sisyphus of Asopia, I swore that I would have my revenge on the first crew of Greek seamen who dared to venture up this river and would kill every man of them? What virtue, do you think, lies in the impious name of Athamas that it should persuade me to alter my intention towards you?'

Echion answered blandly: 'It is fortunate, Majesty, that your words, spoken in anger, were so loosely phrased that you need not consider yourself bound by them in your dealings with us. In the first place, we seamen are not all Greeks, for several of us are of ancient Cretan or Pelasgian stock, and three are Thracians (as their tattooed faces and hemp tunics declare); in the second, we Greeks are not all seamen, for Atalanta of Calydon is a seawoman. As for the name of Athamas, let it ring in your ears as a warning of what befalls those who disregard the orders of the Great One in whose name we come.'

Medea, who had followed her father through the gate from curiosity, caught at his sleeve and drew him aside. 'Father,' she whispered, 'remember your dream and recognize the sign. Do not thoughtlessly drive away the Greek help which the Goddess plainly vouchsafed you last night. Entertain these strangers hospitably, and when you have provided them with hot baths, clean clothes, and the best food and drink at your command, listen attentively to what they have to say. They come in the name of The Mother, not of any upstart Zeus or Poseidon.'

Aeëtes answered aloud: 'If they do not come in the name of Zeus, why does their ship carry a Ram figure-head?'

'Ask the herald,' said she. 'Do not ask me!'

Echion had a ready explanation. The Ram figure-head had been the emblem of Minyan ships for generations, long before the new Olympian dispensation. Why should Aeëtes regard it as having any disturbing significance? He added: 'Among other prime objects of our voyage is that of offering you, on behalf of the present rulers of Asopia and Ephyra, complete satisfaction for the cruel death of your nephew Sisyphus, which has been the original cause of countless distresses in the double kingdom.' Never was known so smooth a liar as Echion, when occasion served. His father Hermes had told lies from the very cradle; or so the Arcadian poets relate.

Aeëtes paused and stared fixedly at Echion, who met the angry gaze easily and unflinchingly, as an inspired herald should. Finally Aeëtes yielded. He dropped his eyes and said: 'Inform Jason your captain that I am grateful to him for the rescue of the four sons of Phrixus, my grandchildren; that he is free to come ashore without fear; and that I expect him to convey to me accurately the message entrusted to him by the Asopian and Ephyran rulers, with whatever other message he pleases so long only as not a word is spoken on the subject of the Golden Fleece of Laphystian Zeus.'

Echion laughed. He said: 'Do not blow old embers into flame, Majesty, by yourself naming an ancient relic of which (I am glad to inform you) everyone in Greece except heralds and poets, whose profession it is to remember everything, have long ago forgotten the very name.'

By this time Jason and the rest of the Argonauts had disembarked and were trooping, two by two, up the broad stone steps that led from the Royal Quay to the city gate. Aeëtes therefore dismissed Medea, not wishing her to be stared at by Greek strangers, and stood prepared to give Jason a courteous welcome. But Medea did not hurry on her way. Where the crooked path turned by a pear-tree, she also turned. Leaning against a balustrade she looked back at Jason as he stepped with youthful dignity, neither too slowly nor too fast, up the stairway, three paces ahead of his comrades.

He was not wearing his dark blue cloak decorated with the history of the Fleece, for that would have been imprudent; but a white cloak embroidered by Queen Hypsipyle of Lemnos with all manner of flowers and fruits, her principal love-gift to him. On his head was a broad-brimmed golden helmet, given him by King Lycus of the Mariandynians, which was adorned with a crest of black horse-hair, and in his hand was the same be-ribboned spear that had transfixed King Cyzicus. Never in all her life had Medea seen a fair-haired man, for her father was already bald and white-bearded when he married her mother and, since she was herself fair-haired, her heart suddenly warmed to him as a creature of her own kind, the natural he to her she. It was as though behind the pear-tree, already in young fruit, lurked the Love Spite celebrated in Atalanta's ballad: he, Eros, pressed the notch of a barbed arrow against the bowstring and drawing it back to his ear let fly at her heart with a twanging sound. For she gasped, and amazement clouded her mind. Then slowly she turned and went on her way again, without looking back.

Aeëtes, though gratified at the rescue of his grandsons, was far from pleased by their sudden return. He had permitted them to sail for Greece chiefly because he wished them to be out of the country when King Styrus of Albania came to sue for Medea's hand. Their only sister, Neaera, was Medea's inseparable companion; and Aeëtes had reckoned that if Medea were displeased by the marriage that had been arranged for her, she would make Neaera a confidante of her misery and Neaera would tell them of it. The four brothers, who were highly esteemed by the nobility of Colchis, would naturally oppose an alliance with the Albanians. The Albanians had once prevented them from pursuing a tiger, which they were hunting, into Albanian territory and abused them with unforgettable insults. They would do all that they could, if only for the sake of pleasing Neaera, to postpone or cancel the marriage. Now all four of them had returned unexpectedly, and Aeëtes was aware that Medea's silence covered a deep disgust of Styrus. To forestall any mischief he must send them off again in the *Argo* as soon as possible; meanwhile, he would command Medea to abstain from making the least complaint about the marriage either to Neaera or to any other person whatsoever. Fortunately, he remembered, Neaera was away from the palace and would not return until midday; she was a priestess of the Caucasian Maiden Goddess, and the festival of the New Moon had been celebrated that night under her direction.

He disguised his anxiety from his grandchildren, folding each in turn in a loving embrace, and offering his hand in friendship to Euphemus who had been the instrument of their salvation. To Jason he behaved with affability and told him: 'The news from Ephyra, my lord, can wait until we have eaten and drunken well. I make no doubt but that you have had a voyage as perilous and exhausting as it was long.'

Jason nodded courteously, but did not know what news Aeëtes meant. As the Argonauts followed Aeëtes up into the city, leaving Melampus and Little Ancaeus to guard the ship, Echion explained to Jason in an undertone the fiction about Ephyra which some god – and who else could it be but Hermes? – had unexpectedly put into his mouth, and which nobody must be allowed to contradict; and he advised Jason that all mention of the Golden Fleece by the Argonauts must be absolutely forbidden.

'Very well,' said Jason, 'if this fiction is indeed inspired by your divine father, it would be impious not to take advantage of it. Return at once to the *Argo* and warn Melampus and Ancaeus to be discreet. Meanwhile, I will pass your words around the company. It is fortunate that Hercules is no longer with us: he would have blurted out the truth before we were half-way up the hill.'

CHAPTER THIRTY-TWO

JASON SPEAKS WITH MEDEA

The Argonauts had been well bathed in warm water and well dried in warm towels by the palace women, who were for the most part Circassian slaves of surprising loveliness. With their heads anointed and chapleted and with clean linen shirts next to their skins they were soon reclining on couches in the royal dining-hall making an excellent repast. Many unfamiliar dishes were set before them, which they sampled with gusto, in true politeness not enquiring what the ingredients were, even though some of them might be ritually forbidden to them, and liable to cause cramp in the belly or death. They took no harm as it proved. But Butes was horrified when the servants heaped his plate with what he knew at once for the roasted bodies of immature bees; he groaned aloud at the sight and tears gushed from his eyes. Idas derided the distress of Butes, and to please his Colchian hosts crammed his mouth with the novel food, well sprinkled with salt, and called for more.

Jason and King Augeas of Elis were invited to eat at the King's own table, which was set on a dais at the eastern end of the hall. There they were introduced to four dark-featured, kinky-haired noblemen, the King's Councillors of State. Phrontis, son of Phrixus, acted as interpreter; for none of these noblemen could understand the Greek language, and Aeëtes, to lull any suspicions that might spring from the Argonauts' unannounced visit, spoke only in Colchian. The conversation was conducted in a formal and halting manner, Jason and Augeas relating slight incidents of the voyage, but disclosing nothing of importance. Aeëtes, who was wearing a gold diadem set with emeralds, and a robe of state, feigned a perfect indifference to Greek affairs. He asked only one question concerning the regions beyond the Black Sea: how had they forced the passage of the Hellespont against the Trojan guard-ships?

Jason replied carelessly that the Trojans had doubtless been forewarned by the Triple Goddess, who was venerated by them under the name of Cybele, that a Minyan ship was due to pass through the strait on divine business. At all events, he said, they had let the *Argo* sail through without challenge.

Aeëtes grunted discontentedly in reply.

However, when Augeas happened to mention the Thessalian traders who had joined the ship at Sinope, Aeëtes, whose treaty with the Trojans prevented him from direct trade with Sinope, listened with undisguised interest. He called down the hall for Autolycus to come and sit beside him, and, when Autolycus came, fed him with dainties from his own trencher, making much of him. Autolycus answered the King's questions frankly and pleasantly (for his trading days were now over), and quoted the prices, reckoned in gold dust, that had ruled in the last annual fair at Sinope. He felt a malicious pleasure in watching the King's face, since it was clear that the Trojan King Laömedon had given his ally a most misleading account of business at the fair.

At this point, Medea's only brother, Apsyrtus, a young man with a cat-like tread and a strong Taurian cast of features, came in from hunting. He saluted his father respectfully and, as Jason judged, affectionately, and sat down to meat without another word. His manner towards Jason and the other two Greeks was distant and unfriendly.

With dessert came the time for Jason to make a formal declaration of his visit. He rose to his feet, stretched out his right hand, first to the King and then to his four Councillors, and said:

'Glorious and magnanimous Aeëtes, it has perhaps already come to your ears – because the Trojans who trade both with you and with us are famous gossips – that our country of Greece has for the last two years been ravaged by a threefold plague: by great storms of wind that have torn down our fruit-trees and set the roofs flying from our houses; by an alarming barrenness among our flocks and herds; and by a great plague of poisonous snakes in our fields and woods. Judging that these plagues could only have been caused by the Ineffable One, and that appeal to any Olympian Oracle was therefore vain, a haggard all-Greek Council that met at Mycenae decided to consult your sister Circe, who is deeply in the Goddess's confidence, and ask her what should be done to propitiate the Goddess. Delegates waited upon your fair-haired sister at her palace in the island of Aeaea; who, after purifying herself and going into her customary trance, induced by a black potion, consulted the Goddess, addressing her as Brimo. Brimo responded that she had sent the plagues as a tardy punishment for the cruelties inflicted by the Achaeans many years before upon Sisyphus of Asopia. She now ordained that Sisyphus should be awarded a hero's tomb and be honoured with rich sacrifices every month, and that his Asopian lands should be taken away from Creon their usurper and restored to the rightful owners, the hereditary Priests of the Sun.

'Since, Majesty, you are the undoubted head of the elder branch of this illustrious clan, I have been desired by the inhabitants of the double kingdom of Corinth to convey you their loyal and humble petition: they beg you to return and rule over them – for your own fair lands, which include the city of Ephyra itself, can (after the thrusting-out of Corinthus, their regent) be reunited under one sceptre with Asopia. But if, they say, Colchis has become so dear to you and you have become so dear to Colchis that you cannot remove, they beg that you will immediately send one of your children – a daughter or a son would content them equally – to rule over them in your stead. Listen pityingly to their plea, for only thus can the kingdom of Ephyra, and all Greece besides, be saved from the disaster which threatens to engulf it.

'So much for the first message, to the accuracy of which Augeas of Elis, head of the younger branch of your illustrious family, will gladly testify. To it is joined another message from the Mare-headed Mother of Pelion, whom I learned to worship during my childhood; for the Centaurs reared me. It runs thus: "Aeëtes of Ephyra, on pain of my displeasure you are to give rest to the soul of my servant Phrixus the Minyan, which still languishes disconsolately between the bones of his unburied skull."'

Then Jason added, using an ancient formula: 'It is not my word, but my Mother's word.'

After a long time Aeëtes answered: 'As to the first message, I will deliberate with my wise Councillors of State and return you an answer within three days; but do not expect it to be a favourable one. For my daughter Medea is already expecting an offer of marriage from a neighbouring monarch and my son Apsyrtus must remain in Colchis as heir to my throne and prop to my declining years. I understand that the Corinthians have not invited me to send one of my four grandsons to rule over them; I could have spared them a grandson. But the Ephyrans do not love the Minyans, and the sons of Phrixus rank as Minyans. This is a pity. Nevertheless, for all the disasters that have come upon Greece since my departure the impious Achaeans and their dupes are responsible, not I; these plagues do not concern me.

'As to the second message, am I to believe that the Ineffable One speaks contradictorily with two different mouths? As the Bird-headed Mother of Colchis she has laid a sacred injunction upon her worshippers that no man's bones may be laid in the holy earth of Colchis; and the King of Colchis must obey this Bird-headed Mother rather than the Mare-headed Mother of Pelion. Let me beg you not to renew your plea; because the question whether the bones of Phrixus should be interred or not was asked by myself at the time of his death and conclusively answered by my priestly Councillors: since he died in Colchis, he was necessarily honoured with a Colchian funeral.'

The kinky-haired Councillors signalized their approval of this speech by drumming on the table with the handles of their knives. Jason kept silent, relieved that Aeëtes had not accepted on behalf of Apsyrtus the imaginary offer of his former subjects, and hopeful that an accommodation could yet be reached in the matter of burying the bones.

That afternoon Phrontis, son of Phrixus, brought Jason a private message from Aeëtes, which was that the Bird-headed Mother had not expressly forbidden the removal of the bones of Phrixus for burial elsewhere than in Colchis; and that therefore, if Jason cared to remove them secretly and at his own risk from the high poplar where they were suspended, he would find the cemetery unguarded on the following night, and could count on conveying them safely out of the country for eventual burial in Greece. For he himself, said Aeëtes, had loved Phrixus as a son and hated to cause his ghost the least pain or inconvenience.

This answer did not altogether please Jason, for the orders of the Goddess were that the bones of Phrixus were to be buried before any attempt might be made on the Fleece. He told Phrontis of this difficulty. Phrontis replied: 'Let me take you privately to the apartment of my sister Neaera, who returned to the palace while we were at dinner. You must not confide to her your design to carry off the Fleece, but merely tell her that you have been ordered by the Goddess to bury her father's bones before, and not after, you quit Colchis. She is quick-witted and may be able to suggest an evasion that will cause nobody any offence.'

Jason was pleased to accept a policy that would bring him into intimate conversation with young Neaera. Phrontis led him by a roundabout way to her apartment, and he learned from her with what repugnance Medea regarded her promised marriage to the old Albanian. For though Aeëtes, after his return to the palace that morning, had strictly forbidden Medea to speak of her marriage, she had already wept out her grief on the neck of an old nurse, from whom Neaera presently learned the whole story. Dark-eyed Neaera was almost incoherent with grief and sorrow. She told Jason: 'O Jason, my far-travelled kinsman, this news is almost too cruel for me to endure: I fear that I shall go mad if nothing is done to thwart the King's decision. A marriage between my glorious Medea and the rank old lice-eater, Styrus, would be like one between a white rose and a slug. Can you and your comrades do nothing to save her? Can you not carry her off to Greece, my lord Jason, and marry her yourself and set her on the throne of Corinth and thus justify the holy Oracle of Brimo?'

Jason answered: 'Be careful what you say, Princess. How can you think either that I should be willing to risk death by stealing away the King's only surviving daughter, or that she herself would be so unfilial as to slip away to Greece at my invitation? I acknowledge that the brief glimpse that I had of her this morning, as she leaned over the balustrade by the pear-tree, pierced my heart through with instant love, yet I should be mad to imagine her to be burning with equal passion for me. Therefore I shall try to forget your strange words, though I thank you for them from the bottom of my heart. Yet, dear kinswoman, to show your kindness to me, give me advice in the matter of your noble father's bones. For the White Goddess of Pelion has ordered me to bury them before, not after, I quit the land of Colchis.'

Neaera answered: 'Only Medea can arrange this matter. But first tell me: have I permission to report to Medea what you have just disclosed of your feelings for her?'

Jason pretended to hesitate in lover's modesty. Then he answered: 'If you swear by your own girdle to report my words exactly, secretly, and to no living being but Medea herself, you have my permission.'

Neaera swore, as she was desired, and then took her leave. Jason asked her as she turned to go: 'What of Apsyrtus? Does he favour the marriage?'

Neaera answered: 'He hates his sister, and is pleased by any event that discomfits her. Consider him your enemy, as I consider him mine.'

Presently Phrontis came to Jason with the news that Medea would visit his apartments that same evening at dusk, if he could absent himself from supper without exciting suspicion. Jason's heart bounded for joy. In a few hours he had already accomplished what he had expected would cost him days, or even months. But he said nothing to any of his companions and joined them that afternoon in friendly athletic contests with the Colchian nobility. The stadium was enclosed with buildings on three sides, namely by the wing of the palace reserved for the Royal Family, by the Guards' barracks, and by the Stables of the Sun, where the twelve white horses of the Sun God (whose backs no man might ever bestride) and the fatal black mare were tended with unimaginable honour.

The Argonauts had agreed to treat Jason, publicly at least, with the utmost love and deference, in order to enhance his glory in the eyes of Medea, who would be watching the games from a palace balcony. They chose him to represent them in quoit-throwing, archery, and leaping, and his performances, though they would not have been remarkable in any Greek city, excited the admiration of his hosts. For the Colchians, though courageous, are an indolent, unathletic people and, like their Egyptian cousins, execrable marksmen with the bow. Aeëtes himself would not watch: he declared that he hated any sight that reminded him of his early manhood in Greece, but also perhaps he foresaw that his Colchian subjects would not gain many prizes in the games.

In effect, the Argonauts were the victors in every contest except that of knucklebones, which they despised as childish but at which the Colchians were marvellously adept. Apsyrtus, who was the Colchian champion of upright wrestling, showed himself ignorant of the simplest principles of the art. When opposed to Castor, he sprang forward at once to catch at his knee. But Castor was too quick for Apsyrtus: he seized his left wrist with the right hand, his left elbow with the left hand, turned rapidly about, drew the whole arm over his own left shoulder and threw Apsyrtus clean over his head. In the second bout Castor, disregarding an attempt to catch and break one of his fingers, secured a body-hold almost at once, shook Apsyrtus off his balance, and tossed him ignominiously on his back.

Jason absented himself from supper at the hall that night, pleading that as a result of his athletic exertions he had been suddenly overcome by a recurrent fever; he must huddle himself in blankets and sweat it out. Since such fevers are common enough in Colchis, he was not suspected of deceit.

At dusk Medea visited him. She came in the disguise of a bent, hobbling old hag fetching him blankets for his fever. He paid no attention to her at all until she addressed him in a quavering old woman's voice, saying: 'My lord, I am Medea.' With that she laughed, wiped the painted wrinkles from her face, unhooded her luxurious tresses of yellow hair, kicked away her shapeless felt shoes, tore off her rusty-black linen smock, and stood up straight and beautiful before him, dressed in a white robe curiously embroidered with golden ivy leaves and fir-cones.

Jason threw off his blankets, hastily ran an ivory comb through his hair, and stood up before her, tall and handsome, dressed in a purple tunic fringed with gold lace and decorated at the neck and shoulders with amber pendants; these were spoils that he had taken from King Amycus the Bebrycian at the sack of his palace.

The two stood gazing at each other for a while, saying nothing, both equally astonished that a close view augmented the beauty that they had seen from a distance. It seemed to Medea that they were two trees: she a spired white cypress, and he a golden oak that overtopped her. Their roots entwined below the earth; their branches quivered together in the same southern breeze. The very first greeting that passed between them was not a word or a hand-clasp but a trembling kiss; yet a sense of shame preserved the decorum of the occasion and Jason did not press his advantage by handling her familiarly as he had handled Queen Hypsipyle at their first meeting.

Jason spoke first: 'Lovely lady, your holy powers have not been exaggerated. There are priestesses of the Mother who have the double-eye and use it to ruin and destroy, but you use the single-eye to heal and make whole.'

Medea answered wonderingly: 'You are the first of your sex who has ever kissed me, or whom I have kissed, since I was a child riding on the knee of my father.'

Jason said: 'Only allow me to hope that none other but myself will ever have this delight again – until one day perhaps an infant son clasps you about the neck, and kisses you, and calls you Mother.'

She said: 'How can this be, my dear love? Do you not know that I am to be courted by old Styrus the Albanian lice-eater, and that for the kingdom's sake I cannot refuse to marry him but must smile on him as he fetches me away to his gloomy mountain fortress in Caspia. O, but I can say no more, nor tell you with what horror and loathing my belly churns at the thought of this union – for my father has strictly forbidden me to make the least complaint.'

'Perhaps,' said Jason, 'the Colchian Mother will strike your old suitor dead at the palace gates if you pray to her with holy fervour; for among the

Albanians, I hear, the Sun God presumptuously makes himself the equal of his Mother the Moon. But it would be dishonourable in me to suggest, as your true friend Neaera has done, that you should forget your duty to your father and steal away with me before this wretch's arrival. And if you are so scrupulous to obey your father in the small matter of making no complaint against the filthy wedlock, the barren slavery, arranged for you, how will you dare to disobey him in a great matter?'

Medea did not answer this question, but raised her downcast eyes to his and said: 'Phrontis has already told me of your courtship of Queen Hypsipyle the Lemnian. He had the story from your comrade Euphemus. Euphemus did not impute any falseness or cruelty to you, but is it not true that you quitted the Queen after only two days, and would not undertake ever to return?'

'It was three days,' Jason answered, flushing, 'and that was an altogether different case from this. I consider Phrontis most uncomradely to have carried an old tale to your ears, knowing how easily you might have misunderstood it and judged me accordingly. Well, I will tell you briefly how it was. This Queen Hypsipyle invited me to share her bed chiefly for reasons of state: she needed a male heir for her throne and wished to provide him with a distinguished father. She showed me and my crew wonderful hospitality during our visit, and I should have been a boor to deny her anything within reason. Thus, certain loving courtesies passed between us which are inseparable from the act of procreation, and I do not deny that my person attracted her greatly. Yet I did not fall in love with her at first sight, as I have done with you, or even at second sight. My feelings for her are fairly proved by my honourable refusal of the throne of Lemnos. How many men do you know, Lovely One, who would refuse a rich kingdom freely offered them even if the gift were burdened with the forced embraces of an ugly old woman? Hypsipyle was young and generally accounted beautiful though a deal taller than you (too tall, in fact, for my liking). She had dark hair, not golden; and a straight nose, not one with your falcon-like hook; and her pale lips did not invite my kisses as do your red ones. It was easy to forget Hypsipyle; but you I could never forget though I outlived the Egyptian Phoenix. At the instant that I first set eyes upon you my heart began a golden dance. Do you know how a sunbeam quivers on the white-washed ceiling of an upper room, thrown up there by a great cauldron of lustral water in the courtyard, whose surface the wind stirs? That is how my heart danced, and is dancing now.'

'Nevertheless,' said Medea, trying to calm the clamour of her heart with a prudent speech, 'nevertheless, if it ever happened, whether because of the timely death of Styrus or for some other reason, that I were free to offer you more intimate embraces than those which we have thievishly enjoyed, I should be bound to exact an oath from you that you would marry me honourably beforehand and afterwards share the Corinthian throne with me; for my brother Apsyrtus has already privately resigned his claim to it in my favour. Also, I should require you first of all to conduct me to the Istrian city of Aeaea ruled over by Circe, sister to my father; she has summoned me to her in a dream.'

Jason knew Medea to be desperate and believed that she could be trusted with any confidence. He said: 'I would take that oath at once, were you to swear at the same time to help me accomplish my twin missions in this country.'

'What are they?' she asked. 'I have, so far, been told only that the Mare-headed Goddess of Pelion wishes you to inter the bones of Phrixus in the Greek manner, and this before quitting Colchis. I will gladly assist you, and already know the means. Ideëssas, the eldest son of the Moschian King, comes here tomorrow with the annual tribute. As usual, he will consult the Oracle of Prometheus, for whom the Moschians have the greatest veneration because the responses committed to me by him always prove to be true. Ideëssas will be told, among other things, that Prometheus loves the Moschians well and will graciously grant them an Oracle of their own which they can consult immediately whenever an unusual event occurs to disturb their peace of mind; that they are there-fore to build a tomb of shining stone, in imitation of the shrine of Prometheus, and are to deposit in it, with such and such ceremonies, the heroic bones that Ideëssas, upon returning to his apartment, will find laid in his own bed. But he will oracularly be warned to conceal these bones from every human eye until they are safe in the tomb; and to conceal their provenience ever afterwards, lest their oracular properties be impaired; and to speak of the hero merely as The Benefactor. And the aspect of the Goddess to whom he is to be oracular hero shall be the White Goddess, Ino of Pelion. I shall not reveal to the prince that under that name the Ephyrans have worshipped Ino, by whom Phrixus was sent to Colchis, ever since by her suicide and the murder of her son she became one with the Many-named Mother.'

'That is wonderfully contrived,' said Jason; 'but who will steal the bones and intrude them into the bed of Ideëssas?'

She answered: 'The trader from Sinope, Autolycus, is reputedly the cleverest thief in the world; Phrontis will instruct him how to act. And now for the other matter. You spoke obscurely of your twin missions. What other divine task have you been set to accomplish?'

Jason demanded: 'First swear by your girdle that you will never, by word, sign, or act, reveal this mission to any living soul until we are safely home in Greece.'

Medea took the oath.

Then Jason said: 'It is to carry off the Golden Fleece of Zeus from the shrine of Prometheus, and restore it to the oaken image of the Ram God upon Mount Laphystios.'

Her eyes widened and her lips parted in amazed horror. At last she said in a whisper: 'You ask this of me, the daughter of Aeëtes and Priestess of the shrine of Prometheus?'

'I do,' he answered, 'and with the explicit authority of the Mother herself.'

'You are lying,' she cried wildly. 'You are lying!' She turned and ran weeping from the room, all undisguised as she was.

He was taken aback and could say nothing.

Fortunately the corridors were empty, because of the supper-hour: Medea regained her own room without having been observed. Left alone, Jason presently stretched out his arms and exulted to himself: 'Was I not wise to say nothing and make no movement to restrain her when she ran out? A man should never run after a woman who loves him; just as a fisherman would be mad to plunge into the water after the fish which he has hooked. This shining fish of mine cannot swim further than the length of my line, which will not break.'

That evening he watched her from his window as, standing upright in a polished car, she drove her mules at full tilt through the streets of Aea and out through the East Gate towards the temple of Infernal Brimo. The reins were wound about her middle and she wielded a heavy whip in her right hand. On either side of her crouched a young priestess, and behind the chariot ran four more, with their light robes kilted to the knee, and each with a hand laid upon the rail. She urged the beasts on with cries of rage and the people fell back to avoid her onrush, shunning her glance. As Jason watched and wondered, a crow chattered at him from a poplar-tree that grew near his window. He asked Mopsus, who was with him, what the crow had said.

Mopsus replied: 'Crows have only two topics – the weather and love. This crow was talking to you about love, assuring you that all was well.'

CHAPTER THIRTY-THREE

THE SEIZURE OF THE FLEECE

After breakfast the next morning, Jason invited King Aeëtes to visit him in his apartment, and when he entered made a show of profound gratitude and respect. He even praised the King's decision to sacrifice his daughter's happiness for the good of Colchis. 'Alas, Majesty,' he said, 'the royal tiara is cruel headgear for many a loving father!'

Aeëtes answered with a frown: 'Why should my daughter Medea not be happy? And is she not free to accept or reject any suitor that I propose for her? Albania is a rich country and the old man will soon die, leaving her to rule as she pleases, for she will be styled the Mother of the sons who succeed him, and in Albania it is the King's mother who exercises the greatest power.'

'I beg you to excuse me,' said Jason. 'I had not known that this marriage was of Medea's own choice, and was ignorant of Caucasian customs. Yet for my part I should prefer to be your meanest subject than sole sovereign of any other land hereabouts, were the choice offered me.'

After enlarging upon the beauty and fertility of Colchis, where all good things spring up without sowing or ploughing, and congratulating Aeëtes on the harmony that ruled between its diverse inhabitants, Jason suddenly displayed the skeleton of Phrixus, falling apart from decay, which Autolycus had stolen out of the horse-hide suspended from the poplar. Aeëtes recognized the skeleton by the teeth (for Phrixus was gap-toothed) and wept over it. The bones had a miserably forlorn look, being furred over with white and green mildew. Then Jason, in the hearing of Aeëtes, ordered Autolycus to convey them with circumspection down to the *Argo* and there secrete them in the locker under the helmsman's seat, which had a false bottom. Autolycus took them away but not to the *Argo*: he went first to the apartment of Neaera, where she and her four brothers piously scraped and polished them; he himself undertook the articulation, boring each bone with an awl and joining it to its neighbour with a strip of leather. When they had done, and had jewelled the eye-sockets with turquoise, Autolycus removed the limber skeleton. He conveyed it to the apartment of Ideëssas, which, as he had hoped, he found deserted. For much the same distraction had been arranged as at the palace of King Phineus: all the

Colchian palace servants, and the Moschian suite of Ideëssas with them, had been drawn out by Orpheus to the fore-court with an inviting jig. They now stood rooted there with delight and amazement around a gaudy booth where Periclymenus the wizard was making magic. Besides the feats that he had shown the Argonauts on their first entrance into the Black Sea, he performed others even more extraordinary. He swallowed a two-handled sword and, as if that were insufficient wonder a long broad-headed javelin, point downwards; and presently voided them both from behind. And he set a wooden duck in a basin of pure water and then addressed the water, which heaved about with such a tempest that the duck was cast clean out of the basin; then, as he made to pick it up, it sprouted feathers and flew away quacking.

When, at a covert sign from Autolycus, Periclymenus at last concluded his performance, the Moschian suite reluctantly returned to their duty; but on re-entering the apartment they saw, as they thought, the figure of their princely master lying between the blankets of his bed, with his head tied in a woollen nightcap and his face turned to the wall. They did not dare address him, but sat on the floor in repentant attitudes until he should awake. They were disturbed and astonished by the sudden arrival of Ideëssas himself, who disregarded their nervous greetings and, going over to the bed, reverently abased himself, well knowing what would be lying between the blankets. He drew back the blankets, and there lay the polished white skeleton of a hero, just as the Oracle had promised. It held a tiger's tail in one hand, which is a good-luck sign among the Moschians, and in the other the staff of Ideëssas himself, as though it intended to go on a journey to Moschia.

Ideëssas closely questioned the four servants: what did they know of the matter? The first answered, his teeth chattering with fear, that none of them had left his post for an instant, the second was bold enough to allege that the skeleton had come walking in at the door without knocking; the third added that the skeleton, unwrapping the tiger's tail from about its skull, had drawn on the nightcap instead – after which, seizing the staff, it had rapped nine times upon the floor and climbed into bed. The fourth then declared that he and his companions, struck with awe at this unac-countable event, had crouched about the bed in silence, reverently guarding the occupant until Ideëssas should appear. For the Moschians excel even the Cretans in lying fiction.

Ideëssas was overjoyed. As a reward for their discreet behaviour he gave each of the four servants a fine Chalybean hunting-knife with an ivory handle, and enjoined them to holy silence. Then he folded the skeleton into a crouching posture, locked it into a chest of cypress wood and went at once to take his leave of Aeëtes. The Oracle had warned him to make no delay.

Presently Jason, watching from the city walls, saw the Moschian embassy winding their eastward way along the river-road of the Phasis, mounted on mules. A great burden was lifted from his heart. It was clear that Medea had given Ideëssas the oracular instructions of which she had spoken; and that not only were the bones of Phrixus on their way to a distinguished burial with full rites, but she had committed herself to a gross deception of her father – for Aeëtes had intended the bones to be buried in Greece, not in Moschia. Jason was convinced that the nearer the day drew for her meeting with Styrus, the more compelling would be her temptation to throw in her lot with his, even if in so doing she must rob Prometheus of the Fleece.

Yet for the three following days Medea gave no sign at all. She refused audience to the sons of Phrixus, and even to Neaera, whom she blamed beyond all others for the turn that events had taken.

On the last of these days Jason was walking through the palace grounds in the early morning when he heard a hissing sound above his head and, looking up, saw a writhing head and neck among the leaves. It was no snake, as he had supposed, but a dappled wryneck, or snake-bird, caught in a fowler's snare. He at once recalled an infallible love-charm, the charm of the hero Ixion, which had been taught him by Philara, the mother of Cheiron the Centaur. He released the bird from the snare and took it back with him to the palace, hidden in his wallet together with leaves of the plant ixias, which, as he expected, he found growing not far off. At the palace he obtained a Colchian fylfot fire-wheel and a piece of willow-heart touchwood and took them to his apartment. With his knife that night he whittled the touchwood into a female doll and addressed it as Medea, with soft words of love, tying a purple rag around its middle for a skirt; this rag Autolycus had secretly cut from Medea's own robe as she walked along the corridor to supper.

Jason fixed the spindle of the wheel into the doll's navel, the seat of love in a woman; then, smearing the wryneck's beak and claws with the bruised leaves of the plant ixias, he spread-eagled it to the four spokes of the fylfot-wheel. He turned the wheel around, whirling it gradually faster and faster, muttering as he did so:

Wryneck, cuckoo's mate,
Not too soon, not too late,
Bring the girl to my gate.

The driving band of the wheel twirled the spindle at such speed that presently the doll Medea burst into flames; and Jason blew gently upon them until she burned down to a fine ash. Then he released the dazed wryneck, thanked it, gave it barley to peck at, and put it on the windowsill. After a while it flew off.

On the fourth night at midnight a tiny gleam appeared to the southeast across the Phasis, in the remote distance: it was a great bonfire of pine-trees lighted by Ideëssas to signal his safe return with the bones. Now at last

Jason could undertake his seizure of the Fleece. He sent a message to Medea by Neaera: 'Loveliest of women, I thank you most heartily for your pious action in the matter of the bones: may the Bird-headed Mother reward you with happiness. But, alas, since you are unable to help me in the other matter of which I spoke, there is no help for it, but I must say farewell for ever. I propose to sail in two days' time, at dawn, empty-handed, and carrying within me an aching heart, the pain of which no other woman's love will ever assuage. Remember me, unfortunate one, on the morning of your marriage.'

Neaera was afraid to visit Medea, because on the last occasion that she had done so Medea had driven her from the room with Gorgon grimaces; but her brothers persuaded her to go.

She found Medea asleep. Medea started up with a cry from terrible dreams and, when she awoke, retched for disgust. She threw her arms about Neaera's neck, clasping her tightly, and cried: 'No, no, I cannot. It is too horrible to endure.'

Neaera answered gently: 'My dearest one, you cannot fight against Fate, for Fate is the Mother herself. Fate binds you to Ephyra and Jason, not to Albania and Styrus. Come, take your serpent girdle and cast it into the air for a sign.'

Medea did as she was told. The golden serpent fell at full length with its jewelled head pointed towards the east.

Neaera uttered a glad cry: 'In which direction does Ephyra lie, and in which do the Albanian mountains lie?' she asked. With that, she reported Jason's message word for word and said: 'Ideëssas has arrived safely back with my father's bones at his city among his Moschian mountains. Soon the poor ghost will be at rest, and I shall be grateful to Jason for ever more. But I pity his forlorn condition with all my heart. Why are you so cruel to him, Medea? Ah, if only I could myself heal the Healer.'

Medea answered, weeping large, round tears: 'I love him, I love him with unendurable passion. I cannot root out his image from my mind. The pain that I feel throbs under my breast-bone close to my navel and cuts deep under the nape of my neck, slantwise, as though the Love Spite had pierced me through and through with an arrow shot from below. Yet how can I thwart my father, to whom my duty lies? He will be undone if, when King Styrus comes to lead me off into marriage, I am no longer here.

'Last night I could not sleep. I rose and dressed myself long after midnight, when even the dogs had stopped barking and no sound came from the city except at intervals the voices of the watchmen calling out the hour. I wanted to go and talk to Jason. But when I gently opened the door into the vestibule where my twelve maidens sleep, and would have passed between their pallets into the corridor, shame drove me back. Three times the same thing happened, and at last in desperation I went to my medicine-cabinet and took out the poison casket, and undid the clasps slowly, one by one. Then it came to me: "If I kill myself, I shall never look upon Jason again with living eyes and he will marry another woman. Nor will suicide advantage me in the least, for every city near and far will ring with my infamy. Colchian women will spit into their bosoms if ever my name is spoken and say: 'She fell in love with a yellow-haired foreigner and died like a fool, disgracing her home and her father.'" So I put away the casket, trembling for fear. I sat down on a low stool beside my bed, resting my cheek on my left palm, and waited for the cocks to crow, thinking that day would perhaps prove kinder to me than night; but that was a foolish fancy.

'O Neaera, what shall I do? My thoughts chase one another faster and faster in an unescapable circle. Break the circle, my dearest friend, with a word, lest I go mad with the chase. Tell me what I am to do. I will obey you, whatever you may say.'

'Go to him,' Neaera answered. 'This love-impulse comes to you from the Bird-headed Mother, and is not to be lightly regarded.' But she did not know of the condition that Jason had laid upon Medea before he would take her with him, and which Medea would not reveal; else perhaps she would not have urged her so warmly to flight with Jason. Neaera had been in awe of Prometheus from earliest childhood and would have loathed to rob him of his golden prize.

It was thus that Medea took her decision, and once her feet were on the new road they never strayed or faltered. She told Neaera: 'Inform Jason that I will do all that he wishes, but only in the name of the Mother, and that henceforth my duty is no longer to my father but to him alone, so long as he offers the Mother no injury; and that I will never fail him, for I believe that he will never fail me.' And she gave her an ointment for Jason to rub upon his body after he had washed himself three times in running water; and told her where he should be at midnight of the following night.

The next morning the outriders of King Styrus, conspicuous for their oblong shields and tiger-skin capes, came knocking at the Eastern Gate of the city, demanding admittance for their master, who presently arrived with the clashing of cymbals and blaring of horns borne on a litter by two frost-coloured mules. Styrus was a benign old man with a scanty beard and small merry eyes. He and his courtiers stank of putrid fish – for the Albanians bury their fish for days before eating it – and of garlic, of which they consume prodigious quantities as a protection against giddiness on their mountain peaks. Aeëtes said privately to his Councillors: 'I shall fumigate this palace with sulphur when the marriage ceremonies are over. Meanwhile, pray bear this stench with Colchian fortitude!'

Medea was presented to Styrus, who was at first surprised and displeased by the colour of her hair, but, none the less, asked for her hand in marriage. She did not either refuse or accept him, being careful of her pledged word; but deceived him by saying submissively: 'My lord, when once I am in your Court I will dye my hair with ink of cuttlefish, or with whatever stain you commend. But meanwhile do not, by dispraising it, hurt the religious feelings of the Colchians, for whom the colour has the lucky connotation of honey and gold.'

Since the retinue of Styrus was larger than had been foreseen, some of the elder men, priests of the Albanian Sun God, were accommodated in the inner hall where the brazen bulls stood; which furthered Medea's plans. When all were lying behind locked doors in drugged slumber on their mattresses that night, Jason and Autolycus entered the inner hall by a window of the musicians' gallery. Autolycus uttered a long charm of aversion, taught him by Medea, and going boldly up to the bulls, gelded first one and then the other with shrewd strokes of hammer and chisel. This terrible task had at first been assigned to Argus, but, being a Bull man, he had shrunk from it because of religious scruples. Autolycus was of the Wolf fraternity and did what was desired to do, grinning. He was the very man for the task, having once been a were-wolf. He had taken part in the octennial festival of the Wolf men, when the guts of a boy are mixed with those of wolves at the solemn pool-side feast; the man who eats the guts of the boy hangs his clothes upon an oak-tree, swims across the pool, and lives as a wolf with wolves until the next festival. Autolycus had been such a one.

Jason unwrapped the bundle that they had brought with them, in which were a double yoke and traces and a wooden plough. He harnessed the bulls to the plough, saying: 'Be oxen now!' Their jewelled eyes seemed to flash red with anger in the light of Jason's torch, but they were powerless to hurt either him or Autolycus, who presently climbed out again by the window of the gallery. Thus the dream that Aeëtes had unwisely revealed to Medea first, before telling it to the Sun, was in part fulfilled; but the incident of the falling star and that of the anguished cry of Prometheus still remained for fulfilment.

Medea, wearing the customary willow-chaplet in honour of Prometheus, waited for Jason in a thicket at some little distance from the hero-shrine. The moon was young, and obscured occasionally with clouds hurrying from the east. Medea's mind was calm now, though every now and then an involuntary spasm shook her, as huge waves still toss a ship after the water-spout has passed. She had sacrificed to Brimo with nameless offerings, and the Goddess had granted her favourable omens.

Soon she heard Jason's stealthy tread along the path. Her heart knocked loudly as she asked in a whisper: 'Is the deed done? Is all well?'

He answered: 'It is done. All is well. Give me leave to kiss you, my fair-haired love, and lend you courage for your fearful deed.'

Her veins, when he kissed her, seemed to run with fire, and her heart to leap out of her breast. She had no strength left in her knees for moving backwards, and a dark mist came over her eyes; yet she thrust him from her, crying faintly: 'Have done, now, my love! Your kisses sting like hornets. O that I had never been born a king's daughter!'

She gave him a woman's smock and shawl for a disguise and put into his hand a basket containing a black cock, a bag of barley-grains, and a flint knife. She warned him: 'Crouch low to conceal your stature, take hobbling steps, shroud your chin in your shawl, show yourself submissive to me. If anyone addresses you, place your finger on your lips and shake your head.'

He obeyed her, and this time did nothing foolish, remembering how badly he had played at being servant to Argus among the Lapiths.

They went together along a well-planted avenue of black cypress until they came to the gate of the enclosure.

There stood two sentries with battle-axes, wearing bull masks and cloaks of black bulls' hide with dangling tails. Medea set her finger to her lips and they admitted both her and Jason, making a reverence to them. Medea passed across the court, looking neither to the right nor to the left, and Jason followed, three paces behind her, until they reached the small bronze door of the inner enclosure. This she unlocked with a bronze key and they entered a paved maze, the walls of which were tall yew-trees planted closely together and confined with bronze railings. Medea led Jason first this way and then that, singing softly as she threaded the windings of the maze. Now and then she stood still, listened and sang again.

Presently Jason heard a strange noise of rustling or scraping. Medea breathed: 'The serpent is issuing from his shrine. He is taking up his station on the tree.'

She led him into the central enclosure, paved with serpentine, which was in the shape of an equal-sided triangle, and as he entered the moon rode clear from behind a pack of cloud. At the furthest angle, behind the round white shrine where the sacred jaw-bone and navel-string were laid up, grew an ancient cypress-tree.

Jason drew in his breath sharply. He had come at last to the goal of his travels, but would willingly have forfeited five years of life to be safely back in Lemnos with buxom Hypsipyle, playing dice with her for kisses under a painted bed-canopy while the birds of morning sang sweetly from the rose-bushes below the window. Before him, tied to the cypress, under a slight canopy of planking, shone the Golden Fleece, hung head downwards as if in mockery of the Ram God; and around the trunk and limbs of the tree coiled the serpent Prometheus. He waved his blunt head slowly to and fro as Medea sang to him in the Greek tongue, and flickered his forked tongue. Jason judged his length to be four times that of a tall man, and his thickness about that of a man's thigh.

Medea took the basket from Jason's trembling hands and opened the lid. She pulled out the cock, unhooded its head, untied its legs, set it upon the ground and poured it barley-grains to eat.

Then she addressed the serpent in a low caressing voice, chanting:

Prometheus, take this gift, this cock,
This black cock gift I make.
Devour it for my sake, Medea's sake,
Fair-haired Medea's sake.
Then sleep, Prometheus, sleep you well,
Sleep well tip dawn shall break.

The great serpent uncoiled his full length from the cypress and came rustling down towards them, but the smell of Jason made him restive and he uttered a sudden hissing sound: for all savage beasts are disturbed by the sour smell exhaled by frightened men. Medea soothed him with gentle words as a mother soothes a fractious child and brought him to obedience. Her voice soothed Jason too; his smell sweetened and gave the serpent no further offence.

The serpent Prometheus perceived the cock and coiled to strike. The cock became aware of the greatness of its peril. It ceased pecking at the barley, drooped its crest and quailed. The serpent drew back his head and drove it suddenly forward like a darted spear.

'Close your eyes!' ordered Medea. 'No man is permitted to watch Prometheus at his feast.'

Jason closed his eyes. When he was instructed to open them the serpent had engulfed the cock – feathers, legs, beak and all. Medea stretched out her hand behind her, searching for Jason's hand. He pressed it to his lips, but neither said a word.

Presently the serpent glided slowly back to his station on the cypress, and Medea sang to him again. Jason observed that he no longer kept time with the music as he swayed, but moved sluggishly. His head sank lower and lower: for the feathers of the cock had been sprinkled with the soporific juice of the tall, two-stalked saffron-coloured Caucasian crocus, that has a root as red as newly carved flesh and is now known as the flower of Prometheus. Medea had cut the root while the moon was full, and let it bleed into a three-whorled Caspian shell.

Now she drew from her bosom a spray of juniper and waved it slowly before the serpent's eyes in a holy figure of eight. Soon he dizzied and a shudder ran through his vast body. His coils relaxed and he hung suspended from the branches with dangling head, as if lifeless, beside the dangling head of the Fleece.

'O beloved Jason,' said Medea, between weeping and laughter. 'Go up now and take your prize. Here is the knife.'

Jason climbed into the cypress, among the huge coils of the drugged serpent, which were cold as death to his touch. He cut the leather thongs by which the two fore-feet and the two hind-feet of the Fleece were bound together about the tree; and took hold of it by the tail, and began to climb down again. Unknowingly he grimaced as though he had drained a hornful of sour wine, yet when he stood on the pavement again the glory of his deed warmed his belly and flushed his face.

The Fleece was wonderfully heavy because of the huge curving horns and the golden fringe. Jason bound it about himself under his smock. Then Medea gave him the basket again, and he followed her out through the maze.

They recrossed the court of the war god, looking neither to the right hand nor to the left. The bull-headed sentries opened the gate to let them pass out and made them a reverence. They trod in safety down the avenue of cypress trees towards the city, Medea leading the way, neither saying a word. Jason wished to run, but Medea's pace was slow and meditative.

CHAPTER THIRTY-FOUR

THE FLIGHT FROM AEA

When Jason and Medea came within sight of Aea again, Jason uttered the call that had been agreed upon, the melancholy howl of a Magnesian leopard, which set all the house-dogs of the city barking together. This was a signal for the sons of Phrixus to begin the bloody diversion under cover of which the *Argo* might sail away undisturbed. They ran through the palace, each through a different wing, yelling all at once so that the cry echoed down every corridor: 'O the villains! O, O! Revenge on the sacrilegious villains!'

Aeëtes sprang from his high couch, half-clothed and bewildered, to ask what was amiss, and Phrontis came running to tell him: 'Alas, Majesty! The filthy Albanian, your intended son-in-law, has desecrated your palace. He has castrated and mockingly yoked with a double yoke the sacred bulls of your Taurian allies. Yet was this not to be expected from a lice-eating aboriginal to whom the Bull is a symbol of all evil?'

The news of the sacrilege spread like fire about the palace, and Medea's stony-eyed Taurian mother, Idyia, sent her son Apsyrtus in haste to summon the Bull men from the shrine of the war god. Soon they came running down the avenue in a swarm and Idyia herself opened the North Gate to admit them. Without a word they ran on into the palace brandishing their axes, to the terrible sound of bull-roarers whirled on long cords. Then battle was joined between the Taurians and the Albanians, Aeëtes trying in vain to keep the two nations apart. The Taurians with their axes soon broke down the well-fitting doors of the inner hall; and when they saw their mutilated and insulted gods they were excited to unspeakable deeds of vengeance. Their axes rose and fell like flails, until the son of Styrus, descending upon them from the gallery with his Albanian spearmen, bloodily drove them out again.

As the tide of battle ebbed and flowed and corpses were piled high in the doorways and corridors, the Argonauts, under the command of Great Ancaeus, slipped stealthily out through the unguarded gate by which the Taurians had been admitted, and making a wide circuit of the city came to the river without discovery.

Argus and Nauplius had moored the *Argo* in a narrow backwater under the shadow of a poplar-grove. This was the very spot where Phrixus had disembarked a generation before, when he brought the stolen Fleece to Aeëtes. Jason and Medea were already aboard when Ancaeus and his party came hurrying to the ship, and all was in readiness for flight. They took their seats hastily, stumbling against one another in the darkness, for the moon was obscured by clouds as well as by the foliage of the poplars; then some of them, reaching for poles, began to push off. But Lynceus, counting heads, cried in a fierce whisper: 'Hold! We are short of a man. Remember our covenant, Argonauts! We cannot sail away and leave a comrade behind.'

'Who is missing? Who?' asked Jason impatiently. And he complained: 'I cannot distinguish anything in this darkness, Lynceus, nor do I believe that you can, either.'

'Who shares the bench with Melampus, son of Ares?' asked Lynceus.

'It is Butes the Athenian,' whispered Melampus. 'You are right, Lynceus. He is not here yet.'

'Butes, Butes, where are you?' called Jason.

'Hiss!' said everyone at once. 'Not so loud!'

Jason called 'Butes, Butes' again in sharp petulant tones. But no answer came. 'O, O, does anyone know where he is?' he asked, nearly weeping.

Phalerus the Athenian answered: 'Alas, noble Jason, about an hour ago, or it may have been less – not long, at least, before Phrontis raised the alarm in the palace – I met my compatriot Butes in a corridor. "Look you, Phalerus," he said. "I cannot bear to leave Aea without first sampling the Colchian mountain honey which Autolycus and his two brothers pretend to be poisonous. Here I have a luscious piece of honeycomb fetched this morning from the high azalea forest. Smell it; it smells delicious. Try some of it, dear Phalerus, as I also intend to do. Together let us prove that these wolfish Thessalians are credulous fools." But I replied: "No, Butes, no! Let Trouble seek me out, I will not go in search of her." Then Butes put the honeycomb to his lips and, first licking it with his tongue, bit off a mouthful. He said: "It has a bitter but refreshing taste. See, I do not swell up suddenly and die! Try it, I beg of you, my Phalerus!" But again I refused to eat, or so much as to taste the drippings. I turned and left him to finish the comb by himself. Since then, I have not seen or heard of him.'

Jason said: 'The God Apollo, when he understands the urgency of the case, will doubtless release us from the oath of mutual assistance that we swore in his name. For if we send back a party to rescue Butes, who is perhaps already dead of the poison, not one of them can hope to return safely; and with many oars unmanned, the escape of those who remain will be impossible. Shall the presumptuous folly of Butes condemn his comrades to death as well as himself? I say no! Cast off, Argonauts! Let Butes, since he is so knowledgeable about bees, escape from the angry hive of Aea from which we have already dared to rob both the golden honey, which is the Fleece, and the young Queen Bee, Medea.'

Some of the Argonauts, though not many, praised this prudent speech. Others indignantly rejected it – not only the Athenians but also Iphitus and Mopsus and Admetus, out of respect for Apollo; for they did not dare forswear themselves of the oath that had been taken in his name.

Augeas of Elis said: 'The law of Apollo is this: "Nothing in excess." Let us please the Far-Darter by not carrying to excess the loyalty that we owe to a fool.'

This speech angered Atalanta, who sprang out of the ship and asked: 'What man of honour dares come back to Aea with me? Because Jason and Augeas are cowards, shall we others leave Butes to a Colchian funeral and to the same cruel fate from which we were sent to deliver Phrixus?'

Meleager followed at her challenge, and Iphitus and Phalerus and Mopsus and Admetus, but not Argus (because of his lameness); and when Little Ancaeus saw that all the rest hung back he offered himself as a seventh. But Atalanta asked: 'Will no one come of those who speak the Colchian language?'

Melanion, son of Phrixus, answered: 'I will come. My hair and features are darker than those of my brothers, and I can pass unnoticed among Colchians. Besides, I am by far the most courageous of them all.'

Atalanta praised Melanion, and they were starting out together, a party of eight, when Jason called them back. He told Atalanta that she was robbing the ship of too many oarsmen: she must leave five of the seven men behind. She therefore chose Iphitus and Melanion as her companions. But Meleager and Phalerus went off with her into the darkness, notwithstanding.

The remainder of the Argonauts waited on their benches in prolonged anxiety. Each man prayed aloud to the god or goddess whom he most favoured, imploring assistance, and making great promises of sacrifices and votive gifts. At last Jason said: 'Comrades, be ready with weapons to assist the return of Atalanta and her party. Mopsus, have bandages and salves at hand for the wounded. Lynceus, go and stand on the mound yonder, called the Ram's Back, and keep watch.' But he himself remained in the ship, to comfort Medea, who was racked with sobs and could not utter a word.

Meanwhile, since the palace guards, who hated the Taurians and the Albanians equally, could not be persuaded to intervene and prevent them from exterminating each other, but stood by laughing, Aeëtes sent a messenger to Jason demanding the immediate assistance of his Argonauts. The messenger came back after a while with the report that Jason was not to be found in the wing where the Argonauts were lodged, and that no Greek at all remained with the exception of the Bee King (for so he called Butes), whom he had found lying insensible in the corridor. Aeëtes at once divined what had happened: the mutilation of the bulls had been a Greek stratagem to set the Albanians and Taurians at each other's throats, and his own grandsons, who had now disappeared too, were Jason's accomplices.

Aeëtes was swift to act. He despatched the captain of his guard with a hundred men to the Royal Quay to seize the *Argo* if she were still there, and himself ran to his brother-in-law, Prince Perses the Taurian, imploring him to call off the bull-headed priests. With great difficulty he persuaded Perses that the Albanians were innocent of the sacrilege and that the Greeks were the culprits. Then, with still greater difficulty, he and Perses together persuaded King Styrus to call off his Albanians, who were now gaining the upper hand of the Taurians. Gradually fighting ceased and order was restored throughout the palace. The wounded were taken up and laid upon couches, where their comrades began dressing their wounds as best they might. Aeëtes tried to soothe Styrus, saying: 'Cousin, wait and you shall see how wonderful a physician my daughter Medea is. She will heal the most gaping, desperate wound within the hour, so that only a thin scar remains to record it.'

No sooner had he spoken than he was overcome by a hideous thought. What of Medea? Where was she, all this while? Could she too have been drawn into the plot? Could she have contrived the mutilation in the hope that the Taurians would avenge their god on the Albanian King, and thus cancel her hated marriage?

He ran to her apartment and looking hastily about found it in disorder, with garments lying on the floor and coffers open and ransacked as if she had gathered together a few choice possessions in haste. 'So she is gone!' he cried aloud. 'My daughter Medea is gone! Not with the impious Greeks surely? Yet with whom else?' He was stupefied.

The captain of the guard returned breathlessly to report the *Argo* missing from her moorings. Aeëtes told him: 'The three war-galleys at the Public Quay, that are always provisioned and manned in case of an emergency: send them down the river at once in pursuit. Jason the Greek must be killed or captured at all costs, together with his crew and as many traitors of my own blood as may be found in the ship. If any of the galley-masters dares to return before this mission is fully accomplished I will first cut off his hands and feet and then enclose him in the scorching hot belly of a Taurian bull, to make it bellow for delight. Go, inform Prince Apsyrtus that he is to command the flotilla. You will find him with his mother, the Queen Idyia, at the North Gate.'

It was just about this time that Atalanta and Melanion re-entered the city, without being challenged, and slipped into the palace by a side-door: he, spear in hand, clothed as an officer of the Royal Guard; she disguised in the same shawl and smock that Jason had used, with bow and javelin hidden under the smock. They hurried unnoticed through the corridors and up the staircase of the wing where the Argonauts had lodged. There they found Butes lying in a faint upon the floor of the corridor, wound about with a long cord as if he were a chrysalis or an Egyptian mummy.

Melanion quickly unwound the cord and reeved one end of it into a running noose. Then he hauled Butes to the window, pierced in the city wall, under which Iphitus, Meleager, and Phalerus waited far below, he tightened the noose under his shoulders and lowered him to the around. But as Iphitus released Butes from the noose, he unluckily jerked the other end of the cord from Melanion's hand so that he could not descend by it.

Meleager was trying to throw the cord up again to the window, high above his head, and Melanion was leaning out to catch it. Aeëtes himself appeared at the stair-head, roaring with rage, a drawn sword in his hand.

Atalanta cried: 'Hasten, Melanion, I will fend them off while you escape. Send Phalerus and Iphitus ahead with Butes. Do you keep with Meleager. I will go by another way if I must.'

Then Melanion, catching the cord at last by the end where the noose was, thrust his spear through the noose, which he drew tight about the middle of the shaft. Then, gripping the cord, he clambered out of the window and slid safely down to the ground; for the spear, being longer than the window was broad, pressed against the wall on either side and supported his weight.

Atalanta did not follow him. Instead, she cast off her disguise, seized her bow and javelin, and uttering her famous laughing scream ran for the stair-head. Aeëtes opposed her with his sword; she thrust him sideways through the bowels as she ran, so that he fell groaning, and his guards raised a wail of alarm and grief.

On she ran as though she had wings, her eyes glaring with the rage of Artemis. Leaping high over the wreckage of battle in the hall below she burst through the mixed company of Colchians, Taurians, and Albanians, like the leather-covered bladder that young men or women hurl about for sport at the baths. One man only, an Albanian Sun priest, dared to lift his hand against her; she struck him dead with the javelin and ran on, leaving him transfixed, then darted through the guards at the main gate like a diving swallow, and rejoined her party with a yell of triumph.

When Perses came rushing out in pursuit at the head of his Taurians, Meleager and Atalanta covered the retreat of Iphitus and Phalerus, who were carrying Butes by turns, and drew off the pursuit in another direction.

Meanwhile Jason and the other Argonauts heard shouts from the Public Quay and the rattle and splash of the three ships that were being launched. This was followed by the beat of oars and the shrill voice of helmsmen shouting the stroke, and presently the war-galleys came rushing abreast past the dark backwater where the *Argo* lay, and threshed onward downstream towards the sea. As the sounds died away in the distance, the dismayed Argonauts heard another noise, that of a running battle coming towards them from the North Gate. Lynceus called out: 'To the rescue,

Argonauts! I can see Iphitus and Phalerus not far off, carrying Butes between them. Atalanta and Meleager are lagging behind. Atalanta is wounded in the heel with an arrow and Meleager is supporting her as she hobbles; but every now and then she turns to use her death-dealing bow. Meleager is also wounded, in the left arm, but not badly.'

At this, not wishing to disgrace himself in Medea's eyes, Jason proved himself more courageous than his comrades had hitherto credited him with being: he leaped ashore and called on all brave men to follow him. In the battle that ensued many Colchians and Taurians and Albanians fell, among them a brother of King Styrus, and Jason was run through the shoulder with a javelin, and the skull of kindly Iphitus the Phocian was broken with a flint axe of the sort that the Taurians use for sacrifice. Yet the Argonauts gained the victory and drove off their enemies and held the field of battle. They despoiled the dead and carried their own wounded into the ship, and Butes, too, who was groaning feebly with his hands pressed against his belly. Then at leisure they unhitched the hawsers from the mooring-stakes and pushed the *Argo* along the backwater into the river, each one of them boasting loudly of his feats.

Mopsus, fumbling for his salves and bandages in the darkness, began to dress the wounds of Jason, Atalanta, and Meleager; but Iphitus was already dead. He was the very first Argonaut who had been killed in battle, and his comrades at least had the satisfaction of carrying off his corpse for burial. Jason, groaning loudly for the pain in his shoulder, entrusted the command of the ship to Argus; and Argus gave the order: 'Out oars and row!' But he added: 'In the name of grey-eyed, cuckoo-sceptred Athena, by whose inspiration I built this glorious vessel, I beg you all to keep perfect silence, once we are well on our way.'

Thus the Argonauts came away from Aea with the Fleece, and despite the number of their wounded every oar was manned; for the four sons of Phrixus were practised oarsmen, and Orpheus had taken the helm from Great Ancaeus, who now set the stroke from the seat once occupied by Hercules.

CHAPTER THIRTY-FIVE

AWAY FROM COLCHIS

Atalanta, not knowing for certain whether she had killed King Aeëtes, said nothing of her encounter either to Medea or to anyone else. Medea ceased to sob after a while. She seemed to be dazed by what had happened and spoke in simple inconsequent language to Jason, giggling softly, making childish grimaces and often asking: 'You are Jason, are you not? You love me, do you not?' When at last she fell asleep she tossed and groaned and muttered in a frightening manner. And once she cried aloud in a heart-rending voice: 'Alas, cruel Love Spite! Why have you clung to my breast, you muddy leech, and drained my veins of every drop of healthy blood?' The Argonauts heartily wished her at the bottom of the river; but they feared the double-eye and dared say nothing against her in Jason's hearing.

Argus asked Phrontis, son of Phrixus, how far downstream in his judge-ment the Colchian war-galleys would go in pursuit. Phrontis replied that they would continue to the mouth of the river, and then pertinaciously scour the coasts of the Black Sea; and that Aeëtes would doubtless send other galleys on the same mission, so soon as ever they could be manned, oared, and provisioned. So the Argonauts rowed on at a good pace, neither fast enough to overtake the three galleys ahead, nor slow enough to be overtaken by possible pursuers. About dawn Phrontis hailed the watchman posted on the quay of a river-side settlement. 'Hey, watchman,' he cried, 'have the impious Greeks been overtaken yet?'

The watchman, taking the *Argo* for a Colchian, answered: 'No, my lord, not so far as I know. The three galleys that hailed me in the grey dawn had not yet sighted the wretches, who must have passed my quay in the darkness without using their oars, letting the current carry their vessel silently by.'

Argus decided that the most prudent course for him to take was to sail by night and hide by day. Phrontis knew the river well, and between this settlement and the next he showed Argus a narrow backwater, where the *Argo* could lie concealed, stern on to the river. There they put in, shipping their oars and wreathing the stern ornament with long green creepers.

Two hours later three more galleys ran past their place of concealment, each with an embroidered white pennant at the mast-head, and disappeared beyond the next bend of the river. But the master of a fourth galley gave the order as he drew abreast of the *Argo*: 'Avast rowing! Make her fast to the right bank.' The galley was thereupon moored to a tree not a bowshot downstream. Her proximity was disagreeable to the Argonauts, since it imposed absolute silence on them. But Euphemus the swimmer presently whispered to Argus: 'Bull man, shipwright, dear Attic friend – pray pass me an auger from your tool-locker.'

Argus passed him a sharp auger without a word. Euphemus stripped, dived soundlessly overboard, and swam under water to the Colchian galley. Catching hold of the stern ornament with one hand, with the other he plied the auger and bored five large holes below the water-line; not pushing the auger home in any one hole until all five had been bored to an equal depth. Then he cut the mooring-rope of the galley with his knife and swam back as secretly as he had come.

The Colchians were all asleep while he worked, even the look-out man, and the first thing that the oarsmen knew was that the river-water had welled up through the floor-boards as far as their ankles and that the ship was slowly sinking. They tore up the planking to find and stop the leak, but with their frightened movements they tipped the galley now this way and now that, so that the muddy water seemed to be swirling in from all points at once. They began to bail, but when the water gained on them some leaped overboard, hoping to make the land, and were engulfed in the black ooze of the foreshore; others climbed up on the gunwales. Only one man tried to swim downstream to the nearest landing-stage; but Euphemus swam after him, stunned him with his fist and towed him back by the hair to the *Argo*. He proved, by his badge of a winged horse, to be the galley-master. The rest of the crew went down with the galley, shrieking for terror. Only the white embroidered pennant remained fluttering above the water, and this Euphemus secured as an adornment and disguise for the *Argo*.

Melanion asked: 'Dear comrades, what prevents the *Argo*, now that the enemy has been sunk without a trace, from taking her place in the squadron? If we keep well astern our identity will not be suspected, and when this captive revives we can threaten him with death unless he communicates to the galley-master next ahead of us whatever messages we may care to put into his mouth. This stratagem will allow us to sail boldly past the remaining settlements, even by day if we keep our distance prudently, and as soon as we are clear at last of the river we can use discretion as to our further course.'

The Argonauts applauded Melanion's reasoning, and Argus agreed to carry out the plan that he had suggested.

To the Colchian master, when he revived, Melanion promised his life on condition that he did whatever he was commanded to do. He proved to be a man of good sense and obeyed Melanion faithfully, for he had a large family of children dependent upon him. His name was Peucon. When the *Argo* came in sight of the galley next ahead of them, Peucon hailed her, as Melanion ordered him to do, and reported that four men of his crew had the fever heavy on them. The other master, suspecting nothing, shouted back: 'Alas, friend Peucon, is it indeed the fever? Then keep a wide berth of us when you anchor tonight, for we are as yet uninfected, blessed be the name of the Mother.'

That night Euphemus proposed to swim out and sink in turn each of the three remaining ships; but Argus restrained him. He argued that so soon as one ship began to sink, the others would be rowed hurriedly up to take off the yelling survivors. 'So much the better,' replied Euphemus. 'In the confusion I will work undisturbed, and you shall see good sport.'

His boldness was applauded, but Orpheus said: 'Comrades, let us not take Colchian lives merely for sport. Let us kill only if dire necessity compels us; if not, let us refrain. The men will drown, but perhaps their ghosts will clamber aboard our ship, conveyed on floating sticks or leaves, and plague us beyond endurance.'

Euphemus listened to Orpheus, being as prudent as he was courageous.

Jason resumed command of the *Argo*. He had recovered from his wound in the most wonderful manner, as also had Atalanta and Meleager; for Medea that morning had unbound the bandages tied by Mopsus and dressed the throbbing wounds with a salve of her own preparation which burned like fire but healed the festered flesh within the hour.

Butes came to his senses at about the same time. He sat up suddenly and asked what had happened, what was the time of day, and where was he?

Idas replied bitterly: 'Your taste of mountain honey has cost us dearly enough, Bee Fool. Because of you, a gentle Phocian has been killed, and the corpse lies under a bear-skin cloak yonder, awaiting honourable burial.'

Mopsus reproached Idas, saying: 'Idas, how nonsensically you talk! Our dear Phocian comrade was struck by a Taurian with a sacrificial axe. Butes was lying senseless on the ground when the blow fell.'

Idas persisted, careless whether the ghost of Iphitus overheard him or not: for he was secretly ashamed that he had not ventured with Atalanta on her glorious task of rescue. But at least he had the good sense not to rouse the ghost of Iphitus by uttering his name. He said: 'But for Butes and his taste for honey, the Painter would be alive today. If anyone denies this to be true, let him guard his head, for my spear lies handy on its rest below the gunwale.'

Butes wept. He daubed his face with tar and dishevelled his hair. But hardly had he completed his disguise when he saw an augury to chill his heart: a gaudy coloured bee-eater alighted on the bulwark above his head, twittered and flew off.

'What did my enemy say, Mopsus?' asked Butes in a trembling voice.

'Nothing, nothing at all of importance,' answered Mopsus hastily.

The incident caused general dismay and it was decided to bury Iphitus with full rites as soon as ever firm land should be reached. They were now sailing through the swamp country and the heat had greatly increased since their first entry into Colchis; the corpse would soon stink offensively and breed Spites or snakes. Phrontis said to Jason: 'The eastward set of the currents along the southern coast of the Black Sea, which favoured you on your outward voyage, continues northwards along the foot of the Caucasian mountains; and the nearest stretch of firm ground, outside Colchian territory, where you will be able without interference to bury your unlucky comrade lies a day's sail northward from the port of Phasis. I mean Anthenios, a settlement of the Apsilaeans, who are hospitable to strangers of all sorts. I propose that when we have passed safely out of this river our course shall be northward, not southward, unless the wind is against us. I have credit with the merchants of Anthenios, and we can there replenish our water-jars with fresh water.'

Jason repeated this proposal and asked whether anyone disagreed with it. Nobody replied. He therefore said: 'Anthenios it shall be, unless the winds prove contrary!'

Augeas of Elis asked: 'Why should we not continue northward and circumnavigate the Black Sea, thus avoiding the contrary current of the southern shore, and being helped along by the powerful currents which, according to King Phineus, pour from the great northern rivers at this season? In this way we should cheat pursuit.'

'Ah, why should we not do that?' many of the Argonauts asked.

The sons of Phrixus declared such a course to be impracticable. They said that the inhabitants of the Caucasian seaboard for five hundred miles or so northward from Anthenios were hostile, treacherous, and poor. If the *Argo* were delayed by contrary winds and provisions ran low on that inhospitable coast it would be impossible to replenish them. Moreover, where the Caucasian range ended the kingdom of the Taurians began: even with Medea aboard it would be as dangerous to venture into their land in search of food or water as to eat beans from a red-hot spoon.

The three brothers from Sinope agreed with this view. Jason accepted it, saying: 'Let us rather face again the dangers that we have already once surmounted than tempt the Gods by attempting new ones.'

They sailed on down the river, always lagging behind the other vessels of the squadron to which they had attached themselves, and on the evening of the second day – for the river ran with a strong current – reached the river-mouth and the port of Phasis, where they were not challenged. Thence they rowed southward, following the Colchian squadron, but only for a short distance. As soon as darkness gathered, they hoisted the dark sail and sailed off to the northward, profiting from a south-easterly breeze. As they went they raised a concerted shout of despair, as though their ship had struck a sunken rock, to mislead those from whom they were parting company.

Next morning, the sun rose beaming above the eastern peaks and shone upon a sea empty of all ships but the *Argo*. Jason, who had been sharing the watch with Meleager, roused his comrades from sleep and jubilantly drew the Fleece out from the locker below the helmsman's seat. He lifted it up shining for all to see and said: 'Look, Argonauts, how magnificent a treasure we have secured and at how small a cost in blood! For this our names will be famous for ever in the royal halls of Greece, and in populous barbarian camps, and even among the all-wise Egyptians whose smooth white-sided pyramids pierce the skies above the floods of the river Nile. As we were greatly favoured by the immortal Gods during our outward voyage, namely Zeus, Poseidon, Apollo, Athena, and Artemis, and in all our doings at Aea, so we may confidently expect the way to be smoothed by them for our return. The *Argo* is now more precious to them than ever as the repository of this holiest of all Greek relics, the Fleece of Laphystian Zeus.'

Immediately Erginus, a man who had learned by defeat to avoid boastful and ill-omened talk, rose and said in deprecation: 'It is indeed a great feat, Jason, for a shepherd to scale the cliff that overhangs his valley home, and rescue a stolen lamb from the eagle's nest; but while the she-eagle soars shrieking above his head, making ready to pounce upon him – as with the lamb slung behind him in a wallet he lowers himself laboriously down the crumbling precipice – O, let him not become forgetful of danger and fancy himself already at home beside the bubbling black pots of his hearth. Put away the shining Fleece, insensate Jason, lest it excite the jealousy of some deity, and let us not look on it again until we have heard our keel hiss sweetly on the sandy beach of Phthiotic Pagasae. For I fear the jealousy of one deity at least, the Great Goddess by whom it was long ago removed from the oaken image, and whose tremendous name you have not yet spoken. Therefore let Orpheus lead us in humble prayer to the Goddess; or, better still, let us beg neat-ankled Medea to do so. Medea is a beloved priestess of the Goddess, and but for Medea we should no more easily have been granted a sight of the Fleece than we could have gathered ripe olives from the flowering trees. Remember, pious comrades, that this is an unlucky time of year, the gloomy time of purification when at home in Greece we go dirty and throw our scape-men into the river or sea, stopping our ears against their screams, and sweep out our shrines with brooms of thorn, and prepare for the glad feast of First Fruits. It is not yet time for rejoicing, you foolish son of Aeson.'

Jason shamefacedly returned the Fleece to the locker, while Medea arose from her seat in the prow and, gazing upwards, spread out her open palms and prayed:

'Mother and Nymph and Virgin, Triple Queen, Lady of the Amber

Moon; who by your sovereignty over Sky, Earth, and Sea are tripled again; to whose Infernal Trinity the priestess of Brimo, my dear sister Chalciope, dying bound me priestess: hear me and forgive.

'Not willingly did I step aboard this vermilion-cheeked ship, not willingly did I rob the Serpent of the Golden Fleece that he guarded for you, not willingly did I disobey my father. You yourself, Almighty, forced me to this madness; I know not why.

'You I obey; you only, you the Dancer upon Skulls; I scorn the upstart Olympian breed. Say the word only, and by the power with which you have invested me I will sink the proud *Argo* – crew, cargo, speaking branch and all – into the dark and lifeless waters of the sea-bottom. Say the word only, and I will plunge this dagger deep into my own breast or into the breast of fair-haired Jason, whom you have impelled me to love beyond all reason. Say the word only, Bird-faced Queen!

'You have warned me by the tumult in my heart that the choice which I have taken may bring me little peace; that the great love for Jason into which I have fallen, though it roars like a fire in a thorn thicket, may presently die in white ashes; that Prometheus may seek vengeance upon me. I demand nothing as my right, I serve you faithfully, I adore you without hope. But bring, I pray you, bring this ship, and the accursed Fleece with it, safely back to Greece; and grant me to be Queen in Ephyra with Jason as my King for as many years at least as I was faithful to you in lovely Aea.'

She ceased and all sat waiting for a sign. Presently three great claps of thunder were heard in the distance echoing and rolling among the snow-capped mountains. Medea sat down again with a long sigh of relief.

Castor was the first to break the long silence that ensued. He asked Pollux: 'Is it not strange, Brother, that our father Zeus should have thundered at this very moment?'

Medea replied disdainfully in halting Greek: 'The Goddess rolled thunder among the mountains of Crete and Caucasus while Zeus was still an infant in the Dictean Cave – how greedily he drank from the dug of the old sow, his foster-mother which the Dactyls fetched for him! And she will doubtless roll thunder among the same mountains when his very name is forgotten among men.'

Nobody dared contradict her.

They sailed past the northern forest swamps of Colchis and at noon came to a broad bay backed with lofty mountains. In the middle was a narrow, deep gorge, with precipices on either side, and far behind they saw a snowy mountain, shaped like a saddle, which was reputedly the seat of the Man-eating Goddess of the Apsilaeans. The whitewashed city of Anthenios (since named Dioscurias) was visible from the south from a distance of several miles. This was the most sacred place of the whole Caucasus. The Man-eating Goddess ruled that no man, on pain of death, might go armed across the broad flowery meadows between the mountain and the sea, nor so much as pick up a stone to fling at a weasel; for which reason no less than seventy tribes made it their common meeting-ground for barter, for the settling of disputes, and for the conclusion of treaties.

Jason beached the *Argo* on a low spit of sandy shore, but did not disembark or permit any of his comrades to do so, except the four sons of Phrixus, whom he ordered on no account to let the Apsilaeans guess that the *Argo* was a Greek ship. They clambered down the ladder in silence and went off, carrying the corpse of Iphitus between them. When they returned in the evening, they reported that they had first waited upon the Governess of the town and asked her permission to perform Colchian funeral rites over a comrade who, they said, had been killed by the fall of a rotten tree as their ship lay at anchor in a backwater of the Phasis. This the Governess refused, as they had known that she would; for the Apsilaeans practise urn-burial and abhor the tree-cemeteries of Colchis. After a show of pleading, Melanion had said: 'Well, Blameless One, it makes no matter. Our comrade was born of a Greek father. Permit us to bury him with Greek rites.' She had replied: 'By all means. If you are ignorant of the ritual there is a Greek trader named Crius living near the jetty, who will doubtless assist you.'

Crius was a Phocian whom the Trojans had once, many years before, rescued from shipwreck off the island of Imbros; but they sold him into slavery at Anthenios. There he had soon bought his freedom, for he was a painter and potter of more than ordinary skill. When the sons of Phrixus revealed to him that Iphitus had been a Phocian too, Crius undertook to raise a stone shrine above his barrow and decorate the walls with paintings in coloured earths. So without more delay they laid the body on a pyre and danced in armour about it, heaped a barrow above the calcined bones, poured drink-offerings, tore out their hair in handfuls, sacrificed a pig, and came away.

Euphemus the swimmer had been born in Phocis and had learned the art of swimming from the Seal men there. He remembered Crius well and urged Jason to let the sons of Phrixus return and fetch Crius off on the *Argo*, for Crius had told them how miserably he longed for one more sight of his homeland. Jason refused, saying that he had come to Anthenios for one purpose alone, the burial of Iphitus, and could permit no delay; besides, if he took Crius with him, the tomb of Iphitus would never be built.

'True,' said Peleus the Myrmidon, 'and since Crius does not know that we are homeward-bound for Greece, he will feel no regret that we have sailed without him.'

So Crius was left behind. Nevertheless, on the advice of Argus, Jason sent Phrontis and his brothers back to him to purchase provisions of dried meat, dried fish, dolphin oil, and fig-bread, offering in payment certain ornaments and jewels that Medea had brought with her. These provisions were presently brought to the ship drawn on ox-carts, enough for a month's voyage when they were added to those already aboard. Argus, who was ordered by Jason to stow them away in a place of safety, found that he could not do so, the lockers being already stuffed with gifts and trophies. He therefore divided everything equally among the whole crew, saying: 'Here are sufficient provisions for a month, comrades; dispose of them how you will, but see that nothing is spoiled by the sun or by sea-water. If we fall in with the Colchians again, as I fear that we must, and find that the strength of their fleet has increased, we may well be forced to take to the open sea, without hope of provisioning our lovely ship again for a long while. For my part, I care not much whether I bring home safely to Athens the rich gifts that King Lycus of the Mariandynians gave me, or the gifts of blind King Phineus, or the spoils that I took when we sacked the palace of King Amycus the Bebrycian, so long only as I come home with a whole skin, a full belly, and the Fleece.'

They stood out to sea again, first putting in at the outfall of the river Anthenios to fill their water-jars. Peucon, the Colchian master, pleaded to be set ashore, but Jason would not let him go, judging that he might prove useful to them yet. Since the wind was still fresh from the southeast, old Nauplius the navigator set the *Argo*'s course due west, and she sailed boldly across the Eastern Gulf, far out of sight of land.

CHAPTER THIRTY-SIX

THE PURSUIT

Ten days later a squadron of fifteen ships under the command of Aras, the Colchian High Admiral, reached the Long Beach on the impulse of a north-easterly wind. It was here that the Thessalians had danced their sword-dances and Atalanta had gone out with Meleager to hunt gazelles. Aras found, drawn up on the beach, not only the squadron of three ships which was commanded by Apsyrtus but, also under his command, the three surviving ships of the second squadron despatched by Aeëtes.

No sooner had Aras stepped ashore than he prostrated himself before Apsyrtus and hailed him King of Colchis; reporting with tears that old Aeëtes had died, in intolerable anguish, of the wound dealt him by Atalanta. He reported, too, that Perses, the Queen's brother, had proclaimed himself Regent of Colchis in the absence of Apsyrtus; that Styrus and he were at peace; and that when Styrus had asked with some impatience: 'When do I marry the Princess Medea?' Perses, with the approval of the Council of State, had undertaken that if Medea could not be fetched back before the summer was out, he should be permitted to court Neaera instead.

Apsyrtus grieved greatly for his father, but still more for himself. He had set his heart upon marriage with Neaera; for marriage between uncle and niece is permitted among the Colchians, so long as there is no blood-kinship in the female line. He knew now that unless he could fetch Medea home before the summer was out he would become involved in a war with Styrus. He had no intention of yielding Neaera to him, whatever promises Perses might have made, because to Neaera, on the death of Aeëtes, fell the possession of the frontier region that had belonged to her Colchian grand-mother and which he loathed that the Albanians should occupy.

He asked Aras impatiently: 'What news of the Greek ship?'

Aras replied: 'None, Majesty.' They both judged it unlikely that the *Argo* had sailed ahead of them along that coast, for each of the squadrons had kept a sharp look-out all day, and the moon had shone unclouded every night, and the natives whom they had questioned had sighted no craft at all since the *Argo* had passed by them on the outward voyage. Apsyrtus concluded that, since Jason had evidently taken the risk of sailing around the Black Sea in the opposite direction, the Colchian fleet should make for the Bosphorus as speedily as possible and there block his escape; for the southern route from Colchis to the Bosphorus is far shorter than the northern, despite the unfavourable currents and winds.

As they were taking this decision, the *Argo* herself came running down the wind towards them, making for the mouth of the Halys river. Lynceus told Jason, while they were still already a great distance away: 'Our Colchian enemies, sixteen ship-loads of them, are taking their ease on the Long Beach. I can see their white pennants fluttering above the curve of the sea, though their hulls are still hidden from me.'

Jason was in a quandary. The *Argo* was well enough provisioned, but the water in the jars had an evil smell and already several of the Argonauts, among them Orpheus and Echion, were sick of the dysentery; and all the others were in a quarrelsome and unhappy mood. For the sun was very hot even for the time of the year. They had hoped to replenish the jars with the sweet water of the Halys, and also to taste roast meat again, if they had luck with hunting, and lie at full length on grass under the shade of trees. Jason could not decide whether he should change course and return to the wild, lonely stretches of mid-sea, or whether he should wait for darkness and then enter the mouth of the Halys, to sail on as soon as his jars were full of good water. He wished to put the question to the vote, but the Argonauts would not vote until they had debated it at length; and while they argued together, discontentedly and insultingly, the *Argo* drew ever nearer to the coast.

Presently the Colchian look-out on the hill sighted her, and Dictys the Vice-Admiral, having climbed up to the look-out post to signal her with smoke, came down again and reported to Aras on the beach: 'She is one of our own vessels. I can just make out the White Horse and the white pennant. But why does she not reply to our signals?'

Aras climbed the hill himself and studied the *Argo* with care. He said to Apsyrtus, who followed after him: 'The pennant and the figurehead are Colchian; but, Majesty, look at the curved stem ornament. No Colchian ever carried one of that shape. She is the Greek pirate in disguise, for I noted her curved stern ornament myself and admired it. She is shaping her course for the Halys. Probably the Greeks are in need of fresh water. They are not so hardy as we are, and would rather die of thirst than drink water that has rotted or is brackish.'

Apsyrtus gave the order: 'Every ship to sea! To the master who first overhauls the pirate I will give his own weight in gold, a pair of green jade earrings for his wife or daughter, and a resonant silver gong.' But by the time that the Colchians were afloat again and rowing out in the teeth of a stiff breeze, the *Argo* had rounded the headland to westward and disappeared.

It now wanted five hours for nightfall and the Colchians hoped to overhaul the *Argo*, which was more heavily built than any of their vessels and slower both with oars and under sail. But the Argonauts, so soon as they saw the enemy's vanguard rounding the headland behind them, and realized that they were being pursued, took to their oars and began rowing vigorously, as many of them as were not incapacitated by sickness. They kept their lead until darkness gathered, but with no hope of rounding Cape Lepte, which lay to their north-west: for the wind continued to blow from the north-east and they were already wearied by rowing.

Autolycus said: 'Here we are back in Paphlagonian territory. What do you say? Shall we beach our ship among friends upon whom we can rely, and disembark and return to Greece by land?'

Argus cried indignantly: 'What! Leave the *Argo* behind and the speaking branch of Zeus which is built into her prow? We Argonauts have sworn a blood-oath never to desert the *Argo* or one another.'

And Augeas asked: 'What? A three months' march through hostile tribes, and in the end to fall into the hands of our enemies, the Trojans?'

Medea said too: 'I for one am unaccustomed to marching. My tender feet would be torn to pieces by the rocks and thorns before evening of the second day.'

Autolycus answered: 'Yet, standing before a choice of evils, we counsel you to take the least noxious.'

Peleus said with decision: 'Let us go ashore where there is water, I care not where, scour our jars well, refill them with clean water, and see what comfort the Gods bring us when we have done.'

So they put in at the Carusan river, which lies in the middle of the gulf between Sinope and the Halys, and there hastily scoured and refilled their water-jars. But Medea went out into the dark woods, which spread down to the water's edge, to pick juniper sprigs and the pungent leaves of a small nameless herb, which are good against dysentery. She soon found what she needed, her nose guiding her, and returned to the ship.

When the water-jars were safely stowed away, Peleus asked: 'Do I not hear a humming from the prow?'

Mopsus went to listen and reported: 'The branch of Zeus is speaking again. It says: "To sea, Argonauts! To sea! Bring my Ram his fleece without delay."'

But Idas mocked: 'Can the old tup want so warm a covering in mid-summer? Now is the season of shearing.'

Medea laughed aloud and Jason was vexed with her, but dared not rebuke her because of the double-eye.

They lowered their sails and put to sea again, using their oars, though they were very weary, and struggled against the wind, which was hard abeam. They puffed, sweated and pulled like plough-oxen when the field is clayey and the ploughman uses a sharp goad; they plant their hoofs deep and roll their bloodshot eyes from under the yoke, but still they pull.

Medea doctored the sick men, putting the rolled leaves of the nameless herb in their nostrils and under their tongues. Then she stood up in the stern, and the moon shone bright on her pale face and yellow hair. She raised her hand to command attention and made the Gorgon face, and ordered every man to ship his oar, to stop his ears with his fingers and to rest his head upon his knees. Then she called Atalanta to her, to act as her attendant.

Atalanta came willingly, for, though in her heart she despised Medea for having fallen in love with Jason and robbed Prometheus for his sake, she knew that only Medea could now save the *Argo* from the power of the Colchians. Medea and Atalanta together sprinkled the ship with juniper sprigs dipped in fresh water. Atalanta then blindfolded the eyes and sealed the ears of the sick men, and afterwards Medea uttered a prayer in the Colchian tongue which Atalanta did not understand, at the same time performing certain intricate gestures with her fingers. Then, between them, the two women hauled up the sail and made fast the sheets to the bulwark; together uttering screaming cries like sea-eagles at play.

The moon was suddenly obscured by a black cloud, and the wind veering obediently to the south-east, filled the sail and drove the ship along, while the men still sat mute with their heads upon their knees. Atalanta took the helm and Medea stood at the prow. Ahead of them in the gloom lay the dark shapes of two Colchian ships. For the leading squadron of the enemy fleet, instead of pursuing the *Argo* to the river, had sailed across the mouth of the gulf to cut off her retreat; and had lost sight of her in the darkness. Medea asked Atalanta: 'Is the *Argo* stoutly built?'

Atalanta answered: 'Most stoutly.'

'Port your helm a little,' said Medea. 'And a little more!' She fetched the ship's pole and held it ready in her hands. There was a crash and a rending of timbers as the prow of the *Argo* drove into the port counter of the nearest Colchian. The Argonauts were thrown forward in a heap, and when they struggled to their feet, forgetting that they should be stopping their ears, Atalanta laughed at them and cried: 'Alas, comrades, we have struck! We have struck upon a wooden rock!'

Medea had already pushed the *Argo* clear of the Colchian, which was settling down in the water nearly out of sight astern. The crew were yelling for help: 'Save us, we are drowning! Save us!'

Medea told Jason calmly: 'The other ship will go to their rescue. Let us sail on!'

Thus they came safely off with the water fetched from the Carusan river, scudded past Sinope and rounded Cape Lepte. But a part of the Colchian fleet was cruising ahead of them at a distance of half a mile, with lanterns shining at the poops. At this they changed their course, steering north-west for the open sea, in the hope that with the help of winds and currents, and by their own exertions at the oars, they might reach the Bosphorus before the Colchians, though on a longer tack.

The next morning, when they were well clear of the coast, and not a sail was in sight, Jason called a Council of War. Having learned not to be the first to speak, he asked the advice of Argus first, and next of Phrontis, son of Phrixus, and next of old Nauplius, and next of Autolycus the Sinopean, and lastly of Medea. Echion the herald, who had been disgusted by the ill-mannered controversy of the previous afternoon, now took it upon himself to regulate the proceedings with his twisted staff; for he had recovered from his dysentery.

Argus said: 'There is only one way out of the Black Sea, namely the Bosphorus. Let us sail there as soon as possible, remaining at a distance of thirty miles or so offshore until the last day. Then, if we find the Colchian fleet assembled to guard the entrance, let us run on boldly. I warrant that the broken planks of the vessel that we rammed last night will be warning enough to our enemies; each in turn will sheer off and we shall come safely through.'

Phrontis, son of Phrixus, said: 'The Colchians are not such cowards as you suppose, Argus. And if the wind proves contrary, or does not blow at all, many ships will crowd about us and hem us in. We shall be boarded from both sides at once and, however boldly we may fight, yet in the end we must be overcome.'

Old Nauplius said meditatively: 'I have heard that the Bosphorus is by no means the only way out of the Black Sea. We have a choice of at least three others. Either we might sail up the Phasis river, and from the Phasis into the Cyrus river, and from the Cyrus into the Caspian Sea, and from the Caspian Sea into the yellow Oxus river which falls at last into the rushing Ocean that girdles our hemispherical world with its blue stream; and so homeward by way of Egyptian Nile – which also falls into the Ocean...

Autolycus laughed: 'Alas, Nauplius!' he said, 'you have been misinformed. To pass from the Phasis to the Cyrus river the *Argo* would have to be propelled on rollers over rough tracks for as long a distance as it takes a train of baggage mules four days to cover. Moreover, the yellow Oxus nowhere approaches within a thousand miles of the Ocean.'

Old Nauplius said: 'I do not believe it. You are retailing, doubtless in good faith, a story long ago invented by the Colchians in the hope of discouraging the maritime enterprise of us Greeks. But let that be, for none of us wishes to return home by way of the Phasis merely for the purpose of proving you a liar. The second route is by the Don, the great river that enters the Sea of Azov near the territory of the Royal Scythians. We might sail up the river, which is very broad, for a hundred days, until we came at last to the White Sea, or Cronian Sea, which is frozen thick for nine months of the year, and –'

'No, no,' cried Jason, 'that will never do. What is the third route?'

Nauplius did not care to be interrupted and, with the consent of Echion, he continued his account of the White Sea and of the witches who haunt it, and of the night of six months long, until everyone laughed at him. At last he spoke of the third route, which he commended as the most practical of all for the conveyance of the Fleece: by way of the calm Danube, along which one might sail for thirty days before reaching its confluence with the lusty Save, easily navigable at that point. 'The Save will whirl us down to its outfall at the head of the Adriatic Sea in ten days,' he declared, 'and from thence to the Gulf of Corinth is no more than seven days' sail in good weather.'

Autolycus gently disputed this: 'No, Nauplius, that will not do either. The Trojans, in search of amber, once sailed up the Danube for as far as they found it navigable; but after twenty days only they reached the Iron Gates, which is a rocky gorge with rapids insuperable by any vessel afloat.'

'I do not believe it,' said Nauplius again, 'the Trojans are born liars.'

Then Medea spoke in tones of authority. 'Autolycus is right in declaring that the *Argo* cannot sail from sea to sea by the waters of the Danube and the Save. For the Save does not flow into the Adriatic Sea; it rises in the Alps and flows eastward into the Danube. Yet Nauplius is right to propose this as the safest route for conveyance of the Fleece. We will go by canoe and on mule-back, Jason and I, taking the Fleece with us. Let the *Argo* sail back by the Bosphorus.'

Idas laughed. 'Ha, ha, Madam! You are a true woman. You intend to come off safely with your lover and your jewels and the Fleece, and leave us to the mercy of the Trojans and the Colchians.'

Here Echion pointed at Idas with his staff and solemnly enjoined him to silence. But Medea stood in no need of a herald's help. She answered with eyes that flashed so green that Idas covered his head with his cloak and made the phallic sign with his fingers, to ward off her curse. She said: 'Do not show yourself an ungrateful wretch, Idas. If Jason and I remain in the *Argo* with the Fleece my fellow-countrymen will kill you all without mercy; for they are bound to overtake you in the end. Truly, I advise you to be rid of us and to sail as soon as possible to Salmydessos, on the coast between the Danube and the Bosphorus, and there place yourselves under the protection of King Phineus of Thynia. The Colchians will fear to offend him, knowing that he can close the Bosphorus to their trade with Troy; therefore Calaïs and Zetes, his stepsons, are your passports to safety, whereas Jason, myself, and the Fleece are mere warrants for a cruel death. The journey that I propose to make will be a hard one for a woman of my delicate nurture, yet make it I must, for all our sakes. I can command the help of that Scythian king whose daughter King Phineus married; he is an ally of my father's and trades with him, giving amber and skins in exchange for our Colchian hemp, linen and other goods. Nor do I intend to rob you of the glory of bringing the Fleece home to Iolcos. I count upon you to circumnavigate Greece and fetch us off from the place to which we will bring the Fleece – namely the island city of Aeaea, at the head of the Adriatic Sea, where my father's sister, Queen Circe, rules. From Aeaea we will all sail safely to Iolcos together.'

Medea's arguments were unanswerable, and since Autolycus and his brothers, as also Phrontis and his brothers, agreed that the mouth of the Danube might be reached within twelve days, if the wind were favourable, Jason gave his order: 'Make it so!'

Melanion, son of Phrixus, had undertaken this very voyage two years previously, and knew what course to steer, checking it by the Sun at midday and by the Pole Star at night. The true bearing was due northwest, but he said that allowance must be made for the south-westerly set of the currents, which were at their strongest at this time of year. Jason entrusted the helm to him.

A bright light appeared in the sky to the north-westward, like fire, and all read it for a sign that the Triple Goddess approved their decisions.

CHAPTER THIRTY-SEVEN

THE *ARGO* IS TRAPPED

When, ten days later, the Argonauts made their next landfall, it was a wooded islet not much more than a mile in circumference, with an unbroken line of steep, low cliffs. Melanion rejoiced and said: 'There lies Leuce, the largest island in the Black Sea, except for reed-covered mud-banks lying in the mouths of rivers. We are dead on our course, and only twenty miles distant from the main northern mouth of the Danube.'

By their reckoning they knew that this was the morning of the summer solstice. Then Augeas of Elis said: 'I am a priest of the Sun, and this is my holy day. I must go ashore to make sober sacrifices to the great Luminary.'

The sons of Phrixus, who also were devotees of the Sun, said: 'We go with you.'

Jason opposed them at first. He was in a quarrelsome mood and wished to show Medea that he was captain of the Argonauts in more than name. Yet he longed for the smell of flowers and leaves and to set his feet on firm ground again. The south-eastern wind that had carried them out to sea was one of great violence and, blowing sidewise against the vast masses of water that were rolling towards the Bosphorus, had produced the hacking waves that are the most disagreeable of any known to sailors: for the sea boils like a pot. Fortunately this wind had blown itself out after two days, and given place to milder winds from the east and south; but for a whole day they had been forced to heave-to and protect themselves from shipwreck by dangling oil-bags over the bows, which exuded dolphin oil slowly and broke the force of the waves. Then when Atalanta said: 'I warrant that there will be game in those woods. Which of us all does not love roast goat-flesh or roast venison?' Jason yielded. He too was weary of dried meats and of raw mackerel caught by trolling. He said: 'Very well, comrades, let us disembark, but not for long. Now is no time for delay. It may be that the Colchians are still in close pursuit of us.'

They ran the *Argo* ashore at a spot on the southern end of the island where the beach had an inviting aspect, and made her fast, and disembarked. Since there was little breeze Jason did not trouble to lower the sail, or it may be that he forgot to give the order; whichever the case, the sail remained hoisted all day. When they stepped ashore the ground seemed to quake under their feet; because they had been so long at sea that their bodies had become habituated to the heaving of the waves. This proved to be the pleasantest day of any that they spent during the whole voyage. First of all, they lighted a fire of driftwood for the pleasure of watching the flames leap and listening to the crackle of sticks; and while Argus kept a look-out to seaward and idly threw pebbles at a mark, all the others, except Medea, went out armed to make a drive for game. They moved across the island spread out at an interval of some fifteen paces, each from each, shouting and laughing like children, and drawing ever closer to one another as they approached the narrow tip of land at the further end. The game fled before them, and for so small an island it was wonderfully well stocked. There were three hares (besides two more that doubled back and escaped) and a herd of deer consisting of a tall stag, two brockets, three does, and three fawns.

The hares they knocked on the head with sticks; the brockets and one of the does, which was barren, they killed with javelins. But the other two does they spared, together with their fawns, because they were pure white in colour and seemed to be sacred animals. The stag they also spared, because his antlers had been gilded, and opened a lane in their ranks by which he might trot off, accompanied by the does and fawns. There were a great many snakes on the island; these also were driven to the one point, but there disappeared into a hole in the ground.

The hares and deer they sacrificed to Apollo of Disembarkations, and while the flesh was roasting at the fire, giving off delicious smells, Augeas and the sons of Phrixus roamed over the island in search of a honeycomb to offer to the Sun at noon. Before long they found a bees' nest in a hollow tree, and called Butes to take out the honey, which he gladly did with the help of smoke and an axe; and when a circular portion of honeycomb had been laid aside for the Sun a double handful remained for every Argonaut – the bees having remained undisturbed in the tree for a very long time.

Then Augeas raised an altar of stones on the beach and set the honeycomb upon it, arranging acorns and berries around it in the form of rays. He led the dance of the sacred wheel, circling the altar giddily in the same direction as the Sun circles the earth, and singing a hymn of praise in which the whole company joined; the sweat rose in beads on their flower-wreathed foreheads, so heartily did they dance in the heat, while from a shady thicket behind them rose the terrible noise of bull-roarers whirled in the Sun's honour.

When they were seated again about the other altar, wearied with well-doing, and drinking wine tempered with fresh spring-water, Jason held a council. It was there agreed that the *Argo* should put in at the Fennel Stream, the northern mouth of the Danube, and sail to the commanding hill, beyond the head of the delta, where the Scythian king had his court;

there Jason, Medea, and the sons of Phrixus would be put ashore with the Fleece. The *Argo* then returning to the sea by way of the Fair Mouth, the southern arm of the river, her crew would touch at Salmydessos to obtain the protection of King Phineus, and to revictual, and would continue thence by way of the Bosphorus and Hellespont into the Aegean Sea. They would circumnavigate Greece and sail up into the Adriatic Sea to the very northernmost part; where Jason's company would be waiting at Aeaea, the island city of Circe, to be fetched off.

Ascalaphus of Orchomenos now recalled an oracle delivered to him at Orchomenos by the Chief Priestess of the great shrine of his ancestor Minyas. 'You have a great voyage to make before you die, Child – before you descend to meet me in the Underworld. You will sail to the furthest East; yet before that same summer is out you will find yourself knocking at the door of the house where I was born, the house of my father Chryses.' Since it was well known that Chryses had founded the city of Aeaea, where Circe was now residing, here was good news – a warrant that the *Argo* would at least reach Aeaea in safety. 'Yet oracles can be deceitful,' said Admetus of Pherae, 'and it is best to put no reliance upon their manifest meaning.'

Oaths were sworn on either side, in the name of Zeus, that the party which first arrived at Aeaea should remain fifty days, if necessary, for the other to appear; but after fifty days would be released from any obligation to stay longer. This matter having been settled, the water-jars were again rinsed and replenished at the spring, which was a tedious business. The spring was a mere trickle, and they had not finished before evening. Jason therefore consented to let his companions pass the night on the island; for this was the night before the new moon, and starlight alone was insufficient to guide them safely into the rushing mouth of the Danube.

Meanwhile King Apsyrtus, observing the *Argo*'s flight to the north-westward, had divided his fleet into two flotillas. One, consisting of eight ships, he had put under the command of his Admiral, Aras, and ordered him to sail direct for Troy, to lie in wait for the *Argo* there; but if he came across her while he was still in the Black Sea, or the Sea of Marmora, so much the better. He was to butcher all aboard except Medea, the sons of Phrixus, Calaïs and Zetes; these were to be spared. With the other flotilla of twelve ships, which he commanded himself, Apsyrtus sailed north-westward in pursuit of the *Argo*, taking Dictys, the Vice-Admiral, with him.

The Black Sea is of enormous extent, a desolate waste of waters. Apsyrtus, losing sight of the *Argo* almost immediately, sailed for the mouth of the Danube, where he expected to overtake her. He arrived off the Fair Mouth on the very morning that the Argonauts disembarked at Leuce, and asked the local fishermen, who were Brygians, whether they had seen or heard of the *Argo*. They could tell him nothing, but later one of his own ships that had been blown northward out of her course arrived with news: as she had laboured along with oars about an hour after dawn that morning, her look-out man had sighted an island about a mile and a half to westward. The rising sun glinted on a white patch at the island's southern extremity – a beached ship with the sail still hoisted – and a light smoke rose near by. The master, recognizing the island as Leuce, had sheered off and shaped his course to the south-westward.

Apsyrtus guessed that the beached ship was the *Argo*. He drew up into the Fair Mouth all his ships but one, ordering the master of the remaining ship to sail as quickly as possible to the northern mouth, the Fennel, and there set two men ashore: they were to lie hidden among the reeds until the *Argo* should appear and to send up a column of smoke when she was well within the river. Apsyrtus was confident that Jason would put in either at the Fennel or the Fair Mouth, the lesser mouths further to the northward being the outfall of shallow and tortuous streams. Other pairs of men from the same ship were to be posted at nearer points along the coast of the delta, to observe the smoke signal and pass it backward.

The Colchian sailed off at once on this mission, and when she returned at midnight her master reported that the men were posted in pairs according to the orders of Apsyrtus.

The Argonauts slept well, unaware that a trap had been set for them or even that they had been observed; for they had all been busied with their pastimes and sacrifices during the brief time that the prow of the Colchian ship had peeped over the horizon.

But Apsyrtus planned, as soon as the *Argo* had crossed the bar of the Fennel, to send a part of his flotilla into the Fair Mouth to intercept her at the head of the delta, while the remainder sailed north along the coast and, crowding up into the Fennel, blocked her escape.

The next day at dawn the Argonauts spread their sail to a northeasterly breeze, and continued their voyage; the sea-water was presently discoloured with the grey mud of the river. As they approached, they steered by a five-peaked mountain, far inland, called the Fist. The coast of the delta was low, flat, and treeless, but covered densely with reeds. In the distance they saw a settlement of rude huts, raised on piles, and light canoes, of willow framework covered with sewn seal-skins, lying in a row on the muddy shore close by. This was the chief village of the Brygians, who wear seal-skin breeches and reek of fish oil; it lies close to the mouth of the Fennel.

The *Argo* crossed the bar, and when she had come a mile or more up the stream, which was flowing at two knots, the Argonauts saw a tall column of smoke rising astern on the right bank; but paid little attention to it, supposing it to be the smoke from a funeral pyre. The stream at this point was half a mile wide, and alive with fish.

At evening, helped on by the same wind, they anchored on the left bank, near a grove of rotten willow-trees, about twenty miles from the mouth of the river. It was a gloomy occasion, because the ground was damp from heavy rain, and Orpheus, who had been weakened by his dysentery, was overtaken by a sudden fever. He became delirious and poured out a torrent of eloquence, so ill-omened, though nonsensical, that his comrades were constrained to gag him; and he fought with such violence that a man was needed to control each of his four limbs. Medea could do nothing for him; for she was unclean at the time, because of her monthly course, and therefore unable to undertake any work of healing or magic.

It was then that the Argonauts heard, for the first and last time, the prophetic lament of King Sisyphus for the Goddess Pasiphaë, which he sang in the quarries of Ephyra on the evening before the stone crushed him; for Orpheus repeated it as he struggled, unaware of the blasphemy.

Dying sun, shine warm a little longer!
My eye, dazzled with tears, shall dazzle yours,
Conjuring you to shine and not to move.
You, sun, and I all afternoon have laboured
Beneath a dewless and oppressive cloud –
A fleece now gilded with our common grief
That this must be a night without a moon.
Dying sun, shine warm a little longer!

Faithless she was not: she was very woman,
Smiling with dire impartiality,
Sovereign, with heart unmatched, adored of men,
Until spring's cuckoo with bedraggled plumes
Tempted her pity and her truth betrayed.
Then she who shone for all resigned her being,
And this must be a night without a moon.
Dying sun, shine warm a little longer!

A crane flew by with a fish in its long bill, but dropped it into the river-mud close to the Argonauts' camp, uttering a sharp cry of distress and then a gabbling sound.

Jason asked Mopsus: 'Mopsus, what does the crane say?'

Mopsus answered: 'It says: "Alas – alas – cut into little pieces – cut into little pieces – they can never be put together again!" But whether the bird of Artemis is speaking of its own private grief or prophesying to us, I do not know.'

Lynceus said: 'If those are indeed the words of the crane, they cannot refer to the dropped fish, which, though dead, is not cut in pieces. In my opinion, the bird intentionally opened its bill to drop the fish and address us; and therefore the words are prophetic.'

'Let us wait in holy silence for another sign,' said Mopsus. 'Let none of us move until a sign appears.'

They waited in silence, and presently a large shoal of a sort of sardine fish came swimming close to the bank where Medea was sitting, and called attention to themselves by making a flurry in the water with their tails. This evidently was the expected sign, but nobody could interpret it plainly, though Atalanta observed that in Thessaly the Sardine is sacred to Artemis, just as the Crane is to Delian Artemis, and judged that some message of protection was being conveyed to Medea by the Goddess.

Melanion, son of Phrixus, agreed with this view. He said: 'Artemis is well known in these parts. Two islands sacred to her lie a little further up the coast, opposite the lesser mouths of the river, called the Thousand Mouths.'

Echion the herald put an end to the discussion. 'It is unprofitable,' he said, 'to torture the mind with surmise and speculation. Let us be content to remember the voice of the Crane and the flurry of the Sardine. Perhaps tomorrow the sense of both these portents will be apparent to us.'

They rolled themselves in their cloaks or blankets and slept, but shortly before dawn Jason dreamed that he broke open a ripe pomegranate with his nails and spilt the red juice upon his tunic and upon Medea's gown. Meanwhile Medea was dreaming that she and Jason, coming together into a hut, tossed a huge crayfish, the size of a man, into a cauldron of boiling water, and that both crayfish and water turned red; and that Jason drew the crayfish out and plucked out its eyes, and trimmed off the lower joints of all its legs with his sword, and scattered them outside in the darkness, crying with a voice like the crane's: 'Cut into little pieces – cut into little pieces – they can never be put together again!'

Medea and he were sleeping at a distance from each other, but both started up at the same instant in common terror. They dared not sleep again, but purified themselves at once in the running water of the Fennel, and remained awake until it was time for breakfasting.

The second day passed uneventfully, though ominous of evil in the first hours, when the sky was so heavy with mist that the sun rose like a vermilion ball and did not show his glory until long after they had breakfasted. About noon on the third day when, wearied with rowing, they drew near the head of the delta, suddenly the flotilla of Apsyrtus bore down on them from behind a wooded rise where the river made a sharp turn.

One ship against six was unequal odds, and Jason immediately gave the order: 'About ship, and row for your lives!' The *Argo* had a lead of about five hundred paces and doubled it as the afternoon wore on because Melanion, who was steering, knew well how to take advantage of the twisting currents, but all the ships were clipping along furiously.

Argus called Jason to him and said with gasps as he rowed: 'Beyond the next bend, as I noticed this morning, there is a stream or backwater which, if I am not mistaken, communicates with the Fair Mouth. At all events it flows out of the Fennel, not into it. Let us quickly turn in there, and hope that the Colchians will hurry on seaward, not noticing our change of course.'

Jason asked Melanion: 'Do you know where that stream emerges?'

Melanion replied: 'Alas, I have never enquired.'

Jason, with a prayer to Athena, to take the ship and himself under her keeping, made his decision.

'Steer her into the next stream to starboard,' he ordered.

A fierce current caught the *Argo* and whirled her past the bend. When she was again in a straight stretch of the river, the stream showed to starboard, its narrow mouth flanked with reed-beds. Melanion steered the *Argo* safely in, and after a few strong pulls the crew shipped their oars as silently as possible and let her slide on into concealment behind a forest of reeds. Behind them they could hear the wild bird-like cries of their pursuers and the measured plash of oars as each of the Colchian ships in turn drove on downstream.

They mopped their brows and spoke in whispers. Melanion said: 'This stream may be a blind alley. The current is so sluggish that I doubt whether it communicates with the Fair Mouth, which is fast flowing. I propose that we wait until the Colchians have rounded the next bend downstream and immediately double back upstream for six miles. We can then row up the narrow tributary which enters the Fennel from the opposite bank; I have been told that after twenty or thirty miles it communicates with the nameless northern arm of the river which breaks into countless small streams, the Thousand Mouths, and debouches behind the islands sacred to Artemis of which I spoke yesterday. If we take that course, the Colchians will never catch us.'

Jason asked: 'Who approves of the proposal that Melanion has made?'

Augeas of Elis said: 'Not I, for one. I am utterly exhausted. I could not row another mile, nor even half a mile, except downstream. It is easy for a helmsman to speak as Melanion does, but in this stifling weather it would break our hearts to contend once more with the current that tried our strength so severely this morning. Six miles, says he! And what then? Another twenty or thirty miles, still upstream, along a narrow rushing tributary? No, no! This stream that we are in may run slowly, but it runs in the right direction, namely seaward. It will bear us to safety before nightfall, I have no doubt. Then as soon as ever we are swept out into salt water, let the sons of the North Wind invoke their father with prayers and promises; we will hoist our sail, and within five days we shall be racing through the Bosphorus. We cannot afford to delay or to return upstream. Our enemies, when they reach the mouth of the Fennel and find no trace of us anywhere, will be at a loss. They will not know whether we have eluded them by turning off the main stream or whether we have scuttled our ship, or whether we have hidden her in a reed-bed somewhere and are now waiting to slip past them into the sea under cover of night.'

Augeas spoke with such passion that he convinced Jason and all his comrades except Melanion and Idas.

Idas, turning about to fix his eyes upon Augeas but addressing the company at large, said: 'I am sorry that you are so easily persuaded, my lords, by the gutless Epian. "No moon, no man", as I have often told you. But I blame his father, not himself, for his cowardice and sloth, and I will tell you why. My dear mother Arene (after whom my father Aphareus named our city) came to visit Hermione, the wife of Eleius, at about the time that she expected to be delivered of her first child. The night was moonless, and my mother therefore said to Hermione: "Dear cousin, in Heaven's name I implore you not to fall into labour until tomorrow night, when there will be a new moon. You know the proverb 'no moon, no man,' and I should be exceedingly sorry for you if you were to bear your bold husband Eleius a tadpole instead of a son." Hermione undertook to do nothing that might possibly precipitate childbirth. However, that same afternoon Apollo, who hated Eleius – as he secretly hates all priests of the Sun for not identifying their God with himself – sent a mouse which ran up Hermione's leg as far as the thigh and made her scream involuntarily; and at once her pangs came on her.

'My mother Arene cried to Hermione: "Lie down on your bed quick, dearest cousin, lie still, do not speak a word and I will delay the childbirth until tomorrow night." So my mother reeved all her own hair, her long fair braids, into difficult knots, and knotted together the skirts of her robe and cloak, and tied nine knots in her amber necklace, and then sat silently down with her legs crossed and her fingers tightly locked together at the door of Hermione's room. This is a sure charm, the same charm that the mother of King Sthenelus spitefully employed to delay the birth of Hercules and thus defeat an oracle. There she sat all night in great discomfort, and Hermione thanked her repeatedly in her heart, for the pangs became fainter and fainter; but could not speak, for fear of breaking the charm. And my mother sat on, cross-legged, and allowed nobody at all to set his foot across the threshold.

'Eleius broke the charm when he returned from hunting very early in the morning. He found my mother seated at the door of his bed-chamber, and wished to enter to fetch fresh linen from the chest, but my mother cast him a Gorgon look. He was a foolish and impetuous man and he shouted loudly through the door: "Hermione, Hermione, hand me a fresh linen shirt and drawers. I am wringing wet."

'Hermione dared not answer or rise from her bed, for fear of breaking the charm, and Eleius, growing suddenly angry, picked up my mother by her elbows and flung her aside. Then he burst into the bed-chamber and began abusing Hermione. He asked: "Why, wife, what ails you? Would you bar your dear husband out of his own bed-chamber when he comes home wringing wet from hunting boar?" At once the pangs returned, and Augeas was born before the night of the new moon, and he is what you see him to be – and all for the sake of a fresh linen shirt and a pair of drawers! And I am sorry, my lords, that you have been persuaded by this gutless Augeas to rest on your oars, when only by a vigorous use of them will we ever escape from the Colchian fleet.'

Had the speaker been any other Argonaut but talkative Idas, his comrades might have listened to him and reconsidered their decision; but since he was Idas, they paid no attention to him at all.

Presently they rowed on at their leisure down the stream, which was muddy and in part choked with reeds, but had not come far before they found themselves in a lake about two miles broad, its calm surface unbroken by any islands or reed-beds. They continued across it in the expectation of discovering a concealed egress at the southern extremity; but found none and sailed back along the reedy eastern shore, confident that the water which flowed into the lake from the Fennel must also flow out somewhere.

They were still debating the question in loud voices when first five, and then six more, Colchian ships nosed into the lake through a reed-bed just ahead of them. Spreading out in a half-moon they hemmed the *Argo* in, allowing her no hope of escape.

CHAPTER THIRTY-EIGHT

THE PARLEY

As soon as King Apsyrtus found that the *Argo* had eluded him, he had heaved-to and anchored his whole flotilla, except for two ships which he sent back upstream to the bend where she had last been sighted; ordering their masters to examine all intervening reed-beds, tributaries, or backwaters, and report to him at once if they found any trace of her. Presently one of them, searching the stream which the *Argo* had entered, noticed some newly bruised reeds and the mark of an oar on a mud-bank. He returned hurriedly to Apsyrtus with this report, and arrived just as the other Colchian flotilla under the command of Dictys the Vice-Admiral came rowing up from the sea. Dictys knew the river well, and when he heard what the master had reported, he hurried to Apsyrtus and pointing downstream said eagerly: 'Majesty, the tributary which you see yonder, flowing into the river on the right bank below the clump of willows, proceeds from a broad lake, called Crane Lake, into which the Greeks have evidently sailed, and it is the only stream that does so. If we sail up the tributary until we reach the lake we shall catch them in a trap.' And this is exactly what had happened.

Now that the *Argo* was surrounded, Apsyrtus behaved cautiously. He ordered every Colchian to hold his weapon in readiness but not to use it until the trumpet should blow for a general attack. He hoped that Jason would surrender unconditionally, after a short parley.

Outwardly the Argonauts preserved their calm, but the chill of doom stole upon their spirits as they reached for their weapons and put on their helmets or body-armour. All eyes were turned to Jason, but he mumbled ignobly: 'What can I say? What can I do, good comrades? I cannot in honour hand the Princess Medea back to her brother after the sacred oaths that I swore to her; yet if I refuse to do so, he will kill us all.'

'That is very true,' said Augeas, speaking in low, rapid tones, so that Medea should not overhear him. 'However, as I see the case, we went to Colchis for two reasons only: to bury the bones of Phrixus and to fetch back the Fleece. The bones are duly buried and we have won the Fleece; but we cannot hope to bring it safely home unless we restore this lady to the father from whose guardianship Jason stole her. Fortunately, she is still a maiden, or so I suppose, and what oaths of love Jason may have sworn to her need not greatly concern us. We can, if need be, depose him from his captaincy and act according to our own interests. We can inform Apsyrtus that if he allows us to keep the Fleece we will give him Medea in exchange, but that if he refuses us the Fleece we will kill her without pity. He will think twice before he refuses us the Fleece, because if he fails to bring Medea back, Styrus the Albanian will doubtless suspect Aeëtes of double-dealing and will make war on Colchis in vindication of his honour.'

Echion the herald fixed Augeas with a stern eye, saying: 'Pray be silent, King Augeas, and leave this matter to be settled by men of greater experience than yourself. Have you no shame? Your laziness and your ignorance are the cause of our present predicament.' Then he asked Jason: 'Most noble Jason, have I permission to speak on your behalf and on behalf of us all?'

Jason said: 'Do your best. But I think that the case is hopeless.'

Echion then bent down to whisper in Medea's ear: 'Gracious lady, do not take to heart any crooked words about you that my divine father, the God Hermes, may put into my mouth today. We Greeks love and honour you, and will never give you up to your brother, whatever we may tell him to the contrary during this parley.'

Then he put on his royal robes and took his twisted rod in his hand, and the parley began. Apsyrtus was obliged to be his own herald, because none of his captains or counsellors spoke Greek, he spoke it haltingly and confusedly, but whenever he stumbled for a word and lapsed into Colchian, Phrontis, the son of Phrixus, faithfully interpreted his meaning to the Argonauts.

Apsyrtus spoke first: 'You have committed four great and premeditated crimes, Greeks, and before I pronounce summary sentence upon you I sincerely recommend you to acknowledge yourselves guilty on all four counts, throwing yourselves upon my mercy.'

'We are unaware that we have wronged you in any way, Prince Apsyrtus,' replied Echion, 'and are much distressed to think that our former friends should have suddenly turned against us, poisoned by base-less suspicions. While freely apologizing for any accidental wrong that we may have done you, we do not find it consistent with our honour to plead guilty to four premeditated crimes, without knowing what crimes you mean, merely because you outnumber us in ships and men. Come now, pray tell us, for example, what is the first charge?'

'The first crime with which I charge you,' replied Apsyrtus, 'is sacrilege. You came to Colchis under the guise of friendship and piety, yet you obscenely mutilated the sacred brazen images of the Taurian bulls in the inner hall of the palace. Do you deny this charge?'

Echion answered: 'Whether this deed was done by a Greek, a Colchian, or an Albanian, who knows? We do not know; though, like you, we have our suspicions. But in any case, was it not well done? The Taurian bulls are obnoxious to Mithras, the glorious Sun God whom you worship and whom the Bird-headed Mother of Colchis loves and fosters. Doubtless it was at the Goddess's own prompting that the Albanians, or whoever it may have been, turned bull into ox.'

Apsyrtus dared not press this charge, knowing upon what insecure ground he stood. The Taurian alliance was hated in Colchis, and on his return there he might be wise to let it lapse. The Albanians, a powerful race, worshipped almost the same deities as the Colchians; and alliance with them, confirmed by the marriage of Medea to Styrus, would immeasurably strengthen his throne. He therefore said nothing in reply.

'What is the second charge?' asked Echion, after a pause.

'The second crime with which I charge you,' said Apsyrtus, 'is the abduction of my well-beloved and only sister, the Princess Medea. You can hardly dare to deny that charge, I believe, for I can see her with my own eyes seated on a purple cushion in the stern of your ship.'

Echion answered: 'We deny the abduction. The Princess Medea came with us of her own free will. Having, with the gracious help of your father, accomplished in Colchis a certain secret and divinely dictated mission, we were just about to sail home with his blessing under the friendly cloak of night, when the Princess came to us and asked for a passage to Greece. Naturally, the request astonished our noble leader Prince Jason, who questioned her closely. He asked, was her marriage to King Styrus already abandoned? She answered: "My father loves me and has never intended me to marry that filthy beast King Styrus, nor have I pledged my word in the matter. Within the hour you will hear a great commotion in the palace, which will be the sound of the Taurians and Albanians provoked to savage battle by my father. Pay no attention to the hubbub, dear friend; but I myself will take advantage of it to slip out unnoticed and come along with you. This is my father's desire." Prince Jason answered: "I can hardly believe your words, Princess; yet if the battle of which you speak does indeed take place within the next hour, I shall take it for a sign that you are deep in your father's confidence." The Princess Medea answered: "A thousand thanks, gracious Greek. I will come to you again with irrefutable evidence of my sincerity." And so indeed she did.'

When Echion lied he not only made his hearers believe him, against their inclination, but he believed himself.

Apsyrtus said: 'This is a strange and fantastic story that you are telling me, though I suppose that, for want of any evidence to the contrary, I must believe that Medea told you what you report her to have told. Yet let me assure you that she wove a tissue of plain lies, and that I blame your captain heartily for believing her.'

Echion answered: 'Prince Jason is young and inexperienced and was naturally inclined to believe whatever Medea told him. He could not imagine that Aeëtes was cruel enough to persuade his entrancingly lovely daughter into marriage with such a stinking old dung-hill as King Styrus. Now, what is your third charge?'

Apsyrtus answered: 'That you impiously stole the Golden Fleece from the shrine of Prometheus. You cannot wriggle out of that charge by any slippery trick of eloquence.'

'I wriggle!' cried Echion in indignation. 'Pray, my good lord, remember the cloak of sanctity with which we heralds are invested in our noble calling! I wriggle indeed! I stand upright and announce finally and fearlessly whatever I am commanded by my divine father to say. In the matter of the Fleece, we have nothing to hide from you. This Golden Fleece is the undisputed property of Laphystian Zeus and was long ago stolen from his sacred image by Phrixus, your brother-in-law. We have been commissioned – and this commission has been solemnly confirmed with oracles, dreams, signs, and prodigies – by the united wills of all the leading Olympian deities, Zeus himself at their head. On our outward voyage we rescued from drowning the four sons of this same Phrixus, your nephews, who understood at once that what had brought them into such peril had been their presumption in sailing, without the Fleece, to claim their paternal inheritance at Orchomenos. They humbled their hearts and offered to intercede with their grandfather on our behalf. Though at first he demurred, his obdurate mood was not long-lasting; and when Medea displayed the golden trophy to the stupefied gaze of Jason, as she climbed up the ladder into the ship, and when she said: "Here, noble Greek, is the Fleece of Zeus, irrefutable evidence not only of my sincerity but of my father's love towards you" – O, then You can guess how gratefully he accepted the glittering gift from her sacred hands! And who else in the world had a right to confer this gift upon him but your sister Medea, the Priestess of Prometheus, who tends his hero-shrine? No, no, my honoured lord, I beg you in good earnest not to regard us as pirates or petty thieves. We are all Minyans, and as Minyans we came boldly to Colchis to demand our own. The Golden Fleece lay under the guardianship of Athamas the Minyan at the time that his son Phrixus absconded with it; and ever since that day a curse has lain upon our clan which only the glorious adventure that we have undertaken can ever wipe away. I warrant that you will find it hard enough, Prince Apsyrtus, to part us from the sacred Fleece, the Luck of the Minyans, now that it is once again in our possession. It will be easier to part our souls from our bodies.'

'Yet I shall not hesitate to do both, unless you yield the Fleece to me freely,' said Apsyrtus sourly. 'And now, as I acquaint you with your fourth and most heinous crime, let me instruct you to address me not as "Prince Apsyrtus" or "my lord", but as "King Apsyrtus" or "Majesty". For Aeëtes, my admirable father, has succumbed to the terrible belly-wound that one of your Greeks inflicted upon him, and with his last breath he named you collectively as his murderers.'

Echion did not conceal his surprise. 'Pray, Majesty,' he said, 'let me condole with you most sincerely upon your loss, of which, as I will swear by any sacred name you please, I have hitherto been wholly unaware – until this instant I did not know that your dear father had been even wounded. Yet at the same time, let me congratulate your kingdom of Colchis upon its good fortune. Bitter as is the grief that the demise of good old Aeëtes will everywhere occasion among his loyal subjects, it will be swallowed up and drowned by the joy of your accession. And is it not possible that the dying King was mistaken in charging a Greek with this extraordinary crime? Was his mind not perhaps clouded by the pain of a wound inflicted by some Taurian or Albanian? And, if not, will you be good enough to name the murderer, who must answer to us, as well as to yourself, for having abused the laws of hospitality in this unheard-of manner?'

Apsyrtus answered: 'The guilt must fall equally upon all of you, as my father ordained with his dying breath, though the instrument of the crime was a single person, the red-haired Atalanta of Calydon. She it was who mercilessly pierced my father's bowels with her javelin as he stood at the head of his palace stairs. I am informed by my High Admiral that he expired four hours later in unspeakable anguish.'

Echion turned to Atalanta and asked: 'Surely, best of women, King Apsyrtus has been misinformed?'

Atalanta rose up and answered calmly: 'It is unlikely that he has been misinformed about the old man's death, but I cannot speak with certainty not having waited for the death-rattle. However, being a Greek by birth, Aeëtes should have been wiser than to oppose a maiden huntress of Artemis with a naked weapon in his hand. I had done him no harm and intended none either. If he is dead, in punishment for his act of sacrilege, let the Goddess answer for his death, not I.'

'Come what may, I must avenge my father upon all of you together,' cried Apsyrtus. 'Do you ask me also to take vengeance on the Goddess?'

Atalanta answered: 'Be careful what you say, Majesty. The Goddess who is reverenced even in these outlandish parts, is the most implacable of all deities, the Bird-headed Mother not excepted.'

Apsyrtus addressed Echion again: 'You deny all the charges, herald of the Greeks; and I reaffirm them. Does this not mean battle?'

Echion answered imperturbably: 'That is not for me to decide, Majesty. I must seek further instructions from my captain; and will return you a plain answer as soon as I have obtained one from him.'

Apsyrtus said: 'I will give you as long a time to answer me as it takes that crane, in the distance yonder, to fly past us and out of sight.'

Echion again spoke privately to Medea, who sat with a face like clay, stunned by the news of her father's death. 'Princess,' he said, 'let me repeat my assurance: we will never give you up, whatever may happen. But we must practise a deep deception and must even threaten to take your life. I beg you to pay no attention to our empty words.'

Medea raised troubled eyes to his face, nodding to show that she understood.

Echion next addressed Jason: 'Prince Jason, take the Fleece from its hiding-place quickly and give it into my hand, and lend me your sharp Magnesian hunting-knife. Whatever I may say, however strangely it may sound to you, assent. The spirit of my divine father is upon me.'

Jason made no answer, but with gloomy countenance he fetched the Fleece from its hiding-place below the helmsman's seat, unrolled it and displayed it glittering in the sunlight. Then he drew his curved hunting-knife from its sheath and handed it to Echion.

As he did so, the crane flapped overhead and repeated the same cry that it had uttered on the previous evening.

Echion laughed aloud, stretching out his right hand to the bird in gratitude for its message. He stood up again in the prow and, lifting up the Fleece for all to see, again addressed Apsyrtus. 'Majesty, even before the crane has flapped out of sight, heading (you may be sure) for the island of Artemis – of Implacable Artemis, to whom the crane is sacred – I have ready the answers not only of my captain, Prince Jason but of your sister, the Princess Medea. And all my comrades, the Argonauts, assent to them without dispute.'

'Say on,' Apsyrtus answered.

'We have concluded,' began Echion, 'in the matter of the mutilated bulls to make you a handsome offer – handsome because it has not yet been established who it was that performed the act of mutilation. Let me remind you that this is a quarrel subsisting not between Colchians and Greeks but between the war god of the Taurians and the Colchian Sun God Mithras, whom in Greece we honour as Helios. We have aboard our ship five devotees of the Sun, namely the four sons of Phrixus and Augeas, King of Elis, who are prepared, here and now, to disembark on the nearest stretch of firm ground and fight to the death with as many champions of the Taurian god as you may care to call out against them.'

Apsyrtus answered: 'Is this not unreasonable? Your challenge could be accepted only by myself, the son of a Taurian princess, and by two old Taurian greybeards who are here in this ship with me. All the rest of my men are worshippers of Mithras. We three should be no match for your five.'

'Evidently,' said Echion, 'you have lost confidence in the might of your god, now that he is unmanned by the gelding of his two sacred images. I cannot reckon you a less bold man than myself, who, were I challenged to uphold the honour of my father, the God Hermes, would gladly come out armed against the whole embattled might of the East and be assured of victory. I presume, then, that our challenge is refused and shall pass on to the matter of the Fleece. For the reasons that I have already advanced, we have concluded to retain the Fleece. We warn you that if you attempt to seize it by force I myself with this knife will *cut it into little pieces – cut it into little pieces* and fling them into the water. The weight of the gold will sink them in the thick black ooze, beyond recovery. *They will never be put together again* and the Fleece will be lost to Prometheus, as it was lost to Zeus.'

'That would not disturb me,' said Apsyrtus. 'I care not whatever may happen to the Fleece, so long as you do not fetch it back to Iolcos and flaunt it there as a proof alike of your enterprise and courage, and of our negligence and cowardice.'

Echion took him up at once, saying: 'I am rejoiced, Majesty, to hear an admission from your lips that you do not prize the Fleece as much as we do, and are indifferent to its fate so long as its removal by us does not reflect injuriously on the honour of the Colchian nation. Doubtless, when the two other outstanding questions are settled to our common satisfaction, we shall reach an understanding upon this also. For I assure you that we value the honour of your kingdom as highly as any men living, having received marks of hospitality from your King and principal noblemen which it would be ungrateful in us ever to forget. Let us therefore pass on to the third question: what is to become of the Princess Medea? Here is our offer to you. We do not insist upon her remaining with us, but neither shall we permit her to be taken back to Colchis against her will. Since, by your own admission, her father Aeëtes is dead, the secret treaty that you made with her, in which you resigned to her your claims to the throne of Corinthian Ephyra, has now come into force. By that act of resignation you set her free to become Queen of Ephyra as soon as ever your father should die, and in return she freely resigned to you all claims to her Colchian patrimony. Therefore, though we admit the right of the King of Colchis, namely yourself, to persuade his sister, a Colchian princess, into marriage with whomsoever he pleases this right can now no longer be exercised. By the terms of your compact Medea has ceased to be a Colchian princess and has become Queen-Designate of Ephyra; and as Greeks we cannot admit your right to persuade her into marriage with a vermin-eating barbarian. For the Queen-Designate of Ephyra, if she is unmarried, is entitled to contract a royal union with the prince of her choice and to disregard the persuasions of the King of Colchis. However, we do not wish to press our view too strongly; the Fleece is our prime concern, not the marriage of your sister Medea. We therefore make the following suggestions. Let us all sail together in consort down the Danube, and set Queen Medea ashore with a suitable attendant upon the island of Thracian Artemis, which the crane in its flight has divinely indicated to us. Let us leave her there until some powerful king – without prejudice, we nominate the milk-drinking King of the Scythians, your ally, as a man of the highest rectitude – shall have consented to act as arbiter between yourself and ourselves. If, after weighing the case scrupulously in the scales of justice, the king decides that your sister must return with you, why then we shall let her go without hindrance; if, on the contrary, he decides that she may remain with us, then you, for your part, must let her go without hindrance.'

'Before I consider this proposal,' said Apsyrtus, 'let me know how you propose to satisfy the vengeance that I require for the death of my father.'

Atalanta stood up again and spoke for herself. 'My comrades Majesty, are in no way concerned in the death of your father, of which they have now heard for the first time: for I said not a word to them of the blow that my javelin dealt him. To butcher them all, in requital for a crime of which they are wholly innocent would be to stock your palace with a swarm of gibbering ghosts: who would haunt you without respite, night and day, until you died horribly at last with twisted mouth and twitching limbs. But if you seek vengeance against me, my advice to you is to consult the Oracle of Artemis on the island mentioned by Echion. I am ready to stand by the verdict of the Oracle; and if I have sinned I will come freely to you for punishment. But if the Goddess approves my action, I warn you to respect her decision.'

Apsyrtus said, gesturing nervously with his hand: 'I have now heard proposals which I should applaud as fair and reasonable had they come from the herald of a fleet as powerful as my own; but since your ship is alone and has no chance of escape either by flight or fight, I cannot regard them as anything but absurd and impertinent. What if I reject them out of hand and give the signal for battle?'

Echion answered in a voice that bespoke perfect assurance: 'For that, King Apsyrtus, I have a ready answer. If you reject them you will lose three things of great value. First, the Golden Fleece, which will be immediately destroyed, as we have already declared. Next, you will lose your sister Medea, for since the signal for battle would spell certain death for all my companions, they would be careful to take her ghost down with them to the Underworld to guide them securely to the mansion of the Great Goddess whom she serves. Lastly, you will lose your own life. For I have resided long enough in Colchis to learn that the King must lead his fleet or army in person, not lagging behind with the rear-guard; and you need no reminder from me that our archers have a deadly aim. At the display in the gardens of your palace you saw with your own eyes how a flying pigeon fell transfixed by three Greek arrows – a feat never before seen or spoken of in your land. Sound your golden trumpet for battle, Majesty, if you dare, but you will be blowing an insistent summons to my father, the God Hermes, Conductor of Souls, to bring you where you would hate to go.'

Echion could see that the King's resolution was weakening. He said, pleadingly this time: 'Come, noble son of Aeëtes, retain your own life and honour and leave us with ours. There is no question in the world that cannot be amicably settled by law or by arbitration, and may I further remind you that to kill us would spell the destruction not only of yourself and your sister but of your entire kingdom? When the line of Aeëtes is extinct, who will rule Colchis? Perses, your Taurian uncle? Were I a vulture of the Caucasus the news of your death would be good news to me: I would summon my long-winged mates from near and far to converge upon Aea, assured that civil war heaps corpses as the first blast of autumn heaps acorns in the woods. Majesty, prudence is a gracious virtue in a young king, and becomes him more even than the valour which you possess in full measure.'

Apsyrtus yielded at last, though with a bad grace, further insisting only that the Fleece must also be set ashore on the island of Artemis, and the question of its ownership submitted to the same arbitration.

Echion pleasantly assented to this article of the armistice, and the parley was over.

CHAPTER THIRTY-NINE

THE COLCHIANS ARE OUTWITTED

That evening the *Argo*, sailing down the Fennel Stream in consort with the Colchian ships, six of them ahead and six astern, reached the sea again. The whole flotilla anchored in line near the Brygian village, with the *Argo* in the middle. Gloomy Melampus of Pylos said: 'Comrades, no man of sense could envy the position of our ship, guarded like a criminal between warders; nevertheless, I do not despair. Which of you sees what I see? To the first man who confirms my presentiment of deliverance I will give my necklace of interlaced-silver rings which every one of you covets.'

For a long while nobody understood what Melampus meant, but at last his comrade Coronus of Gyrton, who had hitherto passed for a man of slow wit, cried out: 'I see what you see, Melampus. Give me the necklace!'

The other Argonauts asked: 'What do you see, Coronus? What do you see?'

Coronus answered: 'I see that Apsyrtus is either ignorant, rash, or extremely careless, since he has added a strange ship to his flotilla of twelve, which is a direct challenge to the Thirteenth Deity, of whose name every wise man avoids mention.'

Melampus handed over the valuable necklace without a word, and encouraged by this omen, the Argonauts grew merry and sang choruses to Atalanta's lyre-music; for Orpheus, though somewhat recovered from his fever, was still excessively weak.

Jason and Medea then concocted their plan of action and presently confided it to Melanion, son of Phrixus (for whose integrity Medea could vouch), and to Atalanta; but all that the other Argonauts knew was that two emissaries – Peleus the Myrmidon for the Argonauts, and Dictys the Vice-Admiral for the Colchians – had gone together to bargain with the Brygians for a large canoe and a crew of three paddle-men who should convey them upstream to the Court of the Scythian King at the head of the delta.

The night passed uneventfully, though the sentinels on both sides were vigilant beyond the ordinary and shouted frequent challenges; the Greeks fearing a night attack, the Colchians fearing an attempted evasion. In the morning all the ships rowed northward in consort again, until they reached the island of Artemis, a low-lying, desolate place evidently formed in the course of ages by the mud and sand carried down by the Thousand Mouths.

However, Jason refused to put Medea and the Fleece ashore until Apsyrtus should have agreed to two conditions: namely, that he would not commit any act of hostility against the Argonauts, nor make any attempt to remove Medea or the Fleece from the island, until an arbitrative judgement should have been delivered by the King of the Scythians; and that he would abide by the judgement without question, whatever it might be. Apsyrtus, confident that the judgement would be in his own favour, since the Scythian depended on Colchis for a great part of his sea-borne trade and had no direct dealings with Greece, agreed to the proposed conditions, and added that he was ready to confirm his agreement with an oath, if Jason would do the same. He found Jason willing enough. Jason proposed that they should take an oath together, in the name of Artemis, on an uninhabited island that lay a short distance off. So the *Argo* and the Colchian ships were rowed to the island, where Jason and Apsyrtus disembarked together, sacrificed a kid to Artemis and swore the oath on its blood, drinking a little of it out of the hollow of a shield and pouring the remainder out upon the sand. They exchanged gifts, Apsyrtus presenting Jason with the skin of a Caucasian tiger, Jason presenting Apsyrtus with the purple-red cloak that had been Queen Hypsipyle's first gift to him at Myrine.

Medea scornfully refused to accept the two male attendants offered her by Apsyrtus for her stay on the island of the Oracle, and insisted on being provided with a single female one. Since Atalanta was the only other woman in the flotilla, Atalanta it had to be; but Apsyrtus would not allow her to go armed.

Medea and Atalanta were then set ashore on the island of the Oracle, and there came under the protection of the Priestess of Artemis. She was a tall, toothless, half-crazed Thracian, whose diet consisted wholly of nuts, berries, and raw fish. This skinny old woman patted Medea's cheeks, stroked her hands, and felt the texture of her robes in a childish ecstasy of admiration; but to Atalanta, when the men had rowed away, she gave a sisterly embrace and they exchanged magical passwords and signs.

The Greeks and Colchians, ashore together on the other island, the uninhabited one, now mixed freely, conversing in the language of signs and playing games together, and Peucon rejoined his comrades. But Melanion, the son of Phrixus, sought out Apsyrtus and led him aside into a thicket out of earshot. He said: 'Royal uncle, I have a secret message to you from your sister Medea, to which I hope to join a proposal and a plea of my own. Are you willing to listen to me, or do you hate me and thirst for my blood?'

Apsyrtus replied: 'Give me my sister's message first. Whether I listen to the plea and the proposal will depend on the nature of the message.'

Melanion, speaking in low, hurried tones, said: 'These are Medea's words: "My nephews Phrontis and Cytissorus have done both you and me a great injury. As you are aware, they and their two brothers decided to escape from Colchis some months ago because of your enmity towards them. An oracle had warned them of our father's approaching death, and they feared that as soon as you succeeded him you would take vengeance on them for obstructing your marriage to their sister Neaera. When their first attempt to escape ended in shipwreck and our father refused to lend them another ship, their one hope lay in winning the favour of Jason. He offered not only to give them a free passage to Greece, but to secure them their Boeotian patrimony, if in return they enabled him to win the Golden Fleece. They struck hands on the bargain, and presently set to work. Phrontis and Cytissorus, the more malignant of the four, forced me to abstract the Fleece from the shrine of Prometheus and accompany them to the Greek ship: they had threatened if I refused, not only to murder me but to poison our father and yourself as well, and then to swear that I had been the poisoner and had committed suicide to avoid punishment. Tell me, brother, what else could I have done but submit to their will?

"'I do not pretend that I love the thought of marriage with old Styrus, or that, to avoid it, I would not gladly sail to Greece, if that were possible, and there accept the throne of Ephyra which you have resigned to me. But I would fear the vengeful ghost of our father if I thus followed my natural inclinations; and I am aware that Styrus will prove a formidable enemy to my beloved Colchis if I do not return to marry him, but a staunch ally if I do. I wish therefore to return and deserve well of my fellow-countrymen, however painful the consequences to myself. Rescue me, dear brother, I implore you. If you abide by the oath which Jason has tricked you into swearing, you and I are both lost. For cunning Peleus the Greek, who has gone to the Court of the Scythian King, will (as I have overheard) present himself there as a son of blind King Phineus of Thynia, whom the Scythian holds in the greatest respect, and has been primed with arguments irresistible to the Scythian mind. The judgement will certainly be pronounced in the Greeks' favour, of that I have not the least doubt.

"'Why delay? The oath which you swore need not trouble you, because the power of Thracian Artemis does not extend to Colchis, any more than does the power of Father Zeus. She is not the ancient Taurian Artemis to whom our mother's tribe sacrifice strangers, fixing their heads on poles above their houses; she is an upstart deity – sister to the Mouse demon Apollo, and born within memory of man on the Aegean island of Delos – whose worship has recently spread to Thrace in the wake of trading ships. Be bold, therefore. Come secretly in a canoe at midnight to fetch me off the island, together with the Fleece, and take vengeance at the same time on the murderess of our father. I will set a lamp in the window of my hut to guide you. Come alone. But do not attempt to take me back with you to the Colchian ships. I fear for our lives should the alarm be suddenly raised and the Argonauts put their hands to their bows. Instead, let us row off southward in your canoe; then let the ships follow after and take us aboard at some distance from the island."'

Apsyrtus listened attentively and asked: 'What proof do you offer that you are Medea's emissary and that what you report is not a fabrication of your own?'

Melanion handed Apsyrtus a lock of Medea's yellow hair, which Apsyrtus accepted as security for her honesty and put into his wallet; just as the priests at Dodona had accepted a lock of Jason's hair as security for his promised gifts to Zeus.

Apsyrtus asked: 'But what is the proposal and what is the plea of which you spoke, nephew?'

Melanion answered: 'I am confident that you will forgive me, Majesty, for my former folly and my enmity towards you. I was led astray by my two eldest brothers. Argeus and I are not malignant, and do not now wish to go to Greece even if Jason could make good his promise to secure us our Boeotian patrimony; for we are the two youngest sons, whom the two eldest have always conspired to keep in poverty. Phrontis and Cytissorus, being given first choice of cities and lands, will, as it were, take the hide, flesh, and fat, and leave us the hoofs, umbles and bones. My proposal is this: Argeus and I will volunteer to stand watch tonight, so that your journey in the canoe may pass unnoticed by the Greeks, as may also the subsequent silent departure of your ships. At the last moment, Argeus and I will lower ourselves over the side of the *Argo* and be hauled aboard your own vessel. My plea is this: that in return for our loyal services you will graciously appoint Argeus your High Admiral and myself the Captain of your Palace Guard.'

'I accept the proposal,' said Apsyrtus, 'and shall consider the plea most favourably so soon as ever I have gained the three things that you have promised me: the Fleece, my sister, and vengeance on my father's murderess. Seeing that Atalanta now makes the Thracian Artemis, not herself, responsible for the murder, I consider myself justified in disregarding the oath that I swore in the Goddess's name. What duty can I owe to a deity who has inflicted this great and unprovoked injury upon our house?'

Melanion returned to the *Argo* and assured Jason that all was well. At dusk Autolycus was sent out to recover the lock of Medea's hair from the wallet of Apsyrtus and to replace it with a long strand of yellow yarn; he accomplished the feat without difficulty, being light-fingered to an incredible degree. It is said that he could rob a man of his front teeth or ears with such swiftness and skill that the victim might not be aware of his loss for an hour or more later. Yet Autolycus was not made an accomplice of the plot against the life of Apsyrtus: only Jason, Medea, Melanion, and Atalanta knew what was afoot.

That evening the Argonauts made a pretence of immoderate wine-drinking. They sang tipsy songs, beat with sticks and bones on the ship's cauldron, and drubbed loudly on the floor-planks with their heels. And Idas was continually crying: 'Jason, Jason, you are drunk!' To which Periclymenus the wizard, in tones indistinguishable from Jason's own, would reply: 'Silence, man, I am as sober as a water nymph!' Soon afterwards, all except Argeus and Melanion, the sentinels, made a pretence of falling asleep.

This performance was a ruse to conceal the absence of two of them: Jason and Euphemus of Taenaron. They had hidden in a thicket just as darkness drew on, and Euphemus, as soon as he dared, had noiselessly plunged into the sea and swam across to the mainland, where several Brygian seal-skin canoes were hitched to a mooring-stake. One of these he took, paddling back with it to where Jason waited. The dark night with rain threatening, suited Jason well: he climbed into the canoe, took up the double-bladed paddle, and guided by the lamp was soon ashore on the beach of the island of Artemis, wordlessly clasping Medea in his arms.

She led him to the hut where visitants to the Oracle were accustomed to wait for the Priestess's pleasure, and said: 'There is the bed in which you are to lie. The blankets will cover you up. Do not let your sword show! He may bring the lamp with him.'

Jason answered with a smile: 'Melanion tells me that he swallowed down your story as greedily as Butes the poisonous honey.'

Medea sighed and bit her thumb-nail. 'We should have abandoned the Bee man to his fate,' she said. 'His greed has led us on from crime to crime.'

'We are innocent of any blood,' said Jason hastily. 'Show no weakness, lovely one, for only relentless hearts can bring the Fleece safely to Greece. Do you not desire to come with us? Your way home to Colchis still lies open. If you choose to return, whether in piety or fear, I will not stand in your way, bitterly though I might grieve at losing you. But understand this much: I must retain the Fleece at all hazards.'

'The Fleece, always the Fleece!' cried Medea. 'I could hate you as I hate the Furies, did I not love you unendurably. No, no, I will follow you to the ends of the world and neither my father's blood nor my brother's shall flow between us and prevent our marriage. Kiss me again, Jason, kiss me! Only from your mouth can I suck courage for the ineluctable deed that lies before me.'

He kissed her again and again, drinking in with his nostrils the aromatic odour of her hair and body. She shut her eyes and whimpered for delight like a little dog.

Presently he went apart from her and, lying down on the bed, pulled the blankets over him. There, alone, with his sword ready to his hand, he awaited the entry of Apsyrtus.

Atalanta was not to be seen. Presently he heard her voice coming clearly from the shrine: she was amusing the Priestess with an account of the voyage. The Priestess liked best the story of the Lemnian women, and Jason heard her cry out with cackling laughter: 'Ah the fools, the fools! Did they not know how well off they were without men!' Then he heard Medea going to the shrine to silence Atalanta, for Apsyrtus must believe her to be in the hut.

An hour passed and, straining his ears, he heard the low sound of voices conversing twitteringly in the Colchian language: it was Apsyrtus and Medea. They were stealing towards him along the path. The voice of Medea was soft and servile, that of Apsyrtus was bitter and vengeful. Jason fancied that she said: 'Have no fear, brother. Atalanta is a woman unarmed.' And that Apsyrtus answered: 'Were it Hercules himself with his bow and brass-bound club, I would not shrink. I warrant that she will not escape me.'

Apsyrtus slowly came nearer. He stood in the doorway and uttered in a whisper what seemed to be a prayer to the ghost of his father Aeëtes, dedicating the sacrifice to him.

The prayer ended, and Jason heard the chink of weapon against armour as Apsyrtus groped his way across the room.

Jason started up, with the sword gripped in his right hand and his cloak doubled about the left as a shield. Apsyrtus stepped back a pace, but Jason, seeing him dimly outlined against the doorway, lunged forward and pierced him in the groin, so that he howled for pain and dropped his sword. Jason wrestled with him, threw him to the ground, and with one deep stab of the Magnesian hunting-knife cut the principal artery of his throat, so that blood spouted out like a warm fountain.

'Bring a light quickly,' Jason called to Medea, when Apsyrtus had ceased to struggle.

She fetched the lamp but hid her eyes from the sight of blood. Jason straddled the corpse and shouted boldly down to it: 'I am innocent, King Apsyrtus. You were the first to break the oath that we swore together. You undertook to offer no violence to any Argonaut, yet you came with steel in your hand against me. I did no more than defend myself against your violence.'

Nevertheless, knowing well in his heart that he had committed a treacherous murder, he lopped off the ears, nose, fingers, and toes of Apsyrtus, and three times licked up some of the blood that came gushing out, and three times spat it back, crying: 'Not I, ghost! Not I!' He had lopped off the ears and nose so that the ghost should be unable to trace him by smell or sound, and now he also nicked out the eyes, to blind it; and he slit the soles of the feet so that it should not pursue him without pain. The fingers and toes he cast through the window among the reeds of a swamp, so that the Colchians should have difficulty in recovering them.

Then he went out, his hands and face sticky with blood. Medea shrank away from him with irresistible loathing, and he said to her reproachfully: 'Princess, there is blood upon your gown also.'

She answered nothing, but called Atalanta from the shrine. 'Bring the Fleece,' she said, 'and follow me!'

The old Priestess came stalking out and asked: 'Did I not hear a cry?'

Medea answered: 'Gracious lady, the Goddess Artemis is avenged on the blasphemer.'

The Colchian sentinels, watching for the return of Apsyrtus, heard the plash of paddles and called out: 'Boat ahoy!'

Medea answered: 'It is I. It is Queen Medea. Colchians all, listen to me, listen with awe and obedience to your new Queen! My brother King Apsyrtus is dead, and I alone remain of the Royal House. Careless of the oath that he swore to Jason the Greek in the name of the Thracian Artemis, Goddess of this place, he came secretly by night to take vengeance on my attendant the maiden Atalanta, whom he unjustly charged with the murder of our father. As he stole into the hut where Atalanta and I were both lying, and as he crept, sword in hand, towards the bed, I witnessed a prodigy. A kirtled woman of extraordinary tallness and marvellous beauty, plainly the Thracian Goddess herself, appeared from nowhere and darted her javelin into my brother's throat, crying: "Pitiful man, would you dare murder a maiden huntress of Artemis upon the very island of Artemis?" Then her firm hand lopped off his extremities, using his own sword, so that he fell in a pool of his own blood. The blood spouted out on all sides, and bespattered my gown.

'Listen again, Colchians! I am your Queen, and whatever orders I give you, they must be obeyed. In the first place, I require you to remain here for nine days, beginning from dawn tomorrow, to mourn and perform funeral rites for my brother Apsyrtus. Assemble his scattered bones with care – not some, but all – and convey them in a white horse hide to Colchis, to my capital city of Aea, where I shall sail ahead of you. As for these Greeks, I intend to let them go free, restoring to them the Fleece that was stolen from them by Phrixus, my sister's husband; and I make this gift not from weakness or cowardice but lest its noxious properties should cause the death of a third member of our Royal House, namely myself. Yet I shall tie a condition to this gift: they must carry me to Colchis with them before they sail homeward to their own land. Sailors, I am aware of your religious scruples and respect them. You consider it unlucky to take a woman aboard any of your ships, and doubly unlucky to take a priestess of the Goddess of Death, and trebly unlucky if her robe happens to be stained, as mine is, with her brother's blood.'

The Colchians listened to Medea's speech with stupefaction, and no one dared say a word. Then she cried out: 'My nephew Melanion, you who stand sentinel on the Greek ship! Wake your leader Prince Jason and ask him whether he will agree to the bargain that I offer him.'

Melanion made a show of consulting Jason and then replied in the Colchian language that Jason assented, but on condition that he might first fetch off Atalanta from the island and then sail up the Danube to overtake Peleus and bring him back: for he could not desert either of these two comrades.

Medea pretended impatience, but acquiesced. She came aboard the *Argo*, crying that the sooner they sailed the better, if they hoped to over-take Peleus. So the Argonauts trundled their anchor-stones aboard and rowed away into the darkness without another word, while behind them rose a slow wail of grief from the leaderless Colchian sailors, like hungry wolves howling to the moon.

Ancaeus steered to the island of the Oracle, and when the keel grounded upon sand he let down the ladder. First Atalanta, holding the Fleece, and then Jason climbed aboard. From the shore came the cackling laughter and repeated farewells of the Priestess, who called out merrily in her Thracian accent: 'Cut into little pieces – cut into little pieces – they will never be put together again!'

The Argonauts shivered when they heard this. They guessed that she had been the crane in disguise, and indeed with her long nose and skinny legs she looked crane enough. They were glad to leave the island of blood astern and to spread their sail to a stiff northerly breeze.

CHAPTER FORTY

THE *ARGO* DISMISSES JASON

At dawn the Argonauts found Peleus waiting for them at the Brygian village. Admetus asked him as he climbed up the ladder: 'Are you still here? And what of the Colchian Vice-Admiral?'

Peleus answered briefly: 'We borrowed the canoe and sailed off in her. But the Vice-Admiral admitted to me that he could not swim.' He paused.

'Ah, I understand,' said Admetus. 'This was another of your unlucky accidents, I suppose.'

'My life has been strewn with them,' Peleus confessed, blushing, 'ever since, long ago in Aegina, my quoit was diverted from its true course by a winged Spite and killed my wretched foster-brother. Yesterday it was the unsteadiness of the canoe and the rapidity of the current which bloodlessly robbed the Colchian of his life.' Then he addressed Jason and Medea: 'Tell me, blessed pair, how have you managed to be rid of our oppressors? Did our Euphemus borrow the auger again from the tool-locker of Argus? And have you brought the Fleece with you?'

As Jason rose up to display the prize, the searching rays of the sun shone on his bloody tunic and smeared legs and on the clots of blood in his yellow hair.

Peleus made a Gorgon face and said: 'It seems, Jason, that you too have had an unlucky accident, and not a bloodless one either. Or have you perhaps been making a midnight sacrifice to an Underworld deity?'

None of the Argonauts, except Atalanta and the two sons of Phrixus, knew that Jason had murdered Apsyrtus, though all knew that he had secretly visited the island to secure the Fleece. The sight of the blood astounded and shocked them, and they waited in silence for Jason's answer.

Jason gave no answer.

Medea smiled down the row of well-filled benches and said: 'Come sail on, dear men, while the breeze is fresh. Let none of you think that I was in earnest when I demanded that you should convey me back to Aea before returning to Greece. The whole kingdom of Colchis may be engulfed by an earthquake or overwhelmed by a deluge for all I care. The *Argo* sails directly to Iolcos. Come, let us push her off!'

No man stirred. All eyes were fixed on her robe, sprayed with blood on the left side.

Atalanta asked: 'Comrades, what hinders you? Why does none of you stir?

The creaking voice of Ascalaphus of Orchomenos broke the long silence. 'I hear a strange singing sound from the prow,' he said. 'Does it perhaps proceed from the oracular oak branch of Zeus that addressed us on a former occasion and dispelled our uncertainties?'

'It is only the buzzing of flies, or the wind in the cordage,' said Echion, who was jealous of all oracles not delivered by his father Hermes.

Mopsus the soothsayer climbed up into the bows, carefully drawing his garments away from Medea as he passed by, so that they should not be defiled. He listened intently and at last nodded and spoke. 'The branch says: "Those who in battle destroy my declared enemies are welcome to sit in due order upon the well-made benches of this ship; but those who are concerned in a treacherous murder, committed in however just a cause, lie under my curse and displeasure. Unless they quit the ship at once, I will blast her and them with a thunderstroke and hurl all the Argonauts together down to bottomless perdition. They must go, they must go, they must go, and they must not return until they are fully purified of their guilt. Ha! I smell blood even on the golden horns of my Fleece. I will accept no bloody Fleece, not though the blood may have flowed from the throats of my enemies. Remove the purple-and-gold from the ship, let it not be brought back to me until it has been washed in seven rivers that flow into seven different seas."'

From the distant peaks of Mount Haemos thunder rolled with a growling noise, though the day was cloudless, and confirmed the authenticity of the oracle.

Without another word Jason and Medea gathered up a few of their possessions, together with the Fleece, and descended the ladder.

Mopsus asked Atalanta: 'Had you no part in the murder?'

She answered: 'I was an accessory, not a principal. There is no blood on my body or hair or kirtle.'

Eurydamas the Dolopian said: 'Yet a spot or two may have evaded your scrutiny. I shall not permit you to remain aboard.'

Meleager said: 'If Atalanta goes, I go too.'

'Go in peace,' answered Eurydamas. 'And take Melanion with you, who, though he did not disembark on the island of the Oracle, is more guilty even than Atalanta, I believe.'

The other Argonauts echoed: 'Go in peace, Meleager!'

Atalanta, Meleager, and Melanion quitted the *Argo*, and Meleager said: 'I go from free choice, not necessity; yet I call you to witness before Apollo that I am no deserter, for I am desired by you all to go in peace. Where do we all meet again?'

Argus answered: 'Where but at Aeaea, the city of Circe? Circe, being the sister of murdered Aeëtes and aunt of murdered Apsyrtus, is the only person alive who can perform the purifying office for the guilty ones. Do you conduct them to her palace, taking the Fleece with you by the route that we agreed upon in our recent council, and persuade her to cleanse them.'

Another distant peal of thunder lent weight to the words of Argus.

Meleager said: 'Very well, comrades. I wish you a happy voyage and a lucky escape from Aras the High Admiral, who is lying in wait for you at Troy, and from his relentless Trojan allies. I consider that you have been unwise to expel Medea from among you, since she alone, as Queen of Colchis, can command the obedience of Aras.'

'I fear nothing for the *Argo*, said Argus, 'so long as no evil thing remains aboard her. We are under the protection of five deities – of Athena, under whose guidance I built this glorious ship; of Zeus, whose speaking branch has just admonished us and whose confirmatory thunder has twice rolled across from Haemos; of Poseidon, on whose trickish element we have sailed and must yet sail; of Artemis, whose crane lately gave us a comforting augury in our distress; and of Apollo, whom Artemis calls Brother, and to whom we sacrificed at Leuce when we went ashore on that delightful island.'

From his blanket in the bows Orpheus reproved Argus, saying in a weak voice: 'Argus, son of Hestor, do not forget the Great Goddess, in whom we subsist.'

Argus answered in haste: 'There is no need to speak her name with our lips; ever since our stay on Samothrace it has thudded beneath our ribs like the maul of a shipwright.'

Then they pushed the vessel off, with farewells only to Meleager, not wishing to earn the enmity of the ghost of Apsyrtus. Argus was elected their captain, without dissension.

They sailed on down the western coast of the Black Sea, meeting with no further adventures. The shores continued low until, on the third day, they came abreast of Haemos; after which they were moderate in height, backed with wild hills. The winds were light but favourable, and on the fifth day the *Argo* rounded a tree-covered cape with sloping yellow shores and came to Salmydessos, the summer capital of King Phineus. All the Argonauts went ashore, and Phineus, ruddy and active again from his change of diet, came tapping with his stick across the courtyard to meet them and wept upon the necks of his stepsons Calaïs and Zetes. When they had told him in brief the whole story of their voyage, 'Hasten home, dear sons,' he said, 'as soon as ever the Fleece is safely laid again upon the oaken image of the Laphystian Ram.'

They undertook to do so, but they said: 'There is danger still ahead. How are we to escape alive from our Colchian enemies and from the Trojans, their allies?'

Phineus answered: 'Atalanta is not with you, nor is Medea, nor is Jason, nor are you carrying off the Fleece. What have you to fear from the Colchians? As for the Trojans, you have no merchandise aboard to rouse their jealousy; and when you inform them that both Aeëtes and Apsyrtus are dead, and that the throne of Colchis is untenanted, they will bless and feast you as bearers of good news. The misfortunes of Colchis will sound merrily in their ears, I warrant, for Aeëtes drove many hard bargains with them and restricted their trade with several peoples of the Black Sea coast.'

Thus reassured and refreshed, the Argonauts continued contentedly on their way. But they sailed without Orpheus, who had been ailing ever since they had quitted Colchis and had not once made music for them during all that time. When Phineus undertook to restore him to health with baths and purges, and to send him safely back into his own country under sufficient escort, his comrades absolved him of his oath to remain with them. On the evening of the next day they came to a desolate place covered with arbutus thickets, rough brushwood, and stunted oak-trees – the outfall of Lake Delcos. There, on a beach of glaring white sand, they sacrificed to the Goddess Athena two sheep that they had brought with them from Salmydessos, beseeching her as the blood flowed out to guide them again safely through the Clashing Rocks.

The current in the Bosphorus ran even more strongly than before, and though they grieved that Tiphys was no longer alive to steer them, Great Ancaeus, relying upon the instructions of King Phineus, took the helm confidently. They swept down the straits without misadventure in three hours or less, and were soon sailing merrily along the northern coast of the Sea of Marmora. Their first stage was the wide, sheltered bay into which the river Athyras falls, in the territory of King Phineus; their next was a sand-bank under the shadow of the Holy Mountain; their next was the bay of Sestos. This was the first landing-place of their homeward voyage to coincide with a landing-place of their outward voyage, and was destined to be their last.

They ran swiftly down the Hellespont one early morning with the sun hot in the sky and the waters as blue as lapis lazuli; but the fresh green grass of the shores was withered and burnt, summer being now well advanced. A column of smoke went up from Trojan Dardanos as they sailed by, and another from a look-out tower a few miles downstream. They looked askance on one another, put on their armour and held their weapons in readiness, fearing the worst.

Soon they saw four or five ships putting out from the mouth of the Scamander river. Lynceus reported: 'They are Colchian ships, the squadron of Aras. But I can see no Trojan ships anywhere about, either beached or afloat.'

Phrontis, son of Phrixus, said to Argus: 'Aras the High Admiral was for many years a prisoner of war at Percote, and therefore understands Greek.

Let Echion the herald speak for us. Doubtless Hermes, his divine father, will put another pack of lies in his mouth.'

Idas guffawed at this, and Echion was offended. He said: 'My father Hermes is not to be lightly derided. His eloquence is such that he can deceive with the truth as easily as with lies. Listen, and you will find that I say nothing at all to the Colchian but what is strictly true; and yet I will darken his vision with an impenetrable cloud of falsehood.' So saying he put on his heraldic robes and, taking his twisted rod of office in his hand, stood up magnificently at the prow. He hailed Aras across the water in a clear voice.

'Excellent Aras,' he called. 'We have good news for you. Your squadron has already accomplished its destined mission without any hazard or bloodshed, and may now return home in honour. Our ship was pursued across the walloping waves of the Black Sea by your dogged and sagacious King Apsyrtus, and trapped at last in a lake – the Crane's Lake – which lies a few miles up the Fennel Stream, the more northerly of the two broad arms that carve out the Danubian delta. When he had us at his mercy, Apsyrtus demanded three things from us: that we should restore his sister Medea to him; and restore the Golden Fleece to the shrine of Prometheus; and grant him bloody vengeance upon our she-comrade, Atalanta of Calydon, whose ungrateful javelin pierced the bowels of your former King, glorious Aeëtes. We were but one ship against twelve. How could we not yield? Yet so vexed with us was your King that blood, royal blood, spouted and flowed before the quarrel could be composed. Therefore, alas, not only are Atalanta and the Princess Medea gone from the *Argo*, but you no longer see Jason among us, heir to King Aeson of Phthiotis, nor Meleager, heir to King Oeneus of Arcadian Calydon, nor yet Melanion, the grandson of doomed Aeëtes. May this mast fall and crush my head if I am lying to you! Come aboard, lord of the salty beard, and welcome, to see for yourself that we are not hiding the Fleece from you or any of the persons whom I have named. Our lives have been spared. We are returning empty-handed to Greece, under another leader, and when the story of our adventure runs through Greece it will excite laughter, do you not think? Be assured, after what we have seen and suffered, none of us will ever wish to brave again the terrors of your inhospitable sea.'

Aras was a suspicious man. His captivity at Percote in the house of Cleite's father, King Merops, had taught him to mistrust all Greeks and to disbelieve all heralds sent out from the College of Hermes upon Mount Cyllene. He desired the *Argo* to heave-to while he came alongside.

Argus hove-to and permitted Aras himself to come aboard, but no other Colchian.

Aras satisfied himself by a thorough search of the vessel that the Fleece was not aboard. He found the false bottom to the locker under the helmsman's seat, but nothing was in it except some amber beads and fili-gree head ornaments, which he recognized as Medea's.

'Here is stolen property,' he exclaimed.

'No, no,' cried Peleus, who was never at a loss. 'They are mine. The Princess herself gave them to me as a present for my wife, in recognition of the kindness that I showed her. For when King Apsyrtus overtook us, Jason threatened to kill Medea with his own hands unless Apsyrtus allowed him to keep the Fleece. But I prevented him.'

Aras ordered two Colchian sailors, who were swimmers, to dive under the *Argo* and report whether the Fleece were perhaps nailed to her bottom, a device which traders often used to deceive the customs-officers of Troy. But the sailors found nothing and Aras was reluctantly compelled to abandon the search. He was convinced that he was being fooled, but could not see where the deception lay.

Echion said: 'Excellent Aras, before we go, will you accept a gift from me? It is a pair of bronze greaves, which will fit your sturdy legs far better than they fit my elegant ones. I took them at the sack of the palace of King Amycus the Bebrycian. He was a man of about your build, but gifted with less intelligence – and this deficiency proved his undoing.'

Aras gladly accepted the greaves. As he climbed back into his ship he said to Argus in as cordial a tone as he could muster: 'Have you, I wonder, heard what has occurred in Troy since your last visit to these waters?'

'No,' said Argus. 'Pray tell me! I am greatly interested in the fortunes of this famous city, with which, as an Athenian, I have traded for many years.'

Aras began 'There is a Greek named Hercules, of whom you must have heard –'

Argus asked eagerly: 'Hercules of Tiryns, do you mean?'

Aras replied: 'I think that he is a Tirynthian by birth. He is, at least the Hercules who came once into Amazonia and killed Queen Hippolyte – a man of colossal size and strength, with a brass-bound club and a lion-skin.'

Argus said: 'We all know that Hercules. He was our shipmate on the outward voyage.'

'Hercules was enraged,' proceeded Aras, 'by the news that his foster-son Hylas had been stolen from him by the Mysians and, for some reason or other, despatched to Troy. He therefore went to the Dolionians of Cyzicos, and to the King of Percote, and to one or two other small Greek settlements in the Sea of Marmora, and collected from them a fleet of six ships. With these he sailed into the Scamander by night, surprised and burned the Trojan fleet and, rushing into Troy itself – his great club shat-tering the main gate into pieces – he appeared suddenly in the palace hall of King Laömedon and demanded satisfaction for his injuries. Laömedon, though frightened out of his wits, was unaware that he had done Hercules any injury, and courteously asked him what his complaint might be.

Hercules began a long story about some man-eating mares which he had entrusted to Laömedon's keeping some years before, and which had not been returned. Laömedon answered that he remembered the mares well, now that Hercules mentioned them. They had been in very poor condition when they arrived at Troy: the truth was that Hercules had not only denied them the human flesh which had been their diet in the stables of their former Thracian owner, King Diomede of the Bistonians, but had over-driven them. Hercules told Laömedon to refrain from insults and confess what had become of the mares. Laömedon answered that they had expired almost at once. Hercules called him a liar but said that he would be content to accept in place of the stolen mares an equal number of the mares of Ganymede. These were Laconian mares sent to Troy by King Eurystheus in compensation for the death of Laömedon's son Ganymede who had been killed in a skirmish with Achaean pirates. With the gift had come the comforting news that the soul of Ganymede had been carried off to Mount Olympus on the back of an eagle – or so the pirates had testified; doubtless Zeus would make him his immortal cup-bearer.'

'I remember the case well,' said Argus. 'But did Laömedon hand the mares over to Hercules?'

'Unfortunately he demurred,' Aras answered. 'This vexed irascible Hercules, who then asked: 'Where is Hylas, you ruffian?' Laömedon replied that he knew no one of that name. Hercules explained that Hylas was his Thessalian foster-son and the most beautiful and charming boy in the world. He accused Laömedon of concealing him somewhere in the city. At this point one of Laömedon's sons, emulous of glory, tried to kill Hercules by toppling a great stone down upon him from a tower. He missed his aim, and Telamon of Aegina, a companion of Hercules, killed Laömedon with a spear. Then Hercules and his men sacked the palace and city and led off the leading citizens as prisoners.'

The Argonauts were marvellously relieved by this recital. Argus asked: 'Who is now the ruler of Troy?'

Aras answered: 'Hercules took a fancy to Priam, Laömedon's infant son. He picked him up and sat him on his father's throne, saying: 'Be King, child. Let the Trojan nation grow up again slowly, as you grow up, and achieve mature wisdom when you do.'

Argus and Aras then parted with many expressions of goodwill. The *Argo* bent her course southward towards Tenedos, and Aras told his captains: 'It is well. We sail home.'

However, at Sestos, on his return voyage, Aras dreamed that Aeëtes came to him, holding both hands to the wound in his belly to keep in his bowels, and cried angrily: 'Aras! Why do you disobey my orders? Bring my murderers to justice. Fetch back the Fleece.'

In the dream, Aras answered: 'Majesty, you are murdered and Apsyrtus your son reigns in your stead. I obey his orders, not yours.'

Aeëtes repeated in hollow tones: 'Why do you disobey my orders? I am dead, but my orders live on. Bring my murderers to justice. Fetch back the Fleece.'

In the dream Aras asked: 'Where shall I find either the Fleece or your murderers?'

Aeëtes answered: 'Sail to Aeaea, to the house of my sister Circe. There you will find Atalanta my murderess, and the Fleece, and my treacherous daughter Medea, all together.'

So Aras, when he awoke, turned again and shaped his course for distant Aeaea, though his captains complained bitterly against him.

CHAPTER FORTY-ONE

REUNION AT AEAEA

Hercules, after sacking Troy, had returned amicably with Talthybius to Elis in the Peloponnese, where he easily performed, within the stipulated period of a day, the Labour of cleaning the filthy stables of King Augeas. He simply compelled the palace servants by blows and threats to divert the course of two neighbouring streams, which, rushing through the stables, cleared away all the filth, and some of the cattle with it. He then returned to Asia to search for Hylas again, and take vengeance on Calaïs and Zetes. Wandering through Lydia, he rested near Sardis at the navel-shrine of the Ionian hero Tmolus, where grows the terrible snake-plant, curving up higher than a man, with crimson lily-cup and a rat-like stench. Here the High Priestess, Omphale, made him her lover and subsequently, it is said, bore male triplets.

He grew envious of her pleasant and tranquil life. 'How do you contrive always to be at peace with your neighbours and friends?' he asked. 'Tell me your secret!'

She answered: 'Contentment here hangs upon three slender threads.'

'What are they?' he asked.

'Guess my riddle!' she answered. But he became so impatient that she told him. 'The slender thread of milk as we press it from the udders of our ewes and milch-goats; the slender thread of gut that I loop from one end to the other of my Pelasgian lyre; the slender thread of wool as we spin.'

'Milk is good food,' Hercules said, 'if drunken in large enough quantities, and I confess that I am not insensitive to lyre-music. But tell me more about spinning: how can mere spinning breed contentment?'

Omphale asked: 'Is it possible that no woman, of all the many hundreds with whom you have companied, has ever described to you the pleasures of the spindle? Why, there is no occupation in the world half so soothing as to sit and to spin. The twisting whorl, the turning spindle, the white wool teased by one's fingers into a firm and even thread – these are inexpressibly pleasant toys. And as one spins, one sings softly to oneself, or chats with friends, or lets the mind wander at will...'

'I should like to try it,' said Hercules eagerly, 'if you are sure that I would not break all your spindles and whorls. As a boy I had no luck with my music lessons.'

So it was that Omphale taught Hercules to spin. He learned quickly and spun a marvellously fine strong thread. He confessed that he had always wished to be a woman, and now at last knew how much pleasure he had missed. Omphale dressed him in female clothes, washed, combed, and braided his matted hair, and tied up the braids in blue ribbons. He was happier at the navel-shrine than he had ever been before, because the ghosts of the children, not recognizing him in his new finery, ceased for a while to plague him. Talthybius lost track of him too, and since the shrine was a sanctuary where even a herald had no right of entry, Hercules might have remained there in safety for months or years, had not the news come from Teos, a town on the coast, that the *Argo* had put in there to refit. In her passage down the coast from Tenedos she had fouled a sunken reef and only by constant bailing had the Argonauts managed to make the shore and beach her; the planking of her bows was torn away on the port side.

When Hercules heard this news he tossed his spindle across the court-yard, tore off his gown, snatched up his club, bow, and lion-skin, and went raging down to the sea.

The Argonauts had nothing to gain by sending Echion forward to propitiate Hercules. Calaïs and Zetes had been warned at Lesbian Methymna that he intended to kill them for having persuaded Jason to maroon him at the outfall of the Cios river. No sooner did his huge bulk heave in view, than they sprang from the ship and rushed at wonderful speed up the river-valley, darting from side to side to distract his aim. Yet Hercules needed only to discharge two arrows. Both men fell, each trans-fixed beneath his right shoulder-blade, and died in their tracks. Thus Hercules was fully avenged, and came smiling to the remainder of the Argonauts to greet them, his blue-ribboned plaits bobbing on his shoulders. He embraced Admetus and Acastus and said: 'Dear comrades, try spinning, I implore you! There is no occupation in the world so soothing.'

They made evasive replies and he was about to compel them forcibly to this unmanly task when a fortunate interruption occurred. Talthybius the herald stepped out of an Argive ship which had just been made fast to the jetty and addressed Hercules at once with these words: 'Most noble Hercules, well met! The compliments of King Eurystheus, and he has a new Labour for you to accomplish. He is not satisfied with your cleansing of the stables of King Augeas the Epian of Elis, because you did not perform it single-handed; all the digging and shovelling and damming was done by the Epians themselves with their own mattocks. You must under-take another Labour instead.'

Hercules cried: 'Holy Serpents, Dung-man, I think that this is the most unreasonable complaint that I ever heard! First, I am forbidden to go in pursuit of Augeas to ask his permission to cleanse the stables, and when therefore, not wishing to offend my old comrade by any act of trespass, I compel his servants to perform the task, I am told that it is not properly performed. What do you say yourself, King Augeas? Did I do well? It is for you to say, not Eurystheus.'

Augeas nervously replied that he had done very well indeed.

'There, Dung-man, you hear what he answers,' said Hercules. 'But after all, what is one Labour more or less? Tell me what your crazy master desires this time.'

Talthybius then ordered him to fetch a basketful of sacred oranges, or golden apples as they are sometimes called, from the islands of the Hesperides – a Labour of his that has already been mentioned. So Hercules warned Augeas that since Eurystheus had refused to recognize the previous Labour as properly performed, and since Augeas considered that it had been performed very well indeed, Augeas must award him a consolation prize: one-tenth of all the cattle of Elis would satisfy him.

To this outrageous demand Augeas had to agree, but without any intention of fulfilling it.

Autolycus, Deileion, and Phlogius, the former comrades of Hercules, did not venture to cast in his teeth a crime similar to that for which he had taken vengeance on Calaïs and Zetes: namely that he had wantonly deserted them, many years before, in the land of the Paphlagonians. Upon recognizing them, he now gave them so cheerful a greeting and slapped them so heartily on the back that they preferred to forget their injuries altogether; and indeed he had benefited them greatly, as it happened, because their enforced stay at Sinope had enriched them for life.

Before Hercules went off he enquired closely from Echion what had become of the Fleece; and since he was not to be put off by double-mouthed answers, Echion gave a plain account of all that had happened, but bound him to secrecy until the Fleece should once more be spread shining from the prow of the *Argo*. Hercules expressed no wonder at any point of the recital, but when he heard of Medea's infatuation for Jason he sighed and remarked with unusual mildness: 'The poor girl, I pity her! Echion, my friend, I have a message for you to deliver, and here is my silver cup in payment. Tell the Princess that I condole with her, as heartily as I condoled with Queen Hypsipyle of Lemnos. Tell her that Jason will treat her no less faithlessly than he treated Hypsipyle, though for his sake she has cut herself off from her own house and people and become accessory to parricide and fratricide. Assure her that when he deserts her, whether it be this year or next year or in twelve years' time, she can steadfastly count upon Hercules of Tiryns either to avenge or comfort her.'

Echion accepted the cup and undertook to deliver the message, after which Hercules looked about him with a beaming face and said: 'Dear comrades, tried comrades, if ever any of you should need my help against your enemies, it is at your free disposal.'

On his way back to Greece Hercules put in at Ephesos, where he found a Phoenician ship anchored, and sent the master and his son in bonds to

Omphale as hostages. They were not to be released until the Phoenicians had ransomed them with a pair of African apes. Omphale had often told Hercules that he reminded her of an ape, and he was determined that she should have a pair to console her for his absence. For fear of Hercules, the Phoenicians sent the apes at once.

Here it may be told what happened to Hylas. He did not long survive his visit to the Woodpecker College at the Ascanian Lake. Being no virile Hercules, he could not easily satisfy the demands of Dryope and her fellow-nymphs, who were all in love with him and would not let him go, however hard he pleaded. He fell into a decline and died about the time that the *Argo* passed through the Bosphorus a second time. Dryope, not wishing Hercules to hear a whisper of what had happened, buried him in secret near the fountain of Pegae, and mourned him excessively. The Woodpecker nymphs continued for many centuries to deck his barrow with flowers on the anniversary of his death. On these occasions they chanted a psalm in praise of the most beautiful youths of all time: of Adonis, son of Cynaras, whom Aphrodite loved; of Endymion, son of Aetolus, whom Artemis loved; of Ganymede, son of Laömedon, whom Zeus loved; of Hyacinth, son of Oebalus, whom Apollo loved; of Chrysippus, son of Pelops, whom Theseus loved; of Narcissus, son of Cephissus, who fell in love with himself; and of Atlantius, son of Aphrodite by Hermes, who was the first hermaphrodite and with whom the whole world was in love. But the refrain declared that none of these was ever so beautiful, so charming, so gracious, or so affectionate as Hylas, son of Theiodamas, beloved by Hercules and the nymphs of Ascania.

The fountain of Pegae is a lovely one, and well worth a visit. The pebbles shine like silver through the clear water, and all about grow blue swallow-wort, fresh green maiden-hair, feathery parsley, and deer-grass that tangles the feet, inviting the visitant to linger.

The *Argo* was delayed for some time, not only by the difficulty that Argus found in repairing her at Teos, where he was not satisfied with the quality of the timber procurable, but by the funeral Games which he felt bound to celebrate in honour of his dead comrades, the sons of the North Wind. Here they took aboard as passengers Telamon, the comrade of Hercules, and five of his Aeginetan kinsmen; Telamon had been a brother of Peleus before Peleus was reborn into the Myrmidon clan, and was concerned with him in the death of their foster-brother Phocus; but now they met as strangers, with haughty stares.

The next point of call was at Miletos, famous for its wool, where Erginus was warmly welcomed by his family and found it difficult to tear himself away from them to continue the voyage. From Miletos they sailed to Flowery Samos, beloved home of Little Ancaeus, and thence to Leros, of which they say: 'All the Lerians are bad, not some but every one – all except Procles, and Procles too is a Lerian.' But who Procles was, nobody can remember. And thence they sailed to the Cyclades Islands, visiting first Naxos, the happiest of all islands in the Aegean Sea; next Delos, the holiest, where they honoured Apollo and Artemis with gifts and dancing; lastly Seriphos of the whetstones, where long ago Perseus and his mother Danaë were cast ashore in the chest that King Acrisius had consigned to the tossing waves – here they put off Telamon and his kinsmen. But the mainland of Greece they avoided, going from island to island – to Cythera, Sphacteria (close to Sandy Pylos, home of Periclymenus), Zacynthos, Ithaca, Corfu – not staying long at any of them.

The weather was clear, the winds light, and nothing remarkable occurred to the Argonauts in these familiar waters. To be brief, they struggled up the coast of Illyria, checked by contrary winds, until on the sixty-first day after their departure from the mouth of the Danube they came in sight of Aeaea, the city of Circe, which lies on a rocky phallus-shaped island, twenty miles to the south-west of the Istrian port of Pola. It is named Aeaea because the hyacinth flower, which grows there in profusion, has this name, signifying lamentation, inscribed upon its petals by the Triple Goddess herself.

To their joy the Argonauts found Jason, Medea, Atalanta, Meleager, and Melanion already arrived at Aeaea after a most swift and laborious journey, and with the Fleece still safely in their possession. Thus the reunited company of Argonauts now numbered thirty-three (not including Medea), despite the loss of Iphitus, Orpheus, Calaïs, and Zetes.

Falcon-nosed, falcon-eyed old Circe, with the jutting chin and the bowed back, had greeted Jason's party with no friendly smile when they crossed over to her island in a fishing-boat from Pola; for the visit had been heralded for her on the previous night by a dream concerned with a cataract of blood. Yet the laws of hospitality forced her to admit them into Aeaea. She had come down to the sea-shore in her linen nightdress to bathe herself in salt water, and since they were the first people whom she met after she had done, she told them without any preliminary greeting that a bloody cataract had been washing over the walls and floors of her house, and that a sudden fire had burst out in her medicine closet which she had quickly extinguished with the blood.

They said nothing in reply but followed the dripping Priestess into the palace. She walked backwards, beckoning them on with her finger. When she offered them polished bronze chairs to sit upon, only Meleager accepted the courtesy and, thanking her on behalf of them all, told her his name and parentage; the others shook their heads and made for her hearth, where they sat down in the dust to show that they were homicides and suppliants, and spilt dust on their heads and smeared their faces with charcoal. Not once had they raised their eyes to her face since their arrival. Circe saw that Jason had lodged his sword in the cracks of the hearth, and Atalanta her javelin. Indeed, they were no ordinary homicides: Atalanta had killed her royal host Aeëtes at the head of his own stairway, and Jason had treacherously murdered Apsyrtus, his host's son, after concluding a treaty with him.

Warned by her dream that, unless she performed the purification that they demanded, all her medicinal herbs, roots, barks, and earths would lose their virtue, Circe at once prepared a sacrifice to the ghosts of the murdered men, though she did not as yet know their names; and Meleager advised her to address them as 'the two royal firs of the East' – for the fir is the alpha of the magical tree-alphabet.

She clapped her hands for four sucking pigs, the throats of which she cut as soon as they were brought in; then she duly sprinkled the blood on the hands of the four suppliants. Atalanta and Medea were escorted by Circe's Falcon maidens to the women's bath-chamber, where they were washed in nine changes of water; and the bloody off-scourings were conveyed outside to a hole in the ground where aggrieved ghosts were customarily summoned to drink. Circe's Pig men similarly escorted Jason and Melanion to the men's bath-chamber and purified them in the same laborious way. Meanwhile Circe herself was offering libations to the murdered men, and burning unleavened cakes of atonement on the hearth.

When the ceremony was completed, Circe went over to the suppliants, who were crouched around the hearth again, raised them up by the hands and led them courteously to the chairs that they had refused before; and they sat down.

She sat facing them on another chair and asked Medea: 'Who can you be, my dear, who resemble so wonderfully the girl that I once was? The amber colour of your eyes is found only among the royal children of Ephyra. And how have you come here with an escort of bald-headed Scythian priests along the rugged course of the river Save? And who is the maiden huntress, your female companion in mischief? And who are your two male companions in mischief, the one so dark both in hair and complexion, the other so fair? And who are these two royal Alphas to whose murders you have been accessory?'

Medea revealed herself to Circe and confessed everything without concealment. She ended by saying: 'And indeed I came at your own summons, Aunt, as you very well know.'

Circe had loathed her brother Aeëtes as the cause of her banishment from Ephyra. She embraced Medea and cried: 'Dear child, you have done excellently well! And I should have been glad of your coming, even without the news that you bring, which makes the air taste like honey. For I summoned you on an important business concerned with our mistress Brimo.'

What business this was she revealed to Medea alone. But it is known that she entrusted to her certain presents for delivery to the Chief Nymph of Cocalus at Agrigentum in Sicily: namely, a bronze tripod, an amber necklace of phalluses, and a sealed chest. Jason, not wishing to cross Circe in any way, undertook to sail the *Argo* there as soon as possible, though Sicily lay far out of his course to the westward. Medea presented Circe with an axe of green jade, one touch of which would cure a man of the kidney pain, and a number of rare Caucasian drugs and simples, of which she stood in need, and which later she used to great effect; Circe gladly resigned to Medea all her rights at Ephyra, since she was childless and did not intend ever to revisit the isthmus.

Circe's Court was constantly visited by secret adherents of the old religion, especially by leaders of the beast and bird fraternities. She was the last surviving priestess, except for those living in distant Gaul, and the island of the Hyperboreans, and Ireland, who was capable of performing the painful ceremonies by which a leader was endowed with the supernatural powers demanded by his rank and was enabled at will to assume at pleasure the shape of his sacred animal.

While the Argonauts remained at Aeaea they were forbidden to wound or kill any creature that they encountered, of whatever sort: for if a wolf howled on the hill, it was likely to be a were-wolf; if a bear burst into the dining-hall and snatched up a honey-cake from the table, it was certainly a were-bear. Lizards, magpies, and such-like, even scorpions, beetles, and ants – all must be respected. Circe's male assistants in her responsible and complicated work were Pig men, the Goddess Brimo's own, whose company all men avoided; even the youngest of them had white hair and white eyebrows, and their eyes were red as Death. Some of them were Greeks, but others were Neurians, Gauls, and Celtiberians. The ordinary tasks of the palace were performed by the Falcon maidens who were native Istrians. There were also several indeterminate creatures wandering tamely about the palace, the sight of which filled the Argonauts with dread – a two-headed red calf, a striped horse, a cock with four legs, and an animal that seemed to be a white ass but had a sharp horn protruding from the centre of its forehead. And on a well-shaved lawn in the innermost courtyard screamed and strutted a glistening Indian peacock – the scrannel-voiced bird, with a hundred eyes in his tail, most esteemed by the Goddess. Circe consulted him in all her most vexatious difficulties.

Circe took a strong fancy to Periclymenus the wizard, who, having been born in an eclipse, had magical powers which she envied. She tried to induce him to remain with her but he would not desert his shipmates, and longed to be home at Sandy Pylos. She grew angry and told him: 'As you wish. But I warrant you will not long enjoy your estate. For I see death coming to you from the bow of one of these same shipmates.'

It was from Circe that Meleager obtained a secret potion that would make Atalanta yield to him in love, when the time should be ripe for him to administer it. His one fear was that Atalanta preferred Melanion to him, for Melanion was wonderfully attentive to her; and during their long, rough, hurried journey from the Danube mouth to Aeaea, by canoe, sail-boat, mule-back, litter, and chariot, it was Melanion who had been the true leader of the expedition, and the spokesman at the Court of the Scythian King and at every other Court or tribal meeting-place: for Jason, as befitted a homicide, kept as silent as possible. Only the oath of loyalty that Meleager had sworn to his fellow-Argonauts restrained him from killing Melanion; but jealousy gnawed at his heart night and day.

As for the Fleece, it had now been washed in two of the seven prescribed rivers: in the Danube that empties into the Black Sea, and in the cold rushing Turros that empties into the Adriatic.

CHAPTER FORTY-TWO

THE *ARGO* IS AGAIN OVERTAKEN

Down the Adriatic Sea with a fair wind sailed the *Argo*, making as many as seventy miles in a single day and fifty on the succeeding night. She seemed like a jaded jennet, that, returning from a long journey with the polished mule-cart behind her, realizes suddenly that she is close to her master's home, pricks up her ears and breaks into a smart trot, straining at the halter. Six days and nights only brought her to Corfu, the sickle-shaped land of the Phaeacians. There, Jason, standing in need of water and fresh provisions, decided to put in at the city of Corcyra, which lies surrounded with pine-woods in the lower curve of the sickle, and pay his respects to King Alcinoüs and Queen Arete. Alcinoüs was a maternal kinsman of Sisyphus the Corinthian. He had emigrated to Corfu when the Achaeans abolished the worship of the hero Asopus, to whom his mother Corcyra had been Priestess. After marrying Arete, Queen of the Phaeacians, a tribe that had been driven to Corfu from the mainland by the Cyclops clan, Alcinoüs had founded this city and named it Corcyra in his mother's honour.

Echion went ashore at dawn and congratulated Alcinoüs upon being the first Greek ruler to hear a wonderful piece of news. The famous Argonauts had safely accomplished their divine and much-heralded mission: after passing through many desperate hazards they had come to Colchian Aea at last, and there had persuaded King Aeëtes to yield the Fleece to them; sailing home in glory, and circumnavigating Greece, they had been purified in Aeaea – one or two of them – of a little blood that they had been forced to shed by the way. It now only remained for them to restore the Fleece to Laphystian Zeus, on whose account they had suffered terrible things. Moreover, Echion told Alcinoüs, Medea, the daughter of Aeëtes, was aboard, come to Greece to claim her Corinthian patrimony.

It may well be imagined what haste Alcinoüs made to entertain his visitors worthily. They were soon seated at dinner on throne-like chairs, well-bathed and anointed, their heads garlanded with myrtle, their knees spread over with warm embroidered shawls. The walls of the hall were painted sea-blue, and fish were swimming here and there, singly or in schools, of a hundred distinguishable varieties; and dolphins dived among them, blowing bubbles, to the life; and shells were painted on the sea-floor. Behind each chair stood a pedestal surmounted by the life-sized statue of a boy in painted wood, and dressed entirely in cloth of gold. When evening came, a lighted torch was set in the hand of each golden boy, all about the table. On either side of the door crouched sacred bronze dogs of Lemnian make, between which it was dangerous for wrong-doers to pass; so that the rear entrance was the more frequented by far. The palace was, indeed, one of the richest and best appointed in Greece, because the Phaeacians were seamen by trade and the chief carriers of the Adriatic Sea.

Jason spoke privately with Alcinoüs, whose garments were stiff with gold thread, confiding a difficulty to him: at Colchis, inspired by the Goddess Athena or some other deity, he had informed King Aeëtes that the Corinthians, because of a murrain and floods and a plague of serpents, had invited him either to return and rule over them or to send one of his children to do so. Medea had come in response to this fictitious invitation, and he was now in honour bound to set her upon the throne of Ephyra; to which she was the legitimate heiress since her father, her brother Apsyrtus, and her aunt Circe had all resigned their rights to her.

Alcinoüs smiled benignly on hearing Jason's story and offered to do all in his power to aid him; he would even, if necessary, send a ship-load or two of armed men to Ephyra to enforce Medea's claims.

Jason thanked him heartily, and undertook in return to see that the worship of the hero Asopus was restored by Medea, whom he proposed to marry so soon as ever he had restored the Fleece to the Laphystian Ram. However, respecting his host's sensibilities as a Corinthian, Jason let him believe that Aeëtes and Apsyrtus were still alive, and made no mention of the Danubian journey either.

The banquet continued all day in friendship and jollity, and might well have continued all night, had it not been that, as darkness began to fall, a prolonged commotion was heard outside, and a servant ran in with a disquieting report. A fleet of eight foreign war-galleys had put into the harbour, Aethiopians by the look of them; the crews had disembarked with their weapons in their hands, formed themselves into several compact columns, and were now closing in upon the palace.

Alcinoüs was not perturbed, because, as he said to Jason whom he pressed to continue with the banquet: 'I have never done the Aethiopians any harm, so far as I know, and they have the reputation of being a just and peaceable nation.' But Jason sweated with fear: he guessed that the Colchian fleet had caught up with him again and that Aras the High Admiral would not be easily fooled a second time.

Aras entered as his own herald, being the only Colchian who could speak Greek. He used no eloquence, but spoke tersely and simply as an Admiral should:

'Majesty, I am Aras, High Admiral of the Colchian fleet. Three months ago I sailed from Aea on the Phasis river, which lies from here some two thousand miles to the eastward. My master for thirty years was King Aeëtes the Greek. He has now been treacherously murdered by his own fellow-countrymen.'

'Murdered,' cried Alcinoüs. 'Oh, my lord, I am grieved to hear of it! He and I were boys together at Ephyra.' He turned enquiringly to Jason, who said nothing, but stared impassively back; and then to Medea, who began to weep silently.

'These honoured guests of mine,' said Alcinoüs, 'have not mentioned the sad event, though they come directly from Colchis themselves; no doubt Aeëtes died shortly after their departure from Aea?'

'Four hours after,' Aras replied. 'My Sovereign succumbed to a wound that one of them had inflicted with a javelin, and I have come to fetch the whole ship-load of them back to justice. These criminals, Majesty, who are now imposing upon your hospitality, came to Colchis under the cloak of friendship and the pretence of pious duty. No sooner had they arrived than their leader Jason persuaded the only surviving daughter of King Aeëtes, the Princess Medea yonder, to steal the Golden Fleece of Zeus from the shrine of the hero Prometheus, and run off with him. To create a diversion, under cover of which they might escape, they then committed an act of sacrilege: they gelded and yoked the holy bull images of the Taurians that stand in the inner hall of the royal palace.'

'Pray wait a moment,' said Alcinoüs. 'Tell me, first, what lien or claim had the hero Prometheus upon the Golden Fleece of Zeus?'

'That is no concern of mine, Majesty,' said Aras. 'The Fleece has been in the possession of Prometheus for a generation or more.'

'Yet it is a question that affects the justice of the case,' said Alcinoüs. 'You must appreciate this: that if my guests went to Colchis on behalf of Father Zeus to recover stolen property, and if King Aeëtes refused to restore this property to them, they were entitled to use force – or so at least they are at liberty to plead now that they are back in Greece, where the law of Zeus runs. And answer me this: how came the bull images of the Taurians to be placed in the royal palace of Aea? Do you Colchians not worship Mithras, the Bull's ancient enemy?'

Aras answered: 'Aeëtes contracted an alliance with the savage Taurians and married their king's daughter; it was she who insisted that the bull images should be installed there for her private worship, and that of her suite.'

Alcinoüs said: 'On the face of it, this mutilation of the bulls seems to be a grievance of the Taurians rather than of the Colchians. And I observe by your demeanour that you do not love either the Taurians or their god.'

Aras continued: 'I was sent in pursuit of the pirates, and at the Long Beach overtook Prince Apsyrtus, the only son of Aeëtes, who had sailed ahead of me. I duly saluted him as King. There he and I joined forces and nearly captured the pirate in the neighbourhood of Sinope; but she eluded us and made off to the north-westward. King Apsyrtus sailed in pursuit; but sent me down to Troy with a squadron of eight ships to guard against her possible escape through the Hellespont; this he did because there is no convenient port at the head of the Bosphorus, or below; and because the Trojans are our allies. I had been anchored in the Scamander river, off Troy, for some days when the presence of the pirate was reported to me by smoke signals from the head of the Hellespont. I sailed out, boarded and searched her, but found nothing of any consequence aboard – neither the Golden Fleece, nor the Princess Medea, nor the maiden huntress Atalanta who struck the blow of which King Aeëtes died, nor Jason the captain. Echion, their herald, lyingly informed me that King Apsyrtus had over-taken the ship at the mouth of the Danube and after a short conflict had overpowered the crew. He had exacted summary vengeance on Atalanta and Jason, Echion said, and had sailed home to Colchis with Medea and the Fleece. But I was later informed of the truth by the grim and bleeding apparition of my murdered King.'

Echion rose and said to King Alcinoüs: 'Majesty, I protest. The Colchian may well have seen an apparition, but he is making a wilfully false declaration about my words to him. I said nothing of the sort, as any man among us will bear witness on oath. If, when he searched our vessel in broad daylight, the Gods blinded his eyes by putting a magical mist over the persons for whom he was searching and over the Fleece, what fault of mine was that? I resent his accusations!' He sat down again.

Aras was silent, for he could not conceive how he had been tricked. He decided that Periclymenus the wizard must have been at work.

Alcinoüs turned to Jason and asked: 'Tell me, my lord, how did you contrive to escape from King Apsyrtus?'

Jason answered: 'Majesty, relying upon the protection of five great Olympians, and especially of the Goddess Artemis, whose sanctuary at the mouth of the Fennel Stream the son of Aeëtes had attempted to defile by a treacherous murder, I killed him with my sword and hacked him to pieces. At his death the Princess Medea became the rightful Queen of Colchis, for Aeëtes had no heirs in the male line. She at once ordered the masters of her brother's fleet, one galley of which we had destroyed by ramming, to return to Colchis; and they obeyed her, or so I suppose. Aras too is bound to obey her orders.'

Aras, though puzzled and no longer so confident as at his first entry, said doggedly: 'I am too old a man to be fooled twice. It is impossible that you should have fought twelve ships with your single ship and come off victorious and without loss. King Apsyrtus is still alive, I am certain, and therefore I must carry out the orders that he gave me. I must bring back the Fleece, and the Princess Medea – who is being courted by King Styrus the Albanian – and I must either capture or destroy Jason and Atalanta.'

Alcinoüs asked: 'Excellent Aras, do you agree to abide by my judgement, which will be an impartial one? The alternative is for you to attempt to take both the Fleece and the Princess Medea by force, in which case you will find yourself at war not only with myself but with the whole of Greece.'

Aras replied: 'Majesty, I will abide by your judgement, if you swear an oath by the Goddess Brimo or Hecate or by whatever other name you may call the Infernal Queen, not to be swayed by the least partiality.'

'That I am ready to swear,' cried Alcinoüs, 'though, by a decree of Zeus, the only Infernal Queen in whose name we are permitted to swear is Persephone, wife to his brother Hades.'

Jason said: 'I also will abide by your judgement, Majesty. But I would have you know that Queen Circe of Aeaea, sister to King Aeëtes, has recently purified both Medea and myself, and Atalanta of Calydon too, from the blood which we shed or caused to be shed: she received us as suppliants in her immodestly shaped island and acted in accordance with a warning dream sent by the Goddess whom she serves.'

'I will bear your words in mind,' said Alcinoüs. Then he desired both Aras and Jason to swear an oath to abide by his judgement; but since Aras set no store by Persephone, they swore by the Sun, a deity common to both, and Augeas of Elis administered the oath. Alcinoüs said: 'Tomorrow at noon I will deliver judgement from my throne. Meanwhile, pray remember that you are my guests and bound in a common bond of courtesy to me. I charge you to do nothing amiss.'

That night the Argonauts all slept together in the echoing porch of the palace, but Medea in a little room next door to the royal bed-chamber. Medea came secretly to Queen Arete and said: 'Queen-Sister, have pity on me. Do not let your husband send me back to Aea. My father, King Aeëtes, is dead and so is my brother, and it is ridiculous for Aras to dispute my sovereignty of Colchis. I am in love with Jason, and we propose to marry so soon as ever we have returned the Fleece to its divine owner; then I shall be Queen of Ephyra and all Corinth, and he will be my King. I could share my throne of Colchis with him if I wished, and he his throne of Phthiotis with me; and I believe that he has acquired sovereign rights in Lemnos too, should he care to exercise them. Your husband must think twice, or three times, before he delivers so royal a pair as ourselves into the hands of a barbarous black outlander. Besides, as you have been told, we enjoy the patronage of all the principal Olympians, and, more than this, of the Triple Goddess herself, whom, I know, you secretly reverence before any of them. Be my friend, Arete, and one day I will reward you, you may be bound.'

Queen Arete kissed Medea and replied: 'Queen-Sister, I will gladly plead your case with Alcinoüs. For I also had a harsh father from whom I suffered many unkindnesses, and a savage brother besides, as I judge yours to have been. And I have fallen half in love with Jason myself. I think that he is the handsomest man that ever I saw, and if you were to tell me that you would rather live with him in a fisherman's hut than with another in a palace, I should readily believe you. It is his wonderful hair, I suppose.'

Medea sobbed for gratitude.

Arete put her arm about Medea's shoulders and said: 'I am sure that you will be very happy with him, for though Jason is clearly not so easy-going or so dependable a man as my Alcinoüs, yet you are as clearly a much cleverer woman than I am, and therefore equal to marriage with him. Of course, Jason is still young, and in time, I have no doubt, he will settle down as a just ruler and considerate husband. I must confess to you that I find marriage a wonderful institution – I cannot imagine how our grandmothers managed their affairs before it came into fashion, when the men were merely their casual lovers and there was nobody but themselves to rely upon. We wives have all the real power now, and little of the responsibility, and most of the sport. I secretly adore the Triple Goddess, of course, but I cannot pretend that I am not grateful to Zeus for making her his wife.'

Medea smiled at Arete through her tears, and she rattled on:

'Sweet Child, how I envy you your wedding-night! It seems only yesterday that my dearest Alcinoüs and I were pelted with aniseed and ate the candied quince and kissed each other for the first time under the many-coloured bridal quilt that my dear mother worked for me! And how delicious the honeysuckle smelt that night! Believe me, my dear, the rapture of the first embrace never recurs; is never forgotten, but never recurs. Ah, the inexpressibly sweet joys that are still in store for you!'

The good Queen's voice faltered for tenderness, and Medea could not bring herself to confess that, in truth, there could be no more miserable woman in all the world than herself – hating what she most desired, desiring what she most hated, far from home, the ruin of her own family, and a traitress to the magnanimous hero of whose shrine she was guardian. But she said: 'Queen-Sister, I thank you for your good wishes, and with all my heart I envy you your contented life with noble Alcinoüs, the like of which I can never hope myself to enjoy. For, as you must know, a sworn priestess of the Goddess is cursed with the double-eye and the double-nature: she plots craftily and bloodily against her own innocence, in anguish destroys those that love her best, and to stave off loneliness peoples her house with liars, weaklings, and ruffians.'

Arete cried: 'O Child, do not speak so terribly, even to ward off the jealousy of God or Spite! Goodness shines from your face; I will not believe you capable of any evil action. May you be blessed with many children, four or five at least; children have a delightfully calming effect on women who are over-gifted with intelligence, as you seem to be.'

Medea answered: 'Excellent Arete, I dare hope for no such blessings, though I am as honest a woman, I believe, as yourself. The terrible Mother hounds me on, possessing my soul and making me the vessel of her implacable rage; until she has done with me, I am as dangerous to any city where I may lodge as a smoking pine torch in a barley-field ripe for cutting. Therefore, Queen-Sister, if in the goodness of your heart you can save me now, that will be a proof of your wisdom as well as of your virtue; but pray do not persuade me to stay with you a day longer than is necessary.

CHAPTER FORTY-THREE

THE COLCHIANS ARE AGAIN OUTWITTED

In bed with Alcinoüs that night, Arete made herself as charming as possible, scratching his head gently for him with her evenly trimmed nails, and kissing him often. She asked him: 'My noble lord, tell me what judgement you intend to deliver tomorrow in the case of our sweet guest, the Colchian Princess. For really it would break my heart if you sent her back to be married to that old Albanian wretch about whom Atalanta was telling me. Imagine, he has never washed since he was born – Albanian law strictly prohibits washing – and is crawling with vermin like an old cheese. Such a beautiful girl as she is, too, and so unhappy, and the orphan daughter of your old friend...'

Alcinoüs was pretending to be asleep, but he could not refrain from answering at this point. 'In the first place, dearest one, I cannot tell you what judgement I shall deliver; it will doubtless be revealed to me in a dream. And in the second place, I find it somewhat absurd for you to try to excite my sympathies on behalf of this orphan, whose own disobedient folly was the immediate cause of her father's death, and it may be of her brother's too – though this is not yet proved against her. "Strong Mind" is my name, and Strong Mind is my nature.'

'My dear,' said Arete, 'I know how kind-hearted you are by nature, though you pretend to be severe. I am sure that whatever might happen you could never treat either of our daughters as Aeëtes has treated his. You must admit that most fathers are all too strict and jealous with their children. Do you recall the case of Nycteus, brother of Orion the famous Theban hunter? He tried to oppose his daughter Antiope's marriage to Epopeus of Sicyon, and when she ran off to Epopeus, actually went to war with Sicyon and brought hundreds of innocent families to ruin including his own; and ended by killing himself. And then there was King Acrisius of Argos, who locked his daughter Danaë in a bronze burial-chamber, and when she became pregnant despite all his precautions, set her adrift on the sea in a chest; but she bore a son, the famous Perseus, who killed him and became the founder of Mycenae. If you want a more modern instance, look at our neighbour Echetus of Epirus, who has blinded his daughter Amphissa for the crime of making him a grandfather, and now forces her to grind iron barley-corns in a dungeon – do you suppose that his affairs are likely to prosper? If you were to ask me, I should say that Aeëtes, though perhaps a discreet man in public (as opposed to domestic) affairs, has richly deserved his fate.'

'That Aeëtes may have behaved foolishly or even cruelly does not justify his daughter in disobeying him,' said Alcinoüs. 'At the most, it merely accounts for his death. Two wrongs, you know, do not make a right.'

'But think,' protested Arete, 'of what will happen if you give your verdict against the Argonauts. They are connected in one way or another with half the royal families of Greece, and have the patronage of at least five Olympians. As for these Colchians, they live at the other end of the world and it is more than doubtful whether Medea has any male relative left whose anger you need fear in the case of a mistakenly generous verdict in her favour. On the contrary, her nephews, the sons of Phrixus, have the deepest sympathy for her and have abetted her in her flight.'

'The Olympians,' said Alcinoüs severely, 'spit a man out like a spoonful of burning hot porridge the moment that he behaves in a treacherous or unjust fashion; and I have no intention of condoning crime merely because the defendant happens to be rich or well-born and to have several accomplices, or because the plaintiff happens to live a long way off. Until the death of Apsyrtus is proved (and I have yet to hear evidence on this point), I am obliged to assume him alive and an interested party. To be frank with you, I do not trust young Jason in the least – he has told me too many half-truths and downright lies; and Echion the herald is too eloquent by half; and that the Princess Medea has fallen in love with Jason may be an explanation of her conduct but certainly is no reason why I should condone its irregularity.'

Arete said: 'My dear lord, it may be that you are right, as you often are, but I swear that I shall not sleep a wink unless I know what decision you are going to give tomorrow.'

'I repeat, dear one,' he said as mildly as possible, 'that I have not the least notion. I intend to sleep upon it.'

'I think,' said Arete with warmth, 'that to go to sleep on a problem which one is too lazy to solve is a most foolish procedure. All that can happen is that on waking up one will forget all the relevant facts in the case and deliver a random judgement.' She stepped out of bed and began pacing up and down the room.

'Come back, darling, come back!' pleaded Alcinoüs. 'I was exceedingly comfortable as I lay in your arms.'

'I will come back,' answered Arete firmly, 'when you have told me roughly what judgement you are going to deliver tomorrow. Only roughly, mind you! I am your wife and I cannot bear, on an occasion of this sort, not to know what is passing through your mind.'

Since Alcinoüs and Arete never quarrelled, Alcinoüs yielded at once. 'Well,' he said, 'roughly, my verdict will, I suppose, be this. Since there is a conflict of evidence as to the alleged death of King Apsyrtus, I must presume him to be still alive and his sister's legal champion, unless she is proved to have already passed under the championship of Jason or some other Greek by an act of marriage – which, for all I know, may have already taken place with due formality and the consent of her father or brother. If she is already a bride, it would be manifestly absurd for me to allow her to be dragged back by Aras half-way across the world for the purpose of a royal marriage. But if she is still a virgin, as I presume she is, judging from her dress, why, back she must go, however unhappy this judgement may make her. For justice must be done. As for the Fleece, who is its rightful guardian? It is Medea, the Priestess of the shrine of Prometheus; wherever the guardian goes, there let the Fleece go too, I say. As for any act of vengeance contemplated against Atalanta of Calydon, that can be no concern of mine; however, I forbid any bloodshed within my dominion, under threat of war.'

Arete climbed back into bed. 'I think that yours is the most sensible and equitable judgement in a difficult case that I have ever heard,' she said. 'Now sleep, my dear lord, and wake refreshed. I will not trouble you again. "Virtue" is my name and Virtue is my nature.'

As soon as ever Alcinoüs was snoring, Arete stole from the room and sent one of her women running to summon her personal herald. When he came in, confused with sleep, she told him: 'Send for your colleague Echion. I have good news for him that will not wait. He is sleeping on the porch.'

The herald blinked at her like an owl, but she dashed water in his face to bring him to his senses. When he went to seek Echion on the porch, he found it deserted. He hurried down to the port and caught the Argonauts on the point of re-embarking, for Jason had decided to leave Medea behind and make his escape with the Fleece, regarding this as his sacred duty.

'Where are you going, my lords?' the herald asked.

'O, nowhere, nowhere at all, Brother,' replied Echion; 'we are doing no more than shift our moorings. Our comrade Coronus of Gyrton, a weather prophet like all Crow men, has persuaded himself that the wind is about to slew round to the north-east; we are merely sailing across the harbour to humour him.'

'My mistress Arete has good news for you that will not wait,' said the herald, 'and if I am right in my guess, you would be prudent to return at once to the echoing palace porch, trusting to your hawsers and anchors to keep that gallant and far-travelled ship of yours off the rocks.'

So back they came like a flock of sheep, the herald trotting behind, like a shepherd's dog who has no need to bark or show his teeth, his mere presence being sufficient warning to the flock that they must keep to the right path.

Echion was brought before the Queen. She smiled graciously as she told him: 'A word to the wise, divine herald. Unless your master Prince Jason has married the Princess Medea before morning, the King's judgement is likely to go against them. Let them make haste.'

Echion asked: 'But, gracious Lady, how can so important a marriage as this be decently celebrated at such short notice?'

Queen Arete answered: 'If it is not celebrated immediately, it will never be celebrated. Now listen to me. King Alcinoüs is asleep and I do not wish him to be disturbed by the music of the marriage-song, for he is inexpressibly weary, and as a dutiful wife I must ensure that he loses no sleep. The island of Macris at the entrance to our harbour is the very place for the ceremony. Have you ever visited the sacred cave there, the cave of Macris the Pelasgian? She was the last priestess of Dionysus at Delphi before Apollo seized the shrine from him, and she ended her days in that very cave. Inform Jason that all the resources of my house-hold are at his command and that of his royal bride. He is welcome to my Court musicians; and my Court ladies will attend the bride, bringing with them as much linen and as many swan's-down pillows as will make a bridal bed of the handsomest. Doubtless Jason will find his own blankets; but I will provide wine and mixing-bowls and torches and beasts for sacrifice and cakes and comfits and quinces – in short, everything that he can possibly require. Fortunately, my ladies went out into the valley this evening and brought their baskets home full of flowers, so I cannot think of anything that will be missing. If Apsyrtus is dead, as you say – and I have no reason to doubt you – the sons of Phrixus are the Princess Medea's nearest surviving male kinsmen and therefore competent, in modern Greek law, to yield her in marriage to Prince Jason. I will provide a priest – my own palace chaplain – who knows well what sacrifices to make to the local marriage deities; and Atalanta here can propitiate Artemis.'

Echion asked: 'But what of Medea? Does she agree to these hasty arrangements made on her behalf?'

Queen Arete replied: 'Naturally, Medea would have vastly preferred a decently conducted marriage at Iolcos in Jason's own house, where the axle of the cart in which she rode could have been duly burned. But better a hasty marriage, and even a hole-and-corner one (as she herself says), than none at all.'

Jason was properly grateful to Queen Arete, and calling his comrades together begged them in a whisper not to reveal to her or anyone else that from over-caution he had so nearly lost this glittering prize. Then they gathered together all the wedding-gear that Arete offered them and brought it down with them to the *Argo*. The Court ladies undertook to follow later with the bride, but the Court musicians clambered aboard with their instruments; and after a few minutes of rowing the *Argo* was beached on the islet of Macris. There in the cave the comrades of Jason laid turves to mould a bridal couch, and festooned the entrance with ivy and bay, and spread trestle-tables for the wedding-feast. While Atalanta propitiated Artemis with the sacrifice of a heifer – being well aware that the Goddess is averse to marriage and takes revenge on those who forget her – Queen Arete's palace chaplain regaled the local deities, Aristaeus and Autonoë, with sober offerings of grapes, honeycomb, olive oil, and sheep's cheese. Butes took a delight in assisting at this feast, because Aristaeus had been not only the first cheesemaker in Greece and the first planter of an olive-orchard, but the first bee-keeper.

The chaplain and his acolytes sang a song in honour of Aristaeus. The acolytes began with the question:

> Whence did you fetch your olive-branch,
> Your fertile olive-branch,
> To graft it on the rank wild stock?

The chaplain answered:

> From my neighbour's orchard
> I fetched the fertile branch
> To graft it on the rank wild stock.

They asked again:

> Whence did your neighbour fetch the branch,
> The fertile olive branch
> To graft it on the rank wild stock?

The chaplain answered again:

> From his neighbour's neighbour's orchard
> He fetched the fertile branch
> To graft it on the rank wild stock.

The acolytes asked, with rising energy, from whose orchard had this fertile branch been fetched; but nine times the chaplain traced it back from neighbour to neighbour, until at last he could answer triumphantly:

> From the tree of Aristaeus
> He fetched the fertile branch,
> To graft it on the rank wild stock.

The acolytes asked how had Aristaeus come by the tree, and were answered that he obtained it by the favour of the Great Goddess. And how had he proceeded? He had grafted wild olive upon wild olive under a rising moon, and the next year had similarly grafted a slip from the growing graft upon the graft again, and in the third year grafted a slip from the newer graft upon the same graft, under a rising moon, calling three times upon the Goddess by name. The Great Goddess had rustled among the leaves, and the last slip that Aristaeus had grafted put out the shapely leaves of the sweet olive and blessed him, when winter came, with the oozy purple fruit.

Butes capped this song with another like it, of his own composition, beginning:

> Whence did you fetch this swarm,
> This honeyed swarm,
> To feed upon my orchard flowers?

and taught the acolytes to ask him the appropriate questions. His first answer was that the swarm was fetched from a neighbour's hive. It was then traced back from neighbour to neighbour until it was found to have originated in the hive of Aristaeus. Whence did Aristaeus himself procure it? Butes answered triumphantly that he fetched it from the dead body of the leopard that he killed on Pelion, as it was attempting to kill one of the Goddess's sacred mares. Aristaeus spurned the carcase three times with his foot, calling upon the Goddess by name, and the third time she answered with a clap of thunder that shook the pine cones down from every tree on the mountain; the bees rose buzzing from the wound in the leopard's flank and swarmed in an arbutus-tree.

So ended the song of Butes. But he regretted that he could not with sincerity extol the Corcyran honey.

Medea was rowed across the harbour in a Phaeacian galley. She was dressed in white linen robes and an embroidered white veil lent her by Arete, who herself was present. The twelve Court ladies, appointed to be her bridesmaids, had already dipped her three times in the holy fountain of Corcyra. Medea burned upon the altar of Artemis, which Atalanta had heaped, the clippings of her yellow hair. To the Goddess Brimo, with whom she had made peace before leaving Circe's house at Aeaea (propitiating her with a black sow and a farrow of nine), she now poured out a drink of clear honey, a great bowlful.

Jason was similarly dipped by his companions, in the pool fed by the fountain of Macris; then he was clothed in his finest garments and chapleted with flowers. In honour of the Fleece, Queen Arete had given the Argonauts rare purple and gold flowers, called pansies, which she grew in tall earthenware pots set in a row in her private courtyard, and it was with these flowers that they wove Jason's chaplet.

Then the sons of Phrixus presented Medea to Jason, who took her by the hand and led her towards the cave, where the twelve bridesmaids sang the marriage-hymn at the entrance and strewed flowers for them, and pelted them with honey-cakes baked in the shapes of all manner of phallic beasts and birds, with comfits of almond-paste and with handfuls of tasty aniseed. Queen Arete herself lighted them in with a torch.

The thirty-three Argonauts and an equal number of Phaeacians took part in the banquet, but no Colchians at all, except for the sons of Phrixus.

The company were very merry and made ribald jests, as is proper, Idas taking the lead in this sport; and presently, on the broad, level ground at the entrance to the cave, Medea's bridesmaids danced the bridal dance in honour of the Goddess Hera, going hand in hand about the rough stone herm that Argus had chipped out for the occasion; and the lovely bridal chant rose and fell, while Jason ate sea-food to increase his virility.

At last Medea went hand in hand with Jason to their couch at the end of the cave, before which a curtain was hung. Queen Arete gave them each a slice of candied quince to eat, and a ripe quince to smell. She said to them: 'Keep your mouths and nostrils sweet, delightful pair!'

Medea unloosed her girdle of virginity and handed it to her bridesmaids to dedicate at the altar of Artemis, and then turned about to look at the marriage-couch. She shuddered and turned whiter than a lily, for as a coverlet over the fragrant linen sheets and the far-travelled blankets, that the Argonauts had heaped over the turves, lay spread the Golden Fleece, the crafty removal of which from the shrine of Prometheus she would then gladly have forgotten.

Jason said: 'Lady, do not shrink from this blessed coverlet. It is spread here so that our marriage may be the theme of song for amazed and envious posterity.'

She smiled wanly at him and answered with lips that trembled: 'May it bring us no ill luck, handsome one!' And against her will she repeated the words of the unlucky song of her cousin Sisyphus, the Lament for Pasiphaë, that Orpheus in his delirium had taught her:

A fleece now gilded with our common grief
That this must be a night without a moon.

Indeed, there was no moon that night; and though Sisyphus had other things in mind when he composed the lines, they were as apt now as they were ominous of evil.

Jason gave her ummixed wine to drink, to restore her spirit, and beneath the Fleece they companied in love, while through the curtain came ringing the jokes, songs, and laughter of the guests; and too soon for both broke the clear dawn.

CHAPTER FORTY-FOUR

TO SICILY AND SOUTHWARD

That morning, enthroned in state, Alcinoüs delivered judgement. He said: 'My lords, Zeus the Law-Giver has put it into my heart to declare to you his unalterable will. Perish those who dispute it! These are the words of Zeus. "The Princess Medea, if she is already married with due formality to Jason, son of Aeson, or to some other Greek, may remain with Me; but if she is not already so married, she must do nothing of her own free will to alter her condition and so displease the lawful rulers of her country. As for the so-called Golden Fleece, this discarded purple covering of My Laphystian Ram was long ago, by My permission, conveyed to Aea in Colchis and there consigned to the safe keeping of the Priestess of Prometheus; and still I say, wherever she may go, there let the Fleece go. If the Priestess now sees fit to restore the Fleece, in the name of Prometheus, to the image which it formerly clothed, she is not to be prevented in this; yet, being the Lord of All Things, I do not greatly care what may become of the golden-fringed gaud. As for the maiden huntress Atalanta of Calydon, I forbid any act of vengeance upon her to be performed in any territory where My Law runs, for she is the beloved servant of My daughter Artemis."'

Aras was overjoyed. He declared the divine judgement to be just and ungainsayable, and pointed out that since Medea could have been married with due formality only if she had secured the consent of her nearest male kinsman, namely Apsyrtus, the consequence of the judgement that Alcinoüs had delivered was that she must return to Colchis without delay, and the Fleece with her.

Queen Arete's face was all innocence, but her Court ladies had difficulty in suppressing their mirth, especially when Aras taunted Jason, asking: 'Well, clever Greek, what do you think of this new turn of fate?'

Jason answered smoothly: 'I like it well. Queen Medea of Colchis is already my bride, and the marriage was celebrated with the common consent of every one of her surviving male kinsmen, namely Phrontis, Melanion, Argeus, and Cytissorus, sons of Phrixus. The Queen's virgin girdle is duly dedicated in the shrine of Artemis of Corcyra, for all to see.'

At this a great roar of laughter went up from all the Greeks present; but all the Colchians except Aras remained silent, not understanding what Jason had said. Aras was first incredulous, then indignant. He naturally supposed that Alcinoüs had tricked him, but courtesy kept him from accusing his host of double-dealing. As he stood there, biting his lip and fidgeting with his sword, Medea came gliding up to him and asked with a disarming smile: 'Why do you linger here, Aras? Why do you not sail at once for Colchis?'

He answered: 'If your royal brother Apsyrtus is still alive, and is King of Colchis, he will kill me when I arrive without having fulfilled my three commissions. Why should I return to a country that lies at so great a distance from here, merely to die miserably at the end of the voyage? But if he is dead, as I now incline to believe – for the sons of Phrixus are upright men and would not make any false declaration in the presence of the marriage deities for whom the altars are heaped – why, then, you are my Queen, and from you I must take my orders.'

Medea laid her hand soothingly upon his shoulder and said: 'Noble Aras, either return to Colchis, if you please; or, if you fear to face the anger of my uncle Perses the Taurian, and of King Styrus the Albanian, and of the Colchian Council of State, why do you not make for Aeaea, which lies opposite to Pola at the head of the Adriatic Sea? There you can safely put yourself at the disposal of my father's sister, Queen Circe, who has a welcome waiting on her island for all fighting men who are loyal worshippers of the Many-named Goddess. But if ever I have need of you, be sure that I will send for you. Be off, Aras, and prosper! As for myself, I shall make my home at Ephyra, where my father's former people live, and Perses may, for all I care, continue as regent of Colchis in my absence – which is likely to be a long one indeed. And I charge you, honest Aras, let my friend Atalanta go free. It was Artemis, not she, who killed my father Aeëtes; and Artemis is a Goddess with whom it is not safe to trifle, as you have seen.'

So Aras was persuaded. He took leave of Medea with a dignified obeisance and his men trooped down to the harbour after him, spread the sails of their ships to a southerly breeze, and were soon out of sight. Jason celebrated the departure of Aras with sacrifices and games, and the country people from all about brought bridal gifts to the royal pair: one a heifer, another a honeycomb, another a fat goose. The Argonauts regretted that they could not immediately sail for Iolcos and thence disperse in honour to their own cities and islands before the weather worsened: but they were bound, by Jason's promise to Circe, first to convey certain gifts to the Chief Nymph of the shrine of Cocalus at Agrigentum in Sicily.

On the fifth day of their stay in the island they said their farewells to the Phaeacians, who provisioned the ship and provided her with a new sail and new tackle; and set out for Calabria in Italy. As a parting gift Queen Arete gave Medea the twelve bridesmaids to take with her; and Medea in return gave Arete some of the most beautiful of her jewels. They also exchanged drugs and charms: Medea giving Arete liniment of mezereum root, good against the colds in the chest from which Alcinoüs chronically suffered; and Arete giving Medea a preparation of the onion-like squill which grows profusely in Corfu, and which is a sure poison for rats and mice, while harmless to other creatures. 'With this in your possession,' said Arete, 'you need fear no plague of mice and rats that Apollo may send against you.'

After a pleasant voyage, with dolphins sporting about the ship from dawn to dusk, the Argonauts disembarked at Calabrian Leuca at the tip of the Iapygian promontory. There they found Canthus, brother of the Polyphemus whom they had left behind at Cios: he was wandering in search of Polyphemus, wishing to tell him that sentence of exile had been revoked and that he might return to his home at Larisa. Jason offered Canthus a passage back to Greece, which he joyfully accepted. At Leuca too, Medea in return for the hospitality shown her by the inhabitants taught the priests the art of snake-charming, from whom it was later conveyed to the Marsians of the Fucine Lake, who mistakenly pay her divine honours to this day under the title of the Goddess Angitia.

Jason now chose Nauplius to be his navigator, for this was a voyage that Nauplius had made a score of times. He brought them safely to Croton, where seals bask undisturbed upon the beach; there the Fleece was washed in the third of the prescribed seven rivers, namely the Aesaros, which empties into the Ionian Sea. From Croton they sailed by way of Rhegion to Catania in Sicily, which lies under the shadow of Mount Etna; there they found the pastures and chestnut forests scorched and the sea thick with floating lumps of pumice which the mountain had belched out two days before. They had seen the flame and smoke rising while they were yet a great distance off, but Medea had told them to fear nothing. At Catania, also, they washed the Fleece in the fourth of the prescribed rivers, namely the Symaethos, which empties into the Sicilian Sea. From Catania they sailed by way of Heloros and Gela to well-watered Agrigentum, which lies midway on the southern coast of Sicily, facing Africa.

As they sailed into the harbour of Agrigentum, very early in the morning, only three Argonauts were awake: namely Idas, taking a trick at the helm for Great Ancaeus, who had been steering all night, Nauplius, and Butes of Athens. As the *Argo* rounded a little headland, keeping close inshore, the fifty nymphs of Cocalus were all sporting together on the beach with a leather ball! They were tossing it from one to the other, in time to a song called the Sirens' Song, and had their robes girded up to their waists for greater ease, so that their bare thighs showed. Nauplius and Butes modestly covered their eyes with their cloaks, but not Idas, who had no reverence or modesty and called out: 'Run off, pretty nymphs, and hide in clefts of the rock! Idas, son of Aphareus, has his eyes upon you.'

Butes, a man of the greatest propriety, rebuked Idas, saying: 'O Idas,

Idas! Keep your eyes upon your course! You will endanger our lives by your folly!'

Idas replied: 'No more than you did, bee-mad Butes, when at Aea your taste for honey destroyed our dear comrade Iphitus, who was killed when he returned to rescue you.'

These words, spoken in a loud voice, aroused the ghost of Iphitus, which, disdaining the funeral barrow raised for him in the territory of the Apsilaeans, had come aboard the *Argo*, hidden in a basket of provisions, to seek revenge. Lynceus had seen the ghost several times since, as it groped blindly from bench to bench forgetful of its name and purposes. Now it remembered all and crept under the handsome Mariandynian cloak with which Butes was covering his face, and began twittering in his ear: 'I am Iphitus, Iphitus, Iphitus, Iphitus, Iphitus!'

Butes uttered a tremendous cry and leaped overboard to escape from Iphitus – for ghosts dare not cross salt water except in a boat or on a raft – and swam away as fast as he could, heading westward. Nauplius called to him to return and, when he only swam the faster, changed course and pursued him. Meanwhile the nymphs, more amused than annoyed, had called upon their Goddess and at once a thick sea-mist enveloped the *Argo*; so they continued with their sacred song in broad sunshine on the beach, and the prying eyes of Idas were cheated. Nauplius thereupon stopped the ship, for fear of running Butes down. He wakened Medea and informed her of what had happened. She at once called out a greeting to the nymphs and asked them to plead with the Goddess to disperse the mist; which they did willingly enough when they learned who she was.

Butes was lost and never set foot aboard the *Argo* again. He was not drowned, however; for some hours later a chance vessel picked him up exhausted but still swimming, and conveyed him to Lilybaeum, the westernmost promontory of Sicily. There he found a honey of such wonderful properties that he remained as a guest of the college of nymphs on Mount Eryx for the remainder of his life. He no longer feared the ghost of Iphitus, having hacked off a forefinger to placate it, and he fathered a number of distinguished children on the nymphs, blessing the mishap which had brought him there.

At Agrigentum, Medea delivered Circe's presents to the Chief Nymph of Cocalus, who kissed her and showed her the authentic jointed image of the Goddess which Daedalus had made. The two conversed in the interior of the shrine for a very long time, while the Argonauts feasted outside under the shade of laden apple-trees. It was then that Meleager shredded the secret drug which Circe had given him into Atalanta's bowl of honey-water. If she had tasted it she would have fallen so passionately in love with him that she would have forgotten all modesty, and even her loyalty to Artemis. But keen-eyed Lynceus, observing Meleager's act, upset the bowl as if accidentally, so that the drug was wasted. Then, drawing him aside, he whispered in his ear: 'Comrade, do not pick a quarrel with Artemis, I implore you!' The lovesick Meleager was thus brought to his senses, but Atalanta remained vexed by his jealousy and his uncomradely taunting of Melanion.

The *Argo* could at last turn her prow homeward. The wind was fair from the west as she sailed back along the southern coast of Sicily, but just as she cleared Cape Pachynon a most violent north-east wind came tearing down the Sicilian Sea. Nauplius advised Jason to let her run before it and take shelter in the harbour of Malta, which has good anchorage. Jason consented, but by some error Great Ancaeus steered too far to the east and passed Malta by in the failing light, Lynceus unluckily being asleep at that time. They drove on all night, through a sea of indescribable violence, fearing that every hour would be their last. The morning brought no relief but only increased anxiety. The *Argo* had sprung a leak from the strain of her terrible buffeting, and Argus called for ropes to frap her, which was done with great difficulty among the huge seas.

Argus told Nauplius: 'The leak is in the part of the ship which we repaired at Teos; the timber was not to my liking but there was none better to be had. We must run for the nearest shore and meanwhile bail for dear life, first casting overboard everything that is not necessary.'

Jason gave the order to lighten ship, but nobody wished to throw rich armour or sacks of gold dust to the insatiable waves. As they hesitated, Augeas cried: 'Come, comrades, let us heave the water-jars overboard. They are the objects of most weight!' So this was done, but they kept a little fresh water for their needs stored in golden pitchers and silver jars.

Those were terrible days and nights, for nobody slept a wink and the twelve Phaeacian bridesmaids were so dreadfully sea-sick that they begged their mistress to toss them overboard after the water-jars and so put an end to their miseries.

At last someone remembered the Mysteries of Samothrace and suggested that the Triple Goddess should be called upon to abate the force of the wind. Mopsus thereupon attempted to invoke her in the manner that the Dactyls had taught them, but in the presence of so many uninitiated persons he could not recollect the correct formula of incantation, and neither could anyone else; it seemed that the Goddess had clouded their minds purposely.

Jason then begged Medea to propitiate the Goddess, but Medea was herself prostrated with sea-sickness and could only groan for answer. So they drove on past the rocky island of Lampedusa, the shores of which shone white with tremendous sheets of spray, but Nauplius mistook it for Pantellaria, which lies a day's sail away to the northward, and so was thrown out of his reckoning. Now heavier seas even than before broke over the *Argo*, rusting the weapons of the Argonauts, spoiling their clothes and forcing them to bail without ceasing until they thought that their backs would break with the strain.

Meleager cried out early on the third morning: 'Comrades, will any of you explain to me why this misery has come upon us? Since all the sins that each of us has committed openly have been purged by sacrifice and lustration, what cause or reason is there for this dangerous buffeting?'

Castor fixed Idas with his eye, an eye no longer clear but dulled with weariness and reddened by salt spray. 'There sits the culprit,' he said 'who insulted the nymphs of Cocalus and thereby vexed the Great One who rules the winds. Were our ship lightened of Idas she would soon float on an even keel, the torn seams would close, the winds would fall, and the kingfisher would skim merrily again across blue water.'

Lynceus answered for his brother Idas, addressing Jason: 'Jason, son of Aeson, did you hear what Castor said? Forgetful of the oath of loyalty which he swore to us all on the beach of Iolcos, and which he renewed on the island of Apollo when first we entered the Black Sea, this madman is openly plotting against the life of my brother Idas. He is attempting to convert his private rancour into public condemnation of the boldest man among you. Why should dear Idas be denied his innocent jests? Has he not earned the right to say whatever he pleases? When the prodigious boar killed Idmon by the reeds of the river Lycos and would have destroyed our whole ship's company with the same bloody-stained lushes, who was it that drove a broad spear home and destroyed the pest? Answer me that, Peleus, you who stood in the greatest danger that morning! Or who was it, when we battled with the Bebrycians, who led the attack along the lip of the dell and, taking the enemy in flank, broke them in pieces? Answer me that, Great Ancaeus, you who followed two paces behind him. If the *Argo* must be lightened of any man, in sacrifice for the remainder, let it be the ungrateful and worthless Castor at whose heart envy gnaws as a rat gnaws at an old black leather bottle in a corner of the cellar.'

Lynceus and Idas reached for their weapons, as also did Castor and Pollux, and all four struggled to come to grips; but the vessel was tossing and pitching so violently that they could not stand upright. The rest of the Argonauts tugged them back by their tunic tails, and disarmed them. However, Pollux managed to come near enough to Idas to deal him a heavy blow on the jaw. Idas, spitting out a broken tooth and a mouthful of blood, said: Pollux when this voyage is over, my broken tooth will demand a whole jawful of vengeance!'

Argus, his face glowing with rage, shouted: 'The voyage will end here and now, dolts and imbeciles, if you do not at once resume your bailing. The leak has gained two fingers' depth on us since this insane quarrel began.'

Then Meleager said: 'Blame me, Argus. It was my fault not to have spoken plainly. I had no intention whatsoever of rousing discord between these proud pairs of brothers. I was about to raise another question altogether, namely, whether the storm and the leak might not both have been provoked by some error on the part of Atalanta of Calydon. At Agrigentum, when we went ashore, I watched her going apart into the bushes with Melanion...'

Argus thrust a brass bowl into Meleager's hand and screamed at him: 'Bail, man, bail, and hold your accursed tongue if you ever wish to see dry land again!'

But Atalanta came to sit beside Meleager and said in a subdued voice: 'Dearest Meleager, let me confess that I love only you, though you weary me by your importunity and by your groundless jealousy against honest Melanion. I see your distress and will not punish you further. Come, dear one, smile at me and we will bail together in alternation!'

Meleager began to weep and implored her pardon, which she sweetly granted. They bailed together, knee to knee, he scooping while she flung away water, he flinging away water while she scooped. Then there was peace in the *Argo* again, broken, to the general surprise, by Ascalaphus, son of Ares, as he sang in a deep, very true voice:

Last night I heard my Thracian Father speak,
'*Warriors, doff your helmets!*
The *Argo* has a leak, a list, a leak,
Warriors, doff your helmets!

'Fear neither bloody axe nor sword nor mace,
Warriors, doff your helmets!
The cold green water gains on you apace,
Warriors, doff your helmets!

'Not goblets now, for yellow Lemnian wine,
Warriors, doff your helmets!
But handy scoops for bailing out the brine,
Warriors, doff your helmets!'

These three verses, and others in the same strain, encouraged the Argonauts to persist with their bailing; the tune was of the sort that runs in the head and cannot easily be expelled. Soon they had the water under control again. Argus found the leak and plugged it with strips of waxed cloth, and gave them hope of coming safely to land, if only the wind would abate a little.

CHAPTER FORTY-FIVE

THE ARGONAUTS ABANDON HOPE

Between midnight and dawn on the third night of their distress, the ninth since their departure from Corcyra, Lynceus, on watch in the bows, cried 'Breakers ahead!' shouting loudly so that his voice should not be snatched away by the wind. Then simple-minded Coronus of Gyrton spoke from his seat near the stern: 'I fear, comrades, that the time has come when we must say a sorrowful farewell to one another, with mutual forgiveness for any injuries or insults of which we may yet nurse the hateful memory in our hearts. Let us recall only the exploits that we have performed in common; for though we may perish now, nobody can deny that we have succeeded in our extraordinary quest and have earned glory that will be long in fading. Yet, alas, Idmon and Tiphys and Iphitus and Calaïs and Zetes, our comrades who have fallen by the way, will be counted luckier than we. Whereas we burned their bones piously and performed exact funeral rites for them, our own bodies will feed the crabs that crawl sideways upon the desert shore of Africa; and what will become of our ghosts, who knows?'

However, Periclymenus the wizard rose up, supporting himself by gripping the gunwale with his left hand, and stretching his right hand into the air thus confidently addressed his father, the God Poseidon: 'Father, whatever other deities may rule the waters of the Black Sea, or the waters about Samothrace, assuredly it is you who rule here. Do you not remember the three men, honoured by you with the name of sons, who, in the spring of this very year, offered you an extraordinary holocaust of twenty unblemished red bulls in the land of the Bebrycians? These same three men are aboard this ship. Preserve them, I beseech you, together with all their companions, and bring them safe to land. In so doing you will confer a benefit upon your elder brother, All-powerful Zeus, whose Golden Fleece lies safely folded in the locker under the helmsman's seat of this ship. If the *Argo* goes down and the Fleece with it, Father, you will not be able to plead ignorance of the accident. The Thunderer will be angry and demand compensation, urging that the Fleece was won back for him by us with incredible labour and hazard. Here is a gift for you, Father, my own gift, this handsome Thessalian bit and bridle that I won from Castor the

Spartan at a game of dice; for you first taught me to rattle the dice-box so that the dice would obey me and fall how I please. Accept this gift and use it to curb your green insensate steeds so they may not cast us in wreckage on Africa's pitiless coast. I give, that you may give in return.'

Then someone cried out 'O!' and pointed astern with his finger. For the God seemed to despise the gift of his son Periclymenus and to be bent on their destruction. A most prodigious wave, a wave of waves, that rose above the others as the snowy ridge of a mountain overhangs a green valley, came rolling towards them at frightful speed. It caught the *Argo* upon its shoulder and rushed onward with her. The Argonauts heard the sucking, grinding noise of shingle and expected instantly to be dashed beam-on against an iron-bound shore; yet when the wave broke with a booming noise and shot them forward in a white smother of foam they felt no shock at all.

The *Argo* slowly lost way: it was as though the fingers of a divine hand caught and checked her to a dead stop. To all the Argonauts the same thought came: 'We are dead. This is how it is to be dead.'

On that strange thought they fell peacefully asleep, so utterly wearied were they, none of them expecting ever again to look upon the rutilant wheel of the Sun.

However, as Dawn swiftly drew the curtain of darkness with her red fingers, the cry of a gull wakened Little Ancaeus, who bestirred himself, climbed upon the gunwale and looked about him. The *Argo* lay on an even keel, safely cushioned in a great mass of seaweed, not having lost so much as a fragment of her stern ornament. Before rousing his comrades to tell them the news, Ancaeus took soundings and found her afloat in a few feet of water but out of reach of the waves, which were still breaking with violence a couple of bowshots astern.

At first nobody could understand what had happened. Nevertheless, Periclymenus, rubbing the sleep from his eyes, arose and gave mumbled thanks to his father for this miraculous rescue. Soon afterwards the wind began to die in a series of fretful blasts. As the sun rose higher, a dead calm succeeded the storm, though the sea still hissed like an angry goose in the ears of the Argonauts. When they recovered from their bewilderment and eagerly looked about them, they saw that the wave had borne the *Argo* over a succession of reefs, any one of which would have cracked her like a rotten hazel nut, and flung her finally over a broad high beach into an inland lake filled with seaweed, its shores hoary with salt.

Someone began to laugh at the drollness of the accident, and soon the whole ship was in a roar. But old Nauplius checked them. 'Comrades,' he said, 'this is no laughing matter. The wave that flung us here has been drawn back into the bosom of the deep, and though we might perhaps with great labour in a month's time cut a channel through the beach back into the sea, we should never be able to lift the *Argo* over those reefs which stretch back row upon row, like benches in a crowded hall, for the better part of a mile. The *Argo* is caught here, a stranded whale, and here her carcase must lie and rot, and we with her; unless perhaps the lake communicates with the sea in some way not yet apparent to us.'

The lake stretched inland as far as the southern horizon and for a great distance to the eastward, but the strand which divided it from the sea to the eastward gradually widened to a great stony plain; while to westward, not far off, it was bounded by a long line of sand-hills.

Jason asked Nauplius: 'Where are we? What lake is this?'

Nauplius answered: 'I cannot say for certain, never having been here before. A large lake lies inland from Hadrumeton, near which, by my reckoning, we now are; but I have been told that it lies many miles distant from the sea, so that I am perplexed. Let us try at once to shift the ship into deeper water, and sail across the lake. It may be that we shall find a river running out of it into the sea.'

Weary and hungry as they were, the Argonauts reversed their oars in the oar-holes, stripped off their wet garments, retaining only their breeches, then clambered out and began to push the ship through the clogging weed. After a few paces she grounded on a sand-bank. They fetched her back and started her on another tack, but almost at once she grounded again. The weed made it impossible for Nauplius to judge where the water would be deep and where shallow. He therefore urged that they should abandon their random efforts and post themselves about the *Argo* at intervals in all directions so that he could see, by the depth in which they were standing, where the water was deepest. They did so, and he was able to mark out a crooked channel with oars; after which he recalled them all and they pushed the *Argo* along the channel, the keel often scraping the sandy bottom. But by the time that the sun was high in the heavens they had not progressed more than two hundred paces and were quite worn out.

Jason reviewed the stores of wine and water. Of water he found somewhat more than a gallon and of wine less than half a gallon, to quench the thirst of thirty-two men and fourteen women. When he broke the news to the Argonauts they all fell silent for a while. Nauplius said: 'It will be two months or more before even a drop of rain falls in this desert. Unless we can find a way out from the lake we shall soon all be either dead of thirst or mad from drinking salt water.'

At this Erginus of Miletos turned to Augeas of Elis and cried: 'Upon you, gold-greedy Augeas, our dying curse will be fixed, and whether you live or die our ghosts shall not cease to torment you for all eternity. Why did you counsel us to heave the water-jars overboard and hoard these useless sacks of treasure? I was a fool to re-embark in the *Argo* once I had set foot again, in the course of our voyage from the Hellespont, upon the flag-stones of my own lovely city of Miletos. Why did I not sham sick, as resourceful Orpheus did, and so escape from your disastrous company, madman of Elis? Never again, I fear, shall I plough with my wooden plough, or harrow with my thorn-harrow, the fertile barley-fields beside winding Meander, where the good black earth contains no stones big enough even for sling-shot and the grasshopper sings all summer long. But some god blinded us all; we should have known better than to listen to you, you tadpole, after the humiliation which your sloth brought upon us in the Crane Lake.'

Augeas answered with spirit: 'You call me madman, I call you a fool, a fool in a striped cloak. How was I to know where your father Poseidon would jokingly toss us? I merely voiced the general opinion of the crew that it was foolish to jettison treasure of which we might stand in need. Had we been cast away on any ordinary shore we could have purchased as much food and water as we pleased with half a handful of gold dust. And why do you fix the blame on me? Jason is our captain. If he had ordered us to jettison the treasure, I should have been the first to obey him. Furthermore, we are not dead yet. It is possible that our gold and silver may yet be of service to us. In fact, I am certain that they will; my honest heart assures me that this is not the end.'

Autolycus said quickly: 'Prove your confidence in your honest heart, dear Augeas, by selling me your day's ration of wine and water for half a handful of gold dust. I am a willing buyer.'

'That is a fair enough offer,' said Echion the herald, 'and I will pay you the same price for tomorrow's ration.'

Augeas was constrained to strike hands on the bargain, but bitterly he regretted it before the day was out; for though they were well enough provisioned with barley-bread and dried meats and honey and pickles and such-like, whatever food they ate without drinking stuck in their dry throats. Of olive oil only a small jar remained, and of dolphin oil nothing at all.

The sun was insufferably hot, and the lake water, being sticky with salt, dried on their bodies with a white scurf. About noon a hot wind swept the desert and they saw the red sand-ghosts dancing in giddy spirals; Idas went out against the sand-ghosts with his spear, but they fled from him, until he ran laughing back to the camp in triumph; then they pursued him menacingly, towering high above him.

Sand in plenty was blown into the Argonauts' food as they tried to eat, and gritted upon their teeth; but the twelve Phaeacian girls did not share in the meal. They lay crowded in a sobbing mass around the supine form of Medea, who had doctored herself with a soporific drug. She was breathing heavily and uttering now and then a slight moan; and once she cried out in a passionate whisper: 'Forgive me, Prometheus, forgive me! Love and necessity compelled me. One day I will make restitution!'

Not greatly refreshed by their midday rest, the Argonauts continued to push the *Argo* through the weed and eased her forward another two hundred paces, along the western shore; a long wide sand-bank to port prevented them from steering into the middle of the lake. Everyone grew gloomy and quarrelsome, with the single exception of Mopsus the Lapith, who was talkative, cheerful, and gay. When Nauplius suggested that the ship should be lightened of as much gear as possible, it was Mopsus who carried out the task.

He went over to the Phaeacian girls. 'Leave your mistress, dear children!' he exclaimed in a bold but tender voice. 'She has no need of your services at present. If any one of you wishes ever again to see the inside of a royal palace, and to sit on soft cushions at her spindle or her loom, with berries and cream in a little bowl on the gilt table at her side, why then, my pretty ones, rise up courageously, the whole dozen of you together, and help me now!'

He made them remove all their clothes but their shifts, and carry ashore on their tender shoulders great quantities of stores and tackle, and the contents of each man's locker, laying all in order upon the beach. The poor girls stumbled under their heavy loads and floundered in the weed and driftwood, and fell often, weeping for shame when they exposed their bare buttocks and Idas mocked at them; but they were willing workers and the ship had risen several inches in the water before they laid off. The men removed the mast, sails, and anchor-stones, and whatever else was too heavy for the women to lift, such as the sacks of gold from Sinope.

The emptying of the lockers brought to light three secret hoards of drink, which amounted in all to twice the amount that had already been declared; these Jason confiscated. The owners, who were Peleus, Acastus, and Eurydamas the Dolopian, looked a little shamefaced, but pleaded that they had forgotten that more than a few drops of drink were left, and pretended to be pleased that so much had been discovered.

The Argonauts slept that night by the lake-side and lighted a fire of driftwood from habit, but had no game to roast at it, nor could they fill the ship's cauldron with fresh water to make a chowder of the small, bony fish that they caught in the lake with their hands. The next day they spent in much the same manner as the first, but the thirst and heat had begun to tell on them: they groaned and whimpered at their labours and by late afternoon the *Argo* had been coaxed forward no more than half a mile from the spot where she was first tossed by the wave.

The sand-ghosts did not dance that day, but far away in the desert they saw a mirage of palm-trees and white houses, and a fleet of three ships sailing upside down. At dusk the Phaeacian girls began weeping softly to themselves; they continued all night, because a jackal was howling in the far distance and they feared that before long he would be feasting on their own shrivelled corpses.

At noon of the third day the last of the wine and water was doled out. Some drank it down greedily, some sipped it frugally, rolling it around their mouths with their swollen tongues; but Great Ancaeus, abasing himself in marvellous humility, poured his cupful upon the sand.

'Dear Deity of this remote country,' Ancaeus cried, 'whoever you may be, pray accept this libation from my hands, knowing well how precious a gift it is that I pour to you. I give of my poverty; do you in return give of your abundance!'

Two or three other men felt impelled to do the same, and among them Jason, as leader of the expedition. But Jason, having swallowed down his own wine and water, poured out the plain water that had been set aside for Medea to drink when she should wake; he did this from no unkindness to her, but because an undrained cup of water would soon have excited his comrades to crime.

That evening, distressed and speechless, they abandoned the ship and began stumbling about at random in the barren desert. Mopsus roared with laughter at them and cried gaily: 'Oho, comrades, what long, lugubrious faces the Evening Star looks down upon! Anyone might mistake you for earth-bound ghosts, or for the population of a doomed city when the images in the fore-courts of the temples sweat with blood, and unexplained bellowings are heard from the sanctuaries, and the genial sun is eclipsed. In Apollo's name, what ails you all? Take heart, comrades, neither Apollo nor any other of the Blessed Olympians will dare to leave us in the lurch after carrying us in safety through so many frightful dangers.'

But Mopsus could not rouse any spirit in any of them. Eurydamas the Dolopian observed to the taciturn Melampus: 'Mopsus will be the first to leave this upper air, I believe. Such exaltation is a certain sign of impending death – an omen more to be relied on than the irresponsible chirpings of wagtails, swallows, finches, and similar small birds.'

'In that case I envy him,' said Melampus. 'For he who succumbs to thirst and heat before all his companions will earn the best funeral. I fear that it will be my luck to survive you all.'

Then the Argonauts, drawn by a sudden compulsion, came together and gazed at the Fleece where it lay shining softly in the starlight. In reverence they handled the heavy golden fringe and the great golden horns. Erginus of Miletos said: 'Nevertheless, when one day our dead bodies are found here, dried and baked black by the sun like Egyptian mummies, the Fleece will also be found, and our great deeds will be remembered because of it. We will be accorded a worthy funeral, all of us together, and our bones heaped in a common grave – unless (better still) our weapons, clothes, and badges declare our several identities and we are conveyed for burial each to his own city or island. I regret having complained against Orpheus and accused him of malingering. I rejoice that he is no longer among us, but has been spared this present misery and returned to his home among the savage Ciconians of Thrace. For when he hears the news of our fate, carried to him by some merchant or exile, or by some prophetic bird, he will weep for us; he will tune his lyre and sing to it, night after night, a great epic of the quest that we undertook and in his company performed – wonderfully composed hexametric verses which will ring around the world for a thousand years or more.'

With this, Erginus began to embrace his comrades, one by one, asking pardon for any injuries that he had inflicted upon them and granting pardon to any who sought it of him. Then he said farewell to them all and strode out into the desert to die alone.

His example was followed by several of his comrades. But Castor and Pollux resolutely refrained from joining hands in friendship with Idas and Lynceus. And Argus waded out to his beloved *Argo* to die aboard her. And Mopsus built a great fire by the lake-side and danced around it merrily in honour of Apollo. And Meleager and Atalanta with a strange look of joy upon their faces went off out of sight, hand in hand down to the seashore where the small waves hissed.

As for Jason, he stayed where he was, with the Fleece at his right hand and the peacefully slumbering Medea at his left. Close to his feet lay a huddled mass of Phaeacian girls, twittering together like wretched fledgelings that have fallen from a lofty nest and lie on the stones below, abandoned by their parents and unable either to find food or fly away.

CHAPTER FORTY-SIX

THE ARGONAUTS ARE RESCUED

Jason wrapped his head in his cloak and fell into a deep sleep, from which he was roused by a sudden remarkable apparition. Three goat-headed women with linked arms appeared, smiling benignly at him, and addressed him in a single bleating voice. 'Jason, son of Aeson, we are the Goat headed Triple Goddess of Libya, and we greatly value the piety that you have showed in pouring an acceptable libation to us of pure water. Your comrades ignorantly poured water mixed with wine, an intoxicating drink which we cannot stomach. Nevertheless, you may inform them that all but one will escape safely from their predicament; we mean all but the slit-tongue fellow, who must die here because he has no fear of death, and because he honours Apollo not ourselves, and because a far-travelled hen-stork once warned him that he must meet his end in Libya.'

Jason looked modestly aside as the Goddess, or Goddesses, spoke to him. He asked: 'Ladies, what must we others do to be saved?'

The Goddess, now united into a single form, answered: 'Only hope. And when you are at length returned to your native country do not forget me, as you forgot me before. Whether I roar to you as a lioness, or bleat to you as a she-goat, or shriek to you as a night bird, or neigh to you as a mare, remember this: I am the same three-in-one implacable Goddess – mother, maiden, nymph – and you may fool the undependable Father of Heaven, or mousy-eyed Apollo, or crop-eared Ares, or even wriggle-wanded, deceitful Hermes, God of heralds: but nobody has ever yet deceived me, or finally escaped punishment for his attempted deceit.'

With that a mist arose between the Goddess and Jason, and when it cleared she had disappeared and he was gazing at the great yellow disk of the moon. Then he slept again, a sleep of marvellous contentment.

When he awoke he leaped up and began to shout to his comrades: 'Argonauts, dear Argonauts, we are saved! The Triple Goddess herself has appeared to me in a vision and promised us all life – or all but one of us!'

The dawn was breaking over the lake with a fiery splendour that portended another day of heat. A lonely Argonaut, who proved to be Melampus, unwrapped his haggard head from the folds of a cloak and answered in a hoarse voice: 'Do not break our last sleep, Jason, by your unseasonable bawlings. Dream your dreams, if you will, but leave us to ours.'

Jason strode out further and came upon Lynceus, whom he wakened with a recital of his dream. Lynceus blinked and looked about him, not yet understanding what Jason had told him. Then he cried out: 'Look, look! Stretch out your hand and tell me what you see at three fingers' breadth to the right hand of the mound of sand yonder!'

'I see nothing, 'Jason replied.

'But I see a man galloping on a fawn-coloured horse,' cried Lynceus. 'He is coming towards us.'

These loud words roused ten or twelve men. They came together with distraught looks and dusty hair. None of them could see any horseman. 'It is the mirage,' Euphemus sadly pronounced.

But presently the better-sighted of them descried a little cloud of dust in the far distance, and presently the horseman came in full view and hallooed to them in a tongue that nobody could understand. Nauplius said: 'He is a Tritonian of the Ausensian tribe, to judge by his white robes and red-tasselled javelins, and by the tuft of hair that he wears above his brow. Can this, after all, be Lake Tritonis, far to the south of Hedrumetum?'

Echion was about to advance and would have made an eloquent address to the horseman, had not Autolycus restrained him, saying: 'Noble son of Hermes, do not think that I wish to deny you your herald's privilege of representing us. But your wonderful eloquence is only of service when those whom you address understand some dialect either of Greek, Pelasgian, or Thracian: it is wasted upon savages. Let me be spokesman for once. At Sinope I became well versed in the universal language of the deaf and dumb.'

Autolycus had his way. He went up to the Tritonian, seized him by the right hand and embraced him; then he made a dumb-show of drinking, pointed to his parched lips and swollen tongue, and began scanning the horizon with impatience.

The Tritonian understood. He made the same dumb-show of drinking, waved vaguely into the desert, and held out his hand for a gift.

Autolycus nodded assent, and the Tritonian pointed to a bronze tripod, with gilded legs and seat, which was lying on its side near by; King Alcinoüs had presented it to Jason, intending him to dedicate it at Delphi on his return.

Autolycus made a show of refusing to part with the tripod, but finally promised that the Tritonian should have it as soon as ever he had led them to the water.

By drawing an imaginary bow and three times thrusting out his hands with fingers outspread, the Tritonian signified that the water was thirty bowshots distant. He then drew himself up to his full height, puffed out his chest, bulged his muscles, roared like a lion, and began banging at a rock with an imaginary club. Then he rippled his fingers in a watery gesture and stooped down greedily, as if drinking, at the same time uttering a sound that was unmistakably an attempt at the Greek phrase 'Holy Serpents!'

The Argonauts looked at one another in amazement and exclaimed with one voice: 'Hercules!'

The Tritonian nodded and repeated 'Hercules', then glowered at them, exclaimed 'Holy Serpents!' again with great vigour, and burst into laughter.

They patted him on the back and followed him eagerly towards the water. When they reached it, not long after – a clear spring bubbling from a rose-coloured rock – they found great fragments of the rock lying in the desert near by, recently broken off by the blows of some powerful instrument, doubtless the brass-bound club of their comrade Hercules. Ah, how they drank and drank of that sweet, restorative spring!

Then one said to the other: 'Hercules has saved our lives, it was Hercules!' And afterwards indeed they learned that Hercules, in sailing towards the island of the Hesperides in quest of the sacred oranges, had been blown ashore not far from that very spot. He was as thirsty as they, but instead of resigning himself to death strode out into the desert snuffing for water like a lion, and as soon as he caught a faint scent of it began striking at a rock with his club until a stream came gushing out. Now the tracks of animals already led to the stream from every direction, and the Tritonian explained with expressive gestures what animals they were: namely the tiny, large-eyed, leaping jerboa, the jackal who feeds on corpses, the porcupine with rattling quills, and the splendid Barbary sheep.

Autolycus persuaded the Tritonian with gifts and promises to return with them to the camp. There he showed him the *Argo*, asking whether she could be extricated from the lake by any means and returned to the sea. The Tritonian assured them that this was possible, because a narrow river ran out of the lake some miles to the east, and the *Argo* already lay in the tortuous channel which communicated with this river. Autolycus gave him brooches and earrings, which all the Argonauts gladly contributed, and promised him a fine red cloak as well if he would assist them to escape. This contented him and he uttered a sudden loud cry between a whistle and a yell. Immediately from a small barren hill half a mile away, as if by magic, a large company of nearly naked Tritonians poked out their tufted heads and came running towards the Argonauts.

Lynceus cried: 'By the Lynx's pads and tail, what a fool I am! Yesterday at noon I saw men and women squatting on that hill, but took them for figures in the mirage.'

These Tritonians, or Ausensians, were troglodytes, living in deep caverns underground, with small holes, like those of a fox's earth, serving for doors and windows. Nobody wandering across that hill would have guessed that he was standing above a populous city; for they are a shy people and seldom dare reveal themselves to strangers. The chieftain had taken the precaution of riding towards the Argonauts' camp from another direction altogether, and as if from a great distance.

Both the Ausensians and their neighbours the Machlyans (who wear their tuft of hair behind, not before) worship the Triple Goddess in the antique style. They do not practise marriage, but couple indiscriminately within certain degrees of kinship; and every three months, at a tribal assembly, any boy that has been born is assigned to the guardianship of the man, of the prescribed kinship, whom he is judged to resemble most closely. The women show great independence of spirit; they bear arms and annually decide who is to be Priestess of the Moon by a furious battle among themselves in which no man is allowed to meddle under pain of dismemberment. To the Ausensians, as to all other peoples of the Double Gulf, the Sun is not a beneficent deity but a merciless tyrant; and they curse it at its rising every day, and hurl stones at it.

The troubles of the Argonauts melted away. Medea awoke suddenly from her trance and led the Phaeacian girls to the spring with empty jars and buckets, which they brought back full, and soon everyone was restored to life and vigour. The Ausensians staked out the further course of the channel, and with their help the Argonauts, after stowing the cargo aboard again, shoved the *Argo* slowly along it, for a distance of twelve miles in all; making two miles or so each day, until at last they found themselves in clear water and able to use their oars. Jason rewarded the Tritonians suitably with pieces of coloured cloth and other slight gifts, and on the tripod Argus incised an inscription of gratitude and friendship for their nation. The Tritonians, shrieking like bats in their delight, bore the tripod underground to some hidden shrine of the Goat-headed Mother, whose triple form Argus had depicted upon it.

The Argonauts waded ashore and built an altar on a knoll close to where the river, called the Gabes river, flows out of the lake. There they heaped sober offerings to the Goat-headed Goddess. Yet on other altars they also sacrificed to the Olympians: two fat Barbary sheep which Meleager and Idas had run down and taken alive, and a gazelle which Atalanta had wounded with a long cast of her javelin.

They had already re-embarked and said a gracious farewell to the Ausensians, and rowed off, when the chieftain remembered a mark of courtesy that he had forgotten: he galloped his horse along the banks of the river, waving a clod of earth. He wished them to accept it as a token that they were welcome to visit his land whenever it pleased them. Euphemus shipped his oar, plunged overboard and swam to receive the gift, which he brought back without wetting it, swimming one-handed. Then the salty current of the Gabes river caught the *Argo* and carried her swiftly towards the sea, after ten days of imprisonment.

Medea made a prophecy to Euphemus: 'Man of the Swallow badge, your descendants in the fourth generation shall be Kings of Africa by the token of this clod of earth, if only you can bring it safely back to holy Taenaron, your home. If not, Africa must wait for the seed of Euphemus until the seventeenth generation.'

But the fourth generation of his descendants, stemming from a son that was born to him by Lamache of Lemnos, was destined to be cheated of sovereignty; for one dark night on the homeward voyage a wave broke over the *Argo* and dissolved the clod into muddy water.

Thus all the Argonauts were saved except Mopsus the Lapith, who had not escaped the fate prophesied to him. Three days before this, at noon, as he wandered by the lake-side, an enormous shadow fell across his path. Looking up, he saw circling overhead a bearded vulture of prodigious size, with pointed wings and wedge-shaped tail. It was crying to him in strange pleading tones and urging him away from the lake with the reiterated cry of 'Gold! Gold!'; hoping (it is supposed) to have lured him to some inaccessible and waterless part of the wilderness, and there feasted at ease on his body when he was dead of thirst. Mopsus was easily deceived. He ran forward with his eyes on the bird, but had not run many paces before he trod on the tail of a black snake that was lying torpid in the sun. The snake turned and drove its fangs into his ankle, close to the shin. Mopsus cried aloud and his comrades came hurrying up to see what was amiss.

He sat on the ground nursing his wound and said: 'Farewell, dear comrades. The bird promised me gold if I followed him. Now I must die, but I feel no excessive pain. Bury me handsomely and speak well of me when I am dead.' Then the numbness from the poison spread swiftly through his limbs, a mist clouded his eyes, and he sank back.

Under the torrid Libyan sun a corpse soon stinks; and the venom of the snake working within the body of Mopsus began to rot the flesh before the very eyes of his comrades and make the hair fall out. They quickly borrowed mattocks from the Ausensians and dug him a deep grave while his corpse was hissing on the pyre that they had heaped and lighted. When all the flesh was consumed they piled a barrow over his bones, and three times marched about it in full armour, mourning grievously for him and tearing out their hair by handfuls; while the shameless vulture circled screaming overhead, baulked of its hoped-for repast.

CHAPTER FORTY-SEVEN

THE *ARGO* COMES HOME

It was dangerously late in the year to undertake a voyage that could not be expected to last less than two months, but the winds and weather proved wonderfully favourable from the day that the Argonauts sailed out into the Libyan Sea by the Gabes river, to the day that they finally disembarked at Pagasae. Throughout their long coasting of the Double Gulf of Syrtis they did not spend longer than could be avoided at any place where they touched; for no cities or other places of attraction were to be found anywhere along the whole length – not even the well-known settlement of Oea was worth a visit. This coast was possessed by savages no less strange than those whom they had visited in the eastern gulf of the Black Sea.

First, in order, they visited the Lotus-eaters, the indolent inhabitants of the large rocky island of Meninx, where the Argonauts went ashore for water. These Lotus-eaters, as their name implies, subsist largely on the sweet berry of the loosely branched, silver-leaved lotus, or jujube bush, that grows spontaneously in every rock-crevice or secluded nook. They own flocks of sheep, besides, for their provision of milk and wool, but consider the eating of roast mutton a loathsome act, worse than canni-balism. From the lotus berry they brew a wine of such strength that it is said to impair disastrously the memory of those who drink it: after only a few draughts they forget the names of their friends and relatives and even of the blessed gods. On Meninx the Argonauts found good water and partook of the lotus berry, compressed into sweet round cakes; but they refused to touch lotus wine, because Nauplius warned them against it. They had learned at last not to invite trouble by dangerous experiment.

Next the *Argo* came to the territory of the Gindanaeans, who are shep-herds, goatherds, and tunny-fishers; they also feed upon the lotus, but do not brew lotus wine. Here for the first time the Argonauts saw date-palms growing, like tall pillars with feathery tops, and tasted the sticky yellow fruit, which is slow to ripen. The Gindanaean women wear about their ankles as many linen bandages as they have companied with men, and are the dominant sex, being the guardians of the wells. They would not let the Argonauts, those who were sent to fetch water, draw even a bucketful until they had companied with them and each provided a strip of linen to bandage his bride. The women were handsome, though exceedingly brown in colour, and the Argonauts, who were commanded by Echion, were pleased to give them the pleasure that they demanded. The Gindanaean men were not jealous of this act, but showed indecent curiosity, resenting to be driven away from the scene; however, at Echion's request the women compelled them to go off and wash themselves in the sea.

The coast of the gulf along which they now sailed was low, sandy, and featureless; and scarcely a vestige of green was to be seen anywhere. On the seventh day they came to Oea, which lies in the middle of the Double Gulf. Oea is an encampment rather than a town. The capacious harbour, protected by reefs from the fury of the North-East Wind, is used by Greek merchants who come to fetch off the local products, such as ostrich-skins, sponges, and herb-benjamin (a condiment of great relish); they can sometimes buy ivory and other outlandish products conveyed in Egyptian caravans. The caravans come in winter-time along the route, connecting the numerous oases of the interior, which ends at this point, and return in early spring. However, since the trading season was over for the year, the Argonauts found only native Macaeans at Oea, not a single Greek or Egyptian. The Macaeans grow a tuft of hair in the very centre of their skulls, shaving the rest. They revere the ostrich and live in skin tents.

At Oea Jason washed the Fleece in the fifth of the seven prescribed rivers, the narrow Cinyps, which empties into the Libyan Sea. His companions also bought Greek water-jars of large size and filled them from the same stream.

From Oea, they continued for two whole days to sail past the territory of the Macaeans, and towards evening of the second day came up with what had seemed in the distance to be three islands; these were three cliffs of a rocky promontory, fledged with palm-trees. In the distance a flock of sheep were seen to be pastured, which gave the Argonauts an irresistible hankering after roast mutton. The three Sinopeans, with Idas, Lynceus, and Canthus the brother of Polyphemus, were at once sent out by Jason to obtain ten ewes or wethers from the shepherds – less would not suffice them. They overtook the flock at dusk, but the Macaean shepherds, rejecting the gifts offered them, refused to yield even a single sheep. In the battle that was then joined, the shepherds, who were marvellously agile, acquitted themselves with courage beyond the ordinary, four men against six; and before Idas could spit them all, one after the other, with his broad spear, their leader had aimed a sling-stone at Canthus, whirling it with great strength and deadly aim, which struck him full upon the temple and broke the bones of his skull.

Sorrowfully they took Canthus up and buried him by the sea, dancing about his pyre in armour and tearing out their hair. They also raised a lofty cairn of white boulders above his bones, so that sailors in after-years might beach their ships close by and pour libations to him. But they themselves had no fear of the ghost of Canthus; it had slaked its thirst well on the blood of four adversaries and a hundred sheep beside, which though thin, the Argonauts found tasty enough. They feasted on well-roasted mutton, with a sauce of barley and herb-benjamin that the Phaeacian girls knew how to prepare.

Next they came to lagoons, salt marshes, and quicksands, extending for a hundred miles or more. This part of the gulf has a remarkably chaotic appearance, being neither firm land nor yielding sea. Some poets say that at the original creation of the world by the Goddess Eurynome she was distracted by the sight of a horned asp which she had involuntarily called into being, and that she left the Syrtis unfinished. Nauplius kept the *Argo* well clear of this treacherous coast.

Next they came to the territory of the swarthy Psyllians, who dare to eat snakes and lizards and, according to the account given by Nauplius, are proof against the venom even of the asp. Nauplius declared that if ever a Psyllian child is bitten by an asp and dies, his mother flings the corpse into the desert without any funeral as being a monster, no true Psyllian. Medea mocked at this story, remarking that the Psyllians are no more proof against snake-venom than any other people, but use placatory charms and anoint themselves with a juice obnoxious to snakes of all sorts. She declared that in their public displays, when they encourage great hooded serpents to bite them, the Psyllians doubtless cheat the populace by first secretly removing the venom-fangs with the jerk of a rag placed between each serpent's teeth. As for the eating of snakes' flesh, she said, that was no wonder; for it is not poisonous, but only disagreeably tough and rank. The Argonauts did not therefore trouble to visit the Psyllians, whom hitherto they had regarded as a marvellous people. They sailed onwards past red cliffs and intervening beaches of white sand, behind which rose coast hills of uniform height, treeless and clothed in scorched grass. Gazelle were sighted from time to time, but no other four-footed animals of any great size.

Next they came to the territory of the Nasamonians, who occupy the firmer parts of the Eastern Gulf. The Nasamonians differ from the tribes to the westward by worshipping a Father God of a sort and practising marriage of a sort. However, the men are not jealous of the chastity of their wives; the husband allows his wedding-guests to enjoy his wife, one after the other in order of rank, so long as each one brings her a suitable love-gift. A rich man marries several wives; but the poor man, who cannot afford to maintain even one, attends all the weddings and is therefore not deprived of the natural pleasures of love. However the Argonauts did not meet with many members of this numerous tribe for the greater part of them were, as usual, spending their summer in the oases of date-palms which mark the desolate interior of Libya as spots do the pelt of a leopard;

they would not return until the rains of winter had reclothed the coastal hills with grass and flowers to plump up their lean cattle.

When the Argonauts went ashore at a substantial settlement in the eastern angle of the gulf, being again in need of water, the leader of the few remaining Nasamonians insisted that Echion, who had come forward as herald, should swear a treaty of friendship with him. The Nasamonian drank water from the palm of Echion's hand, and gave him water to drink from his own. This method of sealing a treaty Echion found most disagreeable. The Nasamonian had filthy hands covered with sores, and the water, which was procured by digging in the sand near the beach, was brackish and tasted disagreeably of sulphur. Nevertheless, Echion behaved with impeccable courtesy, as a herald should.

They were obliged to wait here until the West Wind that had carried them so well and so far should be succeeded by the South Wind; for the coast now curved northward. The Nasamonians fed them generously meanwhile, but upon food that was by no means to their liking – strips of lean beef dried in the sun, and the powdered bodies of locusts mixed with dried milk. On the sixth day the South Wind blew.

It was with pleasure that, not long afterwards, they reached the fertile land of Cyrene, where the soil is deep and all manner of trees and grasses flourish. The Cyreneans, a cultivated and hospitable folk with some knowledge of Greek, entertained them kindly for the sake of the wonderful tales that they told of their travels. Here Jason bought provisions for the next stage of their voyage, which was to Greece by way of Crete, and he and his comrades tasted fresh barley-bread for the first time since they had quitted Corfu. The place from which they finally sailed was Darnis, where they washed the Fleece in the sixth of the prescribed seven rivers, the Darnis, which empties into the Cyrenaic Sea. This sweet-watered stream passes through a deep ravine, the sides of which are clothed in wild olive, pine, and cypress. They found well-tended fig-orchards here and newly planted vineyards, and at a farewell feast the Darnians crowned them with garlands, crammed their mouths with fat roast beef, and would at first take no recompense; but the Argonauts pressed gold upon them for the beautification of their temples.

From Darnis, with a fine south-easterly breeze, they came to Crete by the dawn of the third day, and woke to find Mount Dicte towering before them. They had a mind to land at Hierapytna, a strong town situated on a plain projecting from the coast; but the chief magistrate, wearing a bronze helmet, a bronze breastplate, and bronze greaves, stood on a pinnacle of rock close to the landing-place and shouted roughly to them to sheer off, since Minyan ships were not welcome in Crete. Armed townsmen flocked about him, clashing their weapons together, and pelted the *Argo* with pebbles and stones. The Argonauts debated whether to attack Hierapytna and put all the inhabitants to the sword; but more prudent counsels prevailed when Medea offered to punish the magistrate with a blow dealt from a distance.

They backed the *Argo* out of bowshot and Medea mounted into the bows. Throwing the fold of her purple robe over her head, she made magic beneath it. She could be heard chanting and praying alternately, and at last thrust out her head and gave the magistrate, whose name was Talus, such a Gorgon look, with gnashing of teeth and rolling of eyes and waggling of tongue, that he fainted for fear and fell down from the pinnacle of rock where he was standing. He broke his leg in three places, cut the principal artery of his ankle, and bled to death within the hour; for the townsmen, in terror of Medea, dared not come to his rescue.

The Argonauts rowed away to the eastward, laughing for pleasure, and rounded the rugged eastern tip of Crete. At dawn of the next day they reached Minoa, where Argus was well known to the townspeople, and there revictualled the ship. The river Minos, which empties into the Cretan Sea, was the last of the seven prescribed rivers in which they washed the Fleece. Now it was thoroughly cleansed and acceptable to Zeus.

They sailed at noon from Minoa and continued all night, with a southerly wind filling their sail. The sky clouded over and, though the sea was not remarkably rough, this was the darkest night of the whole voyage, with no moon or stars or any other source of light at all. It was then that Euphemus lost the holy clod of earth given him by the Tritonian chieftain, for they shipped a deal of water about midnight. A black chaos descended from Heaven and nobody had the least notion how far the *Argo* had come or on what course; but they sailed on trustingly. At dawn the sky suddenly cleared and when the first rays of the rising sun gilded the bald cliffs of the island of Anaphe they saw that some deity had guided them well between the two rocky islets that lie off its southern shore at a distance of some four miles. They disembarked on a beach of yellow sand and lighted a fire of driftwood, hoping either to purchase a sheep or to hunt down a goat or some other animal for sacrifice to Radiant Apollo. But Anaphe at this time was not tenanted either by men or by any birds or beasts fit for sacrifice. The Argonauts were forced to pour libations of pure water over the burning brands, which made the Phaeacian girls laugh until their tears flowed.

Then Idas said: 'For laughing at us, girls, I will chastise your over-modest bottoms for you with the flat of my hand!'

The girls defended themselves with lighted brands and handfuls of sand, amid general merriment and much screaming; and Idas chastised each bottom in turn, though the girls burned him well for his pains and nearly blinded him with sand. This incident is now annually recalled by the pious Anapheans in their meatless sacrifice to Apollo; and with 'the hand of Idas', the girls are still merrily chastised in the God's honour.

It was at Anaphe, too, that Medea was led by a woodpecker to a hollow tree, the base of which, because of its bulges and bosses, closely resembled the shape of a matronly woman. Medea understood the language of birds and, on the advice of the woodpecker, desired Argus to fell the tree for her. This he did, and with axe, tar, and minium, obeying her instructions, he converted the base into a frightful statue of Thracian Artemis, which he carried down to the beach and placed, veiled in cloaks, aboard the *Argo*.

From Anaphe they sailed not to Aegina, as some pretend, but between happy Naxos and Paros of the white marble rocks; and in the night left Delos astern on the starboard counter. The three staunchest devotees of Apollo, namely Idmon, Iphitus, and Mopsus, were all dead by this time; had they been living, they would have prevailed on Jason to land on Delos and dance all day.

Tenos and Andros likewise were also left astern, and no adventure befell the Argonauts as, sailing along the holy coast of Euboea, they passed by the land of Cadmus, and Aulis, and the Locrian shore and rounded the flat and lentisk-clothed Cape Caeneon, where Euboea ends; and more than seven months after their departure they re-entered the Pagasaean Gulf and stepped boldly ashore upon the well-remembered beach.

CHAPTER FORTY-EIGHT

THE DEATH OF PELIAS

It was already night; nevertheless, Jason desired his comrades to light a fire of driftwood at once on the deserted beach of Pagasae, while he obtained suitable beasts for sacrifice to Apollo of Disembarkations in gratitude for the *Argo*'s safe return. They could find no dry driftwood, but, at the suggestion of Acastus, broke into a marine storehouse and lighted a fine blaze with the oars and benches that they found inside.

Jason went with Peleus to the same farmhouse from which he had once fetched wine for Hercules to drink, and rapped on the door with the pommel of his sword. The farmer who came, bill-hook in hand, to open the door, blinked confusedly at his visitors, having been aroused from his first sleep, the deepest and sweetest of the whole night; but then let out a shrill cry and tried to slam the door in their faces. Jason thrust his foot between the door and the door-post and asked him: 'Friend, why do you shrink from Jason, the only son of Aeson your King, and treat him as though he were a nocturnal robber?'

The farmer, trembling and stuttering, replied: 'O my lord Jason, you are dead, do you not know that? You were shipwrecked and drowned on your homeward voyage from Sicily two months ago. You are only the ghost of Jason, not Jason himself.'

Jason was vexed. He and Peleus together thrust the door open with their shoulders, and soon convinced the farmer of his mistake by pummelling him with their fists. Still trembling and quivering, he conducted them to his well-stocked byres, where by lantern light they chose two beautiful young bulls for sacrifice. These the farmer led out by their ringed snouts down to the misty beach, which was now splendidly illuminated, because the Argonauts were feeding the fire with tar and turpentine and resin from the storehouse. At once Jason immolated the bulls on the very altar that he had heaped to Apollo of Embarkations on the day that the *Argo* was launched.

When the victims had been jointed, and the flesh was hissing on spits with a savoury smell – they had no reason to placate the God with a holocaust but could confidently seat themselves as fellow-guests at his feast – the farmer, who had previously kept silence lest the sacrifice should be spoilt by ill-omened tears or cries, called Jason apart and gave him heavy news. He told him that his father Aeson and his mother Alcimede were both dead, forced by King Pelias to take their own lives by the drinking of bull's blood. Nor was this all: Hypsipyle, Queen of Lemnos, had lately come to Iolcos in search of Aeson, to whom (as she said) Jason had directed her to go if she ever found herself in distress. She was then exiled from Lemnos, as having preserved the life of old Thoäs, her uncle, when the universal vote had been to kill all the Lemnian men without remorse; for the Lemnian women had not been apprised of her action until the arrival of the Argonauts. When, in all innocence, she told Pelias that she was with child by Jason, he reflected that any child that she bore would be the rightful ruler of Phthiotis, and decided to destroy her as soon as possible; but, warned of his designs in good time, she fled to the shrine of Iolcan Artemis, where old Iphias, the Priestess, gave her sanctuary. However, Pelias protested to Iphias that, since Jason and Aeson were both dead, he was now Hypsipyle's nearest male kinsman, and her guardian; and he forced Iphias to give her up to him. Then he made away with her; but how or where the deed was done, the farmer said that he could not tell Jason with certainty.

It can well be imagined with what horror Jason learned the news of his parents murder and that of his unborn child. He called his comrades to him and told them: 'Let me propound a dark question: A certain evil usurper drives his rival overseas, the son of his bedridden brother, the legitimate ruler of the country; and is thought to have murdered this rival's unborn son; and is known to have forced the brother himself, and his wife with him, to drink bull's blood and die, having disturbed them at a private sacrifice and threatened to kill them himself with an axe and leave their bodies unburied should they refuse. What fate, comrades, does this fratricidal usurper deserve?'

Though none of the Argonauts, even the most simple-minded of them, could fail to understand which king Jason meant, all but three of them replied: 'Death by the sword!' Those who kept silence were Acastus, the son of Pelias; Admetus, his son-in-law; and Peleus the Myrmidon, his vassal. Jason asked each of them in turn: 'Do you not agree that death by the sword is the penalty for such unnatural crimes?'

Acastus answered: 'Let Admetus answer for me, lest by speaking my mind I be adjudged guilty of parricide and hounded by the Furies.'

Admetus answered as follows: 'I am married to the daughter of a king who may be guilty of the very acts of which you speak; for he was suckled by a wolf-hound bitch and has a savage nature in consequence. But before I give the same verdict as my comrades, let me first ask whether driving a nephew overseas is a crime justly punished by death, especially if the nephew goes off joyfully as captain over the boldest champions to be found in Greece and wins imperishable glory in a short time. Next, let me ask whether a child can be said to be murdered before it has been born, and whether a man can justly be punished by death for a crime that has not yet been proved against him. Lastly, let me ask whether a man can justly be punished as a murderer of his bedridden brother and his brother's wife, if these destroyed themselves voluntarily. Had they disregarded his threats, they might be alive still; the usurper would have thought twice before shedding a brother's blood, knowing well that his pious subjects would refuse allegiance to a fratricide. And how much credence should we give to a story in which a bedridden man is said to have been privately sacrificing a bull?'

These words of Admetus pleased some of his comrades, but by no means all.

Augeas of Elis said: 'Jason, we swore to obey you during the voyage in quest of the Fleece, and we have been faithful to our oath. Now that the voyage is ended and we are released from our discipline, I may speak freely. I declare that it would be madness for thirty-one men to assault the city of Iolcos in the hope of taking vengeance upon Pelias. You may be bound that the city gates are well guarded; and when last we were here five hundred men of the Royal Guard stood constantly under arms. Doubtless their numbers have since been increased. I for one am loth to hazard my life in so rash an enterprise as this promises to be. Consider, comrades! The flames of our sacrificial fire have surely been seen by the watchmen on the walls; and Pelias, if he has the least grain of sense, will know that something is astir down here at Pagasae, and will have summoned his trumpeter to sound the call to arms.'

Idas interrupted Augeas before he had well finished, shouting: 'As I told you once before, Augeas was born on a night of no moon; and the saying 'no moon, no man' is confirmed in him. But I, for one, am ready to go up with you at once, Jason, before Pelias becomes aware of our presence. Let us take him by surprise and sack his well-furnished palace. If he believes us to have been cast away in shipwreck, as the farmer here assures us, then the flames of our fire will not alarm him. He will conclude, from the colour of the flames, that a fire has broken out in one of his storehouses.'

Castor and Pollux agreed with Idas, for once; but Autolycus, speaking for the Thessalians in a body, said: 'No, no! Although we stand by you, Jason, through thick and thin, not considering this expedition ended until the Fleece shall have been restored safely to the back of the sacred Ram image of Mount Laphystios, we beg you to be prudent. Let us not go up against Iolcos in a vengeful fury, as the seven champions once went against Thebes, and be destroyed for our pains. Let us rather set on foot a general war against your savage uncle, each first returning to his own tribe or city and there raising a large company of volunteers, so that many columns at once may converge upon Iolcos from all sides.'

Then Peleus gave his answer: 'I am Prince of the Myrmidons, as you know, and a vassal of King Pelias. I will never consent to declare war against him. If you intend to assault Iolcos you must first kill me, who am under a debt of gratitude to Pelias. He is of a savage and treacherous nature, I grant, but he raised me up years ago when I was a miserable suppliant, and I refuse to earn the name of traitor by opposing him. Besides, if several large columns converge on Phthiotis, what will be the fate of my own lands and my wretched subjects, and the patrimony of my dear comrade Acastus? Have you ever seen a herd of wild-boar rooting up lily-bulbs in a peaceful dell? Do you think that the common soldiery will behave with less greed and fury in my dear land, however wisely controlled by their officers?'

Periclymenus the wizard addressed Peleus in winning tones: 'Dear Peleus, an accident disposed of your foster-brother whom you hated, and of your father-in-law whom you succeeded at Phthia as Prince of the Myrmidons. It is a pity, Ant man, that the death of Pelias, whom you have never professed to love, cannot be brought about by another accident of the same sort.'

Peleus grinned as he answered: 'With the drowning of Dictys, the Colchian Vice-Admiral, the triad of accidents was duly completed.'

Nobody else said anything for a while. At last Ascalaphus asked: 'Medea, tell us why you have brought the hollow image of Thracian Artemis here, all the way from Anaphe?'

She answered at once: 'The woodpecker sent by the Mother ordered me to do so. And now that you have asked me this question, let everyone keep holy silence for as long as I keep my head covered in my cloak. When I thrust it out again, listen attentively to my words, which, however dark an enigma at first hearing, will give a single answer to every question that has been propounded tonight. I am about to consult the Mother.'

She threw the purple cloak over her head, and not a sound was heard from beneath it, although the folds shook and flapped and bellied out, every now and again, as if filled with a snake-tailed wind; soon the cloak floated all about her, the folds standing out stiff like the sides of a tent, then fell again slowly, clasping her close. This sight they witnessed by the bright light of the fire. At length Medea thrust out her head and spoke: 'These are the words of the Mother: "Tomorrow, about noon, Pelias shall die a bloody death of his own choosing. Argonauts, you shall be guiltless of his blood; I alone shall exact the vengeance due to me. Abstain from war against Phthiotis, children, and from all acts of violence. Atalanta of Calydon alone of you all shall go up to Iolcos; and she shall go unarmed, under the authority of my servant Medea. Do you row the *Argo* back to Methone, there drawing her up on the beach; disguise her with the lopped branches of oaks; and lie hid yourselves among the thickets, allowing no passer-by to report your presence to Iolcos. A thin red pillar will arise from the smoke-hole of the palace hall when my vengeance is accomplished.

Then come out in haste, row to Iolcos, whipping the water with your oars, and take possession of the city unopposed."'

The Argonauts gazed at one another in bewilderment, yet they had abundant proof of the powers that Medea commanded and none of them had the least doubt but that the Goddess spoke the truth from her mouth. They therefore said not another word, and when Medea began to borrow from them ostrich-skins, bear-pelts, head-dresses of Colchian ibis feathers, and other trophies of the voyage, none of them refused her whatever she might need for the execution of her design. Then they climbed aboard the *Argo* again and rowed away with muffled oars, first smothering the altar-fire with sand; but Medea stayed behind on the beach with Atalanta and the twelve Phaeacian girls, and with the hollow image of Artemis.

When the *Argo* was out of sight, Medea said to Atalanta: 'Dear girl, I am aware that you hate Jason, though causelessly, and despise me for loving him; but let that not prevent you now from obeying the orders of the Mother. I bear you no ill will, for at least we are not rivals for the love of the same man, and I do not blame you in the least degree for the murder of my father Aeëtes, which was the work of your mistress Artemis.'

Atalanta smiled and answered: 'Medea, I am a woman as you are, and though I may causelessly hate Jason I cannot find it in my heart to hate or mistrust his wife. I am well aware that the Love Spite delights in making fools of the most kindly, most intelligent, and most loyal of our sex.'

They kissed each other on both cheeks, and Medea sent Atalanta ahead to give old Iphias a secret warning; the Goddess Artemis was coming to Iolcos in person to punish Pelias for having violated her sanctuary when he removed Queen Hypsipyle of Lemnos from it by force – Iphias must purify herself and be ready with all her Fish maidens to welcome the Goddess into the city at daybreak. Atalanta was to say: 'Do not be afraid, Iphias, whatever marvels you may witness. For the Goddess, who has appeared to me in a dream, is of most frightful appearance. She is coming all the way from the foggy land of the warlike, red-haired Hyperboreans, from the great triangular island lying northward from Gaul and abounding in red cattle. And do not wonder if she speaks with a double mouth, pretending love and affection for bestial Pelias; because the Goddess loves to raise up before she casts down, so that the fall may be the greater.'

Atalanta ran off and entered the city unchallenged by the guards; she knew the secret way under the walls that led to the shrine of Artemis. She warned Iphias, in the exact words given her by Medea, what to expect at dawn.

Meanwhile Medea procured an unblemished male lamb from the farmer of Pagasae and put it to sleep with the same soporific drug that she had used against the Serpent of Prometheus; she then concealed it inside the hollow statue and set the statue on a light cradle which she found in the marine storehouse. She tricked out her Phaeacian maids in the strange disguises that she had borrowed from the Argonauts, first whitening their faces with gypsum and daubing their hands and feet with vermilion dye. Then she led them in procession along the coast road from Pagasae to Iolcos, and they carried the Goddess by turns behind them until they came within sight of the city walls.

They met nobody on the road, for the night was of ill omen in Phthiotis – the one night of the year when ghosts were permitted to walk abroad freely and every prudent man kept within doors. But Medea had no fear of ghosts and at grey dawn she gave the girls ivy to chew, which intoxicated them, and herself uttered a frantic screech and led them raving towards the gate. The face of the statute of Artemis had been painted with a smile of irresistible glee and a frown of implacable fury, and Medea was clothed in all the shining majesty of a Colchian priestess of Brimo and wore a golden kite-faced mask. But under the mask her face was painted with wrinkles to resemble that of a centenarian crone, and she had assumed a perruque with hair of that yellowish-white colour which comes with extreme old age; her hands were also painted with wrinkles and she hobbled on one leg. The frightened sentinels fled with howls from their posts, but Iphias and her Fish maidens came eagerly hurrying out from the shrine to unbolt the gate for their Goddess.

Medea called in a cracked voice to the people of Iolcos to come boldly from their houses and do reverence to Artemis. At her summons a great multitude poured out from every door and alley along the whole length of the street leading from the gate to the palace, and abased themselves before the image. At her command they all kept holy silence, and she informed Iphias in their hearing that Artemis had come down from the foggy land of the Hyperboreans, in a car drawn by a team of flying serpents (now tethered outside the gate), in order to bring good fortune to the Iolcans and their Sovereign. Then she encouraged them all to cheer and dance, and the Phaeacian girls inspired the whole city, thus startled from sleep, into a religious frenzy; raging here and there among the crowd as wildly as the women of the Argive Cow sorority when they perform the gadfly dance in Hera's honour. The Iolcans beat gongs and blew trumpets and, in a word, acted like madmen or madwomen.

Medea hobbled on towards the palace, and when the servants at the gate-house shrieked and fled she burst in without ceremony. There in the hall she found Pelias in his nightcap and with his robes of state loosely girded about him, enquiring in confusion what was afoot. His four daughters were with him, as amazed as he. The Phaeacian girls raced into the hall behind Medea and began dancing crazily on the tables and benches until she sternly called them to order; then the statue of Artemis, upright on her cradle, was borne solemnly in by Iphias and the Fish maidens and set up on a table, fronting Pelias. A great concourse of the commonalty followed behind, but Medea drove them all out and bolted the door after them.

She addressed Pelias, croaking in barbarous Greek, as follows:

'Pelias, Pelias, Pelias, I am the Chief Priestess of Artemis, the Bearish One, Lady of the Lake, Horse-finder, Huntress, Goddess of Good Fame, newly arrived at Iolcos from the giant-breeding land of the Hyperboreans. I and my maidens in a single night, riding in a row astride a pair of winged serpents, have travelled across Gaul of the Druids and over the High Alps and through rugged Istria and Epiros and fertile Thessaly, while the Goddess sat in her car behind us, arms akimbo, urging us on. Ha, what is the Goddess's business here, do you ask? Listen and I will reveal it to you. Listen, I say, and do not fidget, you four slender princesses who crowd about the throne of Pelias. Do not fidget, I say!'

With that she terrified the daughters of Pelias by hurling a silver apple over their heads, which exploded with a roar like thunder against the wall behind them and filled the hall with acrid smoke. It seemed to them that white snakes with flashing eyes wriggled in the air among the wreaths of smoke. They were terrified nearly to distraction, but none of them dared move a finger, for fear of worse things.

Medea proceeded: 'The Goddess, some of whose titles I have declared to you, and whom in our land we name Samothea, called me to her not long ago and said: "Gaze into your crystal ball, eldest and ugliest of my children, and tell me what you see there." Gazing, I answered: "Goddess, I see everything that exists. In this glass I can view the whole extent of the habitable world, your ancient dominions, set like a bright island in the circling stream of Ocean." She said again: "Look carefully again, Kite-face, with a piercing glance, and inform me for my satisfaction exactly where in all my ancient dominions is to be found the most pious of all living kings." I searched and searched for fifty days and nights, gazing ceaselessly into the glass, until at last my eye, that had travelled up the eastern coast of Greece from Laconia and Argolis onwards through Attica, Boeotia, and Locris, passed into the kingdom of Phthiotis and lighted contentedly upon the well-roofed palace of Iolcos, and on the comely person of white-bearded Pelias, son of Poseidon. I said to the Goddess Samothea: "Pelias is the most pious of all living kings. He has rededicated to you, in your name of Artemis, the shrine that hitherto belonged to the outrageous Nymph Goddess, risking the displeasure of the Nymph Goddess by this act, yet asking no reward of you. He has also burned countless sacrifices to your majesty and honours your name above that of all Goddesses in existence, not even excepting Hera, the wife of Zeus." Then Samothea answered me: "It is well, Crook-nose! Let us go up now in our snake-drawn chariot to fly half across the world to Greece, and reward Pelias suitably. Let us divest him of hateful old age and restore his body to perpetual youth, and his impotent member to virility, so that he may reign here at Iolcos for ever, outliving all his rival monarchs and all his subjects. Let him take a young wife to his bosom and beget on her worthier sons than dead Acastus, whom lately I cast away upon the rocky coast of Libya in punishment for an unfilial act of desertion.'"

Then while Pelias marvelled, yet doubted – for he was a shrewd old man and not easily deceived – Medea reminded him of many strange particulars of his life that she had gleaned from Acastus; and from Jason; and from Periclymenus, son of Neleus, the brother to Pelias; and from Echion, the son of Hermes, whose business it was, as a herald, to learn and remember all that was spoken about the private lives of the great men of Greece. Then she said: 'You doubt, Pelias, you doubt, I read your innermost thoughts. Do not doubt; to doubt is dangerous. However, the Goddess has graciously consented that I should give you evident proof of her powers by a transformation performed upon my own person. Child' (here she addressed Alcestis, the eldest daughter of Pelias and wife to Admetus), 'fetch me pure water in a sacrificial goblet of painted earthenware ; for my lips may not touch metal.'

When Alcestis fetched water in a painted goblet, Medea brought it to the image of the Goddess and prayed in the Colchian tongue, which Pelias took for that of the Hyperboreans, being equally ignorant of both; and flames seemed to leap up from the goblet as Medea gulped down some of the hissing water. She shrieked aloud and darted into a little wine-closet near by, the door of which stood ajar; then closed the door behind her and shrieked again terribly, so that tears burst from the eyes of every woman in the hall. Soon the noise of shrieking was moderated, and the sound of low, sweet laughter rose instead. Medea emerged young, beautiful, golden-haired, and without a single wrinkle upon her face or hands. For with what remained of the water and a Libyan sponge she had thoroughly cleansed herself, and had torn off her yellowish-white perruque.

A great sigh of wonder went up from the spectators.

Pelias said, his voice quavering for eagerness: 'I do not doubt. Do with me as you wish, Holy One! I consent in the name of the Goddess. Make me young again!'

Medea, no longer hobbling, went up to Pelias and gazed at him steadfastly. She narrowed the pupils of her eyes until they were as small as sesame-grains, and waved her hands about his face like white weeds that sway gently in the current of a stream. 'Sleep!' she commanded in her most tuneful voice.

The white head of Pelias sank upon his breast, and he was fast asleep in an instant.

'Lay him upon his royal couch!' Medea ordered. The princesses obeyed her and she followed them to the bedchamber. When the doors were closed, she said to them quietly: 'Children, do not be frightened by the commands that I must now deliver to you. Before your father can be reborn as a young man, he must first be cut into pieces and boiled in a cauldron of magical herbs and spices. This act of violence must be performed by his own loving children, because no other persons have the power to work the miracle. Take knives now and hatchets and sharpen them well upon whetstones, so that no deformity will appear upon his new body from any jagged or ill-managed stroke upon his old.'

The daughters, whose names were Alcestis, Evadne, Asteropaea, and Amphinome, quailed. Each looking for encouragement to the other, they refused in a body the task assigned to them.

Alcestis said: 'I am Alcestis. I object. I will never shed my father's blood – no, not though father Poseidon himself should order it.'

Evadne said: 'I am Evadne. I also object. It is the common fate of men to grow old. I should loathe to call a man 'father' who looked younger than I; my friends would deride me. And it is easier for a woman to bear patiently with the spleen of a petulant old man than with the rage of a head-strong youth.'

Asteropaea said: 'I am Asteropaea. I also object. A young father would find a young stepmother to tyrannize over us. As things are now, we super-vise the royal household ourselves, leaving to our old father only the management of the wine, the armoury, and the sacrificial instruments; we lead a happy enough life. Why should we wish for so strange an alteration of our affairs?'

Lastly Amphinome said: 'I am Amphinome. I also object. Why must our father be cut to pieces like an old ram and boiled in a cauldron? It was enough for you merely to gulp at a goblet of hissing fiery water and retire into a wine-closet; you became young without shedding a drop of your blood.'

Medea dismissed Alcestis, saying: 'You are Alcestis, and a married woman. Go far away from this holy spot. Only maidens are permitted to take part in the holy rites of Artemis.' She saw that Alcestis alone shrank in piety and love from the atrocious deed, whereas the other three hated the old man.

When Alcestis had been bound to silence and had gone, Medea said to the remaining princesses: 'I will answer all your objections in turn. Evadne, do not fear to call a young man "father". The Gods are eternally young, and Pelias has never complained, I think, that his father Poseidon is more vigorous than himself and still able to beget sons and daughters. Your friends will not deride but honour you. Besides, if Pelias is often petulant, this is because he suffers the cruel aches and pains of old age; I undertake that when he is restored to youth he will become as sweet-tempered as yourself. Asteropaea, do not fear a young stepmother. So long as Pelias has need of you to manage his affairs he will never consent to let you marry; but as soon as he is young again, I undertake that he will find a splendid match for you, worthy of your birth, beauty, and talents. You shall be a Queen and rule over a rich and populous land. As for you,

Amphinome, you must understand that the magical formula used for rejuvenating old men necessarily differs from that used for rejuvenating old women; nor was my transformation by any means a painless one.'

Amphinome was silent, not wishing to offend the Priestess.

Medea then said: 'Amphinome, you spoke of cutting an old ram into pieces. Tell me now, is there not an aged ram in your palace, the sacred ram of Zeus? Bring him out of his stable to me. I will kill him and cut him into pieces, and boil him in a cauldron with magic herbs. You will then see him reborn as a lamb again, from the worm of life that inhabits the hollow of his spine. Soon he will crop again the rich meadow grass and the juicy shoots of the terebinth; from which he turns now with a sigh of weariness.'

Amphinome replied: 'If you can perform this miracle upon the old ram of Zeus, I will believe that you can do the same with my father. Nevertheless, I am a pious Achaean girl. I will not lay violent hands upon the ram myself, for fear of Father Zeus.'

Evadne fetched the ram, a beast of sixteen years of age, with bleary eyes, no front teeth, a mangy fleece, and a tremendous head of horns. It was Amphinome's daily task to feed him with milk-gruel, and curry him and sweep out his stable.

Medea led the stinking old ram into the hall where a cauldron of pure water was bubbling on the fire, suspended from a hook in the chimney; ready to boil up the customary broth of mutton and barley for the royal household to breakfast upon. It was the very cauldron that Hercules had dinted with his fist and, when filled to the brim, held fifty gallons. Medea dismissed everyone from the hall except the three unmarried princesses. She ordered them to close every door and bolt it fast. Then, uttering long prayers in the Colchian language, she hacked the ram into pieces with an axe of black obsidian and tossed them into the cauldron, together with packets of aromatic herbs and barks which she drew, one by one, from the embroidered wallet by her side. She began to utter incantations and stirred the cauldron with a wooden spoon until at last, uttering a glad shout, she cried in Greek: 'Look, look! The maggot rears his head! The transformation has begun!'

She sprinkled a powder upon the burning brands, so that they crackled furiously and gave out excessive heat. A blood-red light glowed throughout the hall, the cauldron seethed over and thick steam hid the whole chimney-corner from sight.

As the smoke cleared, a sudden bleating was heard and a lamb, six months old, with little horns budding from its forehead, skipped and bucked about the hall in fright, and fled to Amphinome as to its mother. Amphinome gazed at the lamb in wonder and then ran over to the cauldron. Nothing was left in it but a sort of broth and a few sodden wisps of old wool.

Medea spoke again to the three princesses: 'Evadne, Asteropaea, and

Amphinome, you have witnessed a miracle. Hesitate no longer but obey the wishes of your father, and carry out the orders of Artemis. Be sure that when you have done so, your names will never be forgotten by poets. Yet strike all together, that none may hereafter claim the glory of having dealt the first blow; and leave the backbone entire between haunches and ribs, for there the worm of life resides.'

Resolutely returning to the bed-chamber, each with a sharp axe in her hand (taken from the armoury which adjoined the hall), they whetted the blades with a whetstone, passed from hand to hand; and soon Medea heard the chopping sound that she longed to hear and the shrill scream of Pelias as he awoke from sleep.

The Argonauts, drowsing at noon in the oak-thickets of Methone, were aroused by Lynceus: 'Look, comrades!' he cried. 'Red smoke is rising from the smoke-hole of the palace of Pelias.' They started from their hiding-place, ran down to the *Argo*, launched her, and were soon rowing at a furious rate towards the beach of Iolcos. They leaped ashore under arms, and found the principal gate of the city unguarded; for Medea had given orders that nobody should bar the way of the Goddess, who would shortly return by the gate through which she had entered and would resume her seat in the waiting serpent-drawn car. They ran in, and coursed down the main street, silently, like well-trained hunting dogs.

The townspeople wondered at them but nobody opposed them, for their appearance was sudden, and it was only when they had passed out of sight that one neighbour turned to another and asked gaspingly: 'Did you see the same as I saw? Did you see the pale armed ghosts of the Argonauts pass by in a body, with Jason, son of Aeson, and Acastus, son of Pelias, at their head? How is this? Did the night of ghosts not end with the dawn, as we had supposed?'

When they entered the palace, Medea herself opened the door of the hall to them and cried out: 'Alas, Argonauts, you come too late to save Pelias from destruction. His three daughters have turned parricides. They have barbarously chopped him into little pieces and are now boiling them in a cauldron, with as little concern as though they were preparing mutton broth for their royal breakfast.'

CHAPTER FORTY-NINE

THE FLEECE IS RESTORED TO ZEUS

That evening the Argonauts feasted in the hall of Pelias, after first fumigating it well with brimstone and Arabian incense, and sprinkling the walls with lustral water inside and out. The three axes and the great cauldron they dedicated to the Goddess Persephone, in whose shrine outside the city the three guilty princesses had already taken sanctuary. Against Medea they dared to do nothing, but every man and woman except Jason avoided her glance and company: they would pale even if her shadow fell across their path. However, she pleased them well, while they sat at dessert, by rising up and publicly urging Jason to resign the throne of Phthiotis to his cousin Acastus as a free gift, without delay. How could he do otherwise? Had he not once declared before witnesses at a popular sacrifice that he laid no claim to the wealth of his uncle? A king without wealth, she said, is a spear-head without a shaft, and since Acastus would not willingly forfeit his inheritance, would it be prudent or seemly for King Jason to go ragged and beg crusts and scraps of meat from his rich cousin's table? Besides, though she had not been present in the royal bed-chamber when the axes began to fall, she could not risk the displeasure of a certain ghost by taking up her residence in Iolcos.

Jason brooded and would not at first reply. But when his companions playfully pelted him with crusts and scraps of meat he answered that he would follow her advice, though it grieved him to resign what was his own and so appear to be slighting his father Aeson and his grandfather Cretheus; and as a reward for his magnanimity he called upon his comrades to assist him, if necessary, in securing the throne of Ephyra for Medea and himself. This with one voice they all promised to do; for they feared Medea's anger if they refused.

The next day, seated upon the Phthiotid throne, gloriously crowned, robed, and armed with the ram-topped sceptre of Athamas, which Jason himself had put into his hand, King Acastus called for holy silence while he pronounced sentence of perpetual banishment from Iolcos against Medea, Atalanta, Jason, Idas, Castor, Pollux, and Periclymenus, as either instigators of his father's murder or accessories to it, and against the murderesses themselves, his three sisters. This sentence caused no surprise since it would have been unfilial in him to pronounce any other, and he showed remarkable mildness in permitting all of the guilty ones to remain at Iolcos until the funeral Games of Pelias should have been held.

These Games Acastus solemnly inaugurated that same day, and who should arrive, just as they were about to begin, but Hercules, lately returned from the island of Hesperides with the basketful of sacred oranges that he had been ordered to fetch back for King Eurystheus. The Argonauts at once crowded about him, kissing his great dirty knees and hailing him as their saviour from death in the wilderness of Libya.

He displayed the oranges with satisfaction, saying: 'Smell them, if you please, comrades. They confer long life. But do not touch or handle the sacred fruit.' Hercules was not drunk and had not yet dined, but was affable beyond the ordinary: for an oracle of Artemis had informed him that he would soon beget a daughter at last. He seemed to have forgotten the very name of Hylas, for he never spoke of the boy; they were careful not to do so either. When he had feasted at the palace for an hour or two he consented to become President of the Games.

Telamon of Aegina made the longest cast with the quoit; Meleager, the longest cast with the javelin; Euphemus of Taenaron won the two-horse chariot race. And Peleus won the wrestling contest, for Castor, who would otherwise have been the winner, was competing instead in the four-horse chariot race: Peleus twice hurled Jason to the ground with the savage throw called the flying mare – for now that the *Argo* was safely home he needed to show his captain no tenderness or mercy.

Castor's four-horse team outdistanced those of all his Thessalian rivals; yet the team consisted wholly of Thessalian horses, than which there is no better breed in the world, not even the Laconian. Corinthian Glaucus also entered for this race. He was Medea's cousin-german, being the son of Sisyphus. It is still unknown why his team took fright at the first post and not only dragged him out of the chariot but turned on him and began eating great mouthfuls of his flesh. Some say that the ghost of Pelias had baulked them; others that Glaucus had offended Poseidon, Protector of Horses, in some way; but the common rumour is that Medea had poisoned the team with the herb hippomanes, fearing that Glaucus might be an obstacle to her at Corinth if ever he claimed the throne of Asopia. In any case, Glaucus was killed and his ghost has ever since haunted the isthmus of Corinth, delighting to baulk the teams in the four-horse contest at the Isthmian Games.

Pollux won the boxing contest, but too easily to please the better-bred spectators, though the commonalty roared for joy to see the blood spurt from the mouths and noses of his inexpert opponents. Hercules entered merrily for the all-in wrestling contest, and Alcestis, for whom he had the greatest respect, persuaded him to spare the life of his opponent, the Centaur Nessus, when he had broken his leg and three ribs and had him at his mercy. Phalerus of Athens won the archery contest, shooting at a straw doll dangling in the wind from a tree and piercing it through the throat at the very first shot.

The competitors for the foot-race were Argeus and Melanion, the younger sons of Phrixus, and two strangers, Iphiclus the Phocian and one Neotheus. Iphiclus came in first, with a long lead. He was a Minyan, and his winning of this race has therefore misled some poets into describing him as an Argonaut, which he was not; and neither, for that matter, were Iphiclus half-brother to Hercules, or Iphiclus the uncle of Castor and Pollux, as has also been alleged. It would have needed a fleet of ships to accommodate all the heroes for whom the vanity of their descendants has claimed the illustrious title of Argonauts.

Atalanta entered for the hop, skip, and jump; but when Acastus measured out the jumping-pit and had the earth loosened and raked and levelled, Atalanta raised a protest. She declared that Hercules, as President, should have undertaken the task, and that Acastus, though King of Phthiotis, had no right to meddle with the preparations for any of the contests. Hercules obligingly measured out a new jumping-pit, the further edge of which lay at the customary distance of fifty feet from the starting-line, and the nearer edge half that distance. But the fifty feet measured by Hercules were longer by a half than those measured out by Acastus, who was a short-footed man. The propriety of Atalanta's objection was soon proved, when she jumped to the very end of the pit marked out by Hercules: if she had made as long a jump from the edge of the pit marked out by Acastus, she would have flown clean across and broken her ankles on stony ground not loosened by the mattocks. This wonderful jump was no novelty to Atalanta, who was accustomed to keep her legs supple by the buttock dance, leaping up and down on a greased cow-skin and kicking her buttocks with alternate feet: she could do a thousand kicks and more, where any common athlete would have slipped from the cow-skin at the first or second kick.

The sword fight at the barrow of Pelias was performed between an Iolcan named Pilus and Ascalaphus, son of Ares, the Argonaut. It often happens in contests of this sort that one of the swordsmen tries to excite the admiration of the crowd by laying about the other with unnecessary vigour; then play turns to earnest. On this occasion, Pilus foolishly ran Ascalaphus through the fleshy part of the thigh with his sword, narrowly missing his genitals; and the pain vexed Ascalaphus so much that he retaliated with a back-handed sweep that cut off the Iolcan's sword-hand at the wrist. Pilus died from rage and loss of blood, having fought on with his left hand and refused to let his friends bind up the pitiful stump. The death caused general satisfaction, since Pilus was a man without kinsmen to avenge him and the ghost of Pelias drank well of the spouting blood – as keen-sighted Lynceus testified.

Orpheus arrived suddenly, at the close of the Games. He was in settled ill-health and his voice was no longer what it had been. Nevertheless, he sang a long and exceedingly sweet song about the voyage of the *Argo*, not glozing over any unhappy or discreditable event, as many poets have since done; and was by general consent crowned with a chaplet of sweet-smelling bay. He had preserved, as in honey, the memory of several glorious particulars that might otherwise have been forgotten even by the Argonauts themselves. However, the priests of Dodona later complained against him that the song was in part disrespectful to Zeus, and forbade him to sing it again under pain of the God's displeasure; so that only snatches of it now survive.

When the Games were over, the Argonauts made their last voyage in company, sailing down the Euboean Gulf until they came to the town of Opus. There they disembarked, entrusted their ship to the care of the Opians, and marched across the hills until they came to the Copaic Lake and to the famous city of Boeotian Orchomenos; where they made their devotions at the shining white tomb of their ancestor Minyas.

From Orchomenos they proceeded to Mount Laphystios, and there at last Medea, on behalf of Prometheus, restored the Fleece to the oaken image of the Ram in his shrine near the summit, while the others burned rich sacrifices and sang hymns. However, Zeus vouchsafed no sign of pleasure or gratitude, not so much as a distant roll of thunder, which abashed them all. They had counted upon some extraordinary dispensation, in the foolish belief that, because Zeus invariably punishes his devotees for any injury that has been done him, whether voluntarily or involuntarily, he will also show gratitude for benefits conferred.

Hercules had come with them, on his way to Mycenae with the sacred oranges, and, though he did not ascend Mount Laphystios, yet it was he rather than Orchomenan Ascalaphus, or anyone else, who compelled the Orchomenan Council to restore to the sons of Phrixus the inheritance of their grandfather Athamas, and thus make good a promise of Jason's. The sons of Phrixus feasted Hercules well for his kindness.

Then followed the first dispersal of the Argonauts, those of Thessaly and Phthiotis travelling northward on foot, after embracing with tears their comrades in so many hazards. But Hercules, Jason, Argus, and the rest hired Boeotian oarsmen and fetched the *Argo* down the Euboean Strait. They circumnavigated Attica, and set Phalerus ashore at Athens, where they reverently greeted the King and Queen Archons and all went up together to the shrine of Athena, giving humble thanks for her continued care. Then they re-embarked and, passing by the island of Salamis, came to the isthmus of Corinth.

Jason beached the ship at Cenchreae, and sent Echion forward as his herald to the people of Ephyra, to announce the arrival of their rightful Queen, Medea. This was a charge that pleased Echion well, since he wished to convert into truth the fiction which his father Hermes had put into his mouth when he disembarked at the Royal Quay of Aea. He found his task the easier, because there had been a drought and a pestilence in Corinth that summer, much as he had said, and the Ephyrans were weary of the harsh and capricious rule of the Achaean usurper, who had styled himself Corinthus.

Echion stood in the market-place and informed the Ephyrans that Jason, glorious son of Aeson, had fulfilled his quest of the Fleece and, in response to an oracle, had brought home Medea the fair-haired sorceress, daughter of Aeëtes, to be their Queen; and that, freely resigning to others his claims to the thrones of Lemnos and Phthiotis, Jason had consented to marry Medea and become their loving King. Echion told them further that Castor and Pollux, Atalanta and Meleager, Melampus and Periclymenus, Idas and Lynceus, and the great Hercules himself, were on their way from Cenchreae with arms in their hands, to ensure that justice was done, however tardily, to the name of Aeëtes. The Ephyrans listened with joy and made an immediate uprising. The usurper Corinthus fled, and the populace streamed down to the coast to welcome the royal pair.

Echion's one regret was that the people of Corinthian Asopia, the former kingdom of Sisyphus, could not by any means be persuaded to revolt against Creon, their unyielding Achaean King, and thus join the double kingdom into a single one, as he had prophesied; for Creon had married Glauce, the daughter of Sisyphus, and was ruling in her name.

Jason decided to dedicate the *Argo*, with all her oars and tackle, to the God Poseidon, in gratitude for the great wave that had saved her from the rocks of the Libyan shore. He therefore sailed her eastward from Cenchreae to the narrowest part of the isthmus, where she was duly beached, and put on rollers, and rolled inland to the enclosure of Poseidon. There Argus said a proud farewell to his lovely ship, being the last to quit her at the final dispersal of the Argonauts.

CHAPTER FIFTY

WHAT BECAME OF THE ARGONAUTS

Acastus reigned in Iolcos for some years, but fell out at last with his dear friend Peleus. They quarrelled about a flock of one hundred sheep which Peleus paid as indemnity for the accidental murder of a young son of Acastus; however, it was not Peleus himself who had struck the blow but one of his drunken Myrmidon retainers. The flock was set upon by a pack of wolves on the way from Phthia to Iolcos, so that only a few sheep survived. When Acastus demanded more sheep, to replace those that had perished, Peleus refused, on the ground that the wolves had made their attack nearer to Iolcos than to Phthia. In the ensuing war Acastus was defeated, captured, and put to death, and Peleus made himself master of all Phthiotis; but he owed his victory to the powerful help of Castor and Pollux, who brought chariots from Sparta. Peleus lived to a good age and survived his famous son Achilles, an initiate of the Centaur Horse fraternity, who was killed at the siege of Troy.

As for Atalanta, she returned to Calydon in company with Meleager, going by way of Arcadia for the sake of the hunting. Coming to the sanctuary of Artemis on Mount Artemisios, where Hercules had caught the white doe of Artemis and so fulfilled his Third Labour, she resigned from the Goddess's service, hanging up her bow, javelin, and girdle and offering nameless sacrifices. She companied at last with Meleager in a thicket on Mount Taphiassos, not far from Calydon; for desire compelled her against her will. Now, Melanion was journeying on foot from Orchomenos to Calydon, intending to ask Jasius for Atalanta's hand in marriage. By chance he came upon Meleager and Atalanta asleep together in the thicket; but feared to do them any injury. He passed on into Calydon to the palace of King Oeneus, where he spitefully told Cleopatra, Meleager's wife, what he had seen. Cleopatra went in a rage to the apartment of her mother-in-law Queen Althaea, who was not there and searched in the Queen's chests until at last she found what she needed: a charred brand of nut wood. For when Meleager was born Althaea had been warned by an augur that her child would live only so long as a certain brand remained unburned on her hearth; she had seized it, extinguished it, and secreted it in a chest. Cleopatra, vexed beyond endurance, now took up the brand and thrust it back into the fire on the hearth; whereupon Meleager, asleep in Atalanta's arms under a bean-rick not many miles off, uttered a loud cry and began to burn with fever. He was dead before morning. Thus the prophecy of Aphrodite was justified, which declared that the man for whose sake Atalanta first hung up her girdle would die on the same night.

When Atalanta became aware that she was with child she consented to marry Melanion, not knowing that he had been the prime cause of Meleager's death; and the child that was born to her, by name Parthenopaeus, she fathered on Melanion. But upon learning from Althaea what had occurred, she refused to cohabit with him and he won little from his marriage but her hate and scorn. Some say that Melanion defeated Atalanta in a foot-race by dropping golden apples for her to pick up, and so gained her as his bride, but this is a misreading of an ancient fresco of the funeral Games of Pelias shown in the palace of Iolcos. Atalanta is there depicted, crouched on the ground, in the act of winning the jumping contest, and close by her, in a chair, sits Hercules, as president of the Games, with the golden oranges tumbled at his feet, one of which she seems to be picking up; and just ahead of her is shown the foot-race in which Iphiclus the Phocian came in first and Melanion last; all the runners but Melanion have disappeared from the fresco, because a new door has been pierced in the wall at that point, so that Melanion appears to be winning the race from Atalanta. So much for these jealous lovers.

The quarrel between Idas and Lynceus, on the one hand, and Castor and Pollux on the other was patched up for a time, until one day they joined forces in a marauding expedition against Ancaeus of Tegea. They drove off a hundred and one head of prime cattle, pretending that Ancaeus had cheated them long before, at Bebrycos, when the palace spoils were distributed, by withholding from the common stock four valuable neck-laces of amber, emerald, and gold. Ancaeus, whose conscience troubled him in the matter of the necklaces, did not go in pursuit of the brothers; but left the vengeance to his father Poseidon, to whom he had already promised ten of the best bulls in the herd as a gift.

The four marauders sat down together close to the spot where the fron-tiers of Laconia, Arcadia, and Messenia meet, and disputed not very amicably how the herd was to be divided among them. At last Idas said: 'Let us have sport, comrades. I will carve this bull-calf into four equal parts, and roast them on spits, one part for each of us four. Let the man who first finishes his share and leaves nothing but bare bones be awarded half the cattle, choosing the fifty that please him best; and let the one who finishes next take the remaining fifty.'

Castor and Pollux agreed: Lynceus was a slow eater, because he had broken his front teeth in a boxing match, and both twins fancied them-selves better trenchermen than Idas. But no sooner had the hissing joints of beef been taken from the spit and allocated by lot, than Idas began tearing at his joint with teeth and dagger, bolting the succulent beef almost without chewing. He had finished every morsel and sucked the marrow-bones too before the others had well started. Like the loyal brother that he was, Idas then went to the assistance of Lynceus, carving the beef into handy strips for him and swallowing a marvellous deal more himself, so that Lynceus finished second, a little ahead of Pollux, before whom several rib-bones and part of the inwards lay still untasted.

Idas and Lynceus rose up, replete but not incapacitated, and drove off all the cattle with a mocking farewell. Pollux, with his mouth full, called to them to stay, objecting that Lynceus had not finished his portion by himself; but he did not pursue them until, by finishing his own portion, he should have established his claim to half the cattle – for he did not dispute that Idas had justly earned the first choice of fifty. Castor however, who was vexed at being slowest eater of them all, left his joint unfinished and ran off. He took a short-cut over the mountains and laid an ambush for Idas and Lynceus, concealing himself in a hollow oak sacred to Zeus. He guessed that they would pass close by the oak: it grew near the tomb of their father Aphareus, where they doubtless would pour a generous liba-tion of bulls' blood.

Lynceus with his keen sight discovered the hiding-place from half a mile away, for the tip of a swan's feather from Castor's head-dress showed through a chink in the tree. He signed to Idas to creep around behind the herd and spring the ambush. Idas did so; he charged suddenly at the tree with his spear and pierced Castor through the ribs, killing him instantly.

At this moment Pollux came hurrying down the path and heard Castor's death-cry. He drove at Idas with his spear, and Idas, unable to free his own spear from the oak, darted sideways and dodged behind his father's tomb. He broke off the headstone from the tomb and hurled it with both hands at Pollux, crushing his left collar-bone.

Pollux heard Lynceus charging down upon him from behind and turned, wounded as he was, to receive him on the point of his spear. Lynceus fell, transfixed through the belly. But Idas sprang forward and catching up his brother's spear from where it lay in the grass, drove it into Pollux with an upward thrust through the fundament so that he died miserably.

Idas began to dance in triumph beneath the sacred oak, and loudly to blaspheme Zeus the father of the dead champions, laughing until the rocks re-echoed, so that the shepherds who lived in a hut not far off stopped their ears for shame. He continued with his dancing and laughing and blas-pheming, heedless of a sudden thunderstorm that came growling down from the north, until suddenly there was a blinding flash of lightning and, simultaneously, a disastrous crash of thunder. The lightning caught the point of the spear that Idas was brandishing, scorched away his right arm, and tore off all his clothes.

His dead body was found by the shepherds, tattooed all over with the leaves of the sacred oak. They wondered greatly, and fenced off the place where he had fallen, making it forbidden ground; and instead of burning the body they buried it, as is customary when a man has been blasted by lightning.

The Thessalians, Admetus, Coronus, and Eurydamas, returned to their flocks and herds, and for the rest of their lives took part voluntarily in no further adventures, having won fame enough to content them. Nevertheless, they all met with violent deaths, Thessaly being a country where war and tumult are unavoidable even by the most peaceable men; Coronus was killed by Hercules when the Dorians called him in to assist them in a war with the Lapiths; Eurydamas and Admetus killed each other in single combat.

Autolycus and his brothers Deileion and Phlogius had seen enough of Thessalian Tricca by the second summer after their home-coming. Accompanied by Argeus, the son of Phrixus, they paid a visit to Samothrace at the time of the Great Mysteries and there became initiates; after which they returned to Sinope, where the simple Paphlagonians welcomed them with tears of joy. Now that the power of Troy had been broken by Hercules, and the power of Colchis weakened by the death of Aeëtes and the loss of the greater part of the Colchian fleet – for not a single ship had returned from the expedition sent out against Jason – Autolycus and his brothers secured a monopoly of Eastern goods and grew fabulously rich. At their deaths they became oracular heroes.

Phrontis and Cytissorus, the elder sons of Phrixus, went to Iolcos to ask the assistance of Peleus in some dispute that they had with the Orchomenans; but no sooner had they entered the city than he arrested them and sentenced them to death. He declared that Father Zeus had never been paid the debt of two lives that had been owed him by the house of Athamas ever since Helle and Phrixus absconded with the Fleece, and that this unpaid debt was the reason why the God had given so cold a welcome to the Argonauts when they restored the Fleece to his image, and why rain was so scarce in Phthiotis. So Peleus garlanded the two men and called upon the whole city to chase them out with stones and weapons. This the citizens did and Cytissorus soon fell, pelted to death, but Phrontis escaped by running and leaping; and when he returned to Orchomenos he sacrificed a ram to Zeus the God of Escapes. Peleus then issued a warning to all the surviving descendants of Athamas that the same fate awaited them too, if ever they ventured into Iolcos; for the debt to Zeus had been increased by the usurious lapse of time. But Melanion lived on, childless and unhappy, under the same roof with Atalanta, who scorned him and took to fine needlework and grew very buxom.

Phalerus, the Athenian archer, quarrelled about the ownership of a brass pestle and mortar with his father, Alcon the archer, who had once saved his life as a child by shooting to death a serpent that was entwined about him; the arrow, though discharged from a distance, had not done him the least harm. Phalerus did not revile or injure Alcon but went silently away from Athens and died in exile at Euboean Chalcis. The Athenians named their port of Phaleron after him and paid him heroic rites; they reverenced him especially for his wonderful feat of archery that had saved the *Argo* in her passage through the Clashing Rocks, and they considered (though the case never came up for decision upon the Areopagos) that he was right in claiming the pestle and mortar as his own property.

Melampus of Pylos became a soothsayer, by accident. A pair of snakes nested in a tree outside his house, and his servants killed them; but he piously preserved the whole brood of young snakes and kept them as pets in his bedchamber. One day, as he slept after dinner, they graciously cleaned out his ears with their forked tongues. When Melampus awoke, he was surprised to be able to understand the conversation of some wood-worms in the beams over his head, one saying to the other: 'Dear friends, we have now riddled this beam through and through. Let us dance up and down in celebration of our feat, by midnight it will fall and crush Melampus.' He shored up the beam and saved his own life. Melampus presently found that he could understand the language of all insects and worms and of birds as well. This knowledge stood him in such good stead that he ended as ruler of a large part of the kingdom of Argolis, and was awarded an oracular shrine at Aegosthena in Megaris.

Ascalaphus, the son of Ares, died at Orchomenos not long afterwards, drowned in a shallow carp-pool: a strange fate for one who had survived the dangers of so many inhospitable seas and dangerous straits. His grandson of the same name led a contingent of thirty Minyan ships to the siege of Troy and was killed by Priam's son Deiphobus.

Great Ancaeus, returning to his home in Tegea, planted fig-orchards and vineyards there. He kindly gave asylum to Evadne, Asteropaea, and Amphinome, the sisters whom Acastus had banished from Iolcos for the murder of their father Pelias, and he found a husband for each of them. One day as he was setting to his lips the first cup of wine brewed from the grapes of his vineyard, and observing with satisfaction to his wife, 'At last my labours are rewarded,' a messenger came running in to him. 'My lord,' he cried, 'a great boar is ravaging your vines!' Ancaeus set down the cup, seized up his javelin and ran to the rescue; but the boar burst out unexpectedly from a thicket and disembowelled him. Thus the proverb originated that 'There is many a slip 'twixt the cup and the lip.' It is thought that the boar was sent by Artemis, to whom Ancaeus had forgotten to offer the first-fruits of the vineyard. But he earned a hero's tomb, none the less.

Echion the herald was accidentally killed while trying to settle a dispute between the Arcadians, Laconians, and Messenians about the possession of the cattle stolen from Ancaeus by Idas, Lynceus, Castor, and Pollux. The blow was struck by Euphemus of Taenaron who, when he saw that he had killed a sacred herald, returned home in shame to Taenaron, refused food, and was dead within three days. Echion's tomb was much frequented by heralds, and if ever the sacred person of a herald was affronted, his headstone used to sweat with blood and a myriad of winged Spites flew out from below, at his orders, to vex the criminal.

Before Erginus the Minyan returned from Greece to Miletos he made a second attempt against Boeotian Thebes, from the walls of which he had been driven many years before by Hercules. He ran in one early morning with a few Minyan comrades disguised as country-men with goods for sale in the market. But Hercules happened to be in Thebes on a visit, and with his arrows killed all the raiders but Erginus himself. He spared Erginus, who had a well-founded grievance against Thebes for the murder of his father and the mutilation of his tax-gatherers. Then Erginus and Hercules made peace and Erginus returned in safety to Miletos. Hercules went with him as far as the island of Tenos, where he raised a monument for Calaïs and Zetes, as their ghosts had demanded of him in a dream. This is a memorial rather to the strength and precision of Hercules than to any quality of the two heroes: one huge rock is balanced upon another so exactly that it oscillates with the least breath of the North Wind, yet twenty men with crow-bars could not heave it to the ground.

Argus went on a journey to Ephyra to repair the *Argo*, whose timbers, he had heard, were warping and falling apart in the sun because the priests of Poseidon had neglected to raise a shed over her. Robbers waylaid and killed Argus at the approaches to the isthmus, and it is improbably related by the poets that the *Argo* groaned aloud at the news and with her sighs burst all the stout ropes that girded her about.

Nauplius the navigator founded the town of Nauplia, close to Tiryns in Argolis. He died there not long after, and is revered above all heroes by the Argive sea-captains.

Little Ancaeus of Flowery Samos was exiled from his island because he would not tolerate the religious innovations of his compatriots. When the yearly feast for Men of the Same Mothers was displaced by a feast for Men of the Same Fathers, Ancaeus grew angry and unsuccessfully tried to interrupt the sacrifice at the cross-ways. He went in exile to the far west, almost to Spain, and was put to death by the Goat men of Hesperidean Deia at the orders of the Orange Nymph, as has already been related. She honoured him with a hero's tomb, none the less.

As for Hercules, he continued to perform Labours for King Eurystheus of Mycenae until he had concluded them all, within the specified period of a Great Year. His last Labour was to enter the Underworld by the chasm at Lycos in the land of the Mariandynians and there complain to Hades in person about the God's alleged ill-treatment of the ghost of Theseus the

Athenian. In proof that he had accomplished his mission, Hercules brought back a blind and snow-white monster of some sort from an Underworld lake, which Eurystheus supposed to be the dog Cerberus, but which only had one head and did not bark. While he was down below, Hercules met the ghost of Meleager, who, on condition that Hercules raised him a hero-shrine in his native Calydon, revealed to him the name of the one woman capable of bearing him a daughter – Meleager's own sister Deianeira. Hercules undertook to raise the shrine as soon as the daughter was born; and he kept his promise, too.

While Hercules was warming himself with wine at the Court of King Lycus, the extreme cold of the Underworld having parched him, and eating great quantities of food, having wisely refused the food of the dead offered him by Hades, a handsome slave-woman set bread and a cold roast goose before him. She asked: 'Does this cold roast goose taste as good as the one which I once set before you in the council-chamber of Lemnian Myrine, forgiving you the mud-pellet that you threw in my face?'

She was the exiled Hypsipyle, and when she showed Hercules her twin sons by Jason, named Euneus and Nebrophonus, he remembered his promise to assist her. He therefore purchased her from King Lycus with a golden belt and took her back with him to his ship, but did not company with her. Landing on Lemnos, he restored her to the throne from which she had been banished by her women subjects. He also called his sixty-nine little three-year-old sons to him, and ranged them in a company, and made them all together swear to serve and obey Euneus, the elder of the twins, as their rightful King, and to avenge any injury thereafter done to his mother Hypsipyle. It was Euneus who, many years later, provided the Greeks with wine when they besieged Troy under King Agamemnon. But the island of Lemnos was haunted by the ghosts of the men whom Hypsipyle and her companions had murdered. At last Euneus instituted an annual feast of purification, lasting for nine days. All fires on the island are extinguished and blood-sacrifices are offered to the dead; after which a ship from Delos brings sacred fire from the shrine of Apollo.

Hercules, when he had accomplished his Labours and was a free man again, remembered that Augeas of Elis had promised to pay him a tenth part of all his cattle in reward for the cleansing of his stables, but had never done so. Gathering an army of Acadians, he marched against Elis, where he killed Augeas and all his sons but one, Phyleus by name, who had urged Augeas to fulfil his promise to Hercules. Hercules put Phyleus on the throne, and with the spoils taken from Augeas endowed the Olympic Games as a quadrennial event. He then dug a sacrificial pit at Olympia for the ghost of Pelops, by way of affronting Eurystheus: for Pelops had founded the dynasty which Sthenelus, the father of Eurystheus, had over-thrown. Then he marched against Neleus, the baleful brother of Pelias, who lived at Sandy Pylos and had sent troops to the help of Augeas; he killed Neleus and all his sons, except the boy Nestor (who lived to take part in the siege of Troy), and did not even hesitate to attack the Priest of Hades, who entered the battle disguised as a skeleton in the hope of striking a superstitious dread in his heart. Hades had been the enemy of Hercules ever since Hercules had robbed him of Alcestis, the wife of Admetus; but Hercules, undismayed, threw the jaw-bone of a sow at him and wounded him in the side. In this battle fell the Argonaut Periclymenus: not all his wizardry and baffling changes of shape could save him from the unerring arrows of Hercules.

Hercules himself was destroyed by his love of Deianeira, whom he had duly married and who had borne him a daughter, Macaria, on whom he doted. This is the true story. He was about to feast in the palace of King Oeneus, his father-in-law, when he accidentally killed a Calydonian boy whom he was tossing into the air for fun. The boy had poured water on the hands of guests before dinner, and he poured so profuse a stream on the hands of Hercules, because they were wonderfully stained and dirty, that Hercules laughed until the hall re-echoed. He tossed the boy up to the rafters in such excess of joviality that the child cracked his skull against the roof-top. Filled with remorse, Hercules went into voluntary exile with Deianeira. When they came to the flooded river Euenos, Hercules crossed first with his daughter and all the household belongings, leaving Deianeira to be carried over by the same Centaur Nessus whom he had conquered in the all-in wrestling contest at the funeral Games of Pelias; for Nessus now made this porterage his trade. Nessus tried to outrage Deianeira in revenge for his broken leg, and Hercules, hurrying back, killed Nessus with his arrows. But the dying Nessus whispered to Deianeira that she should pour some of his blood into a bottle and keep it as a sure charm for preserving a husband's love. This she did, and later used the charm on Hercules when she suspected that he was in love with a girl named Iole; she mixed some of it with the water in which she washed a white shirt for him to wear as he sacrificed to Zeus in Euboean Caenion. The blood was poisonous and ate into his flesh, causing him the most exquisite pain; he tore off the shirt with great lumps of flesh sticking to it and, being ferried over to Trachis, went raging up into Mount Oeta; where he built himself an enormous pyre and lighted it himself. He lay upon the pyre, roaring for indignation until his body was utterly consumed.

The soul of Hercules rose high into the air, carried by the flame and smoke, and the South-West Wind bore it to Mount Olympus. The poets say that he thumped at the door of Olympus with his shadowy brass-bound club and frightened the Divine Family almost out of their wits. When he refused to go to the Underworld and put himself at the disposal of his enemy Hades, they made the best of things by inviting him to join them as an Olympian. But he refused to become a thirteenth deity declaring himself content to become a porter at the gate, there to eat and drink to his heart's content, as all porters do. Hera, the poets say, pardoned him at last and gave him her daughter Hebe in marriage. What things take place in Olympus cannot, however, be known to mortals, even to the most trustworthy poets; all that is certain is that Deianeira hanged herself for grief when she heard that Hercules was dead, as Marpessa had hanged herself for grief when she heard of the death of her bold husband Idas.

The sons of Hercules, coming together from all over Greece to Oeta for the funeral Games of their father, saw how many and how strong they were and planned a grand assault on Mycenae; but King Eurystheus forestalled them by laying a cunning ambush, and those whom he did not kill fled as suppliants to Attica. Here they were well received. When Eurystheus marched against Attica, the sons of Hercules and the Athenians withstood him, and at the battle of the Scironian Rock Hyllus, son of Hercules, cut off his head, as he had previously cut off the head of Sthenelus; but to gain the victory he had been obliged to sacrifice his sister Macaria to Persephone. So this was the end of Eurystheus, but his head, when Alcmena, the mother of Hercules, had prudently gouged out the eyes with weaving-pins, was buried in one mountain pass and his body in another, to discourage enemies from ever again attempting the invasion of Attic soil. Eurystheus was succeeded by his son-in-law Atreus, who restored the Pelopid dynasty and became father of the famous Kings Agamemnon and Menelaüs.

The end of Jason and Medea was this. They lived together happily enough at Ephyra until the citizens were offended by Medea's attempt to win immortality for the two younger of the five children that she bore Jason, by rearing them in the temple of Hera and never allowing them to visit the outside world. Jason tried to persuade her to abandon this strange ambition, and when she flouted him, he refused to cohabit with her. Creon, King of Asopia, hearing of their differences, sent a messenger to Jason inviting him to marry his daughter, Auge, by which means the double kingdom of Corinth would be reunited under one sceptre according to the prophecy made by Echion; for Creon was old and wished to resign his throne to Auge.

Jason accepted Creon's proposal, forgetting that he had no title to the throne of Ephyra except as the husband of Medea. He divorced Medea by public decree and then celebrated the marriage with Auge. Medea pretended acquiescence and gave Auge a wonderfully worked night-gown as a wedding-gift. But when Auge put it on, it burst into flames which consumed not only her but also Creon, who tried to put them out with his hands, and the entire royal palace with nearly everyone in it, including Medea's two elder sons. The third son, Thessalus, was rescued by Jason, who jumped with him from a window and escaped uninjured. (It was this Thessalus who ruled over the kingdom of Phthiotis after the death of Peleus.) The Ephyrans in rage revenged themselves on the two younger children whom she had bred up in the temple of Hera; and have been obliged to make yearly atonement for the murder ever since.

Medea remembered the promise of Hercules, conveyed to her by the herald Echion, that he would help her at any time during the following twelve years if she were deserted by Jason. She fled to him at Thebes where he was residing, and asked him to restore her to the throne of Ephyra. He undertook to do so; but as they passed together through Attica, Aegeus the King of Athens fell in love with Medea and persuaded her to relinquish her Ephyran throne and become his Queen; and there at Athens, on the Areopagos, she cleared herself of all the crimes with which the Corinthian envoys charged her. In gratitude to Hercules who testified on her behalf, she cured him of his madness, which the Aesculapian priests of Apollo at Delphi had been unable to do, for all their boasting.

Medea soon wearied of Aegeus, or he of her, and one day she sent a message to Aras, the Colchian Admiral, who had continued in the service of her aunt, Queen Circe of Aeaea, that Colchis had need of him. Aras at once sailed to Athens with his Colchian ships, or as many of them as were still seaworthy, and Medea embarked with him for Colchis, which she heartily regretted ever having quitted. For even when her infatuation for Jason was at its height she had hated to leave Aea, which was a glorious place, better situated than any inland city in all Greece and as well built as either Mycenae or Thebes. She had wept to leave her bedchamber with the costly furniture and hangings and ornaments that she could not take with her in the ship. She had kissed her bed and the folding-doors and stroked the walls and her medicine-cabinet and her table inlaid with shells, and promised them: 'One day I will come to you again, dear things!' With Aras also came Peucon, who had been elected Admiral of the flotilla that Apsyrtus brought to the Danube. He and all his comrades had long been settled on the mainland of Epiros, opposite Corfu; for he had not dared to return to Colchis without the complete skeleton of Apsyrtus, some toe-joints and finger-joints of which were irrecoverably lost. But as much as he could find he had wrapped in a white horse-hide and hung up, with Circe's consent, in the island of Aeaea: which has been named the island of Apsyrtus ever since.

When Medea arrived back in Colchis after a prosperous voyage she seized the kingdom from her Taurian uncle Perses, and marrying Ideëssas, the King of Moschia, ruled the two kingdoms until her death; and Aeëtes, her son by Ideëssas, succeeded to the double throne. Neaera, daughter of Phrixus, was the Queen-Mother of Albania throughout this period, and the affairs of Colchis prospered greatly because of the friendship between the two royal houses, and because Medea had placated the Serpent Prometheus by driving the Taurians from the fore-part of his enclosure. The dynasty of Aeëtes is still firmly settled upon the Colchian throne.

Medea on her return voyage is said to have anchored at the place where

Pollux had killed Amycus the Bebrycian, and there to have found a laurel-tree growing out of the barrow of Amycus, the leaves of which had the power of throwing all who handled them into a violent quarrel. A shoot of this Insane Laurel, with a clod of earth around its roots, she towed behind her ship in a little cock-boat, all the way to Colchis. There she planted it and used the leaves to great effect in fomenting disorders among her private and public enemies.

Jason was overcome with grief at the death of his four children, and of Auge; and that he was now undisputed King of the double kingdom of Corinth gave him little comfort. He went down one early morning to the shrine of Poseidon on the isthmus, and there lay brooding under the prow of the *Argo*, wrapped in his figured cloak, and without either sacrificing to Poseidon or speaking a civil word to any of the priests who came out to greet him. They could see that he was plagued with a deep-seated grief; but what was passing through his mind, how could they tell? At last he uttered a number of heavy groans and muttered, as they thought, the name of Iphias the old Priestess of Artemis whom he had once flouted on the road to Pagasae and whose curse had at last brought him there. For though still in the prime of life, according to years, Jason had aged greatly since his quarrel with Medea. His gums had festered and he had lost several of his sharp white teeth; he was lame with rheumatism; and his once beautiful hair had lost its lustre and was streaked with grey.

The Chief Priest addressed Jason, saying: 'Majesty, be ruled by me! Do not sit despondently on the damp ground under the rotting memorial of your former glory. Such a posture can bring you no luck. Rise up, now, sceptre-wielder, reveal your griefs without fear to the Lord of Horses, the Sea-Shaker, Him of the Trident. He will assuage them, I warrant, especially if you bring him costly sacrifices of red cattle, feeding his priests with the tasty roast flesh while reserving the delectable thigh-bones for himself.'

Jason turned his head, but still would not answer. There was a dazed look in his eyes and his mouth stood open, like a child's that is about to cry; though no cry came.

The Chief Priest dismissed the other priests and sat watching from the temple steps, warned by his own heart that some strange event was about to take place that he could neither hasten nor hinder; and there he sat until past the dinner hour, though the rain was falling in showers and the eight snake-tailed winds seemed to be-chasing one another in sport around the whole enclosure, blowing from every quarter at once.

Jason's head sank lower. He fell asleep. And presently the Chief Priest saw from the corner of his eye what he could not have seen directly – the pale forms of a man and a hound coming at a shambling run along the road from Megara. He did not turn his head for fear of disturbing the clarity of his vision, and the two phantoms ran onward together. The man was dressed in the rough sheep-skin dress worn by the Aethics and Phlegyans, and a shadowy bronze spear-head protruded from the back of his faithful red wolf-hound.

The hound made straight for Jason and stood over him, baring its fangs in a snarl, the fur at its neck rising, but the shepherd clambered up into the bows of the *Argo*, as a lizard runs up a wall.

Then, as the Chief Priest watched, holding his breath, the shepherd shoved hard with his shoulder at the curved prow; and as he strained, with his feet braced against a stanchion, the eight winds ceased their sport and all rushed together with a roaring noise along the gunwale on both sides of the ship.

There was a tearing sound, and a loud crash. Down fell the tall prow and the muzzle of the Ram figure-head struck Jason upon the skull and crushed it miserably to a pulp. Yet the prudent Chief Priest did not move from his seat until both shepherd and dog had satiated themselves with the blood and brains of their enemy; for had he baulked these phantoms of their vengeance they would have haunted the enclosure insufferably. Now, however, they trotted away in perfect contentment.

The double throne of Corinth passed to the son of Glaucus, named Sisyphus in honour of his grandfather; but the Ephyrans, disconcerted by the death of Jason, ordained that the stern of the *Argo* should thenceforward be kept in perfect repair, and that if any timbers or tackle rotted they should be replaced with new – only the prow, being publicly convicted of homicide, was laid up as a deodand in a shrine of the Goddess Persephone. Thus the *Argo* became immortal, and remains the *Argo* of the Argonauts, though today not one of her timbers is original, from keel to mast-head. As the proverb says: 'This is my grandfather's axe: my father fitted it with a new stock, and I have fitted it with a new head.'

Orpheus also died a violent death. The Ciconian women one night tore him to pieces during their autumnal orgies in honour of the Triple Goddess. Nor is this to be wondered at: the Goddess has always rewarded with dismemberment those who love her best, scattering their bloody pieces over the earth to fructify it, but gently taking their astonished souls into her own keeping.

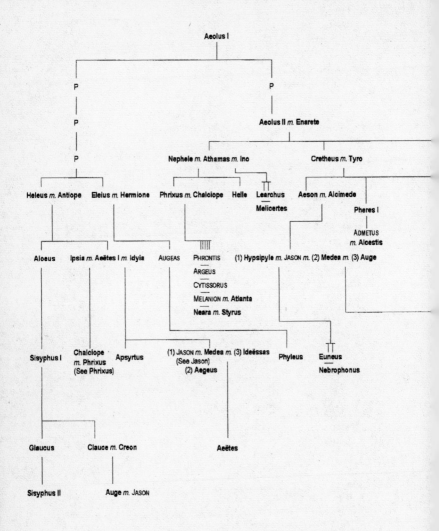

THE STEM OF THE AEOLIANS

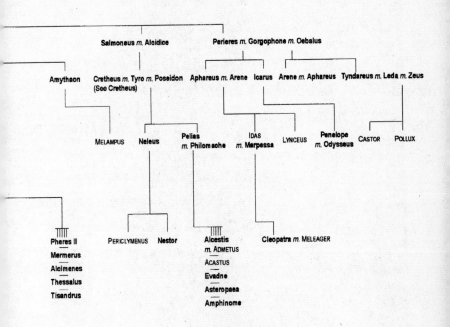

The Argonauts appear in Capital letters

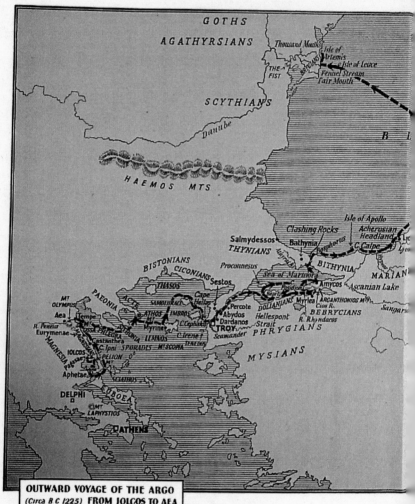

OUTWARD VOYAGE OF THE ARGO
(Circa B C 1225) FROM IOLCOS TO AEA
AND HOMEWARD VOYAGE AS FAR
AS ISLAND OF ARTEMIS
Third week of March to third week of June

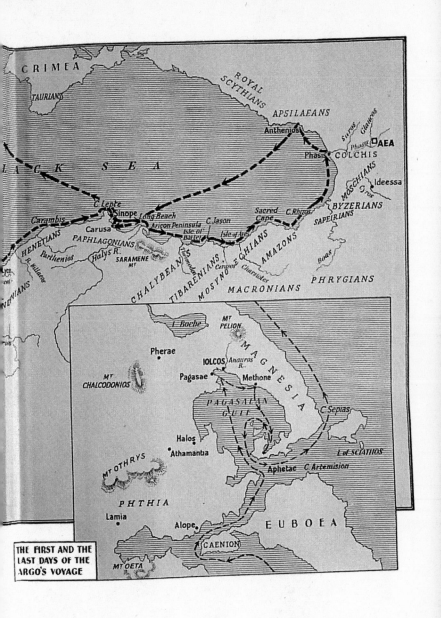

THE FIRST AND THE
LAST DAYS OF THE
ARGO'S VOYAGE

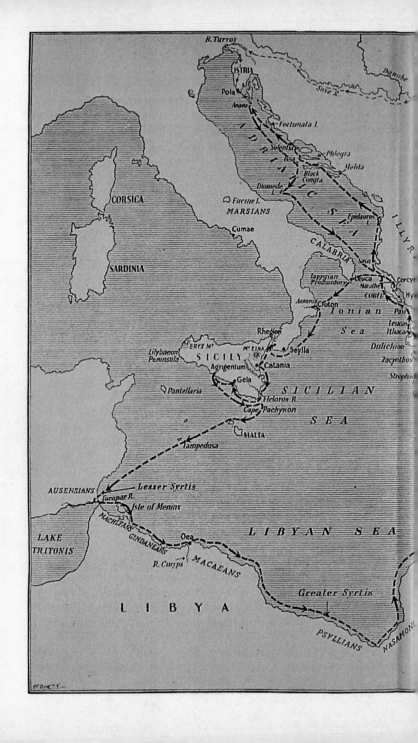

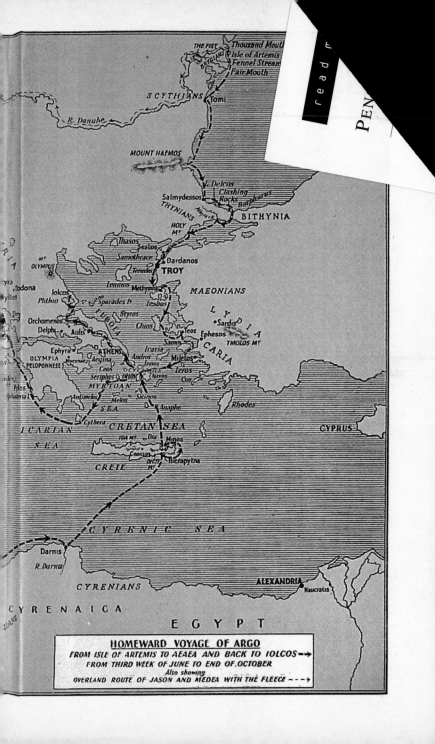

THE FIST · Thousand Mouth
GETTING · Isle of Artemis
· Fennel Stream
· Fair Mouth

SCYTHIANS · Tomi

R. Danube

MOUNT HAEMOS

L. Delcos
Salmydessos · Clashing
Rocks · Bosphorus
THYNIANS · BITHYNIA
HOLY
MT

MT
OLYMPUS
Ilhasos
Sestos
Samothrace · Dardanos
odona · Tenedos · TROY
Myllos · Iolcos · Lemnos · Methymna · MAEONIANS
Phthia · Sparades Is · Lesbos
Orchomenos · Styros · L Y D I A
Delphi · Chios · Sardis
Aulis · Teos · Ephesos
Ephyra · Icaria · Samos · CARIA · TMOLOS MT
OLYMPIA · ATHENS · Andros · Miletos
PELOPONNESE · Mycenae · Aegina · Ios · Leros
Ceos · DELOS · Naxos · Cos
Seriphos
MYRTOAN
Antimeles · Melos · Sicinos
Rhodes
SEA · Anaphe
Cythera · CRETAN · SEA · CYPRUS
ICARIAN
SEA · IDA MT · Dia · Minoa
Cnossos · dicte · Hierapytra
CRETE · MT

CYRENIC · SEA

Darnis
R. Darnis

CYRENIANS · ALEXANDRIA
Naucratis

C Y R E N A I C A · E G Y P T

HOMEWARD VOYAGE OF ARGO
FROM ISLE OF ARTEMIS TO AEAEA AND BACK TO IOLCOS →
FROM THIRD WEEK OF JUNE TO END OF OCTOBER
Also showing
OVERLAND ROUTE OF JASON AND MEDEA WITH THE FLEECE - - - →

GOODBYE TO ALL THAT
ROBERT GRAVES

'His wonderful autobiography' Jeremy Paxman, *Daily Mail*

In 1929 Robert Graves went to live abroad permanently, vowing 'never to make England my home again'. This is his superb account of his life up until that 'bitter leave-taking': from his childhood and desperately unhappy school days at Charterhouse, to his time serving as a young officer in the First World War that was to haunt him throughout his life. It also contains memorable encounters with fellow writers and poets, including Siegfried Sassoon and Thomas Hardy, and covers his increasingly unhappy marriage to Nancy Nicholson. *Goodbye to All That*, with its vivid, harrowing descriptions of the Western Front, is a classic war document, and also has immense value as one of the most candid self-portraits of an artist ever written.

PENGUIN MODERN CLASSICS

I, CLAUDIUS
ROBERT GRAVES

'One of the really remarkable books of our day, a novel of learning and imagination, fortunately conceived and brilliantly executed' *New York Times*

Despised for his weakness and regarded by his family as little more than a stammering fool, the nobleman Claudius quietly survives the intrigues, bloody purges and mounting cruelty of the imperial Roman dynasties. In *I, Claudius* he watches from the sidelines to record the reigns of its emperors: from the wise Augustus and his villainous wife Livia to the sadistic Tiberius and the insane excesses of Caligula. Written in the form of Claudius' autobiography, this is the first part of Robert Graves's brilliant account of the madness and debauchery of ancient Rome, and stands as one of the most celebrated, gripping historical novels ever written.

With a new Introduction by Barry Unsworth

Contemporary ... Provocative ... Outrageous ...
Prophetic ... Groundbreaking ... Funny ... Disturbing ...
Different ... Moving ... Revolutionary ... Inspiring ...
Subversive ... Life-changing ...

What makes a modern classic?

At Penguin Classics our mission has always been to make the best books ever written available to everyone. And that also means constantly redefining and refreshing exactly what makes a 'classic'. That's where Modern Classics come in. Since 1961 they have been an organic, ever-growing and ever-evolving list of books from the last hundred (or so) years that we believe will continue to be read over and over again.

They could be books that have inspired political dissent, such as *Animal Farm*. Some, like *Lolita* or *A Clockwork Orange*, may have caused shock and outrage. Many have led to great films, from *In Cold Blood* to *One Flew Over the Cuckoo's Nest*. They have broken down barriers – whether social, sexual, or, in the case of *Ulysses*, the boundaries of language itself. And they might – like *Goldfinger* or *Scoop* – just be pure classic escapism. Whatever the reason, Penguin Modern Classics continue to inspire, entertain and enlighten millions of readers everywhere.

'No publisher has had more influence on reading habits than Penguin'
Independent

'Penguins provided a crash course in world literature'
Guardian

The best books ever written

PENGUIN CLASSICS

SINCE 1946

Find out more at www.penguinclassics.com